For David
from Cecily
with love
19.1X.15

AGE OF GOLD

AGE OF GOLD

Cecily Paul

Library of Congress Control Number:		2015906170
ISBN:	Hardcover	978-1-4990-9680-4
	Softcover	978-1-4990-9681-1
	eBook	978-1-4990-9682-8

Cover picture *Pleading* by Sir Lawrence Alma Tadema
By kind permission of the Guildhall Art Gallery
City of London

Print information available on the last page.

Rev. date: 09/04/2015

To order additional copies of this book, contact:
Xlibris
800-056-3182
www.Xlibrispublishing.co.uk
Orders@Xlibrispublishing.co.uk
699510

'If a man were called to fix the period in the history of the world, during which the condition of the human race was most happy and prosperous, he would, without hesitation, name that which elapsed from the death of Domitian to the accession of Commodus.'

Gibbon, *Decline and Fall of the Roman Empire*

For Isabel who brought the classical world alive for me.

CHAPTER 1

April 171

Βουλο ιμην κ' επαρουρος εων θητευεμεν αλλω ανδρι παρ' ακληρω ω μη βιοτος πολυς ειεν η πασιν νεκυεσσι καταφθιμενοισιν ανασσειν

I'd rather be the slave of the most miserable wretch on earth than queen in the kingdom of the dead.. Homer Odyssey I 489

There were six in the bed, if a herb-stuffed pallet on a stone floor is a bed, pressed together, sharing secrets. Nerysa, who dared not speak and didn't wish to listen, couldn't help but hear.

Chione loved the stoker's mate. He'd given her a bracelet which all agreed was brass but quite pretty. Iris loved Talos, the carpenter. He didn't love *her* any more but this was no great loss because he was too handsome to give presents. The cooks' boy, who loved Nephele, promised to use his influence to get her promoted to the kitchen but no one believed his influence was that great. Cheimone's soldier loved her thoroughly and often but, so far, hadn't given her a thing. Doubly disappointing because he was a free man. A visitor's slave had wandered into the staff quarters in search of refreshment and seen Aura. Next day, he'd sent her, by the post boy, a brightly coloured bandeau, nearly new, and a message which, she said, was private.

Nerysa had heard this sort of thing, day and night, for three months and it still puzzled her. All she knew of love came from poetry, which didn't deal in its commercial aspects. But she knew Aura had no chance of keeping a secret. Confidences were currency, exchanged on a like for like basis. The cries of, 'Don't be mean, go on, tell!' as the

1

other four tickled her, soared above her laughing and shrieking until Iris squealed above them all, 'The silentarii!'

As the laughter died, Nerysa heard footsteps. Arcs of lantern-light swung under the door curtain and the girls leapt up and stood in line against the wall. The curtain was snatched back and two men stood in the doorway each carrying a lantern and a strap. From the far end of the line, Nerysa watched the lamplight flicker over five outstretched hands. She heard a whirr, then a crack. Nephele winced and cried out. Another whirr, another crack. Cheimone gasped and pressed her hands together. Then came a long whirr and no crack. Aura had snatched back her hand. The silentarius cursed, passed his lantern to his colleague, held her wrist and landed three savage blows on her palm. As Chione's eyes shone and spilled over, Nerysa stretched out her own arm. When the strap fell on Iris, she set her jaw as if she dared them to bully a sound or a tear from her. The silentarius came closer, thrusting his lantern against her face.

'Can't our master grieve in peace in his own house? Or do you think you can riot because the steward's away?'

'No use asking her.' said Iris. 'Can't speak.'

'Don't understand?'

'Mute.'

'Can't make no noise, you mean?' he laughed. 'That's the cheekiest excuse I've heard.'

'Give her a good hiding. See how mute she is.' suggested the other.

'New aren't you?' he shouted. 'Northerner by the look of you. D'you hear?'

Nerysa looked at him. He flinched and his companion pushed past him.

'Got any Latin? Then I'll warn you. Once. I'd know you anywhere. When I catch you again you'll get it for this time, too. Understand?'

'Good. The same goes for all of you. Keep your hands busy in your master's service and your tongues still in your silly heads.'

They marched out. The girls fell back on the bed and the room was silent until Iris gave a wail which Chione stifled with a hand. Iris struggled free and whispered, 'The steward! He said, "The master's grieving." That must be why he bought that new slave, Jacob, for the shipping office - because he knew Demetrius was never coming home.'

'If he never comes home it will break the master's heart.'

As suddenly as they'd laughed, they all began to cry, burrowing their faces into the pallet to muffle the sound.

Nerysa, as confused by their tears as by their laughter, groped for Iris' uninjured hand; the simplest sort of fellowship but the only one possible. She didn't speak because she didn't know how. She'd counted on finding a British slave to imitate but, this being an elegant household, it kept none.

Losing her freedom had been less painful than she'd feared. The sun shone impartially on slave and free, her food still savoured and she slept more soundly than ever. Her fellows were rough but their prosaic cheerfulness steadied her like the grip of a great, calloused hand. True, she couldn't choose when to sleep, what to eat or whether to work but she was a naturally early riser, so energetic that idleness irked her more than exertion and the food was good. The master didn't want his meals served by slaves with rumbling bellies and his cooks didn't know how to make tasteless food, whoever it was for. Most evenings when she reached the head of the queue, Arminia, the florid German overseer, would lay a hand on her head and say, 'Good worker, this one.'

Apicius would beam, cram her fist with bread and fill her bowl to the brim. He made ambrosial soup. Its glutinous richness coated her stomach like balm and its heat coursed through her body, dissolving the stiffness of her limbs to a sensual delight. They'd been wrong, the old men who'd wept and pleaded for an honourable suicide. How could they judge, when they'd never felt hunger or fatigue? She knew now that slavery was not just preferable to death but dealt moments of joy, intense in their stark simplicity. Washing in cold water, the stench and embarrassment of communal latrines, having no books and the threat of the strap were minor irritations compared with the dread of exposure. Terror was mingled with exultation. She was alive, shielded by complete obscurity. And not every change was for the worse. To sit hatless in the sun, without two officious women balancing a parasol over her head, was a liberation.

After three months, the house felt familiar; the dormitory clean and airy, the pallet comfortable and fragrant. The house painter was a genius with a roguish wit and he was a glutton for work. He'd even painted the smoky kitchen. Apicius strode along the frieze, brandishing a bread slice at slaves pilfering sweets and dogs stealing joints; chefs tossed pancakes with varying degrees of success, washers-up juggled pots, servers kissed as they squeezed past each other with trays piled-high.

Because he was in mourning, the master didn't entertain so the girls were limited to fetching water, peeling vegetables, scouring pots and scrubbing the kitchen floor and they were well schooled in these monotonous tasks that left their minds vacant. Arminia, despite her awesome appearance, treated them as a harassed mother of a large family might treat her daughters, quick to threaten but slow to deliver. Once, Nerysa saw a whip cracked but, when the girls fell silent and scrubbed frantically, it was returned to its hook on the wall, limp and cheated. She tried to remember the slaves in Quintus' house. Had they choked back tears? Had they been beaten? She'd never thought to ask. It wasn't as though they were people with feelings; more a sort of moving furniture. Yet these girls were crying, and not for their own misery, but for their master's. Could he really be broken-hearted at the death of a servant? Quintus would laugh at that because he'd disapprove. He'd say it wasn't Roman. What sort of man was her new master?

CHAPTER II

April 171

οὔτε τι μάντις ἐὼν οὔτ' οἰωνῶν σάφα εἰδώς .οὔ τοι ἔτι δηρόν γε φίλης ἀπὸ πατρίδος αἴης ἔσσεται, οὐδ' εἴ πέρ τε σιδήρεα δέσματ' ἔχῃσιν:

He is a man of such resource that even though he were in chains of iron he would find some means of getting home again. Odyssey book 1 203-205

The girls got up as soon as the rising bell sounded. Two shook out the sheet and coverlet while two thumped the pallet and propped it against the wall, hiding their belongings. Nerysa was sweeping the floor when Iris clutched her arm.

'Stop, listen!'

The sounds from the courtyard were new. Louder, more urgent, as if, on ordinary days, an earthly gardener eased the lid from his hive but, on this day, Zeus had struck the summit from Hymettus. Nerysa caught her breath. The hubbub was joyful. It made her want to laugh. They all crowded under the window. Cheimone, the tallest, crouched down and Nephele, the smallest, sprang onto her shoulders. With Cheimone on tiptoe, Nephele could just poke her face into the deep recess, blocking out the grey light.

'What's happening?'

'Everyone's in the yard. They're all hugging each other!'

The six of them hurtled down twisted stone steps, through deserted workrooms, to the back kitchen. Arminia held out her arms.

'My beauties,' she beamed, 'It's true! He's home.'

Having a giant's arms she could hug them all at once. Iris looked toward the yard.

'There'll be a feast tonight.' she said. 'We'll need lots of water.'

Arminia laughed.

'You want fetch water so you wash vegetables? I don't think. But go, yes.'

They shouldered their urns and elbowed their way through the crowd to huddle round the well, wriggling, giggling, patting their hair and looking in every direction except one. Turning in that direction, Nerysa saw a group of men by the brick colonnade that surrounded the yard. One of them was sitting on the parapet. To judge by the deference of the others, he was the leader. The gardener, whom she'd only ever seen leaning on a shovel, came forward and presented him with a sprig of wallflowers.

The gesture stirred her memory. The queen had pressed a bunch of meadow flowers into her hand as they parted and it had seemed to her then that all the sweetness of her native countryside was in those fragile blooms. Then came the soldier's arm around her shoulder, a walk across wrinkled sand to the pilot, and the grey shoreline receding. The flowers were wrenched from her hand and flung overboard. They trembled on the foam and she followed each stem as they bobbed their separate ways.

The leader inspected the flowers, passed them briefly under his nose and nodded. The yard was fully light now and everyone was smiling. Nerysa caught the elated mood. The black clouds of fear and betrayal rolled away. She'd survived the spring she should never have seen and she'd see the summer too. She didn't notice the weight of the urn as she swung it to her shoulder, smiled up into the sunlight and made for the house.

But the careless lift had placed the urn awkwardly. She stopped to adjust it and caught the eye of the man who sat on the wall. He scanned her from eyes to ankles and up again. She felt as if she were a pot he'd turned up on a market stall and this was the first pass to see if she was worth closer scrutiny for chips and cracks. The experience was new and painful. Her fellow slaves had no interest in a mute with stiff manners and outlandish looks. In Quintus Pulcher's house, any slave or freedman who'd looked at her like that would have taken a slap of a gaunt, jewelled hand. If a guest had done so, Quintus would have suggested she retire to her rooms.

This man was not to blame. Pass yourself off as a kitchen slave and people would treat you like one. You had to show them they shouldn't. Her shoulders squared, her chin shot up and she swept past him towards the kitchen. How obtuse must he be to call her back? Only a quickening of her pace betrayed that she'd heard. Footsteps followed. Two men barred her way. The shouting died, birds stopped quarrelling in the crowded eaves, the well handle stopped creaking. The yard fell silent as a fish tank and the gaping eyes and jaws of all the fish were turned on her.

'Come here.'

The soft voice twisted a knot in her stomach. It was three months since she'd heard an educated voice. Careful not to hurry, she turned and walked towards him, curious as to what he might be doing in the slave quarters. He wasn't her master. The master, she'd heard, was fair-haired. Yet if he weren't her master, how dared he look at another man's property as he'd looked at her? She caught a whiff of his flowers, apricot colour, apricot scent.

'The jar's heavy for you.' he said. 'The boy can take it while you talk to me.'

'That won't be necessary, thank you. I bear my own burdens.'

With all the dignity possible in a skimpy tunic with a full jar on her shoulder, she made for the house. Footsteps pursued her but stopped on a word of command. She lowered the urn onto the scullery floor as the other girls fell on her.

'Why say nothing for weeks and then say something so stupid?'

'Arminia, can she help Chione take up the ice for his wine. She could throw herself at his feet –'

'Cry and say she's new –'

'And stupid –'

'And don't know the rules –'

'What is wrong? No use asking you, silly hens. All talk at once. I go find someone with sense.' and Arminia strode under the arch into the kitchen.

'You don't know, do you?' cried Iris. 'Great gods! You don't know who that was. It was Demetrius, our steward!'

'Surely not! He's too young for a steward.'

'Twenty four. But he's clever and the master loves him like a brother.'

'A freedman?'

'Might as well be. He's Mercury's pet. He travels the world and everything he touches turns to gold. He was in Aquileia last autumn when it was *besieged* by *barbarians*. We thought he'd been killed. He never sent word. Just came home in the middle of last night.'

'You never even saluted him and he wasn't angry. Nerysa! Suppose he loves you?'

'Loves me? He never set eyes on me until this morning.'

'Lucky you!' Four of the girls were gleeful but Iris was looking at Nerysa's face.

'Look,' she said, 'there's nothing here without his sanction - no praise, no pay, no promotion. He's got more eyes than Argus and, if he gets a down on you, it's the end. Why am I still in the back kitchen? Because I'm ugly or stupid?'

Nerysa gloated. Apparently, just because she'd offended the insolent man, she'd be left in the back kitchen forever. No exposure. No risk of detection. Out of sight of any but the lowest slaves until Quintus claimed her. And who'd think of looking for her among them?

Arminia came back looking grim.

'Best thing,' she said, 'We all disremember. So will he. Stupid, ignorant girls no interest for him. Little Brit, rake out the ashes and scatter them round my pear tree. And hurry back – we all behind and the master feast tonight.'

Nerysa took as long as she dared collecting the ashes. By the time she took them to the yard it was, as she'd hoped, deserted. Except for the gardener. She asked him why he was digging up the flowers.

'To replant - in master's garden. Came up a new colour – matches summer dining room exactly.'

'But they're *your* flowers.'

'Yes, and I'll be paid for them. I'm glad someone told steward. There's not much he don't notice but he don't come here so often.'

'He's been away, hasn't he?'

'Yes, and if he wants to sit in a garden he sits in master's. Close to master, he is. Grew up together at Horta. So did I, come to that. And it's where we all end up when we're too old to be useful or beautiful. I shan't mind as much as most.'

'Why not?'

'I like the wide open spaces – different from these cramped quarters.'

She started. Even the slave side of the house was the size of a British village.

'Meadows and cornfields,' he mused, 'vineyards and olive groves, orchards, forests and lakes; all master's as far as the eye can see. Takes steward three days to check the boundaries.'

'Does he often go there?'

The sooner the better she thought.

'Five times a year; beating the bounds, haymaking, harvest, vintage, winter ploughing. Is that German giant calling you?'

She wished him good health and ran back to the kitchen.

Shelling quails' eggs required no thought and she was able to give her whole mind to this development. The scrutiny of an educated, worldly man could be dangerous. The house was full of young men with olive skin, crisp black hair and saucy manners. None worth notice. Her survival plan to stay dumb and humble had worked. What was it about him that had provoked her to break her silence? Not his self-assurance; Quintus was self-assured. Unlike Quintus, he radiated energy in an overpowering way, but neither was energy, in itself, offensive. Was it that her wretched circumstances had been bearable before because they'd had no point of contact with her previous life? His speech and bearing filled her with a bitter sense of loss; punched her in the deep, raw spot that ached for Quintus. How dared a slave go about as a parody of a Roman gentleman? There ought to be a law against it. To play dumb wouldn't serve any longer but the situation was manageable with caution. Iris agreed with Arminia. As she hadn't been summarily punished, she would now be ignored.

Iris was wrong. A few days later, Demetrius strolled into the yard as the girls stood round the well, washing radishes. Unusually, for one of his consequence, he was alone and his approach threw them into confusion. He spoke in an easy, bantering way but, as he called each girl by name, her face kindled flame and she simpered into her shoulder. Nerysa couldn't tell if he terrified or attracted them. He dismissed them all except one.

'Let the new girl stay behind.'

She couldn't manage the head deflection or the coy smile but she wiped her wet hands across her backside and folded them demurely. She held his eyes steadily but blushed under the look; longer now and twice as penetrating.

'Tell me about yourself.'

'I'm from the fourteenth gang - the back kitchen.'

'I can see that. What do they call you?'

'My name is Nerysa.'

'Mine, as far as you're concerned, is *sir*. 'My name is Nerysa, *sir*.'

The correction seemed the more offensive for being gently said. She felt a thrill of horror. Never in her life had she called anyone 'sir' and this fellow, for all his pitiful pretension, was a slave. He reached for her hands and ran his thumbs over the palms.

'Not hardened up to the work yet, are they? Where do you come from?'

'From Britain. I'm a Briton.'

This was clearly not a point in her favour.

'It's my duty,' he said coldly, 'to buy the slaves here, one I could delegate, but don't, because I consider it an important duty. Why don't I know you?'

'I think you were in Aquileia when I came here.'

'From Britain?'

To hesitate would only arouse suspicion, he'd find out anyway. She breathed the name, Quintus Fabius Pulcher. She touched a nerve. His face showed surprise, amusement and a flash of raw lust. She drew back and his expression became impassive. Dismissing her with a gesture that implied he was a busy man with no time to waste on kitchen slaves, he strode across the yard, a flurry of flapping pigeons in his wake.

It was the name, Quintus Fabius Pulcher. When she'd said it to Successus, the deputy steward, he'd pursed his lips and shut his eyes. But neither of them knew Quintus as she did, and she knew nothing that should cause his name to shock.

CHAPTER III

April 172

Ότε γαρ πρωτον επεδημησα ύμων τη πολει εξεπλαγην μεν εύθυς ιδων το μεγεθος και το καλλος και των εμπολιτευομενων το πληθος και την αλλην δυναμιν και λαμπροτητα πασαν.

When I first came to your city I was terrified when I saw its size, its beauty, its great population, its power and its general splendour Lucian VI The Scythian 9

D emetrius *was* shocked. Not so much by the name as by the tender pride with which she'd said it. He was broad-minded. If he hadn't been a slave he'd have been called a man of the world. Quintus Pulcher was a poet; rich, cultivated and aristocratic, with an appalling reputation. His house was a temple to vice where boys, in particular, learned more than they should. Strange for a girl schooled in that house to seem so serious but that would add spice to her skill. Interesting. There must have been something to draw him to her so powerfully. No need for her to know how powerfully. He'd shown interest. Her sights would be set on him. She'd be coaxing her companions; borrowing a pretty tunic, scrounging slivers of soap, bartering extra chores for a bracelet. He smiled. She shouldn't bother. He could do more for her than all the kitchen maids in the empire. But he'd make her wait a little.

He had seven months' work to audit that morning but he made time to ask his valet, Polybius, to find out about the circumstances of her coming into the house. Discovering that it was a private deal between the master and Quintus Pulcher alerted him to the need for caution. Lucius Marius hadn't specifically warned him off – hadn't even mentioned her, but, if he'd bought her into the house for his own use, he'd be understandably annoyed if his steward were to help himself first. Then again, barbarous serving maids weren't in the master's style and, unless he was being unusually devious, he wouldn't be hiding her in the back kitchen.

Lucius was about to leave for Ostia to negotiate on a consignment of tin, an errand which should have fallen to Demetrius. But Demetrius had only just come home and the weather was unseasonably hot so the master had volunteered himself for the business and the stay at his client's seaside villa. The night before he left, he dined alone with Demetrius, a habit of his of which the household was, naturally, ignorant - at least, the household behaved as if it was ignorant, which was what mattered. When he judged Lucius had drunk a suitable quantity of wine, Demetrius asked casually if any of the girls in the house was out of bounds. Lucius said not, adding that, if Demetrius unearthed any unknown charms, he should try them and pass on them on in due course.

***

Nerysa wondered why Arminia had sent for her. Seeing her at the far end of the colonnade, she ducked behind a pillar. Arminia was not alone. Nerysa edged forwards the space of two pillars. What could they be talking of, Arminia and the elegant youth? She moved closer, noting his crisply pleated tunic, the sheen of its amethyst silk, his soft hair, shapely legs and polished sandals. Cinnamon and rose wafted towards her and she leaned on the pillar for support. He must be one of Quintus' boys, come to fetch her home. But how so soon? It should have taken years. A word here, a hint of a bribe there, cultivating diplomats, feeling a way through a legal labyrinth, divulging nothing until the pardon was signed and sealed. The boy turned to face her. She didn't recognise him but she didn't know all Quintus' boys. He might be new. But something was wrong. His stare was too bold and Arminia was grinning approval not amazement.

'Good girl!' she cooed, 'Here's Polybius, steward's boy, fetch you up to his master. You go to bath. Get, new tunic. Then he give you good fuck.'

Nerysa clung to the pillar though it spun under her hands. Three months in a slave kitchen had taught her what the word referred to but not what it meant. She loved Quintus as much as one being could love another but she'd never wanted physical intimacy with him. Nor he, she was sure, with her. With a slave, the thought was grotesque. She managed the lamest excuse.

'No, you not.' Arminia said. 'No new moon since last time.'

'Perhaps a little early.'

Arminia narrowed her eyes shrewdly, 'You want I take look?'

Polybius smiled at Nerysa. And winked.

'No need. We can wait.'

When he came again, five days later, she still had no excuse; the suggestions of her twittering companions had gone no further than what to ask for if he allowed her to choose her present. Arminia took her to the baths as promised - not to clean herself, she was expected to do that under the pump at home, but as a mental preparation and a treat.

It *was* a treat. Quintus had never wanted her to leave the house. She'd lived in Rome six years without seeing it. Now it lay spread before her in the sunshine and she wanted to see it all. They were six in the party; Arminia, Polybius, two guards and a boy to carry sponges and scented body oil. Arminia advised bringing one's own oil.

'Bath attendants scrape it off one customer and sell it to the next.'

Nerysa's colouring attracted attention. Her escorts closed in and quickened their pace to avoid the stares and catcalls but she hung back as much as she dared, fascinated by the city and delighted when Polybius stopped to drink at a street fountain. He took his time, flirting with the laundresses, deaf to Arminia's reproaches.

The domus of Lucius Marius Lepidus was on the Quirinal hill - a mixed quarter with fine buildings uncomfortably close to mean ones. Walking along marble porticoes, past gilded temples and towering equestrian statues, Nerysa thought it right that people who lived in such splendour should rule the world. Her tribe had been mad to resist. They'd be crushed by a vengeful conqueror when they might have sat at the feet of a wise teacher, as she'd done with Quintus. Yet she couldn't blame their ignorance. How should they suspect the grandeur of the rough legionaries' home unless someone like herself returned to tell them? They'd battle against an overwhelming force until they were ground to rubble.

Although the surroundings were fit for gods, some of the throng were less than divine and, among the hawkers, loafers and shoppers who jostled them, there were some who didn't smell divine. Between grand buildings, she caught glimpses of festering alleys, tumbling children, washing lines and litter.

In Britain, there were kings and queens, priests, warriors and farmers. They might all eat together in one great hall. But in Rome, there were those who gourmandised on lark's tongues and Falernian, those who saved up for a scrawny chicken, those who ate out because they had no kitchen, those who got gristle and bones from public sacrifices, those who ate bread and garlic and those who starved. Some were carried everywhere, some rode horses, some mules, some donkeys. Some walked, some hobbled, some weren't allowed out at all. Free society had more layers than a leather shield and she was learning that slaves also benefited from a class system. Escape, had it been feasible, wasn't an option. Where would she fit in this maelstrom? Life looked rougher outside the house than in it.

But hiding among slaves was a ploy to save her life. It was no part of her plan to become like them, to touch them, to be contaminated by them. To lose her virginity to one was too disgusting to contemplate. But there'd be some sort of preamble, surely, in which she'd explain that she hadn't sought his attentions and didn't want them? If all else failed, she'd serve him as she'd served the legate on the ship. He'd soon changed his tune.

It amused her to see how Polybius was excruciated by Arminia's Latin. She was pained by it herself but couldn't grudge respect to one who could pluck and draw a row of chickens with verve while kicking slavering dogs from under her feet. Arminia wasn't cowed by his condescension.

'Just you sure to be wait here when we get out. You plenty time for bath - my lucky girl get the full treatment.'

They entered by the women's door and Arminia paid the entrance fee. So this was a private bathhouse. Iris would be impressed. Charming as they were, there was no avoiding the fact that the women's baths were smaller, less grand and, Nerysa suspected, less well-appointed than the men's. Why were there two sets of everything - living quarters, theatre seats, baths - one obviously superior and reserved for men? British women didn't offer sacrifice to a set of lesser gods, nor did they ride to war in second-rate chariots. A king's relict could rule as absolutely as her husband before her. Rome had known powerful women, too, but they pulled strings behind screens. It seemed the more urbane the people, the more passive its women.

The marble changing rooms seethed with people, to whom public nudity seemed quite normal and Arminia lost no time in bustling her out of her clothes. Averting her eyes from Arminia's mountainous, pallid body, Nerysa resented the fact that Arminia didn't return the compliment but stared thoughtfully at her and rolled her flesh between finger and thumb as if she were buying poultry.

Steered into the hot room, Nerysa marvelled at the walls' shimmering seascapes in olive and turquoise. How did they resist the steam, billowing from a vast copper cauldron? She soon fainted and Arminia dragged her into the tepidarium where attendants massaged her with scented oil. The tease of the strigil and the caress of skilled hands taught her the distinction between luxury, in which she'd long lived, and sensuality, of which she was innocent. Close to enjoying it, she reminded herself that she was accepting it under false pretences.

A cold plunge completed the process and she emerged into the sunshine, body glowing and spirits apprehensive. She noticed other attractions; gymnasia, restaurants and a library, and wondered how long it would be before she'd earned enough independence and pocket money to use the library. She was about to make a bad beginning. Arminia seemed disconcerted by her calm. It must have looked like over confidence.

'No need flatter yourself.' she said. 'Steward just curious 'cause you new. If he call you again, give you wine, have you lie on his couch, then you done well.'

'Doesn't he want me to lie on his couch?'

'No, bend over his table, silly, you never see dog with bitch?'

Her legs were leaden as Arminia and Polybius shepherded her down the alley leading from the slaves' quarters into a marble colonnade bordering a garden. A cuckoo called. That was no marvel in the northern outskirts of the city, close to woodland but she'd last heard that call as a herald of happy childhood summers. She swallowed hard and told herself she would be safe. He was an educated man and, therefore, could be reasoned with. But how far could you advance a rational argument while posing as a menial?

A guard opened massive double doors and waved her through. The size and grandeur of the room shocked her. She set her face against the smirks of the scribes as they gathered up their writing tablets and left. The steward crossed the room, his smile fading to a look of intense concentration. She edged backwards and he gave a throaty laugh.

'Steady on, I'm as hot for you as you are for me but, if you want to play the virtuous vestal, you should drop those blazing eyes.'

His hands came down on her shoulders and moved across her chest and over her hips. She jerked her face away so he kissed her neck as he called her 'deliciae', 'darling,' forcing her against his swollen groin.

'We must keep the refinements for next time,' he said thickly, then panting,

'Quick, darling, up with your tunic, 'I'm afraid I can't wait.'

If he'd braced himself for the pain he might have controlled his reaction; taken unaware, he howled and fell, first to his knees and then full length on the floor. She looked down, paralysed with horror, while he searched her face with a puzzled frown. His colour drained as fast as ink into cheap papyrus. Beads of moisture studded on his brow and his eyelids fluttered shut.

She recoiled and backed into a jardinière sending a vase crashing to the ground. Guards, posted outside, paused only to shout for reinforcements before bursting in. They ran to Demetrius who stirred and looked at her. She looked back at him stupidly. Would he order her to be flogged or clapped in irons as a lunatic? The guards seemed to await the same decision.

'Taken ill.' he said, hands pressed to his belly. 'Girl panicked. Have her clear up!'

She knelt in a pool of water, collecting rose petals and shards of bi-coloured glass with shaking hands while he was helped to a couch. Someone asked, 'Is she to pay for the breakage, sir?' As if the hoarded tips of a lifetime could come near the value of such an article. Polybius proposed sending for a doctor in tones of sharp concern that surprised her. Demetrius must have asked to speak to her for she was pulled forward and forced onto wobbling knees beside his couch. For the second time, he took hold of her hands. She looked down and saw that the tips of her fingers were bleeding. He spoke into her ear.

'Go. Quickly. Have the sense not to speak of this.'

He made a slight gesture of dismissal and she found herself on the outside of his great doors.

CHAPTER IV

April 172

Nam ut se ament efflictim folia sunt artis et nugae merae

Making men fall in love with her is the least of her arts Apuleius Metamorphoses I 8

Arminia marched her wayward charge to the head cook's alcove, pushed her inside and snatched the curtain to behind her. Polybius' appraising look was as unnerving as his master's and distinctly less appreciative.

'Tell me, are you mad?'

I don't think so.'

He came closer, dropped his bantering tone and asked, 'Are you a sorceress?'

Nerysa laughed in his face. 'Of course not.'

'Are you trying to hurt my master?'

'Is your master trying to hurt me?'

'Ah, you like cash in advance? You needn't worry, he doesn't cheat - and he's generous. But an old hand like you should know better than to push your luck.'

'I don't understand.'

'Oh, I think you do,' he purred, 'and we understand you, too. I concede we've found you ...stimulating. Himself wasn't unamused. At first. But no game delights forever, so let's talk terms.'

He perched gracefully on the edge of the table but leant no weight on it. She could have kicked it away and left him perfectly poised.

'In fact,' he confided, 'I'd been wondering how I could help things along. Now my master sends me and I can speak with his authority.'

'I've given him my answer. He can't want me to repeat it?'

'The direct approach didn't suit? You like sweet talk and flattery? He can do that but what do you expect when you tease a man till his loins are bursting? And who are you to complain? I suppose my master is fine enough for a kitchen drudge?'

'He chose to lower himself to notice me. Why? No one else bothers me.'

He shrugged.

'Who knows? He could take his pick from a hundred more gracious than you. Curiosity perhaps, or because your coyness piques him.'

'If his reasons are so trivial it shouldn't pain him much to forgo the pleasure.'

'Why should he be pained at all on your account? Look, if my first approach offended you, I can only say I'm sorry but it's not my fault. That overseer of yours has all the finesse one expects of a German.'

'It's not the *phrasing* of the proposal that disgusts me.'

'If it *disgusts* you, you can't have understood me. Our steward has condescended to say he wants to lie with you.'

'I'm not for him.'

'Of course you're not,' he agreed with good-natured contempt, 'but you'll serve to while away an hour at siesta time. By Venus, he deserves a diversion when the sun's hot and he's taxed with work. If you managed to keep his interest longer you might do well for yourself.'

He came uncomfortably close. He was different from her workmates; close shaven, expensively scented, his tunics fine and spotless. He spoke coaxingly, close to her ear.

'A girl in your position...you like sweetmeats and trinkets I expect. You'd wouldn't mind being excused some of your...less pleasant duties.'

'You mean I should lie with him in the hope that he'll give me trinkets?'

'Not the *hope*. I think we can safely say the *expectation*. I don't deny he's taken with you. Come! Don't pretend you find him unattractive. I do well out of bribes I get to help girls throw themselves in his way. Not just girls from this house either – freedwomen and freeborn women too. It's one of the best perks of my situation.'

'I've nothing to give or I'd pay you to keep me *out* of his way.'

'Oh, very good! You think me conceited. But be fair, I didn't exaggerate my powers to that extent. He's the head of the house. He wants something, he helps himself.'

When she'd faced losing her freedom she'd reckoned on many evils, but not this. It hadn't occurred to her. She saw now that she'd been warned. There'd been hints but they'd been veiled and she too innocent to understand.

'What your master asks is impossible.'

'Who do you think you are? What's your price?'

'I'm not for sale. Don't you understand?'

'No one could understand that. Just behave reasonably and I'm authorised to offer his forgiveness – his love even.'

Love! She'd never imagined herself in love and had the vaguest idea of how it might be, but it wasn't to be taken bent over a table by an arrogant bully as heedlessly as he tossed off cheap wine.

'Tell him,' she said 'I should find his love as loathsome as his lust.'

'I wouldn't dare tell him such a thing. But those who have their ears to that curtain - they'll tell him, probably before we've finished this conversation. What are you trying to do? Have you neither sense nor discretion?'

Indeed, she'd forgotten that, for a slave, there was no such thing as a private conversation. She lowered her voice.

'Is he the sort of man who enjoys forcing himself on a girl who detests him?'

He seemed dazed. At last he said slowly, 'No, I think he's not.'

'Then if he has any delicacy whatever, he'll leave me to my grief and busy himself where he's welcome. Will you tell him that?'

His insouciance finally deserted him, his lip curled.

'Of course he has delicacy but I see no call for him to use it on kitchen sluts.'

'Even so, would you ask him, no, beg him, to excuse me?'

He frowned.

'I'll try to make him a reasonable answer but he'll hear of your insolence which he hasn't deserved. You presume too much on his forbearance.'

As she followed him out the crowd shrank away as if her defiance would contaminate them.

Polybius would repeat her scornful words to Demetrius. They might well cool his passion, as she'd intended but, if they made him wonder why his kitchen drudge was arrogant and articulate, she'd be in mortal danger. What would he do about the loss of his priceless vase? Evidently, he was a man of measured response but he'd be no less resolute for that. The penalty for offering violence to a supervisor was death, preceded by torture. Whether this penalty was, like the best baths, reserved for males, she didn't know, never having heard of a master being felled by a maid. But the full story, if public, wouldn't add to his dignity, a consideration that seemed to be giving him pause. He might decide to let the matter drop. She would help by staying out of his way; keep to the back kitchen and the dormitory. He'd hardly demean himself to come to such places.

CHAPTER V

April 171

Contrahere agrestes et moenia ponere utrique convenit sacra Palis suberant ; inde movitur opus

The twins decided to assemble the shepherds and build a city. It was at the Parilia that the work began. Ovid Fasti IV 810 820

Religious observance was regular and strict in Lucius Marius' house. He, or in his absence, Demetrius, presided over daily prayers, attended by superior servants. The humble prayed at their work stations led by their overseers. All prayed together on feast days. The Parilia, or Shepherds' Festival, was an important feast; not because city dwellers cared about shepherds but because it was the anniversary of the founding of Rome.

Standing before an altar in the yard, Demetrius drew a fold of his cloak over his head and prepared to make the traditional offerings. The household was marshalled in awed silence before a forest of statues. Polished marble busts of deified emperors; Augustus, Pius and Verus surrounded the golden boy that was the master's genius. A winged silver Hermes was hemmed in by the gods of the hearth; wood and terracotta, crude but antique. An acolyte held the scroll open because Demetrius wouldn't risk reciting the ritual from memory. If he stumbled over any syllable he'd have to begin again from the beginning and even that might not save the house from bad luck.

As he raised his hands and spoke the solemn but unnecessary warning, 'Favete linguis' 'assist me by your silence', he cast an eagle eye over his troops. In the back ranks eight litter-bearers, of matching, impressive height, torch bearers, grooms and coachmen, stokers and porters, carpenters and plumbers. In front of them cooks, waiters and sommeliers. Next came scribes, secretaries and librarians, then post boys and messengers, launderers and pages. All present. All neatly turned out. All silent and respectful. Next he checked the women; receptionists, florists, seamstresses, nurses, cleaners and skivvies. The master had his personal servants with him but, even thus depleted, the household was almost two hundred strong. Each member could take rightful pride in their particular skill and immaculate appearance. Demetrius felt proud too, not least, of his own contribution to the prosperity and efficiency of the household.

Scanning the rows of bowed, black heads, he missed that white face set in a gilt frame. Her colouring reminded him of the Athena in the Parthenon but the features were alien. The nose, in particular, concave rather than convex, gave her an expression of pert enquiry. If she'd been a statue he'd been charged with transporting, he'd have ordered extra lamb's wool and raffia round that nose, so finely chiselled and fragile.

His stream of unintelligible words dried up. He looked down at the scroll. Where was he? What had he last said? The ritual was in old Etruscan. No one had a clue what it meant. The slaves couldn't tell if he made a mistake. But they'd have noted the hesitation and would have no difficulty connecting it with any subsequent run of bad luck. Besides, he owed it to Lucius to perform his duties perfectly. Back he went to the beginning, hunching his shoulders over the scroll.

Where was she? Her only excuse would be illness, but, in that case, the infirmarians should be with her. He glanced up. They were both in the yard. The guard on his left read his mind. Muttering, 'Little bitch! Absconded!', he lunged forward and ran towards the house. Not to be outdone, the guard on the right shot after him, striking the table a glancing blow with his hip. Demetrius reacted promptly but failed to stop it overturning. He shot out a foot and saved Verus. (Which, he wondered, was the greater sacrilege; to let the god hit the ground or to scoop him onto a servile toe?) Other gods did bite dirt, bouncing and rolling over the cobbles. Acolytes scrambled after them and Successus, his deputy, moved close and whispered, 'Everything will be purified and repolished, sir. With your permission, I'll see to it myself.'

The gods were collected, wrapped in a purple altar cloth and borne tenderly away. Demetrius paced along the ranks of flustered slaves to ensure decorum and, from time to time, checked on the advance of a threatening cloud. As a new cloth was spread and the gods were reverently replaced, he saw Nerysa bundled into line. One guard stayed beside her and the other returned to his place by the altar. Demetrius nodded to Successus and signed to the flautists who gulped for air and played at full blast to cover any extraneous sound. At this third attempt, he recited the prayer flawlessly but, as he arranged the millet offerings methodically on the silver paten, he was conscious that every slave in the house was watching him driven to distraction by a kitchen maid. Beneath their respectfully bowed shoulders, they were hugging the knowledge to themselves until they were released to tattle about it.

It was six years since he'd first come to the house, broken in body and spirit, despised by one half of it and resented by the other. Now he had complete authority and everyone's respect. He must not lose them.

CHAPTER VI

April 171

Tument tibi cum inguina, num si, ancilla aut verna est praesto puer, impetus in quem continuo fiat, malis tentigine rumpi?

If your lust is hot and a maid or boy is handy to attack you won't choose to grin and bear it. Horace satires 1.2.116

Nerysa stood before the steward again waiting for his wrath to descend and thinking that Quintus, who found nothing so amusing as religion, might have warned her that the house was a repository of old fashioned piety.

As the steward was absorbed in a sheaf of bills on his great carved table, she set herself to admire his room. Her eyes wandered over the barrel-vaulted ceiling and down to the wittiest wall paintings she'd ever seen. There was a quayside, unremarkable until you saw that the dockers were cupids with pudgy, pink bodies and filmy wings. They swarmed up gangplanks rolling barrels, staggered bow-legged under cases and dragged sacks. Their burdens landed in the sea more often than on the decks. Their attempts to weigh and measure caused chaos at the customs shed and they let loose a monkey among spice jars and bales of silk in a warehouse. In a banking hall, they scattered piles of coin while they calculated interest on a crooked gold abacus.

Was the artist laughing *at* the steward or *with* him? Off duty, did this man have what passed, among his own kind, for a sense of humour? Surely no one with a sense of fun could take the gods seriously?

In the centre of the long, unbroken wall was a map of the world, where Britain was a squat triangle squashed into the top left hand corner. On the left was a sea-scape where the naked cupids surged up the ropes and sails of a golden vessel, posed astride the figurehead and fought over the golden helm. To the right of the map they were farmhands. Some stood, some sat, under an awning, receiving laden baskets of tribute from the tenants and helping themselves to the choicest morsels while recording rents on huge tablets.

The final tableau was the liveliest and filled the high, arched wall behind the steward's table. Cupids loaded grapes in baskets. Bulbous legs purple to the thighs; they leapt on vats, stirred juice in steaming cauldrons, played pipes and drank like bacchanals. The scene was so vivid, she caught a whiff of grape must and fancied she could stretch out her hand and wipe the bloom from the fruit.

The steward looked up and, fleetingly, his expression softened, as if her admiration of his paintings pleased him. Then he looked pointedly downwards. She followed his gaze to the coils of a leather strap on the table and felt a wave of contempt; sure that he didn't usually keep a whip on his table. He'd put it there to frighten her. And he'd taken care to protect himself on this occasion; guards stood along the walls, still and expressionless as Atlantes.

'What am I to do with you?' he asked. 'Profaning religious rites is a crime against the gods and the state. Ignorance is no excuse. Your impiety could rebound on the whole household.'

He leant forward and, deliberately or not, his tone demonstrated how to hold a private conversation in a crowded room without sounding furtive.

'This is a sober, pious house. Dealing in potions, curses – that sort of thing – is strictly forbidden and carries heavy penalties. Did you know that?'

'All that I know of such things is that they are forbidden.'

'Then there is your public defiance of me in …another matter. What do you mean by that? Do you know that I could have your back cut to ribbons with the lash?'

This didn't seem to call for a reply. He leant back now, perhaps to emphasise that he had a chair with a back, an impressive status symbol. He joined his hands at the finger tips and looked up at her.

'How long have you been a slave?' he asked.

'Three months in this house.'

'And before that?'

'As I believe I told you, I was with Quintus Fabius Pulcher.'

'I understand that gentleman runs an irregular household but, even there, you must have learned what's expected of a slave. Why do you suppose you came here?'

'To work in the kitchen, and I do. I work well – ask Arminia. Why should I have to do...anything else?'

'What you have to do is whatever I say, as soon as I say it, because that's the way this house works. That doesn't mean I want to be cruel to you – or to anyone else, for that matter. What would be the point?'

The question must have been rhetorical. He began again, 'I've often thought it must be hard to be freeborn and enslaved. To lose freedom suddenly, perhaps brutally, might be harder than never having known it. The adjustment must be painful, certainly.'

What an unpredictable man! Sympathy was the last thing she'd expected.

'Perhaps you lost a sweetheart?' he probed. 'It will be easier for you to accept that your old life is over - as if you'd died. You can never go back to it and friends from that life are lost forever.'

She shook her head involuntarily.

'But you haven't fallen on a bad house. Your attitude is your worst enemy. Have you no more sense than a moth that batters broken wings against a lantern? Your enslavement is a fact. Accept it and start to live again.'

'I'm not pining for a lover if that's what you think. I never had one or any wish for one.'

He gave an odd laugh, closer to nervousness than anything she'd heard from him.

'You don't expect me to believe you left Quintus Pulcher's house a *virgin*?'

'Whether you believe it or not, it's the truth.'

'It's no secret he likes boys but he'd hardly deny himself the pleasure of deflowering his own housemaids.'

'As to that, I can't say. As far as I was concerned, he had no such interest.'

'We've been at cross purposes. I thought you willing. But you must see I can't let you make a fool of me in this house. This can only end one way. You open up the grate and I rake out the coals.'

She sensed his unease with his own crude language and knew he used it to remind her that she was the lowest of the low. He embroidered the insult in silken tones.

'Naturally, I'll dismiss the guards while I deal with you but I fear that door is not impervious to prying eyes.'

'I will never, never do that'.

He smiled. 'Oh, I think you will. Once you concede that I give the orders here, not you, we can begin again. You may not find me unforgiving.'

He took up a stylus and moved it idly over a tablet as he said,

'I have an arrangement with our neighbour, Publius Cornelius Surdus. The basement of his house is equipped with all modern instruments of discipline and he, himself, is hard of hearing. Here's a letter, asking him to have you whipped. I'll allow you some time to consider. Consult your fellow kitchen maids. They're hardly professors of philosophy but I think, in this matter, they'll give you sound advice. I'll see you again in...' his forefinger flicked beads across the abacus, 'seven days, when you'll either obey me or deliver this letter. Do you understand?'

'Perfectly.'

'Perfectly...sir. You may go for now.' he said, 'But don't act the tragic muse. It's hardly a calamity - to be noticed by a man in my position.'

CHAPTER VII

April 171

τῷ δ᾽ ἁπλῷ καὶ θυμικῷ πολὺ τὸ ἀνόητον καὶἀλαζονικὸν πρόσεστι καὶ τὸ φιλόκοσμον:
χρυσοφοροῦσί τε γάρ, περὶ μὲν τοῖς τραχήλοις στρεπτὰ ἔχοντεςπερὶ δὲ τοῖς βραχίοσι καὶ
τοῖς καρποῖς ψέλια, καὶ τὰςἐσθῆτας βαπτὰς φοροῦσι καὶ χρυσοπάστους οἱ ἐν ἀξιώματι.
ὑπὸ τῆς τοιαύτης δὲ κουφότητος ἀφόρητοι μὲννικῶντες, ἐκπλαγεῖς δ᾽ ἡττηθέντες ὁρῶνται

Britons are simple, high-spirited and boastful. They're fond of ornament; for they not
only wear golden neck chains and bracelets, their notables wear garments sprinkled with
gold. Strabo Geography 4 4 5

Polybius, the steward's boy, was everyone's favourite. He had
a sweet expression and graceful manners and glowed with
the confidence of a valued servant. The most potent of his charms,
however, was his closeness to the steward. From his makeshift bed in
his master's cubicle, he observed his restless nights and the household
gossip worried him.

Demetrius was touched by the boy's ingenuity. Wherever he went
in the house, he found a girl in a short tunic bending over furniture;
cleaning, adjusting, pretending to be busy. He wasn't amused for long.
He'd lost his appetite for any of them and began to think he must be
ill. One longing gnawed at him, displacing all other interests, even
his work. All night, Nerysa's name throbbed in his ears and her smile
receded into the darkness. In that smile, there had been, beside its
sweetness, something tantalisingly familiar that gave him no peace.
As letters, bills and records mounted on his table he delegated more to
the secretaries, knew they noticed and doubted they were up to it. He
didn't recognise himself. Love, for him, was a series of sudden urges

swiftly discharged. He exhausted his mind with work and his body with exercise, soothed away the day's vexation in well-earned luxury, slept like the dead and woke remade. Love couldn't explain his state of mind. If he couldn't work he must be sick.

Superstition wasn't his first recourse but, once Polybius had begun to mutter about sorcery, he couldn't laugh it off. Dabbling in sorcery by the unskilled could cause loss of reason and perhaps she was mad. How else could he reconcile the poignant sweetness of her smile with the savage violence of her behaviour?

He had her dormitory searched and the staff questioned but he didn't turn up any useful information, any locks of hair or a single owl's feather. The vegetables she prepared were for slaves' pottage. She had no contact with food destined for his table. As a newcomer, she wasn't allowed outside the house. She saw no one but her kitchen colleagues. Her only possessions were a toothbrush and a sweat cloth. It pained him that she'd only two mean possessions. Didn't she realise how much she had to gain from a liaison with him? Perhaps she did and that was why she worked evil magic on him. But, if so, she was doing it without an outside accomplice and with none of the standard equipment. An accomplice inside the house? An unlikely but serious possibility.

His household functioned because everyone accepted its hierarchy, as he did himself. How did a system cope with a misfit who rejected its basic premises? Brutality was distasteful to him and her improbable mixture of defencelessness and defiance made him ache to protect her.

Well, he'd said enough to bring her to heel. When she came to him, docile and trembling, he'd take her to the shelter of his cubicle and surprise her with tenderness. The house gossips didn't need to witness her initiation. Her face, slackened with pleasure, was all they needed to see. Once he'd tamed her, he'd like to get to know her. Remembering that some basic details would have been recorded when she came to the house, he turned up the log book. The entry was in Successus' cramped hand.

12 days before the Ides of January Female servant - Nerysa
Age - 18 years
House born? – no.
Origin - Mona, Britain.

Previous owner - Q Fabius Pulcher - ownership attested.

Health - apparently sound.

Distinguishing marks - hair red.

Temperament - nothing unfavourable declared.

Special skills — none. Defects - none declared N.B. Account not settled.

He read travel guides. Some told him the sun didn't rise in Britain for more than half the year and the ground was frozen until June; others that, although the land never saw the sun, it was warmed by miraculous ocean currents. The natives were vicious head-hunters who practised human sacrifice and they were terrifying warriors - the women even more formidable than the men. Most of this he discounted. But he noted that Britons loved ornament, especially gold.

CHAPTER VIII

April 171

Haec quoque quam poteris credere nolle, volet

She says she won't but she will. Ovid Ars amatoria I 274

Nerysa knew that everything she'd said and done since she met Demetrius had made her situation more dangerous but she conceded that he'd found a good way out for both of them. She'd take a whipping, his face would be saved. She'd be an outcast and left in peace. There were downsides. She might be scarred. Was that so bad? If she was unmarriageable she could stay with Quintus forever, which was what she'd always wanted.

'Take a whipping' was simple enough to say. Britons were renowned for physical courage but hers had never been put to the test. In earlier times it might have fallen to her to lead her people into battle against Romans but what could you do if you were alone in their great city with no army to lead?

The ever-turning cycle of work and sleep calmed her but she dreaded the communal meal with its ribaldry and coarse laughter, most of which was directed at her, and the giggling dormitory where the girls stared at her, trying to discern what it was about her that pleased the man they all wanted to attract, and failing, yet again, to find it.

She prayed to the gods she'd once served fervently and met the bleak void of their indifference. They'd deserted her just as her own people had. To crowd out the terror, she crammed her mind with thoughts; Latin and Greek poetry, her own native sagas, and wondered if philosophy could help soothe physical pain. Perhaps she should have given more time to it and less to literature.

When off duty, she retreated to a corner of the yard. Never inured to the Roman summer, she longed for a dank mist to roll down a mountain and engulf her. She'd conjure one in her imagination and, for a blessed moment, she was bathed in a delicious cool but the illusion soon faded and lukewarm, foetid air filled her lungs again. She watched the play of shadows on the tawny brick wall; fluttering shadows of butterflies, swaying shadows of branches, bustling shadows of passing slaves. A longer shadow fell on the wall and over her. Polybius reminded her of his name and position and held up a small flask in the shape of a tear drop. He spun it, so light shimmered from the iridescent aquamarine glass, then slid it into her hand.

'Nerysa, I wasn't told to say this but you should know this perfume is worth a great deal so, you see, my master sends it as a token of his esteem.'

She laid it on the wall and forgot its existence. The boy's manner didn't deceive her. Because of him, everyone knew what was to happen to her and when. He'd charted every keyhole and crack in the office door and rented them out for the occasion. It was the only topic of conversation until the household was diverted by the return of its master. Of course, the lower slaves didn't see him or even venture onto his side of the house but they worked hard for his comfort and news filtered down to them that his business had prospered. The day before Nerysa was to meet the steward, he gave a dinner for his freedmen and clients. The girls worked all day and then oil lamps, swung from the ceiling, sent shoals of cockroaches clacketting for cover and allowed them to work a late shift. Nerysa swayed on her feet as she made for her bed, her eyes smarting from the smoke. There were perhaps three hours until dawn. It was as well she felt weak, she'd faint sooner under the lash. Iris stroked her arm and whispered, 'Lucky you! I wish it was me. I won't get another chance. I lost my temper once when I didn't know he was watching.'

'Another chance did you say?'

'I went to him once. And the master more than once. He noticed me, at Tivoli, but I was too young and he waited 'till I was thirteen.'

Her face was in shadow but there was no mistaking the pride in her soft voice.

What's the master like?' Nerysa asked.

'The master? As beautiful as the statues of Antinous and kind even to his slaves.'

'And they all love him! Even me. I've never seen him and I'm supposed to love him.'

'Wherever were you brought up that you didn't learn to love your master?'

'I didn't have a master. I haven't always been a slave.'

'That must be hard. They say the freeborn prefer death to slavery.'

'No.' said Nerysa firmly, 'Anything is better than being dead.'

'And life's not bad here, is it? Imagine being on the grand side of the house, wearing fine clothes and meeting elegant guests. I copy those girls; the way they walk, the way they speak. There's something special about you, too. I'm not surprised our steward took to you. You've such pretty ways. Not so grand as theirs perhaps, but the way you tilt up your head before you lower it, the way your fingers flutter; so pretty.'

'I don't want to be on the grand side of the house, just to be near the kitchen and smell the bread coming out of the oven. That's a slave's pleasure. Masters don't go to the kitchen.'

'Mistresses sometimes do - looking for faults to find. There's another blessing – there's no mistress in this house.'

'But there's a garden full of flowers and birdsong. I'll be glad to be alive, even as a slave, once tomorrow's over.'

'You mind it, don't you, being a slave? We don't keep freeborn ones. They're the roughest sort from outside the empire. But Britain's in the empire isn't it?'

'Yes, but my people rebelled.'

'Nerysa, don't offend him again. I'm afraid for you, you're so... unpredictable.'

'Forgive me, Iris, I'll treat with the enemy in my own way.'

'But he's not an enemy! Think what he could do for you!'

'Romans are my enemies.'

'Demetrius isn't a Roman. A slave doesn't have a country.'

'I do.'

'No, you don't. You *were* a Briton, his mother *was* a Greek.'

'His nose is Roman enough.'

'Well his tool's not hooked if that's what worries you.'

Iris seemed to find this thought hilarious and giggled herself to sleep.

CHAPTER IX

April 171

mihi quam profitebar amare laesa est

I've hurt the girl I claimed to love. Ovid. Amores I 7

The master's garden was a blessed place, beloved of those superior slaves whose business took them through its scented porticoes. It was Demetrius' unique privilege to walk on the hand-trimmed grass. He could sit on marble benches under gnarled apple trees, watching the blossom float to a mosaic carpet or stand beside basins of green marble where dragonflies hovered above rippling water and silver carp darted beneath. The garden's sounds were soothing – the birdsong, the rustle of aspens, the drone of bees, the splash of the fountains.

But, on this occasion, he hadn't come for the balm of nature. He was in search of a person; the one to whom he always turned and who always turned to him in times of crisis. Though sure of his master's love, it was his rule never to presume on it or to overstep the limit of acceptable behaviour in a slave. If Lucius had been busy, he wouldn't have disturbed him, so he was relieved to find him reclining on a day bed.

Intercepting the waiter, he took charge of the tray of wine and spice cakes and strode across the lawn. He set down the tray with a carefully judged, slight sound. The master's eyes stayed shut and he lay still as the lizards, basking on his grey stone walls. The travel and the dinner party had taken their toll. It wasn't the right moment.

Demetrius bowed and retreated across the grass. A sleepy drawl brought him back.

'Good of you to play the butler! Have you put away the ledgers for today?'

'Shall I send for an awning, master? The heat is oppressive.'

'Spare me the chatty boys with their clattering tent poles. I'd rather wilt.'

'Would this be a convenient time to speak with you, sir, on a domestic matter?'

Lucius extended a limp hand for the wine cup.

'Provided you can do it here. It would be cruel to move me.'

Demetrius had wanted the seclusion of the locked tablinum where he could, sometimes, even sit in his master's presence. The garden wasn't private. He'd have to stand. Well, he reflected, that might be best. He wasn't proud of what he had to say. At least it was their habit to speak in Greek between themselves.

'Very good. Master, I hadn't thought it necessary to mention it, but we…we had some slight trouble in the house while you were away.'

There was no reply. Lucius, having achieved a comfortable position, blinked into his wine.

'A trivial matter, master, to begin with. A kitchen hand I took a fancy to.'

Lucius shut his eyes. Demetrius struggled to be more concise and became less so.

'I can't explain the effect she had on me. I've considered love potions or sorcery, some such device. She turned out to be a barbarian, new and raw. Even so, I wasn't overbearing. I liked her. I had her taken to the baths, I gave her –'

'Demetrie. let's be clear. Are you saying you sent for a kitchen hand and she snubbed you?'

'More or less.'

'She's feeble minded.'

'I don't think so. She had the wit to make a fool of me. The house was in uproar. I got Surdus' slaves to whip her.'

Lucius exuded boredom. A butterfly landed on his cheek. He eased it aside as though even this exertion drained him.

'Bravo! You want me to commend you?'

'Master, she's badly injured. Thaïs is concerned.'

The patrician brow wrinkled.

'Come to the point, Demetrie. Since when do I interfere with your running of my affairs? Flogging slaves to death is not my style but, if you choose to do it, that's up to you. Providing you tried and sentenced her legally?'

'Of course, master; insolence, insubordination, disruption of religious rites, assaulting a superior...'

'Hermes, Demetrie! Why do you keep a slave like that in my house? I doubt if she'll be missed but, if she is, replace her. I expect you'll find one even more attractive. Had I noticed her, by the way?'

'You knew of her. You took her at New Year from Quintus Pulcher.'

Lucius swung down his legs and set the cup on the tray in one lithe movement.

'God's thunder, Demetrie! What have you done? She's not my slave.'

'N..not yours, master?'

'She belongs to Quintus Pulcher.'

'Still belongs to him?'

'While you were in Aquileia, he asked me to lodge her. I don't remember exactly how the matter stands. I should have mentioned it when you got back but we had to other matters to discuss.'

Only a barbarian invasion! When did that last happen? Three hundred years ago?'

'I was sick with worry over you. Could you really not have sent word that you were alive?'

'There was no one but myself to send it with.'

'Well, I probably didn't listen properly to Pulcher. He asked me to take the girl off his hands and I did. He wouldn't have got past you so easily. Mind you, he never said she was wild, just a misfit. The wonder is that he should care. I'd better see the damage for myself.'

'They've put her in the preserving room but there's no need for you to go, master. I'm sure the women have exaggerated.'

Lucius was already hurrying across the garden.

The bustle and the murmur of voices stilled as they entered the room; the slaves saluted and all but Thaïs, the chief slave mistress, fell back against the wall. Demetrius watched Lucius survey the scoured wooden table, white snood, white neck and slight prone figure under a white sheet. It looked an unlikely source of uproar. Lucius signed to Thaïs to draw back the sheet. He flinched and looked up sharply.

'How many lashes did you order?'

Demetrius gripped the table.

'Six.'

Lucius whistled. 'A fair number for a small girl.'

'Not in view of the seriousness of the offence, master. But I didn't expect…she could have…why would anyone *choose* this?'

'What puzzles me is how six lashes could make such an appalling mess.'

'That's what I've been trying to tell you, master. I can't understand.'

'Either Pulcher or I has an action against Surdus, but we must send for a surgeon whoever pays. I might, perhaps, persuade Pulcher his girlfriend deserved beating to death but he'd take a dim view if she died without a surgeon.'

'Marcus Archias is on his way, master…I took the liberty..'

'You did take a liberty and how you - of all people…'

Demetrius winced. Lucius was furious. Not for the girl's plight but for his own embarrassment. Thaïs replaced the sheet over her body which had begun to twitch.

'Master, would you permit me to withdraw? I'm not well.' Dismissed by the slightest wave of his master's hand, Demetrius fled and, with no time to reach his own quarters, hurled himself into the slaves' latrines and vomited as though his guts would turn inside out. Between bouts he dared not leave but sat, shivering and sweating, on the stone bench, from where he couldn't fail to see the graffiti. A surprising amount of it referred to the love of stewards for kitchen maids. His name and Nerysa's were coupled with a variety of obscene symbols. Crude sketches of her were daubed with an orange mane and the blue paint the artist evidently thought of as her national costume. He was startled, though not displeased, by the supposed size of his own endowment.

He was aware, too, of slaves occupied on other seats, who could be relied on to broadcast what they'd seen. So well that, by the time he reached his room, Polybius had already prepared a mouthwash. The boy was silent, at a loss for anything inoffensive to say. He poured wine, prepared the bed in case his master wished to rest and averted his eyes from his master's shaking hands.

Demetrius dismissed him, sat and lowered his head into his hands. Fleetingly, he caught the scent of the precious oil he'd used that morning which led him to compare the day he'd planned with the day as it had turned out.

After all that had passed between them, he would have been shy of conversation but, with his body, he must have shown her how completely she obsessed him. No woman could have resisted such a tribute. Later, he'd have advised her how to earn promotion and escape drudgery. She was disoriented by the change in her fortunes and who better than himself to help her make the best of them? By now, passion spent, they should have been holding each other, sharing sweet wine. Listening to her history, probing and comforting by turns, he would have dispelled all misunderstanding. He'd chosen the day deliberately; the first day of the Floralia, a festival when it was the custom to spoil one's women. On the seventh and last day he'd planned to take her out and buy her some jewellery.

But now she was dying on a kitchen table. Her bones, whiter even than her skin, would be slid into an urn. Every year, when he took the slave family to the monument to pray for the spirits of their dead, his eyes would stray to that urn in its niche and he'd remember. He grasped the jug and gulped the wine undiluted, bullying his brain with the same questions. Why had he wanted her so much and why had she schemed to attract him, only to bring disaster on herself?

The flurry of activity due to the surgeon's arrival broke in on his thoughts. Without conscious intent, he followed the party of slaves accompanying Archias and his assistants. The crowd fell back for him to enter the room but he signalled his wish to wait outside. For as long as he could remember, the room had been used for preserving. A subtle perfume of rose petals, fruit, honey and sweet herbs had seeped into its walls. It floated out to him and choked him with nostalgia. A stool was set in the alcove and the wine he ordered came promptly. He was surprised to hear Lucius' voice inside the room.

'Not here, Archias, at Surdus' place. Questioning his people, it seems Demetrius did give written orders, but the word 'servant', abbreviated, could refer to either sex. One of Surdus' own slaves had an order for thirty lashes and the notes got confused. We can't sue because our orders weren't clear. The men admit they didn't check the signature though they were shocked to have to punish a girl so harshly and they drugged her first.'

'They did well, but the effects are wearing off. I'll give another draught straight away. What does your excellency expect? I'm a medic, not a magician.'

'I don't expect miracles but she's not my property. I can't let her die without a surgeon.'

'I'll make her comfortable and then see if there's anything else worth doing. You'll want the wounds salted to prevent festering if she survives a few days? Festering wounds...smell bad...make nursing unpleasant.'

'I never saw an army surgeon use salt. Have you nothing kinder?'

'I've copper and alum certainly but it's expensive. I couldn't cover her back for less than six hundred.'

'Do it. I suppose a barbarian might feel pain almost as we do.'

Demetrius struggled to his feet as Lucius swept past then fell back on the stool. He couldn't enter the room but nor could he leave the threshold. Polybius, having missed him all night and all the next day, consulted with the master. Lucius could imagine the effect on his household if the major domo stayed unwashed and unshaven outside a menial's sickroom. He shed his elegant languor like a stale tunic.

'It's no use trying to sleep with such excitement in the house.' he told him. 'Tell them to fill the lamps and leave out my tablets for lucubration. I may as well draft a speech. Take him a flask of his favourite with enough hellebore in it to keep him under until the... unpleasantness is over.'

CHAPTER X

April – May 171

Qui nimis cupit solvere invitus debit ; qui invitus debet ingratus est.

He who is too eager to pay his debt is unwilling to be indebted and he who is unwilling to be indebted is ungrateful. Seneca Morales III IV xl

It was the eighth hour and the house was heavy with sleep. Shutters banned the light but not the heat, or the flies, which Polybius was warding from his master's face with a swan's feather. He slid from the bed, took a pole, prodded open the shutter and eased back the curtain, allowing a narrow stream of light onto the polished floor. Coming back to the bed he looked down at Demetrius and, after a moment's hesitation, bent and kissed him full on the mouth, not with the light-hearted mockery he used for women, but with a solemn tenderness. He smiled as Demetrius opened his eyes.

'The best of health to you, dear master.'

Demetrius pressed a hand to his forehead and worked his mouth sluggishly. Polybius mixed water and wine and gave it to him.

'The girl?'

'She's being cared for. Marcus Archias is quite taken with her. Says she's as brave as a bear - or something equally primitive.'

'How long have I slept?'

'Best part of two days.'

Demetrius stood and grasped the bed frame to steady himself.

'I'll see Archias myself.'

Polybius reached for the razor.

'Our Lucius wants you as soon as you're fit to be seen.'

Demetrius felt ill at ease in the tablinum. Its seclusion allowed him a degree of informality but it was the sacred hearth of the clan and he didn't belong. It seemed that the ancestors didn't fully cede the hallowed place even to Lucius; as though the love between them didn't draw Demetrius into the family so much as estrange Lucius from it. The gentlemen of the busts and portraits stared coldly down at them and, when they lay laughing in each other's arms, disapproval seemed to coalesce into a single, chilling frown.

On this occasion Demetrius must first appease even Lucius. Other projects depended on how well he could do that. He waited an hour before visitors were ushered out and he was admitted. To his relief, Lucius signed to him to bolt the door and tapped the couch, inviting him to sit.

'I trust you slept well.'

'Too well!'

'I've been busy enough for two.' Lucius said. 'Pulcher doesn't claim the girl – says he meant her as a present. However, under the circumstances, we'd better pay him the market price. Draw up a bill of sale and get the cash to him today. Then, he'll have no right to ask questions, whatever he hears.'

'I will, master.'

'Attend to it personally will you? And delicately. To settle a small debt so promptly might well offend him and he's a senior senator.'

'I'll see his steward myself. Quintus Simo, I think, a freedman.'

'He'd be grateful, by the way, if we didn't mention to anyone how we came by her and, indeed, I wouldn't want this to get back to his people. Ill-treating slaves – not a reputation one aspires to.'

'Master, I'm wretched - the whole affair - I didn't manage it as you've a right to expect.'

'Demetrie, what have I ever had to reproach you with? Only that whim about buying your freedom which keeps us both waiting on the thing we want most. I don't blame you for this. Barbarian women can't be tamed, even with kindness. They're more difficult to handle than their men folk. Remember those Germans killing themselves and their own children rather than give service in civilised houses? Extraordinary!

'I'm sure you did your best with her. But send your boy down to ask after her. Then forget her. Even if she survives, those scars won't be pretty.'

'I never thought her pretty, exactly. I don't know why she obsesses me.'

'Don't you? I do. She didn't fawn on you. Being Pulcher's minx gave her delusions of grandeur.'

'She wasn't Pulcher's minx. She says she's a virgin.'

Lucius laughed until he gasped for breath.

'Coming from that house, she wouldn't know the meaning of the word! Demetrie, you were never that gullible, even as a boy.'

'We're not boys now, master. You're burdened with your career and I with your fortune.'

'If that's a burden you've only yourself to blame since you keep growing it. As for my career, you'll be proud to know I'm appearing in court again next month, in defence of my client, Marcus Marius Bibulus.'

'Has that scoundrel a reasonable case this time?'

'Not a bit, so a successful defence will be the more impressive. He's pursued by a certain Varus, a small-time building contractor who happened to stroll along the street below Bibulus' flat.'

'Don't tell me! Bibulus emptied his pisspot on him.'

'Well, it's alleged that someone on the balcony let a pot and contents fall on Varus' head. Bibulus claims he was in the country and had let the flat out.'

'Who to?'

'He can't remember.'

Demetrius groaned, 'How many people actually saw him in Rome that day?'

'Varus will bring witnesses to say they visited him at home that very day. But he maintains he's been unable to work since the accident and claims loss of earnings, whereas our witnesses have seen him many times, hodding bricks, driving carts and going to the games, seemingly in the pink of health. I think we'll be able to discredit him so completely he'll lose the case and forfeit even his medical expenses.'

'And his laundry bill?'

'That too. And, of course, the law allows him nothing for his broken head since the body of a free man is beyond price. Let's write the speech together. Your reason and my passion. Always a winning combination.

'Zeus! It's time I heard you laugh again. Here's a scurrilous verse I had from Quintus this morning. By the way, he made me a handsome offer for your Polybius. No, don't look dismayed; you'd have to gamble away half my fortune before I'd want to make money that way!'

CHAPTER XI ·

Vae victis!

Woe to the vanquished! Livy. History V. xiii 9

Nerysa floated in and out of consciousness uncertain as to which house she lay in. The screams of her fellow sufferers still rang in her ears. As long as she held still, the pain felt strangely far away and, through it, new truths pierced her consciousness. A free man was guilty when a jury had sifted the evidence and heard the blandishments of his patron. A slave was broken on the rack until he confirmed his master's suspicions. Slaves were whining and deceitful by nature but how should they be otherwise?

Her injuries were not battle scars in an epic struggle against oppression. They were the shameful, indelible marks of slavery. Quintus had been right. Death wasn't the ultimate evil. She'd been so sure of herself. Yet all she'd had to do was lie low and she'd failed, letting a clash of wills with Demetrius draw the curious attention of the whole house. But he was also to blame. His life was comfortable and secure. Need he have trampled on the ruins of hers?

It was typical of Quintus not to have emphasised the danger of her plan to himself but, if she were discovered, he would be ruined. Though she was beyond rescue, Quintus shouldn't suffer because of her misjudgement. She must keep her secret, if only to protect him.

Get back to the kitchen and stay dumb and humble until she was forgotten.

As her condition improved, people stopped whispering round her. High ranking slaves, like Thaïs, disappeared and were replaced by the two seamstresses who doubled as infirmarians. Arminia came and clucked over her maternally, which made her squirm. She couldn't look her in the eye but forced herself to ask, 'Did they punish you because of me? Did they...?'

'Just my savings they fine but they not much. No matter.'

Nerysa understood. There wouldn't be too many open handed gentlemen coming to the back kitchen to tip you for running errands or getting them access to the master.

'I'll pay you back one day, I promise.'

'The kitchen miss you, dear. You good slave whatever they say. No need be afraid. Arminia keep eye out for you. When they say you back on duty?'

'No one's said anything yet.'

'No, well, slaves good treated in this house - not made get up and serve when they sick. We have you back very pleased.'

'Thank you. I hope it's soon.'

She never saw the steward but Polybius was often at the doorway. Once he came into the room.

'Well!' he said, shaking his head. 'You gave us a nasty fright.'

'*I* gave *you* a nasty fright?'

'You were very poorly, you know. My master wants to give you a present. Tell me what you'd like to have.'

'I'd like to have an unscarred back.'

'The reason you're impossible to deal with is that you're too dim to see your own interest. Don't you understand he'd give you anything reasonable you asked? I don't say he'd buy your freedom but, if you'd any sense, that's what you'd be angling for.'

'How generous of him! I'm not worth much - especially with a scarred back.'

'It would cost him more than your miserable worth. He could hardly throw you on the world to earn a living. He'd have to give you an annuity or a dowry.'

'I don't want his patronage.'

'You're not thinking clearly. I'll come back when you feel better.'

Archias came every day with his students. He told them how to make scars fine and neat, how to control pain and bleeding, the danger of contaminating wounds. Fascinated, Nerysa couldn't help interrupting, 'In Britain we have a vegetable juice we rub on skin to stop battle wounds festering, But you use copper ointment. Two quite different things for the same purpose. How is that?'

He turned to her with raised eyebrows but he didn't say that medical lectures were for the benefit of students not patients.

'There are many ways to prevent suppuration; heat; as with poultices or cautery; salt, honey, wine, even lavender oil. I hope you're as grateful as you should be. Your master bought you the best treatment there is.'

It was frustrating that she wouldn't be able to join the students and inspect her own back to see the ointment's effect. How long before the bandages could be removed? He laughed into his flowing beard.

'Time is the doctor's most powerful remedy but he can only use it if he also has patience.'

When the day came, the students assured her that their master had performed a miracle and that her back would be almost as good as new. He renewed the dressings and pronounced her fit for any work she could do sitting down, though not yet strong enough for the kitchen. She was eager to work. Boredom only focussed her mind on her uncertain future, her injuries and her muscles, stiff from bracing her body against the blows.

Thaïs found her a cubicle and a pile of mending, equipped her with a bronze needle and demonstrated stitches so slowly and carefully Nerysa inferred that she thought her dim-witted. She applied herself. From gossip round the bedside she'd learned exactly how much the master had paid for her treatment. Hard work was all she had to offer in return and she didn't grudge him that. Thaïs was delighted.

'Why didn't you say you were an expert? I don't suppose you do embroidery?'

Nerysa blushed as she lied.

'No, only professionals and ladies' maids do that. I wonder if our Demetrius would want to have you apprenticed? Not yet, perhaps. When you've been here longer and learned to be loyal to the house.

Apprentices live out, you see. Did Quintus Fabius teach you to sew? They do call him the old lady.'

'But not the old seamstress.' Nerysa protested. 'You must know he keeps women in his house who know their needlework.'

'They taught you well. If your manners were more pleasing, I really think you could do well here.'

'I'd like to be apprenticed and live out.'

'Well, there's something to aim for. Work hard and stay out of trouble.'

When Polybius next came to the door, Nerysa beckoned him in.

'You mentioned a present' she said. 'Perhaps not quite freedom but... to be apprenticed and live out?'

'No longer on offer, I'm afraid.' He shook his head. 'Himself has other plans for you.'

CHAPTER XII

Saepe te mihi dixisse scis quaerere te quid maxime faceres gratum mihi. Id tempus nunc adest.

You know you've often asked what you could do that would give me the greatest happiness? Well, now is the moment. Marcus Aurelius to M. Cornelius Fronto C143 AD

D emetrius was in an interesting position; sprawled on the tablinum floor, tugging at his master's knees. It was the correct posture for a slave and a suppliant but it was new to him and Lucius was shaking with laughter.

'Is this a joke or are you trying to embarrass me?'

'No, master. I'm trying to ask you an enormous favour.'

'At last!'

Lucius plunged to his knees and threw his arms around Demetrius. His smile grew from small, incredulous twitches to a sunburst of joy.

'Demetrie, little brother,' he choked, 'this is the happiest day of my life!'

'Master, I didn't know it would be possible.'

'But you know it is. You know I've longed for it for six years – no, longer. It's the earliest wish I can remember, that you were free. I understand why you've refused me so often but you shouldn't have.'

He punched Demetrius in the ribs and said with mock severity, 'How dare you come begging for something I've been hurling at your feet?'

Demetrius retaliated and they were both tumbling on the floor, rolling over and over each other and laughing. Demetrius felt as if he were ten years old again and the bitterness of later years had never touched him. Their chests were heaving and eyes streaming before Lucius asked, 'Why are we lying on the floor?

'Get up,' he ordered, scrambling onto the couch, 'and stop mocking me.'

Demetrius felt the air warm with affection and nostalgia. Now was the moment. Pulling the stool from under the couch, he sat astride it and leant forward. He opened his mouth and shut it. Lucius waited.

'I heard lately that some generous masters had allowed it but have you ever heard of a slave being allowed to marry?'

'Why? Who wants to? Oh no, not you, Demetrie!' Another splutter of laughter. Less infectious. 'Marry? You're teasing me! It's not as if you've a family name to perpetuate. I shall have to, it's my duty. But I'll postpone the evil day as long as I can.'

'I don't know why I want it, just that I do.'

'Then it's as well I'm going to free you. No sensible freedwoman would risk her status for love and you don't want one who's not sensible.'

'I don't want to marry a freedwoman.'

'Yes, you do! I never ask how much you've stashed away but I bet it's not far short of your market worth. You'll buy your freedom soon without me waiving a penny of the price, just as you've always wanted. We'll find a rich freedman's widow who's wise enough to let you control her money and go into partnership as friends and brothers.'

'I didn't plan to leave your service once I was free.'

'I'm relieved to hear it. But you'll have business on the side. You manage my money so well it's only right you should play with some of your own – you'll buy and sell me one day.'

Lucius laid a hand on Demetrius' arm.

'As long as we live there'll be that social distinction between us but, by Zeus, there'll be none between our grandsons. I'll plan your marriages as carefully as my own. There's no reason why you couldn't eventually aspire to a woman of free, even gentle birth.'

Demetrius should change the subject deftly now. It was the wrong moment for his bizarre request and he'd perfected the art of choosing his moment many years since. Why did he blurt out, 'It's your slave, Nerysa, I want.'?

Lucius dropped his hand. Not from anger, Demetrius sensed, but from from bitter disappointment – and alarm.

'You're out of your mind.'

'Master, do you remember you once said you'd give me anything that would make me happy.'

'That couldn't make you happy.'

'I don't think I could ever be happy without it'

'Happy! Quartered with a clumsy, dim-witted barbarian! Think of your beautiful vase. Yes, of course I heard about it.'

Demetrius' cheeks flared and he kept silent. Lucius' arm stole around his shoulders.

'She's bad, Demetrie. You said it yourself, she could be a witch. Let's get rid of her!'

'But you've only just bought her from Quintus Fabius. Passing her on so quickly might offend him. If she's a liability, best make me responsible for her.' Demetrius hesitated. It would wound Lucius to explain the affinity he felt with her, because of her suffering and her endurance. He managed, 'She has at least courage - perhaps I know better than you how much – and firmness.'

'A Thracian gladiator has courage and a mule is equally stubborn. Are they qualities to charm a man like you? Why not take one of our own girls, born on the estate, well trained and eager to please?' Lucius' face convulsed with disgust. He took Demetrius' hand and spoke with gentle earnestness. 'She's wild, Demetrie, and she's a greasy, smelly, back-kitchen slave.'

'She's what I am.'

'That she's not. You're my slave by your own choice, for now. To me you're not, never were. I love you as dearly as a blood brother, you know that.'

'And I you.'

'Then how could you persist in this, seeing how it pains me?'

'I don't know. Naturally, I want to be a free man. You think it poor-spirited of me but I can wait. I was born to servitude but I'll discharge myself if you'll be patient.'

'No, *you* be patient. Give her half rations of black bread and water. Assign her the heaviest, dirtiest work and let's see how quickly she comes to heel.'

Demetrius shook his head involuntarily then bit his lip. It wouldn't help to betray frustration.

'Demetrie, you're going to Ostia?'

'Yes, master, you've four ships due in any day.'

'Then let the litter-bearers soften her up while you're away. By the time you get back she'll be all too pleased to be passed on to someone as suave as yourself.'

'I don't want her softened up. I want to have charge of her. I think she needs guidance.'

'Demetrie, you're a master of the understatement.'

'I could shield her from the rougher element. She didn't excite much interest before: unusual looks and that forbidding manner –'

'She sounds irresistible.'

'Well, she will be now. Perhaps I want to make amends.'

'For what? You didn't confuse the instructions.'

'When did you know me to write a sloppy, imprecise order? If I'd written maid instead of servant...'

'So, you're a little less than perfect. Who isn't? Look, lock her in an outhouse, if you must, and visit her at night. On second thoughts, she'd probably cause trouble even there. I know what! We can rent a room for her down in the Suburra.'

'And send Polybius to live there, to keep an eye on her?'

'By all means, if you're that jealous. Demetrie, don't keep me on the rack. Make me happy. Take your freedom, gratis.'

'And I buy hers?'

'So you can begin your career by contracting legal marriage with a lunatic? A thousand times no!'

'Then we shall all have to wait.'

'You'd buy freedom for a girl who'd rather be flogged to death than love you? Thirty lashes won't have sweetened her view of you.'

'But she's yours to give. With respect, master, the solution would be for you to give her to me, in such a way that everyone knows she's mine, entirely and absolutely. Then she won't be troubled – and neither will you.'

Lucius' eyes opened wide.

'Hermes, Demetrie, you'd mind, wouldn't you? You're safe from me at any rate.'

His jaw tensed and he turned his face away.

'We could spend our time together more profitably than this, surely? Until then, I imagine you've work to do.'

Demetrius had miscalculated. This was not merely a dismissal. It was formal notice that the subject was closed and could never be reopened. At the very least, Lucius thought him guilty of eccentricity. He'd been a fool to ask.

CHAPTER XIII

May 171

quaeso hercule quid istuc est? seviles nuptiae?

By Hercules! They *marry* do they, the slaves round here? Plautus *Cisitina* prologue

Nerysa lay late in bed because Archias was coming to remove her dressings for good. But for them, she was naked under the sheet. Hearing footsteps, she sat up to greet him but it was a large group that squeezed into the poky room and, although she'd never seen him, she knew her master had condescended to visit her. She snatched the sheet to her chin.

It had been a comfort to Quintus that he'd been able to place her in the house of Lucius Marius Lepidus and he'd spoken warmly of him. At twenty three, having had the conduct of his own career and patrimony from boyhood, he was already being noticed in the right circles, as much for his learning as his wealth. He had the happy knack of winning the approval of his seniors and the affection of his peers. It had mattered to Quintus to believe him enlightened and kind. To Nerysa, he represented the race and class that had laid waste her country. And he owned her, now, as he owned his dogs and his shoes.

Iris had hardly exaggerated his beauty; taller and slighter than Demetrius, his bearing was proud yet graceful. His eyes were dark but his hair was blonde and soft. Whether the artlessly tousled ringlets were natural or not, only his hairdressers could have said. There was an aura of power about him; everyone in the room, indeed, everyone in the house, had but one purpose in life; to please him. He sat without troubling to feel for the chair he knew would have been placed behind him and, if her scrutiny annoyed him, he was too dignified to show it. Having taken a report on her progress from the bobbing, blushing nurses he turned and addressed her directly.

'Do you know who this man is?'

She felt rather than saw the brooding presence of Demetrius behind his chair.

'He's the procurator.'

'Which means he's the head of this house and my other houses, my farms and my business affairs. He was my boyhood companion. I trust him, and, I'm not ashamed to say it, I love him. What are you?'

'Your kitchen hand, master.'

Someone stifled a laugh. He continued serenely, 'The procurator tells me he wants to marry you.'

There was no audible gasp, only a sudden deepening of the silence as the crowd held its collective breath.

'You may well look appalled. You could hardly be more so than I am but I've given my word. We'll have to train you up. I'll perform the ceremony myself.'

'Wouldn't you need my consent to a lawful marriage?'

'My will is the law here. Do you think I'll have my house thrown into confusion by a creature worth less than a fistful of coppers? The situation bores me. I'll resolve it as Demetrius asks or I'll move his base to Horta. I don't need to point out the resentment that will cause. There are two hundred slaves here who'll know how to punish you. I shan't interfere. You are beneath my notice.'

'If you please, master, wouldn't it be easier to send *me* to the country?'

'Be silent! I dictate the terms in this house - and have the grace to lower your eyes in my presence.'

Correcting slaves' manners was a task so far beneath him he seemed surprised to have been goaded into it. He stood, his chair was whisked away and his entourage followed him out of the room.

The two nurses sidled up to the bed; one was as dark and dumpy as the other was wan and willowy. They'd told Nerysa repeatedly which one of them was Olympia and which Cynthia but she never remembered. One each side of the bed, they smoothed the sheet and stared down at her.

'You work in the kitchen, don't you? Are you a chef?'

'No. I fetch water, scrub pans and floors and –'

'Then you're a *mediastina*?' The word was whispered to lessen its offensiveness. The short nurse bounced down on the bed and sat studying her plump fingers.

'We're skilled, so we count as ordinarii, but there are a hundred grades between us and him. He...well, he's never sick but, if he were, we wouldn't get the chance...it'd be the court physician and a year's convalescence by the sea.'

The other disagreed.

'The master couldn't spare him a year. They say he won't ever free him in case he grows rich and proud and leaves him.' She giggled, 'Odd, isn't it? He could buy a hundred of us and maybe a thousand of you but he couldn't buy himself because he's too expensive. The emperor could though.'

'Best thing for him.' said the dumpy one. 'A year or two inspecting taxes. Emperor comes to trust him. Freedom with a knighthood.'

'Never!' squealed the other, 'Not our Demetrius!'

'Why not? It's happened before.'

The same thought evidently struck them both. Their eyes converged on her and the dumpy one spoke it, 'Why does he want to marry you?'

'He doesn't. He wants me in his bed.'

'But he could have that anyway. Easily.'

'Perhaps not as easily as he thought.'

Archias came late, without his retinue of students. He dismissed the nurses and soaked off the bandages himself, which put Nerysa on her guard. On the point of leaving, he asked if they might talk. She placed a chair for him.

'Nerysa, you know I was once a slave?'

'I guessed so.'

'You know the slaves' motto?'

She smiled, 'Do as you're told, eat what you're given and mind your manners.'

'Good, I see you don't lack knowledge, just understanding. Perhaps we can make progress.'

'Towards what?'

'Nerysa, civilised life is based on a system. At first sight, it may not seem entirely logical but it works, because everyone accepts its conventions. Of course, Demetrius is stronger, physically, than Lucius, as well educated and at least as clever. There are two hundred slaves here and one master. He couldn't beat them all at once. A handful could overpower him. They don't because they work within the system. Those who don't are cast out from it. Is that such an achievement? You fought for that life of yours. Do you want to spend it chained to a stone slab in some downtown sailors' brothel?'

'The master said I should stay here.'

'For how long? Once Demetrius is out of the way or cured of his infatuation you'll be sold to another house. If you don't suit there, you'll be sold again, at a loss, into some inferior establishment where the slave buyer is less fussy or on a tighter budget. You'll finish in the place where you decide to co-operate with authority and make the best life you can for yourself.'

He looked at her, gauging the effect of his words and went on as if encouraged.

'You must have seen how well ordered and prosperous this house is. Lepidus is an able man and a kind master but his affairs run on wheels because Demetrius runs them - without raising his voice for the most part, let alone his whip hand.'

'He's a slave.'

He flinched from the disgust in her voice. She regretted wounding him and revealing so much of herself. Why didn't he make the obvious retort?

'He's a man. An immensely talented one who'll make a good life for himself. I've been a slave and I know that a command doesn't have to be insulting and compliance isn't necessarily demeaning. Take Demetrius; when Lepidus asks him to do something, he does it as if he's chosen to because it gives him pleasure to be of service. No one's fooled. Lepidus commands, Demetrius obeys, but both with grace.

'Now Demetrius has made it plain he wants you to fall in love with him. You've no more choice than he has when Lepidus gives him an order, so why not pretend you've been poised to fall in love with him for months, only waiting for him to sanction your presumption?

Because that would be deception.'

'Which wouldn't worry you surely? Who, for instance, knows you speak Greek?'

Her heart stopped, then slammed into her ribs. How much did he know? What had she said in her delirium? Enough to stimulate his curiosity but not to satisfy it, obviously, for he coaxed, 'Doctors swear on oath to keep their patients' secrets.'

She avoided his eyes and kept silent, hardly daring to breathe.

'Well, if you want to keep that one, don't react to what you're not supposed to understand, even with your eyes.'

'That's good advice, thank you.'

'Here's some more. You'll like living in Demetrius' rooms. Pulcher obviously gave you a taste for the finer things of life. He taught you to speak exquisite Latin by the way. I keep expecting you to burst into poetry.'

'Archias, are there *books* in this house?'

'Why, yes, your master has a magnificent library.'

'Does Demetrius have books?'

'He has the use of his master's. Does he know you can read?'

'He has no reason to.'

'Perhaps that's a good secret. Play the raw recruit. He's shrewd enough to discover very quickly that you're not stupid. You'll need some excuse for your mistakes and you're so headstrong you'll make plenty. Have you seen the house?'

'The slave quarters, not the main part.'

'You'll like it. It's more spacious than Pulcher's. The Palatine may be exclusive but it's cramped compared with the Quirinal. The house is magnificent and I suspect the art collection will please you.' He smiled, 'I'm one of Demetrius' oldest friends and the only one who approves his choice of bride.'

'Save your approval until I *am* his bride.'

'Nerysa, let's come to the point. You shouldn't fear his lovemaking, he's not a brute. You know, surely, that he never intended you to be so badly beaten?'

'I've been told so.'

'You both suffered. Regret hurts too. Look, life is a game of dice. Stop quarrelling with the throw and use your wit to make the best of it. You've few options and only one worth taking. Like it or not, you're a slave and you won't find a better master than Lepidus.'

His departure meant that she was officially recovered but Olympia and Cynthia continued to wait on her and make it politely plain that they couldn't allow her to leave the room. She didn't challenge them. There was nothing to be gained by arousing suspicion. The room had grown suffocating, the night never cool enough to freshen the air before the next day's heat built upon the last. All surplus effort, including conversation, was avoided. But she thought; about the various kinds and purposes of marriage and about slavery. A slave was a defective being of course, but what, exactly, was the nature of his defect? Had *she* changed? Not yet. That would come gradually, surely – the coarsening effect of servility she'd resist with all her strength. She thought about the system under which a slave lived in greater state than a king did in Britain and a man claimed to love his brother while he kept him in bondage.

Her suffering and scars had gained her nothing. Marriage was their euphemism for rape. She'd be just one in a long line of British women raped by Romans. They usually committed suicide afterwards but it would make more sense to do it before. A suicide less pleasant than the one she could have chosen six months earlier. Then she would have died a virgin among friends. Now, supposing she could find the means and the privacy, she'd die alone, scarred and violated. Had fate defrauded her, she wondered, or had she defeated herself?

CHAPTER XIV

Manus, dentes, oclos, bracia, venter, mamila, pectus, osu, medulas, crus, osu, pedes, frontes, uncis, digitos, umlicus, cunus, ulvas, ilae defixo

I curse her hands, her teeth, her eyes, her arms her belly, her breasts, her chest, her bones, her marrow, her legs her mouth, her feet, her forehead, her nails, her fingers, her navel, her cunt, her womb, her vulva. Inscriptiones latinae selectae 8751

Lucius was appalled. They'd shown him an outlandish, wild-eyed creature, a barbarian from the fringes of the empire. Chalk white skin and flaming hair produced a garish effect that repelled him. Worse still, she'd no idea how to behave. He was so used to deference he'd been unsettled by not receiving it and uncertain how to react. She'd looked him straight in the eye and challenged him on the nature of legal marriage. And she'd touched the point with a needle. The arrangement would be a domestic one, recognised in the house and by those outside who wished to gratify its master. It could have no legal significance. Yet, if he chose to pretend it did, how dared she question him? How dared she speak at all without permission? Was she so brutish not even whipping had chastened her? How would she make out as consort to the head of his household? A disaster. She'd bring Demetrius endless misery and embarrassment before he came to his senses and dismissed her.

Demetrius had mentioned sorcery. He'd better examine the evidence. There had to be some explanation when a sensible man suddenly lost his reason. It was disappointing that a slave, even when most carefully reared as a gentleman's companion, had no true sense of values. He was liable to unpredictable errors of judgement, such as a child or a woman might be. That was common knowledge, of course, but it had never before seemed to apply to Demetrius. If he had a fault, it was obstinacy. Lucius remembered him turning up a filthy, old dish in the flea market and rubbing it with chalk all night, heedless of teasing. When it turned out to be Etruscan silver, worth a small fortune, he'd smiled briefly and presented it to his master as a gift. Lucius thought fondly of him. He should have looked to him; steadied and guided him until the madness had passed. As it was, he'd actually promised to perform the ceremony – had said so decisively to disguise the fact that he'd no idea what kind of ceremony would serve. Foolish to have given his word! Perhaps he could go back on a promise to a slave? No, a promise was binding on an honourable man, not because of the person *to* whom it was given but because of the person *by* whom it was given. It was up to him to find a way to extricate his favourite without losing face.

'My foolish boy thinks she's a virgin,' he told Thaïs. 'He's got the bitch's own word for it. Satisfy yourself and report back to me. Did you ever hear of an eighteen year old virgin?'

'Perhaps a Vestal, master?'

'Quite right, and if I wanted to find one, I'd search the Temple of Vesta before Quintus Pulcher's house.'

***

Nerysa assumed Thaïs had come to check the mending and that Archias had sent his midwife to ask after her health. She didn't recognise the other two women but wasn't suspicious until four litter-bearers filed into the room and Thaïs coughed.

'I'm sorry for this, but it's necessary. The master must satisfy himself that you really are a virgin.'

Nerysa looked up at the athletic young men, two in the doorway, one either side of it.

'What's it to do with them?'

'Nothing if you don't give us trouble. I'll make them face the wall.'

Each in turn, the women tunnelled under her tunic. The stretching felt like a burning brand, her legs trembled and she feared they would think she was struggling. Abruptly, it was over and they nodded to each other.

'Good girl. We can tell your master you didn't lie.'

She looked at the muscular litter-bearers. They'd turned to face the wall and not looked at what they were forbidden to see – at least you could rely on that in a well-disciplined house. They all trooped out. She sat stabbing the linen with a furious needle. The worn sheet was patched in six new places before she heard footsteps cross the threshold. Cynthia and Olympia melted away and Thaïs stood looking over Nerysa's shoulder.

'Your stitches are larger than usual, Nerysa.'

'I was disturbed this morning, perhaps I lost concentration.'

Thaïs flushed and made to leave but it seemed she'd not said what she'd come to say. After some hesitation she sat down.

'It will soon be your wedding day. A great day for everyone.'

'Everyone?'

'Of course. For the master, because he's indulging his favourite, which he's been longing to do, for the steward, because he'll get his heart's desire and for all the slaves and freedmen because they like to see their patron happy and they'll be feasted royally.' She bent her head over the linen, 'I can recommend him, as a lover.'

'*You?*' Thaïs was a fine looking woman but she must be at least thirty five, and radiated efficiency rather than allure.

'Why not? When he first took up his place as head of the house he was about your age - eighteen aren't you? And I wasn't quite thirty. I knew the house whereas he was more used to the country estates. I helped him over a few difficulties. He was good to me. He won't hold your defiance against you because he's generous and, believe me, you'll faint with pleasure in his bed.'

'Who else in the house is his lover?'

'By Venus you're a silly girl. Do you think there's anyone here he hasn't noticed or who wouldn't give up all hope of freedom to change places with you?'

'I wish they could. I'd gladly change places with any of them.'

'It's as well for you fell on this house. If you feel such disgust for a good-looking young man I can't think how you'd have reacted to an old, perverted one and there are plenty of them in this city. Come to think of it, you came from one, didn't you? Don't tell me you preferred him to our steward!'

Nerysa drove her fingernails into her palms to contain her rage until Thaïs' footsteps had faded away. Then she rushed out of the room. She couldn't deal with these servile beings. She must find Lepidus and explain. He'd see that it would be an outrage to couple her with a slave.

But he'd also see that he'd been imposed on and that he was committing treason by harbouring her. An ambitious young man on the brink of a public career would be bound to denounce her and she'd have betrayed Quintus as well as herself. She stopped running. There was no point. She'd thrust herself into a tunnel. To retreat was impossible. To proceed was fraught with danger. Every act of defiance drew attention to herself and risked exposure. At the very least, she'd be sold on, to a house where slaves were kicked awake at the start of the day and could count on a beating before the end. And she'd have severed her last, tenuous link with Quintus. She'd contrived her own fate and she must submit to it, sacrificing herself for him.

In Britain she'd helped to prepare beasts for sacrifice. She knew of the human sacrifices of the past and the principle that one might be surrendered for the good of others. When it seemed that the gods had abandoned their tribe, a Druid prince had come to them from across the sea. The gods, he said, rejected old, disfigured victims and he offered his own perfect, young body. So the priests had smashed his skull and slit his throat. But the Romans had still come.

The corridor she'd reached was unfamiliar, wider than the ones she knew, the cubicles curtained off, exuding a hint of musk. A group of girls emerged, the sort Iris envied, with towering hairstyles and faces as painted and haughty as temple statues. Humble in her coarse grey tunic and bare legs, she drew back against the wall for them to pass but one of them spotted her.

'Look! The red-haired witch who put the evil eye on the steward!'

They all turned to stare. The tallest stiffened and her black eyes flashed, then narrowed as she started forward. Nerysa felt a warning flutter in her stomach and eased herself along the wall out of her path. As they closed in on her she marvelled at how ugly they had suddenly become with their bared teeth, flared nostrils and clawed hands.

'The Hyperborean! What's she doing here?'

'Man stealing!'

'Did you know, she's so wild, she can't braid her own hair.'

'That's not all she needs to learn.'

She scanned the ring of hostile faces in abject terror, cowed as she hadn't been by Surdus' men, who shook their heads and said it was a shame to lay the rod on her pretty back. They'd had an unpleasant duty to perform but they were in control. These girls weren't. She shrank against the wall until the roughcast cut into her still tender back. She heard her own quick breath, felt the creep of her own sweat. But she held those smouldering, black eyes steadily and swerved as the girl sprang forward. A hand slapped onto her forehead and the back of her head slammed into the wall. The other hand came up. The girl spat on her thumb and began to scrub and scrape at Nerysa's temple. The others pushed so close she could smell the myrtle from their tooth powder.

'You were right. Those veins aren't painted on!'

'Told you. Couldn't be. She hasn't any paints.'

'Can you see her double pupils? Can you see?'

'They're enormous! Y..Yes! Two lights in each eye. No doubt about it.'

As they drew back, crossing their fingers to avert the evil eye, Nerysa saw her chance. She dodged between two of them but was pulled up short by a searing pain. The tall girl had her by the hair. She looked up and flinched from the hatred in those blazing, black eyes.

'Why do you want to hurt me?' she pleaded. 'I've never hurt you.'

'Listen to her! Hoity-toity! The kitchen slut talks like a senator!'

'They said she couldn't talk at all.'

'She can do anything she wants. She sprouts feathers at night and flaps around the ceiling to call her demons! And they drive our Demetrius mad. Why else would he notice a rod-spoiler?'

Nerysa's nose and eyes streamed as the girl twisted and wrenched at her hair and, with a yelp of triumph, thrust a hand full under her nose.

'Got you, see! Your magic's not the strongest in this city. I'll get you cursed by an expert so all your hair falls out and your breasts shrivel and drop off and your privates too.'

Nerysa ducked and pressed her hands to her scalp. The girl lunged at her again but her friends pulled her back.

'Don't mark her while she still has him bewitched, Aglae, why earn yourself a whipping? He never keeps the dim ones long. Wait till he's tired of her. Then she's yours.'

Footsteps sounded on the stone staircase. She broke free and, in panic, ran breathless on jelly legs, up many a blind alley until she found her room - no longer a prison but a sanctuary. It had been Archias' step on the stairs. He took her pulse and advised delay.

'I hope,' he said, 'you're not brewing up another fever. I'll check tomorrow but we should wait ten days at least. June is the luckiest month for weddings.'

CHAPTER XV

June 171

Amor... sternuit appprobationem Nunc ab auspicio bono profecti mutuis animis amant amantur

Cupid sneezed and, beginning from this good omen, they live in mutual affection. Catullus XLV

Lucius was up by first light to oversee the frenzied activity in his house. He'd bidden his freedmen and poorer clients to the feast and prevailed on some of his shabbier business partners to come too. They wouldn't refuse a good dinner and, by their presence, they'd be recognising the strange affair and conferring a certain status on it. He prided himself on achieving a balance between what was commensurate with his love and what was due to his dignity. The union of his favourite with a worthless drudge was wormwood and gall but he downed it with defiant relish, daring the world to laugh. If he owed Demetrius a debt from the past, it was good to have settled it so comprehensively. The more he understood that the event had no legal significance, the more he embellished it with extravagant trappings.

As she was led through the atrium to the guest bedchamber, Nerysa was engulfed in a tide of scent from the jasmine, lilies and roses, spiralled around pillars, spilling from huge vases and worn by everyone. Except for Aglae, she didn't recognise the women in the room but she took them for high status slaves, kept to wait on guests. Remembering they were all supposed to have shared the steward's bed, she saluted his energy and wondered how they left him time to run four houses, three farms and a world-wide trading operation.

Sly fingers loosed the pins at her shoulders and her tunics slid to the floor, leaving her naked before twenty cold stares. She turned her face to the wall then violently away from it. The erotic paintings were sickeningly explicit. Suddenly she was on her back; arms and legs splayed, being attacked with tweezers.

'Goats grow hair in the groin and armpits. Hold still while we civilise you.'

Sweating and flinching while eight slaves worked at once, she felt she was being plucked for the steward's table.

Next, she thought, *they'll send for Arminia, to wring my neck and douse me in fish sauce.*

Sure enough, a cauldron clanked across the floor. They hauled her to her feet and slapped dank-smelling mud over her. Shivering under feather fans, cracked and brown as an old pot, she stared down at herself and wondered whether to laugh or cry. The mud was scrubbed off and her angry, blotched skin had to be soothed in milk. The jug and basin looked innocent but, as their use was explained, heat surged to her skin and her ears hummed. Next she was lying on the floor, a circle of anxious faces peering down at her, Thaïs forcing the rim of a wine cup between her teeth.

'Girls who don't douche fall pregnant. Try again.' And, supporting her with an arm, she coaxed her through the hygiene routines of a courtesan, saying, 'I wish you'd pay attention. Do you want to be put out after one night? You'd be a fool to neglect the douche because he's a fastidious man. Quick! Put on this tunic and sit down, here's Phoebe at last!

'We're so grateful to you, Phoebe. The master wants everything to be just like a real wedding.'

Phoebe didn't wear the house livery and her self-importance subdued them. A plump purse vanished into the folds of her cloak and a silver comb came from them.

'Don't fuss, Thaïs. Who do you think had the dressing of our young mistress for her wedding? Lucius Marius will find nothing to complain of, I assure you.'

Draping her cloak over Thaïs' outstretched arm, she advanced into the room as though she owned it.

'So which is she? Hmm, I see the problem. Well, a bride's hairstyle's so old fashioned there's nothing to it. Two straight partings each side, so...', as though scoring a plank with an adze, 'and plaits... here, take this one. Jump to it, girl!'

Nerysa thought six tight braids springing from her head like daggers uncomfortable enough until Phoebe grasped them all in one hand and wrenched them to a tight hub.

'Where are your pins? Why do you sit there gaping?'

'We've no *ladies'* hairdresser here.' Thaïs apologised, handing them over. 'We do the best we can for ourselves. None of us has ever seen a wedding.'

Phoebe crammed her mouth full of pins and contrived to carry on grumbling.

'You'll see one soon enough. It'll be Lucius Marius next and there'll be some torn backs and cheeks here when you've a mistress to please!'

While she anchored the veil and myrtle garland she helped herself from the trays of quails' eggs and apricots that were passed around. Nerysa waved them away with a shudder. The older women, amused, patted her taut scalp. Their lurid reminiscences made her stomach crawl up her throat; did they think she'd no Latin or no modesty?

Lucius' chamberlain, Cyrus, scratched at the door and an alabaster jar of perfume was borne in shoulder high. Its slender neck was snapped to squeals of admiration for it was an absurdly extravagant present, not intended to please the bride but to overwhelm the groom with the prodigality of his master's love. The slaves said it provoked them to a frenzy of desire. They were at a loss to describe its likely effect on Demetrius. It certainly had an effect on Nerysa, sending her into paroxysms of sneezing. The old women muttered 'Jove bless you!' but everyone else cheered and counted. Sneezing was the best possible omen and no one had heard of a bride sneezing fifty seven times. Hers was sure to be the happiest of marriages.

Directed by Phoebe, they draped the bridal gown around her, tied the girdle in the traditional knot, slipped gilded sandals on her feet, stood back and congratulated themselves. Under the veil, they conceded, she was hardly a typical Roman matron but neither did she look like a reject from the slave pen. Exotic, they said, but enchanting. Demetrius would be well pleased with their efforts. They showed her off to Adrian, the most supercilious of the secretaries, come to explain that there was no official form for slave marriage.

'When citizens marry they simply join hands. There's trust between them, you see.' He shook his head. 'You know what it means to swear before the gods of hearth and state?'

'I think so.'

'The steward wants you to swear an oath of loyalty and obedience to him.'

He had her repeat it, one word at a time, after him, mouthing each syllable with painful clarity and expansive gestures as if he were conducting an anthem. It promised no less than perfect fidelity, obedience and submissiveness for as long as it pleased the steward to live with her and ended by calling on all the gods to punish her for failing in any particular. She heard it through once, then floored him by repeating the whole by heart.

'Ah! The illiterate have good memories.' he sneered.

'We've well-trained memories, because our sacred teaching isn't written but lives in the hearts of the faithful.'

'Not one scribe among them, I fear.'

'Our language could be transcribed but we wouldn't permit it. To write it down would profane it.'

'If I were you, I wouldn't tell our steward that literacy is a profanation. He thinks of it as the glory of civilisation.'

'It probably is the glory of *your* civilisation, having no competition from the arena, the war machine and the slave market.'

'The most useful thing I could do for you, before you go to your new master, would be to bite out your tongue. But on second thoughts,' he bent and hissed in her ear, 'you'll need it - to lick his arse.'

Thaïs took her trembling hand. The old women put their arms around her.

'A virgin always cries on her wedding day, but widows laugh because they know what's coming!' They chuckled and popped the customary slice of quince on her tongue - to sweeten her breath they said.

Still crowing with laughter, they threw open the doors to the crowd of waiting torchbearers, flute players and singers, all freshly bathed and aglow with nard and excitement. The wooden doors of the tablinum were folded back so that, but for a clearing in front of the dais, the vast space from the front door to the far side of the peristyle was packed with cheering guests. A roar of approval ran round the room. The bride had sneezed fifty seven times!

An outsider would have taken the smiling Lucius for the happy bridegroom. Demetrius stood with him and Polybius under an awning. With a swift look, Nerysa took in a dogged expression under a garland of anemones and noted that his poppy-red silk gown had set-in sleeves; a modern affectation Quintus despised. Waving and stamping greeted the master as he settled himself unhurriedly on the dais. The haruspices dispatched a squawking cock with a slick proficiency that impressed her and had hardly begun to dissect the belly, when they looked round significantly at Lucius and beckoned. Demetrius tensed and Nerysa had a fleeting hope of adverse omens until Lucius, smiling complacently, announced, 'Everything is exceptionally propitious.'

He bowed before the altar and scattered grains of incense on the fire. The flames leapt heavenward with his prayers to Juno and Hymen. Seated again, he turned to his steward and spoke with precision.

'Demetri, for your loyalty and service, I am giving you this woman for yourself, in the presence of witnesses, in every way *as if* under the law for the getting of children.'

Nerysa felt a wave of nausea and told herself that the blood of slaves was not miscible with the blood of kings. There was a general sigh as Demetrius promised her protection and the recognition due to a wife. She looked round at the slaves, drooling for their feast; all born, forced or sold into slavery. She was the only one who had deliberately chosen it. Resolved to live with the consequences for Quintus' sake, she spoke the vow. Thaïs caught up her hand and a shout went up from the crowd. Demetrius grasped it and thrust a ring onto her fourth finger, from where, tradition held, a thread led directly to her heart.

The cupbearer brought him a golden goblet, representing the wine of life they should share. As he passed it to her, their eyes met and he gave the ghost of a smile. Barely moistening her lips she returned the cup and he surprised her by draining it in a single gulp and holding it upside down aloft. The crowd cheered him to the echo and, looking at the sea of flushed faces, she knew, with sudden insight, that no one in the house would sleep alone that night. The steward's passion had infected everyone.

When the din subsided, Lucius asked to see Demetrius kiss the bride and she froze as he brushed her brow with his lips. Lucius forgot himself so far as to offer his hand to his slave who was dazed enough to grasp it and they hugged each other with joyful ebullience. Thaïs stepped forward.

'Congratulations, sir, I'll bring your bride to your room when she's ready.'

He kissed her with a warmth he'd spared Nerysa. Polybius offered his hand and good wishes and, suddenly, there was a forest of hands to shake and backs to slap. Hazelnuts rained down like hailstones. Nerysa was an outsider; all thoughts were with the beloved head of the house, being congratulated on his new toy.

The merrymaking could be heard in the bedroom where the women combed out her hair, offered chamber pot, water jug and towel and murmured of blessings that the gods would begrudge the ungrateful. Stealthy hands slid under her tunic and fondled her breasts. She made no protest. She felt dread of a slave's embrace as an overpowering nausea. She shut her eyes as the room lurched and her stomach heaved. Oily fingers crept between her thighs and she heard excited whispers.

'They've got jugglers and tumblers in the dining room and flute girls.'

'There's no room left on the benches. Slaves are squatting all over the floor.'

'Demetrius is reclining with freedmen.'

'No he's not. He's on the master's couch. Thaïs, the lips don't swell and they're dry.'

'That's often the way with virgins, carry on.'

'It's not working, I'll chafe the skin, it's bone dry.'

'Pass me the oil flask. She's overcome by her good luck, it's understandable. She won't be able to walk. Go and find one of the litter-bearers – Atlas or Dion, even Mysius - whoever's sober. He'd better carry her the back way.'

Her eyes were shut against the nausea but she felt the lamplight play over her face. Sandalwood and cinnamon, a faint aura around his person, were potent in his room, as if his essence had been concentrated and forced up her nose. Rustling silk and wafting air plotted the women's' movements and conveyed their impatience to finish their tasks and be off to the feast. Coarse cloth was pulled under her, fine linen drawn over her and, one by one, they kissed her and left. Thaïs stayed; Thaïs who, as a slave, was beneath confidences but who, as the highest placed woman in a house where Nerysa was the lowest, was too grand for them. Nerysa clung to her.

'Please don't leave me.'

'Don't be foolish. When the steward comes to enjoy the reward the master has given him, would I be here to hinder him? You must know I wouldn't dare.'

'What will he do?'

'You've lived with Quintus Fabius. You know exactly what he'll do.'

Nerysa thought of the times she'd surprised couples in the broom cupboard. The girls writhed and moaned more than she had under the rod. Yet they were willing enough. How was it for the unwilling?

'I don't know, I don't know anything.'

'By all the gods, Nerysa, did he keep you in his house with a sack over your head?'

How to explain she'd lived in her own private apartments, shielded from coarseness by a man as capable of delicacy as depravity? To hint at her past would cost her her life and, to her surprise, she still wasn't ready to let it go.

'You're a strange one.' Thaïs said, 'They whipped you and all you complained of was that they'd taken your clothes off. But, you'll see, love sweetens pain.'

'This isn't about love. It's about power.'

'Yes, it is. Power to bewitch a good man and drive him to distraction. He could have had you served up any way he wanted, you wicked girl. What drove him to this?

'But I shouldn't have said that. If the steward chooses to honour you in this way, and the master sanctions it, it's not for me, or you, or anyone to question it.'

'If he touches me, I'll die.'

'No you won't. And you won't offend him. You're not really his wife, of course, you're his underslave. Don't ever forget that. You wouldn't want him to have to remind you.'

'I lied to you. I can do embroidery. Perhaps, instead of...' But Thaïs was already hurrying out of the door.

A hollow victory - to side-step the executioner's sword and be pierced by the lust of a slave. On the battlefield she would, at least, have had the option of flight. Here defeat was a foregone conclusion. The guests were already roaring the victory song.

CHAPTER XVI

June 171

Nihil postulavit pro sua verecundia nisi quod probum honestumque sit et tibi datu et sibi postulau

As was to be expected of his modesty, he has asked nothing but what is right and honourable for you to give and him to receive. Marcus Cornelius Fronto to Lollianus Avitus 161 AD

The success of the celebrations and the warm glow of his own generosity had brought Lucius back into perfect charity with Demetrius. The slave looked magnificent in his silk gown and garland. There was a complacency about him that was vaguely provocative. In an attempt to see him grin, Lucius referred frequently to *your wife* but only succeeded in seeing his lips twitch almost imperceptibly with suppressed pleasure. Wine always intensified his yearning for them to be on more equal terms. He leant forward and refilled the cups himself.

'I must have you drink a bowlful to each letter of her exotic name.'

'Would you, just this once, drink to her?'

This was aking too much.

'I'll drink to the day you marry legally with a Roman citizen. Though I doubt you'll find one more prettily spoken. Do you suppose all Pulcher's maids speak poetic Latin?'

'Simo's pedantic. Perhaps he taught her. There's something about her. I don't know what but I'll find out. At any rate, she was never in a kitchen. Arminia says she knew nothing when she came, though she soon learned.'

'She can learn! Then have some overseer teach her to keep her eyes on her sandals, it's unnerving the way they drill through your head. We don't know what she was to Pulcher, why he sent her here or why she's such a troublemaker. But she's your problem now. When you buy out I'll give her to you with a dowry, if you still want her. But if she makes trouble or there's a hint of sorcery, she goes and you must accept it.'

'You're the best master a man could have. You've done this for me against your judgement. I'll never forget that and never forget to be grateful.'

'Grateful! Let's hope she is. I should think she'll behave – if she can. The omens were favourable.'

'Were they truly?'

'Remarkably so. Did you think I dissembled? I wouldn't have. If they'd been adverse I must have postponed the ceremony. Ask the priests yourself but, for now, I imagine you'd like to retire?'

'Not while you need my company or service, master.'

'For tonight, little brother, I have you out on loan - to Aphrodite.'

CHAPTER XVII

June 171

Την μέν θαλαττιου τινος ερωτος παραφορον τε και αγριαν και κυμαινουσαν έν ψυχη

A love like the sea, frenzied, savage and raging like stormy waves in the soul. Lucian after Plato In Praise of Demosthenes 13

The shouts and laughter of the bridegroom's party grew louder. An unruly crowd gathered outside the door and refused to go away. They sang the usual tasteless songs in chorus and offered their uncensored suggestions one by one, each endorsed by a tumult of laughter. Polybius grinned as he folded Demetrius' tunics and picked up his own bed roll. He'd sleep on the outside of the steward's door - the end of an era for both of them. Demetrius reflected that it was a pity the boy should have to couple in a corridor.

'By the way...'

'Master?'

'If you can find someone to deputise for you for a few hours, I shan't mind, so long as there's someone reliable in attendance.'

'Thank you, master. A goodnight to you,' he laughed, 'and a peaceful one!'

He opened the door a crack and squeezed through. Demetrius bolted it against the surging crowd and turned towards his prize. He sat on his bed and drew down the sheet, releasing her girdle and parting the folds of her tunic in one practised movement. Her white body, ethereal in the flickering light, made him pause in sudden in awe. There was a shout from behind the door, 'Come on, Demetri, tell us if her brush is as red as her nob!'

He touched her bald pubes. She stirred. Passion, so long contained, swept through him as a raging torrent. He kneed her legs apart and battled to enter her. With the first successful thrust, a roar of approval from outside the door drowned her cry and he gave a soft crow of triumph. But he'd heard that sound before - a piercing scream of surprise, then a grunt, deep in the throat. He'd heard it from a woman in the agony of the childbed. He thought that, once the honeymoon was over, he must take care how he spilled his seed into her. Pregnancy wasn't a common problem but a highly significant one. Childbirth was bloody and dangerous and abortion hardly less so. He wouldn't want to have to choose between them.

***

Nerysa felt a hot surge of fluid inside her and a steady, viscous trickle down her thighs. This must be blood. Didn't a sacrificial victim bleed? But Iphigenia had been swiftly dispatched, her own ordeal would last longer. He slept, then, half conscious, reached for her again. Penetration was less of a struggle but she was sore and the process more prolonged. When he woke again near dawn she flinched away involuntarily and he caught her round the waist and pulled her backwards towards him laughing, 'Don't run away, I shan't hurt you this time.'

What happened next was a shock. She'd never dreamed than anyone would use a woman in that way. She retched and crammed the sheet into her mouth, stifling protest and vomit. He kissed the nape of her neck and whispered, 'You're torn in the front, this way is kinder.'

She turned over and saw that dawn was breaking. So, was that it? This love people made so much of? The throbbing of the poet's lute, the ardent scenes of the bedroom walls; were they just the prelude to searing pain and sticky fluids that smelled of a fresh kill?

Light poured through the open shutters. It was well past the time for work to begin. Though she felt stained to the core, she refused to hang her head but looked him straight in the eye. Surely he didn't wink? He said, 'I expect you'd like to wash.'

He helped her down from the high bed and led the way across the room to a closet which must have been his own washroom before a more modern one had been built alongside. He swept the curtain shut and she was alone for the first time in six months.

There was a tap on the inside wall of the lean-to, a luxury she'd never heard of, and water drained across the sloping floor to a gurgling outlet which, judging by the sponge on stick placed by it, could also serve as a latrine. The side wall was lined with shelves, neatly stocked with clean tunics and towels. The room had been thoughtfully supplied by someone who knew how to please women, with strips of old linen for her monthly problem, toothpowder, oil and perfume; comforts she'd renounced six months before. She'd survived without and wouldn't have bought them back at such a price.

She felt more positive about the set of tunic pins. Pretty pins were the first luxury a slave girl aspired to and she'd been despised for still wearing the standard issue. Realising he'd pitied her for the same reason, she flushed with annoyance. These weren't extravagant, but of good quality; silver with a delicate beading trim. She tested them against the tip of her thumb and found them sharp enough not to damage fabric. *Nicely judged,* she thought, *to be a little too good for her.* Beside them lay an ivory comb, hairpins and, the ultimate luxury, a burnished bronze mirror. She took a swift look in it, curious to see if loss of innocence was branded on her face.

Walking was painful because dried blood stuck her thighs together. Glad now that they'd plucked her hair, she was even grateful for the sight of the dreaded jug.

Her body was shamed and broken but it could have been worse. She imagined it exsanguinated on the pyre; Quintus setting a lighted brand to it. She wouldn't have preferred that. Shivering, she reached for a tunic and shook out sprigs of rosemary from it. It reached her ankles – the steward's 'wife's' legs were evidently not for general show.

Hearing creaking of trolley wheels and conversation, she twitched back the curtain. Two youths were changing the bed linen but Demetrius, already dressed, was surrounded by admirers; his scribe Philemon, Polybius and three of the men who'd been with him in the yard the day she first saw him. They had the stained sheet between them and he looked exultant, as if they'd all been hunting and he'd slain the biggest boar.

'Make sure the master sees it before it goes to the laundry.'

'Never fear, sir, the whole house will see it.'

He turned towards her and his triumphant expression made her sick with loathing.

'Thanks for your service and good wishes. We've everything we need.'

They saluted and left. He made an expansive gesture towards the couch.

'Come, breakfast is served.'

His couch was wooden and plain but it was of exquisite line and, in its understated elegance, as pleasing a piece as Quintus' ivory and gold set. He brought the table to it and reclined, motioning her to a stool beside the couch. He rested his left elbow on an embroidered cushion, leant his glistening, perfumed head on his hand, drew up his right knee and balanced his arm across it. Quintus used to recline in exactly such a pose yet this man looked so different; his grace couldn't conceal the energy that radiated from him and repelled her.

'What shall I pass you?' he asked, hand hovering over the dishes.

'Thank you, sir, I'm not hungry.'

'But you need strength. We've a day's work ahead.'

Didn't she belong in the kitchen? What work could they do together?

'Today,' he announced, 'we serve Venus herself and we owe her a thousand kisses before tonight. You'll have some fruit, at least.'

'Since you wish it, sir, a cherry.'

He dangled it playfully before her lips but, as she made no move toward it, he presented it on a fluted silver dish and she stared at it, wondering how to make it disappear. To swallow it was out of the question. He ate bread moistened with wine and a quantity of fruit, without taking his eyes from her. Suddenly aware that he was looking significantly at his hands poised above the finger bowl, she reached for the jug and drizzled water carefully over them as Quintus' slaves had used to do. He nodded in brief approval and wiped them on the edge of his napkin.

'We'll leave the tray,' he said, 'you may tell me when you're hungry. If anything's missing in the washroom just tell the boy. Shall I show you my room?'

She stood promptly to forestall any offer of help and surveyed the room. It was surprisingly austere; panelled in olive and magenta with a mosaic floor to match and sparsely furnished with fine pieces. He had a carved sandalwood chest and a great, studded, iron one on which stood a bronze of two youths wrestling. Thrilling vigour and movement was compressed into their muscular bodies; they were obviously original and valuable. Above them hung a remarkable picture. She moved involuntarily towards it and he took her hand and led her closer.

'Do you like it? I was lucky to come across it in a sale of bankrupt stock. Perhaps you think it too fine a piece for a slave?'

It was a study of Demeter, goddess of the earth's bounty, sitting in a corn field, diaphanous robes and golden hair lifted by the breeze. On each knee sat a sturdy boy child reaching out for poppies and pomegranates. It was an important work. She could guess the artist - certainly the school, but resisted the temptation to stun him by telling him. Correctly placed, she thought, it might well command the price of his freedom but he wouldn't part with it. He was, above all, acquisitive.

'Look, by all means,' he said, 'but, perhaps, better not to touch my things.'

Her eyes fell on a book.

'That's a book,' he said, 'by Virgil, Rome's greatest poet. It's about the country. I love the countryside - if you liked, I could read some to you.'

Nerysa couldn't precisely gauge the enormity of his condescension but she knew heads of households didn't read Virgil to scullions. She couldn't think how to answer him and he registered lack of interest.

'But today,' he continued quickly, 'we've another purpose. We should go to work now.'

Abruptly, he picked her up and carried her to his bed.

Lucius' two masseurs provided a welcome respite. Rose and citron diffused through the room from oil, warming in their cupped hands. Nerysa found the skilled touch of the masseuse soothing after a wretched night. Her breathing deepened and slowed as tension drained from her body. Hovering in a twilight between sleep and full consciousness, she conceded that Lepidus' house was comfortable because everyone in it took pride in their skill. Fate had predestined her for the house. If Quintus couldn't rescue her, she would live, serve and die in it. With a convulsive effort of will, she resigned herself. She would try to be a good slave, a good scullion and a good wife though she doubted her capacity to be any of these. She would even study to please this hateful, overbearing man. She'd weighed all the possible alternatives. They were even less appealing.

The masseurs were collecting their jars and towels and Demetrius, sitting clothed on the bed, was looking down at her.

He handed her her tunic saying, 'They're bringing lunch.'

She blinked in dismay at oysters, anchovies, asparagus, mushrooms stuffed with pine kernels and every other aphrodisiac the kitchen slaves recommended with a snigger. They ought to have served him a sedative. The food looked and smelled good but it was hard to swallow under his scrutiny and her throat was as dry as her vagina. He mixed the wine and water himself and she reached for it eagerly, saw him frown and laughed to herself. She'd made him suspect her of a weakness for drink and put him to the unnecessary trouble of marking his flagons with charcoal to catch her out.

With the day's heat at its fiercest, they lay facing each other, her face flushed with wine.

He stroked her breast with his forefinger and said solemnly, 'This is a new beginning for you with new responsibilities. You're my wife and we live here very publicly. Other girls don't see why you were chosen and they weren't. It's only natural they should try to discredit you. It would be best to distance yourself a little and not confide in them. But don't let them find you arrogant.'

'You mean be aloof and ingratiating at the same time.'

'Well, in as far as you can. I hear you were with Quintus Fabius long enough to learn to sew.'

'I'm told I learn quickly.'

'I could keep you in my room and hire in someone to teach you embroidery. But I work long hours and I'm often away. Girls get lonely.

Out in the house, it will be easy for you to embarrass me or, worse still, to embarrass the master. If you do that, I'll have no choice but to correct you. Do you understand?'

She lowered her head.

'I don't punish honest mistakes but, once your duty has been carefully explained, I expect you to do it. I'm happy for you to ask me about anything you don't understand – you might have to choose your moment of course – but I don't want to give you orders without explanation. You're ignorant, not stupid and bright people work best when they understand what they have to do. Don't be afraid to bring me any questions you have.'

She had several but none she could pose. Did he take her with such ferocity to convince himself of his dominance over her or expressly to humiliate her? Why did he actively wish to believe her ignorant? How soon would he tire of her and let her go?

As he stroked her nipple she felt it tingle and watched in detached surprise as it swelled and rose, as if drawn by a lodestone, to salute his teasing finger.

He's content to control my body, she thought, *a paltry victory without my mind or heart, but good enough for him.*

He was looking into her eyes – a look at once candid and questioning. She looked away. Whatever his faults, he was honest. Her sole purpose must be to deceive him.

'One final point. When we're alone in this room you're my darling girl. Outside, I'm the head of the house and you're a kitchen hand. Is that also clear?'

'Of course.'

'It's common gossip that, when the tablinum door is locked, I'm the master's brother. At all other times I'm his respectful slave. Our relationship will be something like that. It would distress me to humiliate you in public by reminding you of your place, so I ask you not to make that necessary.'

Her lips cracked, she traced her tongue hesitantly over them.

'Darling,' he said, 'I'll wet your lips for you.'

His tongue circled her mouth then invaded her throat. She held her breath until she thought she'd suffocate and, as the kiss led inexorably to a new embrace, a knot of hatred twisted in her, tensed with each new indignity and braced her spirit. She resolved to drink all the wine he offered but found it disappointingly thin. Not being a regular drinker, she was susceptible even to the diluted mixture he allowed her. Her second night of marriage was more comfortable than the first. And shorter.

CHAPTER XVIII

June 171

Daunius Libycis bulbus tibi missus ab oris, An veniat Megaris, noxius omnis erit.

Onions, wherever they come from, will do you no good at all. Ovid. Cures for love. 797-8

With the first clang of the bell he roused her for a normal working day. He'd changed. There was nothing of the lover in the brisk way he told her to braid her hair and coil it on the back of her neck. As she stepped back into the bedroom she knew she'd failed.

'Is this intended as a joke?'

'I beg your pardon, sir?'

'I thought you had a mirror.'

'I do.'

'Then go and dress your hair properly. I don't wish to see a hair out of place.'

Blushing, she stumbled back into the washroom but no matter how firmly she scraped her hair back, curling tendrils sprang out from her temples. Eventually, she discovered that wet hair could be plastered down onto her scalp. He pointed out that her tunic was taken up unevenly by her girdle so the hem was not level and one of her pins was out of line. It was late, footsteps were scurrying outside. He replaced the pin and asked if she had make-up. She hadn't.

'I don't really like it on any woman, especially not on a slave unless she's an actress or a prostitute.'

She wondered what was the precise distinction between her situation and that of a similar girl who happened to have been sold to a brothel keeper. It eluded her.

'You'd better eat quickly.' he said.

'I don't need to eat, sir.'

'I've decided you will continue to work in the kitchen under strict supervision. It's in your own interest that you have no chance to put a foot wrong. After work you will come straight back here. If I am out you will do as Polybius suggests. I shall see to it that, within these constraints, you will be happy and have everything you need. Do you understand?'

She nodded.

'Then you may go.'

***

It would be unwise, he thought to show interest in her lack of appetite. He'd find out if she ate at work. If so, there was no problem, if not, he'd give the matter some thought. Should he have called her back and insisted on the usual salute? It was bad for discipline not to but hadn't he said that, within his room, he'd treat her as a lover? He'd have preferred her to show him such deference without prompting. A less primitive girl would have sensed that.

Dismissing her from his mind, he went to his office. A great deal of work would have accumulated in two idle days and he had appointments in the city. They were necessary but they'd hardly be a penance. He'd be congratulated and presented with gifts wherever he went. He disliked to be the centre of attention but there were occasions when one should bow graciously to the inevitable.

***

To walk to the kitchen was a challenge to Nerysa. A day and two nights in bed had left her back stiff and the bruising of her private parts forced her to walk with her knees apart. Her head throbbed from the comb, the pins and the wine. From every door and opening, slaves stared at her, some openly laughing. A pimply youth ran in front of her yelling, 'Our steward's little Brit can hardly walk! He's got the sturdiest shovel in the empire!'

What did it matter if a slave laughed at you? A slave was a non-person. She forced her head high as she walked through the kitchen to the scullery and found Arminia and the girls. They stopped working and stared. No one smiled. No one spoke until Iris edged forward looking at the floor. Nerysa put out her hand. Iris touched it with the tips of her fingers.

'What's it like?' she whispered. 'Is it wonderful, over there?'

Nerysa leant towards her and fell against her. The tension of her body dissolved in weeping. The girls pushed her to a corner where she couldn't be seen from the main kitchen, crooned to her, petted and cuddled her but nothing staunched the effortless flow of her tears.

Arminia slipped away and returned with Apicius. He moved nimbly despite his bulk. His dignity suggested *the* Apicius, the famous gourmet, but he hadn't been born Apicius. In their youth, Lucius and Demetrius had amused themselves choosing apt names for the slaves they bought. They called the messengers Hermes - numbers one to six - the boiler man Vulcan and the doorkeeper Hypnos. They declined to buy Apicius' woman, who was fat and unfresh, or her infant twins. But the girls were ten now, ready for work, and she was a good laundress. Demetrius had negotiated the purchase of all three and brought them into the house. Apicius would have walked through fire for him. His first priority was to hide the girl's distress, especially from Demetrius, so he wasted no sympathy which, in his experience, only encouraged weeping in females. He left, returning moments later, dragging a net of onions hardly smaller than himself. Relishing his heavy, Hispanic aspirates he said, 'Your task for today, girl, his to peel hand-chop these honions.'

It was a master stroke. She could cry all day and no one would think it untoward. He mentioned how he would punish all seven of them if anyone spoke about the affair and left them to Arminia.

Nerysa worked doggedly. Her nose streamed as freely as her eyes and the ache in her face soon rivalled her other discomforts. Passing water felt like passing white hot nails and she needed to do it every few minutes. Because she was crying, she couldn't be seen outside the kitchen and had to submit to the indignity of the chamber pot. Beyond the scullery precincts she heard the cooks slapping pastry on the wooden table and grumbling. The master of the kitchens, they said, had capriciously changed the evening menu and ordered onion tarts.

At lunch time, the girls brought her the barley cakes they knew she liked and she ate greedily through her tears. It was hot and the work was well forward so a midday rest was allowed. They settled down on their mats and Arminia snored. By the time the whispers subsided, Nerysa had learned that he'd done to her everything a man should do with a maid, that her condition redounded hugely to his credit and that her tears were proof of her stupid ingratitude. This was a new insight. His conquest of her was not about love – or even lust. Nor was it about power. It was about his credibility with other men.

The steamy afternoon gave way to the cool of evening. The onions went through to the kitchen and, when she thought of returning to Demetrius, her heart pounded but her tears miraculously dried. Arminia splashed her face with ice water.

'If he complain your eyes red, tell him because of onions.' she said

It was a relief to find Polybius alone in the bedroom. He apologised.

'Himself is burdened with work. Freshen up and be patient. He'll join you for dinner but it will be served late.'

To wash was soothing. The white sound of running water calmed her. She adjusted her hairpins and flattened the rebellious curls with wet palms. The fragrant linen felt good to her skin. Was she being too prodigal of clean tunics? No one had said how often the laundry would supply a fresh pile. But she'd only be wearing the new one for an hour or two - not even her bosom band had been allowed in bed.

Fading light drove her back to the bedroom where Polybius had lit the lamps, laid out the steward's clean tunics, draped the tables and drawn down the bed sheet. The bed looked inviting but she decided to be nowhere near it when Demetrius returned. She toured the room and noticed that, as well as a bronze bath, his washroom had a window. It looked wide enough to squeeze through and, if she stood on the stool, she could reach it. It must give onto the back of the property. In case Polybius noticed her interest, she looked away and sauntered to the chest. An educated sniff at the wrestlers confirmed her first impression; genuine Corinthian bronze. Beside them were other trophies; a dragon with separate scales of polished jade, an ebony carving of a woman's head, an ivory elephant.

A table was drawn up to the couch with a lamp ready lit and beside it a drum-shaped leather book case, obviously brand new. Two scrolls, removed from their covers, lay open. Feasting her eyes wasn't enough, her fingers itched to stroke the smooth, shiny paper with its neat, scarlet margins and elegant, black lettering. From the embossed silver tags, she learned that it was a complete set of the four books of the Georgics. If they belonged to Demetrius, they must be his pride and joy. She daren't touch them nor let him suspect they meant anything to her but she carried the lines in her head, phrased as Quintus had taught. Sitting on the floor, she closed her eyes and heard them in her heart.

When Demetrius came in, she jumped up and hurried to remove his sandals, colliding with Polybius, who warned her off with a scowl. He was allowed to settle his master comfortably and dismissed. Demetrius tapped the couch and, as she sat beside him, he caught up her hand, raised it to his lips and dropped it in disgust.

'Hermes!' he said, 'Your hands stink of the kitchen. Go and scrub them.'

She groped around in the gloom of the washroom, held her hands under the tap, rubbed them on a towel and smeared them with perfume. When she returned, dinner was already served and the waiters had gone.

'I've a present for you.' he said, handing her a package. She turned it over in her hands mechanically, unable to summon the slightest interest. 'Aren't you going to open it?' he said.

It wasn't a question but a command. She obeyed.

'It's the custom, after the wedding night, for a man to buy his wife a present, in exchange for her maidenhood.'

She looked down at the gold bead necklace. Pretty enough in itself, lavish for a kitchen hand. It was the price of that bloodstained sheet. She wanted to tear it with her teeth, link from link. Turning away her head must have given the impression that she tilted it coquettishly for him to clasp the necklace round her neck, which he did. He'd send her out wearing it to face the household. He might as well have hung the blooded sheet around her neck.

'Do you like it?'

She kept her face averted and made him no reply.

'Well, before I buy you another, I'll discover which sort you prefer.'

'I hope you won't trouble yourself, sir. I don't care for necklets.'

Swiftly but gently he removed the offending item from her neck and stared at it with a puzzled frown.

'Then you shall come with me to the jeweller and choose something you *do* like. That way I'll learn what pleases you.'

Her belly tensed in alarm. The less he learned about her the better.

'You'll want to try one of these onion tarts,' he said, hand poised over the dish. 'Our poet Ovid observes that onions sharpen desire.'

Laughter rose in her as from an underground spring, uncontrollable and incapacitating as her tears had been. It burst forth in a gurgle, a splutter, then a torrential hysteria. He watched impassively as her shaking body rocked her stool on the uneven floor. When the attack had subsided into occasional gulps, he withdrew his hand from the dish and flicked the crumbs from his fingers.

'If you wish to eat something,' he said stiffly, 'no doubt you'll ask. But you'd better leave the wine alone tonight.'

CHAPTER XIX

June 171

Tibi enim parcis cum videris alteri parcere

You are merciful to yourself when you are seemingly merciful to another Seneca On Mercy I V 1

As soon as she was back in the kitchen Nerysa began to cry again. Apicius mopped his brow. His onion tarts were popular but he couldn't serve them every day. He ordered onion soup and spiced meatballs and grumbled to Arminia that the bad business couldn't go on. There'd be congestion in the latrines. The ageing system barely coped with two hundred people as it was.

Peeling onions was vile. She tried desperately to control the attacks, which never came on her in Demetrius' room but only in the kitchen when she saw the other girls and smelled smouldering charcoal and proving dough. They lasted for a shorter time each day so, after five days, Arminia gave her salsify and clucked with relief.

She still couldn't eat in Demetrius' presence. A whiff of his breakfast sausage banished her appetite until midday, though he'd discovered she liked barley cakes and these humble items duly appeared on every tray. He knew everything she did and everything that happened to her. Because, to her fury, he'd set other slaves to spy on her.

To live under his keen observation was to court discovery. Each evening he would take her up on his couch and attempt conversation, an uphill task with one who had so much to hide. Her days were taut with anxiety. He had an eye for detail and evidently believed that faults left uncorrected would multiply and were best rooted out when small and unobtrusive, like weeds in a cabbage patch. His manner was gentle but his incessant, considered analysis of what was wrong with her was demoralising. He set about to change the tilt of her head, her level gaze, her direct manners; objecting to anything that distinguished her from the rank and file. It was true that he sometimes praised her but she disliked him too much to value his praise. He didn't use these inept management techniques on anyone else so she assumed they arose from possessiveness. She was his and so must be perfect; like his figurines, his painting and his other slaves.

Polybius was an archetype of the perfect servant; the supply of wine, oil, matches and clean linen never failed. Demetrius would have been incredulous to be offered unsponged sandals and never troubled to ask for anything. He opened his hand and whatever he wanted was immediately placed in it. The merest hesitation in obedience from any of his minions wouldn't have angered so much as puzzled him. Polybius guarded his duties so jealousy that bodily presence was all that was ever required of her. He had a sixth sense of his master's homecoming and he chivvied and worried her so, whenever Demetrius returned, she was groomed and ready, ranged alongside the footbath and the wine-cup.

He had absolute possession of her for as long as he wanted - an overwhelming victory. Each night she endured agony and humiliation; sleepless and shrunk against the alcove wall like the wife of a garlic addict. Regular relief didn't calm his lust. The more he exhausted it the more fevered it grew. Her very reserve seemed to goad him to drive his knee between her trembling thighs and prise them apart. But she dared not offend him because he stood between her and the house bullies. Aglae was not the only slave harbouring jealousy and resentment. Them, him, flight into the unknown through the washroom window or death; these four revolved constantly in her mind as she threw herself into her work. Taking on extra chores made her more popular with other slaves and longer hours in the scullery meant shorter hours in the bedroom.

Late one evening, as she was leaving work, she looked into the kitchen. A poultry knife glinted in a shaft of late sunlight on the scarred wooden bench. Without conscious decision, she looked around her, snatched it up and thrust it in her bosom band. In her washroom she clawed out mortar, freed a loose brick and hid the knife behind it.

Next morning there was panic in the kitchen. When a general search failed to uncover the missing knife, guards were summoned and the slaves lined up to be strip-searched. Demetrius appeared and swept Nerysa into the pantry. She was close to fainting with fear, more on account of his fabled omniscience than her own guilt but, when he began to remove her tunics, she took heart. If he didn't know where she'd hidden it, she could deny it. He passed the tunics through the curtain for the guards to shake out, then snatched it shut, gave a long sigh and leant her over a shelf. She arched her back and submitted. He put his arm through the curtain, recovered her tunics from the waiting guard and pulled them over her head. She marvelled that he wasn't embarrassed to step out into the kitchen and face his staff but he was as cool and assured as if he'd been making an inventory of the preserves.

After he left, gloom descended because the knife was still missing and everyone was under suspicion. Demetrius didn't linger over dinner and drank sparingly.

'Go to bed.' he told her. 'I'll be late. I lost time over that missing knife.'

'Couldn't Apicius have dealt with such a trivial matter, sir?'

'I dealt with it myself because it's not trivial. Good quality Norican steel is expensive. A knife's a lethal weapon and either theft is a stranger to this house or it will be rife. Think of a girl treasuring a present from a lover. A slave hoarding tips to help his freedman son set up in business or as a dowry to get his daughter respectably married. The old gardener's savings. Do you want to live in a house where such things aren't safe? No one else has a strongbox like mine.'

'What if it isn't found?'

'It will be.'

'What will you do to the thief?'

'It depends on the circumstances. I doubt it was stolen. It was probably mislaid. But if it's not found, I fear the deputy cooks must be whipped. They're to blame. The occasion makes the thief.'

She flinched and looked away. He squeezed her hand.

'Don't fret,' he said, 'It's bound to turn up - behind a sack of flour or in the pig swill. Slaves can be so careless of their masters' property.'

She waited for him to fall asleep. When his breathing was slow and regular she slipped the knife from under the mattress. She didn't know if she meant to kill him or just to comfort herself with the knowledge that she could if she chose. How easy it would be to slide it between his ribs and touch his heart. Perhaps the whole household would like to see the sheet in the morning? She eased around towards him and stopped dead at the sight of his naked back in the moonlight, pierced through with a fearful anguish; whether pity or disgust she couldn't tell. Tracing trembling fingers over her back, she reassured herself that her own scars were less ugly. Even as she hesitated, he murmured and turned over and she mocked herself. What kind of barbarian was she, who couldn't kill a sleeping Roman in his bed?

Gradually, she became aware that the dull thud she could hear was not her own heart but a tapping on the door. It wasn't the first time she noticed how inconsiderate the staff were of him, apologising abjectly for needing his advice yet never making the least shift to do without it. He woke, stood straight up and, to her amazement, pushed his feet into his sandals. What man, possessed of a slave, ever put on his own shoes? Did she respect him less or more for not calling Polybius to perform this basic service? He'd pulled on his tunics and left before she reflected that she'd never known him disturbed at night. Could someone have seen her take the knife and come to warn him? She ran to the washroom and thrust it back behind the loose brick.

Crossing back to the bed she saw light through a crack in the office door. Listening at doors, however unworthy, was her only chance to hear good conversation. Demetrius and his contacts used sophisticated language, spiced with wit, speaking as no one spoke to her any more.

Putting an eye to the crack, she felt a flood of relief to see Jacob, the shipping manager from Ostia. She'd only seen him once but recognised him easily. His domed forehead gave him a scholarly look and she was fascinated by his gestures; not those assumed by trained orators, but fluid and instinctive as if his hands were outposts of his mind. If she could have loved a slave, he would have been a more likely choice than the aggressively physical Demetrius.

Jacob wouldn't have come from Ostia in the middle of the night to tell his superior tales about his wife and, if he had, he wouldn't be slumped on the floor clutching his knees. She strained her ears to catch the rapid Greek.

'Not public auction, sir. The shame would kill me. If you could place me privately in a good family, even for menial work, you'd spare me and honour yourself.'

'A strange request. And an even stranger time to come making it.'

'God help me, sir! I had to find you alone. I'm ruined.'

His voice faltered. She took her eye from the crack, pressed an ear to it and made out the word 'cargo'.

'Small deals with Decius before....offered me the big one...Leather mostly, due in from Marseilles....matter of days... selling at a discount because...cheap corn at the port... needed cash straight away –'

'The ship went down?'

Jacob was hoarse. She had to squash her ear flat against the door to hear him.

'Limped into port today, sir; no mast, no rigging, no cargo. The loss is bad enough but I've the strangest feeling that he already knew - though how could he?'

In the silence that followed she took her ear from the crack and put her eye to it. Jacob's face was barley grey in the lamplight and the sweat glistened on it. A shudder rippled the length of his long robe and her whole heart went out to him. Her husband's power appalled her and she'd no doubt he relished the exercising of it. He seemed so cold. Did he feel anything? A strange bargain formed in her mind. If he helped Jacob, she'd be able to forgive him much of what he'd done to her. She put her other eye to the crack so as to see him. Light flickered over his face but it was immobile, inscrutable. He stretched out an unhurried hand and Jacob placed a scroll in it.

'This is dated seven days before the Ides and the ship, you say, reached port two days before. I take it this is your signature, correctly witnessed?'

'Alas, sir!'

'And the sum, I note, within your peculium?'

'Just.'

'Did you think to send for me to confer on this?'

'Ask you to leave Rome, sir, when you're barely a month married?'

'Then I'm to blame? I did wrong, indeed, if I let you think my own pleasure was more important than my master's business.

'But perhaps my own unexpected return from Aquileia prompted you to try to make your mark here. What funds do you have of your own?'

'Nowhere near this sum. My credit is good for a small loan. I did have savings, of course, but, before I came here, I bought my mother's freedom.'

At last, Demetrius showed a flicker of warmth.

'Where did you settle her?'

'In Brundisium with my brother, a freedman but poor.'

'You questioned the passengers and crew, of course?'

'Storm off Corsica, it was a miracle the ship wasn't broken up. Every man, woman and child was bailing out, with bare hands some of them.'

'And the freight went overboard?'

'Most of it. One merchant refused to part with his. Said he was better dead than bankrupt. His slaves drew swords. The captain offered them the life raft.'

'Without a pilot?'

'He sent one of the crew with them.'

'Then that's it, isn't it? Blown ashore further north, fast ride down the Via Aurelia. We can't touch them but at least we know how they did it.'

'How did *I* do it? Throw away a good position and my master's trust.'

'Who said you did? Have your men hang round the bars in Ostia and keep their ears open for a sailor boasting of a lucky escape. Our Lucius may be able to get a warrant for his arrest. But be quick - and quiet. If Decius is ahead of us he'll free him so he can't be tortured.'

'He can't be forced to testify against his own master, surely?'

'No, but if we can convince a magistrate there's been a deception, we'll get a compulsory purchase order on him.'

'I hope you recover some of the money. You'll have no further use for me, of course.'

Nerysa held her breath. Finally, Demetrius said, 'I was raised as Lucius' companion and given a liberal education; literature, mathematics, rhetoric. At eighteen, I found myself running farms and trading. People said I couldn't do it. They asked how I learned. Between ourselves, I learned something by watching more experienced men but, mainly, I learned by my mistakes. A man who's made a mistake is wiser than one who hasn't. Why would I sell you to someone else for him to profit from the experience you gained at our expense?'

'Sir, – I never expected – you mean I'm to stay –'

'I shall fine you, of course. You'll know how much is suitable. Enough to sting but not enough to crush.'

'But, sir, my peculium is accounted for in the deed of sale. You know exactly what I have.'

'I do but what I don't know is the extent of your obligations.'

'But Lucius Marius –'

'I think we may have to tell him you were acting on my instructions. He'll think it out of character but he'll forgive me. Sleep here an hour or two but be sure to leave before dawn.'

Nerysa stole back to his bed mindful of the bargain she'd made and found that his embrace, though distasteful, no longer caused physical pain.

CHAPTER XX

July/August 171

Peculium, quod servus civiliter quidem possidere non posset, sed naturaliter tenet, dominus creditur possidere

The slave's peculium which the slave, of course, cannot possess at civil law, but can hold only in fact, his owner is held to possess. Justinian Dig.41.2.24 Javolenus 14 epist.

Nerysa's working life improved. She felt Demetrius' protection like a cloak swathed around her. It couldn't soothe jealousy or dislike but it stopped them being openly expressed. For every one who referred to the steward's 'wife' there were two who referred to the steward's 'woman' but the steward's 'baggage' and the steward's 'copper top' were muttered under the breath.

She was promoted to the bakery team and, progressing rapidly from dog biscuits, began to specialise in bread, pastry and the animal-shaped honey cakes offered daily to the household gods. The tasks were simple but they engaged her interest and commitment. There was a science to the work and scope for self-expression in decorating pies and fancy loaves for the master's table. Pounding dough and slapping it against the table released stores of pent-up aggression. Kitchen life was fast and exciting and she learned at a vertiginous rate. The women wore tightly coiled hair and plain grey tunics severely girdled, but the men, more often stripped to the waist, were a forest of brown, hairy trunks streaming sweat. There were foods such as peas and celeriac which she didn't recognise because their raw state bore no relation to their appearance on an elegant table, but there were slave rations, like barley, which comforted her with the long lost tastes and smells of childhood.

Craftsman, rather than slave minder, Apicius didn't carry a whip. If he had, he'd have been forever mislaying it. Goaded past his fragile patience, he seized whatever came to hand; marrow, rolling pin or pig's shank which, gaining momentum from being swung above his head, shot through the air and descended on the culprit to excellent effect. His most offensive weapon was his mouth. He'd suck up sauce and blast it to the corners of the kitchen, spluttering, 'Like barley water! Add fish sauce. Smidgeon at a time, you're not dousing a fire!' Or, 'Like a salt lick! Drown it in honey and the pig might eat it.'

She watched him spin pies on his left hand, edging and sealing them with a flourish of a potter's crimping tool with his right. When work had finished for the day, he let her take the tool from its box and practise, which diverted her and delayed her return to the bedroom.

Demetrius never talked down to her and shared even the finest food with her. He gave her her own napkin but, when she dabbed her pursed lips with it, she saw his eyes widen and knew she should have used the back of her hand. When she dipped her bread in the sauce bowl, he grinned and winked as if he approved the neat turn of her wrist. He leant down towards her so his hair tickled her temple and asked softly, 'Do you ever lapse into the vernacular? I can't wait to hear you.'

After that she became more laconic than ever. But a single, thought provoking word of hers never failed to elicit an interesting argument from him. As the days drew to a close, she'd look forward to dinner even though she dreaded his bed. Perhaps it was the wine, perhaps she felt less angry or more at ease in his room; perhaps the sight and smell of rich food reminded her of suppers with Quintus. For whatever reason, food, wine and conversation disarmed her. One evening she wondered if it was his birthday, for the succession of exotic dishes served was fit for an imperial banquet. He seemed particularly alert and kept up a steady flow of small talk while she savoured each course and feared he would think her greedy. But, although he was looking at her intently, his look was not disapproving; indeed he seemed pleased with her - or with himself.

He began to occupy himself with the empty dishes, arranging them in a row across the table. She looked down at them. There, drawn up in order, were the rectangular soup spoon, the tiny scoop for prising snails from their shells, the slender winkle pick, the dainty fork fashionable ladies used to spear dormice and the miniature sauce ladle. She'd wielded them unconsciously and with assurance. Iris wouldn't have known what to do with any of them. She broke into a sweat. He'd set a trap for her and she'd pranced straight into it.

For a foolish moment she thought of throwing herself on his mercy, groveling at his feet, begging him to keep her secret. She looked up into his steady, penetrating gaze and knew it wasn't worth a try. He laid down his own spoon, leant back on his cushions, an arm curved above his head and said conversationally, 'I've rumbled you, you know. A few discreet inquiries – quite simple, really.'

Her heart gave a hollow, sickening thud. This was the end – for herself and for Quintus.

'I seem to remember Quintus Pulcher's house is in the old style, is it not?'

Eyes closed in despair, she nodded.

'So it has a separate wing for ladies.'

She held her breath.

'His mother and grandmother, who retired from the world years ago, they lived on that side of the house, didn't they? You weren't his mistress. I know that. But you weren't his skivvy either, were you? A lady's maid who can ape her mistress to the life. That's what you are. No, don't blush. I like play acting too. I'll buy us both silk gowns and we can play act together.'

Giddy with relief, she saw that he'd explained her speech and manners to his own satisfaction and it would be safe to talk. The next afternoon, biting into a peach to cover her nervousness, she blurted out, 'Sir, what's a peculium?'

He looked up and smiled. 'An odd question. Why do you want to know?'

'I've heard you say you have one.'

'No, I have two.'

'Two then and they say the master's friend, Gaius Julius, has exceeded his. So I wondered what it was.'

'Same word, three different things. We call the wealth of a Roman family the patrimony; it's made up of real estate, jewellery and plate, slaves, investments and so on. One man controls it, the father of the family. Lucius has it because his father's dead. Gaius Julius won't get it until his father dies. In the meantime he has his peculium, his allowance, to spend as he likes.'

'And yours?'

'My two are different. I've no legal right to the money I earn. It belongs to Lucius. But, while it pleases him, it goes in the inventory of his wealth under the heading of money for me to use as I please. My other peculium, the third kind, comes about for the same reason. In the course of my duties I need to spend money every day. I may need to buy equipment for the houses and farms, or slaves, or commodities to trade or to charter a boat, say to Marseilles or back from Corinth. I'm thinking of exporting wine to Britain by the way. What do you think to that?'

'You couldn't sell it there, sir, Britons have their own mead.'

'Well, my sources tell me there's a fashion for Italian and Gallic wines among the sophisticates of the south but I'll remember what you say.'

She disclaimed hastily, not wanting to be blamed for bad advice. He acknowledged her with a wave of his hand and continued, 'It would be tiresome for Lucius to have me constantly asking for cash or a signature, so I'm allowed to spend his money, pledge his credit or draw on his bankers, here and abroad, up to a certain limit. That's also my peculium; the amount of his money I can spend on his behalf without consulting him beforehand.'

'Supposing you overspent, inadvertently, of course,?'

'My dear, I hope I'm never inadvertent.' He broke off, flushing darkly and she remembered Archias saying that regret was painful. 'At least,' he resumed, 'I'm careful not to exceed the peculium because, if I did, my transactions would be illegal and unenforceable, my correspondents couldn't recover their money and Lucius would never be able to employ me in business again.'

'That's why you keep records?'

'Well, I keep a tally in my head. The records are so, any time he asks, he can see how things stand.'

'And check for discrepancies?'

'He's no fear of that. But he has business acumen himself and likes to be involved – not in detail, but in a general way. Then, for tax reasons, we keep records and in case the books are questioned. I need to know who owes us money and prove that my accounts balance. Because they do, I'm entitled to call myself "pariator".'

'Thank you. I used to think kitchen work was complex.'

'Kitchen work's hard. I don't plan to leave you there forever. But I think that whether or not your master's friend exceeds his allowance is not a suitable subject for you to be discussing. When you hear such things, by all means ask me about them but don't add one word of your own to the tittle-tattle you hear. What you say may be more significant than you think because people may think your views reflect mine - I must go, I have to throw a ball at Lucius.'

'Why must you do that?'

'To help him work up a sweat before his bath.'

'Doesn't he have ball boys for that?'

'Of course, but they don't make him sweat like I do.'

Was it the lightness of his step or the glint in his eye that told her he felt smug? She envied him. Not the ball games but having something meaningful to do with his leisure. He seemed to think constant grooming the only suitable pastime for her. To be kicked and beaten would have made her feel like a slave but the tacit assumption that she existed for his convenience made her feel more like an inanimate object. He was even-tempered, however, and tossed her an endearment or a titbit often enough to make her resentment seem churlish, even to herself.

CHAPTER XXI

August 171

Si saevitiam, si impietatem, si feritatem permissam nobis contendere possumus, eamus in amphitheatrum.

If cruelty, depravity and savagery are permitted to us then let's go to the amphitheatre. Tertullian De Spectaculis XIX

D emetrius meant to train his wife much as he trained a hound but couldn't find the right rewards to make her sit up and beg. He certainly intended to exploit any tearful scenes in which she asked if it was right that other girls should have this or that when the steward's wife had not but, to his surprise, that never happened. When the household went to the Coliseum for the spectacle he hesitated to refuse her first request but she didn't ask. He had to broach the subject himself.

'When I've time, I'll take you to the theatre. That would be more suitable. There's literary merit in some of the plays. Actors are scoundrels, of course, but they're skilled. Now in the arena there's no need to create an illusion. People die for real.'

Seeing her frown, he hastened to add, 'I don't care for it myself but it pleases the common herd.'

'Why do you let them go, sir?'

How could he answer that? He thought the games distasteful and there was no doubt they unsettled the slaves but it had never crossed his mind to ban them. He felt an unwonted need to justify himself.

'I impose enough on them without imposing my aesthetic taste. A slave's life is drudgery. They get food, a jug of wine a day, the odd word of praise and an occasional treat. If I were to forbid that I might not be obeyed. Would I want to make going to the games a flogging offence? It would be thought very singular. Besides, if I'm disobeyed in any matter, people will begin to question their habit of obedience. Even I can't order anything, however unreasonable.'

The August afternoon was eerily quiet, even the dogs were asleep in the heat. He'd never felt burdened by his charges, in spite of their noise, their qualms and their petty squabbles but it seemed to him that the house was all the finer for being deserted and he wanted her to see it. Its magnificence must surely reconcile her to her place in it.

**

Full of curiosity, Nerysa let him lead her by the hand across the bright garden to the summer dining room. Entering this arcade, facing due west, she felt as if she were stepping into the setting sun. Swirling mosaics covered the walls and floor. The tesserae of coloured glass were interspersed with carnelian, coral, sardonyx, tourmaline, fire opal and garnet. Touches of gold and citrine glittered in the sunshine so the walls seemed to dance in flame. The room was an obvious sign of new wealth yet the palette was so restricted and the whole effect so harmonious that the most carping critic couldn't have called it gaudy or detected the least hint of vulgarity. There were heirlooms, too, though not so numerous as in Quintus' house, which was almost a private museum. Curious as to which of the city's famous architects had designed the room, she refrained from mentioning any by name, observing only that it must have been professionally designed.

'No,' he said, 'Lucius has the general concept. I fill in the detail and engage the craftsmen.'

'You're a good team.'

'We understand each other.'

Quintus had arranged couches in groups of three but here were modern semi-lunar units, purpose built in perfect proportion to the spacious hall. With ten guests to each, more if some were women, and their attendants crowded onto benches below, there could be fifty to be served. The dining room prefect must have the marshalling skills of a military commander. Demetrius drew back the heavy cloths to reveal the feathered grain of the citrus wood tables and she took care not to breathe on them. High gloss now meant but one thing to her - elbow grease. He opened cabinets displaying embossed gold dishes and Alexandrine crystal. Admiration was not enough; she learned the purchase price, the current value and the penalty for dropping one.

The winter dining room seemed to her a masculine room, smaller and spare, fitted with silver lamp stands and panelled in black marble, spangled like a starling's breast. They strolled through it to the atrium. On the previous occasion she'd been there, she'd noticed nothing. Now she gasped as she tilted her head to follow the colonnades of glassy, rose granite to the azure ceiling. Sunlight burst through the central opening and she squinted at the dazzling blue Hymettian marble walls and the sparkling waters of the impluvium. Demetrius boasted that the domus was larger than when Lucius inherited it. Adjacent property had been bought up and incorporated. At first, she listened patiently to the inventory but she began to find it distasteful. Curiously, her unease was on his behalf, as if the vaunting of his master's wealth somehow diminished him.

'I don't think owning things is important.' she ventured, 'It's the capacity to enjoy them that matters. The master couldn't get more pleasure from his paintings than I do, just because he owns them.'

He stared in blank amazement as though at a loss to explain the pride of possession to one so penniless and so primitive.

'Well, for instance, suppose I didn't own you?' he said, 'You'd be a torment.'

The shrine was an elaborate ivory piece with carved pillars and solid gold doors which he unlocked to reveal the household gods. The Priapus with its distended phallus made her blush and stare at her clenched toes but Demetrius didn't share her embarrassment. He explained that this god was the guardian of the family's prosperity. A figure of a youth was the master's genius who would ensure that Lucius had an heir, to discharge his duties to the gods and his clients and increase the patrimony. Next was a finely wrought silver statue of the winged messenger, Hermes. She was surprised to hear they'd brought it back from Spain.

'A year's military service.' he said ruefully, 'It was expected of Lucius. He wasn't cut out for a soldier nor was I born for a batman. He was happy for me to do the minimum polishing up his breastplate and spend my time in the forum setting up deals. We got by without disgrace but it wasn't a distinguished year for us. We bought silver mines, or rather, the rights to work them.'

'Do you run them too?'

'Nominally. I went last year but I shan't be going this year; not while there's a war on. The local manager's excellent. I don't need to breathe down his neck.'

He kissed his hand to the silver statue. Roman religion baffled her. Her gods were spirits who pervaded nature; stirring waters, fanning flame and haunting whispering forests. These figures were artefacts made by mortal hands. Did Demetrius believe they were gods or did he think his gods resided in them? She didn't dare breathe the word 'druid', knowing he'd find it sinister and alarming. He took flame and incense and prayed solemnly for her, that she'd find fulfilment and tranquillity in being a dutiful wife to him, while she squirmed with embarrassment.

He brought out family portraits and wax death masks, at pains to inform her that the collection hadn't been acquired with the house but were the images of eminent men of Lucius' own family. She discerned a resemblance to Lucius in several of them, but then Demetrius also resembled Lucius somewhat, not in colouring but in feature and, especially, in expression. Did slaves grow to look like their owners after years of patient imitation?

'It's strange,' he said, 'that you've belonged to two bachelor houses. They're rare. If Lucius' parents had lived, he'd be married by now. He needs an heir. But he's ambitious and rich enough to take senatorial rank. I'd expect him to do that first and marry into that class. He'll make a considered choice. He wants his son to grow up in a stable family as he did.' He frowned. 'It will be an upheaval. No aristocratic lady will want to be simply absorbed into this household. Her slaves will belong to her, of course, not to Lucius, but they'll have to live alongside us. Then, Lucius would insult her not to give her authority over the house, so there, at least, I'd have a mistress instead of a master.'

Sensing his unease, she offered up a silent prayer for him, to whichever of his gods cared to listen.

The library was at the front of the house where, according to Demetrius, there had once been shops. Its outer walls had been reinforced so the room was cool and remarkably quiet; the retreat of a rich man who loved books. Tables and benches were arranged about the light well. The only decoration was the gilded stuccoed ceiling, the walls being entirely lined with shelves and pigeon holes for scrolls and leather scroll cases. The collection was extensive. Demetrius couldn't resist cataloguing it, even for the benefit of an illiterate, barbarian woman. Half the volumes were legal reference texts but there were also histories, travel guides and works on natural science. The rhetoric section included every published speech of Hortensius, Cicero and Fronto and scores of textbooks. She noted all the well-known and many obscure philosophers, the standard Greek dramas, together with Plautus and Terence and poetry from Sappho to Statius. It was an ordeal. She daren't raise her eyes lest their scanning seem purposeful to him or betray that her hunger, even for a single volume, caused her physical pain. He must have caught her wistful mood.

'Reading is not a mere utility.' he said. 'To some of us it's a source of great pleasure. Maybe, one day, you might like...you don't lack the wit...'

She looked up in panic and he said, 'But not yet, of course, there are too many new things in your life already.'

Could he really mean to guide her hand round a template of the alphabet? Was she equal to such a protracted deception? She was touched but determined to give him no encouragement. She saw the swift frown as his eyes lighted on a glue pot left uncovered and had no doubt the careless bookbinder would be disciplined. For once, she approved his severity. Stale glue spoiled books.

CHAPTER XXII

August 171

ἐπεὶ δὲ ὁρῶμεν ὅτι αἱ παιδεῖαι ποιούς τινας ποιοῦσι τοὺς νέους, ἀναγκαῖον καὶ παρασκευασάμενον τρέφειν οἷς τὰ ἐλευθέρια τῶν ἔργων προστακτέον.

We need to train the slaves we've bought if we want to make them overseers Aristotle the householder 1 5 1

Despite the inexplicable gulf between his behaviour in bed and out of it, Nerysa could no longer think of Demetrius as a brute. From the number and variety of decisions that made up his daily life, she understood why he was so valued. Lucius couldn't have replaced him with three men.

Of his commercial and rural duties and the companionship he gave his master, she knew nothing but she observed his day to day running of the house. He rarely had to exert authority because he inspired everyone with his own single-minded devotion to his master. Painstakingly fair in his judgements, he was patient beyond belief with stupidity.

One suffocating day, when the office door was propped open, she watched him dictate two separate letters to different scribes while adding columns of figures and answering questions. Imperturbable when everyone else was excited, he was always rational and practical. His omniscience rested only partly on the network of spies. Whether it was a stain on a wall, a pitcher left out by the well or shutter blowing in the wind, he would point it out politely, sometimes with a joke. But nothing went unnoticed. Besides the two hundred slaves in Rome there were the same number at Horta and in Sicily, others at Ostia, Tivoli and the Spanish mines. People said he had a shrewder idea of what each was capable than the individuals themselves. It would have been extraordinary if he'd treated them all to their entire satisfaction but she saw that, broadly, the machine worked; that the strengths and skills of each person were dovetailed into those of the rest so a thousand souls lived in plenty and harmony. It had never occurred to her before that a slave might be estimable and she resisted the uncomfortable conclusion as long as she could.

Her over-riding ambition was to stay alive but, along with it, she began to have new ones, among them that this man should not despise her. She couldn't tell him who she was or show him what she could do. The qualities he would value in her were the very ones he must never suspect. How to make him see that she was more than a plaything? She'd left her own world, where he would have been beneath her notice, and entered his, where there was only one way to impress him; on his own terms, by being a good underslave.

It was uphill work. She'd blithely imagined it would be the easiest thing in the world to impersonate an unskilled slave but his standards were high and she was a novice. There were at least ten wrong ways of doing the simplest thing and no hope that the least of her imperfections would escape his notice. Regret, admiration and fear of detection mingled uncomfortably and made her gauche in his presence. He treated her as a possession but a cherished one and, while she shrank from his touch, she was glad of his friendship. He'd come in from the office or a trip to Ostia grey with fatigue and make a noticeable effort to recount something amusing that had happened during the day or to acknowledge any action of hers that had met with his approval.

His brow was furrowed for his age and, when the creases deepened, she would have liked to share his concerns but that would have been inappropriate. She was kept as a diversion not a confidante. By contrast, he took a great deal of interest in her affairs. Did she need anything? Had she any complaints of Polybius? Was he polite and helpful? Did she still hanker after her past life or anyone particular from it?

'I'm sorry,' he said, 'if you looked to me for promotion. Your new situation is a strain in itself so it's wiser for you to stay in familiar surroundings, less exposed to comment. Do me credit there and I'll move you on.'

He laid a hand on her shoulder, so gently she didn't flinch.

'Poor girl.' he said. 'You don't know how to behave because no one has taught you. The master said you should be trained. I'll remind Thaïs.'

Nerysa suspected that Thaïs disliked her and couldn't spare the time, so she wasn't surprised when Xenia was proposed instead. Xenia was old but alert and agile and had lived in the house longer than anyone could remember, having been the old master's nurse. Like Demetrius, she was a stickler for discipline. Nerysa thought that, if anyone could teach her how to be a satisfactory underslave, Xenia could. Though her frame was spare and her complexion like cured pigskin, her black eyes were gimlet sharp. She sat erect and prim on an upturned pail, smoothing her tunic over bony knees, evidently seeing Nerysa, standing to attention before her, as a challenge.

Nerysa didn't care that she was hungry and tired, that the midday heat weighed on her or that her fellow workers were lying on their mats enjoying a siesta. Xenia held a treasure house of knowledge that she was keen to plunder. She forgot to keep her eyes lowered and smiled.

'Thank you for teaching me. I think Demetrius wants to move me on.'

'So he will as soon as he's tired of you,'

'No, I mean promote me.'

'Promote you?' Xenia snorted. 'An ignoramus that jumped from nowhere and landed in the steward's bed? You might have been freeborn but you're a slave now, a vicaria at that, and the sooner you accept it, the better. Do you even know what a vicaria is?'

'A slave's slave – an underslave.'

'And you're not the only one here, are you?'

'There's Polybius and Philemon – and Idumeus and....the African girl –'

'Niobe, Thaïs' maid. We called her Niobe because, when she first came, the silly thing cried all day. Happy enough now, as you'll be when you've learned to please your master. To understand your duties and know you perform them perfectly; that's happiness for a slave.'

'Please tell me how.'

'Don't expect me to spell out what he likes. It's your job to study him. Notice what seems to please him and what makes him frown.

'If I'd *my* way, we'd have our country wenches breed more and staff the house with home-grown slaves. They take in meekness with their mother's milk. You imports are all the same - no self-control.

'If you're tired or bored you don't show it. You swallow yawns and coughs and sneezes and you don't break wind until you're under the bedclothes, or in your case, not even there – especially not there! How do you think it is for the guards to stand against the wall for hours without moving a muscle? Do you think it's fun to run panting beside the master's carriage? We girls get the best of it.'

To Nerysa's amazement, there was a glint from the black eyes and a leer from those thin, bloodless lips.

'But, man or woman, a slave's feelings don't matter. The only thing that matters is pleasing your master. In bed. That's the only use he has for you.'

'Nothing else?'

'Well, you might sail to Egypt and negotiate a keen price for silks and spices. Huh?' Xenia cackled. 'Or supervise the slaves at their tasks and settle their disputes and grievances. Perhaps you'd draw up the accounts every month and make his debtors pay up?'

'No. but I thought there might be something I could do that he might like.' Nerysa said, feeling suddenly small and worthless.

'You could learn to hold your tongue for a start.'

Xenia did, at least, perfect Nerysa's salute, teaching her to raise her right hand palm forwards while inclining her head and sweeping the ground with her eyes. After exhaustive practice, the gesture became instinctive and graceful yet, when she tried it on Demetrius, he frowned.

'No, not here in this room,' he said, 'but always, without fail, outside it.'

Over the coming weeks Xenia analysed all the ways in which a slave could fail to please, taking the view that the eventuality for which one was unprepared was the one most likely to occur. The situations she described were so improbable Nerysa took comfort from the sheer number of interesting blunders that even she was unlikely to commit. But it was frustrating, since she was eager to learn, that Xenia taught her nothing to the purpose. A repertoire of servile turns of phrase and stereotyped behaviour didn't help her understand him or much else about her situation.

After a month of daily monologue, Xenia was still speaking slowly as though to a foreigner of dim wits. Since she had long since given up all hope of learning anything useful from her, Nerysa assumed a posture suggestive of rapt attention and escaped into her usual trance. When a fly landed on her brow she jumped and shook her head.

'Don't fidget.' snapped Xenia, 'It's disrespectful.'

The fly buzzed through her hair and settled on her nose. It wasn't quite still. She supposed it was stroking one antenna with the other as flies do. It didn't hurt, why was a tickle more difficult to bear than pain? Xenia's litany droned on.

'Respect. Always respect. Respect your master. Show respect...'

Nerysa had the strange thought that she did respect him though only in so far as he allowed her to respect herself and not for any of the reasons Xenia advanced. He was clever but Xenia had said it wasn't clever of him to choose to live with a savage in defiance of the master.

Dislodged, the fly circled her head and she screwed up her face to deter it from landing. The air was suffocating, her body crawling with sweat. She pulled herself erect. He ran the house efficiently, she thought but Xenia wasn't so sure..

'Things seem relaxed here but the prefects know how keep order, however indulgent the master may be. Now, in his father's time we didn't have slaves taking liberties and carrying on like Saturnalia all year round.'

The fly landed back on Nerysa's nose, enjoying a refreshing dip in her sweat. To touch her nose in the presence of a superior would not be disrespect; it would be a studied insult. She clasped her hands tightly behind her back, clenched her arms and bit her tongue to distract herself from the itch.

'Why should you respect him, stupid girl? She ticked off the reasons on her gnarled fingers while Nerysa clenched her teeth to stop herself screaming. 'Because a woman naturally looks up to a man;

because a menial defers to the head of the house and, in your special case, we must also consider the respect a wife owes a husband...'

A dribble of sweat meandered down Nerysa's nose. She turned her head and lifted her shoulder, straining to press her sleeve to it. Sensing inattention, Xenia raised her voice.

'Feeling respect is no use unless you show it.'

The fly buzzed onto Nerysa's brow and settled back on her nose. She wrinkled it. She blew down it, dislodging the bead of sweat which reached the tip of her nose and clung on, trembling, irritating to madness. She looked towards the doorway, desperate to escape.

'Now tell me how you can show him respect. Think now.'

Reckless and feeling a delicious frisson of malice, Nerysa threw back her head and said,

'I could kick him, perhaps, - in the balls?'

Xenia froze, growled like a mastiff poised to spring, and struck out. Nerysa clutched her stinging cheek and peeled off the squashed fly. There was a ripple of activity outside and Demetrius stood in the doorway with what seemed like half the household behind him. For the first time ever, she heard his voice raised.

'No one,' he said, 'handles my wife. If you weren't so insensitive you'd see she's foreign and untrained and doing her best. She should be guided with kindness and understanding. You're not fit to have charge of her.'

Nerysa slumped to her knees beside the prostrate Xenia. Her defiance dissolved in rivers of ice flowing down her back as she waited for the old woman to speak but, after a long, tingling pause, it dawned on her that Xenia was too terrified to defend herself and she was ashamed.

'Sir, if you please,' she whispered, 'I did deserve it.'

'If you were at fault, it was for me to punish you. Come, stand up. I'll see you back to the kitchen.'

The crowd melted away as they walked around the cloister.

She said, 'I was to blame, sir, I'm sorry.'

He stopped, looked down at her and said slowly,

'I think...you do your best.'

Suddenly his arms were around her, his kiss brief and gentle, unlike the hungry, crushing kiss she knew. Far more terrifying.

God help me. she thought, *What's he trying to do to me now?*

She pulled back in panic as her lips furred, her knees faltered and her heart fluttered like a stricken bird. He owned her body. She'd come to terms with that. Rape was bearable because her spirit had learned to escape her body while he mauled it. But his kiss had become a threat and she'd find ways to avoid it.

CHAPTER XXIII

September 171

Esse tibi videor saevus nimiumque gulosus Qui propter cenam, Rustice, caedo cocum. Si levis ista tibi flagrorum causa videtur, Ex qua vis causa vapulet ergo cocus?

If I seemed to you greedy and brutal to beat my cook for spoiling the dinner, then tell me, do you know a better reason to beat a cook?Martial. Epigrams VII 23

Over the coming days, Nerysa came to realise that Xenia dared not betray her. And she hadn't lost credibility with Demetrius. He even trusted her with an important commission,

'Tell Apicius from me that the master will be out from dawn until late,' he said, 'so today would be an excellent day to kill the pig.'

And he prevailed on Thaïs to teach her. She couldn't commit to regular lessons but, when she had spare time, she sent for her. Nerysa still reproached herself.

I'll never be credible as a slave, she thought, *if I can't be servile.*

Yet, she reflected, *he* wasn't servile. She understood the hierarchy and saw that the way out was up. The higher up the system you were, the fewer people you had to grovel to. Even for someone who still dreamed of a return to freedom and privilege, the top of the slave pile was the more comfortable place to wait. Thaïs was clear and clever. Nerysa snapped up everything she said and memorised it. Bustling out of the kitchen to a lesson, she caught Iris slinking in from the scullery.

'Why are you always trying to come and see me here?' she asked

'Why are you always stopping me?'

'Because you're supposed to be working. So am I.'

'You kitchen girls think you're too good for me.

'Of course I don't. I'd love to talk but I can't. Thaïs is waiting for me.'

'Thaïs is it? Chief slave mistress. Wants your advice, does she?'

'You should go. Apicius sees everything and there are ..other people, too, who…we'll both be in trouble'.

Her lesson was absorbing and she forgot about Iris. She hurried back to the kitchen, head bowed as she ticked off facts on her fingers. Household consumption per diem; olive oil, three amphora; wheat, two hundred libera; barley, one hundred. A sudden roar came from the direction of the kitchen. She looked up in annoyance. 'Barley, one hundred; Wine, six amphora - ' Another roar, a scream, wild cheering; definitely coming from the kitchen.

'Where are those silentarii?' she muttered. 'Never where you want them.'

Once in the kitchen, she saw why they weren't there. It was easy enough for two to cane five small maids but they could hardly quell a riot. Discretion was the largest part of their valour and they had gone for reinforcements.

A hybrid monster was careering around the kitchen, skidding on pools of grease and ricocheting off the walls and shelves. Four stamping legs and anklets and four flailing arms and jangling bracelets meant that it consisted of two girls fighting; spitting, grunting and screeching insults as they rolled over each other. Supporters cheered and jeered. Some had bowls of slops at the ready but couldn't discharge them because the two were so entangled and moved so unpredictably they couldn't be sure of hitting their intended target. Apicius, red hot bread slice poised above his head, was in the same dilemma. Twice he shied, once he slammed it down, only to deflect it on to the ground at the last moment. Finally, he scored two blows on the same rump. There was a sizzling, a smell of burning flesh, a blood curdling scream and Iris shot from the tangle and hurled herself into the scullery.

Much as Nerysa liked Apicius, Iris was the closest thing she'd ever had to a girlfriend. She exploded in righteous indignation with the force of a cartload of chestnuts tipped on a bonfire. With inspired eloquence, she maligned his judgement, his fairness and his competence to preside over a kitchen. An excited crowd added their comments. From the vantage of the pastry table she thrilled to the power of the demagogue, demanding in scathing tones, 'Do you think you earn respect by tossing the highest pancake? How vulgar! Can't you see that leadership is showing your people you care for them!'

This was received in uneasy silence and, looking beyond the rows of wary faces, she saw Demetrius, flanked by men she'd marked out long since as his informers. His stillness seemed to cheapen her shrill performance. She faltered and clutched at the one brave hand that dared to offer help down from the table.

He told her, 'Wait for me in my office.'

Alone in his office, she could justify herself. Criticising a superior was a fault but hardly as grave a one as injustice. She squared her shoulders as he approached and he shook his head.

'Bristling with defiance, as usual, but you mistake the enemy. You think me powerful? No doubt my magnificence dazzles kitchen hands but understand this; I have complete discretion to run my master's house as he pleases. Beyond that I'm a slave, the same as you.'

She looked into his eyes and winced to see receding depths of pain.

'I wonder if you can imagine the shame I should feel to send my wife out with a gag in her mouth?'

She swallowed hard but looked at him levelly.

'I'd rather you beat me.'

'Of course. Because you fear humiliation more than physical pain. You're not the only one to hate the fist more than the rod. Perhaps Apicius does? A master craftsman who earned his position with years of loyal service. *I* wouldn't speak to him like that in front of his staff. What possessed you?'

'He was unjust. You don't approve of that. And she's my best friend.'

'Don't you think it might be dangerous to have brawls in a crowded kitchen?'

'Then he should have punished them both.'

'Really? I'd expect him to punish the one who started it.'

'Why assume Iris did?'

'Come! You must know Talos, the shapely carpenter who deserted Iris for Acte. Acte is still weak from her miscarriage. Iris attacked her before and bruised her face. She was warned that, if she did it again, she'd be severely punished. Didn't you know that? And you such a close friend! Perhaps you feel you should apologise to Apicius?'

He told her exactly what to say and sent for Apicius. Mercifully, he admitted no one else. She could hardly believe this latest twist of fate; that *she* should kneel on the ground and beg pardon of a common cook. But she looked at Apicius, sweating and tugging at the neck of his tunic and her sense of the ridiculous came to her rescue. The poor man didn't want a turbulent tyro in his kitchen. He just wanted to do his job and stay out of trouble. She got to her knees and forced the revoltingly servile words from her mouth.

'Are you satisfied with this apology?' Demetrius asked.

'Yes, hindeed, sir.'

'Do you wish me to impose a punishment on her?'

'Ho no, sir. She's no trouble really, 'Hi'm used to the questions.'

'Questions?'

'How does leaven make dough bigger? Why does it do it faster on hot days? Where does green mould come from? Why does more come when it rains? Why do raw onions sting the eyes when cooked ones don't? How does sauce grow skin? I say, "It does, it just does," hor when I'm busy, "providence disposed it that way just so *you* could pester *me* with damn fool questions." You see, sir, the rest of them do their work but, while they do it, they think about… other things. But she thinks about the work all the time and the questions never stop.'

'It may be good to think about the work,' Demetrius conceded, 'but, in your position, you should not be cross-questioned. Have you told her to be silent?'

'Ho no, sir! Hi'd miss those funny questions!'

'If you've any further problem with her, however small, I want to know. I needn't keep you now.'

Apicius saluted and left. Nerysa stood up but hung her head, conscious of his disappointment.

'You may go too,' he sighed, 'but strive for some self-control. A slave can't survive without. That's why barbarians never beat Romans in battle, for all their courage; they never stop to think before they hurtle into danger.'

'I didn't know you were acquainted with any barbarians, sir.'

'I don't need to be. I read geographies. Civilised people learn things from books.'

'It's true I don't always think before I speak. I'll try harder. I'm grateful for your advice.'

'On the contrary, you resent it as much as ever. You shouldn't. It's kindly meant. And stay away from Iris. Such a pretty girl should have been promoted to the atrium long since. She won't be because I won't expose my master's guests to slaves with no self-control. I hoped for better things from you. You don't stay in the kitchen because I want you there but you must be seen to earn your way out of it.'

He let her reach the door before calling her back.

'Don't you think you should give me the customary salute? Your husband is used to such dismissive treatment but the head of the house expects better manners in a slave he's had cause to rebuke.'

He wanted a bodily sign of her respect for him. Could she give him less than she'd just given the cook? She fell on her knees, her forehead barely above the ground.

***

For Demetrius, the episode was a serious setback; not because she'd been insolent and insubordinate but because it would be bound to filter up to Lucius. He looked down at her, exasperated.

'I hope this isn't meant as an offensive mockery.' he said, 'The usual salute will do. And you may, perhaps, remember that I suggested you bring any questions you might have to me.'

Strange! He'd often tried to draw her out but now, when he'd nothing in mind but reproof, she jumped up and gave him a brief glimpse of the smile he dreamed of. It was the moment he'd hoped for, though nothing had prepared him for the sweet earnestness of her expression.

'Boiling softens vegetables, doesn't it, sir? And bread and meat and fruit skins and almost everything?'

'Of course.'

'Then why do eggs go hard when you boil them?'

'Well...they just d...that's to say...it must be...in the nature of the atoms.'

'"The nature of the atoms." Thank you, sir. Would that be the same reason soda turns cabbage green?'

'*Cabbage?*'

'Yes. Leathery old leaves, black as seaweed. A pinch of soda in the water and they turn the colour of young leeks. Why? Could anything else do that? What if I boiled lots of pans of cabbage and added a different spice to each, just to see?'

'Hermes! Don't ever dare add anything to the cooking unless you're told to. Do you want to be accused of *poisoning*?'

He'd have been less entertained but more comfortable, with conversations about who, in the house, was in love with whom and why it wasn't the moment to indulge her in the latest rage in earrings. But he couldn't imagine such conversations with her. She was wild and proud. Roman aristocrats were proud but not in that fearless, uncompromising way. Barbaricum must breed this free, unbending spirit, this utter and inappropriate lack of deference to anything or anyone. He ought to have been repelled by it but he wasn't. He was fascinated and full of helpless longing.

It hadn't been his intention to yoke himself to a woman who disliked him. He knew he'd made a bad beginning and that discomfort would limit her pleasure at first but he meant to apply himself to seduce her. Why not? Never before had he failed to delight. But her indifference intensified his hunger for her. He was behaving like a starving beggar co-opted to a civic banquet and was bewildered by himself. Her submission didn't satisfy as he thought it should. He seemed to meet her fleetingly, in moments of truth between them or when she showed sympathy to her fellows but she was never so distant as when they lay together. He wanted to strengthen those fragile bridges of communication and make them routinely accessible. But relations were not as he wanted and he didn't see how, left to themselves, they ever would be.

CHAPTER XXIV

September 171

Simia est simia, etiasmi purpura vestiatur

An ape in earrings is still a monkey. Roman proverb

'Kitchen tyrant!'
      'Pudding head!'

Nerysa looked up from the dough she was shaping. Gluco's moon face was blank. Suavo's habitual sneer had vanished. Hearing a suppressed laugh, she looked to the end of the table but couldn't identify the culprit. Each time she lowered her eyes, the taunts began again in a crude parody of her own patrician speech. Hunching her shoulders, she kept her eyes on her work and her strangely clumsy hands.

'"Less sense than a stuffed pigeon". That's a good one!'

'Expensive! Worth six of the best, I'd say'

She studied the dough intently and pummelled it hard.

'"Couldn't supervise two snails on a cabbage!" That'll be another six.'

'What about "Couldn't carve a ham even-handedly!"'

They winced and shook their heads. She remembered saying some of these things, others, she could hardly believe she'd said but supposed, in the heat of the moment, she must have done.

'Hoity-toity ain't she?'

'Won't look so haughty tonight when steward's playing chess on her backside.'

'He'll have his cane out that's for sure.'

'Ram her insolence down her throat'

'Chase it with molten lead.'

'And when our Lucius hears she'll be out of the house.'

'Slave training station? Best place for trouble makers. Trainer doesn't pull his punches; he's just after his fee. If the poor sods die under the lash he pays a fine and that's the end of it. Trash like that don't even get buried.'

The workers grinned at her as they trooped past to get their rations; some threw an arm over their shoulder and thumped their backs to suggest a vigorous beating. Tears burned her eyes. She'd disgraced herself and Demetrius. She lingered on at work until Apicius came and dismissed her. She'd thought herself too proud to ask but the words came tumbling out.

'When am I going to be whipped?'

'By Jove, not hat all.'

'Tonight, when I go to my husband?'

'Course not. Didn't he say so? He don't want to hurt you more than he has to. You couldn't know why only one got hit, they're both tiresome henough.'

'But Acte's ill. I shouldn't lose my temper when I don't know the facts.'

'Whatever you know, you shouldn't be so free of speech. People think you lash our steward with that tongue of yours. Why don't you learn from him? There's a man with complete command of himself.'

'I do try. It's difficult. We don't keep slaves in Britain.'

'No slaves! Who carves the meat? Natives tear it with their teeth, do they?'

'A man's sons carve for him.'

'Hand I suppose his wife scrubs his house. His that what you want Himself to do when he comes home from the law courts; cook his banquets, wash his clothes and sweep his house while his hex-slaves starve on the streets?'

'Of course not.'

'Then you'd do it with hincantations. You'd say, "Pot, go to the well and fill yourself with water." Haway he'd run on his curved iron legs and when he got back you'd say "Now kindle a fire and jump on it! Joint and vegetables hop in the pot and boil yourselves!" Now Lucius Marius hain't no sorcerer so he needs slaves. Hagreed?'

'Yes'

'Hand he can't keep two hundred in idleness and riot. The slave gets security. A lifetime of knowing where the next meal comes from. Hif he does his master's bidding he gets his dinner and he don't get beaten. Hif not, he don't get his dinner and he do get beaten. He don't need Latin to understand that. Do you know an unhappy slave in this house?'

'Iris isn't happy.'

He spat. 'She's stubborn. Talos don't love her. So what? Plenty other boys do.'

'But slaves sometimes have to do other things for the master. Things they may not like, that aren't …necessary.'

'Ha grateful slave wants to do what pleases the master. Course he does.'

She looked at the ground.

'Why don't I want?'

'He bruised you. You're not ready, yet, to love him. He don't blame you. Now we've talked long enough. Some busy tongue will be telling him you and me are sweethearts.'

She was incredulous but he was serious.

'There's always some fool around to mistake a situation. Be careful with Polybius, with hall the boys, especially when he's away. That's when he'll have you watched. Be sure you're no more cold to him than to any other man. Best get back to him. Make your peace.'

Instead, she ran to the dormitory and, drawing right inside, took a long look at the lime washed, roughcast walls, the high unglazed window and the pallet on the floor. Did she still want Demetrius to tire of her and send her back there? Seeing it again, she knew she didn't.

Iris cried easily and tears suited her. She was like an April day. There was a lustre to her dark hair and a gleam to her skin, her green eyes like raindrops twinkling on ivy leaves. But now there were no tears; only harsh, dry sobs of impotent fury.

'Curse her! Curse her eyes and hands and teeth, her breasts and her womb and her c...'

'Curse who Iris?'

'That girl! I've worked three years - in the scullery - lowest place in the house - for a woman - can't be moved 'cause she's in the kitchen and - can't keep my hands off her - she's got my promotion - and my man - now I'll be scarred - never get another lover!'

Nerysa looked down at her blistered buttocks. Someone had smeared them with lard. She didn't know if they'd scar. Slipping a linen rag and a pot of eye black from their usual place under the mattress, she spat on her fingernail, dipped it in eye black and wrote in Greek on the linen.

'From Nerysa to her esteemed doctor, greetings. My friend has a serious burn. How should I treat it? Reply secretly. I'm grateful. Always. Farewell.'

Hearing footsteps on the stairs, she rolled and knotted the linen into an innocent-looking bundle as a girl paused on the threshold, eyeing her suspiciously.

'What's *she* doing here?' asked the girl. 'She's trouble!'

'I only came to ask how to get this to the doctor's house. On behalf of a lady.'

Iris gasped, 'Thya here - one of the messengers - her lover.'

'You've a steady hand,' Thya said, pushing the bundle under her belt, 'considering the trouble you're in. I answered back once. I never will again.'

Iris looked up. 'The cellar?'

'Like an ice house, only stinking and slimy. Too dark to see my own feet. I screamed myself hoarse but there was only an echo and the rats scurrying. I don't know how long I was there but, any longer, and I'd have gone mad. When our Demetrius asked if I meant to be polite in future, my teeth chattered so much I could hardly say, "Yes, sir." He told them to give me a hot bath, a rub down and clean clothes and said he hoped next time I came to his notice it would be on account of my diligence.'

Iris snorted. 'Wasn't though, was it?'

'No. One August when everyone else was out, Polybius called me and, when I realised it wasn't for himself but Demetrius, I was terrified in case I didn't please him. But I did. He asked if I wanted this bracelet or to have some money in the family bank for my future.'

She patted her gold wire-work bracelet, stroked its cameo medallion with a forefinger and smiled.

'Well, the future was a long way off and I wanted something to show the others. He fastened it on my wrist and said, 'It's worth a bit. Take care you're not cheated if you sell it.' And then I got promoted to the kitchen.'

'Smart decision. You've had the pleasure of it and you can turn it into cash whenever you need, no questions asked.'

'I only go with boys who swear to be careful. Fall pregnant and you're sent to the farm. After five years nursing a child and working in the sun, who'd want you back here with no figure and no complexion? Arminia fetched me pennyroyal from market last year. I couldn't get off the floor of the latrine for three days but it did the trick. Otherwise, I'd have lost my bracelet to the wise woman.'

The next afternoon Thya sidled past the pastry table and slipped Nerysa a small pottery jar.

'The doctor said to tell the lady in question it would be better not to keep secrets from her husband.'

'Thank you,' Nerysa breathed, tucking it into her bosom band. 'I'll tell her.'

She anointed Iris tenderly.

'I can't tell if you'll be scarred. I hope not. The most painful burns heal best.'

'This one's painful.'

'You never told me about Talos.'

'I talk about my conquests, not my defeats.' She looked up and smiled.

'How is it with the steward?'

'Strange.'

'You look tired. He's energetic isn't he? Algae, one of the atrienses, went with a famous gladiator once and said he was no match for our steward.' She looked down. 'They say he still loves you.'

'He doesn't love my hair. I wet it to make it lie flat but as soon as it dries it springs up again.'

'Silly chicken, use oil. Do you still call him the enemy?'

'Did I say that? Yes. He seemed to me to be every Roman soldier who ever torched a British village or raped a British woman.'

'That's ridiculous! He couldn't be a soldier. It's against the law to send a slave into battle. That's what the word servant means - someone who gets pre*served* in wartime.'

'Well, I saw the deputy governor the day I left home and Demetrius reminds me of him; not so much his looks but his bearing and his manner.'

'What presents have you got from him?'

'None.'

'That's a bad sign. Or perhaps not. Do you remember Cheimone was seeing this old soldier who never gave her anything? Well, he's got no children and, when she asks him for money for the wise woman, he goes straight to our Lucius and buys her off him and frees her and says he'll marry her! Best present of all. Perhaps he plans to give you something special when he lets you go.'

Nerysa looked away, her stomach somersaulting.

'Why would he marry me with all that ceremony just to let me go?'

'Ah, marriage! That's class. He's playing at being a freedman. What does a freedman have that a slave doesn't? A toga, a patron and a wife. The patron he has, in all but name, the toga will be next. Then he'll need a rich wife. Perhaps he'll pass you on to the master.'

'I hope not.'

'Well, you belong to the master really. One way or another, you'll serve him all your life. I'd rather lie groomed and scented on his soft couch than be up to my armpits in his greasy dishwater, wouldn't you? Sh! Someone's coming, It's Cheimone to fetch her things.'

Cheimone filled the doorway. She stood tall, elegantly dressed, transformed. Impulsively, Nerysa reached for her hand and cried, 'Congratulations! I'm so happy for you.'

The reaction was so unexpected she'd no time to flinch. She pressed her humming cheek in bewilderment.

'Don't speak to me, dirty British scum!' screamed Cheimone, 'Don't you know I'm a free woman? Pick up my bags, slave!'

Nerysa handed them to her and she flounced out of their lives without a goodbye.

'She was scraping turnips two days ago.' Nerysa said. 'She's soon got high and mighty.'

'No, she looks like a freedwoman but she doesn't feel like one. Slapping a slave convinces her she's free. I wish I was her, all he same. Nerysa, could you spare me a little of that potion you use on the steward? It must be very powerful. Talos wouldn't need much.'

'You know better than that. If I had magic wouldn't I have used it to escape him?'

'Very well, if you won't. But I know where to get resin that takes off hair painlessly without tweezers. You'd like some of that wouldn't you?'

'Yes, I would and, if I ever get any money, I'll buy some for both of us.'

She pressed the jar into Iris' hot, wet hand and said, 'Get one of the girls to put it on twice a day and don't say where you got it. I can't come again. My husband wouldn't like it.'

CHAPTER XXV

September/October 171

Quid mihi maesta die, sociis quid noctibus uxor, Anxia pervigili ducis suspiria cura?
Statius Silvae III 5 1-2

Why are you so sad, wife, all day long. Why are you sleepless and sighing through the nights we share?

It was dusk but the office was still hard at work. Adrian, the snidest of the secretaries, glanced through the window across the yard and asked, 'Sir, are you having your wife trained up as an outdoor slave?'

Demetrius went to the window and saw Nerysa, a square of linen round her head, scurrying through the home farm gate. He sent a passing slave to order her back to her quarters. Nine months in the house, three months married; she knew house slaves didn't mix with outdoor slaves. Was she trying to embarrass him?

During dinner, she kept one side of her face turned away from him. He took her chin between finger and thumb, turned her head and stroked away the dusting of flour on her cheek.

'Who hit you?'

'I slipped and fell on a doorpost.'

'Minion, don't lie to me.'

He felt the flush spread under his fingers. She'd have hung her head but for his thumb under her chin.

'Cheimone didn't like being congratulated her on her freedom.'

How did he explain? Even the most litigious master wouldn't sue if his slave was cuffed on the cheek. It wasn't considered insulting to a slave.

'I can't stop a vulgar freedwoman slighting you. But I hold the purse strings here and I'll be ready for her husband when he comes begging for a loan. For now, all I can do is keep you out of her way. Where did you see her?'

She looked straight at him. *Not defiant* he thought; *just too proud to be furtive.*

'I went to see Iris in her dormitory. I suppose you'll punish me for that.'

'I think Cheimone already has. But that reminds me. I can't think of a good reason for you to go to the farm. Can you?'

She lay in his arms that night as stiff as a javelin. Hearing an occasional moist snatch of breath, he passed a hand over the damp bolster, sat up and lit the lamp.

'Forget her. She's not worth your tears.'

'It's not her.'

'Then what?'

'Sir, a goose broke its leg trying to fly in the yard. The cooks would have roasted him but Archias told me how to mend limbs and I made a splint for him. He's in a basket in the tool shed but I didn't get to feed him today, so either he'll starve or he'll make such a racket someone will wring his neck. You see, in my country we don't eat geese, they're -'

'Kept as guards?'

'Perhaps, but mainly for company and friendship.'

'As *pets* you'd say?'

'That's right, sir.'

An unexpected sidelight on the ferocious Britons he thought, as he pulled on his outer tunic. Taking two woollen cloaks from the chest, he gave her the smaller, reflecting that it had been long on him when he was twelve - not the happiest year of his life, though not the most wretched either. He took the set of master keys from under the bolster, a lamp from the stand and bread from the supper tray. Even though they went out through the office, Polybius woke and struggled to his feet.

'Is that you, sir?'

Demetrius cleared his throat. 'We're going for a...walk.' he said, suppressing a laugh at the boy's incredulous, 'Of course, sir.'

Touring the outbuildings in the dead of night was a novelty. He cursed as the tool shed key grated in the lock and again when no one challenged him. If the noise woke neither man nor beast, security was not as tight as he'd thought. Even the gander, false to the reputation of its kind, slept on in the basket. When Nerysa checked the splint it stirred, rubbed its beak against her arm and took bread from her hand. He watched her stroke its neck with a curved forefinger, saw her smile and heard her voice, throaty with tenderness. His body and soul yawned with longing.

When the gander objected to her leaving in cries of mounting panic, he imagined waking the household, to be discovered in an outhouse with his wife and a goose. He made a swift decision, picked up the basket and set off to his quarters.

At first, it seemed a good decision for the bird, ushered into the bedroom by Polybius, seemed to approve it. All was well until he made to join Nerysa in bed when it reared up, fluttered out of the basket and stood on one leg, wary but quiet. Each time he moved closer to the bed it skidded towards him with fluttering wings and baleful honks. He'd just concluded that the best ploy was to put out the lamps when there was a knock at the door and Polybius' respectful voice enquired, 'Can I be of assistance, sir?'

'You can come in and try.'

Together they rolled the bird in a cloak and stuffed it into the basket which Demetrius presented to Polybius.

'Take this creature to the under-gardener and tell him to take good care of it.'

The boy blinked into the velvet darkness.

'Would you wish me to do that now, sir?'

'Straight away. You may take the lamp.'

'In my opinion,' he sighed, falling on his bed, 'a goose is not a suitable pet.'

He'd been counting on a good night's sleep. At first light he'd leave for Horta to preside over the grape harvest. He wasn't looking forward to the country break and thought of the complaisant farm girls with less enthusiasm than usual. It seemed to him that seven nights was a long time to be away. But there would be a full moon on the last. The porter would have to wait up for him but the porter didn't have a hard time, by and large. No one in the house worked as hard or as long as he did himself. His pulse quickened as he thought how abstinence would sharpen his appetite and he was impatient to be away and home again.

CHAPTER XXVI

September 172

Passer deliciae meae puellae

My girl's pet sparrow Catullus 2.

At daybreak Nerysa squeezed onto the precarious attic loggia and watched the grooms lead the horses to the front door. Adrian and Idumeus mounted from a wooden block held by houseboys but Demetrius sprang from the step, landing neatly between the saddle pommels. Nerysa saw him down the cup of travel wine, catch the cloak Philemon tossed up to him and speed off without a backward glance. As the valedictory shouts of the crowd around the door died down, she groped her way down the steep stairs. There was that soreness again, deep between her thighs.

Ignore it. It would go away.

Polybius followed her into the bedroom and stood watching her expectantly. Her eyes lighted on a wicker cage.

'Himself had it brought here this morning. He told me to say he hoped it would please you.'

The starling was young and poignantly thin, its throbbing chest downy soft, its back shimmering green and black, like shot silk. It regarded them gravely with a cocked head and a bright eye then scrambled onto the reed perch, shrilled at them and clattered with its beak. Nerysa ran for honey cake and offered crumbs from her finger. She thought he might like to be let out of the cage but Polybius disagreed. The bird might fly away. He might not know what was good for him. In any case, the experiment must be postponed. He took up his toilet bag. His morning's work was done and he was off to the baths.

'I usually have to go on these country jaunts.' he confided with a shudder. 'It's remarkable how Himself loves them. He even used to try and convince me it would be fun to squelch barefoot on wet skins. Naturally, I declined. I sit under a shady tree and watch everyone else making fools of themselves. Even His Excellency some years. This time I'm excused because I have to keep an eye on you.'

He bowed ironically and she bridled.

'Why keep an eye on me?'

'Someone might annoy you, you never know. It's obliging of me. I'm a cubicularius not a nurse maid.'

'So it's not your job to spy on people?'

'You wouldn't ask a cup-bearer to light a lamp or a hairdresser to fold a toga would you? Do you grind the knives or feed the chickens?'

'I do as I'm told.'

'Well, praise to your Juno! Keep it up! That's the way to stay out of trouble. And don't get into a scrape while I'm out. I can't be watching you *all* day.'

'*If* I get into a scrape, I shall naturally arrange to do it while you're out on the town or fondling some girl at the back of the wine store.'

He hooted with mirth.

'So you can see round corners, little minx! I may have to tell Himself how I caught you rolling out his book.'

'Please, *please* don't tell him that! I was only teasing.'

'You and I should cooperate. We could keep Himself comfortable and ourselves too. I intend to have a little holiday of my own these next few days.'

'I'll be good.'

'Well, when you *do* get into trouble, tell me quickly, so I can sort it out before His Excellency hears. What we want is a nice, quiet time. No wild scenes in the kitchen, no rumours to disturb His Excellency, no bad reports when Himself gets back. Then I get my tip.'

'And what do I get?'

She could have bitten out her tongue. He laughed significantly.

'I think we both know what you'll be getting when Himself comes home after seven days. I'm not expecting any sleep - even the floor outside will be bucking like an unbroken colt.'

She flushed and recoiled. She felt the pain again, sore and sickening as in the early days of her marriage. Polybius regarded her irritably.

'Not very appreciative are you? A generous man likes to think his girl shares his pleasure. Can't you thrash about and moan a bit?'

She shook her head miserably.

'Come on! You do the best imitation of a haughty senator's wife I've ever seen.'

'I can't pretend.. that sort of thing.'

'Well, you'll just have to hope the farm girls take the edge off his appetite.'

He leant negligently across the table and selected himself a choice cluster of grapes.

'He told the kitchen not to send inferior food up here just because he's away. Perhaps you should think about that and be more grateful. If you're good, I'll see you get hot water before dinner, like he does.'

And, with an admonitory wag of his finger, he was gone.

She hadn't expected to miss Demetrius but life was flat without his odd flashes of humour. The bed seemed strange without the warmth and firmness of its owner. She was changing and her certainties were failing her. She'd even begun to see Quintus in a different light. Suppose his pretty play-fellows were as unwilling as she with Demetrius. How would he know? How should any master learn the truth from slaves who only told him what he wanted to hear? She was almost looking forward to his return except that the soreness of her private parts had become acute. She couldn't account for it and her sanguine thoughts of his homecoming turned to dread.

CHAPTER XXVII

October 171

Estne novis nuptis odio Venus an quod aventum Frustrantur falsis gaudia lacrimulis ubertim thalami quas intra limina fundunt? Catullus. LXVI

Must new brides always hate sex, quenching their husbands' ardour and drowning the bedroom in crocodile tears?

Demetrius reached home, dusty and unshaven, having ridden forty miles without a break. Lonely, dark roads weren't safe and, throughout the journey, he felt Adrian's mute disapproval. He contained his impatience while he roused the porter who'd dozed off but, by the time Polybius had helped him freshen up, he was hungry for his wife. When she pulled sharply away, his hand shot up to strike her but he felt her tremble and drew back.

'Are you ill?'

'Something's not right.'

He lit the lamps, lifted the sheet and saw her soft, secret parts livid and swollen.

'How did this happen?'

Her cheeks flamed. She looked away.

'I don't know, sir. I douche every day but it hurts.'

He decided to reserve judgement. If she'd been unfaithful, he could rely on his aides to report it.

'The girls in the house have had me cursed.'

His belly tensed in alarm. 'Don't be ridiculous!' he said. 'No one here has had you cursed. No one would dare.'

The next morning, as he transferred money from his safe to a wallet, strapped against his body, an imperious voice demanded, 'What do I get? What do I get?'

He spun round. Nerysa had gone to work. Her voice sounded strange and the question was most unlike her. Again, it echoed in the empty room.

'What do *I* get?'

He scanned the room. The starling turned its head sideways and challenged him with an unblinking eye. Then it opened its beak wide and spoke again.

'What do *I* get?'

Demetrius laughed and threw a cloth over the cage.

That morning he had several ports of call in the city but made a detour to Archias' house. Archias refused payment and when Demetrius, resenting his condescension, tried to insist, he said brusquely, 'You're a stiff-necked fellow, Demetrie, but you'll have to swallow your pride. I honour your wife as a queen among women. I won't take your money for treating her.'

Demetrius remembered his position and his manners and thanked him graciously, relieved to know Archias would attend his wife without charge. He, himself, never troubled doctors but women, he knew, had special frailties.

In the cool of the evening he ushered Archias into his office. The scene was stilted. He hesitated to sit in the presence of a freedman but Archias refused to sit while he stood and he found himself giving way again.

'You'll have wine?' he asked, filling two cups.

'What do *I* get?'

The voice made them both jump. Demetrius pointed to the cage and laughed and the tension eased. He handed Archias a cup saying, 'Polybius has taken your people in search of dinner.'

'Thanks. I'll remember to tip him.'

'If you wish but I've seen to that, and so, I should imagine, have they. Is my wife very sick? Is it her fault?'

'No and no; she has a common condition that will respond to douching with sour milk.'

'She's inexperienced. Perhaps she didn't take proper care of herself.'

'This malady can affect any woman. I've treated it in the palace. Neither of you is to blame. But, my friend, what have you been about? The girl is four months married and reacts like a virgin.'

Archias had been a staunch friend in his hour of need. He was looking kindly at him. Demetrius couldn't snub him. Bereft of everything but the truth, he said, 'I've never been with a woman who was what you might call… respectable but I suppose that's what she is. No great fault in a wife, perhaps.'

'If you can't come to Venus try Minerva. Talk to her – as you do to me – art, poetry, philosophy…things that interest you.'

'Spare the poor girl your satire. She can't help what she is.'

Archias' penetrating look led Demetrius to think he would say something significant but, after a tantalising pause, he only shrugged.

'Well, in a few days, she should be able to resume her…duties in comfort.'

Archias downed his wine and departed rather more abruptly than friendship required.

Demetrius felt his pulse quicken and rued his dependence on her. Why did nothing savour any more unless he shared it with her? What of Lucius; puzzled, neglected, perhaps hurt? Lucius was the pivot of his life. So, now, he also had a liaison with a barbarian woman. He had better keep it in proportion.

CHAPTER XXVIII

October 171

Cogita filiorum nos modestia delectari, vernularum licentia

Reflect that our sons please us by their modesty, our slave boys by their forwardness
Seneca Moral essays On providence I 6

Nerysa never opened conversations with the other pastry cooks but curiosity drove her to ask, 'Whatever's that commotion?'

'They're bringing Philodespotus. That'll be fun !'

'Why would they bring the master's cup bearer to the kitchen?'

'He *was* the master's cup bearer. Now he's apprentice to the meat cooks.'

'Why?'

'Too old. Down on his top lip or showed an interest in girls.'

The unruly band burst into the kitchen, some pushing, some dragging the boy. Nerysa stared in frank admiration. He was like Quintus' boys; beautiful, finely dressed and gently mannered.

'It's all up with you now, little pretty boy.' crooned his tormentors, pinching his cheeks,

'Got to do a man's work.'

A woollen cloak flew across the kitchen and they caught it with a shout. The four brawniest seized the corners while the rest stripped the boy of his silk tunic and pushed him, incoherent with terror, naked but for his loincloth, backwards onto the cloak. They tossed him gently at first, then ever faster and higher. Nerysa was sure he'd hit the roof, then that they'd fail to catch him, then that they wouldn't be able to break his fall and he'd be dashed to the ground. Philodespotus clearly thought so, too. His screams echoed from the rafters. Nerysa started forward, angry words sprang to her lips. She pulled herself up short, covered her mouth with her hand and blinked back her tears. She would stay in control. She despised herself for not defending a child from bullies but, she realised, Demetrius was more important to her than Philodespotus.

At last it was over and he was pulled onto splayed and trembling legs. Apicius bustled up. One look at his gleaming knife and the boy made to run away but his captors roared with laughter and tightened their grip. With each rasp of the knife a silvery curl joined the scented pile on the greasy stone floor. Girls snatched them up and ran off squealing in triumph. Nerysa, who would not have shrunk from causing hurt if necessary, was shocked to discover people for whom another person's pain was a source of delight.

Shorn and dressed in a coarse tunic he stood at his place by the brazier, shoulders hunched, face streaked with smoke, sweat and tears. A short time before he'd been a joy to look at. Nerysa watched him as, alternately, he sniffed or dashed a hand across his nose. When she had stowed her batch of loaves safely in the proving cupboard, she went up to him.

'Don't cry. That's the way to make them tease you more. The kitchen's not a bad place to work, once you're used to it.'

'How could you understand?' he raged. 'Not to be with Himself! To live this side of the house and never see him. To know he doesn't love me anymore. To be with this brutish, common rabble.'

She put out her hand to comfort him but was prevented by Apicius, ordering her back to work with an oath. She darted to her place, hurt that he'd spoken so roughly, for she didn't neglect her work nearly so much as some.

That evening Demetrius said with studied lightness, 'I hear you comforted young Philo today.'

Her jaw tightened. 'I did. But I wish I'd spoken my mind to the beasts who bullied him.'

He grinned. 'Tossed him in a cloak, did they? Well, it's usual and harmless enough - a shock to him though. Slaves can be indulged as children - especially if they're pretty. Some masters even encourage boys to be pert. They think them cute. Once they grow big and hairy everything changes.'

'That seems hard.'

'What would you do? Should they be harshly disciplined from birth and never shown tenderness? Or pampered and spoilt until they're senile?'

'But the change is so abrupt and brutal.'

'So it is for everyone. If Philo were freeborn he'd be off on military service – a harder life than that of a cook in Lucius' kitchen and a more dangerous one.'

'Was it like that for you? Were you tossed in a cloak?'

She'd trespassed on forbidden ground. He spoke as if picking his way over thorns.

'My boyhood was unusually privileged. That wasn't a blessing either. It would have been better for me if I'd been brought up to know my place. Seeing clearly ahead makes life easier.'

'Yes, I think so too. Isn't it strange how most people prefer *not* to see things as they are?'

He must have thought realism too strong a medicine for her. He frowned and said, 'Don't cry for the new cook. Tonight his workmates will get him drunk. Tomorrow he'll have a sore head and, by the time it wears off, life will look more promising.

'There'll be no more high spirits in the kitchen for the next month. We're giving a dinner to celebrate the emperor's victory in the north – not a free meal for clients and freedmen but a high society affair and woe betide us if the slightest thing goes wrong. If you're still concerned after that, I'll place him somewhere else.'

'He only wants to be with the master.'

'Perhaps he will; as a serving man, perhaps one day as a valued freedman but never again as a pet. The break must be made and he must adjust. The kitchen maids know how to console him.'

She fancied he was remembering his own youth and, as he took her, she wondered what consolations he was revisiting.

CHAPTER XXIX

November 171

οποταν ανεπιστημονα ταμιειας και διακονιας παραλαβουσα επιστημονα και πιστην
και διακονικην ποιησαμενη παντος αξιαν εχης

When you take an ignorant girl in hand and make a useful, dependable housekeeper of her, you double her value and make a treasure for yourself. Xenophon. Oeconomicus VII 31

The starling grew plump and bold, acquiring a repertoire of chirrups from the wheedling through the querulous to the imperious. He was a sociable soul and couldn't bear solitude. Rather than leave him to pine, Demetrius would have the cage brought to the office. If the secretaries disapproved, they knew better than to show it and, when Demetrius' dictation speeds were uncomfortable, its reiterations were helpful.

The slaves talked of nothing but the dinner party. Apicius toured the kitchen garden and earmarked produce nearing the peak of perfection. Snails, crammed into clay pots, gorged on milk; hens and guinea fowl, confined in dark cages, grew fat on barley meal and honey water. In the sty, a blissful sow ate herself into a stupor. The menu was cunningly chosen, not just for cost and rarity of the ingredients, but to display precious tableware. The culinary creations and flower arrangements would be feats of engineering and artistry, the public rooms would gleam and smell like a flower market. Free time was a fond memory.

On the great day, Nerysa rose before the first cock crow. Her back was stiff from bending over the sink, her throat dry from feather dust and her fingers raw from vicious mullet scales but she hurried eagerly to work.

There was something strange about the kitchen. She could see to the far end because the usual steam and smoke haze hadn't formed. Only a small, subdued group had gathered. She turned to Gluco, the senior pastry cook, who was slumped over the wooden table.

'Where's everyone?' she asked.

'Sick.' he burped. 'Been puking up all night myself.'

Nerysa scanned the room and asked herself how standing around in huddles was supposed to solve the crisis.

'Let's make a start,' she said, 'so when the others get here we shan't be behind.'

As if everyone had been waiting on the suggestion, the work swung into action. Fires crackled under cauldrons, whirling pestles sprayed a film of pine nut and herbs over every surface, the cleaver kept up a steady thud on the meat block. But, without the three senior cooks, there was no direction. No one knew the fine detail of the plan so, when problems arose, everyone had an opinion but no one could make a decision.

Nerysa saw the dinner heading for ruin. Sheltering in the alcove by the courtyard door, she hitched her tunic through her girdle. No one would recognise the steward's wife in a short skirt. With the spare fold pulled over her head and clutched under her chin to hide her hair, she dashed across the yard. Head down, she bumped into a post boy playing with a ball.

'What was the last hour the clock boy announced?' she asked

'Second.' he panted, rushing after his ball.

Seven hours, just seven short, winter hours to make a banquet. Apicius' rooms were on the far side of the courtyard. The first was empty but for a rickety couch and a stout stick against the wall. And Apicius was known as a devoted family man! She burst into the inner room where he lay on his bed, clutching a bucket, eyes revolving in horror.

'Get out! If someone tells you come halone to my quarters, the steward he kill us both with his bare hands.'

'No one saw me. You've got to come to the kitchen.'

'Can't. Not even on stretcher. Guts strangled. Dying.'

He clapped his hand to his mouth, his forehead dripped sweat. She grabbed a wine jug from the floor and forced the liquid between his chattering teeth. Then, gripping him by the shoulders, she said, 'You're not dying and, if you are, then so is half the house.'

'Hepicurus sick too? So, no dinner.' He fell back on the pillow, moaned and closed his eyes.

'But think of the waste and the expense and all our hard work. Apici, open your eyes! Talk to me! Tell us what to do.'

He flinched. 'Don't hit me! Not my fault. Gods don't always smile. No one worked harder than me. Planned for weeks! Himagine!' he spread his shaking hands. 'Merchantman of almond cake on froth of honey cream; crepe sails, cargo of jewels – grapes and gilded nuts. Talk of Rome it would have been.'

Indeed it would, she thought. *Famous for its vulgarity.* She beamed at him.

'What a marvel! But it wasn't the only dessert. I saw a baked ham dressed.'

'Oh, that! Cheese in wine, quince tarts, pears in elderberry custard – simple stuff hanyone could do.'

'Not to compare with your ship, of course. I can't think what main course would have been worthy of it.'

'Hepicurus sick you say? What an artist! He can make anything you like from of slices of pork. He was going to do a sturgeon and a peacock.'

Another happy loss.

'What do you want done with the mullet?'

'Don't pester me. Can't you see I'm sick?'

'But the fish cooks are well and they want to cook it before it goes off.'

'They can stew it with onions in wine but they can't send it up without two sauces. Where's that lazy Linus? I bet he's not really sick.'

'He's not. He's working. So are Botulus and Bulbus.'

'The hidiots who overcook vegetables. They need watching every minute.'

'Oh, yes, and there's a basket of squash in the store. What's it for?"

'Squash with laser. Have you any idea how much a pinch of Persian laser costs?'

She shook her head, and assumed an expression of great interest.

'More money than you'll ever see. That's why it's locked up. Thanks to our steward's travels we've got the best spice store in Rome. But no need to waste it on greedy senators. I keep pine nuts in the laser jar and when I grind them into a dish and I get a good strong taste of laser without using any at all!' He chuckled to himself then looked at her severely. 'Don't dare tell a soul! Hanyway, steward can't complain. *He* got the real thing for his wedding feast.'

'Dear Archimagire,' she sighed, giving him the official title he gloried in, 'that's two spectacular courses. What about the first course?'

Smothering a belch, he shot from the bed, seized the bucket and dived into the outer room. She heard him being violently sick and took the opportunity to revise the menu in her head. As she rearranged his pillows, her hand knocked against a key. She grasped it and thrust it under her bosom band. He staggered back to bed. She waited until his eyes opened before suggesting, 'Perhaps we could manage the simple things.'

'No you couldn't!' he wheezed. 'Do you want the master to be disgraced in front of the city prefect! Tell the steward to cancel.'

'But he's in court all day with the master.'

'Then find Thaïs. Don't say you don't dare. You came here bold as brass. Tell her to send messengers to the court, then to the guests. Don't pout at me, little minx. Get this dinner called off or, hif I ever get well, I'll bake you in a tart - after the steward's flayed you alive.'

She promised and told him to be well. The merchantman cake was no loss. Talented as Apicius was, it was clear he wasn't used to entertaining the nobility. As a modest young man, taking his first tentative steps in high society, Lucius should not be ostentatious. She could imagine Quintus and his friends deriding him for an upstart puppy. Perfect ingredients, lightly cooked and simply served would be most becoming. Could a reduced staff achieve that? She hoped so because last minute cancellations were annoying for whatever reason, and cancelling because the cooks had gut rot would ensure that future invitations were politely declined.

First she looked for Linus, the sauce chef, encouraged to see his apron already spattered with damson juice. She sniffed the heartening aroma of honeyed fruit rising from his pot, drew out the key and dangled it under his nose.

His eyes widened. 'Good! These plums are begging for cloves.'

'Apicius says he's relying on you for the sauces.'

'Sauces is all very well but it's nearly midday and the cranes haven't come from the market.'

'I'll ask Lucullus. Maybe he knows about them. Do you need help?'

'I'll have Sikon when he gets back from the lats. Arminia's girls could chop me some onions.'

She turned to go and tell them but was surrounded by a crowd staring stupidly at the key in her hand.

'Can't you think of anything more useful to do, when we're all behind, than stand and stare? We've got six hours 'till the city prefect gets here.'

Somewhat to her surprise, they all saluted her and skidded over oil and fruit juice to their work stations. No problem, then, getting their obedience. A sudden wordless, heart stopping thought hit her. Serving staff. Were they sick too? She turned to the vegetable cooks.

'Bulbe tell the scullery girls to peel and chop your vegetables as well as washing them. And send someone to the dining room to see if the staff are there. Bolete, show me the spice chest and I'll give you some pine nuts from the laser jar.'

He took her to the head cook's alcove and reached down the chest from a ledge.

'How many do you need?'

'Thirty would do.'

His offhand manner and the glint in his eye alerted her to a second hand market in spices.

'Make it subtle.' she said, counting out ten. 'Have you nuts to replace them?'

He funnelled them into the jar, which she sealed and shook. He winked at her.

'What about some ginger for the apple and pumpkin?'

'How much?'

He opened his other hand.

'Enough to cover a sestertius.'

Lucullus had cubes of pork hopping in his pans. The showy peacock's tail was hanging from a nail on the wall. Nerysa came alongside him, keeping her distance from the spitting oil and wine.

'Epicurus is too ill to make the sturgeon and peacock,' she said, 'Apicius said to do something simpler with the pork.'

'Linus is making a damson sauce – tell him to knock up a honey mushroom as well.'

'Do we have enough honey?'

'Hades! Vats of it in the store. And Spanish fish sauce and olives and oil. You wanna see?'

'Not just now. Have we got sausages?'

'Yes and anchovies.'

'Then I guess we've no problem with the first course because the thermidospores will fry them in the dining room.'

Linus wheeled round shouting above the sizzling of his pans, 'Anyone seen Carbo and Cineas? Phago, go find them.'

The elephantine Phago lumbered off across the oily sawdust towards the yard and collided with two messengers who rushed past him bawling, 'No cranes! No cranes!'

Lucullus removed the pork pan from the fire, grabbed the first messenger by the throat and shook him.

'Ten cranes I ordered.. What happened?'

'Stop choking him and he'll tell you.' said his companion, backing out of range. 'They should've been collected first thing. At the third hour, when no one had come, the butcher was offered a good price. It's not everyone can afford crane and he didn't want them left rotting on his hands.'

Lucullus gave his victim a final shake that sent him flying and hurled the pan at him. Nerysa replaced its scattered contents and laid it back on the range. She saw he was shivering and sweating.

'I'm sorry you're ill,' she said, 'but it must be past the fourth hour. Work now, sleep later. Apicius is counting on you. Our Lucius is counting on you. We may not have cranes – but we've dozens of guinea fowl. Get their necks wrung and have Arminia draw and pluck them. We're short of time but she's nifty.'

Lucullus worked his mouth. She pulled back assuming he was going to vomit. He spat.

'Do you think *guinea fowl* will impress senators?'

'Luculle, do you want the guests to talk about how much the meat cost or how exquisite your sauces were?'

He pursed his lips, head to one side. 'My apricot and lavender is special, it's true. But it needs cumin.'

'There are preserved apricots in the fruit bowls. Let's have them out and put in some more apples instead. Is the cumin in the spice chest?'

'And there's that caraway and ginger I've been wanting to try.'

'Philo,' she said, 'mop that floor before someone else skids on it.'

Philo pouted 'When Himself asked me for anything he used to say "please".'

'I've done better than that. I've told you why you should do it. And I'm not the only person here who doesn't say please. Do it before I box your ears.'

She wiped the sweat out of her eyes. Phago arrived back alone, panting.

'Servers are fine but Carbo and Cineas are too ill to come. I did my best to make them.'

'Luculle,' Nerysa laid a hand on his arm. 'If Linus helps with your sauces can you fry the anchovies and sausages in the kitchen?

Phago said, '*I* can. I fry as well as them. I'm just not allowed in the dining room because I'm… not beautiful.'

'Let's go and find someone to fetch the braziers in here and make sure we really do have sausages.'

To her relief they found serried ranks of them hanging in the smoke house, individually wrapped in bay leaves. Suavo's voice floated towards them and she pulled Phago back inside.

'Aren't you going to put a stop this?' It was Gluco.

'How could I?' replied Suavo. 'She's mad and, where she's concerned, so's the steward.'

'But let her manage a formal dinner? She's never smelled one!'

'Got the key to the spice chest though. That's authority, no matter how she came by it. There'll be ox-hide laid on tomorrow or when Apicius next checks the spice chest and, if she's asked for it, that suits me. Do exactly as the bossy little know-all says and let her take the blame.'

She flinched back against Phago's comforting bulk. She'd been a fool to interfere. If the dinner was a failure it would be her fault. Better to have cancelled, no matter the expense. This was what Demetrius meant when he said someone rushed into something with unwashed feet. In his book, impulsiveness didn't excuse a crime; it compounded it. Keeping behind Phago she followed Gluco and Suavo back to the kitchen and confronted them.

'Apicius says we can't do the merchantman. He wanted to refer to the master's voyages but it's just too complicated.'

'Master don't do voyages,' said Gluco, 'Our Demetrius does. Master writes speeches.'

'I think I once saw scrolls made out of fine pastry.'

'In squid ink! Let's send out for some. And I'll roll them up in truffle paste.'

'But what could you do for pens?'

'Shaved cinnamon sticks, of course. Are you allowed to take anything you like out of the spice chest?'

'I suppose so.' *Might as well be flogged for a sheep as a lamb.*

Suavo leaned forward, suddenly eager. 'We could still have a boat, you know. Imagine half a great gourd on a sea of pureed peas.'

'No, we've got the cress we were going to use for the sturgeon.' said Gluco. 'What else would we do with it?'

Nerysa said, 'What about lots of small ships? We wouldn't want the guests to think our master was boasting about the size of his ships.'

'We've got pears in the fruit bowls. Half a pear scooped out makes a good boat.'

'I know what! Fill the boats with snails as cargo.'

'And we can still use the vanilla pods for the oars if we cut them shorter.'

They were now completely absorbed in each other and their plans. Nerysa left them.

'Phago,' she said, 'do you know what this stuff's supposed to taste like?'

'My palate's not a slave.' he retorted. 'It's the very twin of the master's.'

'Then take this spoon and come round and taste. It's all too spicy for me.'

'Not that spoon! You can't expect anything to taste right if it's not on a silver spoon.'

When he'd toured the kitchen tasting, with eyes rolled upward under closed lids he suddenly asked, 'Who did you get to put up the dinner tray for the musicians?'

'I didn't. Who normally does it?'

'I do. Their food doesn't tempt me.'

'Oh, should we have set out different grades of food for the guests, too?'

'No. There's no low life coming tonight.'

'Thank the gods. We can do without that complication. Would you put out something for the musicians and check the wine's up from the cellar?'

'If it is, shall I see if the steward's come home to taste it?'

'Yes, and while you're that side of the house, find out the time.'

He turned back at the doorway. 'Seventh hour, I'd say, by the sun.'

Two hours to go then. First course; ham; done. Sausages; ready to fry. Anchovies in wine; ditto. Main course; pork in damson sauce and honeyed mushrooms; guinea fowl in apricot with lavender; mullet with onions and carrots, squash with laser; all in hand. *Hades, I can't breathe in this heat!* Dessert; pastry rolls in squid ink; snail boats on watercress puree; better check. Fruit bowls, Hades! Refill them. Quince tarts; honey cakes; in the cupboard. Cheese in wine; in jars in the store. Elderberry custard; find out where it is. Bread baskets. Bread baskets! We haven't baked any bread!

'I'm in the bakery team,' she moaned, 'and I've forgotten the bread!'

She scanned the room, blinking into the smoke. There was no one to mix dough, hardly time for it to rise and no one but herself free to shape it. Gluco and Suavo were working frantically. She daren't ask them to stop and bake bread. In desperation, she ran to the scullery. Not because Arminia could help but because she was solid and comforting and didn't know how to panic. She stood, puce and panting, in a snowstorm of feathers, tossing the last bald fowl onto the cloth held out by Iris and Nephele. Two buckets of entrails stood ready for the sauces.

'No bread bad.' she agreed. 'Go shops buy some. Tell Thya to find the Hermes. They'll need try every bakery on the hill. No one shop have enough.'

Nerysa, dropped her sweat soaked head in her hands and began to cry.

'Don't!' said Arminia, 'Start that again and I'll take the whip to you.'

'Then I won't.' she gulped. 'But thank you, thank you.'

She looked through the open door and saw the shadows were lengthening. No time to cry. Cry later. Seizing the buckets, she followed Iris and Nephele into the kitchen where Lucullus was about to slide the birds into the oven.

'Thaïs came while you were out.' he said over his shoulder. 'Said she'd heard a rumour we'd had a disaster but she could see we hadn't so she went off again'.

'I think we're doing well. There aren't enough of us to get in each other's way. Who shall I get to refill the fruit bowls?'

She swooped on Nebula and Chione who were coming in from the scullery with trays of split leeks and tiny purple carrots. They promised to put out apples and pears, figs and preserved apricots. Everyone cheered when they heard running in the yard and the six messengers burst into the kitchen each carrying a sack of loaves.

'Luculle, take those chickens out for a bit,' said Gluco. 'and put the bread in. Cut out the bakers stamp and serve it warm and the guests will think it's home baked.'

Thya squealed, 'They're here, they're here! I looked out from the attic. The road's blocked with litters and carriages and grand folks and torchbearers!'

'Phago!' Nerysa screeched, 'Start frying the sausages now! Boys, over here with those bread baskets!'

The dishing up and the final touches were even more fraught than the cooking. Apicius' strictures about overcooked vegetables rang in her ears and she was standing over Bulbus and Boletus, to make sure they drained them promptly when, from the other end of the room, she caught sight of a tarnished silver dish being carried out. With a shriek, she ran the length of the kitchen and dragged the porters back. So stupefied were they to be ordered to scrub a dish with chalk, they did it without protest.

But the reliable boys had already handed over the bread and were now stationed either side of the door to add the valedictory shake of the pepper pot to every dish. A seemingly endless procession of trolleys and trays set off for the dining room, each a source of sharp anxiety.

Only when the guests were reported to be lingering over cake and fruit could she relax. She could have no idea if her exertions in the kitchen had met with approval in the dining room but the focus of attention shifted. Sweeping and scouring were tasks she understood and, once they were underway, she longed for her bed. But, for that campaign, she'd been the general and she sensed that her army, ill and exhausted, would be demoralised if she left so she stayed until the last pot had been replaced on the shelf and the last scrap washed from the floor.

She wasn't sure her legs would carry her as far as the bedroom until they actually had. Polybius had been asleep on the threshold but he scrambled dutifully to his feet and opened the door. The lamps were still lit. Demetrius hadn't retired but had dozed off on his couch. He poured wine for her, observing with a raised brow, 'You're very late.'

'Some of the slaves were sick so there was more work for the rest of us. How was our dinner?'

'I think it was the most successful dinner I ever attended. The food was excellent but not so showy as to distract from the conversation. And what conversation! Philosophy, politics, ethics; elegant, well-informed. The whole event showed Lucius in just the way he wants society to see him.'

'Did they send you any of the lavender sauce?'

'Exquisite. Most original. I did save some for you to try but you were so late I let the waiters clear up and get to bed.'

They'd experienced the dinner from opposite ends of the servile social scale. She'd not left the kitchen. He'd overseen operations in the best dining room, where he hadn't even had to direct the action, only to dignify it with his presence. His face relaxed.

'I thought we might have a problem when I heard some of the slaves were sick but we didn't. Lucius is delighted. He's ordered tips for everyone.'

This was said with a yawn and she reflected that largesse was easily ordered by the master but was a chore for Demetrius who must decide the sum due to each and see it disbursed. He would be scrupulously fair but not everyone would think him so. He looked so weary she dared to suggest retiring and he readily agreed.

By the next morning, she was ill herself and afraid that the sickness might have spread to the master's guests. Demetrius was attentive until midday when he succumbed himself and they lay side by side taking turns to dash to the washroom. She felt she'd never be quite so shy of him again after spending such an embarrassing day with him.

CHAPTER XXX

Emere malo quam rogare.

I'd rather buy what I want than beg for it. Cicero In Verrem II 4 12

D emetrius struggled to get up for the next morning's reception but it was noon before he could stand steadily. He'd no appetite so, as soon as Polybius had smartened him up, he went in search of Lucius to present his excuses in person.

'Are you well, master?'

'Never better. Yourself?'

'Fit now, thank you. Have you heard from any of your guests?'

'None of them is ill as far as I've been able to discover.'

'With one or two exceptions, only the lowest slaves have been affected.'

'And their rations, I suppose, are kept separate.'

'Yes. It's interesting that most of those who took sick drink from the well in the yard. Most of those who didn't from the fountain in the lobby.'

'Demetrie, aren't you forgetting something? Distasteful as it is, there's a possibility we can't ignore - that we have a poisoner in our midst.'

'But, master, who would bother to poison a few dozen low ranking slaves? What could they hope to gain by it?'

'Look at it this way. Half the kitchen staff out of action the day I give the most important dinner of my life. And there's a strange girl in the kitchen, from the land of magic and demons, who, as we both know, has cause to feel resentful.'

Demetrius was baffled. Then he met Lucius' gaze, tinged with distaste, and took his meaning like a sock on the jaw.

'My wife! She works herself ragged in the kitchen. And she's been ill too.'

Lucius shrugged. 'Be vigilant, Demetrie, that's all I ask.'

Demetrius returned to his office to find Apicius waiting for him, shifting from foot to foot. His tortured paraphrases suggested it was no mean feat to praise the steward's wife without provoking jealousy and suspicion. He'd obviously calculated that he couldn't avoid telling him and had better do it before someone else did. His account of Nerysa's success and his tentative suggestion that the steward might see fit to promote his wife and exploit her powers of leadership did gratify Demetrius. Lucius was wrong. You *could* make a useful slave out of unpromising barbarian material, by applying the correct methods.

'I also hope she's capable of something better. I plan to move her around a little so I can discover what suits her best.'

Having dismissed Apicius, he sent for Nerysa, happy to have the opportunity to praise her. Perhaps he'd see her smile. She kept her head bowed and, when she looked up, her face was anguished.

'Sir, they're saying I showed it only takes half of us to serve a banquet so you'll be putting the rest up for sale.'

He got up and went towards her.

'Nonsense! Say we keep half of them and the next time we give a banquet, half of *them* take sick. What then?'

As she lifted her head, he smiled but there was no answering smile from her.

'Besides,' he said, 'the number of slaves a house keeps isn't based on need. Any fewer and Lucius' reputation would suffer. People would call him frugal – which isn't a virtue in a millionaire. I should, perhaps, overstaff more than I do but busy people are easier to manage than idle ones.'

He turned away. 'I could wish there were fewer people to tell me how to run this house. Some folk have been foolish enough to say that they'd rather work for you than Apicius which means I can't send you back to the kitchen. To outshine your betters is a grave mistake. But you're not the only one who's had to learn that. Tomorrow you must report to the laundry.'

This last he said brusquely to pre-empt argument. She wouldn't welcome a move away from friends and familiar work with no promotion. But she took it without protest, as if she'd accepted that her life would be spent at the disposal of others. He gave her her tip - a generous one. He explained that for prudent people, money was for saving not for spending and offered to keep hers for her. Again, she made no objection and he warmed to her thrift. Saving money, he realised, was a habit they could share, though not on equal terms.

As he locked the strongbox, he told her she could expect to be rewarded for exceptionally good work, just as Lucius rewarded him when a shrewd investment yielded well. He had other sources of income that weren't available to her; forwarding business for other men who paid him generously because he knew the most efficient ways to pack antiques for shipping, which sea captains were the safest pilots and kept the best fed crews. He went in for some speculating, especially if he had inside information, and took commission on slaves he bought or sold.

All this was easy to say. What he was amassing this fortune for, was too private and too complex to explain. He didn't fully understand himself, why he was determined to pay the full market price for his own freedom. His ability to manage and create wealth made him an extremely valuable slave and the price on his head increased steadily in proportion to his experience and achievement.

He sat her beside him on his couch and told her how he and Lucius had begun trading. Seeing he'd caught her interest, he recounted how, barely out of boyhood, they'd planned meticulously, learned from their mistakes – some small, one near fatal - and turned a handsome inheritance into a vast fortune in six years. He did the leg work. It didn't suit Lucius' dignity to soil his hands with business, but the planning was a pleasure they shared.

She looked up at him, eyes bright with curiosity, her words fast and fluent, her hands alive. Quite unlike the wooden creature who usually sat beside him.

'I see now how you go on. You have a pile of money and you invest some and make a profit and maybe you lose some but never as much as you gain so the pile keeps growing. But how did you begin and what with?'

'Our first big break, you mean? That was in the very year Lucius came into his patrimony. The emperor wanted traders to join his mission to China. We hired a ship, stocked it and sent it with the delegation. We couldn't afford the exotic items most merchants sent; rhinoceros horn and tortoiseshell and such, but we thought a remote people might be interested in things that were ordinary to us; glass vases, cameos and gold coin. We were right. They took everything we sent and gave silk in return. We send ships regularly now, sell most of it in Kos and bring some on here.'

He still felt a thrill remembering how much they'd made. There was no point mentioning actual figures to her but he did say that the rewards that pleased him most were large ones from risky ventures, especially ones Lucius had been sceptical of.

'When I suggest something speculative,' he said, 'even if I've carefully researched it and point out all the advantages, sometimes he's not convinced and won't sanction it. I don't press it. I play a waiting game. He comes round in the end and, when my hunch pays off, he's generous.'

'Do you always succeed?' She sounded awed.

'Almost always. The cargo from Alexandria that came back in May brought in two million. He gave me a half percent.'

'You made two million for him, he gave you ten thousand and you call that generous?'

'It was ten thousand more than he need have given me Besides, he gave me you as well.'

A lucky guess, he wondered, *or was mental arithmetic another of her talents?*

'Is your labour worth so little?'

'Whatever it's worth, it belongs to him already. And the increase in wealth is his because the substance is his.'

'Then is nothing due to a craftsman who fashions a beautiful ornament from a plain gold bar?'

'The law is clear on that. Whoever has commissioned the work pays the goldsmith but the ornament melts down to a plain gold bar again, so it belongs to the owner of the gold. Wine is different. Grapes can't be recovered from wine so it belongs to the vintner. But money is like the gold ingot; we turn it into cargoes, antiques, wheat, slaves and so on, but we can always liquefy it into cash again – so any increase belongs to Lucius.'

He didn't think he'd been indiscreet. In his enthusiasm, he'd given her an idea of the riches in his safe. But he'd noticed that, though wildly unpredictable, she'd never been free with information she'd gained as a result of her private life with him. Indeed, he'd sometimes let fall scraps of unimportant information, precisely to see whether, and by what route, they'd surface. He was equally sure that she wasn't a thief - or a poisoner. She was like a bran tub. Whenever he delved into her mind she gave him a surprise. Sometimes it was a sting or a burning brand but, more often, a honey cake or a jewel. Lucius would come to see that he'd misjudged her. Not yet. Pygmalion's masterpiece still had rough edges that needed to be sanded and polished. But, in the end, he'd be proud to have given his steward such a wife and she'd be glad to serve a generous master.

CHAPTER XXXI

November – December 171

ὂυδεν γαρ απρεπες εν εόρτή λεγεσθαι πας δε γελώς, καν περιεργός ή πανήγύριζειν δοκει

Nothing said on a festive day is unseemly and any jesting, even if carried to excess, is thought in keeping with the holiday spirit. Lucian vol VIII

From first impressions, the laundry was not so different from the kitchen. Both were hot as Vulcan's forge and all that Nerysa could see from the entrance was a cloud of fumes and spray. But the smell of the kitchen made her mouth water; the stench of the laundry made her retch. Peering through the acrid steam she saw, to her right, three huge copper cauldrons set over wood fires. At the far end of the hall, she made out the bulbous shape of Erotion and began to pick her way over the slippery stone floor towards her. Suddenly, she was drenched in a cascade of foul water. She stopped, wiped her eyes with her fists and looked to see what had happened. Three enormous vats were sunk into the floor against the left hand wall, a naked youth crouched in each. Two of them stomped up and down in the vats, slewing water over the sides and the third leapt high in the air and landed like a tidal wave.

That can't be necessary. she thought, *especially in this heat. What a show off!*

Erotion brought her a bucket and mop.

'Keep the floor mopped, dear.'

It was a Sisyphean task. The launderers' enthusiasm mounted until the hall floor resembled the deck of a hapless ship battling through the Bay of Biscay. Rushing around the floor shunting water, stopping every few steps to bend down and wring out the mop, she made no impression on the flood. She flinched as a sudden deluge hit her and she lost her balance and skidded against a vat. The occupant seized her around the chest, caught up her tunic and perched her over the edge of the vat.

'Let it go, my lovely, all contributions welcome.'

She soon stopped beating with her hands and kicking with her feet because his grip only hardened.

'Don't be tight with it.' he urged. 'Makes good bleach, don't you know? But, if you want to shit, wait 'till the shift's over, or you'll get a brush up your backside to learn you better manners.'

'I thought you bought...that sort of thing from contractors.'

'Buy it! Spend the master's money on piss! Perhaps her ladyship thinks it'd smell sweeter if we shipped it from Arabia!'

Erotion descended on them brandishing a mop and shouting, 'Fool! Don't you know better than to handle the steward's woman? If a job on the farm's what you want, just ask her. She'll put in a good word for you.'

She waved to two other girls to mop the floor, took Nerysa's hand and led her to a series of tanks at the far end of the hall. Water was piped from the highest on the left and spilled through all the tanks to the lowest on the right into which a slave tossed tunics he'd carried over a mop handle from one of the vats. Erotion took the handle and stirred them round in an evil sludge of chalk, urine and dirt. But, as they progressed up the series of tanks they became steadily cleaner until, to Nerysa's amazement, in the highest tank, they floated soft and snowy on limpid water. Erotion summarised, 'Water flows downwards left to right. Clothes get moved upwards right to left. Keep saying it under your breath, dear, you'll soon get the hang of it.'

She fished in the top tank with the mop handle and caught a tunic, then pointed to a stone bench facing the open drain that ran along the wall.

'Sit there and wring it. I'll leave the pole against the wall so you can reach the rest.'

Nerysa sat listening to the slopping, running, splashing and dripping of water. Before she came to Rome a flowing stream was where you washed clothes. In Quintus' house, a maid had whisked away her dainty dresses and returned them fresh as new. *Could they have been through a stinking hole like this?*

Her hands were small. Twisting stiff cloth for hours on end made her arms ready to fall from their sockets. Worse was to come. Turning the giant screw on the press made her pant and sweat and, when she'd done her utmost, any one of a dozen other slaves could shame her by forcing the screw an extra turn. At least, the winter day was short but the best moment of it was when she was dismissed. She met Phago lurching across the yard. He greeted her with a grin and a belch.

'A day's holiday,' he said, 'feasting on the leftovers and tips all round. Shame you weren't there.'

She shrugged. 'A slave's lot.'

Her muscles trembled at work and twitched all night with fatigue. Steam tightened her chest and made her hair spring into unruly curls. In the kitchen, she'd succeeded in pleasing Demetrius. She knew, because she'd learned to notice when he pursed his lips to suppress a grin, when his eyes danced as he made a dry remark and when his touch was on the gentler side of bracing. Now he'd sent her back to the bottom of the pile. He wanted her to learn all the various kinds of women's work in the house so, eventually, he could promote her.

'To manage people,' he said, 'you need to know their work as well as they do. I don't say you must have done it for as long or do it as well but you must *understand* it as well so, when they say the linen is moth-eaten because the chest was cracked you point out that it should have been strewn with Artemisia to repel moths. If they say the meat is tough because they weren't given enough time to boil it you ask them what marinade they used to tenderise it. That way, they respect you and don't waste time trying to fob you off with lame excuses.'

It was some consolation that he meant to move her on but how soon would he do it and how would she stand it until then? A few bearable moments were spent in the gorge that was the laundry yard, spreading clothes over lavender bushes. The dried flower heads lingered on brittle stems. When she lowered the damp fabric onto them they gave up the last of their fragrance. But the delight of breathing cool, sweet air filled her with despair. When Demetrius detailed Polybius to present her with the seasonal gift she wilted at the sight of the combed woollen shawl and he hissed, 'If you don't thank Himself nicely and wear it every day I'll know how to make your life a misery. Warm too. Save you taking a chill in the laundry yard.'

How could she get out of the laundry? Should she wash less carefully? If she took the stink home to him in her hair, he might move her sooner. Or could she could pretend to be sick? Relief came unexpectedly.

One crisp morning, the rising bell didn't ring. Demetrius enjoyed his conjugal rights and a leisurely breakfast and told her to rest as long as she liked. He said he was going to escort Lucius to a public feast and would bring her home some treats. He clapped his hands under her nose and shouted, 'Io Saturnalia!' then snatched up his cloak and was gone. When Polybius came she remembered to clap and wish him 'Happy Saturnalia.' He looked sour and she knew he'd had to stay back because of her.

He recovered his good humour when Demetrius and Philemon came home, wearing ivy wreaths. Each had an enormous knotted napkin which he opened and shook over the table. Showers of sausages, olives, figs, dates and cakes landed on it. Demetrius poured wine and they dined together. Nerysa looked from one smiling face to the other, heard the gentle sonority of their conversation and was glad that slaves should have such an aura of peace and dignity about them. As Demetrius led her to bed she was able to say, 'Thank you. That was a lovely day.'

He grinned. 'Tomorrow will be better. Io Saturnalia!'

The next morning they dressed in the costumes they wore for play acting lord and lady. They made their way to the atrium hand in hand, tripping over squatting figures rolling dice. To Nerysa's amazement, no one made way for them. The atrium, ablaze with torches and festooned with greenery, smelled of pine and roasting chestnuts. Long trestles were arranged along three sides. Shiny new coins rained from the ceiling and the household jostled and collided as they vied for them. Slaves passed along the tables with trays of presents. When these had been distributed and unwrapped, brisk trading began until almost everyone had something they liked. Nerysa swapped a toothpick for a bronze thimble and laid it on the pointed freedman's hat she'd been given, together with a neat pile of the coins Demetrius had caught for her. The bowl of wine, passed down the table for each toast, was so heavy he had to hold it to her lips.

Loud cheering broke out, the company lurched to its feet and Apicius and Erotion progressed to the places of honour at the centre table. Judging by their clothes, they were playing lords and ladies too. Apicius waived to everyone to sit and beamed at the procession of slaves bearing in steaming beet soup, roast goose, pork with crackling, turnips and baked apples. Everyone burst into song.

In Saturn's day we used to play
In plenty and in pleasure
No care, no coil, no want, no toil
Earth offered up her treasure
No slave, no free, no work, no fee
But love and peace and leisure

She blushed when she thought she heard some bawdier variants then again, more deeply, in case she hadn't and people should think she'd construed obscenities herself. Soon there was no doubt. The song grew more thunderous with each repetition. Clapping, thigh slapping and table thumping kept time and the odd forehead hitting the table added some syncopation. Horrified, she turned to Demetrius.

'I think they might be drunk.'

'Of course, it's Saturnalia.'

'Aren't you going to do something?'

'Of course not, it's Saturnalia.'

'But isn't it bad for discipline?'

'No, it's Saturnalia'

Saturnalia with the ladies of Quintus' household had meant a new clay doll, lighting ritual lamps and offering cakes to Saturn. She wondered, for the first time, what had gone on in other parts of the house. What shocked her even more than the anarchy was Demetrius' relaxed attitude to it. At last he reacted.

'Hermes!' he said, 'Just look at our Lucius. His seventh Saturnalia as master of the house and he still can't imitate a keen servant. Excuse me, he needs help.'

Tearing off his fine gown, he tossed it on the bench and ran to the serving board, wearing only his under tunic. Lucius, ridiculous in short tunic, long apron and wounded dignity was looking from trays heaped with meat to two hundred gaping mouths and back again. Apicius hurled a loaf at him catching him in the belly.

'Look sharp! I want my meat before it's cold.'

Demetrius pushed a tray at Lucius, took two long forks himself and they ran down the lines tossing meat onto plates followed by boys slamming down vegetables. Demetrius had just returned to his place with Lucius standing close behind him, when the gong sounded and Petosirus, Lucius' official master of ceremonies, announced that Talos was the winner of the knucklebones competition. Talos sprang to his feet, acknowledged the deafening cheers and ran to the top table.

'What's the prize?' Lucius whispered to Demetrius.

'A set of silver knucklebones in a leather case.'

'Handsome - and appropriate.'

Petosirus then announced, to a chorus of boos, that the loser had lost every single game he'd played in the tournament. A diminutive post boy was dragged before Apicius and silence reigned while he considered the forfeit. A grin widened on his face.

'Now, what would we hall like to see? Phago, on your feet! Your forfeit, boy, is to carry this gentleman haround the himpluvium.'

The boy looked Phago up, down and round. His dismay was good for a laugh but some were disappointed that he'd have to be let off. Others maintained he should at least try and some said that even the Lord of Misrule had no right to impose impossible forfeits. It seemed that only Lucius could resolve this question. Chin in hand, he paced the room while everyone waited, still and silent, for his decision.

At last he said, 'Good people, I listened attentively to the sentence and it does not seem to me that it was specified that the task in question should be undertaken without assistance.'

To a roar of approval, the litter-bearers sprang into action. Phago was lifted just so high that the post boy could reach up to touch him with the tip of a finger. The nine of them ran several times around the impluvium then lowered their burden onto the edge of it and kicked him into the water. His spluttering and floundering sent the company into convulsions of merriment. Tears ran down their cheeks, they held their shaking sides; they fell on their backs on the floor and flailed their legs

Nerysa looked to see if Demetrius was laughing as heartily as the rest. He was staring vacantly at the ceiling but, as though he felt her eyes on him, he turned and looked at her. She blushed and looked down in case she wasn't allowed to meet his eyes in public, even at Saturnalia. But she blushed hottest of all when she declined an almond pastry. Some looked like sausages, others were shaped like cowrie shells. There was no doubt, even in her mind, what they were supposed to represent and, had she still worked in the kitchen, she'd have been required to fashion them.

After five more days the riot ended abruptly. Everyone reverted to their obedient, servile self and she was back in the laundry. It had taken six weeks to reduce her to despair but, after six days rest, a single day returned her to the same state. Exhausted though she was, she couldn't sleep. Neither, it seemed, could Demetrius.

'Is there a dog in the room?' he whispered 'Do you hear that noise.'

'No, what noise?'

'A sort of whistle, like a fat, old dog asleep.'

'It's not a dog. It's me. It used to come on - at work sometimes. Now it's most of the time.'

'Hermes! The fumes in the laundry! I remember a slave years ago. He got so sick we had to send him to the farm. You must stay out of there.'

'Well, I'm not good at the work yet but I think I know about it.'

'What you learned is a waste of time because you can't go back there – ever.'

Then he asked, accusingly, she thought, 'Why didn't you tell me?'

The next morning he told her to report to the linen store. She was intrigued. In the kitchen Apicius had kept an eye on her and, there was no doubt, Erotion, his wife, had performed the same function in the laundry. Who, she wondered, would be chief spy in the linen store?

Thaïs greeted her with a smile and, to Nerysa's delight, Apicius' twins, Flora and Filix were bobbing about behind her, skinny and jerky as crickets. When Thaïs called them to order, they ran to Nerysa and each took her by a hand. She laughed. They were the best spies of all. They would never willingly be separated, either from her or from each other.

The linen store, where clean washing was mended, folded and packed away strewn with sweet herbs, was cool and tranquil. Demetrius had improved her lot. She was grateful – and aware that she did little for him. He didn't turn his naked back towards her but the occasional glimpse of his ugly, puckered scars stirred a tenderness towards him. She knew her body, wooden though it was, brought him comfort that he couldn't find elsewhere and, gradually, she stopped grudging him that comfort. What he conveyed to her was not dissatisfaction so much as a restless hopefulness. His dream of loving her was not of a coupling such as theirs, but what that dream was or how she could help realise it, she'd no way of knowing. If her hem or her tunic pin had offended him he'd have told her precisely what to do, but on this crucial subject, he was silent. It was as if he expected her to converse with him in an unknown language. She saw the dalliance that went on everywhere in the house and knew she couldn't imitate the arch looks, pouting lips or languorous gestures in any way that would be convincing.

She must be at fault. His embrace was probably no more offensive than the next man's. Other girls yearned for it. She was deficient, unresponsive, less of a woman than the lightest feather-brain in the scullery. He'd see that and reject her, because he'd come to want of her the thing the scullery girls called 'love'. What was it? She felt much for him but not what he felt for her or what Iris felt for the carpenter. And, although it tamed her rebelliousness and made her struggle to conform to his ideal of servile behaviour, it didn't help her suffer his touch without a shiver.

CHAPTER XXXII

February – May 172

Odi quae praebat quia sit praebere necesse Siccaque de lana cogitat ipsa sua

I hate girls who give themselves grudgingly and lie unmoved, thinking about their knitting Ovid Artis Amortariae II 685-686

Lucius was surprised and hurt that Demetrius never talked about his marriage. From boyhood they'd compared notes. If it was for one of them to become too dignified for confidences, it was surely not for the slave. An intangible barrier had grown up between them because Demetrius had changed; he seemed taller, broader, more deeply assured.

They hadn't shared Saturnalia the way they usually did. Demetrius hadn't neglected his duties but, having discharged them, he'd returned promptly to the sour faced companion Lucius had been so indulgent as to give him – so he could ape the upwardly mobile freedman that he denied Lucius the pleasure of making him.

It was absurd to feel neglected by a slave. He decided to fill the void with a sweetheart of his own. They could both be intense and reserved. The project required thought. He was wary of the responsibilities of marriage, too ambitious to blight his career by seducing the wives of influential men and too proud to join the following of a fashionable hetaera.

He bought himself a Parthian girl; a private purchase that cost him a fortune. Roxana was in a different class from Nerysa; conventionally beautiful, olive skinned with dark, shining hair and lustrous, onyx eyes. Reared for the ornamental market, she was most genteelly incapable of anything except a little embroidery and a lot of coquetry. Nor was she a virgin as the vendor had delicately hinted, (actual false description would have been actionable) but what she lacked in innocence she more than made up in expertise.

From the first, she behaved perfectly. He went several times to the vendor's house to watch her. She must have been aware of his interest but she never looked directly at him. The day he beckoned to her she came hesitantly and he said, 'Would you like to come home with me and be my girl?'

Not daring to lift her eyes, she'd breathed, 'If you please, master, I should like that very much.'

She felt just as she ought. Demetrius seemed to enjoy re-enacting the rape of the Sabines. Lucius couldn't see the attraction. The right girl was the one who melted gratefully into your arms. Roxana wasn't intelligent but so vivacious no one else suspected that. Indeed, his household was impressed. And he was ready to be infatuated. He showered her with presents, indulged and privileged her until he did just wonder if she might grow vain.

He thought it odd that she was drawn to Nerysa so that she came to his notice again and he was able to compare them. He supposed the attraction was that they were of an age and Nerysa's situation compared unfavourably with Roxana's. Both were less than concubines but Nerysa served a slave rather than a Roman knight, was put to menial work and was low in the hierarchy. He'd placed Roxana not so much high in the hierarchy as outside it. She did envy Nerysa's wedding ring for, to his amusement, she worked on him until she had several rings for each knuckle. Beside Roxana's brilliance, Nerysa could, at best, have seemed eccentric, but he found her severe hairstyle and dogged expression less appealing than ever. He was guilty of a thrill of satisfaction. Demetrius must be regretting his headstrong decision. Of course, he couldn't have expected to own a girl like Roxana but, if he'd been more tractable, he might have taken his turn. No doubt it was through pique that he stinted his praise. He'd even suggested to her face that she should be less rough with her maids and Lucius had had to exert himself to soothe her wounded pride.

'Damn your impudence!' he said to Demetrius. 'My girl a problem when yours is an untamed savage? If my girl forgets herself occasionally it must be because she's learning tricks from yours. I've warned you, lick her into shape or we'll get rid of her.'

Demetrius, who was about to leave for hay making, went looking for his wife to order her, in the strongest terms, to have nothing more to do with Roxana. He found them together in the master's garden. A striped awning was slung between two pillars and, under its russet shade, they sat with the starling's cage between them. Roxana, he saw, was not as talentless as he had supposed. She was a brilliant mimic. With her shawl wrapped around her as a toga, she was unmistakably Lucius, stifling yawns and exchanging pregnant looks with Demetrius while receiving a delegation of vulgar clients. Demetrius felt as if he'd taken a sharp blow to the head. He ordered his wife out of the garden and Roxana turned her fury on him.

'Lock her up, why don't you? She's desperate to get away from you. Perhaps I'll do her a favour and ask Lucius to give her to me. He'd give me anything I asked.'

'If you wish to keep him in that frame of mind, I suggest you exert yourself in his bed and leave his staff to one who's managed them for seven years, to his entire satisfaction. You'll not improve your position by making an enemy of me.'

It took all his force of personality to bring the interview to a broadly satisfactory conclusion. The naked malice in her look didn't concern him. He was above her power to harm. But, crossing the garden to his room, he had the disturbing thought that Nerysa was dazzled by her new friend and might be led on to imitate her. It struck him, for the first time, how surprising it was that she'd never tried to make capital out of her marriage. He must, at all costs, prevent her from beginning now. Behaviour that passed in the master's mistress wouldn't be tolerated in a menial; she'd be sold on; sent to a strange house with no one to protect her and he'd lose her. Would she ever behave like Roxana? He couldn't be sure. She was an enigma, his precious, alien girl. But she was far from stupid. He could make her understand.

'Why should a master keep slaves; feed, clothe and shelter them, so they can laugh at him behind his back? Nerysa, are you trying to have yourself sold away out of my reach? I couldn't excuse such behaviour, even at Saturnalia. How can I think of setting you over other slaves who would look to your example? Take away a slave's reverence for his master and you take everything that makes his life bearable. What does he live for but to please his master and what satisfaction is there in drudging for a worthless fool? If his master's nothing, he's less than nothing. Have you heard of the slave wars? Three hundred miles of the Appian Way and, every thirty paces, some mother's son writhing and choking on a cross. That's what happens when you incite slaves to revolt.'

'We weren't trying to start a rebellion. We were just having fun.'

'Fun! Anyone watching that offensive display would have taken our master for a vain, empty-headed, idle snob. He's not. You don't know him. You can't begin to imagine how gentle he is, how refined.'

'How long would he stay that way if he were taken by pirates and sold off as no better than us?'

'I'm not interested in hypotheses. If I find that you have been in Roxana's company while I'm away, I shall punish you. Is that understood?'

CHAPTER XXXIII

May 172

πως ποιεις, οταν των οικετων τινα τοιουτον οντα καταμανθανης; κολαζω πασι κακοις, εως αν δουλευειν αναγκασω.

What would you do with a slave like that? Beat him and make his life a misery until I force him to serve me. Xenophon. Memorabilia. II 16-17

When Demetrius had been away ten days Nerysa asked Polybius, 'How long does it take to make hay?'

'It varies. Depends on the weather I think. You look worn out.'

'I've had a difficult day. Flora has been crying all the time.'

'Silly child. What for?'

'Well you know they've made a new team to wait on Roxana? Filix has been drafted in as a wardrobe maid. They've never been separated before.'

'Alike as two eggs aren't they? Same as horses; a matched pair's more valuable than two singletons. They'll be worked in harness again. Look, I've finished for today. We could play draughts.'

'I've never played so I shouldn't be much of a challenge. But, thank you, I will for a bit.'

They knelt, opposite each other, sat back on their heels and balanced the board across their knees. Polybius shook the pieces from the linen bag, took the jet pieces for himself and set them out. Scooping up the moonstone pieces and copying his arrangement, Nerysa said, 'Roxana will be sending for me soon.'

Polybius looked up sharply. 'Nerysa, didn't Himself tell you to stay away from her?'

'How can I?' Nerysa shrugged. 'She'll complain to Lucius if I don't go and Demetrius dreads Lucius hearing bad reports of me. It'll just be, "Carry this here" or "there" or "Go and tell so and so such and such." She'll stop asking for me once he's back.'

***

Demetrius, who returned that night, confirmed Polybius' opinion of twins and matched pairs so Nerysa was able to comfort Flora the next morning. They spent a tranquil day pacing to and fro folding sheets. *This is the best work,* Nerysa thought. *I could do this comfortably for the rest of my life.*

'This one's still stained,' she said, dropping it onto the stone flags. 'Back in the wash.'

Flora passed her another from the basket.

'Oh, look how thin and worn this is. We'll put it aside for now and later we'll slit it down the middle and join it down the sides. See, here where it's still strong. Then we'll hem the raw edges and we'll have a sheet with years more life in it.'

Flora looked doubtful. 'But there's a hole in it – here.'

'So there is. You've sharp eyes. But we can darn that. I'll show you how.'

'I'd love that. Perhaps, after work, I could teach Filix so, when she comes back, she'll know already.'

'That's a good idea. We'll ask Thaïs if you can borrow a needle – you know we have to count them every evening.'

But Flora wasn't listening. The room was suddenly still and all the women were looking at Polybius who was standing in the doorway, a hand pressed to the lintel. His eyes scanned the room for Nerysa. She moved towards him, a knot of fear in her stomach, suddenly realising how much she would care if anything had happened to Demetrius.

'Himself wants you.' he said, 'Now.'

He took Flora's hands, unclasped them from Nerysa's skirt and pushed her away.

Demetrius looked well enough. He was sitting, not reclining, on the couch because he was still wearing his sandals. Nerysa hurried to loose them but he waved her back. His voice was soft as usual but strained.

'Did you see Roxana while I was away?'

'Only when she sent for me. She would have complained to Lucius –'

His hand shot up, index and middle finger raised, in a gesture Quintus was wont to use to forestall interruption. She bit her lip.

'Did you run errands for her?'

'Sometimes.'

'Outside the house?'

'Never.'

'Did you go to the atrium?'

'Not since I went with you.'

'You could have spoken to visitors elsewhere?'

'No….possibly. I don't remember.'

'Did you handle money for her?'

'No, sir.'

'Sealed packages, perhaps?'

'All the time. To carry from one place to another.'

'What dealings have you had with a man called Marcus Marius Bibulus?'

'I've never heard of him.'

He paused. She wanted to ask where all this was leading but, one look at his face, made her think better of it.

'Bibulus is not a man I enjoy dealing with but I'm grateful he had the discretion to bring this to me. It seems he gave money to one of our maids to deliver to Roxana. It was to be used to bribe a jury. Do you understand what I'm saying?'

'Yes, sir.'

'I wonder if you do. Bibulus is satisfied with the outcome of yesterday's hearing but puzzled to find that the jurors voted purely on the merits of the argument and are none the richer for having done so.'

'What is this to do with me, sir?'

'Do you know the penalty for perverting the course of justice and abusing a client?'

She shook her head.

'Death. Given the emperor's lenient disposition and our master's blameless record, that might well be commuted to a period of exile and social and professional ruin. But, try to understand, that's not the reason he wouldn't do it. He wouldn't because he's a man of the highest principle. The very suggestion of bribery would be abhorrent to him.

'What it has to do with you is that Roxana says you were the courier. Not only that, she says it was you who suggested the scheme to her.'

'Do you believe her?'

'If I did, I wouldn't be laying the matter before Lucius, who'll hand over her staff to the city magistrate for interrogation.'

'No! Not magistrates! They'll torture them.'

'Of course. That's the way slaves are questioned. There is no other way.'

She was back in Surdus' cellar, rigid with terror, waiting, a seemingly interminable time, to be whipped. Through a jagged gap in the brick wall she could see a fellow sufferer. For the first time in her adult life, she was looking at a naked man but she only saw bulging eyes, flared nostrils, bunched sinews and bared teeth. She pressed her hands to her ears to muffle the creak of the rack and the howls.

Bounding forward, she cried, 'Sir! You can't do that! They're innocent and they'll be mangled to death! Some of them are hardly more than children.'

He shrugged. 'One of them, at least, is not innocent.'

'Only one. There are ten of them.'

'I will have the truth. If that's what it takes, so be it.'

Flora's sister! she thought, *Filix is her laundry maid.*

'If it was me, just me and Roxana, tricking money out of Bibulus, what would you do?'

'I should buy this man's silence and teach you a lesson you'd never forget.'

'Then you'd better teach me!'

She expected contempt. His dismay scythed the ground from under her feet. There was no doubt that he'd believed in her innocence and would have done whatever it took to prove it. She'd yearned for his respect. In a single instant she'd been sure of it and lost it forever. How could she reassure him, avoid punishment and still save the maids? She'd retract, pretend her confession had been a tasteless joke. But, if she changed her story a second time, he wouldn't believe her and he wouldn't spare any of them. She watched him swallow again and again. He couldn't stop. His voice, when it came, was hoarse.

'You took money to bribe the jury that was going to hear your master's case.'

She braced herself and looked him straight between the eyes.

'Yes.'

'They promised you a cut?'

She lifted her chin. 'Of course.'

'Bring me the whip from the chest.'

She obeyed promptly, hoping to avoid the meticulous enquiries he was apt make before ordering punishments.

What do I say, she thought, *if he asks me what this Bibulus looks like?* He might be red-nosed and bleary-eyed but, then again, the soubriquet might be inherited from his grandfather and he, himself, a model of sobriety.

'Are you well?' he asked as he took the whip and got up from the couch. 'You're not indisposed today? Is there… anything I should know before I do what is necessary?'

Not trusting herself to speak, she gave a jerk of her head. It was enough that he should think her depraved. He shouldn't think her a coward too.

She came to, prone on the bed and pressed her hands to her wounds to blunt the pain. He pulled them away and ranted at her, as if it was *she* who'd injured *him*.

'As soon as our Lucius comes to his senses, that bitch will be out of the house. And you, with her, if I can't protect you. I told you to stay away from her. In future, you do as I say, without hesitation or question because what your master orders is always right, however wrong it seems to you. By all the gods in heaven I don't know what a man is supposed to do with you. You're impossible!'

She pressed her sides again. He seized her wrists and held them in an iron fist.

'Don't, I said! You'll make the wounds fester.'

His grip numbed her hands while, loud and long, he cursed Quintus Pulcher, in whose disorderly house a slave couldn't even learn how to escape whipping. There was a scratch on the door. His grip slackened and she was able to writhe and press her sides alternately into the mattress.

'What do you want?' she heard him growl, 'Where's Polybius?'

'The baths, sir.' It was Philemon's voice. 'He said you told him to make himself scarce.'

'I want him here as soon as he gets back.'

'Very good. Sir, the master's asking to see the draft of those warehouse leases.'

'Before dinner?'

'That would suit him. He's dining in his bedroom with Roxana.'

'Say I'll have them ready.'

He reached for writing tablets, wrenched out the leather binding string and lashed her wrists to the bed head.

'I can't hold your hands all night,' he said, 'and I'm not going to tell our Lucius I'm behind with my work because my woman's giving trouble.'

He sat at his work table grinding his teeth. His girl lay torn and bleeding while Roxana, no less guilty, took supper; because Roxana's master was a free man and Nerysa's was a slave. Someone powerful must have protected her in Pulcher's house because she was unruly down to the bone yet she'd come to him unscathed. Unscathed but not unpunished. A lady's maid sent to a strange house as a kitchen hand. He could imagine why; some indiscretion in the heat of the moment. How to control her? Weals on olive skin were commonplace but ruby wounds on stark white skin unnerved him. He'd have no comfort of her that night. Whipping had been a necessary and judicial act but to take her in such condition was unthinkable.

From the moment he knew he couldn't have her, desire mounted until it was a throbbing tumult that swept away all power of thought. He shouted to Philemon to find him a girl, any girl. Philemon ran off with a salute and an impassive expression and he stood over the table, his wayward phallus lifting his tunic, his face on fire and his breath torn from him in painful gasps.

A girl came promptly and ran across the room hoisting up her tunic. He seized her in a shuddering grip but, as he thrust home, he heard a crash from the bedroom and a suppressed cry. He cursed, broke free and blundered after the sound. Nerysa lay on the ground tethered by the wrists, in a pool of water and broken pot. He strode to the dinner tray for a knife, slashed through the bonds and lifted her with shaking arms. She whispered, 'I'm sorry.. water. I needed..'

He went to the table, spilled wine neat into a cup and pushed it against her teeth.

'We are slaves.' he said. 'Never forget that, even in your sleep.'

Feeling his face twitch, he turned it sharply from her and stumbled blindly out of the room. The lights guttered in the office. The girl was still bent over the table, waiting. He swore at her to take herself off. The sight of her disgusted him.

CHAPTER XXXIV

June 172

Rocket seed so dulls the senses that whips and torments do not give any grief. Andres Leguna after Dioscorides

Nerysa struggled to marshal her thoughts. Her mind raced in countless directions; a thousand nameless fears tormented her and fled before her mind could engage them.

The pain won't last, she told herself. *I just have to bear it till it fades*

But would it fade? She stopped pretending that Quintus could get her a pardon. He'd held out the possibility because he couldn't bear to send her away without hope. She saw now, he'd never believed it himself. Her old life was gone and the new one was slavery, with or without Demetrius. She didn't blame him. He'd done what the system demanded of him. During the year she'd lived with him, he'd never once raised his voice or his arm, to her or Polybius. In general, he was even sparing of the foreman's aid – the slap on the cheek that hurt and humbled in one economical swipe. Knowing what she thought of someone who'd trade her master's reputation for money, she knew what he now thought of her. And that wasn't her only fault, perhaps not even the worst. She couldn't love him in his bed and couldn't help showing it. Her body throbbed in every atom but the pain in her mind was keener.

Polybius whispered, 'Nerysa, do you want anything?'

'Water!'

'I thought you might.' He had water from the depths of the well in a double clay pot. 'Not so fast! You'll be sick. Did he give you rocket seeds? He should have. Here. Chew.'

He pushed seeds into her mouth. She bit into them and they exploded in her head. Her nose burned, her eyes streamed. She made to spit but he was too quick for her and clapped a hand over her mouth.

'Keep chewing.' he said. 'It helps.'

It takes your mind off the smart in your back, she thought, by giving you a fire in the throat..

'You certainly know how to put him through it. What did you do to make him so angry? No one held his interest a month before and he's kept you a year without looking at another girl, even when you're out of action.'

'You even tell them that, don't you, so they know when to make eyes at him?'

'Is it my fault if they want to pay for little things I know? Much good it did them until you spoiled everything for yourself. But I'll be sorry to see a new girl in here. You never tried to make trouble for me.'

'Why would I make trouble for you?'

He looked puzzled. 'Why wouldn't you? I wish I understood you. Himself is the best, the kindest master a slave could have. Why rub him against the grain? Why shrink from him as if he were a leper? What's the strategy?'

'I try. You don't know how I try. I work hard. I'm respectful. And obedient – mostly –'

'Do you think a man keeps you on a goose feather mattress in silk sheets for housework?'

'It's all I can do.'

'Then he won't keep you.'

'I know.'

Then, at last, tears came. Polybius knelt beside her, thoughtful.

At last, he said, 'I'll look out for you then. If anyone bullies you, I'll tell Himself.'

'You are kind.'

'It's what Himself would want me to do. Now here he is. Lie still and don't fret him any further.'

He drew a table up to the couch, lit the lamps, placed a screen between the bed and the lamplight and left without meeting his master's eye. Demetrius muttered over his tablets. She heard the regular refilling of his wine cup and the creaking of his couch when he changed position. The rocket seed must have been effective because she dozed. A muffled sound woke her. It took time to work out what it was. She'd never heard a grown man sob.

Dawn broke before she heard regular breathing followed by the sound of tablets thudding to the floor. He didn't approve of wasting lamp oil in daylight. Clenching her teeth, she bent to retrieve the tablets, laid them on the table and snuffed the lamp, willing him not to wake. She could bear the pain, but not him watching her bear it. More than anything, she wanted to be alone but the linen room was preferable to his bedroom.

Perhaps it was the smell of the smoking wick that woke him. Why did he insist she stay in bed? No one would marvel that he had whipped a disobedient wife; the general wonder was that he hadn't done it sooner. But, if he was trying to avoid gossip, then he was still trying to protect her. She felt a flood of gratitude. And guilt that she'd disillusioned him. Then she remembered Flora's eager, upturned face and thought that, instead of learning to mend sheets, she could have been mourning her twin. She'd hurt Demetrius. She'd hurt herself. But, she thought, we're not children. She had...how had he put it? She'd done what was necessary.

Would he put her out of the house or just out of his life? Would he tell her himself or would it be Polybius who told her to take her things and go? Perhaps she'd be sent away empty-handed. She decided to avoid him as much as possible. If she wasn't in his presence she couldn't be on his nerves and provoke the final rejection. Perhaps he'd keep her out of habit until someone else caught his eye. A spent passion wouldn't rekindle but she hoped she could help it dwindle to a benign indifference and not turn to hatred and bitterness.

CHAPTER XXXV

June 172

Titulus servorum singulorum scriptus sit curato ita, ut intellegi recte possit, quid morbi vitiive cuique sit, quis fugitivus errove sit noxave solutus non sit.

Take care that the bill of sale for each slave be written so that it can be known exactly what disease or defect each one has, which one is a runaway or a wanderer or not innocent of any offence. Aulus Gellius Edict of aediles from attic nights 4 2 1

The deed was done. Demetrius knew it had had to be done. And more would have to be done. He must lay everything before Lucius. Once he did, Nerysa would be sold and her crime declared in the bill of sale. With such a record, it wouldn't be possible to place her in a good house. To keep Lucius in ignorance would be disloyal to a kind master, a foster brother and a friend. Getting up from his couch was like clambering out of a river. His body was leaden and he shivered. He walked out of the office and towards the atrium but his steps grew ever slower until he stopped.

He couldn't do it. He remembered the hunger, the emptiness, the loss of concentration until Lucius gave her. If he lost her now they would dog him again with the added anxiety about her fate. He wouldn't be able to function, which was hardly in Lucius' interest. He would never reach the mystery at the heart of her. Never win her over.

What alternatives did he have? Roxana and Bibulus wouldn't incriminate themselves. Lucius couldn't hear of the matter from anyone but himself. Could he stake Lucius' career on the chance that whipping had reformed her? He wouldn't have done it otherwise. He'd hurt her enough to make her hate him but perhaps not enough to make her obey. She had the animal courage of a barbarian.

But her defiant admission showed more than courage. It showed she didn't understand what she'd done. He could have explained. He felt passionately that a master had obligations to a slave and he owed him more than board and lodging and a smart uniform. Since the wretch couldn't be happy unless he pleased his master, he should be taught to please. If he understood his duty and declined to perform it, he deserved all the misery he brought on himself but to be left ignorant of how to please was to be cruelly cheated. In this respect, he himself was as guilty as Pulcher.

Stupidly, he'd come to trust her and stopped having her watched. A careful master denied his charges the opportunity to offend. He did not, through neglect, bring on himself the cruel necessity of chastising them. Well, he could deny her access to the master's side of the house. He could have her footsteps dogged and order a daily report on everyone she met and spoke to. When he travelled, he could take her with him.

He would have felt comfortable with this line of action if he'd had the remotest understanding of why she'd done what she did. He usually avoided punishing a deed without exposing the motive. What a difference twenty four hours made to how one saw a situation! In the first shock of discovery, her depravity had appalled him, now he only pitied her ignorance. That was one reason why a master should wait a night before punishing a slave. Another was to demonstrate, by commanding his own anger, that he was a fit person to command others.

Had she wanted money to buy fripperies she was too proud to ask him for? It wouldn't have hurt to indulge her more. He reviewed everything he'd heard her say and seen her do but he couldn't remember a single instance of her being either greedy or malicious. Bibulus and Roxana had imposed on her ignorance. She wasn't wicked. She needed to be protected from bad influence. He convinced himself it would be unjust to banish her for something that wasn't her fault but his own.

Why hadn't she cried? He knew how to console girls who cried. He'd stayed wakeful all night in case she needed him but she'd retreated into herself so completely he didn't exist for her. She'd no idea how much he'd demeaned himself to choose her or how great the risks he ran in keeping her. His passion left her unmoved. Perhaps she despised him for it.

Her dumb suffering stirred repressed memories, black times he'd pushed to the deepest oubliette of his mind and refused to revisit. Remembering how he'd felt and behaved in those days, he suddenly recognised her wooden indifference, her mute acceptance, as signs of implacable hatred. How had he reacted to those who'd tortured him? He'd despised them so much he wouldn't show them anything of himself, even the fact that he suffered. He knew, then, that she'd never smile at him, and knew, with shattering insight, that it wasn't because of anything he'd done. She'd hated him on sight, before he'd done anything to hurt her, when his only purpose had been love. He was as baffled as he was miserable. Once before he'd provoked blind, irrational hatred, but not in a slave who'd everything to gain from his favour.

But, since she was his slave, he could claim from her whatever he could command. He gave his master those things: deference, obedience, diligence and loyalty but he gave him so much more besides; admiration, affection, blithe generosity and an empathy that flayed him raw. Did they amount to love, he wondered, these things one couldn't exact? Could a woman give them? He sensed that *she* could and one day she would, but not to him. What then? Would he be generous enough to release her? Unthinkable.

He needed ointment for her. He couldn't face Archias but there was another doctor of good reputation who had a small loan outstanding. So, today would be the day he made calls on his master's debtors. He kept doggedly walking all day. Adrian was left to do most of the talking but that didn't matter. To those who owed Lucius Lepidus money, the mere presence of Demetrius in their house or place of business was terrifying enough. Professionally speaking, it was a satisfactory day.

When her wounds had healed, he hardly saw her except when he spied on her unawares. He'd always liked to do this because, when he saw her with other people, he felt he saw her as she really was. With him she always seemed on her guard. He heard no complaints of her.

Though pretentious in speech and manners, she wasn't squeamish of the work she was given. She worked long and late, usually on nights when he did not. He knew her too well to think this a coincidence but didn't interfere. It would be so easy to do more harm than good. He continued to exercise his marital rights. They brought him physical relief and mental anguish. He couldn't deceive her with his body. Pride urged him to match her cold indifference but the frenzy of his nightly tribute stripped him before her scorn. She took it with the inscrutability of a marble goddess receiving offerings from her priest.

He took offerings regularly to the temple. The image never inclined toward him but, in his life, there was the odd sign of favour: the calming of a storm at sea, a stroke of luck in business, an answer to prayer precisely timed to revive his flagging faith. In the same way, he persevered with his wife, watchful for the smallest sign of unbending. He'd overshot the mark. Twice. But he'd loved and given freely. Would she never forgive? He began to despair. Her hatred raised her to a sort of equality; she was a worthy adversary - one therefore, who need be given no quarter. He was no simpering poet to be kept shivering on a mistress' doorstep. Her submission, at least, he would have. He'd paid for it with the derision of his underlings and the betrayal of his master.

CHAPTER XXXVI

June - July 172

Αλλ' επειδη μη θελεις εραστου μου πειραν λαβειν, πειραση δεσποτου.

If you won't take me as a lover then you'll have me for a master. Achilles Tatius. Clitophon and Leucippe VI 20 3

Nerysa noticed that she was being watched again. No doubt to prevent her associating with racketeers and bringing her master to ruin. Though she'd confessed to it, she still felt hurt that Demetrius had believed it of her. His presence, when she couldn't avoid it, was painful. He'd always spared praise and lavished constructive criticism; now he became a Momus. His censure was carping and his sarcasm winded her. A year of his training and example had taught her more self-control than she would have thought possible. She was able to bow her head and accept his taunts dumbly until it dawned on her that her passivity enraged him further and that he'd be increasingly bitter until he stung a response from her.

'I think I may have suggested,' he said one evening, 'that you tell my boy if you needed anything.'

'You did, sir, but I have everything I need.'

'Am I to infer you think me miserly or merely frugal when you neglect to mention that the perfume jar is empty?'

'But it isn't. It's just that yesterday I came in late and I was tired. I did wash but I forgot the perfume – or, at least, I thought you wouldn't mind.' She felt suddenly reckless. 'And I don't think you would mind if I pleased you in bed. Why don't I? Think! When I came here I could do nothing. Now, at least, I can scour pots, bake bread and press linen. Why? Because I was taught. I don't know how to please you in bed. Why don't you have someone teach me?'

His face flushed. Dumb with fury, he lashed out and struck her on the mouth. She staggered and fell across the bed, more from shock than from the force of the blow.

'How dare you?' he shouted. 'I've always treated you with respect, let you lie at my side like an equal, never complained that you were as stiff and proud as if I wasn't fit to touch your shoe. So you need instruction to return an honest man's love? Or do you say I kept you like a whore? If that's what you want, I know well enough how to use a whore. Fetch the perfume.'

Lying back on his cushions, he told her to strip off her tunic, something he'd always done for her, and anoint herself, which she'd always done in private. She supposed other girls would have managed this seductively but, even in these simple tasks, she was clumsy and self-conscious. Next, she must do the same for him, at least for his front for he didn't turn her his back. Overcome by shyness, she skirted over his skin as swiftly and lightly as she dared. She saw that his frame was taut, his limbs athletic, his neck supple but these were facts she noted without emotional response. If he'd been a statue, she would have admired his beauty. But he wasn't a sculpture. He was her master and he was raging with a hurt she'd inflicted, for reasons she didn't begin to understand. She put the jar on the floor and waited without daring to look up.

His voice made her shiver.

'Interest me. You have a mouth and two hands. Use them.'

She looked up at him, helplessly ignorant. In curt, crude language, whose meaning she guessed from his explicit gesture, he told her what a paying customer expects. She obeyed mechanically, without resentment or disgust, without any feeling at all but exhaustion. Only desperation to appease him sustained her when her thighs seemed to have liquefied. She could barely stagger to the washroom, her legs splayed and trembled like a new born foal's but her mind was racing.

A master who sold his slave to a brothel was generally despised. Surely, he wouldn't do that to her? At that point she would, at last, be ready to die. He'd used her like a Corinthian temple prostitute because he could find no more offensive way to insult her. But that was because, in her clumsiness and ignorance, she'd mortified him. He'd shown her the difference between a man overwhelmed by passion and a master being serviced by a slave and, now she knew, she was ashamed she'd needed to be taught. Forgiveness or reprisal didn't seem relevant. She only saw that something was wrong and longed for it to be right.

A sliver of lamplight still showed under the curtain and she waited as long as she dared in the dark closet but, when she came out, he stood facing her, rigid with contempt.

'I hope I've taught you what you wanted to know. In the advanced class you'll learn to serve with a smile instead of a snivel.'

She stumbled and fell on the floor. His voice hit her like a switch.

'I don't know who it is who's taken your fancy. You hide it well enough the pair of you. But make up your mind; I'll never let you go and I'll make you obey me.'

Despair overcame fear and she cried out, 'Sir, you've mistaken me, horribly.'

'How have I mistaken you?'

'Everything I do is to serve you. All I want is to please you. You never treated me like this before. Whatever have I done?'

Sobs choked her and he was on the floor beside her, cradling her with a tenderness that dissolved her shaking limbs.

'I thought you'd show me what love is.' she said. 'That wasn't love, was it?'

She tried to search his face but he hung his head, shaking it over and over.

'I need to know,' she persisted, 'to know if I feel love.'

'If you did,' he sighed, 'you wouldn't need to ask. Love rears up out of nowhere and knocks the breath out of you. You never felt that for me.'

She was desperate now to understand; to tear down the veil of unknowing that divided her from the rest of the world.

'Suppose you felt it in your mind but not in your flesh? At least, I do feel something in my flesh, so strong it frightens me, but I don't know what it is or what to do with it.'

'Nerysa, who is this man? I swear I won't harm him.'

'Who but yourself? You don't believe me? Look, if I admired your reason, your ability, why should I have to show it by hitching up my skirt and smirking at you? That's so...paltry. You had the esteem of a rational being but all you wanted was a sycophantic leer and a histrionic moan.'

'Not at all. But I'd be a strange fellow to thrive on neglect. Even your poor bird sees nothing of you. You're never here before I cover his cage.'

'But I was terrified of provoking you! I thought, when you'd sent me away, … just to catch sight of you in the distance would make any day special for me.'

'That's not possible! How could you have thought that without my knowing?'

'No one *does* anything in this house without your knowing but don't you think it might just be possible for someone to *think* something without your knowing?'

'I tried to be good to you. You rejected me because you blamed me for your fate. I see that. But was that just? I didn't make you a slave. I don't make the rules. I impose them on you, as I do on myself, because I've no choice.'

Her misery resonated with his and she wept for them both. The fears and sorrows she'd suffered since she'd been sent to Rome as a child welled up in her breast and she sobbed them out of her body and her mind until both were drained. He said nothing more, only held her, but there was boundless comfort in the compelling touch she'd resisted for so long. She'd never again look over her shoulder with foreboding. Either she'd be safe in his unyielding arms or indifferent to anything that fate could hurl at her. When she had no more strength to cry, he laid her on the bed. She watched him take a phial from his safe and mix it with wine. He held the cup to her lips.

'A friend gave me this once,' he said, 'to make me forget. I didn't want to, but you must.'

CHAPTER XXXVII

June – July 172

Nunc scio quid sit amor.

Now I know what love is! Virgil Eclogue VIII 43

Daylight filtered through the slatted shutters. Demetrius bent over his breakfast tray. He took a barley cake and laid it in the centre of a silver dish then he set it back on the tray and selected another, more symmetrical and evenly browned. Picking over the cherries he chose the plumpest on double stems and arranged them either side of the cake. He put down the dish and broke two soft pieces from the inside of a loaf. With his thumb, he pressed a hollow into each and spooned honey into them. Then he took the dish to the stool beside the bed, sat and waited.

Nerysa lay white and still, her face tranquil as a child's. The anodyne had wiped the shame from her memory. He hadn't corrupted her. He hadn't lost her. And she'd said she wanted to stay with him. He'd do better now. She opened her eyes and put up a hand to shield them from the light.

'What happened? I must be late for work.'

He held out the dish.

'I sent word you'd be late.'

He watched her eat, then took the empty dish to the table and asked, casually, over his shoulder, what she remembered of the night before. She looked down. He felt fear as a sudden void in his belly as he watched a crimson tide creep over her face and neck. Her eyes were fixed on the damask quilt and her forefinger traced small circles over it.

'Tell me.' he said. 'Everything.'

She told him in a whisper. He pressed her for every detail; forcing himself to hear it all before he gave in to despair.

'I must let you go. We don't need to divorce. Our marriage was only ever a charade.'

'What's divorce?'

She was so innocent! He'd loved that about her. He might, at least, have left her that. But his punishment would be savage. He was going to lose her.

'Nerysa, I don't seem able to train you kindly. No respectable woman should be used as I used you last night.'

She looked up at him then, her eyes wild and uncomprehending.

He said, 'I know a freedman, in comfortable circumstances, who'd take you gladly. Wouldn't it be better for the master to give you to someone who can treat you well?'

She slumped to the floor, wailing like a child.

'Why can't you understand me? I only want to serve you. Can't I ever learn to please you?'

Could he believe that? He wanted, at least, to hear more. He knelt and groped for a form of words that would leave them space to negotiate.

'Do you think it might be possible.. for us to begin again.. as though we'd just met?'

He felt their future hang by a hair. She breathed the sigh that reset its course.

'Sir, I should like to try.'

Her face was bright and eager but her eyes were wary as if she wanted to give him something but hesitated in case it shouldn't please him. She was human at last; more vulnerable than he could bear. He put out a hand to touch her cheek and his mouth sought hers with a gentle reverence. As he drew back the smile he'd yearned for trembled on her lips, small and hesitant at first, then wide, generous, radiant. He pulled her to him in sudden terror.

'Nerysa, my darling, don't ever look at me like that except when we're alone.'

'Why not?'

He couldn't tell her the world was vicious that, if people knew what you loved, they'd use that knowledge to hurt you or control you. He couldn't tell her that when she looked at him with love light in her eyes.

'Dearest girl, it's safer. Let them think I'm harsh to you, that you're just a submissive wife. This miracle is ours. Don't let the vulgar breathe on it.'

When he'd made her promise, he left her to dress and went out into the peristyle. He needed to think.

The problem was unlike any he'd faced or even imagined. He understood her to mean that she valued him but couldn't desire him. She'd never desired any man and thought that was an innate defect in herself. That might be or it might be that the two austere matrons she'd served had stolen her fire and left Scythian snow in its place.

Why not continue as before? His own lust sufficed for two. Her unresponsiveness only troubled her because she thought it troubled him. Well, it did trouble him. After all, when she'd first come to him, she'd had no appetite yet she'd learned to share good food and relish it. She'd been mute yet now conversation was a pleasure they shared. He meant to teach her to read and spread the world of literature at her feet. So why not try to release this faculty also? Because his own behaviour had made it unlikely he would succeed.

If he tried and failed she'd assume the fault lay with her, which would cause her great sorrow. Nor would it guarantee that, some day, some other man might not succeed. Until they failed, they could hope. He was turning these thoughts over in his mind when Polybius passed with the lunch tray. He gave him orders, then went in search of Thaïs because he didn't keep such a thing as a woman's veil.

***

Polybius, almost hidden behind armfuls of roses and myrtle and carrying a wicker cage containing a pair of white doves, met them in front of the temple. Demetrius took the flowers and cage in one arm, nodded approval and dismissal at Polybius and slipped his free arm around Nerysa to guide her up the four steep flights of steps to the entrance.

Inside was tomb dark, the air chill and thick with incense. He stood just inside the massive bronze doors until he could make out the way ahead. The ceiling was too high to see and the walls shrouded in blackness and haze so he felt rather than saw them. Nerysa shivered. He smiled to encourage her but realised she couldn't see him smile and squeezed her hand. As they approached the statue of the goddess, his own heart raced in awe and hope. He laid his offerings on the ground, covered his head, raised his arms and prayed,

'Venus, Queen of Heaven, Mighty Cyprian, Lady Dione, Great Bringer of Victories, Guardian of Beauty, Patroness of Lovers, Mistress of Fortune, Thou who turnest hearts and inspirest love…May it please –'

He felt Nerysa tug his tunic. He bent his head to tell her to be silent but she whispered. 'Mother of the Archer God.'

Thank all the gods for her quick thinking! He could hardly have put the goddess in an indulgent frame of mind by omitting one of her titles, especially one so pertinent to the business in hand.

'Mother of the Archer God,' he continued, 'and let me also greet thee by whatever titles thou desirest, at this time, to be addressed.

'May it please thee to accept these offerings which I have brought on behalf of my wife so thou wilt cease to shun her and take her under thy strong protection.'

Willing Nerysa to join her silent prayers with his, he left her, head bowed, before the altar and found the priest who, as expected, loomed out of the darkness, hand extended for Demetrius' purse. It was a handsome rather than a prodigal offering. Only gratitude would release the full spate of his generosity. The goddess would understand that.

He waited before putting the goddess to the test. He had to behave as one should with a virgin and that was outside his experience. Virgins were scarce and he'd always come second in the queue, after Lucius. On the other hand, he shouldn't delay until his offerings slipped from the divine memory.

The day he kissed her and her lips parted under his, he mixed wine, honey and water in his silver jug. He felt exultation and fear in equal measure, knowing that the time of trial had come. Would he be able to give her pleasure or only pain and disgust? It did seem to him that Venus was stirring but could she, even she, destroy the barrier they had built?

When he kissed her again, he felt the tip of her tongue tentative against his. He drew back and her wistful look made him ache to console her. Taking her hand, he led her to the bed, setting the branched lamp standard close by. When he'd eased off her tunic he held her in the crook of his arm. Her eyes, tawny in the lamplight, brimmed over as they found his. She was humble under his hands and he felt, and shared, her dread of failure.

He whispered that he loved her, more than his own eyes, more than his life. He kissed her brows, stroking her eyelids shut with the tip of his tongue. His lips traced her soft throat and the dome of her breast until they brushed her nipple. She tensed and he pressed more firmly, afraid he'd tickled her. Her breathing was even. A lamp flickered and hissed but she didn't stir. Still holding her close, he reached for the oil flask and inverted it over his palm. When he'd warmed the oil against his thigh he began to slide his hand, in lazy circles from her chest over her belly to her groin, thoughtfully, the way he would stroke a bale of silk; partly to judge its quality, partly because he loved the feel of it. With the lightest pressure, he drew the tip of a finger nail across her skin as he did when testing marble for invisible flaws. All the while he watched her face and listened to her breathing. His hand stole downwards, imperceptibly slowly he thought. But, as it came to rest on her crutch, she whimpered. A great shudder ran though her whole body and he let her go.

'Don't be afraid.' he whispered. 'We don't need to do this. I'll never hurt you again.'

He sat up, hands locked around his knees, despair and loneliness in his heart. He was full of resentment but not towards her; towards Pulcher whose house reeked of vice, towards the two old shrews sequestered there, towards his clumsy self. The silver jug winked at him in the lamplight, reproaching him that he had forgotten to pour the wine. Perhaps that was as well. It might comfort her now. She clung to the cup as if it were a life line but, as she sipped, her grip relaxed so only her fingertips touched it. She swayed and leant against him. He took back the cup. Warm and with renewed confidence, he laid her down again and rested his hand between her calves. She was still and she had a look of intense concentration. He couldn't tell if she strained to connect with his loving or distract herself from it.

He asked, 'Beloved, how is it with you?'

She said, 'I think –'

'Don't think.' he said, 'Feel.'

She shivered and gave a long sigh. Miracle of miracles, her thighs drifted apart, open to his caress. Like dewfall on a petal, he felt the sap that would glide him into her and he came alive. He'd sworn to hold back but he couldn't. He sounded her with insistent rhythm and gasped as he felt her sheath clasp him. She thrust down her hands to push him away.

'No, she cried, 'it's too strong. I can't bear it.'

He forced the depth and pace and urged her with what voice he could muster.

'It's the goddess! Don't be afraid. Let her take you up. Fly in her chariot.'

Her spine arched and her torso rose off the bed as though she really was being snatched away, then she fell back, lifeless. Then he saw her as he knew no one had ever seen her; naked in unselfconscious bliss. Fluttering lashes fanned her bright cheeks, she caught breath between parted lips and, on her heaving breasts, mottled rose dispersed in Parian marble. She was a new being; his own creation. He sighed. Whether from joy or renewed longing he didn't know.

She whispered, 'This is the best day of my life. I can never feel this again.'

He grinned. 'Yes, you can. Every night if you want. There's no need to think of anyone else. I've made you hungry but I can satisfy you.'

'Anyone else?' she looked bewildered. 'What do you mean? I'm your creature.'

'I know girls,' he said, 'who'd hang round my neck and say they preferred my kiss to Jove's but none who'd forgive what I did to you… that night. Are you sure you can?'

She seemed to tread warily, as if she feared he'd think the less of her for bearing such an insult. At last, she said, 'I don't think you'd ever willingly add to my pain again, nor I to yours.'

CHAPTER XXXVIII

August/September 172

Dicta est aliquando a senatu sententia ut servos a liberis cultus distingueret ; deinde apparuit quantum periculum immineret si servi nostri numerare nos coepissent

A proposal was once made in the senate to distinguish slaves from free men by their dress. It then became apparent how dangerous it would be to let our slaves compare their numbers with ours. Seneca On Mercy 1 xxiv

How had she lived so long without any inkling of this phenomenon? Nerysa looked at everyone with new eyes. Had they discovered it? Did they know? Why did no one say? People laughed, winked or said they'd had a good time or worn themselves out in the service of Venus but no one said you were shot to the summit of Olympus and left oscillating among the shimmering clouds. No one hinted at a spiritual experience more intense than any to be found in a temple.

She knew, at last, why she'd refused to die – because she'd sensed dimly that she'd never lived. She hadn't known what she wanted yet he'd given it to her. In that moment of surrender, he could have asked her anything about herself and she couldn't have deceived him. A timely warning. She was armed against that now. As to his need to hide their love; he called it caution but she saw it as a facet of his acquisitiveness. He could only feel her love his by keeping it from everyone else. But how to pretend indifference? If she saw him around the house she hung her head lest anyone should see her cheeks flaming or feel the heat of her short breath.

She was the better actor. Demetrius learned not to follow her with his eyes but, whether it was errors in the accounts, a careless breakage or a mud shower from a passing cart, nothing wiped the grin from his face. No one knew where the happiness came from but joy spread like an epidemic and everyone was in love. The household ran on greased wheels of cooperation and good humour. Lucius found his home pervaded by an elusive fragrance. The peevishness of his mistress was out of tune with everyone else and, sensing his passion cool, she reproached him, sulked and cried. Seeing Demetrius salting away his sale commission Nerysa thought, *She schemed to get me sent away but she's the one who's gone.*

Demetrius busied himself with the lock of the strongbox and said without looking up.

'Why did you let me punish you for something you didn't do?'

'She told you?'

'You let me whip you. You were innocent.'

'You were going to have her slaves tortured, remember? Filix is twelve.'

'Why are you always busy on behalf of someone else? A slave looks out for himself. After all, if he doesn't, who else will?'

'Forgive my presumption,' she laughed, 'I thought you might look out for me.'

'Let me near you,' he said, crushing her to him. 'and I'll protect you, even from yourself. Now she's gone I can promote you to the atrium.'

Panic must have showed on her face.

'What is it?' he asked, 'My precious girl, what is it I don't know about you?'

She forced a laugh. 'What do you want to know about Rome's furthest colony and rebellious hoards lurking in dark forests? We didn't used to – we had houses and villages but you Romans didn't see them as houses and villages, you saw them as targets so we abandoned them. But I'm not one of them anymore. I'm house trained.'

'You are and quite up to the third team.'

She looked in her mirror. *Would anyone recognise Quintus' house guest in a plain tunic, simple hairstyle and humble circumstance?* They'd have to look hard. In his house, she'd taken more notice of the furniture than the slaves. For the most part, it was more interesting and more valuable. If someone saw a chance resemblance they'd think it just that. Who'd believe she'd chosen slavery over an easy death? So she joined the back ranks of the superior slaves who assembled each morning to greet the master. And it did seem that young lawyers and elderly poets moved in different circles for, although it was her duty to greet visitors, she never saw a familiar face.

Flower arranging, one of her duties, meant shopping in Trajan's market; a spectacular, tiered crescent of marble halls clinging to the Quirinal cliff. It was thrilling to go there and, even more, to be one of a select few, out and about with their master's purse, trusted with his business and free to go about some of their own. The only downside was Demetrius' insistence on her wearing a veil. She tripped over its voluminous folds, fell backwards, laughing, onto his couch and protested she couldn't wear it.

'Then you can't leave the house.'

She tossed her head. 'Isn't it against the law for a slave to get herself up like a matron?'

'You recognise a slave by his behaviour, not his clothes. For instance, no slave sits in his master's presence.'

He threw out a restraining hand as she scrambled to her feet.

'Except in special circumstances.' he said. 'Now, if I were to wear a toga, I'd be breaking the law because I'd be passing myself off as a citizen, but a veil only shows you have menfolk able and willing to punish anyone who insults you. Women who dress so and behave modestly are never molested. Women who don't, will be sure to get what, no doubt, they're angling for.'

She eyed his own showy tunic and he threw up his hand to admit that she'd scored a point.

'At home, Lucius likes me in feathers as fine as his but I'd never outshine him in public. The most indulgent master tires of arrogance in his slave. You see some silly fellow take his master's fancy, puff up with conceit and insult free men because he knows his master's opinion of them. A brief blaze of glory, then - banished to the farm.'

'Better not to be noticed at all.'

'Much. Some men fix iron collars or armlets on their slaves or brand them like cattle.' His lip curled. 'That's not our way. Our staff wear uniforms for elegance, not security. Lucius' family isn't a faithless rabble. They're conscientious people who know they're appreciated and cared for. But some men feel more pity for their dogs than their slaves. They can't see that even the lowest of them is a fellow human being.'

'Perhaps such men have more in common with dogs. Plague makes no distinction. It takes master and slave together. It doesn't take dogs.

'I hadn't thought of it like that before but it's true. Plague took Lucius' parents and Archias' wife and two sons all in the same month and then a hundred of our slaves.'

'When I became a slave I used to wonder what was the essential difference between slave and free. I still don't know.'

'I think it's simply that fate has determined their circumstances differently.'

'I think it's that they have more self-control – they have to have.'

'Most do but every master fears violence at the hands of his own slaves. He's heavily outnumbered. Firm training is a safeguard. Would a man who never raised his eyes to his master raise a fist to him?'

'Managing slaves must be the most difficult of all the things you do.'

'To do it well I agree, though any crude brute can crack a whip. A slave's not a machine or even a beast. A person has more to give than a whip can force out of him. Now that's what I love about Terence; his slaves are so human. But if I praise him any longer we'll miss his play!

He tossed her veil to her and tucked a scroll into his belt. From the back of the theatre, where slaves sat, he'd miss some of the repartee without a text to follow.

After the play, they went, as usual, to the gardens behind the theatre. No one else in the house enjoyed Terence so they were sure not to be seen. They could stroll hand in hand, just like any other pair of young lovers and search out shady grottoes and leafy bowers where they could be private.

'That Antipho character's as soft as a wet wash leather.' he said. 'His girl would be lost if she had to rely on him.'

'But what can he do? His father and uncle oppress him so.'

'Said with feeling. Were you ever tyrannised by parents?'

'No.'

'Me neither.'

They looked at each other. Each wanted to understand the other's past but neither dared to disturb old grief.

'The slaves are the best characters, by far.' she said. 'I love to see them run rings round their masters.'

'And Terence gets thousands of slave owners laughing indulgently at their insolence. Imagine them doing that in real life!'

'You know, you make me feel like one of those frenetic factotums. As soon as I get comfortable in one gang, you move me to another.'

'I have my reasons.'

'To stop the grass growing up between my toes?'

'You're so quick, so bright. When you know all about women's work, I can make you up to overseer.'

'But why? I only want to be your vicaria.'

'However low down you start, there's no limit to how far you can climb if you're clever and careful. Thaïs needs a deputy but I'm not filling the post yet, you need to learn to read and write.'

'I couldn't be her deputy. She doesn't like me.'

'You're mistaken. She likes you very much.'

You mean, Nerysa thought, *she likes **you** very much.*

CHAPTER XXXIX

September / October 172

Capillum semirasi et pedes anulati, tum lurore deformes et fumosis tenebris vaporosae caliginis palpebras adesi atque adeo male luminati, et in modum pugilum qui pulvisculo perspersi dimicant farinulenta cinere sordide candidati.

Heads shaved, feet shackled, eyebrows eaten away by filth, blinded in the smoky half-light and covered in layers of dirt and flour like wrestlers doused in talc. Apuleius. Metamorphoses. IX 12

Nerysa thought it inept of Demetrius to sweep into the atrium without warning as she was jerking a polishing rag to and fro round a table leg. Thaïs pushed her forward as he settled himself on the master's official chair and a crowd gathered. He never spoke fondly to her in public but his manner now was so cold, she no longer felt part of the conspiracy. An hour before, they'd been a single being. Still drugged from his loving, she resented him treating her as a stranger. She knelt, dazed, running her eyes from the toe of his gleaming sandal, along his lithe, brown leg, over the crisp white folds of his tunic to his groin, willing it to swell.

Coughs and shuffling told her the whole room was waiting on her reply. Because he'd always mentioned her promotion in a carefully casual way, she knew it was desperately important to him. Little as she wanted to be an overseer, she wanted to disappoint him even less.

'Would it please you, sir, to repeat the question?'

Her mind cleared and, though she couldn't find all the answers, she thought, by the end, she'd acquitted herself reasonably well. He turned to Thaïs.

'I'm surprised you wasted my time on this. You know better than to present slaves half trained.'

Everyone said he'd been too demanding. She knew more than most and was only being put forward as a junior overseer.

'You were easily good enough,' said Thaïs, 'but he wouldn't give anyone the chance to accuse him of favouritism.'

'He ambushed me because he was so sure of me and I let him down.'

'If only you'd known where to find the fire buckets!'

'I did remember the one in the kitchen.'

'But the hose system and chain of buckets for the pool in the atrium – he's proud of that. It's odd he's obsessed with fire drill because we never have a fire. I know houses where they have fires all the time and can never find a sound bucket.'

'Well, he's the sort of man who can always put his hands on a sound bucket – probably because he'll have you punished for putting it back in the wrong place.'

'But it's true what he says – there's no poverty like not having the use of your own things because you've mislaid them.'

He didn't want her to try again and, though he spoke gently, he wounded her nonetheless.

'You're a stranger and you've not been here long but I'll find an opportunity to promote you quietly.'

'Please don't. I want to hold up my head in this house. Do you think I like to be called a barbarian and hear your judgement questioned?'

He frowned. 'Who says that?'

'What use is it if you stop them talking? Only I can stop them thinking, by showing I know more than any of them.' He understood. They were never together during the working day so he taught her in bed and each fact and figure came with its corresponding caress. When Thaïs presented her again she'd no thought of failure. And she knew what the first question would be. 'Why are we celebrating today?'

'Because today is the birthday of the deified Augustus.'

'When do we honour the ancestors of the family?'

'Eight days before the first of March.'

'How much olive oil does the house use daily?'

'Three amphora; one each for lighting, cooking and grooming.' She reeled off figures for sauce, wheat, barley, wine, salt and beans, discoursed on their transport and storage and realised she'd sounded glib. He wanted to justify promoting her, not have her resented as a know-all. She pretended to hesitate over the science of preserving and basic household remedies but, seeing him frown, became fluent on the cult of the household gods and told him more than he cared to know about the teams in which the slaves worked; who did what, who had precedence over whom, who could hold keys to the wine cellar or be given charge of a purse. As she expected, he explored class distinctions; how to tell a senator from a knight and how to sum up the social standing and suitable reception of any conceivable guest. His eyes gleamed, he stroked his chin and produced the trick questions.

'When may a slave leave the house?'

'Never without permission from a superior. When he goes out, he must tell the porter where he's going and why and who has authorised him.'

'So, if he sees a passer-by steal a statue from the portico?'

'He gives chase as he shouts to the porter to call the guards to follow him.'

His lips twitched as they did when he suppressed a smile.

'How would you organise flowers for a reception?'

'I'd check first with the gardeners what might be taken from the garden.'

'Yourself?'

'Certainly not. I'd send a houseboy. The master loves roses so I'd have lots of them and lilies in the atrium and calendula and wallflowers in the summer dining room.'

'You're serving at a dinner. A client's wife is so immodest as to put her feet on the couch. What would you do?'

'Bring her a footstool and arrange some cushions on it. I might suggest politely she'd be more comfortable that way. If she didn't take the hint, the cushions would hide her feet.'

Her knowledge was encyclopaedic and he displayed the full range of it. No fair minded person could deny she deserved promotion. He sighed, pursed his lips and conceded she'd satisfied him. She was ecstatic. Slaves crowded round to shake her hand but the only praise she wanted was from him.

'He slipped off.' said Polybius. 'Jacob sent for him. A cargo of marble's come in damaged and they've got to find a buyer for broken slabs and recoup what they can.'

She was disappointed that he hadn't stayed to congratulate her but she couldn't resent it. He'd taken pains to prepare her and not entirely because he wanted to promote her without showing partiality. He'd understood that she needed to prove herself.

'Barbarian.' he'd repeated, 'Well, I've been called worse than that.'

She'd had to probe. He'd found the word difficult to say.

'What did they mean by *parasite*'?

'That I wasn't worth my daily ration.'

'That's laughable!' she'd said. He hadn't even smiled. He was the master's foster brother, favoured from birth. Who'd flayed open his back? It was more important to know that than to know ten ways of repelling moths. She went to collect her new uniform and cornered Thaïs in the linen store.

'He's the head of the house,' she said, 'and his back's rutted like a cart track. Who and why?'

Thaïs busied herself with the piles of linen, picking out the turquoise tunics embroidered with silver, reserved for the women prefects.

'I couldn't tell you even if I knew. Slaves don't ask each other that sort of thing. And we don't make personal remarks about our steward.' Nerysa lifted her chin. 'Very well, I'll ask him myself.'

Thaïs spun round, her face white.

'Great gods, Nerysa! Why are you such a troublemaker? Pretend you haven't seen his back.'

'How could he believe I haven't seen it?'

'Turning a blind eye and a deaf ear to life's little unpleasantnesses is something every slave learns.'

'Well I shan't. How do you come to terms with things you don't see and don't hear?'

'Nerysa, he could not bear you knowing that.'

'How would he know I knew?'

'Because you blurt out everything that lands on the tip of your lively tongue.'

'That's not fair. I can keep secrets if I need to. Who knows the slightest thing about my life before I came here – except what you can read in my slave log book?'

'This is a dangerous secret. He's a proud man.'

'He has every right to be.'

'I'm glad you think so.'

'Are you going to tell me or shall I find someone else who will?'

'Do you swear, on your hope of freedom, never to repeat what I tell you?'

'On my hope of freedom and a long life.'

Thaïs pushed back a pile of linen and sat on the edge of the shelf, motioning to Nerysa to sit beside her.

'You know, of course, that Demetrius' mother, Zoe, was the master's nurse?'

Nerysa nodded.

'She was freeborn like you but her father went bankrupt and had other troubles, political I think. She was the ideal wet nurse for Lucius; a native Greek speaker with a baby of her own. But she didn't make the proper distinction between the master's child and her own. She died when Demetrius was twelve.'

'Go on. Thaïs, what's the matter? I didn't mean to make you cry. Was she your friend?'

Thaïs shook her head. 'I hardly knew her. I was thinking of my sister. She wouldn't... if..'

'If what?'

'If I'd been here to calm her. But I was helping the mistress make a sacrifice at her family shrine. When the news came about Zoe my sister forgot herself - said the master should have cared enough to send her a midwife. She was sold and out of the house before I got home.'

'Haven't you seen her since?'

'By chance. Then we managed to meet a few times before she left Rome.'

'Sold again?'

'Sent to the contry. When she heard Zoe had died, she must have known she was pregnant herself. That's why she took it hard. And she went the same way. Her child survived her, at least for a time. Demetrius did try to trace it. It's so long ago I don't know why it still makes me cry.'

'And Demetrius and Lucius?' 'They stayed at Horta until Lucius came of age. Then the master brought them both back here and the trouble started. Demetrius was trained to stand behind Lucius, treat him with exaggerated respect and speak only if questioned. Neither of them could take it seriously. Lucius was the worst offender but they were both at fault. Every lesson was a farce; they'd be helpless with laughter and the overseers in despair. The old master was furious, he always hated Demetrius.'

'Was that when…?'

'No. Oddly enough, he made his worst mistake in deadly earnest. He understood the estate, knew every worker and tenant, how everything was run, better than Lucius did. Lucius was conferring with the master, the bailiff and lawyers. Demetrius was there to carry bags but when changes were mooted which he thought unwise and unfair, he said so. The master ordered him to be silent but he would persist.'

Nerysa's stomach churned as if these long past events still hung in the balance.

'What did they do to him?'

'Public flogging.'

'What do you mean, *public?*'

They made us all watch, the whole household. The master made Lucius give the order because Demetrius was his slave. A hundred lashes, then they threw him in the cellar and left him.'

'Someone helped him, surely?'

Thaïs retched. Nerysa, feeling weak herself, took the linen from her, pushed it back on the shelf and slipped an arm around her. They huddled together.

'I went down and saw him lying on the stone flags. He looked like a heap of diced beef ready to be scooped into a pie.'

'He should have died.' Nerysa said.

'The master said a slave was better dead if he couldn't learn to know his place but we got some help to him.'

'Archias?'

Thaïs nodded. 'He was still a slave here then. He risked his own skin to do it. Demetrius was young and fit and he survived. He must have wished he hadn't. As soon as he was on his feet, they put him to work; the heaviest, most degrading they could find. Slaves who'd envied his gentleman's education and his privileged position gloated over it. They'd gather round to mock him.'

'And Lucius let them?'

'He wasn't here, he'd been packed off to the university in Athens. After six months as the lowest slave in the house, he went to Horta as a labourer. They chained him to the bar that turns the millstone and put the donkey out to grass. Calm yourself, my dear, it was a long time ago.'

'How could anyone do that to him? He's so...*special*.'

'Don't you think that's exactly what they didn't like? Within the year the master and mistress died of the plague and Lucius was back in Rome. He sent for him straight away and made him his procurator, a challenge for a boy of eighteen. There were some who felt slighted and said he wouldn't succeed. There were even legal moves to appoint a guardian for Lucius but, by the time they could have come to anything, Demetrius had everything running smoothly. He had absolute power here then. You could smell the fear in the house.'

'What did he do?'

'Nothing. I remember the day he came back, stiff and limping slightly. He took up the running of affairs in the same quiet way you see him do today, never mentioned the previous year to anyone and treated us all the same.'

'How strange!'

'No. It was the only way to run the house. He couldn't afford to have it split into factions. He'd learned the hard way, you see, that privilege excites jealousy. And he was inexperienced so he didn't sell slaves, though Lucius would have let him get rid of any he wished. So many had been freed in the old master's will or died of the plague, we needed those who were left. As far as the estates were concerned he'd been right. He managed them far better than the old guard. He's more than doubled the revenues in spite of treating the tenants more leniently.'

'And he's made a fortune in business.'

'That too, and he and Lucius are as devoted as ever. But perhaps you see why he won't let Lucius give him his freedom. He'll pay the full price with his own money. That won't be long now, a year or two.'

'Why won't he take it?'

'Because Lucius needs to give it. If you asked him if he forgave Lucius, he'd say there was nothing to forgive. Lucius wasn't to blame. But, if he really thought that, he'd take his freedom and put the past behind him.'

Thaïs slipped her hand into Nerysa's.

'When you…you…he said it all came back to him and he could feel the blows on his back, feel what you were going through, knowing it was all his fault.'

'But it wasn't. There was a misunderstanding.'

'He wrote an order that could be misunderstood. So unlike him and about you, of all people. Our Lucius had him drugged because he was afraid he'd lose his reason.' Thaïs squeezed her hand. 'I'd do anything for you,' she whispered, 'because you make him happy.'

Nerysa looked her in the eyes, 'As far as it lies in my power, he will not be unhappy again. I swear to you.'

So he'd been there too. That well of despair where, stripped of dignity and hope, one confronted one's essential self and found it surprisingly free and inviolate. She ached to share that experience with him, knowing she never could.

CHAPTER XL

October 172

Romae dulce diu fuit et sollemne reclusa Mane domo vigilare, clienti promere iura
Cautis nominibus rectis expendere nummos

At Rome it was long a pleasure and a habit to be up at dawn with open doors to
set forth the law for clients, to pay out to sound debtors money under seal Hor. Epist 2 1
103-105

Instead of making her second in command of a team, as she'd expected, Demetrius had Nerysa trained to wait in the dining room. Having kept her out of the master's eye so long, he was now determined to bring her forward. Behind his impassive mask she glimpsed something of his tender pride in her and dreaded letting him down.

'I'll never please him.' she protested. 'He said I wasn't worth a fistful of coppers, remember?'

He grinned. 'No master admits to being wrong. But it can suit them to forget things they've said.'

First, he sent her to the triclinium to observe the protocol, effacing herself against the wall or as close as she could get without touching it. Then he drilled her himself, teaching her to stand with one leg crossed in front of the other, poised for instant response. She might wait for hours with nothing to do but when an order came she must react instantly.

Her first attendance on the master was nerve-racking. The art was rapt concentration and inspired anticipation. The servers must be tingling with awareness of him so the instant he finished with a dish, wanted to have his hands rinsed or his cup refilled, they would be ready. If he had to indicate his needs by a word or a snap of the fingers, they would already have failed. After each course, two slaves removed the table top and another two lowered a new one onto the carved pedestal, laden with fragile glass and embossed gold.

To Demetrius' smug satisfaction, Nerysa was a success and worked in the triclinium until she was thoroughly at home there, when he moved her and gave her the subpraefecture of the atrium. Her exotic looks, now combined with city manners, made her an interesting novelty for a rich man's house.

The girls she supervised were friendly, Aglae poignantly obsequious. A new girl, Charis, joined the team. Nerysa saw straight away why Demetrius had been able to acquire her from a senator's wife. No lady who valued her husband's attentions would keep such a beauty on her staff. She combined the grace of her Greek ancestors with the proud carriage of her former mistress. Nerysa thought her exquisite. So, she imagined, did Demetrius. But, however exalted her previous position, she'd been a dresser with no experience of an atrium and Nerysa had to train her.

'Just after dawn is our busiest time.' she told her, 'We start at first light brushing the walls and benches and waxing the floor. Because, when those great bronze doors are flung open, it's like a dam burst. People flood in so fast the room fills before you've time to breathe in.'

Charis nodded demurely.

'I know you've held a high position in a great household but you served a mistress personally and you could judge when you'd pleased her. We serve the master by looking after his guests, which is very important to him.'

'So important he has barbarians receive them.'

'I beg your pardon?'

'Forgive me. I've never seen a Briton before. There were none in the senator's house.'

Looking down her long straight nose and narrowing her almond eyes, she looked exactly like girls on antique Greek vases, only with attitude.

'Well,' said Nerysa, 'you're in for a shock here. You lived with aristocrats but, as a receptionist, you'll have to meet all types and be polite to them.'

The long nose wrinkled. Nerysa thought of the ragged and unwashed. This girl would have nothing for them but condescension.

'The master's particularly sensitive about his poor clients.' she said. 'He thinks rudeness would affect his own dignity more than theirs. So, if we give hand-outs to shabby folk, we try to do it without making them feel uncomfortable.'

Charis bridled. 'I think I know how to give satisfaction.'

Nerysa thought *We'll see.*

'By the time our Lucius arrives, Petosirus will know who's just come to greet Lucius and who's got personal or legal problems to discuss with him. And he'll know which ones Lucius wants to talk to out here and which, if any, he wants to have shown into the tablinum. Then he'll announce them and we can start serving the refreshments.'

Charis yawned the most elegant yawn Nerysa had ever seen.

'How long does all that take?'

'Maybe to the third hour. We can't hustle them out but it's frustrating if they hang around because, until they've gone, we can't clean and restock, plump up the cushions and check on the flowers. We always have strongly scented ones because some of the clients – well, you know. Later, if the master's in, friends and social callers will come. That's more of a steady trickle than a flood but these are all important people and quite exacting. When they've gone we just prepare for tomorrow unless there's a dinner party. In that case we have to clean and restock before the ninth hour when we start to receive dinner guests.'

The almond eyes narrowed to slits. Charis smiled.

'Why don't you write all this down for me?' she said. 'I can read, you see.'

A stinging retort flew to Nerysa's lips. She checked it and swallowed it hard.

'I don't give written orders. If you can't remember what I've said, watch the others.'

She took a deep breath and led her up to the wall.

'I'm going to show you how I clean this painting.' she said. 'It's very old and valuable but the lamp black has stained it here. So, a smear of warm oil on the sponge, press… and lift.'

Charis' voice was penetrating.

'How interesting. Is that how the natives of Britain clean paintings?'

Someone giggled. Nerysa snapped, 'It's how it's done in Lucius Marius' house, which is all that concerns you.'

She wound a strip of fleece around her forefinger and began to stroke the dust from the beard of a marble bust. Charis imitated her perfectly, saying conversationally, 'How do you clean real ones?'

'What do you mean?'

'Human heads that Britons string up in their huts.'

There was a gasp from beside her, then whispers. Then all the girls were laughing behind their hands.

That set the tone for the days ahead. In wide-eyed innocence, Charis asked questions which created diversions, delayed the work and exposed Nerysa to ridicule. The girl was far from simple and she was hostile. Nerysa wondered why. *Was she trying to discredit her with Demetrius?* Once she saw her crossing the peristyle. The only rooms on the far side were Demetrius' rooms and the secretaries' office. It made more sense to have the girl as a friend than an enemy. She pondered what to do. She needed Demetrius. But, in this matter, she wasn't sure of his support. If she complained to him, she'd be criticising a purchase he'd made and perhaps a love interest. He might even think her jealous. They dined together and, when the meal was finished, he put down his wine cup and said, 'I think I'm going to have to speak to you about Charis.'

'What about her?'

'I hear she makes a fool of you.'

'I suppose you couldn't..?'

'I could; and show the whole house I've no confidence in you.'

'Petosirus?'

'He supervises the men but you're responsible for the women. Discipline is part of the job. Are you saying you're not up to it? I'll send the guards but the order has to come from you.'

'Is there no other way? Must life be so violent?'

'Violent! This house? When did you see our Lucius with his hand bandaged from striking a slave? He has the self-command of a true philosopher. You're a strange one! Your people are cannibals and you're so squeamish and high-minded.'

'Where did you hear such rubbish? My people aren't violent! We're gentle, even with our beasts. If we're bloodthirsty, it's when we're roused by injustice.'

He took his arm from around her.

'Injustice is hateful to everyone. If there's any in this house I'm to blame and you know I regret it.'

'She's so lovely and she has such a beautiful name.'

'As to that,' he said scornfully, 'the name means *gratitude*. If I were you I'd give her some firm guidance to be grateful for.'

She steeled herself to order the caning and watch it. The effect was dramatic and baffling.

'Ever since,' she told Demetrius, 'she follows me around, insists on carrying things for me and looks all the time for ways to please me. It's perverse.'

'She's a pretty woman.' he shrugged. 'What do you expect? Rational thought?'

Nerysa was on her guard. He was the second most powerful man in a houseful of women desperate to make themselves available. She prepared herself mentally for the anguish she would feel when the inevitable happened. She loved him, so whatever delighted him ought to please her. That was logical but it didn't feel comfortable. When she found him in the office with Thaïs sitting at his feet, her head in his lap, the surprise was only that it was Thaïs; so much older and a flame from the past. Thaïs lifted a radiant face and Nerysa bowed in resignation. Why was the pain keener than anything she'd rehearsed? She'd always known this moment would come. But the anguish was not confined to slaves. Queens had born it with dignity.

'May I tell her?' Thaïs whispered.

He smiled indulgently, 'It will be common knowledge soon enough.'

Thaïs crossed the room to Nerysa, arms wide.

'Be happy for me - Demetrius is bringing my niece to live with us.'

Thaïs' sister's girl was alive. Demetrius had traced her and paid for her and, the next day, he'd send slaves to fetch her home to her aunt. Realising she'd seen an outpouring of gratitude, not passion, Nerysa was as happy as Thaïs.

Demetrius dismissed them both and sent for Adrian, the crease between his brows not entirely due to errors in the accounts. He was hoping Thaïs wouldn't encourage Erinna to be intimate with Nerysa. He didn't fear she'd be another Roxana; he just thought it wise for Nerysa to keep herself to herself, and to him.

Erinna took a fever, as slaves often did when moved from the country to the city. After work, Nerysa hurried to the sickroom to relieve the nurses and support Thaïs. Demetrius found himself dining alone and wasn't slow to complain.

'You're overworking yourself.'

'She's very poorly and Thaïs is so worried she hardly has the strength to nurse her. Olympia and Cynthia can't keep up with the rocking and purging and purifying the air and the rubbing down and the massage and the enemas and the medicines and infusions and the gruel. And, as soon as we've done them all, it's time to start again.'

'Hermes! Shouldn't you let the poor girl get some sleep?'

'Archias thinks she has the type of fever that needs to be weakened. He even thinks she might benefit from bleeding.'

'*Marcus Archias* attended her?'

'Of course not. I sent him a message asking for advice. Shouldn't I have done? Why not?'

'Because it's not seemly for my wife to send messages to other men. Why didn't you ask me to ask him?'

'You don't have time to scratch your ear. I didn't like to trouble you.'

'Well, I'll trouble myself to send for Archias and pay his fee. If he needs extra staff in the sick room I'll roster them. You hold a responsible position here. I don't give anyone free time for their comfort. We rest so as to be full of energy for our work.'

Of course, it was easy to allow rest and refreshment in a house where two hundred slaves looked after one master and each other. Demetrius didn't concern himself with those sordid little establishments where a couple of slaves struggled to service an entire family and the porter sat in his sentry-box shelling peas.

But he was right. She'd never been so tired. It was a struggle to get up in the morning. Her muscles were weak and liable to cramp. Fatigue nauseated her and the smell of his breakfast sausage, to which familiarity had reconciled her, became a problem again. She'd heard of being sick with tiredness and, when she missed a monthly bleed, she assumed that was also due to fatigue. It was three months before she acknowledged what had happened to her. Then she felt awkward because she'd been silent so long and surprised Demetrius hadn't noticed because her belly was hardening and her breasts were swelling like gourds. Each time she braced herself to tell him, she decided to wait. Once her condition was obvious, she'd be sent to the country. Other girls would console him. He might not want her back.

CHAPTER XLI

November 172

Ecce lapis Parius ... signum perfecte luculentum... procursu vegetum introeuntibus obvium

A brilliant statue in Parian marble seeming to run to greet you as you entered.Apuleius metamorphoses II 4

A slave ought not to listen to conversations while serving the master. It was too seductive. He'd lose concentration and make mistakes. When Demetrius wanted conversations overheard, he sent in sufficient staff for the business in hand and an extra two whose only task was to listen. Nerysa was insatiably curious and always kept her ears pricked. To her annoyance, Lucius had ushered a shabby stone mason into the tablinum for a private audience. He should have known to keep that sort in the atrium; stooped, as yellow and stringy as an old boiling fowl; hair, beard and clothes coated in dust. Even the hairs springing from his nose were hoary with it. She watched the grey flecks swirl in a hazy beam of light and wondered irritably how much of it would have to be beaten out of the cushions after he left. Lucius renegotiated his loan and made routine enquiries after his health, his family and his business and she marvelled that he treated this miserable dependent with such courtesy and concern. She reflected, too, on the continuity. The man's father and Lucius' grandfather would have had similar conversations in that same room.

'Times are hard, Excellency. Folk take no pride in dying these days. Still, winter's always good for business. And I got the commission for the hall of the perfumers' guild.'

'I hear the work is much admired.'

'You saw my Venus?' He milked the air with cupped hands. 'Toast of Rome! And I'll tell you something no one knows. My own daughter was the model.'

'You must be very proud. Have you found a husband for her?' Lucius made a sharp, slight curl of his finger in Nerysa's direction and she stepped forward with the wine cups.

'Ah! That's the trouble, Excellency.' The mason took the wine, gulped it down and bumped his way further up the cushions towards Lucius. 'There's this widower, comfortably off, would take her as a concubine - without a dowry! She'd be made! But she'll have no one but a neighbour's son she's known since primary school.'

'So, what are his prospects?'

'They're undertakers, no better off than me. Imagine people so unthrifty as to rear three sons! And him the youngest! How could he take her with no dowry? I won't blame the widower if he changes his mind. I've tried beating her. The boy's father's tried the same; I don't know how it will end.'

Nerysa refilled his cup, conceding that his throat was probably as dusty as the rest of him. Lucius leaned forward and she willed him to keep his pristine toga out of range.

'I wouldn't want to undermine your authority in any way.' Lucius sounded tentative but Nerysa sensed this was a command couched as a suggestion. 'But if we saw her behaviour as loyalty rather than stubbornness, we could reward it, surely? With your permission, I'd gladly loan her a dowry if he's a diligent young man and otherwise acceptable to you.'

'Excellency, I'm deeply touched but I couldn't repay you for years.'

'You think me impatient?'

'I hope Your Excellency doesn't think I was angling for a favour. I shouldn't have mentioned the matter if Your Excellency hadn't asked.'

He jabbed at his brow with a limp grey sweat cloth, discharging further clouds of dust. Nerysa retrieved the wine cup, set it back on the marble side table and picked up a dish of figs.

'I know that. But you would oblige me by accepting my offer.'

'With all my heart! I'll bring her to you this evening, if you're at leisure, to express her gratitude. She's beautiful, she won't disappoint you.'

Lucius smiled. 'Marry her first. Her husband may bring her later.'

Well done! Nerysa thought. Demetrius was right. What stopped a powerful man from exploiting his dependents? Only the standards he set for himself. She felt proud to belong to him.

'If your business isn't prospering,' he added, 'You could do worse than have Demetrius look over the books. If he thought it prudent, I could take you into partnership. You're a talented mason but perhaps you need a more commercial approach?'

CHAPTER XLII

November 172

nihil est super mi vocis in ore Lingua sed torpet, tenuis sub artus flamma demanat, sonitu suopte tintinant aures, gemina teguntur lumina nocte

My tongue won't move, I've no voice, a flame is spreading through my limbs, my ears are buzzing and my vision dimmed Catullus LI

The mason bowed himself out and Lucius hurried to follow, for the interview had lasted longer than he'd intended. His escorts were already gathered around the door. As he passed Nerysa, she lifted her face and smiled at him. He was used to ingratiating smiles but it was half a lifetime since a woman had looked at him with such spontaneous, warm approval. It had been a trifling act of self-denial which had cost him nothing but it pleased him because it was one the common man wouldn't understand. Had it pleased her, the dour virgin he'd given to a man she hated? He turned back. She dropped her eyes and he watched her slender, white fingers tremble on the watery, green glass of the fig dish. A steel clamp locked around his chest. His ears rang. His eyes swam. He walked back to her, awkward as a recruit in his first pair of greaves.

'You're the steward's wife, I think? Will you be in the dining room tonight?'

'If you wish it, master, I'll tell Thaïs.'

As he took a fig from the dish, he brushed her hand, as if by accident. Forked lightning shot through his arm. He went out, cradling the burning fruit in his hand.

He didn't linger in the forum but went to the baths as soon as they opened - to the surprised delight of his escorts. Agreeably aware of his body, he warmed it with exercise, taxed himself in the wrestling hall and luxuriated in the pool. He hired a private room for massage and a range of unnecessary skin treatments. Swathed in woollen wraps against the autumn air, he strolled home and bought a garland from a street florist, dazzling her with his charm and generosity.

He lay on his ivory couch, relaxed yet curiously aroused. There was a suppressed sensuality about Nerysa he'd not noticed before. Odd, because he was usually attuned to such signals. His hands often rested lovingly on those who served him but her, he did not touch. He lingered over his meal, deliberately delaying the moment when he would dismiss the rest and be alone with her. Having achieved a delicious frisson of excitement, he detained her with the merest flick of his forefinger. She stood against the wall, poised for instant obedience and, though her face wore the mask of an automaton, he fancied her eyes were wary, as though she expected a reproof for having been bold enough to look up at him. He tossed a cushion onto the floor against his couch and laughed at her confusion.

'Your husband has been known to sit *on* my couch, why shouldn't you sit below it?'

She blushed and sank into a kneeling position she must have thought ambiguous enough to satisfy him. So, Demetrius had taught her the rules, now it was for him to exempt her. He insisted and she sat as if on a nettle bed. There was nothing wrong with her looks he realised, only her hairstyle. He drew out the pins and a tawny rope dropped into his hands and tugged him back to boyhood. It reminded him of the times he'd pricked his fingers on a spiked chestnut case to plunder its shining fruit. Her hair was of the same shades; ripples of sunshine baked to a glaze.

He murmured, 'I like your hair loose.'

A talented man with graceful manners, Lucius was in demand socially. He liked to keep a balance; accepting invitations, especially from those of superior social standing, hosting occasions at home; with congenial equals for pleasure, with clients and business contacts from duty, and spending the odd evening quietly at home with Demetrius. Now he made space in his life for Nerysa. When she helped serve his meals, he dismissed the other slaves early and kept her back, ostensibly to peel fruit or pour wine, in reality, because she enchanted him. He lived a full life but, unlike Demetrius, although there was plenty he could do, there was little he couldn't postpone. He had the luxury of time for reflection and his thoughts were all of her. The most captivating girl he'd ever met was living under his roof, his own possession and he'd only just discovered her. The piquancy of it stirred him. Of course, he could take her body whenever he pleased but he set himself a greater challenge; she had a heart and mind; he'd win those too.

He knew from household gossip that Demetrius showed her no partiality, demanding the same military deference from her as from everyone else. Some even said he'd whipped her for misunderstanding instructions. He was sorry that he'd given her against her will but he could rescue her. What a joy it would be to do it! He thrilled to imagine her surprise, her delight and her gratitude. Of course Demetrius must be considered. It seemed unlikely his heart was still engaged but his pride might be. Lucius wasn't a clumsy man. He planned an elegant takeover. He was in no hurry and, indeed, he couldn't indulge in private dalliance every night.

CHAPTER XLIII

November 172

'Αλλ' ουκ αν κατ' εμε.» Τουτο σε δει συνεισφερειν εις την σκεψιν, ουκ εμε. συ γαρ ει ο σαυτον ειδως, ποσου αξιος ει σεαυτω και ποσου σεαυτον πιπρασκεις.

Whether or not I would do that is irrelevant. Only you know your own worth. Different men sell themselves at different prices. Epictetus. Book I ii 11

At large gatherings, Nerysa found that months of intensive training had prepared her for the exalted task of removing guests' shoes and washing their feet before they drew them up on the couch. Next she circulated with a fresh ewer of scented water and a silver bowl to catch the water trickling from greasy fingers. Sometimes, she was trusted with the bread basket or even the wine jug but that was high status work, more often given to boys.

With forty guests at five couches, their own slaves on benches below them and Lucius' cooks and servers, the winter dining room was crowded. The air was thick with smoke and steam from the braziers. Plumes of heat rose from the bustling bodies of the workers and the glowing flesh and vinous breath of the diners, who retired regularly to change silk gowns that clung to their tacky skin.

Nerysa had been hard at work since dawn and it was the fourth hour of the night. Her chest was tight from the smoke. Her eyes wouldn't focus through the shimmering haze. Pouring wine into raised gold cups, she moved mechanically, sickeningly faint and biting her tongue to keep alert. She was about to refill a cup when its owner unexpectedly transferred it to his other hand and, as she leaned over the couch to reach it, he grasped her breast. With a will of its own her breast surged under his touch and her nipple shot out like a serpent's tongue and flicked against his palm. Mortified by his attentions and even more by her own response, she felt a scalding flush creep over her. A maid servant was a chattel, displayed, like furniture and tableware, to impress the master's guests. It was unthinkable she should object. She clung to the edge of the couch with her free hand, her struggle back to full consciousness helped by the blast of garlic and wine on her face and the tickle of his lisp in her singing ear.

'When are you free tomorrow, sweetness?'

'I'm not free tomorrow, sir.'

'You look to be a resourceful girl. Contrive to be sent on an errand. Where can I see you?'

She looked down at his brown, hirsute hand; a tarantula on her breast.

'I'm not allowed to leave the house, sir.'

She disciplined herself to stay absolutely still as he found his way under her tunics and bosom band and kneaded both her breasts.

'Quick, who's the overseer in charge of you? When my boy has greased his palm, he'll serve you up to me happily enough.'

Suddenly Thaïs was beside her and took the heavy wine jug, hissing, 'Back to your quarters. Now!'

'I meant no harm. I -'

'Don't argue. Go.'

Hollowed out with shame, she tried to lose herself in the milling crowd, sure that everyone had seen her dismissal and the reason for it. Should she pass the linen room on the way to the bedroom and collect mending? Demetrius would have seen her cause an incident in the dining room, she didn't want him to reproach her with idle hands as well. On the other hand, initiative had led her into trouble before. It was better to obey instructions exactly.

Polybius looked up expectantly; she handed him the wreath from her head and he splashed it with water. He'd sell it next day to a needy dinner guest. At her request, he sent for the sewing and she bent over it diligently but her fingers trembled and, every so often, she dashed her wrist across her eyes.

'Nerysa, what's the matter?'

'Oh, one of the guests handled me and Thaïs sent me out of the dining room.'

'You didn't embarrass a guest?'

'No, I don't think so.'

'These things happen all the time. Young bloods, wine flowing, pretty girls. What do you expect? What goes on here's nothing to what goes on in other houses. Our Lucius is such a prig.'

'How do you know what goes on in other houses?'

'When Himself's away or busy, our Lucius often takes me in his entourage. Your little Polybius has seen life, you know. You wouldn't believe how often I'm propositioned. It's bearable, sometimes even enjoyable and one's always rewarded. One day, I'll buy my freedom.'

Her throat felt suddenly parched. She breathed, 'I'm sorry.'

'Well, you needn't be,' he said cheerfully. 'It's life. You're not bad looking and you've filled out a bit lately. Hasn't this sort of thing happened before?'

She clenched her hands over the needlework, no longer pretending any interest in it. He said with sudden inspiration, 'You're afraid Himself will think you encouraged the man and blame you.'

A sob confirmed his suspicions and he put out a hand to comfort her, thought better of it and lowered himself onto the edge of his master's couch.

'Nerysa, may I give you some advice?'

Though a sniff was the only encouragement she offered, he persisted.

'If Himself *should* be angry with you, it would be best to cry and beg his forgiveness - show him you're afraid and you'll try harder to please him. To cringe, grovel, plead for mercy – that's how a slave behaves – that's what a master expects. But, when he's angry, you're so haughty and cold, he couldn't indulge you, even if he wanted to.'

'Do you cringe and grovel? I've never seen you.'

'Well, I've served him seven years, since I was fourteen. It'd be a poor show if I didn't know how to please him. I do everything just as I know he likes and he's forbearing because that's his nature and because he knows I'd never willingly be at fault. He cares for you, you know. With you he's...like I never saw him before.'

Familiar footsteps crossed the peristyle. He jumped up, smoothed the couch, and leapt towards the table, ready to pour wine. She plied her needle feverishly. Demetrius tossed his wreath to Polybius and dismissed him with a jerk of the head. She put down her work and stood. He took her in his arms and she clung to him trembling.

'Come!' he laughed. 'These tiresome incidents happen all the time. You must have seen them in Pulcher's house. You weren't to blame.'

'But you dismissed me.'

'You couldn't stay on duty and avoid one of the guests. That would be insulting. But I didn't dismiss you. Lucius did. I was looking for a chance to get you away. I was sure I betrayed no concern but he must have sensed it. That was good of him. You're not to serve at table again unless he's alone or the company's select. And that's just as well if you allow this sort of thing to upset you. Really, there's no need.'

He looked thoughtful, put out his hand and fondled her breast as if reliving the scene. That night his loving was as it had used to be; an assertion of his sole possession of her. Nothing else could have reassured her.

Early the next morning, she began the long day's work to purge the dining hall of the night before. It felt friendly in the morning light, full of industrious people sprinkling roasted millet on the floor and sweeping it up with the dirt. No one volunteered to wash crystal – a task demanding concentration and silence. Everyone wanted to beat cushions with broom handles. She helped to strip tables and couches of their gold drapes and air them in the peristyle. Long before Demetrius returned from the forum, the law courts and a dinner with his master's patron, Maecianus, she was in bed, weak and sick. The next morning, he was ebullient. Sitting up in the bed, leaning back on his hands, stretched out behind him, he smiled down at her.

'You made an impression on Severus - he offered Lucius a staggering price for you.'

'Is that his name? It doesn't sort with his behaviour, does it?'

'It depends on the occasion.' he shrugged. 'A party at a friend's house is hardly the centumviral court.'

'Did Lucius tell him I was married?'

'Of course not. Slaves don't marry. We live as man and wife in this house for just so long as it pleases Lucius that we should. Beloved, don't look so frightened. He's a generous man. He's more than a master to me and I'm more than a steward to him. We're safe enough – but people outside wouldn't understand.'

Nerysa sat up and laid her head on his chest. 'If he hadn't already given me to you, would he have sold me to this Severus?'

'He might. He doesn't need the money. But if Severus offered you a privileged position; say if he wanted to keep you as his favourite, Lucius might have thought the arrangement would benefit all three of you.'

She shuddered and he put his arms around her, sinking his chin into her hair.

'Oh, he's not vicious. Just hot blooded – he's African after all. He was prosecuted a couple of years ago, a scandal involving someone's wife. Conducted his own defence and was acquitted.'

She laughed in spite of herself. 'And our dear Lucius has such touching faith in the law.'

He pursed his lips. 'If Severus was acquitted, it means he was innocent, doesn't it? I shouldn't have mentioned it and I forbid you to repeat it. But you're right. You wouldn't have suited – not docile enough. Give him his due, he spotted that. Apparently that was the attraction.'

She understood. It would have been the diversion of a few weeks to break her spirit then he'd have wondered why the little creature had begun to bore him.

'Your spirit, he mused, and your magnificent breasts. That shames me. That Severus should need to come here and remind me my wife has magnificent breasts. I've been gazing at your face too long, my darling, because I love to see you blush. By Venus and Cupid, how you blushed when he touched you! What a credit to the house of Quintus Pulcher!'

Slithering back down onto the pillows, she drew the coverlet up around her neck. He turned towards her.

'If Lucius had meant to sell you, he'd have done it. He's made his decision. He won't go back on it.'

'But Severus is more powerful. Lucius daren't offend him.'

'Didn't I tell you he had refinements you didn't dream of! To express a refusal so elegantly it seems like a compliment – that's his stock in trade. Look, I don't understand why it is, but I've come to see that you can't be made servile. You'll be safer as a freedwoman.'

'Anyone can be made servile, surely.'

'Yes, a man could break you - no sleep, next to nothing to eat, cowed by the whip until you crouched warily and flinched every time the wind rattled the door. He'd have to be brutal to achieve that because you have extraordinary courage. It's not your fault. You try. You're just not reliable. It only takes some overseer to be less than just to a slave and you forget yourself and behave as if it's you and not Lucius, who owns the house.'

'Can you afford our freedom?' she asked. 'You must have had a profitable season.'

'Well, not specially,' he admitted, 'but it's a ritual with us. Every Saturnalia Lucius begs me to take my freedom and I beg him to wait until I can afford to buy it outright. This time I'll take it, pay him what I can, and become his debtor for the balance.'

She put a hand over his. 'Don't do this because of me. I know it's not what you want.'

'But it *is*. I've been slow to realise that it's what I should do. Freedom was something I thought I couldn't take as a gift from any Marius. I didn't want charity, even his - least of all his. You won't understand, but I've lived for the day when I'd spill the gold in his lap and say, "Here's the price of the servitude I owe you. Take my money and let me go." Then I'd look him in the eyes and shake his hand and we'd be friends in the way he wants us to be.'

'That's quite understandable.'

He rounded on her in astonishment.

'You understand that? No one understands it. He's closer to me than my own shadow and can't understand it at all. I yearn for freedom; he wants me to be free. So why don't I let him lift his little finger and put everything right?'

'Because it wouldn't put anything right. Because self-respect is even more precious than freedom. That's why people can easily convince themselves slaves are subhuman, because they've no self-respect.'

'Exactly! But self-respect is an expensive luxury. That's what Epictetus meant when he said different men sell themselves at different prices. That's why you preferred to be flogged than give your body without your heart.' His eyes fell. 'If I'd understood you better, I should have behaved differently.'

She laughed. 'But if I'd understood *you* better, so should I. You'll have the money in two years. Surely I can keep out of trouble for that long since you've given me the best of reasons. Don't you think I could do willingly for love what I could be forced to do from fear?'

'There's no need. It's not important any more. To be free and legally married and to let you be your true self; that will be more than satisfaction, it will be the greatest joy I can imagine.'

Not knowing how her pregnancy would affect their sale, she decided to tell him after Saturnalia. When they were free and legally married, she'd thank him for her freedom and offer him something equally precious, a child of his own, freeborn and legitimate.

CHAPTER XLIV

December 172 – January 173

Ei mihi, non tutum est quod ames laudare sodali. Cum tibi laudanti credit, ipse subit.

It's not safe to praise the object of your love to a friend. So soon as he believes your praises he slips into your place. Ovid Ars amatoria I 741-2

Everyone had looked forward to Saturnalia. The last, misruled by the homely Apicius and Erotion, had been a riot. Demetrius and Nerysa hosted the dullest on record. He had the habit of command and, arrayed in crimson silk tooled with gold, lacked nothing of his master's noble bearing. So distant and dignified was he that no one liked to suggest ducking him in the impluvium or that the loser of the knucklebones competition should carry his wife round the atrium.

In fact, he was preoccupied, making rapid calculations. With only himself to consider, he could have handed over every last copper to his master. Now the situation had changed. He must rent somewhere to live. Not large but reasonably salubrious and close to the domus. He'd need two boys; one to accompany him to the baths and go shopping, the other to stay home, keep house and guard his wife. Polybius was well beyond his purse but he must have two bright, dependable boys and they wouldn't come cheap. His wife should have a maid, but that would have to wait. After buying his freedom, he'd have little money left to run his own establishment.

Charis had dressed Nerysa's hair; not cut and crimped at the front for, after Saturnalia, she must return to her simple style, but in a myriad of tiny braids around her face. She wore the flounced dress of a lady; ivory, with deep borders embroidered in the shade of green that edges the snowdrop and trimmed with pearls. It hadn't come from the store of festal clothes in the attic. Lucius had bought it for her in a fashionable dress shop in the Saepta.

Aloof in his short tunic and apron, he looked with approval on both of them, assets for a gentleman to be proud of. He was surprised they hadn't dealt better together. At first, he'd blamed Nerysa. Demetrius had been besotted; she should have had him eating out of her hand. But, now he knew her, he didn't blame her. He watched her presiding over his household like a queen. He remembered her at the Saturnalia the previous year and marvelled at the transformation a fine gown could make. No wonder it had cost a fortune. His own plans for her were maturing but he was in no hurry. She wasn't going to run away. He sensed she'd be a big experience and it wasn't in his nature to plunge headlong. He didn't exactly hesitate but he savoured the anticipation. And he neglected to offer his steward manumission.

***

Thaïs sent Nerysa to the dining room often because she was always available and a good worker. But she noticed that, if Nerysa were absent, the master asked for her. She opened her eyes wide then and was amazed. Lucius had lost control of his discreet campaign; he was being dragged helpless behind passion's chariot. It was whispered all over the house that the master was panting for the steward's wife. No one whispered it to the steward. It seemed unlikely he didn't know and no one liked to scratch a raw wound. Thaïs tried in vain to gauge his reaction. He was ambitious; perhaps he'd schemed to have his wife in the master's bed so as to double their joint influence over him. Perhaps he no longer loved her and didn't care. Perhaps they'd come to an agreement. They'd shared a nurse and regularly shared girlfriends; they might have agreed to share her.

***

Nerysa and Demetrius were serene in the eye of the storm. The master treated her kindly but he was naturally kind and loved her husband. Perhaps he was grateful that she'd made him a better wife than he'd feared. Though noted for his powers of observation,

Demetrius couldn't observe what he wouldn't have believed. Lucius hadn't opposed his marriage merely on grounds of expediency. He'd found Nerysa physically repulsive. Mediterraneans generally felt distaste for northerners - their wan, sweaty flesh, weakness for alcohol and unsophisticated behaviour. He was a gentle, courteous man but there was no denying he was an inveterate snob. Demetrius couldn't imagine him putting a half-tamed Briton between his silk sheets. He'd have been as likely to put a frog there. So, for them both, the revelation came as a bolt from a catapult.

Demetrius, pale and tight around the mouth, handed her an exquisite crystal jar.'

'The master sends you that with his compliments.'

'Please thank him for me, sir, but why does he send it?'

'It's a fashionable variety. He prefers it, now, to the one he sent us as a wedding gift.'

'But there's no occasion to give it me, is there?' Had some obscure festival slipped her memory?

'That's for you to judge.'

'How so, sir?'

'Don't play the innocent. You know what favours he wants to reward.'

She searched her memory. Only her long hours of work distinguished her from the other slaves.

'Wash and use the perfume, then go and serve his meal. When he retires he'll take you to his bed.'

He must have been drinking, the joke was in such poor taste. But Demetrius was never in poor taste, even in his cups, and he was hardly ever that. She looked up into his face. It was clearly no joke to him.

'He's proud of the gift he gave me. He wants to sample it to see just how good it is.'

'How could he sample my love for you?'

'By enjoying your love for him.'

'But I don't love him.'

'Of course you love him, he's your master. And he hasn't just picked you out in a crowd and summoned you with the crook of his finger. It seems he's taken pains to make himself agreeable to you and waited on your response. Tonight you'll reward his patience.'

'I'll do no such thing.'

'You'll do as you're bidden.'

'I *will* do as I'm bidden. I was bidden to marry you and be a chaste wife to you. I was made to swear it before the gods - not my gods, your gods and his gods. How clever of you to make me call down vengeance on my own head if I was forsworn.'

'You're not forsworn if you go to him in obedience and not in lust.'

'So, as long as I suffer, you're content but if it's a pleasure to obey you, I'm at fault.'

He bit his lip and made no reply.

'The master gave me to you as a gift, you say. What's a gift? A loan until the giver changes his mind? You should have bought me, Demetri. If you'd given him a couple of ases for me it would have spared us this trouble and I should have had *some* value.'

'You are of value, to both of us. In your case, I think we wouldn't want to be so crude as to put a figure on it.'

'I've been a present once. How often do you want to exchange me? Clap hands, Happy Saturnalia!'

'You were always his slave. What he allowed me was the use of you.'

'The *use* of me?'

'In the same way he'd let a man plough and sow his field or invest his money. The ownership rests with him.'

'What about what *I* gave? My whole self.'

'Beloved, it wasn't yours to give.'

'Oh, yes, it was! There's a body that drudges for him but, inside it, there's my true self. He can't have that. I gave it all to you.'

'Your people aren't monogamous are they? Gaius Caesar wrote that the Britons shared wives in groups of ten men.'

God! More travellers' tales! It was the standard smear on foreign peoples because Romans thought they had a monopoly on decent family life. She struggled to keep her temper.

'I've heard Romans say that of Scythians, too, and Libyans. Queen Boudicca destroyed two legions to avenge her daughters' honour. Do you think, for one moment, they weren't her husband's children?'

'You're being ridiculous. There's no need to look as if you're ready to take on two legions yourself. You can't make war in a house – especially not in the master's cubicle.'

He led her to the couch and she felt his hand shake.

'Look, you're Lucius' slave and so am I. He's been gracious enough to allow us a recognised union but that doesn't mean you can't oblige him from time to time. When he visits Horta, the farm manager's woman warms his bed. It's natural. He's paying her a compliment. She'd be offended if he slept alone, - so would the manager.'

'But you don't feel like that. You can't tell me you don't care.'

'I'm not saying that. I'm saying I've no *right* to care. You're making too much of this. It's not the first time we've shared a woman. We always did before you. Boys, too, come to that. You'll come back and I'll still love you.'

He wouldn't. He'd hate her. If she went willingly now, how would he believe it was the first time? How would he even be sure that the child she was carrying was his? Already, he wasn't being straight, either with her or with himself. What hope had they, if in deep trouble, they couldn't be honest with each other? His patience snapped.

'Will you go now or must I thrash you first?'

'Don't you think I'd rather be thrashed than lose my honour?'

'A slave has no honour to lose.'

Useless to argue. She took the perfume to the wash room and stayed there until Successus called for him to make their routine tour of the house. Then she stole paper and pen. A message on wax was too ephemeral. Rolling up her letter, she slipped it through her wedding ring and left it on his bed. Stepping through the door in the yard she abandoned the house that had been her sanctuary for two years. There were people who thought even slaves should be allowed to be chaste, if they wanted to be, and she knew where to find them. Pulling her cloak round her, she put down her head and hurried along, because the streets weren't safe.

CHAPTER XLV

January 173

Ancilla fugitiva quemadmodum sui furtum facere intelligitur, ita partum quoque contrectando furtivum facit.

A runaway slave girl is deemed to commit theft of herself and she makes her child stolen property by handling it. Justinian Digest of Roman law Africanus 47.2.61

'My true self, I gave it all to you.' Her words broke over Demetrius like a heady perfume, balm for the misery that was coming. He had her love and, in some way, ill-defined yet quintessential, he'd always keep it. When she came back, he'd suppress his jealousy and they would be the same as before. His own feelings weren't a problem, he could discipline them.

He toured the house mechanically, returned to the office and applied himself to his work but the jealousy he claimed he could control gnawed at him. He concentrated on the aspects of the case that puzzled rather than pained. Lucius wouldn't have sent for her unless he thought he'd had encouragement. But to encourage him and then refuse him was the sort of capricious behaviour no master could be expected to tolerate.

The knock was respectful but the door burst open and six guards fell into the room. He stared in surprise as they saluted, fidgeted and looked from him to each other and back to him. One cleared his throat and took a step forward.

'Forgive the intrusion, sir, our orders are…to escort you to the dining room.'

Why would Lucius humiliate him in front of his staff? But, if they had to insist, the last shreds of his credibility would be lost. Demetrius led the way out. Passing his bedroom door, he saw it wide open and people moving around inside.

The triclinium was crowded but, through the frenzied activity and the smoke, he saw that Lucius was the worse for drink and looked around anxiously for Nerysa. The guards fell back leaving him standing alone before his master's couch.

'Demetri!' drawled Lucius, 'You mongrel in the manger! Where's the girl?'

'She's on duty, master, she should be here.'

Lucius looked at him in contemptuous disbelief. Sensing that to lower his eyes would make him look guilty, though, of what, he didn't know, Demetrius looked levelly back. Lucius threw back his head, bared his teeth and bellowed, 'Get out! All of you! Useless prying fools!'

For an instant, no one moved, as if they couldn't believe that their amiable master was raving. Then the guards rallied and routed the servers. Carvers, cup-bearers, waiters, knives, comfit dishes and ice pails converged on the doorway and the panic-stricken stragglers, whipped in by the prefect, impelled them through. The guards fell on Demetrius and pushed him backwards. He felt his splayed limbs hit the wall with a sickening flood of memory as Lucius advanced on him with clenched fists.

I've come full circle,' he thought. *I'll be chained in the cellar before the night's out.*

A tap on the door broke the tension and, as Successus entered, Lucius stopped in his tracks and recovered himself with a shiver. He took the scroll Successus held out to him, slipped it out of a ring which he pushed onto the tip of a finger, and retired to his couch. Demetrius moved not a muscle but fixed his eyes on his master, reading each change in his expression. Eventually, Lucius looked up and spoke softly.

'Leave us!'

When the guards had gone, he pointed to the door and Demetrius, understanding the familiar gesture, lowered his arms stiffly and went and bolted it. Lucius handed him the letter. It was an elegant, educated hand but he couldn't identify it as his wife's because he'd no idea she could write. That was the first of many shocking facts he had to absorb. She'd defied them both; she was a fugitive and she'd left evidence incriminating herself. He needed to sit down, to go somewhere private and think. Lucius drew up a bench - a sober and different Lucius.

'Demetrie, what shall we do? Her appearance is so unusual she'll be found. Advertise a reward and we'll get her back.'

'Master, a naive girl, alone in this city, at night, for however short a time...'

'Zeus! You're right! What a simpleton! Preserve her chastity by wandering the streets at night? But we can't send the guards, we might as well tell the whole house.'

'I'll go, master.'

He knew how completely Lucius would have to trust him to allow that.

Lucius said, 'We'll both go.'

'Master, you can't go out without guards.'

'Demetrie, how lucky we are that I was born the master and you the slave. With you at the helm, life would be insufferably dull.'

Demetrius was gratified that the slaves he passed saluted him as readily as ever. He went to Lucius' cubicle, sent his man, Cyrus, on a spurious errand and snatched up a toga and a pair of boots. He took a torch, a stout stick and a dagger from the store, and his cloak and a purse from his rooms, locking them from the outside and praising his genius for the vanity that had prompted him to give Polybius a night's leave.

They left openly by the front door, telling Hypnos they were going on a social call. It was years since they'd roamed the streets at night. Perhaps they made Hypnos feel young again. He shook his head and smiled indulgently as he lit their torch from the flambeau in the hall. Doubling back to the postern gate, they found it pushed to but unbolted. Demetrius winced. He'd made an inspection. He should have noticed. It was another crime to be listed against her; leaving her master's house open to thieves. Why was he searching for her? She'd come to grief alone in the city but what had she to come home to but grief?

Footprints in the dusty lane petered out in the main street. He racked his brain for a favourable construction he could put on her behaviour while Lucius badgered him about her friends, favourite haunts, anywhere she might have gone, clearly irritated by his ignorance of her habits yet unsurprised, assuming his indifference. Although that was precisely the impression he'd set out to give, Demetrius found the assumption hurtful. Reaching the edge of the escarpment, they looked down the precipitous stone stairway to the swirling torches below.

'Would she know to avoid the Suburra?' Lucius asked.

Demetrius thought of the disorderly inns and filthy streets full of half-naked prostitutes, brutish pimps and thieves.

'I never mentioned such places to her...at least...not by name.'

'She should have had a maid to keep an eye on her.'

'Marcus Archias, master! She trusts him.'

'Didn't he once offer to take her as an apprentice?'

'Something like that.'

'But he wouldn't hide a runaway.'

'Of course not. But, if you did still want to conceal this business, it would explain her absence if you'd sent her out as an apprentice.'

Lucius stopped and turned in the direction of Archias' house. When footsteps approached out of the ebony darkness, Demetrius tightened his grip on his cudgel but, as he thrust his lantern in the faces of the approaching men, he relaxed.

'It's old Timothy, master! Deputy steward in your father's time.'

Lucius swore under his breath, gave a curt nod and carried on walking as he spoke.

'Good evening. I don't believe I've seen you since you were pleased to put on a freedman's cap and carry my father's bier.'

'Indeed, I pay my respects every year, Excellency, and always have cause to praise your generosity. I shouldn't think it right to trouble you more often, since I'm not in need.'

'Then you know how to be content with little. I hear crowds gather in your shop, stay hours at a time and seldom leave with any purchases.'

'Alas, Excellency, you're well informed. Permit me to present my friend Stephanos.'

'A happy and most prosperous New Year to you, Excellency!'

'The gods be pleased to send you the same! Marcus Timothy, if you were coming to present me with a New Year gift, be good enough to excuse me until tomorrow. I have pressing business.'

Lucius quickened his pace but Timothy was not to be shaken off.

'I needn't trespass on your time, Excellency, if you allow me to accompany you.'

Demetrius knew he was supposed to rid them of this unwelcome intrusion but he was far from his resourceful self and Timothy seemed determined to speak, though in no hurry to come to the point.

'Excellency, I was born under your roof and served there thirty years. I won your father's trust, and, I hope, yours. I think you must know I'm a Christian?'

'A Jewish sect is that?'

'If you say so, Excellency. Do you think there are any Christians in your house?'

'I guess there are some in every house. As far as I'm concerned, if a slave works well and attends household prayers, his private superstitions are his own.'

'We've a girl, Excellency, whom we have reason to think is yours. She may have come by mistake, thinking we had a meeting. When we discovered she was absent from your house without permission, she asked for sanctuary, afraid of punishment I suppose. Please believe none of us enticed her. I would have brought her straight back but I hoped to prepare the way, say what I could in her favour. I think she's not wicked but confused.'

'Who has seen her?'

'Two widows of our congregation, Excellency, most pious and discreet. They have her under lock and key.'

'Show me.'

They hurried to a dingy back street. Timothy led them through a shop front and disappeared into the storeroom behind. Demetrius stood in the centre of the room, under the lamp, hoping that the girl who came out would be Nerysa and praying she would not. She slipped in, her face radiant.

'You've found me! We don't have long. Timothy has gone for Lucius.'

He felt Lucius retreat into the shadows. Nerysa held out both her hands and, when he didn't take them, she stepped back and said, 'I've something to tell you. I should have told you long ago but I didn't know how. We never spoke of it but it's natural when a man and a woman live together. I hope it will please you, sir.'

He made no sense of it. Lucius was more intuitive.

'Demetri,' he said, 'she means her girdle's tightening.'

CHAPTER XLVI

January 173

Eripere ei noli, multo quod carius illi. Est oculis seu quid carius est oculis

Do not take from him what is dearer to him than his eyes Catullus LXII

As Lucius spoke, Nerysa spun round and peered into the darkness towards him. He saw her face contort in horror and her hair heave like a fox's brush. As she sank towards the ground he sprang forward, caught her as she fell and achieved his ambition of holding her in his arms. It wasn't as he'd imagined; she wasn't yielding but inanimate. His people had deceived him. She dreaded him and trusted Demetrius. Disbelief and hurt swept over him. And frustration, because she'd put herself beyond even his power to pardon. Unless.... he pushed her towards his stunned and wooden servant.

'Take her, she's fainted.'

He saw that he'd have to think for all three of them.

'Get her home! Send someone from here to hire a cart. Go in by the postern gate. If it's bolted, go in the front way yourself but bring her through the back, the way she got out - a window, I suppose, and make sure no one sees you. And Demetrie....'

'Master?'

Demetrius was spent but the last faculty to desert him would be that of hearing and obeying his master's commands.

'Don't *you* punish her. That's my right. And take care no one knows she left the house. If she can't hold her tongue, lock her up. You'll give her my orders?'

'I will, master.'

'There's no call for *you* to be harsh with her. Just make her understand what it means to be a fugitive. Take what you need from the purse and leave it me.'

'Are you coming home, master?'

'I'll send you word tomorrow. Make an inspection first thing and tighten up on your security.'

Lucius felt spiteful and it wasn't often he could fault Demetrius. He wanted to speak to Timothy about Christians. Comfortably close to the top of society's pyramid, he was a conscientious practitioner of the state religion but his mind wasn't closed to the variety of religions on offer throughout the empire. Whenever he had an ethical problem, he debated it with Demetrius. This time he couldn't. Timothy enthused about his God, who he called 'the Lord', and what he said of the Lord's teaching had some appeal. A priest of the new religion, he took a professional approach to Lucius' problem, teasing out the strands of the argument methodically.

'The girl is subject to you, under the law and in the eyes of the Lord. She may not disobey you, desert you, or show you disrespect – we've told her that.'

Lucius approved.

'But Demetrius is your faithful servant and, as you say yourself, your friend and brother. You wouldn't be proud of yourself if you hurt him.'

Lucius couldn't deny it.

'The so-called slave marriage has no significance in law, as you know, but in the Lord's sight it might have, if both parties gave free consent. Naturally, she'd defer to you so we can assume her consent. Now, as to vows made to gods, we worship one true God but becoming a Christian doesn't cancel vows you already made. If you believed in the old gods when you swore by them, you will be bound in the Lord.'

Lucius asked how Christians gave in marriage.

'We think it best not to marry but to live for the Lord. If marriage vows are made, they bind for life. We don't divorce. Our widows don't remarry.'

'Never?'

'There is a circumstance where divorce is allowed. Paul of Tarsus ruled that a wife could divorce her husband if he tried to stop her being a Christian.'

'Ah! There we have him, I think. Demetrius wouldn't allow his wife to do anything singular and he's devoted to the gods of the Roman state.'

'Indeed! I don't recall him being pious as a boy.'

Lucius winced. Timothy certainly remembered them both as anything but.

'He is now. He sees religious observance as an aid to discipline and good order.'

Holy Timothy pursed his lips.

'We could summarise the situation this way, Excellency. You couldn't honourably wrest this girl from your brother. But if she was married against her will, or if he gave her up, you could take her with a clear conscience.'

Lucius wouldn't blindly accept the moral judgement of his own freedman or of an obscure foreign sect but Timothy's assessment matched his own. And he saw the strength of his position. For the present, Nerysa was reconciled to her husband but she feared him and, reasonably, feared his master even more. Demetrius was an exacting man. He'd end by crushing her spirit and, when he did, the indulgent master would be standing by to comfort her. Once Demetrius had explained the seriousness of her crime and the severity of the punishment she'd been spared, she'd feel deeply in his debt. A waiting game suited Lucius. Especially one he couldn't lose.

CHAPTER XLVII

January 173

Quid enim terrisque poloque parendi sine lege manet? Vice cuncta reguntur alternisque premunt.

What, in all the world, is a law unto itself? All things either rule or are ruled. Statius. Silvae III iii 45 -

Demetrius had no confidant. Nerysa's flight had shocked him to the core. It had been so unnecessary; he could have spoken to Lucius, pleaded for delay. Some arrangement could have been made; anything but this infamy. But she hadn't known that. She'd seemed to learn quickly but she'd learned superficial information without any understanding of the loyalty a slave owed a master. And he'd bullied her. He should have explored her reservations and advised her. Jealousy had blinded him to everything but his own pain.

Fugitive! When Lucius said the word it had struck him like an arrow in the eye. A word so vile he could barely frame it in his mind, let alone utter it in connection with his wife. Runaways were unheard of in Lucius' house so Demetrius had no experience of dealing with one. He'd seen a few outside; depraved wretches, the stigma branded on their foreheads, their guilt indelible. The crime was as horrific as the punishment, for who, but a mindless ingrate, could be so heedless of a master's care, so callously indifferent to his anxiety and loss?

He imagined a red hot brand hissing on her snowy brow. It was almost certain Lucius was incapable of ordering that but it was the 'almost' that caused him to wake at night, his heartbeat tumultuous and his body streaming sweat. Perhaps Lucius would opt for a less disfiguring mark such as having her ears slit. Her hair would cover them and only he would see her mutilation. But would he see it? What if Lucius sold her on?

From the beginning, they had practised strict division of labour. Lucius had his career. Demetrius supervised the businesses and the farm and managed the slaves. But Lucius now reserved to himself the right to punish Nerysa. Did he suspect that Demetrius, out of partiality, would be too lenient? It would be inept to sympathise with her. He'd put himself out of favour and lessen his bargaining power. Besides, if the master came home and found her wretched, he might pity her. He sought out Thaïs. Although she could not and must not know his problem, he needed her calm presence and her even voice.

'Nerysa is pregnant.'

She suggested abortion; he thought it was too late.

'So she was ill when she didn't report for duty yesterday?'

'She isn't well. But she should have asked to be excused.'

'Our Lucius won't be hard on her, surely?'

Hard? thought Demetrius, *by rights, she should be chained in prison.*

'She's locked in my room.' he said. 'See she has what she needs to clean it.'

Thaïs stared coldly. It was useless to prolong the conversation, having lost her sympathy. He went and sat in the peristyle and stared into the driving rain.

***

Demetrius ordered his washroom window to be boarded up, on the pretext that the weather was unusually cold. The bedroom doors were locked from the outside and Nerysa's stool disappeared. Twice a day he gave her a meagre portion of black bread and a crock of water, making her stand against the wall and wait for permission to eat. She understood. He blamed himself for doing the very thing he'd tried to avoid, promoting her too soon, before she'd learned the ground rules. Now he was forcing her to learn them. It was a harder lesson than he knew because only food assuaged her nausea. But a slave's rations were his own, to hoard, barter or sell. She kept back pieces of bread to settle her stomach during the day and, given the chance, pilfered from his tray and wept tears of shame.

If he spoke, it was to give a curt command or to read a lecture, while she stood before him, struggling against faintness. Since she was a slave, he reasoned, she had a choice; to be a good slave or a bad one. For the good slave there was the satisfaction of giving valued service, the approval of the master, and – the ultimate reward - eventual manumission. Be a bad slave and she would be wretched and she would still be a slave.

'Everyone,' he argued, 'is subject to someone. Why not you? Ship's passengers take the captain's orders just like the crew. Freeborn children put their hands under the schoolmaster's rod. Soldiers obey their commanders. Even our master daren't flout the code of behaviour expected of Roman knights. Do you imagine he enjoys getting up at dawn to receive hordes of stale-smelling clients, hearing their troubles and advising them patiently?'

'I know he doesn't.'

'Have you ever heard of him slinking out through the postern gate to escape the tedium of it? Do you think he likes spending his days in court defending scoundrels? No. He feels he's on trial as much as the defendant.

'Does he ever tell us to deny him, even to the most beggarly petitioner? No. Because, unlike you, he understands what duty is. Duty's not just for soldiers. Even a civilian, once he's stationed at his post, ought to stick to it.'

'Exactly! That's why I should be faithful to you. I didn't choose this marriage but I committed myself to it. I'm not a toy for any man's pleasure.'

'He's not *any* man, he's our master. A slave isn't separate from his master; he's a projection of him. And this master, remember, paced the streets at night looking for you. Not to recover his property - the police could have done that – but because he was afraid for you.'

Not even her tears mollified him. He said he didn't flatter himself that his words penetrated to her heart, she wept for her own misery not for the injury she'd done her master. In truth, she wept tears of despair. She'd known exactly what she did but nothing had mattered so much as to spare him the pain of seeing her in another man's arms.

She'd misjudged him. He didn't prize her loyalty. The only quality he could value in her was obedience. If he sensed how much a soft word would have comforted her, he resisted the temptation to offer it. It was Polybius who took the heavy bucket from her.

'Don't help me.' she warned, 'You'll earn yourself a beating.'

'By my genius, one night off and, when I get back, His Excellency has fled the house, you're shut up scrubbing floors and Himself has lockjaw. Is anyone going to tell me why?'

He looked over his shoulder as Charis slipped in and coaxed the door shut.

'Hades! I'm surrounded by crazy women! Don't you know better than to come here?'

'No one saw me. He's gone to check the warehouses after the rainstorm.'

'Don't you know he can be in two places at once and always where he's least expected?'

'Mistress, you're working, so you're not ill. Is it true what they say, you're in disgrace?'

Nerysa slumped over her scrubbing brush.

'Tell her I can't talk.'

He pressed a finger to his lips.

'I'll ask the questions, you can nod I suppose. Did His Excellency send for you? Thought so. Oysters in ginger, raisin wine and a flute player - always means a new girl. I assume she didn't please him.'

'And is Demetrius angry because of that?'

'Not angry; afraid.'

'Our Lucius isn't cruel but he's spiteful if you bruise his pride.'

'Spite's got nothing to do with it. How is he master in his own house if he can't have his steward's woman?'

'No man knows how hard it is for a woman to lie with one man when she loves another.'

He laughed. 'That's not *her* problem. She doesn't want it with anyone. Ice in the veins. Out you go! And don't come back, we've enough trouble as it is.'

He bolted the door behind her and knelt beside Nerysa.

'I'll make sure she doesn't talk. Don't you think that floor's clean enough now?'

'I know every stone in it. Did you see my ring? I thought it might have rolled off the bed but, if it had, I'd have found it.'

'Took it off to go to His Excellency? Tactful. He'll calm down. That's why he's gone. Demeaning to have his anger out of control. He should go out of town - change of air.'

'Where is he?'

'With Publius Severus where he'll get more drink than sleep. Sent round for Cyrus, hairdressers, cash and clean linen.'

'Demetrius doesn't sleep.'

'How do you know?'

'I don't either. I don't find a pallet on the floor as easy as I used to. He tosses and turns and calls me.'

'Nerysa, when your master calls, you go to him, day or night.'

'I do, but he always says he didn't call me and sends me away.'

'Well he's ordered me back in here so I'll get up to him.'

She was relieved of her last wifely duty. There was nothing now but heavy work, bread and water and rejection. And the strange unease she'd felt for some days, like moths flitting over her bowels. It came again and she realised it must be her child stirring. Two years before it wouldn't have entered her mind that she could be pregnant by a slave. Hurling herself from a high roof to her death would hardly have covered the shame of it. Now she couldn't summon up any sense of outrage. Instead came a glow of pride in her child who would be as brilliant and beautiful as its father and who would be a living link with her lost family.

CHAPTER XLVIII

February 173

Cum volet accedes cum te vitabit abibis

When she's willing go to her when she shuns you depart Ovid ars amatoria II 529

A curious letter summoned Demetrius to Ostia. He was so baffled by it he actually discussed it with his discredited wife. Naturally, he didn't voice an opinion that their master had run mad but he did venture to question his judgement.

'They ask him to open the games every year. He never does. He just funds them.'

'Who invites him?'

'The town council. Because he's their patron. He owns estates around the town, you see. It's a provincial affair and he hates the games anyway. When he has to go here, he keeps his head stuck in a poetry book.'

'He can't do that if he's officiating, can he?'

'Certainly not. That *would* offend the worthy burghers. But he mustn't think of a sea voyage from Ostia in February. There's no commercial shipping out at present. He's having difficulty chartering a boat and imagines I can help.'

'Can you?'

'I know who's reliable but I couldn't find a sensible captain to make that journey before the beginning of April. He'll have to go overland to Rhegium, wait for a fair weather day and persuade a sailor to cross to Messina. If he breaks his journey with friends at Cumae and Buxentum it'll take three weeks to make Rhegium. The sea should be safer by then.'

'It sounds a tedious journey.'

He bit his lip to restrain himself from saying it was folly. The next day he hurried to Ostia with two carts full of baggage and the litter-bearers. There was only a momentary awkwardness between them before they embraced. Demetrius made all the arrangements carefully, hoping to be rewarded by an assurance that his wife was pardoned. Lucius didn't offer it, merely repeating that Demetrius must not mention the affair and must not punish her himself. So he rode home in the same unease as he had come. Crossing the peristyle to his room, he fell in with Archias, walking in the same direction.

He watched as Nerysa stood with drooping head and Archias moved his hands over her belly. They retired to the office and left her to dress.

'I'll write to Lepidus,' Archias said 'but, if you see him first, tell him there's no sign of complication so far. The birth should be in May.'

'When the time comes, would you send us your midwife?'

'Lepidus has asked me to attend myself.'

'My mother died in childbirth.'

Archias might have meant to sound bracing but, to Demetrius, he sounded brusque.

'Remember that many women survive and don't regret their ordeal once it's over. She won't lack for anything I can do or that Lepidus can buy for her.'

Demetrius had lost control of his wife to men who had greater powers to protect her. He felt less anxious on Lucius' account. His insistence on discretion didn't necessarily mean he intended to pardon her; more likely he didn't want the intolerable insult his slave had offered him to be generally known. But he'd hardly take such care of her just to brand and sell her. As he fretted less over her disgrace, the shadow of her confinement loomed larger. He never passed the shrine without a prayer and stood over her to insist she drained the cups of bitter herbal tea Archias had prescribed.

Anxious to spare her heavy work, he remembered she could write and sat her on a scribe's bench at simple copying tasks. He watched, fascinated, as her hand glided quickly and surely over the papyrus, charmed when her brow puckered in thought and she pressed the pen to her parted lips. He ached to lay her along the bench, loosen her girdle and take her there and then. But that would undermine the severity he must assume.

He soon had her making copies of documents. She suggested, to save time, he needn't draft everything on tablets. He could dictate at normal conversational speed. Using a system of her own, she'd write rapidly on wax and produce a fair copy later.

'Where did you learn tyroism?' he asked in amazement.

'With Quintus. He used to pace about the room, composing poetry aloud. I took down everything he said so it wouldn't be forgotten.'

'By my genius! You've been Quintus Pulcher's secretary and you'd demean yourself to be mine?'

'Well, naturally, I'm anxious to ingratiate myself with you, so I may perhaps escape a whipping.'

'That's the master's decision, not mine.'

'You'll put in a good word for me though, won't you?'

'I'll do more than that.'

'Shall I make fair copies of these letters now, sir?'

'Yes. No need to be turning them into hexameters. Such refinements would puzzle my correspondents.'

'You're safe from me there, sir. I've no such skill.'

'Wife, you disappoint me.'

With this Parthian shot, he left her. His face was grim but his heart sang. A pretty young girl trained as a private secretary was an unusual and prestigious possession, one calculated to appeal to Lucius. He might punish her harshly but he wouldn't part with her.

CHAPTER XLIX

February 173

Servis ad statuam licet confugere Even slaves have the right of refuge at the statue of a god. Seneca On Mercy I viii

Nerysa sensed Demetrius unbend toward her. That evening he tapped his couch, inviting her to sit beside him. He wore his silk tunic off one shoulder and, smelling the fragrant warm fur of his chest, she longed to drop her head and lose her face in it. She stayed primly upright watching him break off a piece of soft white bread and stir it round the dish to soak up the sauce. It smelled so good her mouth flooded and the pit of her stomach yawned. He looked up at her with no hint of a smile, drained the bread against the side of the dish and held it out to her. Her eyes misted gratitude. It was the first kindness he'd shown her since her disgrace. She was encouraged to speak.

'Is Lucius going to have me whipped when he comes home?'

A shadow of such pain crossed his face she wished she hadn't asked.

'My poor girl, when you were taken into slavery you must have thought you'd sunk as low as you could, but you hadn't. Even a slave, if he justifies his master's confidence in him, can be respected. A fugitive is a common criminal.'

She lowered her head, feeling no shame but sensible of his.

'Would he..would he want to have me punished before our baby is born?'

'I think he'd be more likely to wait until afterwards.'

'If he didn't wait, would it hurt our baby?'

'Don't fret. He might sentence you to whipping but you won't take it.'

'Why not?'

'If whipping's necessary to save his pride, I'll take it. He owes me that. I can persuade him.'

'I couldn't let you suffer that for me, it would be unjust.'

'It'd be interesting to see how I bear the rod on my back after twelve years.'

He laughed at her protests and stroked her bowed head.

'Don't you think a man would be proud to suffer for his wife's honour?'

'Slaves don't have honour, you taught me that.'

'And you taught me something. A slave may have honour if he has courage and a just master.' He hesitated, adding softly, 'And a good wife to inspire him.'

She blushed and didn't know how to reply. He held her in his arms and prayed, 'Let's hope he comes home in a forgiving vein.'

'Couldn't you raise a loan for the balance of your freedom?'

'I wouldn't want it just for myself.'

'I thought he promised that, when you bought yours, he'd give you mine.'

'Nerysa, dearest, he couldn't give it you now, even if he wanted. He couldn't reward a fugitive with manumission. Don't you see, it's the futility of it that's insulting to him. Why do you think slaves so seldom desert even the worst of masters?'

'Because they've no initiative.'

'Now you're being disappointingly stupid. Why would anyone willingly desert their home? Isn't Lucius' house our home as much as his - for most of us the only one we've ever known? Aren't we as attached to it as he is? Don't we miss it as sorely and lighten our step when we turn back towards it?

'We're privileged, of course, yet even for the miserable slave of a cruel master, loyalty is by far his best option. Let's look at yours, for example. If you fell into honest hands, you'd be returned to your master for punishment. Dishonest hands and it would be the brothel or the wine bar. The wine bar's the worst.'

'Why? Serving wine's not heavy work.'

'The bar girls have to take the customers upstairs but only after they've served all the dinners. They don't get anything to eat themselves until all the customers are…satisfied. You've no idea what your life might be like outside this house.'

'I met Severus.'

He laughed. 'Severus is an educated, civilised aristocrat. There are men out there worse than animals.

'I ordered an inventory, you know. You hadn't taken so much as a thimble. How did you think you were going to eat?'

'I didn't care. Or I thought perhaps the saints –'

'The Christians? Well, you know now they won't harbour you. Even they have too much respect for the law and, incidentally, for Lucius himself. Would you join a band of brigands? Do you think their manners would be gentler than his?'

'Couldn't I seek sanctuary in a temple?'

'You could, or you could apply to a magistrate. You'd hardly say you were trying to escape your master's bed, since every other maidservant in the empire is tumbling over herself to get into it. You'd have to convince the authorities your master was brutal and inhuman. How could you do that without telling wicked lies? Suppose you succeeded? They'd order you to be sold to a new master and the proceeds given to Lucius.'

'Severus?'

'If he got wind of it he'd be at the head of the queue and looking smug for the price would be most attractive. It always is in such circumstances. But you don't need to claim sanctuary to get yourself sold. Fugitives are almost always sold.'

'Doesn't that just reward their crime?'

'No, It's because we know from experience that a slave never absconds once. If they do it at all, they do it often. It's their nature - incapable of loyalty. The owner usually wants to cut his losses. The buyer is warned and the price reflects the fact that the goods are flawed. A new owner would have a sharp eye kept on you. You'd hardly expect him to give you the chance to seek sanctuary again and start telling lies about *him*.'

'But I *am* capable of loyalty. There's a conflict of loyalties and I can't accept your judgement as to which takes precedence.'

'You're my dearest love, my wife and my subordinate and you can't accept my judgement. I must be a singularly unpersuasive fellow. It's as well *I* don't have to plead in court.'

'I've never seen Lucius in court but they say he's effective because he pleads with his heart as well as his head.'

'Trust my head. It's more rational and concerns itself only with your interest. To serve a man like our Lucius, who's worthy of your loyalty and knows how to value and reward it; isn't that better than rebellion? If he lets you near him again you must fall at his feet and hold his knees and say – no, don't say anything, just cry. That would be best.'

CHAPTER L

May 173

Cede tuum pedem mi, lymphis flavis fulvum ut pulverem…bluam, Lassitudinemque minuam manuum mollitudine. Pacuvius.

Give me your feet and I'll wash the amber dust from them in shining water and soothe their weariness in my soft hands.

The master came home without warning. Life in the house was more leisured when he was away and there was a good chance of catching his staff on the hop. It wasn't that he was severe, just that he loved to tease. Knowing no one would work on the last day of the Floralia, he planned to complain of neglect.

Everyone had gone to the races. Demetrius was in Ostia; no business could be conducted so it was a chance for him to confer with Jacob. Xenia was left at home to defend the house and Nerysa had volunteered to be portress. She sat chained to the porter's chair and the guard dogs at her feet snored and wheezed through the long afternoon.

So, when the master sprinted up his marble steps to his great bronze doors and peered through the grille, the first thing he saw of home was Nerysa and she was the first to greet him. He thought she was a miracle; softened, rounded and shimmering in the fractured sunlight. He sent Adrian for the keys and released her from the chain with his own hands, shed the ripples of his toga into the waiting arms of Cyrus and calmed the frantic greeting of his dogs. Then he led her by the hand into the sun-flooded atrium. Her swaying gait, like a ship in sail, echoed in the depths of his memory; heartbreaking yet strangely soothing.

Xenia brought towels and steeped silver fronds of artemisia in water and, when she'd served him wine, Nerysa eased off his stiff boots. She applied iced compresses to his aching soles, rinsed the dust from his feet, and massaged them. Attar of rose mingled with the scent of new leather as she slipped on his sandals.

She dignified the lowly task with a grave earnestness untainted by servility, yet he sensed fear, tangible, as if even the child within her shrank from him. As he gazed down on her fragile, white neck, his heart brimmed over with good intentions. He'd planned to make her wait some days before he sent for her and chastened her with nothing more than well-chosen words. He'd dreamt of drying her penitent tears and forgiving her with the forbearance of selfless love. The unexpected meeting thwarted his plans but he didn't regret them.

'Should there be any dinner for me tonight,' he murmured, 'you must serve it. No one else.'

'Master, there'll be a splendid dinner. Everyone will be home soon and overjoyed To see you well.'

'Are *you* well, Nerysa?'

'Thank you, master, I'm very well.'

The staff were aghast to think of his meal being served by one heavily pregnant girl but he wasn't in a critical mood. She sat below his couch peeling an apple and he asked rhetorically,

'I've been in Sicily. Would you like to hear about it?'

He'd visited his estates, been fêted by his tenants and slaves and entered the town in a grand litter at the head of a procession to open the games.

'Ten thousand people in the arena.' he told her 'Their acclamation was like the roar of a mighty ocean. But when I raised my hand and spoke the dedication, you could have heard a petal fall on the sand!'

She looked into the distance as though she saw the scene as he described it. Her mouth opened. He leaned forward to catch her words as she whispered to herself, "'In the presence of a great man, the rabble falls silent and subdued."'

'Zeus! Where did you get that from?'

'Virg...just something I heard my old master say.'

'Pulcher? Did he quote poetry to you?'

'He was always quoting - himself or someone else.'

'And you remember the lines?'

'My memory bristles with them.'

'Now I shall bristle - with curiosity, to know what's running through your mind while you change my sandals and fill my cup. Do you quote poetry at Demetrius?'

'Oh no! Never.'

Why was she suddenly confused as if she'd said something she shouldn't? She *was* afraid of Demetrius. Did he ill-treat her behind the bedroom door? He'd never asked himself how Demetrius kept the slaves cooperative. He was firm, of course, stern when necessary, he supposed, but he'd never thought of him as cruel. And the girl quoted Virgil! He wouldn't share that with him. If he hadn't discovered it for himself, he didn't deserve to know.

He said, 'Are you unhappy?'

'Master, I'd be an ungrateful wretch, to be your slave and unhappy. And if I were, wouldn't it comfort me if a great poet had felt the same and expressed sorrow so nobly he made it seem more glamorous than joy?'

'Do you share the poets' sorrows?'

'Some of them - but they weren't slaves. That must make a difference.'

'Some writers were slaves though; Terence, the playwright and Epictetus the philosopher, and Diogenes, of course. Their masters rewarded them with freedom.'

He took her chin in his hand, compelling her to look up into his eyes and take his meaning.

'Surely,' she breathed, 'every slave lives to please his master. Some are lucky enough to succeed.'

'Not by luck. Now you disappointed your master. What did you mean by it?'

She dropped her gaze.

'Not to offend you, master. I wanted to do the right thing but it's difficult to know what's right.'

'I shouldn't punish you for trying to do right. I should rather teach you. But there's time for that. You shouldn't be troubled while your health is delicate.'

The next day, he ordered that she should rest in his own garden whenever she wished. Polybius disclosed that she and Demetrius no longer shared a bed and that was balm to his spirit. From Archias, he had the same assessment Demetrius had already heard. She was young and healthy but childbirth was a risky business. Nothing could be guaranteed but everything possible would be done and they must pray for the gods' blessing. It was pointless to press him further. He ordered sacrifices and twice daily prayers to the goddess Lucina.

He looked for her in the garden as she moved slowly through the long days. There was an aura of tranquillity about her he found consoling. As he sat with her one heavy afternoon, her belly heaved under her muslin dress and he whispered, 'Is that the child?'

She laughed, 'He's playful, sir, I can't sleep for his acrobatics.'

Fascinated, he laid a hand on her belly. The child found his exploring hand and leant against it and, as often as he moved his hand, the answering pressure sought and found it again. A sob caught in his throat. He felt as he had felt in the temple the day he came of age and assumed a man's responsibility; as though he'd stumbled on a presentiment of eternity.

'Were we really like this once,' he asked, 'imprisoned in a belly?'

'Both alike, master, I was freeborn as you were.'

She looked up at him and her eyes glittered. Surely not with tears? Their expression seemed to rake his soul.

'Do you want something?' he whispered. 'You may ask.'

She shook her head and looked down. He thought her lip trembled.

Well versed in the minutiae of the law, he knew he could grant her manumission one day and revoke it the next but, if he freed her for a single day of her pregnancy, her child would be born free of the taint of slavery. For a long moment he sat in the still garden and wavered. But it went against the grain to give the greatest gift in his power so soon after her defiance. It wouldn't be just, either to his own self-respect or to his more deserving servants. Better to hold it back for when she yielded to his dearest wish. Time for that, he thought, when it's *my* child in her belly.

CHAPTER LI

June 173

Continuo exponetur: hic tibist nil quicquam incommodi

It won't inconvenience you in the least. It will be exposed straight away. Terence. The Mother-in-Law I III 40 v400

Nerysa knew she'd been tactless. In an unguarded moment, she'd told Lucius that the child disturbed her sleep. She should never have given him cause to think it would be a nuisance. He was the one who would decide its fate.

Demetrius seemed to think she'd been pardoned. He took her back into his bed and bodily closeness comforted them both. No one, he insisted, must ever suspect her crime; not Charis, not Thaïs, not even her own conscious memory. He allowed her back to the linen room to work, sending Charis with her. He said it was more suitable for her to be with the women than the secretaries but he chose her company and she noticed.

'I went to the laundry yesterday to find Erotion. They said she wasn't there, but she was -I saw her. When I went today she wouldn't speak to me. Was it because she thought you didn't want her to?'

'Why did you want to speak to her?'

'She has two daughters.'

'So?'

'She could tell me what it's like to give birth.'

'What could an ignorant, old slave tell you? She'd just alarm you with her exaggerations and superstitions. In any case, she's no idea what it's like to be confined in the care of a fashionable doctor and midwife.'

When he'd accompanied Lucius out to dinner, she asked Polybius. 'Polybi, where do babies go to?'

'I've never seen one close to. They're born in the country, or farmed.'

'In the country?'

'Not that sort of farm! City people who raise and train slaves.'

'What sort of people?'

'Thrifty people. Raising a child isn't cheap and so many of them die they need a good price for the survivors, so it wouldn't be in their interest to knock them around too much, would it? They might talk though. Exposure's safest for babies with the wrong father.'

'What's *exposure*?'

'Slaves take them after dark to...to special places.'

'To starve?'

'Not unless they're ill favoured. Slave trainers pick them up and the best of it is, they don't know where they've come from; no chance of anything coming to light to embarrass you. You never know exactly what...you can hope for the best and never know the worst.

'Take me. I might have been spawned by an emperor. You've seen statues of Verus? Do you mark the resemblance? Well, if I grew a beard you would.'

'But why not keep it with me and train it myself?'

'Look, everyone knows His Excellency...awkward for him if people thought it was his, humiliating if they thought it wasn't.'

***

Hay making began and Demetrius was needed at Horta - not to supervise the farm manager, who knew his job, but to represent Lucius; swear in the labourers, preside over the religious rituals and approve the work. Not all the hands were Lucius' slaves, some were free men hired in for the season. And he had to make calculations; correlating the fodder stored with the number of animals to be overwintered and the portents of harsh weather.

He put off his departure again and again. Nerysa was embarrassed. It was encouraging that Lucius had seemed eager for the birth and she was afraid his interest might cool. He hadn't sent her to the country and now it was too late to move her. But nor had he summoned a country woman or engaged a wet nurse. He only spoke of his prayers for her safe delivery and the joy he looked for afterwards. Did he guess it would break her heart to lose her child? Would he care? Demetrius reminded her she'd forfeited any right to beg favours and to do so could be fatal. A request denied was one that could never be repeated. He promised their baby would live and they would not lose touch with it but, 'I've my own plans.' was all he would say.

If his plans failed, she would defy him and plead with Lucius herself. She'd grovel and cry and clasp his knees and behave as she'd thought she never could. But it was impossible to imagine a baby in his sophisticated house and the birth seemed as far away as the emperor's return from the front, postponed for yet another year. Demetrius had been away five days before she suddenly buckled in pain.

'Erinna, get one of the litter-bearers to carry her up to the new room above the office and send the messengers for Archias.' Thaïs said while pulling off her apron and smoothing her hair. 'I'll go and tell the master. How unlucky that this should happen while the steward's away!'

Between pains, Nerysa felt a fraud because she could have gone on working but, when they came, she could think of nothing but the fact that labour often lasted several days. The pains of the morning were twinges compared to those of the afternoon and the intervals between them, which she used to regain her composure, became ever shorter until she was racked without pause. Hot poultices pressed to her belly caused irritation rather than comfort. The women fussed and told her the usual lies; there was nothing to be afraid of, she was very brave, it would soon be over. They served refreshments throughout the day. Prayers and refreshments were the punctuation marks of life in the house. Nerysa thought that, if the city were devastated by earthquake or barbarians were beating down the gates of Rome, Lucius' staff would carry on serenely serving wine and cake, indifferent to anything but their rituals. With the dinner tray came news that the steward was home.

Nerysa knew she must die. There could be only one outcome of such agony and overwhelming malaise. But what would become of her baby without her to plead for it? She gasped, 'I want Demetrius.'

'I'm here.' sobbed Charis, squeezing her hand.

'No! Demetrius!' she shouted as her ears rang and the world went black.

Archias was firm, 'He can't come here now. He'll come to see you when it's over.'

She forced up her head.

'I'm dying. Can't I see my husband before I die?'

He spoke as if to a difficult child, 'He can't come here now, it wouldn't be suitable.'

What did he mean, 'suitable'? Whenever she'd been ill or injured Demetrius had tended her. If he were wounded or sick she wouldn't be prised from his side. She was wild with frustration, desperate to tell him that she loved him lest, after she was dead, he shouldn't be sure.

In the first light of the new day, she was dragged backwards across the floor. As her heels bumped over wooden boards she realised why she'd only heard accounts of slave and freedwomens' confinements. No freeborn woman would submit to this agony and indignity. Then she remembered that the empress had borne fourteen children. Her mind wanted to laugh but her muscles wouldn't oblige.

They lowered her onto a strange chair with a rim for a seat. Looking down, she saw the midwife warming oil in her hands, crouched in front of her. Her body was wet linen wrung by giant hands that shook towards the end of each wrench so her viscera quivered. Her cries and guttural grunts of effort sounded alien, remote. Between them she gasped in outrage and trembled with exhaustion.

Archias urged, 'Good, but try harder. We can't do the work for you.'

She'd no strength to expel her baby into a hostile world but was powerless to prevent it. The sensations were so rapid and confused she couldn't say she felt the birth but the tearing sensation faded and a slipperiness escaped her. The crouching forms of Archias and the midwife hid the baby from her sight. She heard the rasp of a knife through grit and Archias' voice, harsh with anxiety, 'Get it out of here before it cries.'

He wanted to shield her from the loss of a child on whom she'd once looked with love. Meddlesome fool! That decision should have been hers. His ambiguous words didn't even tell her if she was bereaved of a son or a daughter. She watched the midwife's retreating back and her soul went with it. Charis bent and kissed her, her body racked with sobs.

'Don't cry! I was exposed as a baby and think how happy I am now.'

'One more word, girl,' snapped Archias, 'and I'll have you put out of the room.'

He pushed Thaïs' hand hard against Nerysa's belly and whispered, 'Press here. Hard. Lepidus let his steward play at marriage. Let's see if he wants him to play mothers and fathers.'

Thaïs mumbled, 'Do you know the risk? Suppose..'

Archias looked back over his shoulder and shrugged. 'I'm in a gambling mood.'

CHAPTER LII

June 173

Meus ille, meus. Tellure cadentem aspexi atque unctam genitali carmine fovi poscentemque novas tremulis ululatibus auras inserui vitae. Quid plus tribuere parentes?

He's mine! All mine! As soon as I saw him on the ground fighting for his first breath I gave him his name and ushered him into the world. Could a natural parent have done more? Statius. Silvae V v 52-78

D emetrius found haymaking all but over. It had been a good year. There was no reason to linger once he saw his master's barns full. Even before he opened the door of the house he caught the excitement within. Old Hypnos rose unusually promptly, his chain chinking jauntily, his step light and quick across the hall. He wept as Demetrius stepped into the cool of the house.

'The master will be right pleased to see you, sir, Marcus Archias has been with your wife since the third hour.'

As he washed and rubbed him down, Polybius said anxiously, 'Our Lucius has been asking for you.'

Lucius was prowling around the tablinum, fraught from fourteen hours of solitary dread. His relief at the sight of Demetrius seemed tinged with resentment. Leaving the door ajar, they paced the room together, straining their ears for every sound. Each plied the other with wine. Demetrius sensed he was expected to say something soothing and tried, 'Master, remember Tiresias. The gods had him live as man and woman so he could tell them which sex had most joy of love. He came down on the distaff side.'

'Did he bear a child?'

'I don't know, perhaps not.'

'That must even the score. Didn't Medea say she'd rather serve three times in the front line than bear a child? But then, she never tried the front line, did she? How do you suppose it compares, say with battle wounds or flogging?'

'The screams are worse.'

'Is she screaming? Would we hear it?'

'I can't imagine her screaming.'

'Can't you? I can. It would be unjust to blame you because I gave her to you but you can't imagine what this is like for me.'

Cyrus and Adrian were too slow for Iris. She burst through the door, screaming and flung herself at Lucius' feet.

'Master, make them stop it! She's in agony and they sit there doing nothing. Make them give her a draught.'

Lucius seized her with feverish strength and hurled her into the atrium.

'Take her outside,' he thundered, 'and beat some manners into her.'

Demetrius bolted the door.

'Master, the girl's excitable. Don't let her alarm you.'

'Perhaps she should have a draught.'

'Master, Archias is a pupil of Galen. You couldn't have done better by her. Remember, even without help, most of them don't die.'

'What do I care for most of them? I care about my own girl, my beloved. I remember you asking me for her, praising her courage, her endurance - as if you were buying a horse. You've no idea what Propertius meant by 'reading in the arms of an educated girl.' Did you deceive me, I wonder? No, I don't think so. You just never knew her. Do you feel anything for her?'

Demetrius lowered his eyes. 'I've no complaints of her.'

'But I've complaints of *you*. You made a drudge of her and whipped her and now you're killing her. No, don't look like that. I said I don't blame you. But try to understand. If she…you've lost a well-trained underslave. I'll buy you another, as red-haired and docile as you like. But I worship her in my very marrow. I couldn't replace her. If she.. she'll take with her everything I respect in myself.'

'You were a good man, master, before you loved her. The gods don't persecute the just. They'll spare her for your sake.'

***

They played tabula for hours, Lucius mustering sufficient concentration to win a hundred sesterces off his slave. When they heard footsteps in the ala, he set his face and walked with measured pace into the crowded atrium, wishing, not for the first time in his life, that it was his place to follow Demetrius. But Archias directed his smiling nod beyond him and, as Demetrius made to leave before waiting to be dismissed, laid a restraining hand on his arm. Relief gave way to annoyance. Couldn't the fellow tell which one of them had borne the waiting in the purest agony? Had he forgotten who'd be settling his bill?

Prefects cleared a space and the midwife laid the child naked on the ground before him, the child who, yet unborn, had played with him in the garden. Eyes, wide with intelligence, gazed up into his; calm and enquiring. An overpowering emotion swept through Lucius; an affinity, an unbounded empathy, as though this new spirit, unabashed by its own helplessness, was his second self. He'd give his life to defend it and die of rage if hurt should ever touch it. Nor could he bear, for another moment, that it should be enslaved. He bent and scooped up the warm, wet bundle, sense of occasion to the fore, his voice vibrant. 'I declare this boy is free. He is Lucillus Marius Sciens, the darling of this house and the delight of his patron. May all the gods favour him.'

He turned to Demetrius. 'Take him to his mother. She will raise him for me. She will be my chief slave mistress, responsible only to me.'

CHAPTER LIII

June 173

Ὁ χρόνος οὖν ἡμιν βοηθει. Δυνασαι γαρ δοκειν επταμηνιαιον εκ Διονυσιου τετοκεναι

Time is on our side. We can make it look as though it's a seven month child.. Chariton. Chaereas and Callirhoë 2.10

D emetrius was stunned by the ease with which his master could transform a life on a whim. He felt no jealousy, only elation that Nerysa had survived. Normally, he'd have been shy to enter a birthing room but, with a duty to perform, he didn't hesitate. Nerysa lay ashen in the bed. Exhaustion he'd expected, but not that look of utter defeat.

She came alive when she saw the baby in his arms. He repeated the master's words with due ceremony so they were heard by all the slaves crowded into the room. Nerysa took the baby and put him to her breast. She didn't seem to have understood. *He* understood and was overwhelmed with gratitude. Lucius hadn't been able to save his brother from abuse but he'd stretched out his hand and removed his brother's child from all possible harm. He tried to explain but her whispered replies were indignant.

'He's not Lucius' son. He's *your* son.'

'You've been alone with him. Everyone thinks the child is his.'

'But *he* knows he's not.'

'Let's imagine what would happen if he were. He was slave born. Lucius couldn't recognise him. He couldn't adopt him or make him his heir. He could only do as he's done.'

'But you're still his father.'

'I'm not and you must never say I am. He's the master's favourite.'

'Then who's his father?'

'He doesn't need a father, he has a patron.'

'So what are you?'

'I'm to be his tutor, a post I'm honoured to hold.'

She was still protesting when Lucius arrived. Seeing the three of them on the bed, he frowned. Demetrius shot to his feet.

'Demetri, why is my slave mistress giving suck like a peasant? Didn't you think to hire a nurse?'

The baby, handed to Thaïs, began to scream. His face, contorted in rage, flushed dark as a rowanberry and he howled like a pack of hounds on a bare montain. Thaïs looked inquiringly at Lucius who looked back at her in dismay. The favourite was passed to his mother but his fury only increased. Eventually, he found his own way to the breast, seizing it between qivering jaws and drawing comfort as though from Nerysa's toes. Then his face drained ethereally pale, the only sound in the room was of gulps and contented snuffles and Lucius said with decision, 'We shan't need a nurse. My darling must have whatever pleases him.'

He stayed to see his pet fed and swaddled and put to sleep in his mother's arms. The admiring crowd retired and Erinna, Charis and Flora bedded down behind a screen; worn out with excitement and pounding up and down the back stairs with hot oil and old linen. Demetrius sat on the bed and held Nerysa's hand in the flickering light. She kept her voice low but insisted on discussing her son's status. She mentioned Lucius' cupbearers and letter carriers; not an ugly or straight-haired one among them. Her voice trailed off in confusion but eventually he understood she was asking if Lucius meant to keep her son as a catamite.

'Nerysa, he's let everyone believe the child is his. He'll bring him up with devoted care. Don't you understand? Our child will never know slavery. He's a free man. He'll be rich, loved and secure. Aren't you happy for him?'

'If the arrangement pleases you, I won't cavil at it.'

But he thought she did. For the next few days, she was seldom not in tears. The child attacked her hungrily every hour. Uncomfortable and exhausted, she feared for his health and her own, convinced she'd lost her husband's love and her master's favour. Reason couldn't reach her. Only Charis' sleepless devotion seemed to bring her a degree of comfort.

***

At nine days old, Lucillus was bathed, expensively oiled and dressed in silk. Demetrius, in his wedding clothes, came for him. Nerysa knew her fears were irrational but that didn't make them less real.

'Promise you won't let anyone hurt him?'

'No one's going to hurt him.'

'Lucius hasn't changed his mind?'

'He hasn't.'

'Tell me again where you're taking him.'

'Lucius has to make a sworn statement of his birth and freed status before seven witnesses so he'll be able to claim citizenship when he comes of age. After that we're going to have a party.'

He was gone for hours. She was too morbidly afraid to be reassured by the sound of his wails as they crescendoed up the stairs. Demetrius handed him back with a guilty look.

'He was happy until a moment ago. Lucius was sure a drop of old Falernian couldn't hurt him.'

'You gave him *wine*? You're thoroughly irresponsible. The pair of you.'

She took the baby anxiously and gasped to see a gold locket around his neck. The bulla was the badge of freeborn childhood. He wasn't entitled to it but it was the pledge that Lucius would sweeten his life. She gazed in wonder while Demetrius sat on the bed and cracked hazelnuts.

'Publius Severus sends you his warm congratulations.'

'Severus? Where did you see him?'

'Here in the house. He's just witnessed your son's manumission.'

'Then he thinks, that when he asked Lucius to sell me, I was already carrying his child.'

'What else should he think?'

'Does he think he offended Lucius?'

'He thinks he's a very dark horse. Masters do sometimes free a slave born child and love it as their own. Everyone's told his slave or freedman sired it and everyone pretends to believe it. Now Lucius hasn't claimed to have got your boy but he hasn't denied it. That's what's causing the sensation.' He shook his head in obvious concern. 'I fear he's not being prudent. His friends rejoice for him but he's flouting convention and society won't forgive him.'

'Couldn't you deny it for him?'

'What? Humiliate him publicly and sour his affection for the boy. Why would I do that?'

She was out of her depth. Clinging to his hand, she felt as though he were comforting her as she drowned rather than pulling her to safety. She waved away the silver bowl of festive nuts and wept more uncontrollably than ever.

CHAPTER LIV

July 173 - June 174

Tolerance of adultery is infamous on the part of a free man. On the part of a freedman with respect to his master, it is the effect of a proper sense of gratitude. On the part of a slave, it is duty pure and simple. History of private life P Ariès & G Duby

D emetrius marvelled at the cavalcade of luxuries borne across the peristyle to the new room. Hip baths of transparent alabaster, embroidered linen in sandalwood chests, carved tables and jewelled cups followed the high-backed chair and footstool designed for the enlightened modern lady who nursed her own child. He was disturbed by the gold earrings she was given on her birthday and the magnificent garnet necklace at the Saturnalia. For the Matronalia, in March, it was a rope of Indian pearls, plump and milky as mistletoe berries. What disconcerted him most was the diaphanous, apricot silk dress, thoroughly unsuitable for a matron, which came for the feast of Venus in April.

A short time before, he'd been harrowed with fear for her. That she should be alive and well enough to gratify her master would have crowned his dearest hopes. But his hopes and fears were changing. Lucius had never spoken of any woman as he'd spoken the day Lucillus was born. His feeling ran deeper than Demetrius had suspected and wouldn't be satisfied in a single night. All reason argued for complaisance but something fierce and unservile had stirred in him and rebelled against it. He wouldn't leave her to struggle alone without the comfort of his body.

Ambivalence was the agony. He couldn't bring himself to plead his own cause but neither could he plead his master's with enough conviction to sway her. The more he insisted he could condone her adultery, the less she believed him. Nor could he have described to Lucius her extraordinary indifference to his gifts. Every woman in Rome, from the lowest drudge to the noblest lady, knew the price of her favours. She was being tempted as if she were a senator's wife and didn't seem to understand the value of anything. When he pointed it out to her, she suggested they sell the presents to raise the price of her freedom. Ingratitude so brazen it made his head spin.

'You forget yourself, Nerysa, your master invites where he could compel. He's indulgent, that's no reason to be offensive.'

'Then what shall we do with these?'

'They're too grand for my wife. When you're his mistress it'll be a different matter. I'll keep them in the strong box.'

Had he refused freedom so often just to rebuff Lucius? If so, it had been unworthy and he was justly punished. He and Nerysa were caught like beasts in a trap. Lucius wouldn't free either of them unless she accommodated him and she was adamant she wouldn't. He could afford to buy his freedom but only if it were on offer. He could argue that it was unreasonable of Lucius to refuse the sale and ask some free man of standing to intercede on his behalf or even bring a lawsuit. But who could be persuaded to insult Lucius by helping his own slave to defy him? Besides, the law frowned on masters who freed slaves under the age of thirty and Lucius would have a watertight case. It was unusual to free anyone who'd had control of his master's finances. If irregularities were found in the accounts after he was freed, he couldn't legally be tortured and there'd be no way of getting to the bottom of the matter. Then there was Nerysa. Absconding, a fault that would have to be declared on sale, had wiped thousands off her value but she was still a luxury item. He couldn't afford her. They'd have to continue as they were, camped on the edge of a cliff.

Nerysa remained respectful and loving to him except for one act of defiance over staffing the nursery. Charis, Flora and Filix he approved. He even endorsed the odd proposal that Xenia should be taken on as an adviser. Xenia was overjoyed, having never thought to be useful again, and he saw that she was useful. She'd been a martinet with slaves in training but she was indulgent with the baby, rocking him and crooning, hour upon hour. Iris was the one he vetoed.

'She caught our Lucius' eye once before. She'll be trying it again.'

'I hope she succeeds.'

'And takes over all this?'

'I don't want it. I just want us to be as we were.'

All six women slept in the nursery and he'd have felt himself a bachelor again if Nerysa hadn't slipped up and down the backstairs so often. She worked in the office for longer periods as the child grew. He wouldn't have imposed the work on her but she said it made a welcome change from nursery routine and he was too cheered by her presence to discourage her.

'I've never heard,' he said, 'of a tutor being forbidden access to his charge.'

'Lucius didn't forbid you. He just said, as you've so many other duties, you might consider the post an honorary one and not come unless you're sent for.'

'And who'll send for me?'

'I shall. Often.'

'Don't risk offending him. We've all too much to lose, especially the boy.'

'His obsession with Lucillus has nothing to do with me. It's something extraordinary that happened between them.'

'I think he even begins to believe he could be his own child.'

'He couldn't possibly think that.'

'We know you missed your bleed in September, before you were alone with him. You carried ten months because your blood is cool. Perhaps Lucius thinks he was a seven month child.'

'Why won't you believe me? He's never touched me and he knows it.'

'Don't cry, beloved, it's not important, either way.'

CHAPTER LV

June 173 – May 174

Incipe parve puer risu cognoscere matrem.

Little boy, begin, to recognise your mother with a smile. Virgil Eclogue IV 60

Lucius marvelled at his own patience with Nerysa and saw it as proof of a unique attachment. But there was another love in his life - an exacting tyrant. Wet clay in those tiny, in-coordinate hands, he haunted the nursery to dandle and admire, worry and instruct. In other men's houses, he consulted matrons and venerable nurses and hurried home to insist that their suggestions be carried out, even where they were conflicting or mutually exclusive. One frightening fact he learned was that baby boys could develop a rupture from crying. He never criticised Nerysa but he dealt summarily with anyone else who brought tears to the child's eyes and often heard the nursery staff muttering prayers to Cuba, the goddess who keeps children quiet in their cots.

The regime was clearly ideal for the child thrived under it. Every day he'd a new skill which Lucius rewarded. The house was swamped in rattles and bells, soft balls, hoops and sticks, quoits and, for quiet moments, model animals and soldiers. He was twenty days old when Lucius brought him a silver drinking cup, spinning it before his eyes so the metal fired in the light. Lucillus ignored the silver, instead he held Lucius' eyes for a long moment and his face broke suddenly into a wide, toothless smile. Lucius felt his knees dissolve.

'Did everyone see that? He smiled at me!'

'Oh no, master,' said Xenia, 'he just burped.'

With withering scorn, he eyed Xenia from her shrivelled face, down the length of her stained and spotted apron to her toes, writhing with embarrassment in her open sandals. He gave a jerk of his head and she vanished.

'What's the stupid old hag doing here anyway?' he asked irritably. 'She looks about ready for the columbarium.'

'She's very diligent and careful of the infant, master,' Nerysa said gravely, 'and she was your father's own nurse.'

'I hope she'd more sense then. Wind, MeHercule!' He searched her face, 'Do *you* think he burped?'

'I think, if it were wind, he'd do it randomly. But he smiled when you smiled at him and held you so firmly with his eyes I'm sure he must have smiled for you.'

'Does he smile for you?'

'Sometimes, when I smile at him.'

'And for Demetrius?'

'No, master.'

Lucius courted those smiles with unremitting zeal. He was only ever firm on two points. Lucillus liked to move freely. Lucius was awed by his rages but knew that, if he were not tightly swaddled, he wouldn't grow straight, he'd be misshapen. Lucius couldn't have borne that for him, so he gave orders that he should be tightly swaddled, added the problematic rider that his appalling wails should be calmed, then retired to the deepest recess of his library. Lucillus grew straight bones, strong muscles and teeth of piercing sharpness. Before he was a year old, he bit his mother's breast. A wet nurse was instantly engaged and Lucius hardened his heart in anticipation of fearful protests. But Lucillus accepted her graciously, another willing slave for his retinue.

CHAPTER LVI

October 173 – July 174

O genus infelix humanum, talia divis cum tribuit facta atque iras adiunxit acerbas

Unhappy humans who ascribe such actions to gods and attribute bitter wrath to them as well. Lucretius De Rerum Natura V 1194

According to Demetrius' theory, blatant privilege should have earned jealousy and spite from the household but Nerysa found the reverse was the case. Lucillus was adored and everyone, however poor, brought him presents. He was carried aloft around the house and given everything his prehensile hands stretched out for. As he grew, he'd unrestricted licence to crash around the atrium in his wheeled baby-walker. His minders were terrified he would fall into the impluvium and almost as terrified that, if they tried to prevent him, his protests would earn them a beating. As soon as he could toddle, he appeared at dinner parties, rattling his ivory money box at the amused guests who never denied him an offering. Demetrius expressed misgiving; it was cruel to teach a child to expect what life couldn't fulfil. Lucillus was a freedman; he wasn't a princeling and shouldn't be reared as one. His attitude wounded Nerysa. He made the routine enquiries expected of a conscientious tutor but he wasn't affectionate. If he visited the nursery, it was her he came to see.

She'd recovered from her confinement and knew she was expected to fall in love. Lack of privacy in the bustling nursery gave her some protection. She worked tirelessly for Lucillus and also as a scribe and reckoned Lucius would hardly send for her to wait at table as well.

He had the room adjoining the nursery fitted up as a day room and visited her there. He lent her books, bringing them himself and staying to discuss them. She always knew when to expect him. One of the nursery staff would spy him striding across the peristyle, a present for Lucillus in his hand. That gave her time to wake Lucillus and put him to the breast.

At last, he caught her unawares. He'd sent her grape juice, the first of the new pressing, filtered through snow and she sat sipping it as he came into the day room. She jumped to her feet putting the cup aside and he seized it, pressing his lips to the rim in the place where hers had been. There was no mistaking the passionate gesture or the accompanying look. The closed season was over.

He made the usual enquiries about Lucillus and about her health. For the first time in her life, she stooped to exaggerate minor aches and pains; complaining of sore breasts, lack of sleep and backache. The deception was well punished. She was put to bed, the room was filled with flowers and Archias was puzzled to be called out on an unnecessary visit. But, after this brief respite, he made his wishes increasingly plain. She was able to slap him down firmly at the Saturnalia. Even during a wild game of hide and seek when he trapped her in a broom cupboard, she resisted him haughtily without offending him in the least. Confident she must inevitably fall to him, and soon, it seemed to amuse him to play the suppliant teased by a disdainful lady.

Everything she enjoyed was his gift. Sitting in his armchair, she ate the dainty food he sent and wore the fashionable clothes he'd chosen. Lucillus was a living reminder of his generosity. She couldn't feel his arms around her neck, hear his sweet lisp or smile into his adorable face, without reflecting that Lucius could have had him left on the public rubbish dump by a mere wave of his hand or a single word of command.

The freedom of his garden was a joy. Strolling along the colonnade, she passed the alley that led to the slaves' yard, where she hadn't been for a year, and heard its distant bustle with gratitude and a pang of guilt.

A sudden crack above her head made her look into the tangled branches above. A swallow flew out in alarm, a wisp of straw in its beak but a bird couldn't have cracked a branch. She heard footsteps on the pergola. The canopy of rosebuds swayed and parted as a round, red-faced man dropped across her path and collapsed at her feet. *Fat men ought not to walk on pergolas,* she thought. Then she recognised him. The cook she'd once employed as a taster.

'Whatever are you doing, Phago?' she asked, her fear turning to anger. 'You're out of bounds.'

He began to writhe and moan, seizing the hem of her dress and mouthing it as if he meant to eat it, whimpering that he'd be whipped unless she pleaded with the master for him.

'Why? What have you done?'

'Truffles...from master's plate. Kitchen empty. I thought, "They look good but are they really succulent enough for Himself? Perhaps I ought just to... check." It was! You can't imagine! I thought, "Supposing they aren't all as good? Perhaps.. just to be sure..." Misery! Apicius was behind the door.'

Odd, for the kitchen to be empty! And why hadn't Apicius punished him summarily? It was a trivial matter to come to Lucius' ears and certainly not a matter for her, who remembered stealing bread from Demetrius' tray.

'Phago, that was wrong. Trays of pork and prawns and cream cakes come back from the dining room all the time but we never touch them unless Apicius gives them out. You're not a novice, you knew that. A slave keeps his eyes, hands and tongue under strict control. Whipping's not the worst of it. The master won't trust you again in any matter, great or small.'

He lurched to his feet, his face cracking into a winning smile.

'I don't expect you to help me for nothing! Look!' and, snatching a leather bag from his belt, he jingled a fistful of silver coins, spinning one onto the ground to prove it rang true. He tore out trophies in feverish triumph like a mountebank at a country fair.

'Look! Gold anklet! Pretty isn't it? And a charm from the temple of Isis. Powerful magic!'

'Phago!' she whispered, 'Did you steal all these too?'

'Oh no! The money's mine.. mostly: Rhea gave me the anklet, Acte left it her. Carbo gave me the charm. Everyone'll bless you for helping me!'

She felt sorry for him, he was a sensuous youth. A sturdier soul would have taken the whipping and hung on to his savings.

'I'll speak to my husband. He knows you helped me once. He might choose this time to reward you.'

He wailed again, 'It must be you! Himself will only do it for you.'

'It's not my place. But I promise to speak to my husband.'

When she mentioned it to Demetrius, his reply puzzled her.

'You were adroit but do you think it's wise to thwart Lucius so flagrantly?'

'I don't understand.'

'Don't you? He doesn't give a ball of fluff whether this fellow's flogged or not but he'd toss you his reprieve as a love gift and show everyone in the house he's yours to command.'

She blenched and he spoke with forced lightness.

'An unusual gift – a wretched slave's undying gratitude! He can see jewellery doesn't impress you.'

'Then he sees more than Phago. He offered me an anklet. It looked valuable. He said Acte left it to Rhea but surely slaves can't will things, their property reverts to the master when they die.'

'Lucius lets his slaves dispose of their possessions, within the house, and respects their wills as if they were legally valid. It's an enlightened practice but not without problems. Gerion, the old doorman for instance. His wits left him long before his life. He used to will things and forget. After he died, we found dozens of pieces of pot, all signed and witnessed, giving the same things to different people. I had deals worth half a million on my table but the house was in such turmoil, I had to shelve them and dispose of cheap beads, cracked lamps and leaky oil flasks as fairly as I could. No doubt I committed injustices that still rankle in some quarters.'

'If the bequests had the force of law, it sounds more like a problem for Lucius.'

'I did ask him.' he laughed. 'He said, "Demetri, you're the procurator; whatever you order here is right, so how could you make a mistake? Just get on with it and let's have a quiet house."'

'That was helpful.'

'I couldn't blame him. I'd only the house and businesses to manage and he'd given me control of them. He was fending off prospective guardians and slighted relations, forging his way in society and getting onto a career path. I went everywhere with him, of course, but I could only stand behind him and keep my eyes and ears open.'

'That's a great help – to be someone's eyes and ears.'

'Except that my presence seemed to rile some people – especially his relations. When we took over, the house was in chaos. The plague was rife – we'd two or three deaths and ten new cases every day. I'll never forget Successus coming to take my orders for the first time. The old steward was dead. Timothy, his deputy, had been freed and opted to leave. Successus was next in line. I don't know what he expected but it can't have included having a raw, country lad set over him. From the way his nose curled, I guessed he could smell dung on my feet.

He said, "Sir," - the word was too big for his throat. "Sir, I need to know what provision you've made for the disposal of the corpses."'

'I hope you didn't laugh at him like that.'

'Hermes! No! I was terrified. In those days I felt as though I'd been thrown astride a bolting horse and had to master it before it plunged over a cliff.'

'That's how I feel now. Tell me what to do.'

'I know what *I* must do. Find 35,000 quickly. I'll go to Ostia tomorrow. I don't know how this will turn out but, if he should have a moment of madness and offer me the chance to buy my freedom, I don't want to be short of the full price.'

'Why Ostia?'

'There are men there who buy my services and I can speculate a bit – carefully, of course.'

'Will you leave me alone here?'

'You're safe. Why would he force you when he'll get everything he wants by waiting? Shall I tell him you'll cry if Phago's flogged?'

She didn't sleep in the nursery that night but stayed in his bed through the hours of darkness. She'd dreaded him going away but her fears were groundless. Lucius visited Lucillus but was cold and distant to her, making it obvious he knew where she'd spent the previous night. Polybius wouldn't betray Demetrius. It must be one of the women she'd chosen. Not Xenia. Lucius ignored her. Perhaps Flora, too innocent to understand the significance of what she said.

For several days, the nursery had neither visit nor word from him. Then Iris was summoned and returned to announce that the master would come that afternoon. Nerysa bathed Lucillus in scented water, oiled his wriggling body and dressed him to delight his patron. Her loosely girdled tunic slipped low off her shoulder as she splashed and wrestled with him. Iris ran her fingers along the fine scars on her back and began to remind her how she'd once felt about Demetrius, how she'd nearly died of the beating he'd ordered and how Lucius' care had saved her. Nerysa stared in amazement, why was she bringing up old history? Iris warmed to her theme, contrasting Demetrius with Lucius, who was so generous and forbearing. Nerysa struggled to keep bitterness out of her voice but Lucillus, sensing her distress, began to whimper. She comforted him, then whispered, 'I trusted you as my friend and you betrayed me to the master.'

Iris began to cry, 'He said if I persuaded you to love him I needn't be sent to work on the land in Sicily.'

She'd been roughly handled the day Lucillus was born. Adrian and Successus had beaten her brutally. Of course, she was terrified of Lucius. Nerysa took her hand.

'Then tell him,' she said, 'that I love him but I'm afraid the gods will punish me if I break my marriage vows.'

Iris drew back her hand and Nerysa noticed a new amulet. Looking up, she saw the matching necklace.

When Lucius came he was smiling. Lucillus toddled to him with outstretched arms and cries of joy and he swung him up into his arms, kissed him and passed him to Charis. Taking Nerysa by the hand, he pulled her into the dayroom and leant against the door.

'Now,' he said, 'what's this nonsense about you fearing impiety? I bound you in your vows. I can release you.'

'Master, I didn't swear to you, I swore to the immortal gods whose wrath is more dreadful even than yours. They could punish me with death, a disfiguring disease or the loss of my little son.'

'No, beloved, you won't succumb to sickness and desert your master. You're too strong and brave for that.'

He drew her to him and she trembled like a puppy feeling the force of his master's foot for the first time. Not, in truth, because she feared the gods but because she was suddenly conscious of his power to harm Demetrius as well as herself. He smiled indulgently.

'Of course!' he murmured, 'I always forget, you're foreign. You don't understand religion. I can explain.'

Lucillus, who couldn't believe he was being wilfully neglected, battered the door with his fists. Lucius could never resist him. He let him in and they spent a calm family afternoon together.

After that, he came regularly at Lucillus' siesta time with treatises on philosophy. They discussed the reasons for pain and suffering and their relation to the gods' displeasure. She inclined to the view that such misfortune as people did not actually cause themselves or each other was distributed randomly but she was interested in his attempt to trace a moral pattern in the workings of fate. It seemed a man's actions did bear on his fortunes but only as one variable in a complex formula he didn't fully explain. Educated people, it seemed, believed in one god, Zeus, who sat outside the universe, immersed in contemplation of himself. Of mankind, he was oblivious, though, presumably, not entirely unaware of those who blasphemed or neglected their religious duties. She strove to keep him intellectually stimulated and his mind away from dalliance but it was a strain. Passion appeared to stimulate his wit while hers was dulled by the certainty of ultimate failure. He proceeded patiently as one who craved her affection and admiration and knew that, if he behaved badly, he wouldn't get them. He demonstrated, to his own apparent satisfaction, that she couldn't offend the gods by giving her master the devotion due to him.

She thought of Iris, terrified, threatened with banishment, then decked out in jewellery to console her for betraying a friend. If she couldn't break his expectations on the rock of her constancy they would all be cast adrift, rudderless, into a whirlpool of lust and jealousy.

Iris was radiant. She spared no detail of the bliss she'd regained in the master's bed, catalogued his skills as a lover, compared them favourably with those of his steward and intoned the old proverb, 'There's no shame in doing what the master orders.' Nerysa, unwilling to listen, escaped to the secretaries' office, having work to finish. She started violently as Lucius entered and dismissed the other scribes. It was unheard of for him to come to the secretaries' room.

'Demetrius talks about you.' he said, 'Boasts, I should say. He says, for instance, that you take shorthand.'

'Well enough to satisfy a steward, perhaps.'

'I need to draft a speech; not just the words but the tone of voice and gesture I plan for each phrase. You must note them too. Let's see how you keep up.'

She took the dictation on wax and said she'd need the afternoon to make a fair copy. He said he'd wait and paced the room inspecting records in a desultory way. Even standing bent over her work, she felt his eyes on her. He made a turn of the room and then stopped behind her, peering over her shoulder. She heard his quick breath then felt a sting as his lips cleaved to the nape of her neck. She pulled away. The room spun violently. She looked up at him, puzzled, and crumpled to the floor at his feet.

CHAPTER LVII

July 174

δει μαλιστα τουτω χρησθαι......τον ανδρα και την γυναικα......μη σπειροντας εξ ων ουδεν αυτοις φυεσθαι θελουσιν

Don't sow where you don't want to reap. Plutarch. Advice to Bride and groom.

D emetrius rode home to a storm. The master was beside himself with rage and the house quaked. Summoned to account for himself, Demetrius stayed outwardly calm. Did he consider how it affected the dignity of a chief slave mistress to be forced to breed like a caged dormouse supplying the table? There was more in the same crude vein and Demetrius' face hardened into impassivity. He would absorb his master's rage dumbly. But when it was put to him that he cared nothing for his wife's health and had shown contempt for the generosity of his master's gift; when he was accused of wanting to see her dead rather than in her master's bed, he was stung into reply. Sick at heart and bewildered, he could offer only the truth. He had been careful. Since Lucillus' birth, he hadn't even trusted himself to spill his seed in time. He'd loved her like a boy. Lucius was hoarse with dismay.

'Demetrie, could she have played us false?'

Demetrius knew that she'd never been alone except with himself or Lucius so they were back to the beginning. He was to blame; so clumsy and incompetent he'd spilt himself like a peasant slobbering his pottage into the rugosities of his toga.

'Great gods, Demetrie! How often do we send a girl to the country? Two or three times a year? This one twice in two years and you weren't trying?'

Ingratitude was the bitterest reproach a man could fling at any dependent; child, freedman or slave. Lucius flung it without restraint. Demetrius was made to feel he had illicitly borrowed the master's crystal and clumsily smashed it to pieces. But when the recriminations were exhausted, they agreed on the remedy. It was not simply a question of Nerysa's safety. Lucillus was unique. There would be no other child in the house to share his consequence.

Nerysa lay in the room where she had been prepared for marriage. Her arms were bandaged because Archias had bled her. A brisk bleed often provoked miscarriage but, in her case, had not, so herb water was steaming in the hip bath. Potions and pessaries of increasing strength were ranged on a table. She would sit in scalding water and wait for her pains. When she was in the grip of agony, Archias would be called. Meanwhile, the household prayed for a safe outcome. She was privileged. Ladies were protected in this way from the dangers and discomforts of childbearing. Slaves did their duty and increased their master's stock.

Demetrius held her hand, enumerated the reasons why this was the sensible course and begged her forgiveness. She lifted a feeble hand to his face, feeling it was she who should apologise for her exceptional and embarrassing fertility. When Thaïs warned him that the master was approaching, he left through the side door that led to the bathhouse. Lucius kissed her hands and wept, telling her how deeply he felt for what she must suffer. Demetrius had put her in dange; *he* was trying to rescue her. She couldn't doubt his real fear for her.

'I've borne one child safely, master, Apicius' woman has borne twins.'

He was not so sanguine; he and Demetrius knew of many women who'd survived a first confinement only to perish at the second.

'The empress has fourteen children! How dare we rail against the gods when we're bereaved if we, ourselves, show that we don't value life. I knew a girl – Acte - who worked in the kitchen here. She had an abortion and she died, not straight away but she was never well after, then she died.'

He was silent. They both knew abortion carried its own dangers and that, if she was unlucky, she could be dead before nightfall. He lost his nerve.

'I can't constrain you in this matter. Do what seems best to you. Whatever you choose, you'll have expert care.'

He left the room, shaking with emotion and she got up from the couch, still faint from the bleed, and went back to work.

CHAPTER LVIII

July 174

te regere imperio populos, Romane, memento, (haec tibi erunt artes)) pacique imponere morem, parcere subiectis et debellare superbos.

Roman, you are to rule the whole world with your power, remember, this will be your special genius; to impose peace under the law; to spare the humble and subdue the proud. Vergil Aeneid VI 851-3

Lucius had one purpose; to be away from Rome for at least a year. If fate dealt harshly with his girl he needn't return straight away, he could distract himself abroad until the vividness of her presence had faded from his house. If she survived he would come home and claim her.

It had often been put to him that he should further his career by taking a foreign posting. Before leaving for the northern wars, four years before, the emperor, Marcus Aurelius, had singled him out as just the sort of young man, from exactly the stratum of society, he wished to bring forward. Being on friendly terms with influential men, Lucius soon had letters of recommendation and meant to deliver them to the emperor by the fastest route.

He wouldn't take Demetrius. Though he'd be less comfortable without him, he wanted to indicate that his behaviour had made him unserviceable. Besides, he wasn't looking for comfort. He had plain tunics packed, rough leather cloaks and heavy boots. His party attached itself to a group of official couriers making whirlwind speed along the Via Flaminia. With fresh horses every ten miles they didn't wait behind slow moving vehicles, they simply drove them off the road. They made Ancona in two days and had a smooth passage to Split. After Split, the journey became less agreeable but the military road carried them through the mountains and high above the Danube marshes.

On the second day after his arrival in Sirmium, around the eighth hour, he came into the imperial presence. Three men stood behind the seated Marcus who was thumbing through scrolls. Lucius recognised Pompeianus and Pertinax. The third, a swarthy individual, he took to be Severus' brother, Septimius Geta. All were soldiers. He'd expected an administrative post. If he'd thought he might be offered a military one, he would certainly not have come. He knelt and Marcus held out his hand for him to kiss his ring then signed to him to stand.

'Greetings, Lepide,' he said with a smile. 'At long last, you've decided to put your talents at our service.' He turned to his aides. 'You know Lepidus, by repute, at least. I must confess I'd begun to think him too fond of his warm bed on a cold morning to volunteer for a post.'

The skin crinkled around his eyes and their expression was gentle. Lucius smiled back.

'My Lord, I do want to offer my services, such as they are.'

'These letters of recommendation are impressive; intelligent, pious, diligent, modest, trustworthy, judicious – they read like eulogies not testimonials.'

Pompeianus laughed. 'He's only two faults and one of them is about to be rectified.'

'We know it all already.' said Marcus, tossing the scrolls onto the table. 'Indeed, I often tell my son I want him to grow up to be like you.'

A shadow passed over his face. Lucius remembered that this sole surviving son was thirteen and already giving cause for concern.

'Like me, Lepidus lost his father young.' Marcus observed. 'But unlike me, no adoptive father came forward to sponsor him. It's a self-made man you see here.'

Lucius saw, from the approving smiles that he was to be popular, by imperial command.

'So Maecianus was your law teacher?' Marcus asked.

'Yes, my lord, and a kind patron.'

'He was my law teacher, too, so we've that in common. And you're shaping up well, winning your cases.'

Lucius wondered whether to confirm his reputation for modesty or make a bid for a legal post rather than a military one.

'My lord, I have been so fortunate as never to lose a case.'

Marcus seemed to suppress a smile. 'Well, don't take it to heart when you do.'

'How old are you?' asked Pompeianus.

Ah! They'd worked round to the second of his faults. He marshalled his defence.

'Twenty six, sir. I'm of full age to be married but not quite of age for a quaestor's position...so I planned to wait until -'

So! You want to be like Pompeianus here, the first in your family to become a senator. Well, be patient. It's an equestrian post I have in mind and one too onerous for a new bridegroom.'

Equestrian means Egypt, thought Lucius, *and there's a war on there.* One year in the army had been enough and he hadn't even seen action. Marcus stood. Beside his generals he was slighter than Lucius remembered and his manner less formal than it had been in Rome.

'We're about to go to the bath.' he said. 'Then I'll conduct the sacrifice and we'll have dinner. You'll join us, I hope? You don't despise campaign rations?'

Lucius regretted his Spartan packing but Cyrus and his team rose to the height of their game and sent him out looking quite fine enough for the barrack room meal that awaited him. From the trimmed beards and clipped hair of the other guests, he knew this was a working dinner, so he wouldn't get to meet the empress and admire her fabled beauty. His place beside Marcus favoured private conversation. He looked around the bare room in amazement. Marcus had been fabulously wealthy even as a private citizen. To call the meal frugal would have been to flatter it. Lucius couldn't have persuaded Apicius to serve such plain fare, even to the sick bay. Only bread was in ample supply; coarse black bread at that. There was a dish of beans and flakes of chicken in an onion broth, mixed leaves Lucius couldn't identify, some wild cherries and goats' cheese. Even so, it was many hours since breakfast. Lucius stretched out his hand then snatched it back. Marcus should help himself first. He spread out his napkin. Marcus looked at him with sweetness in his smile.

'Well, you've guessed something of what I have in mind?'

'From what you said, Lord Emperor,' you're thinking of Egypt.'

'There's a job to be done there. You might be the man.'

Lucius nodded, trying to seem neither eager nor reluctant.

'You're continuing your studies?'

'Yes, my lord, Maecianus recommended teachers to me.'

'And what do you value in a teacher?'

'Guidance on interpretation I think. After all, a parrot could learn to recite law codes.' Marcus' eyes widened. Lucius thought, *I'd better qualify that.*

'I mean, my lord, every child learns the twelve tablets but could they apply them? The cases that come to court don't seem to have read the text books. At least they make no effort to conform to the models.'

'You're right, of course.' Marcus said. 'Let's hear what you think to this one.'

Lucius tensed. Here was the test.

'A mother left an inheritance to her two sons and stipulated they were not to come into it until their father, her ex-husband, had died.'

'That's understandable. Anything they received while in their father's power would, technically, be his. So she wanted to make sure her ex-husband didn't get his hands on her money.'

'Exactly,' Marcus nodded. 'The will was sound. But the father and sons came before me to ask that the sons should receive their money because the father had legally emancipated them and set them free from his power. Would you grant their plea?'

This was obviously the trick question but Lucius couldn't see where the trick lay. His heart raced, he felt tight around the neck. He temporised, watching Marcus' face.

'Well, since the testator's intention was to prevent her ex-husband getting any of her money and he's given up his right to it, I imagine... Well, if she'd known he'd do that, she'd have been happy. So, yes, I'd allow them their inheritance.'

'Would you now?' Marcus pierced him with a look. 'Suppose the sons needed the money urgently and offered the father a cut to persuade him to emancipate them? In that case, wouldn't your judgement be to frustrate the woman's intentions and make a mockery of the law?'

That was it, Lucius thought. He'd failed the test and probably put himself in the front line of battle. But failure freed him to express what he thought about the law to someone who felt as passionately about it as he did himself. He could hardly make things worse.

'Lord Emperor, at the end of every case I've been involved in, I've asked myself if it's truly been resolved or if the seeds of future discord are buried in the judgement itself.'

'A sore skinned over?'

'Yes, my lord, or worse. So, I think, in this situation, there's no love lost between the parents or, probably, between the father and his sons. But they've met and cut a deal. If I allow them the money, they'll split it as they've agreed and live in peace. If I leave the sons with a vested interest in their father's death, I may be not so much honouring the letter of the law, as sowing mischief.'

'Young man, that's the judgement I gave and for exactly that reason! You've a subtle mind and more wisdom on those graceful shoulders than one could expect of your years.

'We can't tolerate civil disobedience in Egypt any longer. My dear friend, Cassius, will quell it with his usual thoroughness but...'

Marcus leant forward. Was he going to take some food? No. He lowered his voice and leaned closer to Lucius.

'In my view, rebellions don't happen by chance. Officials are not always as I could wish. If they're overbearing or even dishonest and unjust they spark revolt. Once Cassius has restored order, Rome must show her gracious face.'

The soldiers were eating all before them and their empty dishes were being replaced with full ones. How embarrassing, Lucius thought, if his guts were to rumble. When would Marcus help himself?

'I've too few men I trust to send abroad, ones who care about the happiness of the people we govern. I don't need testimonials to tell me you won't take bribes, despoil free-born virgins or steal civic art treasures. I just need to look into your eyes to see you're deep dyed with the love of justice, which you'll try to temper with mercy.'

'Then you do have a legal post in mind for me, my lord?' *Hermes, would Marcus never eat?*

'The appointment of deputy to the Registrar is in my personal gift. Lucian is old. I made him Registrar so he could enjoy a comfortable retirement. He needs a proxy to do his work without eclipsing him.'

'Lord Emperor, I am deeply honoured but I fear you have been led to overestimate my capabilities.'

'Eat, Lepide, put some heart into yourself.'

Marcus took a crumb of bread and a rocket leaf. Lucius had lost his appetite.

'Effectively, if not in name, I'd be the highest legal power in the province.'

'No one will question your judgements so it will fall to yourself to see that they're sound. Don't be afraid. Just make a bee-line for the truth. That comes naturally to you and truth can't hurt anyone.'

'The truth, as it seems to me, sir, is that I am wholly inadequate to the task you propose.'

'And you know it! Which makes you one in a million. I like this appointment, Lepide, it will do well. You lack experience but you've the right instincts. Better that than vice versa. Never be happy with surface appearance. Delve as deep as you can. Pay the closest attention to everything that's said in your court – I'm sure you always do; but try to get behind the words and into the speaker's mind. As soon as your concentration flags, adjourn.'

'Lord Emperor, I should work blithely, night and day, under a worthier man but I cannot –'

'Cannot, or will not? Lepide, are you going to refuse me?'

There was no hint of command; just a winsome smile and a cajoling in the eyes.

'My lord emperor knows that I couldn't refuse him anything, however small.'

'Don't despise small things. I promise you, no detail is ever unimportant. But, let's be realistic. You and I aren't going to bring about Plato's republic in this world, so rest content if the smallest thing goes well because the good of the commonwealth is made up of a multiplicity of small events, just as the universe is made up of atoms. Now we'll drink to your success.'

The dishes were removed and the wine was mixed and served.

'Don't be ambushed.' Marcus said. 'Arm yourself as I do. Every morning, when you wake, tell yourself, "Today, I shall meet villains, rogues, toadies, liars, cheats, the unwashed and the stupid." You mustn't be harsh with them. They can't help it. Some men are as naturally full of wickedness as figs are full of juice. Govern your temper. Allow free speech where you can.

'Now I must send you on your way with my blessing. You won't be alone. If ever you don't see clearly, stop and take the best advice you can. There's no shame in accepting help.'

'Am I to consult with Lucian?'

'He's slipping into dotage. Odd flashes of brilliance pierce through the miasma. Catch them. He won't explain. If you ask him, he'll have forgotten. But you can safely take inspiration from them because he's a good man and still steeped in wisdom.'

The party broke up when everyone had come forward to shake Lucius' hand and congratulate him. Septimius Geta hovered until rest had left, then said, 'Is your boy, Demetrius, with you?'

'No, he's not.'

'Or perhaps he's your freedman by now?'

'He's not.'

'Are you minded to sell?'

'My slave is not for sale.'

'When he is, may I have first refusal?'

'The question is academic.'

Lucius turned on his heel. He'd been ungracious to a social superior. He'd failed to govern his temper. That was a bad omen. He rode home in a daze, overcome by the enormity of the task that had been thrust on him.

Secretaries, scribes, hairdressers, cubicularii, litter-bearers and sixteen guards would accompany him to Egypt. Clothes and personal effects for all of them were packed and dispatched to Ostia.

'Nerysa, are you sad to see me go?' Lucius asked.

'All your slaves are sad, master, but they're happy for you and proud of your grand appointment. I'm happy for the Egyptians because they'll have a just and kindly judge.'

She looked up into his eyes. 'It's hard for an occupied people to live under a conqueror's yoke.'

'Egypt's been part of the empire for two hundred years. They must be used to it by now. Rebellion only brings chaos and makes life harder for everyone.'

'Those whose lives are already intolerable have nothing to lose.'

'I see that. I shall hold your words in my heart.'

He kissed her lips, delicate as petals, inhaled the scent of her hair and asked her to cut him a lock of it. To Demetrius he said nothing until, as he put his foot on the gang plank, he turned and saw him squinting out to sea. He felt suddenly foolish, bereaved and full of foreboding.

'I would take you,' he said, 'but someone must look to her and the child.'

'Master, everything of yours I shall look to and keep safe.'

CHAPTER LIX

JULY 174

The extremity of the isle is a rock, which is washed all round by the sea and has upon it a tower that is admirably constructed of white marble with many storeys. Strabo Geography XVII 30

D emetrius and Nerysa felt guilt and relief. A golden age dawned for them. Demetrius reasoned that he'd been unaware of her first pregnancy for nearly five months and she'd come to no harm, her second shielded them from detection. They worked together, slept together, revelled in each other. The shadow that hung over them had receded and they basked in the sun, their joy in the reprieve heightened because it was only temporary.

He took her to Ostia to see the harbours. She kept a memory of sapphire sky, sloping cedars and tawny brick so, whenever he stayed there, she could picture him working in the shipping office, sleeping in the flat above, strolling along the quayside or through the warehouses.

'You serve Lucius well.' she said, seeing another aspect of his work at first hand. 'Will he free you when he comes home?'

'Dearest, let's not deceive ourselves. He's no intention of freeing us.'

'Whatever *I* may have done, he promised *you* – to let you buy your freedom and give me a dowry. I don't care about the dowry. But he owes you so much. Why won't he relent?'

'Because he knows I'd rent a flat, however mean, and take you out of his house. I shouldn't leave his service. Even if I did, I'd still be his freedman and wait on him daily but he'd never see you again.'

She giggled, 'Wouldn't you take me to the third rate dinners he gives for his most vulgar clients?'

'Certainly not, but you wouldn't starve – I'd bring you home your share in my napkin. If I were a free man I'd make our fortune. We shouldn't have to live in an insula for long.'

He couldn't imagine living in a squalid tenement for so much as a day and the same thought evidently struck her because she smiled as she sank into his luxurious bed.

Within two months, he was summoned to Alexandria. He went to Ostia and arranged a passage, returning the same night to pack and delegate his duties. As he was to leave Polybius behind, a junior cubicularius was hastily briefed. Darius was a willing youth of unquestioned loyalty but hardly as supportive as the well trained and devoted Polybius. Nerysa was almost too stunned to take in his careful instructions. He seemed embarrassed that her work in the office, which had been voluntary, would now, in the absence of himself, two secretaries and a scribe, become necessary.

'I haven't had time to buy a new scribe. Adrian will look out for one but, in the meantime, you'll be sorely needed. He's in charge of the office; so, although your rank is nominally above his, when you work there, I must leave him authority over you. He'll be anxious and overbearing with me away. He knows he may not strike you and I know you won't take advantage of that but he may discipline you in other ways and you must defer to him absolutely.'

'I'll give him no cause to complain of me and, if he corrects me, I'll try to bear it meekly.'

'I'll be grateful for that. If you need to get a message to me, a rider can be in Ostia in two hours. Ships will sail daily until mid-November and, with a fair wind, they'll make Alexandria in ten days. I expect Jacob will hear from me often, since Lucius must have sent for me to do business.'

'Do you think so? I rather think he wants you away from me.'

'Perhaps he sees that as a convenient result but it's not the main reason. Alexandria's bristling with trading opportunities he hasn't time to follow up because of his official duties.'

She tightened her arms around him.

'He'll be away for a year or more, will he keep you that long?'

'I fear so. If I can make a case for accompanying some valuable cargo you may see me briefly, either here or in Ostia. It's possible but I can't promise.'

She bit her lip to check its quivering and pressed her face against his chest to hide her tears. He held her tightly before he drew back and spoke urgently.

'Archias will attend your confinement and send me word. If Lucius sends no order, keep the child here, as discreetly as possible. If he sends you orders to expose it, you can trust it to Archias. I've arranged with him to have it cared for and signed a contract for the wet nurse. He'll contrive for you to visit secretly.'

It was hard to believe he'd be gone so soon and for more than a year. She thought of the months she'd wasted, indifferent or dreading his presence and longed to go back and live them differently. He didn't mean to hurt but his parting words were a stab in the heart. 'Look to the child, Lucius loves him as his very life.'

She watched from the upper storey loggia for as long as the plume of dust hung in the air. Then, pulling her silk wrap around her, she made her way down the staircase like a sleep walker. At the bottom, she met Lucillus, asking his usual sing-song question.

'My lord come home?'

She lifted him into her arms and knew now why it didn't comfort him to be told, 'Lucius Marius is about the emperor's business.' How unfeeling she'd been to have thought him tiresome and badly behaved in the last two months, too absorbed in her own happiness to notice his despair. She'd make up for that now. They must console each other.

***

Demetrius soon regretted leaving Polybius, who had a feather-light, unerring touch with the razor. He knew many free men envied him his unscathed complexion; some gave up the struggle and grew a beard like the emperor. It didn't flatter Darius that his first encounter with his master's chin was on a pitching ship. He spat convulsively on the whetstone and sharpened his knife for a tediously long time. When he finally steeled himself to turn toward his master, his hands were shaking. Anxious not to undermine his confidence, Demetrius wet the stubble himself and set his face like a stone. He flinched no more than a stone but he bled more and the operation took so long he risked growing a new beard while the first was still being shaved. Time passed slowly on board ship and there was no one but the sympathetic captain to comment but his new servant had better learn from his mistakes before they reached Alexandria. He sighed and took up his tablets so the ship would return to Rome with a letter for his wife.

Demetrius had sailed into Alexandria many times but the sight of the lighthouse still quickened his pulse. It was a work of man to rival the works of the gods. Five hundred years had hardly darkened its marble face, dazzling white as if hewn from salt. It rose a hundred metres from its platform and could be seen from seventy miles away; first as a twinkling star, then as a ball of fire, its galaxy of burnished mirrors flashing arcs of light across the sea. He stood on the swaying deck, looking from the massive base up the elegant octagonal tier to the round tower. Bending backwards to salute the statue of Zeus, he scanned the outstretched arm to the very tip of the fiery sceptre.

A momentary giddiness made him lower his eyes to the base with its familiar inscription in huge granite letters, 'Sostratos, the Cnidian dedicated this to the saviour gods on behalf of those who sail the seas.' No one knew if Sostratus had been the donor, the architect or the contractor, but such a proof of human ingenuity went some way to make one feel safe in a fragile barque at sea. Demetrius screwed up his eyes against the amber glare from the water and murmured a grateful prayer.

The ship dropped anchor in the open sea, waiting for clearance to pass under the swing bridge and enter the congested harbour. The huge grain ships took precedence over all other shipping. They were the floating granaries that brought wheat to Rome because Egypt was Rome's breadbasket. No wonder it was close to the emperor's heart. The restive poor of the city were kept satisfied by those grain ships. Half the citizens of Rome claimed the dole. Demetrius knew there were few free men who lived in the style he did himself. Most were wretched. Slavery had its sorrows but freedom in poverty held no charms for him. To his surprise and pleasure, Lucius had himself rowed out to the boat by a solitary oarsman who spoke only Coptic.

'MeHercule! What happened to your face? Did you fall foul of a gladiator or has Polybius taken the shaking palsy?'

'Young Darius is with me. I shan't take him to see Alexander's tomb until he improves.'

Lucius wrinkled his nose. 'That triumph of Eastern vulgarity! For a man of a ten year reign. Philosophy, literature and the law, now, they're the things that last. Sostratos had an eye to posterity.' He waved towards the Pharos. 'The dedication, you know, he covered it with a layer of gypsum where he put Pharoah's inscription. That weathered away in a generation and left his own instead.'

Demetrius was shocked by his master's appearance. He was worryingly thin, no doubt from fever, but that didn't explain his pallor or the unnatural glitter of his eyes. His laughter was excessive and brittle and he talked more animatedly than Demetrius had ever known, at him rather than to him, as though to ward off unwelcome questions. He asked him if the city was hot for September. No, it wasn't the heat, it was the flies and the people.

'These Alexandrians are shockingly impertinent. First day in court, I presided over a civil case. A man had pawned his slave as security for a loan and, while in the pawnbroker's custody, he was stolen - or absconded more likely. Allegedly, the slave was worth more than the debt so he was suing the pawnbroker for the difference. When I invited him to sum up his case he came forward and lectured me about "Roman occupation", demanding that Egypt should have its own senate, if you please.'

'So he lost his case?'

'Didn't mention it. I think he made up the whole story, just to get the chance to air his politics in public. By the way, did you know Rome will fall in twenty years' time?'

'Did he say so?'

'All Egyptians say so. Take the Greek letters that spell Rome, substitute the numbers those letters stand for in Greek arithmetic and you get nine hundred and forty eight. So, according to the prophecy, Rome will fall nine hundred and forty eight years from its foundation.'

'I'm sure that bothers you.'

'Less than it bothered me to be called tyrannical, dishonest and crude.'

'Hermes! Did you have the fellow crucified?'

'Flogged. And imprisoned until he made a public apology. Then I let him go.'

'Master, was that wise?'

'Perfectly. Undercover agents followed him home and they're watching him and his friends. I'd be surprised if he turned out to be a problem. Alexandrians are all the same: boastful and ineffective. You remember about cats?'

'If you see one lying in the street you give it a wide berth, throw up your hands and shout, "It was dead already!"'

He laughed but Lucius didn't.

'Yes, and if you accidentally injure a cat, then by my genius, you'd better show a clean pair of heels. These people really would lynch you.'

They were silent for some time, listening to the pulling of the oars through the water, the squealing of gulls and the distant shouts of the dockers.

Suddenly, Lucius asked, 'Lucillus, was he well when you left?'

'He was and very lively, asking all the time when you're coming home.'

'Can he say so much?'

'He has ten new words a day. He's forever begging someone to hold him up to kiss your statue on the lips.'

'Was *she* well?'

'She's stronger. She's working in the office.'

'Is that wise?'

'She's a scribe, master, and you need one.'

'Adrian won't work her beyond her strength?'

'They're hard-pressed in the office but he has clear instructions. I think, master, she wants to be useful.'

'She shouldn't neglect the boy.'

'She doesn't. She's raising him as we were raised.'

'I challenged Quintus about her, you know. Asked him why he planted his secretary in my kitchen. I think it was a private joke at my expense.'

'At her expense, surely?'

'He wanted to see if I could find a diamond in my own haystack. Imagine how he'd have laughed if I hadn't! Oh, he intended her for me. I detected a certain grudging respect that I'd passed his little initiative test.'

'Why should he do that to her? Had she offended him? Why didn't she tell us?'

'If she'd felt able to confide in you, she might have done. Demetrie, would you have said I was qualified for this post?'

'None better, master. You won your first case when you were seventeen and you've been in practice ever since. No one raised an eyebrow at your appointment, in spite of your age.'

'Legal theory and practice? Irrelevant. Here, there's a tariff of bribes applied to every case. I'd hardly arrived when this fellow came to my rooms and handed me a purse – bold as a jackdaw, in front of my slaves. "Your share of the pickings." he said. I sent him packing. I don't know whose slave he was and I've never seen him since.'

'Imperial slaves used to work a system like that. Still do probably – it's impossible to stamp out. Everyone pays into the kitty, it's distributed according to seniority. Everyone benefits so no one talks. But free men - legal officers! That's why Marcus sent you here – to clean up the service.'

'If it was just the legal staff, I could, but it goes right through the administration. If an Alexandrian doesn't want loutish soldiers billeted in his house, he pays. He wants his son exempted from military service? He pays again. If he wants a government contract to sell paper or marble from his quarries or if he wants a fair tax assessment, it costs him more. When someone brings false charges against him, bribery's his only chance. If he can't pay, the ever-helpful officials lend him money at rates he can't afford, foreclose and strip him of everything he owns.'

'You'd seem to be saying that the functionaries are tyrannical, dishonest and crude.'

'I'm saying exactly that and more. Of course, I knew something of the sort went on in the provinces. Men are less honourable away from home. I knew there were opportunities to line one's pockets on foreign postings, and not all above board, but I never dreamt of corruption so systematic. Zeus! I blush to think how naive I was just three months ago.'

'What of the Registrar? Does he countenance this?'

'Old Lucian is eighty-five. He's nowhere near as senile as Marcus thinks but, as a registrar, he makes a fine satirist. The high point of this tour has been reading his books. I'll pass them on to you.'

'But he rails against philosophy! I'm surprised the emperor approves of him.'

'Not against philosophy, against bogus philosophers. I can't tell if he's oblivious of corruption or if he sees it and doesn't mean to do anything more than take a sideswipe at it in his next book. He seems more interested in life on the moon than life in Alexandria. But he's frail, living out his last days in peace. It wouldn't be fair to embroil him in this. Marcus sent me here to relieve him of work.'

'Does he resent that?'

'Not in the least. He approves my judgements and speeches and records them exactly, though he claims that, to be truly eloquent, one must be very old.'

'As old as him, no doubt!'

'For the rest, they're all unctuously civil but I'm a disappointment. My slaves have been offered bribes. I've foiled some attempts to compromise me. Now someone's trying to kill me.'

'Master, they wouldn't dare. You're not a provincial upstart. You're a Marius and the emperor's envoy.'

'Oh, I shan't be murdered, I'm going to have an unfortunate accident. We were caught up in a street brawl two months ago, Dion was hurt. We defended ourselves, got away, thought no more of it. The next day I dined in the mess as usual. A soon as I tasted the meat, I knew I'd been poisoned. I don't remember the next few days. Cyrus called in an Egyptian doctor. Zeus! It left me weak. When did you know me carried to court on a litter? Next, it was snakes in the bedroom. I still go to the mess but I don't eat. I dine with Lucian when he's up to it, otherwise I send out to sausage sellers, a different one each time.'

'And the guards sleep in shifts?'

'Of course. I've made a new will. Lucian has it. If necessary, he'll appeal to the emperor to uphold it.'

'Why should he need to?'

'Because I haven't left anything to my dear uncle. I've not forgotten that, when I made you my steward, he tried to have me put under guardianship. He'll get nothing. I find that satisfying. He's been hankering after my inheritance since before I was born. I'd sooner the emperor had it.'

Demetrius flinched. If the emperor inherited the estate, the slaves would be quickly turned into cash.

'If he grants exemption from the quota regulations, as I think he will, then all my town slaves will be freed, with bequests for any who can't make their own way and for my freedman, Sciens. Pulcher is my executor but he'll only need to advise Nerysa and give her to a good man in marriage. Your savings I take to be around half a million?'

Demetrius made a gesture of assent.

'You won't survive me. At least, we'd better hope you don't. At the very least, you'd be charged with failing to protect me. You'd forfeit the manumission I'd willed you and better you die with me than face execution as a slave. Half a million!' He whistled. 'You've done well for yourself. You couldn't legally will it to her so I've left her the same amount. A handsome dowry, Pulcher should be able to place her well on that.'

'Nonetheless, master, if I'm not to survive you, I must insist on coming to your enemies before they come to us.'

'Yes, but by due legal process. What I need is evidence. I don't know who or how many are involved and I can't find out because I spend all day chained to that wretched official chair.'

They came ashore and made for a wine bar in the Egyptian quarter. Sprawled on sandstone seats, they ate swordfish in oil and citron washed down with resin wine. The tang of the salt breeze gave Lucius an appetite for the first time since his illness. They'd escaped the rigid protocol of home and not yet submitted to that of the palace. Nerysa was far away. They were together and in trouble. They were boys again.

***

As a helpless infant, Lucius idolised Demetrius who could crawl. By the time *he* could crawl, Demetrius toddled. Soon they ran together and tussled like puppies. Side by side, they learned to recite two alphabets, swim, sit a pony, drive a donkey cart, fence and shoot. They tumbled together into boisterous boyhood; a time of freedom and irresponsibility, sanctified by the beauties and wonders of nature. They remembered it as a pageant of long, hot days spent stealing eggs from almost inaccessible nests and cakes from the kitchen and tormenting school masters. At night, they crept from their shared bed, eluding the vigilance of devoted minders and lay hand in hand on the riverbank, watching otters sport in the milky dawn. They trained dogs and tamed squirrels, trapped deer and fished trout from streams.

Singly, they could have been beaten into submission but united, they stood firm against all authority. No pedagogue, nurse or school master could break the unholy alliance. The boys were wild - a law unto themselves.

They went together through the bleak tunnel of despair that was bereavement which only served to add another sturdy strand of affection to the cord that bound them. They underwent metamorphosis from boy to man; the disconcerting process in which one's body didn't seem to be the same size or shape from one month to the next, one couldn't be sure exactly how one's voice would sound until one uttered and each day brought a new skin blemish. They came through it with mutual sympathy and good humour, bursting joyously into the full franchise of manhood, with limitless strength, boundless enthusiasm and an unshakeable conviction of immortality. Prodigal of new-found strength, they wrestled a crooked furrow behind the oxen and scythed hay with Herculean vigour, pounded grapes with their strong brown feet and revelled through starry nights at harvest festivals. There were intellectual pleasures too, as they encountered poetry, art and philosophy and realised, with breathless surprise, their power to stir and delight.

Their first sexual experiences were, naturally, with each other, tremulous and hesitant at first, later full hearted and lusty. Then they began to fall in love, frequently and fickly, sometimes with the same girl, sometimes a pair of sisters, sometimes unrelated girls but always synchronously with each taking as much interest in the other's affairs as his own. For fifteen years, they flourished in harmony, every experience shared with joy in life and each other. It was an equal relationship because their natural endowment was evenly matched.

With brutal suddenness, they learned it had all been a mistake. One of them was the cream of society, the other less than fully human, fit only for servitude. One was to be indulged, the other humbled and deprived. Each must learn his place. They never questioned the system. The system was correct. They were at fault. But they couldn't be brought to deny their love for each other or believe that it was shameful. Both were keenly intelligent and cooperation was a lifetime's habit. After Lucius succeeded to his patrimony, they often travelled. In hotels, rented rooms and the homes of business contacts they could dispense with much of the rigid protocol they observed at home. At home they evolved a unique way of life which observed the formalities due to the gulf in their status yet allowed for the fact that each was still, essentially, an eager boy who loved his brother.

CHAPTER LX

October 174 – March 175

Respondi, id quod erat, nihil neque ipsis Nunc praetoribus esse nec cohorti Cur quisquam caput unctius referret.

I told them straight that no one came home more solvent than he went. We had a pig of a governor who didn't care a straw for his staff. Catullus. X

Returning to the palace, they found that Demetrius' baggage, delivered to a dormitory designated for slaves of officials, was being unpacked by Darius. Urging caution on each other, they went their separate ways. Demetrius blamed himself. It was his fault that Lucius had left his comfortable home for a thankless task abroad. Their partnership, burgeoning wealth and Lucius' promising career could end abruptly with death on foreign soil. All because he hadn't shared a woman with the master who'd been generosity itself to him. Better to have given her up than left her forsaken.

From the beginning, he was taciturn with the minions of the other officials but his sharp ears and eyes missed nothing. He and Darius took turns to feign sleep. He cursed his master behind his back and was surly in is presence. One sultry afternoon, he allowed his fellow slaves to ply him with cheap wine and prise out of him the reason for his brooding depression; his master had taken away his woman and got her with child. Her loveliness, her courage in defence of her virtue and her agonies in childbirth he could describe from the heart. Once he added the fictitious rape, the tale was doleful. The wine, the heat and self-pity worked him into a maudlin stupor and he fell on his pallet, breathing stertorously. His fellows laughed, he'd be in no condition to wait on his sanctimonious master at dinner.

***

The mess room was magnificent; high above ground, with triple aspect, commanding views over the eastern and western harbours, the lighthouse and the sea. Lucius, surveying the couches, side tables and braziers and the numberless palace waiters and personal attendants swarming around them, understood the dismay of the Alexandrians. A poor bargain to exchange the glamour of the Ptolemies for these imperial functionaries - at best boorish, at worst brutish and oppressive.

He felt shabby and depressed. Would it have been noble to meet his fate alone, leaving Demetrius and Nerysa to mourn him in Rome? That would have been to betray his forebears and the gods of his hearth, leaving them without an heir or a future. He'd thought of his departure as a benevolent gesture, to call a truce during her pregnancy. Now he saw he'd acted from pique and brought disaster on them all.

He took his place and surveyed his reclining colleagues. Some were Romans on foreign posting, on their worst behaviour. Most were Roman citizens from the provinces, parvenus who probably behaved almost as badly at home as they did in Alexandria. To a man, they loathed the perfidious Alexandrians and delighted in fleecing them. He suppressed the impulse to scan the room for Demetrius but felt uneasy when he didn't present himself. A strange, boot-faced fellow came to serve him and he asked sharply, 'Where's my boy, Demetrius?'

The man rubbed his nose, failing to hide an insolent grin.

'Too sick for dooty t'night, Hexlency. Sent me to fill in.'

Lucius was dismayed. Demetrius must be very ill to leave him to be served by a potential assassin. If he was, how could they keep up the deception? How could he not rush to his bedside and send for the best doctors in the city? But, if not, he shouldn't risk blowing their cover, leaving them in even more danger. How long could he safely leave it without visiting him? Some fevers could kill in a day. Why hadn't he sent a message? Was Darius sick too? Had they been attacked? He passed his hand back and forth to the dishes and frequently held them out to be rinsed but he swallowed nothing and ignored the entertainments. One of the dancers was drawn to him. She came close, wobbled her abject, pendulous breasts under his nose and flashed him the gaping smile that never reached her weary eyes. He repulsed her and wondered why this seemed to cause general amusement.

As soon as he decently could, he withdrew, telling Cyrus to go to the servants' quarters at dawn to see what he could discover. He couldn't sleep but tossed feverishly around the bed, racked with anxiety and indecision until Cyrus returned to say that neither Demetrius nor Darius was in the dormitory. He splashed his face, pulled on an outer tunic and went down to breakfast where, to his relief, he saw Demetrius, looking well enough, but scowling blackly. He came forward, adjusted the table and hissed, 'Strike me, master!', stiffening his jaw in invitation.

Never in his life had Lucius struck Demetrius in anger. He thought back to the night Nerysa ran away and tried to summon the rage that had fired him then. The blow was barely forceful enough to impress the spectators but Demetrius picked himself off the floor and shot him a look of such virulent hatred he flinched.

***

Officials began to take an interest in Demetrius. He stayed sullen but gradually allowed scraps of information to be bribed or blandished out of him by their slaves and, in spite of their caution, convinced them he was their man. Of course, there were many in Alexandria, of the merchant class, who remembered him and Lucius from happier times but imperial bureaucrats didn't mix in such circles and, if they had, the story that a woman had come between them and soured their affection was a plausible one, painfully close to the truth. They didn't suggest immediately that he should help them murder his master but they used him in a variety of ways and rewarded him. They were watching their chance and, when his master was found dead, he, as the guilty slave with an obvious motive, would be crucified with the minimum of formality. Demetrius felt his head slip ever deeper into the crocodile's mouth. Without his master's protection, the best he could hope for was the chance to kill himself, which he probably wouldn't get.

He could identify those who were bent on removing the emperor's legal officer but hearsay was no use. The evidence of a slave must be extracted under torture to be admissible in court and, even then, wouldn't serve to condemn influential men. They must be charged with corruption and condemned by their own hands. He ran errands for them, delivered their letters and kept records of how they divided their spoils.

During the voyage, he'd pictured himself strolling along the porticoes of the emporium where the merchants of three continents mingled. He smiled ruefully as, instead, he skulked in the shadow of the warehouses on the western waterfront. He glanced over his shoulder before diving into the shabby brothel where he'd hired a private room. With a mixture of gum and powdered marble, he'd made himself a set of duplicate seals so he could open and copy every document that came his way. The copies he delivered. The originals were for Lucius. Since they could only communicate publicly, he respectfully enquired of him at what hour he wished to study in the library and Lucius, who until that moment, had had no thought of visiting the library, growled irritably.

'I said the sixth hour, you heedless half-wit. Is it your ears or your brains that need tickling with the whip?'

The famous library was a lofty cloister within the palace complex. It was the most extensive collection in the world - no one need wonder that a studious young man should read there. Demetrius went early, located scrolls for study and slid the evidence inside them. When Lucius arrived, he directed him to the table he'd prepared and stood respectfully aside waiting for him to be ready to depart. He accompanied him along the covered marble way back to the mess for dinner but they took care that no one spying from behind an obelisk would see them converse more than a harsh master and his disaffected slave might be supposed to.

They learned more than they'd bargained for. Among creative new ideas for extortion and proof that even the governor's son, Faustinianus, was involved, were rumours of a coup d'état. It was said that Avidius Cassius, the emperor's staunch lieutenant, was now so out of sympathy with the emperor's style of government, that he was minded to wrest power from him and have himself proclaimed by the army. He commanded a large division, flushed with success and a heady sense of its own power.

The intelligence, though unconfirmed, was welcomed by the imperial staff. Cassius was a stern disciplinarian who detested baksheesh. He desired men to be honest as fervently as Marcus Aurelius did but, whereas Marcus only permitted himself to lead by example, Cassius meant to be effective. So, it was argued, if he were emperor and on the northern front, he'd make less of a nuisance of himself in Egypt. No one in Alexandria would lift a finger to foil the coup.

This was no routine matter to be filed with prosecution papers. Demetrius thought they needed to discuss it and judging by Lucius' expression as he scanned the note in his scroll, he agreed. Demetrius wondered about a visit to the baths. The background noise and the intimate nature of the tasks he would perform for his master should give them the chance to arrange a further meeting at least. He decided to take another look at the baths.

Crossing the forum deep in thought, he didn't react as soon as he might to the cries of, 'Seize him!'. Seeing soldiers converging on him, he ran for his life and was sent sprawling. As he struggled up and flung himself on his assailant, a metal knee-guard struck in the small of his back. His head was jerked back, then smashed into the pavement. His back teeth skewered his tongue and it welled blood. As he lifted a hand to his jaw, his arms were wrenched behind him and iron bands snapped to around his wrists and ankles. A kick on the rump and a cudgel under the armpit propelled him to his feet. He was struck across the face and ordered to 'Quick march!'

The soldiers didn't seem to know the shortest route to the prison. As he was paraded round the city, he felt virulent hatred for the scum of Alexandria who jeered at him and he railed against his murdered master through tears of rage. What sort of idiot couldn't keep safe behind sixteen guards? When he'd been thrown, rather than marched, down a stairwell and chained to a mildewed wall, fury gave way to depression. He mourned the waste of his master's promising young life and dreaded the punishment that was coming to him. Who would break it to Nerysa that he'd ended his life strung up on a gibbet for passers by to mock his death agony? Would she believe he'd murdered his master? His limbs throbbed and the blood in his mouth went rancid. By the time a key rasped in the lock, he was hoping for just one thing - water. Afraid the hope would be dashed, he kept his eye on the ground and stared stupidly at two pairs of boots and greaves and voluminous purple silk billowing over the slimy floor.

'Ungrateful wretch!' said a petulant, upper-class voice. 'I treated you like a brother and would you try to murder me?'

As he raised his eyes from the dank floor, his master, returned as from the dead, commanding in his regalia, seemed little short of a god. He sobbed at the sight of him and the fervour with which he grovelled at his feet was not feigned. Lucius backed away, drawing the hem of his robe out of range and dismissed the guard.

'I'll turn the key on him myself but, before I do, I want to hear him howl. Leave me a torch.' His voice softened. 'I'm sorry for the rough treatment. It was unavoidable.'

'I forgive you everything if you can get me some water – and a skin of wine.'

'Wine? My dear Demetrie. This cell is in the bowels of the building where no one ever comes. When I leave, you'll be left to rot.'

'Master, why?'

'So no one asks after you when you've gone to Tyana.'

Demetrius scanned the windowless stone walls; six foot thick at least.

'Gone where?'

'Tyana. And you'll need to find a crazy sailor to take you in February.'

'Which Tyana'

'You're going to Martius Verus.'

'Cappadocia?'

'Correct. I trust Verus, whereas, Statianus, the governor here -'

'Whose son is up to his neck in the racket -'

'Father and son are both close to the emperor. Even closer to his friend, Fronto, I can't be sure he wouldn't try to destroy me and my evidence. So he has to know Verus has already sent it on to Marcus.'

'What about the coup?'

'Say nothing. If I warn anyone, it should be the emperor. He says the truth can't hurt anyone.'

'Hermes! Do you think he really believes that?'

'Dion tells me this device opens most commercially available fetters. I wonder how many masters know how easy it is to come by. Throw off that tunic. Here's a wallet; documents and enough money to get to India and back. Officer's uniform. You'll look more martial in it than I ever did, damn you.'

'All that under your robe. I thought you looked majestic.'

'None of your disrespect. And pull your helmet over that eye, it's an ugly sight.'

***

In retrospect, it looked easy but they were shaken to think how different the outcome might have been. They went down to the quayside to see the prisoners stowed. Slaves and Egyptians, Lucius had tried and condemned himself but the Roman citizens had appealed to the emperor and opted to face trial in Rome. Demetrius had chartered the vessel at the state's expense and prisoners weren't the only cargo for he'd been shopping, filling every last cranny with crystal, spices, bales of linen, and papyrus. There were presents for Lucillus and letters; for Jacob, Adrian and Nerysa.

Waves slapped rhythmically against the granite quay. The wind was fresh and favourable. Demetrius looked wistfully westward and Lucius had one of his happy inspirations in which generosity mingled with expediency.

'If you don't make haste and send for your baggage, you'll miss the sailing.'

Demetrius looked up, incredulous, guarded against disappointment but Lucius wasn't teasing.

'Greet her from us both, little brother,' he said, 'but if she comes through this time, she'll be mine. There's no difficulty surely? You've had five years. I'll wager that's more than you expected when you took her. Now it's my turn.'

His voice was throbbing and insistent, his arm slipped around Demetrius' aching shoulders in the familiar way.

'Don't you feel how close she'll bring us? I value her most of all for your sake. I love her. I have more to offer her. You don't grudge her what I can give?'

Demetrius looked at the dancing waves. He felt the prosperous breeze straining towards Rome and fancied he caught the scent of her in his nostrils. She must be very near her time. He swore to give her up to Lucius and, in the temple of Neptune on the quayside, he sealed his vow.

CHAPTER LXI

March 175

O quid solutis est beatius curis Cum mens onus reponit, ac peregrino Labore fessi venimus larem ad nostrum Desideratoque acquiescimus lecto

Is there anything more wonderful than to come home after a weary journey, set down your bags and fall asleep in the bed you've longed for? Catullus XI

When the ship docked in Ostia on a keen, blustery morning, Jacob was already pacing the wharf, waiting to deal with the customs formalities. The centurion in charge of the prisoners saw them disembarked and Demetrius hurried to the temple of Ceres with an alabaster vase; a thank offering for his safe voyage. When he returned to the quay, the dockers were already wrestling sacks down the gangplanks. The crew pressed him to join their feast but he pleaded his wife's condition and, before the sun hissed in the Tyrrhenian Sea, he was sitting in the marble cool of the atrium. Slaves crowded round, vying for the honour of washing his hands and feet and rubbing his head with oil. They served wine, cake and apples and told him his wife was well and not yet brought to bed. Lucillus asked, 'My lord home?'

Demetrius smiled, 'Soon he'll be home but, for now, the emperor still needs him. He's sent you presents. They'll be brought up from Ostia in a few days.'

'Mama cried 'cos her starling died.'

'I'm sorry for that but your lord will give her a pair of white peacocks when he comes home.'

Head inclined, Lucillus reflected, 'No good. Wants her starling back.'

Charis whispered to him and he threw back his head and extended his hand with aplomb.

'Welcome home, Demetri.'

Demetrius marvelled at him, not two years old and entirely self-possessed. He looked for his wife. None of the scribes had come to greet him, though news of his arrival must have reached the office. On his way around the colonnade, he stopped to look through the high office window and followed Adrian's hawk-like scowl straight to her. So, he'd refused her permission to come and greet him. He resented that but knew better than to undermine the authority of a deputy. A shaft of sunlight caught her; her face shone translucent and the knot on her neck gleamed gold. Fortune had blessed him; she was well and he'd made it safely home to her. Impossible to be angry with anyone, even Adrian.

Dismissing the crowd of followers, he slipped into the room and signed to the scribes to continue working. Adrian pushed forward the new scribe, Melissus, a lad of fifteen; bright-eyed and quaking in his sandals, before the head of the house where he was determined to succeed.

Adrian was on his mettle too. Trusted with a significant purchase and eager for his superior's approval, he recounted where he'd bought him, his history and education, the sales pitch he'd been given and how he'd cunningly caught him out and proved he was less skilled than the dealer claimed. While he described how he'd haggled over the price and negotiated a hefty discount, Melissus hung his head and squirmed. Demetrius approved. The boy was sensitive; he was probably intelligent. He reached for his hand and clasped it.

'Welcome to the house of Lucius Marius Lepidus! You come at a time when we're sorely pressed. His Excellency has scribes and secretaries with him in Alexandria. I, myself, stay only for tonight. Give us good service at this difficult time and I'll know how to value you.'

Melissus stammered his thanks and good intentions as Demetrius crossed the room to his wife. He looked over her shoulder and started in surprise. The air between them quickened. His pulse raced. He sensed hers responding. Her fingers, poised over the inkpot, trembled slightly but perhaps from fatigue; she would have been writing for twelve hours. When she'd finished her letter, he looked meaningfully at Adrian, gratified to see him dismiss her without checking it, merely rolling and sealing it and signalling to Melissus to light the lamps. The implication was that everyone else would have to work late because one of them had retired early. She cleared away her pens and ink methodically and he led her out, shocked by her heavy footfall and laboured breathing.

In the warm, well-lit bedroom, he put her to lie down and resigned himself to Polybius' joyful ministrations. The boy took such pleasure in every attention he paid him, it would have been churlish to dispense with any, so he submitted to washing, shaving and rubbing with oil until his body glistened. He was robed and given new sandals, dinner was served and, at last, they were alone. If he'd hoped for a rapturous welcome from her, he was disappointed. He couldn't coax her to eat or speak except in monosyllables. There was a matter he wanted to take up with her but meant to defer until after their meal. She was less self-controlled.

'Did you tell Melissus you'd only come until tomorrow?'

'Tomorrow morning, early.'

Her vehemence startled him.

'Why did you come at all?'

'I needed clean linen. And I wanted to see you. I hoped you'd like to see me. Aren't you pleased to see me?'

'Not for one night. I'd got used to being without you but to see you again and part so soon, it's too painful. I think you're cruel.'

He took the outburst calmly. It was due to her condition. She was tired and Adrian had given her a hard time. Life would be far sweeter for her as Lucius' girl. But she should know why he must leave her so near her time. Whenever there was need for absolute discretion, instinctively, his voice sank low and he began to think in Greek, which reminded him of the other matter he wanted to clear up.

'That last letter you wrote.'

'About the surgical instruments, sir?'

'It was in Greek. I assume you've not learned Greek in my absence?'

'No, I did know before.'

'If you write it, and so beautifully, you must understand it.'

'Tolerably well.'

'How many conversations have you overheard in the last four years that weren't for your ears?'

'I never heard you say anything unworthy.'

'You must have heard much that I didn't want repeated.'

'Nor have I repeated it.'

'Dissembling minx! You'd better give me a full account of your accomplishments.'

'Well, I read and write Latin and Greek and speak my own native language, of course.'

He dismissed this last accomplishment with a wave of the hand and she tossed her head.

'Do you want me to bray like an auctioneer?'

'Just answer my question.'

'I can figure, reasonably well. I take dictation and have a fair memory for messages. I sing to the harp.'

'You play the harp? Pulcher took pains with your education. What persuaded him to part with you? No, don't tell me! I can guess. Too squeamish to begin a relationship with an injury, was he? Delicacy, you called it. Did you wish I'd been more delicate or that he'd been bolder?'

The screen came down before her eyes in the chilling way he'd almost forgotten. So, those memories weren't for him to share. He had secrets from her, of course, but she should have none from him. How could he protect her otherwise? He sluiced the wine around the cup, studying its turbulence, and asked, 'Can you understand, when you keep something from me, I wonder why; are you're holding it in reserve to use against me or as a private joke at my expense? Why didn't you tell me you were a scribe, right from the beginning?'

'People need kitchen maids. They're not fussy how many they keep. Not everyone wants a girl scribe. You mightn't have done.'

'Were you so keen to stay here?'

'I heard Lucius Marius' slaves were hand-picked and seldom sold on. I wanted to settle down.'

'I can understand that. But you shouldn't have cheated him.'

'How did I cheat him?'

'A raw import, unskilled, under twenty five, in good health...worth around sixty sesterces. A scribe, ten thousand; secretary for Greek correspondence, at least twenty. For the novelty value of a female, add thirty percent, maybe forty if she's pretty. Double that for a virgin. A bargain at fifty thousand all in.'

'Just what did you pay for me?'

'I see no need for you to know that. Pulcher named his price, we didn't quibble.'

'If Lucius paid for a kitchen maid and got one I don't see what he has to complain about.'

They laughed and the tension eased though he was painfully aware that, while he accused her of evasion, he hadn't told her of his pact with Lucius. If she accepted it calmly he'd hate her for it. But he couldn't face wrangling with her now. There was time enough. She had her confinement to come through, Lucius might never come home or come with an Alexandrian beauty in tow. He needn't tell her yet. But there was something he *would* tell. He felt under his cushion for the scroll.

'Here, what do you think this is?'

Her eyes widened. 'It seems to be a warrant for *you* to use the imperial posting service.'

'To Sirmium. We suspect the Syrian legions are plotting to overthrow Marcus.'

'Heavens! In whose favour?'

'The governor of Syria, Avidius Cassius.'

'What sort of man is he?'

'Stern. Effective. A good soldier.'

'In place of *Marcus*? He's been no friend to me – to my country that is, but I see why the nations adore him. Isn't this the golden age Plato foretold, when a philosopher should rule the world?'

'Marcus is ill. His heir's a fourteen year-old of doubtful merit. It seems even the empress might prefer to throw in her lot with Cassius, rather than risk the free for all after Marcus' death. And Marcus is so gentle people think he hasn't got a grip on affairs. He's tolerant – to a fault some would say, even with the stupidest slave.'

'So are you.'

'Up to a point but, if a scribe asked me how to write Antoninus, I doubt if I'd spell it out for him letter by letter with no sign of annoyance.'

'You'd have him flogged, of course.'

'Perhaps not, but I'd move him – outdoors probably.'

'Why doesn't he?'

'Because, as the most powerful man on earth, he doesn't choose his scribes, the ab episulis does, just as the head chef decides what he has for dinner, his secretaries book his engagements and his ushers say who he will or won't see. He just gets to make the really unpopular decisions. That's another problem. The Pertinax appointment. Imagine, a freedman's son, consul!'

'I imagine the patricians are stung to the quick.'

'Not our place to comment. But Lucius thinks he should be alerted, at least to the possibility that Cassius is disloyal. And he hasn't trusted his letter to official couriers. It's your own husband who'll put it into the emperor's hand.'

'My poor love, nine days at sea and now how many in the saddle?'

'Nine or ten. But if the empire were saved by a slave? Aren't you proud of me?'

'I was proud of you before. You're no less capable and honest for being a slave. The empire's run by slaves and freedmen.'

'No, that might have been true a hundred years ago, not today. Marcus runs it single handed. He barely eats or sleeps. That's why he's been five years on the northern frontier, fighting to protect it. My darling, I hope you don't discuss politics with anyone but me.'

'I might have done but I won't in future if you dislike it.'

'Your ideas are interesting but unorthodox. I'm not offended but other people might be. Pulcher and friends are, no doubt, free in their conversation. In less liberal times, some of them would have been invited to commit suicide.'

'Are there brigands on the road to Sirmium?'

'Probably. I can take two guards but the other two are needed here. The office seems busy. Is Adrian making heavy weather?'

'Well, we've had ships in from Marseilles already and the calendar's full of debts falling due this month. Philemon and I had to take the dictation, Melissus is only trained to copy. Adrian's busy auctioning the Praxiteles Venus by correspondence and he's obsessed with the accounts.'

Adrian wasn't good with figures. Demetrius frowned, knowing he'd have them all to correct when he got back.

'Oh, please don't complain.' she said. 'He's done his best. If he'd been in the least receptive, I'd have offered to help.'

Balancing accounts was high status work. Adrian wouldn't let anyone near it, least of all a woman. He winced to think of the offence she could have caused.

'But I knew I shouldn't escape a beating if I offered.'

He looked up and she answered his unspoken question with a weary smile and a shake of the head.

'Does he beat Melissus?'

She wrinkled her nose. 'To begin with, but he's discovered the boy works faster when he isn't trembling like a jellied fig.'

'Adrian's talented. He drafts exquisite letters. His facility with figures is less special. I didn't say that of course, you noticed it yourself. When I get back and relieve him of the accounts, life should improve for you all.'

That night he clung to her, still sensing the pitching of the ship. Her body radiated heat. As he breathed ever more deeply, the familiar scent of her hypnotised him to a deep serenity. Tension drained from his limbs and he knew how it felt to be a contented cat, stretched out on a sun-drenched doorstep in Alexandria. Even the nagging fear of her confinement left him. He put his trust in Archias.

In the event, Archias came too late. Nerysa woke in the dead of night already in strong labour and Demetrius roused Thaïs, who told him to send for the midwife, at least, without delay. By the time help arrived, a little maid lay in the crook of her mother's arm, blinking up him. Nerysa was exultant. She said she'd had an easy, exhilarating time and would happily enjoy it again the next day. He was too relieved to argue. Later in the morning than he'd planned, he took leave of her and his daughter, saluted the lares in their ivory shrine and set out for Sirmium with two guards and Darius.

CHAPTER LXII

March 175 – March 176

Ne quid res publica detrimenti caperet.

So that no harm comes to the state. Cicero. Pro Milone XII xii

Nerysa lay cradling her baby, suddenly desperately afraid. Why had she insisted on bringing this small being into a world of bitter suffering? She looked into her daughter's placid face. What sorrows lay in wait for her? Six months working under Adrian had taught her how much Demetrius had shielded her from the common afflictions of a slave's life. She could have lived like Melissus. Throughout the long working day, he daren't even clear his throat for fear of the lash. If Adrian hadn't been in awe of Demetrius, he'd have served her the same way. Not because she was a bad worker but because he happened to dislike her. She wouldn't be able to protect her child from such circumstances because it didn't belong to her. If she and Demetrius were freed and left the house, it would stay behind because it belonged to Lucius. Even that wasn't the worst that could happen. When he returned, Lucius might refuse to keep her in his house. As she confronted the reality of her daughter's position, her motherly pride dissolved in tears of helplessness and dread. The bustle around her bed brought no comfort; only the sight or sound of Demetrius could have done that. But she saw that the one who might protect her baby was Lucillus. He was free, he would be rich. She resolved to do everything in her power to foster affection between the two of them and, while he was still young, to instil in him a resolve to protect his sister.

***

The official pass secured Demetrius changes of horses and accommodation along the roads. He regaled his companions with a story about the controversial new consul, Pertinax. As a young man, promoted prefect of a cohort and travelling to Syria to take up his commission, he'd mislaid his pass and tried to use the posting service without it. The governor of Syria had forced him to finish his journey on foot. The prudent Demetrius had no such problems and reached Sirmium before the end of March.

Having expected a frontier camp, he was impressed to find an established colonial town with a fine imperial residence and luxurious houses for courtiers and prominent citizens who came seeking legal judgements. His pass smoothed all difficulties and he was conducted down the echoing corridors into the presence of the most approachable of emperors. From Lucius' description he identified the emaciated figure flanked by burly generals and fell to his knees before it.

'Lord Emperor, greetings from my master, Lucius Marius Lepidus, by your favour, Juridicus in Alexandria.'

Only then did he slip the scroll from the wallet strapped to his body and place it in the emperor's hands. Marcus broke the seal and passed it to the secretaries for decoding. Demetrius was thanked and dismissed. The tribunes' slaves looked after him and, when he'd rested from his journey, he was shown around the camp. He felt no nostalgia for his army days but a growing admiration for Marcus, who wasn't a natural soldier nor even athletic. The rigours of campaigning were ruining his health and distracting him from the intellectual life he loved. Only duty kept him, year after year, at the front.

The next day Demetrius was summoned and humiliatingly strip-searched. Then, in an unprecedented move, Marcus saw him alone. Realising he'd been in Alexandria and was as conversant with the situation as his master, he questioned him shrewdly on every point of Lucius' assessment. He had the haunted look of a man who cannot eat without pain. Demetrius looked into his unnerving, pinpoint pupils and wished he could spare him the truth.

'Why should I believe this?' There was strain in the gentle voice. 'Avidius Cassius is my dearest friend!'

'I do not think, Lord Emperor, that news is necessarily false in the same measure as it is unwelcome.'

'True, and one who loves truth must be grateful to be proved wrong. But, even if Cassius were my enemy and not my friend, I hardly think he'd attempt rebellion with three legions.'

'My master thinks Statianus, in Egypt, might support him.'

'Your master should take care how he slanders my friends. Perhaps he says Martius Verus, in Cappadocia, is also traitor?'

'No, Lord Emperor, he's sure Cappadocia is loyal but fears Palestine and Arabia might not be.'

'Mortal men will not decide this question. If Cassius is disloyal, Divine Providence will judge between us.'

'Lord emperor, if I were to see Cassius, now, advancing on your back with a dagger, would I leave it to Divine Providence to disarm him?'

'Hold your tongue! Reflect how unseemly it is for you to make these accusations and how offensive to Cassius to know I'd listened to them. But I will not be angry because I see that you speak from misguided loyalty.'

The weary eyes seemed to probe his very soul. The voice softened in sudden menace.

'I'd be thought unwise to trust you. Ought I to...detain you?'

Demetrius shut his eyes. Had he exchanged a dungeon in Alexandria for a dungeon in Sirmium? How long before Lucius negotiated his release? If there was a coup, Lucius might not survive. With nothing to lose, he looked unflinchingly into the emperor's eyes.

'My master sent me, Lord Emperor, because, slave or free, there's no one he trusts more.'

'I believe that, and I've heard good reports of you myself. Then you must be convinced; we're dealing with an idle rumour. We shall take no action and maintain absolute secrecy, knowing how it would hearten the enemy to think Rome divided against herself.'

Demetrius had expected to be challenged on the detail but was unprepared for blank disbelief.

'But my Lord Emperor, my master sent proofs with his letter; papers, signatures…'

And I have had them burned. Unopened.'

Demetrius opened his mouth, desperately marshalling arguments, rehearsing the evidence. But he saw the emperor's brows contract and his mouth tense and thought again. He was a slave; a means of delivering letters. He bowed in silence. Who, in Sirmium, could have vouched for him, he wondered. The 'good reports' must be of his master, surely?

Marcus continued. 'Nor do I blame Lepidus for his excessive zeal. I'm grateful for his pains, at least. And for yours too. You made good time - Rome to Sirmium in less than ten days.'

'Thank you, Lord Emperor. I could, perhaps, have arrived a few hours sooner but a daughter was born to me in Rome the morning I left.'

Then Marcus showed his most human face. His congratulations were tender and sincere. His own daughters had brought him more joy than his sons. Four-year-old Sabina was with him in the camp and her presence made every day a holiday. He drew a delightful picture of the joy Demetrius could expect from his daughter and asked about Lucius' dealings with his slaves, whether he avoided separating families by sale or gift. Demetrius was proud to say that Lucius was a considerate master but Marcus still looked grave.

'We live in an uncertain world. If you should ever find yourself driven to desperation you may apply to me, or to the empress if I should.. not be available. The imperial service needs talented men… especially if they're *discreet*. We could find places for your child and your woman.'

'Thank you, Lord Emperor, she'd be useful, she's a Greek secretary.'

Marcus raised his brows. 'Remarkable! Lepidus must be well served by you both.'

The interview ended on that cordial note. Demetrius noticed that special commands had been given regarding him. His horses were ready, everyone was helpful and smiling and said knowingly that he must be anxious to be home. At the barrack gates, an official hailed him down. 'You're the slave of Lucius Marius Lepidus, aren't you? The emperor commands me to give you this, as funds for your journey and a personal reward for your efforts. The empress sends this gift for your daughter.'

Money was always welcome to Demetrius but it was the tiny, chased silver bracelet that touched his heart - that *his* daughter should wear a bracelet given her by an empress.

'Could you find me a tribune who would condescend to write to their majesties on my behalf?'

'I could, but you're a steward, you read and write surely?'

'A slave doesn't presume to address a letter to the emperor.'

Darius held the horses and a helpful tribune was located, an aristocratic youth who was probably finding the battlefield too close for comfort. He readily agreed to compose a letter conveying the heavy obligation felt by the slave, Demetrius and his daughter Zoë and begging the emperor to reconsider their master's letter in the light of his devoted loyalty.

From the moment he'd lifted his daughter from the ground, Demetrius had planned to call her Zoë. It was a name he longed to have on his lips again and it might soften Lucius towards her and move him to be kind to her for her grandmother's sake. Back in Rome, he found everyone calling her by her mother's name and it occurred to him that Lucius might object to the name of his beloved foster mother being given to an unwanted slave child. That name and those memories were not his alone. They belonged equally to Lucius. Lucius loved the baby's mother too. She might be better served by her mother's name.

He slipped back into his old routine; overseeing the farm, negotiating in Ostia and managing the day to day affairs of the house and office. He was dismayed by the failure of his mission. Rebellion would mean civil war. He feared for the imperial family and for Lucius; stranded in Alexandria, no love lost between him and Statianus, and Cassius in charge. Rome itself was threatened. All available troops were with Marcus on the Danube. If Cassius marched on Rome, he'd find the garrison sorely depleted. His wrath would fall on the poor and defenceless whom Marcus was committed to protect. All because Marcus couldn't bring himself to think ill of his friends.

Demetrius asked himself repeatedly what more he could have done or should still do. Who would listen to a slave?

'Someone who knows you.' Nerysa said. 'One of Lucius' friends. They might not sit down to eat with you but they respect your opinion. What about Publius Severus?'

'He's capable and well connected. As tribune of the plebs, the city prefect would have to take him seriously. He's known me since he and Lucius were in law school. Strangely enough, I ran across his brother, Geta, in Aquileia a few years ago and made myself useful to him. He might believe me.'

'You used to tell me a slave should do exactly as he's told, no more no less.'

'That's the general rule. It may seem arrogant but I always felt different from the common run, as though my duty went further than that.'

'Duty to whom?'

'Good question. Marcus? But I gave him the facts. The empire? That's more his responsibility than mine. Lucius then; yes, because I'm his procurator, his property's at risk and I can't look to it if Severus has me clapped in gaol.'

He halved the rations and restricted permission to leave the house. Gladiators were expensive and almost unobtainable, so many had been freed and conscripted but he invested in four and had them train every male slave between fifteen and fifty to defend the house. For Lucius himself, he could do nothing. If he were suspected of betraying Cassius, he was a dead man and his slaves would most likely go under the hammer with the rest of his estate. If the will were upheld, he and Nerysa would be free and comfortably off with their children yet Demetrius never hoped for that. He couldn't imagine a life in which he didn't serve Lucius. He led prayers and offered sacrifice daily for his safe return. While he stood before the shrine in private prayer, Charis dared to disturb him to say his wife had a fever and had cried out when she put the baby to the breast.

***

Looking up from the cup of wine and opium, Nerysa saw the steel blade flash in the lamp light and made to jump off the bed.

She couldn't let Archias put a knife to her breast, she couldn't have borne him to breathe on it. Demetrius held her down with implacable strength and Archias' face loomed over her. She fixed her gaze on the cleft between his shaggy brows as if she had to draw it from memory. When the knife plunged in, she struggled in vain. There was a momentary relief as pus spurted from the abscess, then Archias' finger thrust deep, raking pitilessly. His face shimmered and faded out.

When she surfaced, her first thought was for the baby. Could one breast satisfy her? Iris laughed at the question.

'The little guzzler's with nurse already!'

Nerysa felt Demetrius and Archias tense - the wet nurse was retained by Lucius for his favourite - but Iris only laughed again,

'Lucillus was minding the baby and, when she cried, he dragged her up the back stairs and said, "Feed my sister 'cus ma's ill." And nurse said, "Certainly I will, chicken, but you shouldn't have brought her upstairs yourself." and d'you know what he said? "Best carry her not leave her alone."'

Knowing her baby was safe, Nerysa allowed herself to faint again. She sank down to a world of confusion and angry voices which blended with reality as she came to and saw Flora's tear-stained face flicking from Demetrius to Iris, who was making desperate signals from behind his back.

'I wouldn't have left the children, sir. Dorcas made me go to the linen room.'

'*Made* you go?' Demetrius put out his hand and waited until she blushed, fumbled in the folds of her dress and laid two copper coins on his palm.

'They're hard-pressed in the linen room.' volunteered Iris, 'All the old tunics to be packed up and sent to Horta and Olympia and Cynthia helping the doctor.'

'Yes, and Stimula in the dining room.'

Iris' frantic dumb show was obvious even to Nerysa. It wasn't lost on Demetrius.

'And what was Stimula doing in the dining room?'

'Minding the silver, sir, because..'

He silenced Flora with a raised finger, then rounded on Iris, 'There are nine men and a boy in that team. We haven't given a banquet for a year. Are you telling me *they're* hard-pressed?'

'Every afternoon they're having to learn to fight, sir, and they don't see why. They had to get out. They haven't been to the barbers for a month!'

***

Demetrius was in a quandary. Whatever the excuse he couldn't wink at it. If he did, there'd be no one at home at all the next day. But, if he had them flogged, they'd be in no condition to defend the house. Rumours came home with them; thick, fast and contradictory. Marcus was dead. Cassius had been proclaimed by the Syrian legions and by Statianus in Egypt. Marcus was not dead but Cassius had thought he was. Cassius had landed at Ostia. Marcus had secured the loyalty of the northern legions and was on the move; the show-down would be in the east.

The senate, in a rare show of spirit, declared Cassius a public enemy and confiscated his property, which threw the city into panic. Everyone expected him to march on Rome and avenge himself with his usual savagery. No doubt he'd prepare his way by cutting off the Egyptian grain supply, which he now controlled. There were wild tales of comets and swarms of bees hanging from temple roofs. A senator went into an assembly with black hair and came out with white. Priests slew victim after victim but couldn't get favourable omens. The city was doomed. Reinforcements were promised but it was hardly reassuring that the young prince, Commodus, left Rome and joined his father on the Danube,.

The familia of Lucius Lepidus was no more resolute than the rest of the city. Firm discipline proved powerless against hysteria. Unable to make anything coherent of it, Demetrius bent anxiously over his wife.

'How do you feel?'

'Wobbly. I shan't run very fast when Cassius comes.'

'Dearest, you won't need to run. Do you think I've no plans? He'll land in Brundisium or Ostia. Either way, we'll get word while the routes north are still safe. I'll send the women and boys to Horta. It's a rough life there but better than Rome under siege. I'll lay a goose feather mattress on the barge and have you floated up the Tiber, like Cleopatra on the Nile!'

'I won't go and leave you.'

'I'll be here with a hundred men, I shan't be lonely. Come, we're only expecting seven legions. Don't you know I was in Aquileia when it was besieged by barbarians?'

'I can't bear to be apart from you again. Couldn't I hide in the cellar?'

'I'll have enough to do without running down to the cellar with food parcels. You'll go to Horta with the women. Remember, our Lucius holds you responsible for the boy.'

'The emperor has his wife and son with him at the front.'

'For reasons of state. Commodus must be ready to succeed his father at once if necessary, which may all the gods forbid. If your fever's down tomorrow, I must go to Ostia. The grain's come from Sicily and Jacob thinks it's spoiled.'

'Can't they do anything at that shipping office without you?'

'Jacob's an accountant, you can't expect him to diagnose wheat weevil.'

The next day saw him lying on his belly on the warehouse floor sifting grain through discerning fingers.

'It's weevil alright. I hope it got there in transit. If the threshing floor's infested, it'll have to be relaid.'

Jacob looked beyond the sunken silos to the cluttered warehouse floor.

We could clear some space and winnow it - try and separate out the pests, but is it worth the effort? With price controls as they are, growing grain's more of a public service than a business.'

'That would spread the infection. I doubt if it goes more than a hand deep. Just layer off the top. The rest should be saleable. Worth a fortune in a siege.'

Marching footsteps advanced along the wharf and, to his own disgust, Demetrius flinched. Panic was more infectious than he'd thought. He and Jacob struggled up and stood to attention as the officer and his guard swept into the building. He wasn't their usual excise inspector. He eyed Demetrius' travel-stained tunic and dusty limbs with contempt.

'Are you the steward of Lucius Marius Lepidus? Tell me why you should be honoured with a letter in the diplomatic bag from Tarsus? I hope Lepidus isn't making frivolous use of the postal service?'

Demetrius ran a forger's eye over the scroll.

'This seal has been tampered with.'

'Naturally. Everything that comes from the eastern provinces is subject to scrutiny, as are the recipients.'

'His Excellency, my master, may mention this irregularity to the emperor.'

'Oh, really?' He gave Demetrius a piercing stare. 'Which one? I'll just make a routine search of this warehouse. You can tell him that as well.'

The letter was long and insufferably pompous, no more than a string of bizarre commands. There was a list of assets to be disposed of including every house slave over the age of forty. Cruel and stupid! He must know Rome wasn't exactly a seller's market. Evidently he did; 'For whatever price they can fetch.' There was sufficient intimate detail for him to know it wasn't a forgery. Had illness or anxiety affected his master's mind? To make sense of it he'd need to re-read it carefully but the tone was so insulting he was in no hurry.

In his office in the cool of evening, he steeled himself to open it again and grimaced in distaste. Lucius had spread his neat hand over the fine paper as expansively as he might have stretched his pampered limbs over his ivory couch. Demetrius leapt up and ordered a fire kindled in the brazier – a sufficiently unseasonable order in July to send rumours flying round the house that he'd taken a fever. He ordered everyone from the room and passed the paper through the smoke. As he'd suspected, Lucius had written in citron juice between the lines.

'Lepidus to his dearest, most cunning brother, greetings. When you hear C is dead – slain by his own troops - believe it. I escorted the severed head to Sirmium. A fruitless exercise, you might think, since Marcus wouldn't look at it and ordered it to be decently buried. Some say C's correspondence was burned to protect the empress – preposterous - but you can imagine how it distresses Marcus that such things are said.

'I shall reassure you that my health is good before alarming you by saying I'm on my way back to Alexandria where the situation is chaotic. But Marcus has been acclaimed there and Verus is going to Syria to take control. The emperor has graciously promoted your happy brother to the rank of Knight Illustrious and addressed him by the title, 'Splendide'. You know his reason. He intends to be merciful to the officers in Alexandria for my sake. Ironic, don't you think, since I've been at such pains to have them punished? He says he would even have pardoned C if the assassin hadn't robbed him of the chance.

'The court leaves Sirmium soon and I'm to receive them in Alexandria by the end of the year. Marcus wants to stay there as far as possible like a private citizen and has given me a list of the scholars he wants to meet. For all that, we shan't avoid tedious embassies, official receptions and all the sort of pomp he hates.

'Don't be the first to publish this but, as soon as you hear it from another source, confirm it vigorously. Then you'll do well to report my good fortune and instruct my people to refer to me by my new title. They may need a donative to help them remember so don't hesitate to be generous.

'Charisius should file this letter with those we intend for publication. Having had the good fortune to witness such momentous events at first-hand, I've reason to hope my memoirs will find a modest readership.

'I was glad to hear that Lucillus liked the presents I sent and happier still to know they don't console him for my absence. He's full young and you can't remind him too often how much his patron loves him. Imagine my impatience! Nothing but imperial command keeps me away when I yearn for home and for her. Do you speak to her of my love and longing? You yield more in generosity than obedience, for her sake as well as mine, but I shall reward you, believe me, with more than my love.

'I'll write again to tell you if the Empress is as beautiful as she's reputed but, whatever duty may move me to say, you may be sure she doesn't compare with the one who holds my thoughts, waking and sleeping.

'I long for you, best of brothers, almost as much as I long for her. Keep them both close to you and in the best of health. To have them in your faithful care is my greatest comfort. Keep well!'

Demetrius caused further alarm by rushing from the house, intent on selling the gladiators while the price was still rising.

As surely as he knew Lucius would come safely home, he knew he would honour his vow and give Nerysa up to him. But not until. He took her as his own scribe. She was happy to escape Adrian's charge, on one condition. Someone must protect Melissus.

Adrian had grown careless and welts on the boy's legs showed beneath his tunic. Questioned, he confessed to speaking without permission. Demetrius ordered him to remove his tunics. He blushed and looked up at him beseechingly but Demetrius coldly repeated the order. When the tunics lay on the bench he silently indicated the loincloth. Melissus stood naked before them. He was a singularly beautiful boy but he didn't bare his body with pride because it showed that he'd failed to please his superior. Demetrius had him turn slowly round, noting each weal and bruise and every fading scar. The boy looked up at him again, desperate to promise improvement, to beg for more time to learn. Ordered back to work, he held his head thrust upwards so his eyes shouldn't spill the caustic tears of despair. Demetrius called Adrian to his office to present the accounts. They were by no means perfect but he made no complaint. When they had wrestled them to a balance he asked pleasantly, 'The lad, Melissus, did you make a bad buy there, my friend?'

'I'm sorry if you think so, sir. If I could persuade you to be patient...give him a little more time. I think he'll serve well enough.'

'He seems to need heavy correction.'

'I thought it best to be firm at first.'

Demetrius raised his brows.

'..and I may have been a little hard on him, sir.'

'Not a bad price if he's satisfactory. Did you take five percent?'

'Ten, sir...the price was so low.'

'If he's suitable, he can be managed without the whip. If not, you forfeit your commission.'

Lucius wrote again to say that he would never meet the empress Faustina. She'd died, on the way to Egypt, in her fourteenth pregnancy. Demetrius was quick to tell Nerysa. Whenever he'd fretted about the dangers of child-bearing she had cited the empress' large family. Now she wouldn't be able to. She dismissed the gossip about Faustina, assuring him that any woman who had borne sixteen children in thirty years and whose body had been bloated by two sets of twins, couldn't have had the energy for so very many lovers, let alone the time. He was glad, for the emperor's sake, to bow to her superior knowledge.

The threat of war lifted, the domus relaxed in a languorous autumn. Golden quince and pears and jars of honey arrived from Horta by the wagonload. The children romped in the peristyle and their joyous shouts echoed through the house. The master's return was delayed yet again. Demetrius kept his own counsel but he loved his wife with that desperate intensity with which a man loves that which he is about to lose.

CHAPTER LXIII

March 176

Sine me tibi ductor aquarum Thybris et armiferi sordebunt tecta Quirini.

Without me the Tiber, prince of rivers, and the lordly roofs of the Quirinal will lose their charm for you. Statius Silvae III v 111-2

Lucius returned by the first boat out of Alexandria. Against the odds, his posting had been a triumph and he was coming home to his beloved. When he stood in his marble hall, head covered and bowed, making the thanksgiving sacrifice to the gods of his hearth, he was glad he hadn't achieved his girl before he went away. Delay had honed his longing until its sweet pain was almost unbearably sharp. Her loving surrender would crown his achievements, his trials and his patience and would come with his brother's free consent. If she gave him her heart, as well as her body, he'd reward her generously. There were even moments of giddy irresponsibility when he thought of freeing her and taking her as his official concubine.

When he saw Lucillus, the magic of their first meeting worked again. The boy had lost all but the vaguest memory of Lucius' face but he knew the touch and scent of him. Swung up into his arms, he squirmed and sobbed with delight. Lucius was weak with joy that his boy had flourished and still loved him. Remembering the lost lives and ruined careers of the past two years, it seemed miraculous that the fragile bond between himself and a child had survived and strengthened. Even when he was receiving colleagues or dispensing legal advice, he never rejected the sticky hand insinuated into his and he patiently answered a hundred questions a day as Lucillus referred everything he'd ever been told to his oracle for confirmation.

Lucius couldn't begin a love affair with Nerysa by banishing her baby. He didn't want to see or hear of it but he thought of a use for it. Lucillus had no appetite for the breast now. He took his meals with Lucius who lifted him onto a footstool to offer portions of food at the shrine and recite the ritual prayers. But if he should fall ill and refuse solid food, it could be lifesaving to have a wet nurse still in the house with abundant milk. The baby should work those breasts and keep them active against the boy's needs.

***

Nerysa's chest was bound. She was given dry food and nothing to drink, so her milk dwindled and dried. Philemon reappeared in Demetrius' office. The strain of having the house besieged with callers and holding nightly celebrations seemed to be telling on Demetrius who grew daily more distant and preoccupied. She asked why, when all the staff were stretched, he kept her idle.

'If you really want to help,' he said, 'take this list to the porter's room and check the musicians' instruments for tonight.'

They were all in order; aulos, castanets, cymbals and harp. It was five years since she'd seen a harp and it beckoned irresistibly. She drew it lovingly to her shoulder and tuned it to her own native modes. She didn't care that the strings chafed her fingertips, tender with disuse for, from the first tentative sweep, memories of home came flooding back to her. As long as she sounded them, she was lost in a blessed vision of mountains, sea and mist, and faces seen in a blur but felt with piercing sharpness. Hypnos had to shake her arm to make her aware that the master and steward were in the room. Lucius, smiling graciously, poised himself on the porter's stool.

'Play for us.'

She wasn't in practice but she'd boasted to Demetrius she could play the harp and play it she would. Not one of the salon pieces she'd learned in Rome. A desolate Celtic lament came to her and, as she played, every note and syllable and every nuance of feeling flooded down the years to her, richer, more intense since she'd lived and suffered. The pain of exile needed no language. It throbbed in every cadence. When she fell silent, the three men were still, eyes focused on the distance. She felt she'd done her people credit. Appreciative sounds from the crowd around the doorway encouraged her to look up.

'Was it well, master? Would you like me to play tonight, for your guests?'

Flushing darkly, Lucius turned on his heel and left. Demetrius followed him without a word. It was evening before she saw him again and said, 'The master didn't care for my music.'

'On the contrary, he cared very much. He's bought a harp for you. But I should think you'd want to make yourself scarce tonight. The guest of honour is your old friend Severus.'

'Is Lucius working for him now?'

'He will be; he's the praetor's assistant and Severus becomes praetor at the end of the year. A cosy arrangement."

'Is it? Wouldn't Lucius like to be praetor himself?'

'He's too young. He'd need to be over thirty and a senator. I think he feels the way I used to feel about freedom. He's happy enough it'll come eventually but he doesn't need it now. Of course, you're right. Effectively, he was doing a praetor's job in Egypt. But to do it here in the glare of publicity and under the emperor's eye, that's make or break. He wants to get experience, see how Severus does; make sure that, when it's his turn, he shines.'

When Lucius sent for her to play, she recognised the harp. It was the one she'd played in Quintus' house. As a friend, Quintus would happily have given it to her but, for the use of his slave, her master had bought it. This small detail brought home to her the immensity of the gulf that now separated her from Quintus. The Styx was no wider - as Demetrius had once told her.

The next day Demetrius spoke to her. He began by warning that his freedom was no longer there for the taking and that hers would have to be earned. Face and voice expressionless, he told her he'd given her up to Lucius. He hadn't spoken before because he hadn't wanted to cast a shadow over their last months together. He added that he still loved and wanted her as much, indeed more, than ever but that he'd made the wisest decision in the circumstances.

Because this was all delivered in the tone he normally used to list the contents of a warehouse, its full significance took time to penetrate her consciousness. He asked her to spare him the embarrassment and herself the humiliation of pleading with him. His intention was fixed and he was bound by oath. There was no time to excuse herself. She ran to the washroom, crouched over the latrine and vomited. He'd abandoned her and she'd never felt so alone.

For days, they lived an unreal life, calm and formal on the surface, apprehensive and resentful below it. Outwardly, he was completely self-controlled. His equanimity deceived Lucius but not her or even Polybius, who tiptoed round the room unable to look either of them in the eye. She felt Demetrius' pain so keenly she was hardly aware of her own. He needed the balm of silence. Words pierced straight to the throbbing sores of jealousy and loss, denuded them and doused them in gall. But she needed words to express her anger and unite them in common grief. She slipped her hand into his and asked, 'Is a slave's oath binding?'

He looked wearily at her. 'Legally yes. Morally, isn't that precisely the point that troubles you? It needn't. Our marriage was never more than a charade. Between you and Lucius, if he freed you, there could be, not marriage, of course, but a legal contract. If he felt sure of your loyalty, I think he might offer you that.'

'I don't give a fig for a legal contract. I tell him I'm afraid to break my marriage vows but that's not the true reason.'

Her look challenged him to ask the reason and when he did, she pressed his hand and told him. 'I only want you, it's you I love.'

He held her gently by the shoulders and looked down into her eyes.

'If it weren't for me, you'd go willingly to Lucius. I still think you'll be happy with him. You've closed your mind to him and not given him a chance. He's the sweetest, most amiable of men. He has everything to make you happy.'

'He hasn't the first essential, he's not you. Why are you giving me up without a fight?'

'One man has absolute power over another. That's where we start from. A prudent man obeys before he's forced.'

'Yes, if the order's reasonable. But you know there are things you couldn't make me do.'

'I could make you do anything I liked, by forbidding you to do it in a sufficiently provoking way. A resourceful man doesn't shout his mouth off. He goes somewhere private and thinks. I'm as quick as the next man to reach for the oar when the wind drops. If there was a way out of this, I'd have thought of it.'

'There are a hundred women in this house and no slave in Rome he couldn't buy. The only reason he wants me is because I'm yours. You've caused this with your dissembling! Make him understand how we feel. If he knew how he's hurting you, he wouldn't persist.'

'He would. He loves you. He has hordes of friends and followers but, apart from Lucillus, there are only two people in the world he loves. How do you suggest we tell him they're deceiving him with each other?'

'That's my point. We shouldn't deceive him. We should tell him plainly that I love you and you love me and there's no room for him between us.'

'He's found the girl he's waited all his life for, the one he's destined to love. Do you think he's going to stand down in favour of his own slave? He's been good to you. If you can't feel love for him, you could at least feel gratitude.'

'I do! And I serve him with all my strength; train his staff, write his letters, raise his favourite and I'd willingly do far more. It's only this one thing that's not just of him to ask.'

'He's every right to ask it and we always shared. Think how much of his gracious life I share. Shouldn't I divide the blessing I have with him?'

He spoke as if directing the question to himself but she had the answer.

'Then I suggest you give him a half of one percent. When he dines out does he lean over and help himself from his neighbour's plate?'

'No, but if a senator dined here and admired an *objet* or a slave, I'd be sent round first thing the next morning to present him with it.'

'Look, we are nothing and we have nothing except this one thing which is so precious he can't buy it at any price. Are you going to let him just take it?'

'I don't give him anything of your love for me. But for him, you must feel something.'

'Exasperation! He thinks, because you have me and are a happy man, that he'll be happier if he takes me away from you. Is this man two years old or eight and twenty? Lucillus has more sense.'

'You're perverse. You can share your master's bed. Why cling to a slave?'

'Perhaps you won't be a slave. Perhaps you expect me to wheedle your freedom out of him.'

He cried out in alarm. 'Great gods Nerysa! You'll ruin us. That's something a slave never asks. The motive for freeing a slave is the pleasure a man takes in his own spontaneous generosity. It could never come in response to a request – much less a demand. It's as well I'll be in the house to advise you.'

'Why shouldn't you be in the house?'

'He thought it might be easier for me to live at Horta or Ostia, at least at first, but I'd rather live under the same roof as you. We must meet as colleagues though, and take care not to make him jealous.'

'For a night...or two – a month even – to heal his pride, then I'll be back.'

'I don't think so. I've seen women come and go but now he's in love. And the longer he lives with you, the more he'll find to love. He's my other self. I know what you'll be to him. What I don't know, is how I'll go on without you.'

'How long have we got?'

'Until tomorrow.'

The next afternoon she asked for the apricot silk. She'd decided to adorn herself for her master. *Once he hands me over to his women, they'll make a painted doll of me soon enough,* she thought. Demetrius flinched at the sight of her but his reaction was muted, as if he'd set her apart as someone removed from his sphere. Conducting her through the peristyle, he was already the respectful escort of his master's mistress.

The opulence of Lucius' bedroom surprised her. The softness of the drapes and rich hues of the tapestry cushions, heaped on couches and tumbling onto layered Persian carpets, contrived an oriental splendour that Demetrius had declined to emulate. Against the walls were ornate tables bearing pyramids of fruit and cakes, wine cups and cascades of flowers. Lamps hung from four massive bronze standards, burning scented oil and casting warm, dancing light on porphyry vases and gilded statues. Her throat tightened at the sight of the great bed strewn with roses. Wherever had he found roses in March?

The room was eerily still, emptied of the army of busy people whose constant care it must be. Only the walls were peopled and they made her cheeks throb; Bacchus and Ariadne, Venus and Adonis, Cupid and Psyche; legendary lovers, naked and shameless. She looked away from them towards Lucius, gorgeously robed, garlanded with laurel and flowers, quietly radiant. He signed to Demetrius that he might take a last kiss. She held his hands until they steadied. Then he put her hand into Lucius' hand, saying, 'Master, the greatest privilege you ever allowed me. Take her back with my gratitude and my dutiful love to you both.'

Abruptly, he was gone and she was alone with her owner. He sighed and raised her hand to his lips, his touch so gentle she easily escaped it and backed away until a couch separated them. She held her head high and her voice steady.

'Master, I believe you've made an arrangement with my husband concerning me. I must tell you straight away that I'm not a party to that arrangement and I don't consider myself bound by it.'

He stared incredulously.

'Surely, Demetrius has explained his wishes in this matter?'

'He's explained *your* wishes. You've complete power over me, of course. Use it. I shall resist with all my strength.'

He shook his head.

'It was like that with him. Between us, there can only be tenderness.'

'It's you who have the power and you must exercise it, not use Demetrius to do it for you. Can't you see it's breaking his heart?'

'I can't hurt you. You're too dear to me - for your own sweet sake and as the mother of my boy. We've an agreement. He swore to it.'

'He's delivered. He's brought me here and ordered me to submit to you. What more could he do?'

He crossed the room and took her hand. 'I don't want your submission. I want your love. I offer you mine in return. Doesn't that seem right? Haven't I earned your love?'

'Master, you have it and my admiration, my gratitude and my deepest regard.'

He pressed her hand.

'Demetrius wants this Nerysa, he wants it for you. Pulcher wanted it too.'

Quintus wanted it? If he, Demetrius and Quintus were all of one mind, it was a bold step to oppose their collective wisdom.

'He planned it, of course. He knew us both, knew that, if you were living in my house, I would be bound to find you and fall in love with you.'

'Master, you have wealth, beautiful houses, influential friends, hundreds of slaves. There's no woman in Rome you couldn't have, one way or another.'

'Pretty faces, shapely bodies – I can buy them in bulk. But, if a woman's face charms me, I'm repelled the moment she speaks. She's alien. Her mind, so far as I can sound it, shallow and uninformed, vindictive even. But when you speak, you thrill me. It's not your face but the beauty of yourself that draws me. I want to measure my soul against yours.

'Don't draw back. Let me explain. The banks of the Nile are crowded with temples, faced with marble, studded with gold and jewels. They dazzled me. But when I penetrated to the sanctuary in search of the god, it always turned out to be a monkey or a cat. I couldn't love a woman like that, not after you. Of course, I must marry a Roman lady to have legitimate children. But not yet, not before I've known what it is to live in love.'

'Master, think of all you have already. Demetrius has his savings, two statues and a painting, your love and me. Can you find it in your heart to take me away from him?'

'I'm not taking you away from him for ever.'

'You'll take away all his delight in me for ever. Supposing it was wrong to do that? Tell me the law. Must a slave obey if his master commands him to do wrong?'

He took the bait, sat down and deliberated, as if from his official chair.

'A slave is the agent of his master's will, not the judge. Yet, in the cause of right, maybe he can, or even should, disobey. A man could be praised for risking the consequences. But a woman? No, surely, a woman is always safe in obedience. Obedience justifies her actions because the strength to defy authority can't be expected of her.

'Nerysa, we're talking about a man who abused his authority over you, whipped you, could live with you without even discovering you were literate. I've waited four years for you. Am I to be brushed aside to spare the feelings of my own slave?'

'When you gave me to him I was a bad slave. He did have to school me with the whip. Because you told him to. Can you imagine what that meant, to both of us?'

'*I* told him to?'

'"Lick her into shape or we'll sell her." Isn't that what you said?'

'But I didn't know you. Now I do, I couldn't raise a finger to hurt you.'

'Because he's moulded me to your taste, you want to take me away from him.'

'Because I can give you a better life.'

'But you'd take me not as I was but as he's made me. Now I know the law on this point.' She stood up and smiled down at him, confident that on a point of law, she could win the argument, if not the day. 'I'm the finished artefact. The raw, untrained girl can't be recovered from me now. I belong to the craftsman.'

He stood and ran his fingertips tenderly over her neck as though she were indeed a work of art and smiled indulgently.

'But she *is* recoverable. Her master and her husband have advised, even commanded her and she's as stubborn and rebellious as ever. The craftsman only covered her defiance with a veneer of meekness. Let's give her to a more skillful one who can bend her wholly to his mind.'

She tensed and his voice dropped to a whisper, 'This craftsman has no whip. He only uses love and delight. Beloved, I couldn't bear to force you. Come to me in love. Why not?'

'Because it would hurt Demetrius.'

'But he'll get you back. As a free woman. I don't like you to be a slave, or him either. But, if you want me to do that for you, you have to do something for me. Why should that hurt him?'

She stepped back, looked at him levelly and leapt the Rubicon.

'It would hurt him more than any hundred lashes.'

'The double-crossing little cock! I - I'll have him gelded. He told you that to turn you against me. He's clever but it's himself he's thinking of, not you.'

'Master, that's not true. He doesn't know I know.'

'Then how do you know?'

Rather than betray Thaïs, she twisted the knife in the wound resolutely.

'It's common knowledge in the house, master.'

She watched him buckle. He wouldn't expect her to forgive him for what had happened to Demetrius. He hadn't forgiven himself. He choked on his words as he barked them at her in broken bursts.

'Send him to me. Get out and hold your tongue. Because if I find anyone in this house - who thinks you rejected me – I'll take you publicly and he can watch.'

His threats didn't frighten her. She knew he didn't mean them. But such coarseness, from a deeply courteous man, startled her. Now she understood Demetrius' ambivalence. It wasn't that he didn't love her. He couldn't bear his brother's grief. Neither could she. She took a step towards him opening her mouth to speak and he rounded on her, yelling, 'Get out!'

Didn't he realise she'd yielded? He screamed again, 'Get out, you ungrateful bitch, before I give you what you deserve.'

She found Demetrius stretched out on his bed. When she crossed the room, he made no reaction, seeming not to see or hear. At first she thought him strangely still but, coming closer, she saw that the muscles of his forearms were bulging, the pulse in his neck bounded violently and the corners of his mouth twitched. Dismayed that she could have come so close to betraying him, she placed a trembling hand over his clenched fist and whispered, 'He hasn't forced me. I haven't lain with him but everyone must think I have.'

He turned to her, eyes wild with horror. Seeing him sway on his feet as he stood, she guessed he'd been drinking. He steadied himself, checked his appearance and left her with the awesome thought that she'd been offered his freedom and rejected it as a thing of no importance.

***

Lucius sat rigid with fury as Demetrius knelt before him, defending Nerysa in a stream of incoherent excuses. She was ignorant and wild. The fault was his alone but, given time, he'd bring her to a proper frame of mind. Lucius watched him struggle for self-command. Many times in his life, he'd turned to Demetrius and found him like a rock. To turn to him now and find him abject, distracted and the worse for drink was shocking and Lucius veered giddily between pity and rage. If Demetrius had been honest about his feelings, maybe he could have stifled his own before they'd grown ungovernable. She too; she'd thrown up a bewildering array of excuses but she'd never said that she loved Demetrius or that he loved her, until she reproached him with breaking his heart. He saw, now, that they were still in the springtime of affection. He hadn't seen before because they hadn't let him see. Two chattels of his who owed him a lifetime's gratitude had deliberately shut him out. And they'd not only hurt him, they'd made him look ridiculous.

He lifted a forefinger to command silence and said that a certain slave was unpardonably insubordinate and must be punished but, for her husband's sake, she would not be harmed or sold. The slave's gratitude trembled between whisper and sob, a further grievance to the master, who knew himself to be the wronged party. But the consciousness of his own nobility uplifted him. His beloved thought him a heartless tyrant. He wouldn't stoop to confirm her opinion. He pronounced sentence. She would be banished to Horta. Demetrius would stay in Rome. They would live apart and reflect on their depraved ingratitude.

CHAPTER LXIV

March 176

Vides ut alta stet nive candidum Soracte.

See where Soracte stands deep in snow. Horace. Odes I ix

Archias came to wish Nerysa goodbye and brought her two books. She said defensively.

'These will be my only leaving present. You know I'm in disgrace.'

'Can't anything be done? Lepidus isn't a tyrant. Try to see him and beg his forgiveness.'

'I'm not allowed in his presence. And I've nothing to say. This is the only course which offers us a hope of happiness. Any other way and we should all have hated each other.'

He made no reply. She couldn't tell if he assented or merely declined to argue. She opened the scrolls; Galen's latest text book and a materia medica, both inscribed, 'Copied by M. Marius Archias for his pupil.'

'You've been to a lot of trouble for me. I'm grateful.'

'You're interested in the healing arts and you'll have a chance to use what you learn. There's no doctor at the villa and people will look to you as the bailiff's wife. You'll do good.'

'How could I? I know nothing.'

'By knowing you know nothing, for a start. There are so many fools giving out lethal advice with complete conviction. Often, the wisest thing to do is nothing but it's difficult to persuade the ignorant of that. Give them simple harmless instructions to follow and protect them from worse.'

'I'm interested in medicine but I'm not so presumptuous as to practise it.'

'I think you've aptitude. In other circumstances, I'd have been pleased to negotiate with Lepidus to take you as an apprentice.'

'Can a woman be apprenticed to a doctor?'

'Of course. They work as apprentices, then as assistants. Some of them become almost as proficient as their husbands.'

She looked up at him in amazement and saw that he'd said more than he'd intended and regretted it.

'Forget that. You have a husband. The very one I'd have chosen if I'd been disinterested. Books and your own observation must be your main teachers but don't forget the courier service. I'll answer your questions by letter. Only on medical matters, of course.'

'Then you'll grow tired of my letters, Archias. I'm so hungry to understand why, to...to.. "Know the causes of things"'

He laughed, 'Lucretius. Virgil agreed, "Happy the man whose mind can probe the causes of things."'

'And Propertius wanted to, "study nature's ways."'

'What a scholar you are, little one! The mystery is long, compared with a life. But you're right; we must begin by framing the right questions and never stop asking them. I pray the gods to keep you safe.'

Cradling the precious scrolls in her arms, she walked round the bedroom, stopping at intervals to fix each well-loved feature in her mind. When she closed her eyes in a strange bed she must be able to recreate that room. She'd come to it an unknowing child and would leave it a woman.

***

Demetrius and Archias were in sombre mood. Demetrius couldn't understand how Nerysa had the insolence to slight her master, still less why she should want to.

'You must have trained hounds that wouldn't serve a new master.' Archias said. 'When they hang back whining and fawning on you that's when you kick them hard, to break the bond and ease the parting. You should have rejected her more bitterly and saved her from herself.'

'I should have locked her away in my room from the start. It was pride; stupid, stupid pride. I wanted to force him to admit how fine she is. I might, at least, have secured my freedom first.'

'What difference would that have made? A freedman defers to his patron as a slave to his master.'

'She wouldn't have had to live under his nose, would she?'

'So you *did* plan to leave the house. You've been playing with fire, Demetrie. How could you be so careless of her?'

'I think he'll relent. He's hurt. But he's been patient. He deserves her more than I do even if I were his equal on other terms.'

'He's shown commendable forbearance, so far. But, if I loved her, I wouldn't rely on it. Why should she pay for your possessiveness?'

'Tell him what you told me. She can't love twice, it's not in her nature.'

'I've said as much as a freedman dare say to a powerful patron. He knows anxiety is bad for her health and that he shouldn't force her while she's pregnant or nursing. Do you mean to keep her always in that condition? That's what he thinks. Once she'd borne four children, he'd be thought unusually harsh not to free her. It'll be easier when she's out of the house. He won't visit Horta. He'll want the household to think he's lost interest. You do realise how humiliating this is for him?'

'"A good slave feels the blow that strikes his master." Do you think I don't?'

Demetrius rode to Horta, returning with two farm wagons and mule drivers. The ingrate could hardly leave her master's house in a carriage. The sight of the carts brought home the reality to Nerysa.

'What shall we tell Lucillus?' she asked Demetrius.

'I thought we'd tell him what we told him about Lucius – that you have to go away – for a time.'

'It's hard to lose your mother at any age but he's so young. When he's hurt or wakes in the night…'

'He has a wet nurse and an army of nursemaids. Lucius is devoted to him. And…he has me.'

'He doesn't often cry for me because he knows where I am if he should want me but, the first time he cries for me and can't find me – he'll be so hurt and frightened.'

'Suppose I were to go to Lucius and tell him you'd come to your senses and agreed to be his girl. I think he'd take you back, even now.'

***

The day of departure was blustery and wet. They had to leave the city before dawn. The cart was cold and uncomfortable but Nerysa was oblivious of bodily discomfort. She revered her aristocratic master and loved his beautiful, well-ordered house. She was bruised from her parting with Polybius.

'So you even froze the balls off our genial master.'

He'd heard of ice like her in the Alps. It never melted and it scorched human flesh on contact.

'Himself doesn't know how to make you obey. You should've had the master I had before I came here. He'd have known how to go to work with you. I served Himself for months before I stopped studying his legs to get early warning of his kicks. At first, when I was still a boy, he'd hold me in his arms at night and say, "Why are you so afraid? I'll look after you." By the time I believed him, he'd stopped saying it. That galls you, doesn't it, to know I shared his bed? Why don't you go and lie with the master and even the score?'

'No, that doesn't trouble me. That sort of thing's usual with boys. It was what he said to you. He didn't say that to me.'

'Hadn't he turned his life upside down for you - made himself laughed at by every menial in the house because of you? He was engulfed by you, bewildered and lost in you. And you as cold as a melon fetched up from the cellar. At least, now, we'll be at a safe distance. You'll have to turn your skills to souring the milk and spoiling the corn.'

Then he wept and begged her not to report his bitter words to his master. She comforted him, pointing out that Demetrius would still be based at the domus.

'You'll see more of him than I shall.'

'The last five years were the happiest of my life. Now Himself will change, everything will change. Why couldn't you have tried to please the master? It's not so difficult as I recall.'

'And if I had, do you think nothing would have changed?'

Polybius only saw that Lucius was looking to hurt Demetrius and that he himself would be a convenient instrument. His world had collapsed and her heart ached for him.

'Lucius wouldn't sell you, he'd more likely take you into his own service. If not, it'd be up to Demetrius to place you and he'd do it with the greatest care.'

'I've no cause to complain then. Suppose I said to you, "Himself is going to sell you, but don't fret, he'll take care to find you a good master"?'

'I'm his wife, Polybi.'

'So what? I love him more than you do.'

'Don't be ridiculous.'

'I love him more and I've never caused him the heartache that you have, curse you! Who knows as well as me how he suffers? When I rub him down, don't I feel every knot of tension in his body? Don't I pluck out his grey hairs, smell the sweat on his discarded tunic? I'll never understand it! A man like Himself with the world in his fist. Along comes a girl with a small skill on the harp, a smattering of Greek and an absurdly imperious air and he's completely thrown off course and now he's ruined. Curse the day you came here!'

She didn't try to explain her decision. He couldn't have understood it. They clung to each other, wept and parted friends, his forgiveness an added reproach.

Most of all, she felt for Demetrius. His life had been gracious and secure. Now it would be uncertain and uncomfortable. He'd said her rebelliousness would ruin them. Why had she doubted it?

The baby, attuned to Nerysa's mood, wailed incessantly. As they passed the imposing mausoleum of Augustus, Demetrius stopped the carts, pointed out the monument to the girls in the cart behind and consigned the baby to their care. Except for the driver, they were now alone in the jolting vehicle. He cradled her in his arms and soothed her.

'Don't cry,' he whispered, 'we've so much to be grateful for.'

'I *am* grateful, for myself. I've suffered less than I deserved but he's punished you so unjustly.'

'I've no complaint. I see life, I read history and poetry and it's clear love's a beguiling trap. So bright and welcoming it seems, like a beacon. No wonder those who've had hard lives take it for their rightful consolation. But it lures them into greater misery. Their love is punished as unlawful, soured by infidelity, cut off by death or separation. It has its way with them and they pay the price, a hundredfold for every fleeting pleasure. Lucretius was right, "Bitterness wells from the very fountain of delight."'

She'd brought him to these depths of disillusion and she felt beyond forgiveness but he held her closer and persisted.

'I've lived, worked and loved with you. You've shared my board and my bed, brought me joy and eased my sorrow, not just for an unforgettable day or month but for five blessed years. You've borne two children safely. There's no luckier man on earth. We must show gratitude to the gods and our master for, when the day of reckoning comes, we've a large account to settle.'

Now was the moment to explain herself.

'I thought I couldn't bring you such joy if I wasn't ...*exclusively* yours.'

'You understood me better than I did myself. But he can't keep me away. He needs me in Horta - hay time, harvest, vintage – and, if someone is to keep a watch on you, it suits us both if it's me. We still have each other and our daughter. No reasonable person could ask more. But we must give up all hope of freedom, unless we survive him and perhaps not even then.'

'Is he so bitter?'

'He's not bitter but we've given him no reason to free us. We haven't shown the devotion that manumission is supposed to reward.'

'If it weren't for me, you'd be free by now.'

Then he said something so extraordinary shock checked her tears.

'I'd rather have slavery with you than freedom without you.'

The thought was too awesome for her to process immediately but she treasured it up to savour in private and, seeing her calmer, he took the opportunity to brief her.

'Life will be different for you. No more pouring Falernian wine for urbane senators or adjusting roses in alabaster vases. It'll be putting up bread and windfall olives for the farmhands and scraping clods off the hall floor.'

She felt suddenly hopelessly inadequate, as ignorant and clumsy as the day she first found herself in Lucius' scullery.

***

Before daybreak, Quintus' faithful freedman had released her from the locked cell. His red-rimmed eyes glittered and misgiving showed in every line of his body but he gave her the heavy cloak in wooden silence and handed her over to Lucius' escorts. Except for the two short tunics she wore and the winter cloak, she took nothing with her from the house. She still remembered the steep climb up the Quirinal, the eerie light and the sequential sounds of the great city awakening.

Entering the domus by the postern gate she was taken straight to the scullery, where Arminia was thoughtful enough to ask if she'd had breakfast. The symbolism of this wasn't lost on her. She felt, like Persephone, that the first time she ate his bread under his roof was the moment she came to belong to Lucius Marius. Dressed in his livery, she began the long morning's work; unaccustomed work in a new place full of strange people, coarse yet oddly cheerful and unnervingly noisy. She'd been too disorientated to be afraid. At midday, Arminia took her to Successus, who sat and questioned her and took notes. She gave her name, age and place of birth but admitted to no skill for she'd none relevant to her new life. He'd given her a look compounded of pity and disgust and, remembering it, she flushed hotly, knowing now, what he must have surmised. He advised her to be respectful, hard-working and obedient and condescended to shake her hand and wish her well in her new situation.

The days that followed were long and confused with so much to learn but, once the unfamiliarity had worn off, she'd been at peace until the steward had noticed her. Words couldn't express the gratitude and tenderness she felt towards him or her remorse at the pain she'd caused him. But she took heart, because the present reverse in her fortunes, whatever it held in store, couldn't possibly be as complete as the ones she'd already survived.

But, as the day dawned, glimmered briefly and faded, the weary hours on the hard, jolting bench wore her down. She was thankful when Demetrius called out and the cart lurched to a halt. As he helped her down, she saw a huge menacing shape lowering over them and shrank back into his arms.

'Whatever's that?'

'Only a mountain covered in snow. You have snow in Britain surely?'

'Will it melt in the spring? Will there be grass and grey boulders and sheep?'

'On the lower slopes. And bells and shepherds and howling wolves. Why does that make you cry?'

'It will be like home.'

And yet, she wondered, where was home? Not the unknown place she was going to, not Quintus' house nor the domus. Nor yet that far northern corner she would never quite forget.

'Soracte's not an evil mountain.' he was saying. 'It's friendly. I can see it from the top of the Quirinal and think of you behind it and you'll look up at it and know I'm just the other side.'

Trembling now, she smiled up at him with brimming eyes.

'I'll be a credit to you here. No one will say I'm a bad slave and I shan't mind the hardship because I know why it's necessary.'

'You'll learn a lot from Italia, the farm manager's woman, if you don't pull rank and alienate her, as you're much too kind and clever to do. She may not unbend until Lucius comes to stay but if she's sent for to his bed and not you, she'll be your friend.'

'What's she like?'

'Very pretty, much younger than Georgius, the farm manager.'

'Did Lucius choose her for his manager?'

'How very perspicacious of you, my darling, I'm sure he did. But he's gracious. You won't be living in the villa rustica with the other slaves but in the villa urbana, his own residence.'

'Why's that?'

'I grew up in the villa urbana with him and, even now, he can't find it in his heart to banish me from it. I may keep the room we used to share. That's to remind me of the happy times we spent, how we loved each other and how good he's been to me.'

'He calls in his love with compound interest, doesn't he?'

'You challenged him to force you and he doesn't accept the challenge. You can hardly blame him for using any other ploy he can devise. What would you have said of him if he'd treated you as I did when I first knew you?'

'You didn't take me for love either. You took me so as not to lose face in the house. But you covered me with the dignity of marriage. I'd have died of shame otherwise.'

'Ashamed? Of my love? You dreaded my touch. I knew it even then though I wouldn't admit it to myself. Archias said you'd been stung by the bee without tasting the honey.'

'Well, 'I've been devouring the honeycomb ever since. You must believe I never tried to make Lucius notice me the way the other girls did.'

'You weren't to blame, it was bound to happen. We always wanted the same women.'

'But he didn't care for me at first. He only began to want me once he saw you were happy.'

'No, he thought we were *un*happy. At least, he thought you were. His mind was closed to you at first because you destroyed his dream. We planned for me to marry a rich freedman's widow so we could go into business as more equal partners because my share of the capital wouldn't have been his gift. We'd shared that dream ever since we could remember and suddenly I gave it up. He felt rejected and blamed you. But he hadn't seen you then, had he?'

'No.'

'I thought not because, before he went to Ostia, I asked him if there were any new girls he was keeping for himself.'

'And were there?'

'No, he told me to reconnoitre and if I found anything interesting to pass it on to him.'

She laughed and imitated Lucius' most reproachful tone. 'Demetrie, that was five years ago and you've still not handed it over. What a dishonest, disobedient, *ungrateful* slave you are!'

'Don't laugh, my darling, that's an irreverent summary of his point of view but I fear it's not too wide of the mark.'

But she did laugh and he laughed with her.

Her first impression of the villa was of orderliness. Poplars lined the approach road like rows of spears, guarding fields symmetrically striped by the plough. Olive trees grew in ranks and files, vine frames stood skeletal against the leaden sky. Each area of activity was rectangular and demarcated by fence, wall or hedge. Square white buildings were topped with neat orange tiles and the pleasure garden was as geometrically precise as the kitchen garden.

Peasants mobbed the cart. A wineskin was thrust through the window and she seized it because her throat was parched with dust and sobbing.

Once inside the villa, she saw it wasn't a gentleman's country mansion but a working farm; clean but unpretentious and rustic. No doubt, in summer, nature adorned it with ripples of light and shade, sweet scents and trailing blooms but, in the winter, it had no need of adornments because its master wasn't there to enjoy them.

Demetrius didn't share her reservations. At ease with the smiling staff who flocked to greet him, he shook hands, calling them all by name, a friendly comment or concerned enquiry for each. He'd had too tiring a journey to make a false show. It must be genuine. She was ashamed of her own behaviour by contrast. The household's intense interest made her stiff and shy.

A meal was served. The house was even colder than the cart. Breath froze as it left their bodies. Demetrius summoned the stoker who was a flurry of hands and excuses; the ageing system, inadequate repair budget, sickness among the slaves. The bathhouse relied on its sunny position. It was never intended to function in winter. Warm water could be supplied in jugs. Demetrius kept his cloak on in bed and told her to do the same. After his avowals in the cart, she'd expected something more passionate than a curt goodnight and a turned back, but she supposed he was tired.

Early the next morning he wanted to show her the estate. They walked ahead of Georgius and his team, following the stream towards the Tiber. Nude elder, wild fig and white willow clustered along the banks like clients round a millionaire and, beyond the estate boundary, the path disappeared under a tangle of saplings, ivy and brambles, where the last of the shrivelled berries still swung.

'This vacant farm's a disgrace!' Demetrius grumbled, seizing a fallen branch and beating a path with it. 'If the heirs have no more public spirit than to leave it a breeding ground for weeds and pests, it should be confiscated. I must remind our Lucius to speak to the magistrates again.'

They passed a bend in the river and Horta came into view. Built mainly of tufa, it boasted few marble facings but, in the hazy sunshine, it looked to Nerysa like pearl and ivory rising from the jade of the Tiber.

'You never said it was so beautiful!'

'Beautiful? Horta? A self-important little port. The river's smelly down at the wharf and the tufa's slimy around the waterline. But you're right, it looks pretty from here today. Hermes! What's going on down there?'

The next instant he was halfway down the bank, Georgius and party after him. He shouted over his shoulder, 'Those are our turnips!'

Slithering down, clinging to overhanging branches, she saw a laden barge tied to a willow trunk and two bargemen careening along the towpath towards it. Hearing shouts, they lurched into a run and, recognising Demetrius, fell on their knees with a loud snapping of twigs and crackle of dry leaves.

'There was a clear night, last night, sir, with a full moon.'

'And a sharp frost.' snapped Demetrius, examining a turnip in each hand.

'We thought we'd bring the barge this far so as to be early to market.'

'But it seems you will be late.'

'Slipped into town, sir. The watch arrested us...'

Demetrius was white around the mouth. 'Get those turnips down to the port.' he said to Georgius. 'Take these two home and have them chained up.'

He turned back towards the villa. Nerysa was hard-pressed to keep up and disappointed to have missed exploring the town. They trudged through fields in silence and caught up with the plough. The oxen were not the stocky, brown British breed. They were massive and milk-white and, judging by the defiant snorts and head thrusts of one of them, tricky to handle. Demetrius signalled to the ploughboy to throw him the rope and was edging towards the beast when it lowered its head and charged. Nerysa sprang forward. Georgius clamped his hands around her chest and held her back as the beast thundered past and she felt its hot, rank breath on her face. 'Don't move.' he said in a low, tense voice. 'Our bailiff knows what he's about.'

She followed his every duck and weave but she only saw him pale and still, laid out for burial, and the house in wailing grief. She imagined life without him. After several agonising failures, he had the rope secure around the cruel horns. Then it was a routine task to subdue the beast, pushing it with all the force of his body, raining blows on its rump with his stick and shouting in a voice she'd no idea he had. The boy guided the plough alongside. Its short burst of defiance spent, the ox stood passive and obedient beside its fellow. Georgius released her apologetically.

'I meant no disrespect. It would have been unsafe for you out there and for the men to be distracted.'

Demetrius grinned and panted at the mortified ploughboy.

'It's a knack - you'll master it — then it'll be your turn to impress a novice. But never use a goad on a bull - makes him unpredictable - use your voice — failing that a stick - a whip even - but throw away that goad.'

Exercise had dispelled his anger and lightened his step. Taking her hand, he led her towards the hollow thud of mallet and chisel, scooping tree trunks into cattle troughs.

'When I'm gone,' he said, 'look at Soracte. I'll be looking at it too.'

'Go to the Tiber. I'll tear off great boughs of blossom and float them down to you.'

'Don't leave messages in the cargo or write anything to me you wouldn't want Lucius to read. After all, the couriers are his slaves not mine.'

'Then I shan't write. What I have to say is to console you, not to divert him.'

'But if you don't write, you'll deprive me of pleasure and lose the chance to include the things you want your master to know.'

CHAPTER LXV

March – May 176

Etrusci nisi thermulis lavaris Illotus morieris, Oppiane Nullae sic tibi blandientur undae.

If you don't bathe in the warm springs of Etruria no water will charm you. Martial. Epigrams VI 42

Light was fading in the yard but men were still roasting grain and whittling staves, sending flurries of shavings into the biting air. One came forward and saluted.

'Georgius says the bargemen are chained up, sir. He's not sure they went to the brothel but they admitted going to the wine bar.'

Nerysa saw why urban slaves dreaded rustication. Here, everyone worked from dawn to dusk and carried on by acrid candlelight. In Rome, one day in eight was a feast day and religious observance dictated that these were rest days. Such piety was impractical in the country. There was a long list of chores that could be done on feast days without offending orthodoxy and taskmasters to see them done. There were no luxuries, no public baths, nowhere to go for amusement. Nerysa was better off than most. She'd found a box of books under the bed and, even when Demetrius had removed the unsuitable ones, there were plenty to look forward to. But she missed her washroom. His passionate words in the cart had made her long for his touch. She wanted him to leave his sting in her; a part of himself to nurture. Her pulse raced when he said,

'Tell your women to bring soap, oil and linen. The carts are waiting.'

But, instead of the Horta road, he took a track through forest. When the cart emerged into wintry sunlight and crossed the via Ciminia they tracked a stream, foaming over a grassy bed, to a grove, numinous with swirling vapour and roar of stream and spring. Disappointed, the girls undressed slowly and held back, shivering in the last vestiges of underwear until Demetrius chased them, shrieking, into the spring. Then they squealed with surprise. The hot water warmed them to the marrow and they leapt on the scalding stones, soaping one another and laughing themselves breathless. In the covered cart, they dried, dressed their glowing bodies and believed they'd never be cold or dirty again.

'Who heats the water?'

He shrugged. 'That's how it comes out of the ground. Some say Vulcan's forge is underneath.'

He sent Iris and Charis home in one cart with the drovers telling them, 'I've business in Ciminia.' and drove on deeper into the forest.

It was late afternoon before they reached the lakeside. He made a driftwood fire and they sat astride barrels eating baked fish. He tapped his barrel and said smugly, 'Salt eels are sustaining. You won't see meat except on feast days and then just fat and offal.'

Ragged sedge framed the glassy surface of the lake. The winter sun slipped over the horizon, tipping the rippling indigo with filaments of white gold. She winced at the beauty of it, her eyes widened in roguish delight and she laughed.

'Is this his idea of punishment?'

'It's not punishment. It's an exercise in persuasion. When you're ready to crave his pardon and do as he wants, just tell me.'

'You think he'll break me?'

'I think he'll bend you 'till your white brow presses his boot. But he won't break you because he couldn't bear to see you broken.'

She tossed her newly fragrant head and laid a hand on his thigh. He held it briefly then replaced it deliberately in her lap. One by one, then group by group, stars took their appointed places in the heavenly arena, the grand luminaries and the infinite distant companies, until the black void pulsed with light.

'Like us men and the atoms that up make our being,' he said, 'a teeming multitude, each in his rightful place.'

'Doesn't anyone ever find himself in the wrong place?'

'How could he? We each have the place that providence assigns to us. But stars are so faithful, so punctual, you can sow your seed and steer your ship by them as men have done since time began.'

The fisherman's hut, built out on stilts above the lake, was dank and uncomfortable. They left early and reached home by noon. Nerysa went to the bedroom. Horta was a strange place, she thought. Here, she'd seen Demetrius white with rage, in mortal danger and passionless, all for the first time. She took a linen bag from its hiding place beneath a loose floor board and drew out its contents. Hot tears fell on Lucillus' swaddling bands, a lock of his hair, and a wooden soldier whose painted cheeks were dulled from his kisses.

Please God, let him forget me quickly, she thought.

Hearing footsteps on the stairs, she thrust her keepsakes in the bag and stowed it just as Iris came running in, overwrought and officious.

'Come quickly! To the barn! Himself wants you there.'

The barn was so still she could hear the ferrets scratching in the straw. Labourers stood in silent huddles. Demetrius, sitting on a makeshift dais, flanked by overseers, was looking at the two bargemen, shivering in loin cloths. She saw Iris' nostrils flare as her eyes followed the ropes, from their wrists up and over the massive ceiling beams. It would be an impressive flogging. Why did he want her to watch? As a crude display of power or to warn her that country life was brutal?

'You've wasted common goods and your fellows' labour.' he said 'You've nothing to say in your defence. Flogging and a year in chains on half rations.'

She looked down, wanting to cover her ears to block out the rasping of the rope over the beams as the guilty pair were hoisted up. The shadow of the weighted fetters swung in and out of her sight as the floggers stood waiting for the signal from Demetrius that didn't come.

'I see my wife is not happy. Has she some objection?'

She stood petrified, sensing all eyes on her.

'You think me unduly harsh?'

She bit her lip, determined not to fail such a public test of loyalty.

'Very well,' he snapped, 'call me a fond husband. Six months - not a day less. Flogging deferred until your next offence.'

The ropes were slashed, the men slumped to the ground and she opened her mouth to disclaim.

'Not a word!' he snapped, 'Any more from you and I'd be rewarding their crimes.'

The slaves filed out of the barn and a biting wind swept in. Demetrius stood alone, shoulders hunched against the cold and she caught a glimpse of how he might look in old age. With a sudden rush of tenderness, she ran to him.

'Sir, you misunderstood me! Of course I accept your judgement. But I'm glad you were merciful.'

He laughed. 'Mercy is it? How long do you think it is before I can get heavy work from a flogged man? Miserable wretches. Cheated in the bar and their purses stolen in the brothel. That's why they're not allowed out - too stupid. Say goodbye now, and no tears.'

'What do you mean? You can't go now. It's going to snow.'

He glanced out at the turbid sky. 'It is, but not just yet. I'll make it back before the worst.'

At first light, she put on all the clothes she had and went to look at Soracte, imagining behind its looming blackness, the warmth, light and bustle of the domus. Standing among blades of grass jagged with hoar frost, she heard, out of the frozen stillness, the smack of clogs on iron ground and the creak of leather jerkins. The work gangs were marching to the coppice, single file behind their overseers. The last two, dragging chains, caught sight of her, turned back and saluted. Their companions did the same until, threaded over the grey landscape, were groups of ghostly men with raised arms.

What a showman! she thought, laughing and crying, *He never meant to give them more than six months'*

Their gratitude humbled her. A night on the town had cost them six months chained in prison, brought out for hard labour on a pound of bread a day. How much was a ton of turnips worth? Less than a vase of roses out of season. She didn't blame Demetrius who'd told her he imposed the rules on her as on himself, because he'd no choice. He'd passed the sentence on behalf of Lucius who would never know anything about it. Lucius' inclinations were good. There was no malice in him, perhaps because he'd never encountered any. He was sublimely unaware of the misery that ensured his own comfort. But she wasn't.

She'd lost her innocence. There was a yawning gulf between 'them' and 'us' and she'd crossed to the other side. It no longer seemed right that the energies of a thousand people should be directed to the happiness of one, however noble and well-intentioned. To suit him, she'd been forced into marriage, ordered out of it, parcelled up and sent to Horta because he thought she wouldn't be able to stand it. Her jaw clenched. She'd prove him wrong.

A golden crocus cup gleamed at her from the cracked ground and she knelt and scraped it free with an icy stone. Replanted in a cracked clay lamp, it cheered her room and told her, 'If I can bloom here alone in the cold, so can you.'

Did fate have any purpose for her, she wondered, other than amusement? At twenty three she'd lost three lives; her childhood, her Roman girlhood and her marriage. All had left tendrils binding her heart. Demetrius had left her, as a parting gift, the devotion of every slave in the villa. The snow-capped mountain with its promise of wild flowers and sheep evoked her native countryside and Quintus' poetry flowed in streams of consolation through her mind.

But life was bleak. Winter returned with vengeance. No one could remember such a raw April. Slaves wore all their tunics, one over the other, even in bed and still their bones ached with cold. Demetrius came to her in vivid dreams. She'd wake happy and wonder why she felt vague foreboding. Then memory washed back with its drift of grief. She was still in the rhythm of Lucillus' routine; his mealtimes, his playtimes, his walks and his bed times still punctuated her day. Often she savoured a thought to share with Demetrius, then remembered she wouldn't see him until it had been forgotten or lost its relevance. She couldn't tell whether it was an afterglow of his presence or a tangible sense of his absence that dogged her like an incubus. Her flesh ached and her womb wept for him.

Spring slipped late and haphazardly into her lime and magenta veil, like a girl who'd overslept and dressed in careless haste. Charis and Iris cast off their heavy cloaks, laughed at their coarse unflattering uniforms, saw themselves and cried. They were vain enough to care that their bellies ballooned on black bread and beans.

'This isn't food,' Iris squealed, 'it's fodder!'

Boredom was adding to their misery and Nerysa confronted Italia.

'You haven't given us any work.'

'I've no orders to make you work. Just to lodge you. I could ask Georgius if he wants a scribe in the farm office.'

'No. I want to work with the other women.'

Italia shrugged and produced three aprons. The villa's copper pots were assembled outside and they scoured them with pine cones, sand and salt until they spangled in the pallid sun like the tiny wild jonquils on the hillside. Nerysa trembled with fatigue but slept soundly for the first time in weeks. From then on, she filled her life with toil and slept from sheer exhaustion.

Iris objected, 'We're not here as farm hands.'

'Nor are we parasites. I shall earn my keep.'

'You don't understand the master. He doesn't want you for a drudge. How could scrubbing floors atone for the wrong you did him? He only wants you to be sorry.'

'Perhaps I am.'

'Then, dearest, just say so and he'll be straight here, jump from his horse and run into the house and call you. You'll fall at his feet and wash the dust from his sandals with your tears. He's too good to reproach you. He'll just sweep you up in his arms and take you home.'

'And if I don't?'

'What do you mean?'

'If I just carry on working here and don't complain.'

Iris' face took on the frozen horror of a mask from the tragic theatre.

'Then we'll all be stranded here for ever! You can't do that. You're cruel and mad!'

A sharp kick sent her pan of leeks bouncing down the grassy slope and a chopping knife went flying after it as she rushed into the house.

'Is that what you think?' Nerysa turned to Charis who shook her head and sobbed.

'She says you play your own games with our Lucius and don't care that we suffer for it. But she was stuck in the back kitchen until you brought her into the nursery. She should remember that. Why do you let her speak to you so rudely?'

'Because she's not my servant any more; she's my gaoler.'

Routine and hard work numbed their despair. They came to terms with their fate. Charis wrote letters, Iris cajoled the messengers. Fashionable clothes, cosmetics and perfumes found their way from the domus. If there was no one at Horta worth attracting, to care for their appearance was second nature and luxury items were valuable currency on a country estate.

***

Applying all his powers, it took Lucillus two months to defeat Lucius. The struggle and the journey exhausted him. He lay drained and limp in Nerysa's arms. It was bliss to bury her nose in his soft curls and press her cheek to his.

'It wasn't the crying all night or asking ten times an hour, "When's Ma coming home?" ' Demetrius explained. 'It was when he went off his food and then we heard of a case of plague in Ostia. Lucius panicked. But sending him here was like cutting off his own arm. It'll be the same for Lucillus. He'll wake up tomorrow crying for Lucius.'

He didn't stir as she laid him in the cot beside his sleeping sister. As she turned to Demetrius, her thighs slid apart involuntarily and the liquor of desire streamed obediently down them.

'Well,' he asked, 'what do you want to ask me for?'

She blushed, the question was bald.

He frowned. 'Hasn't anyone given you petitions for me?'

'Oh, that. Yes, lots of them have.'

He took up a tablet and lent against the doorjamb, stylus poised.

'Georgius wants to go to Perugia to see a threshing machine. He can't get there and back in a day so he needs permission to stay away for a night. Amemone says she should be exempt from work because she's had four children but Georgius says the one that was born dead doesn't count. One of the prisoners says his gaoler kicks him and gives him short rations. There's so much of it I made a list.'

'Let's go through it. Were you offered any inducement to appeal to me?'

'I'm sorry, should I have taken bribes and passed them on to you?'

'No, it's good to keep debts alive. Who knows when you might need to call them in? If our people here love you, it makes it more difficult for Lucius to…Has Georgius been hunting?'

'I think so. I saw a hare hanging in the meat store.'

'Make sure he knows you noticed. If I don't mention it, he'll be grateful. I could wish you hadn't taken on that girl, Iris. You know she spies on you?'

'She's no choice. Yes, I know we'd see we had a choice but she doesn't.'

Throughout his visit, he was friendly but cool. Reflecting wryly that she'd been adept at repulsing advances but had no idea how to encourage them, she dealt directly.

'When we came here in the wagon, we talked about the honeycomb. But since I praised it, you've given me none.'

She shrank from the contempt in his face. 'Do you plan to staff Lucius' estates with slaves?'

'I'm not afraid or ashamed to bear children, sir. It's the lien of my sex. When I look at our children, I can't regret them.'

'I'm glad you're satisfied, there'll be no more.'

She gasped as though he'd struck her. Had she rejected Lucius for this? It was *because* she'd rejected him. Demetrius was punishing her on his master's behalf. Or repulsing her in deference to him.

She said, 'This is *his* doing. We must take no pleasure in each other in case it pains him to think of it. But why shouldn't we? Isn't exile a heavy enough price to pay?'

'A trivial price compared with the hazards of childbearing.'

'You don't care about that. You'd love it if I bore twins like that famous Lycian girl; one a copy of her master and the other the image of his steward. What a tribute to your mutual affection! The truth is, neither of you loves me, you love each other. I'm just a toy you like to squabble over.'

'There's no squabble. It's settled. I'm to choose a girl and move her into my room.'

'And. have you?'

He lowered his eyes. 'I haven't found one yet, to suit.'

'And he thinks a bitter, rejected woman would make him a good bed mate.'

'He'd console you.'

'Of course! A few shopping trips to the Saepta, a rope of pearls and I'd have forgotten you entirely.'

'Not entirely, I hope. But it's a poor sort of love that can't convince itself it must be requited.'

'Demetrie, you should look to your master. Confine him to his room and consult his relations. He's insane.'

'Of course. Love is madness. Aren't we all mad? You'd think me mad if you knew how much I've been offered, to say nothing of my freedom which is worth half a million.'

'Then let me go! I swore to be faithful to you for as long as you wanted. Look me in the eyes and tell me you don't want it.'

He looked up at her, then down at the floor. His lips writhed in an agony of effort but no sound came.

'Suppose a widow's life doesn't suit me? Suppose I move some one into *my* room?'

'Who do you think would risk his hide for that?'

He went out early and she didn't see him again that day. In the evening, Charis came with a tray and orders to eat in her room. She never knew where he spent the night but lay sleepless and weeping for him until dawn rustled behind the shutters and he came in, clothed for outdoor work. A swift look was enough to tell her she hadn't been forgiven.

'Put on your cloaks and boots,' he said, 'and come.'

Taking her hand, he pulled her downstairs, out of a side door and into the keen morning air. She stumbled as he hurried her to stand beside the villa rustica under a great yew whose branches swept the ground. He pointed up at the gable, his voice thick, she thought with suppressed rage.

'Do you see that window? My mother died in that room. Lucius and I stood here for three days listening to her die. We heard, desperate, unbelieving screams, then moans, a few whimpers, then silence. We thought she was sleeping until they came and told us she was dead.' His voice cracked and he swallowed convulsively. His hand crushed hers. 'The child they cut from her belly was dead too. We cursed her.'

'Why curse her?'

'She'd no right to leave us. It was her duty to care for us, we needed her.'

'You were only children then, but later when you talked...'

'We've never talked about her, never since that day. If you die here like that, it won't be on my account. I've sworn it. Not, as you so charmingly propose, because Lucius would reproach me with the loss of his property but because I don't want to live without you as I've had to live without her. If you tempt me, I'll put you out of my bed and my room.'

Her own pain seemed suddenly small and unworthy. Slipping both arms around him, she pressed him close.

'My dearest, I'm so very, very sorry.'

He didn't draw back. He seemed to need to stand in that very spot and be held by her, just as, the last time he'd stood there, he'd held Lucius. The sun rose higher and its rays penetrated the awning of the tree, bathing them in dappled light and consoling warmth. She lowered her eyes and whispered, 'Do you remember, once, telling me to take you in my mouth?'

He raised a hand to strike her but lowered it as she flinched in surprise.

'You're not to blame, you were innocent before I corrupted you. A respectable woman knows nothing of such acts. A respectable man doesn't practise them.'

'Then, when you're back in Rome, could you ask Archias if he knows a way to avoid pregnancy?'

'I have. He knows several but none he can guarantee, so none that's acceptable to me. There's no doctor in Horta and none he recommends in Narnia. We couldn't expect Lucius to send him from Rome or that he'd come in time to help you. I'd be a thankless man if I couldn't content myself with your company, your affection and your good health. Can't you be content with the same of me?'

It was no mean compliment he paid her, to want her as his friend for life. Once she would have welcomed that. She'd been unawakened, indifferent to physical pleasure until he intruded on her maiden serenity, roused her and made her pulsate with the lust he now declined to satisfy. Where would he take his own lust? To any woman in the house except her. Remembering her terror when he'd struggled with the ox and her brief vision of life without him, she made no reply. But she mourned his loving and the children she'd never bear. Returning to the bedroom, she found a bolster placed down the middle of the bed. She pushed it towards her own side. He shouldn't have to do heavy work after a cramped night.

***

Lucius had decreed that his favourite must be accompanied by his familiar attendants. Only Xenia was excused. Not because she was too infirm to travel, though she was, but because he'd never thought her of the slightest use to Lucillus. She was bereft. Grief toppled her into second childhood and he soon had the satisfaction of consigning her to the columbarium where he'd long thought she should be.

For Lucillus, at least, Demetrius thought the move beneficial. The master's doting affection had made him spoilt and overbearing by the age of three. A freedman, however rich and well connected, was a third class citizen. Arrogance would earn him nothing but ridicule. The kindest service he could do him was to give him a clear view of his station in life and help him suit his behaviour to it. He didn't underestimate the difficulty.

As for Nerysa, she'd survived two confinements. He'd never risk her again. Where did that leave him? He could hardly philander about the town house where his wife's stubborn fidelity had caused the master such grief. But to single out one girl would be divisive. It would create tensions distorting the finely balanced matrix of relationships that supported the general comfort. Besides, he didn't want an involvement with any other woman. He wouldn't consider the indignities of the brothel at his age or affront his neighbours by trespassing on their territories. His world had contracted, his range of possibilities narrowed to a vanishing point. But there was work. Its horizon of opportunity receded steadily and it yielded satisfaction in proportion to his investment of himself. He pounded the road between Rome and Horta so hard and so often that he and the horses could make the journey asleep.

CHAPTER LXVI

July 176

Iam mihi, libertas illa paterna, valle. Servitium sed triste datur, teneorque catenis Et numquam misero vincla remittit amor.

Farewell freedom of my fathers! I'm given over to miserable servitude. Love never slackens his cruel chains. Tibullus II iv

Zoë had died before the ravages of the plague made it necessary to outlaw private burial on country estates. Her grave was unmarked but memories were long and, when Demetrius asked, people showed him where his mother and her child lay. He would take a camp stool and sit there, gradually releasing his bitterness towards her.

Nerysa brought wine and incense and, together, they hallowed the place. She thought it a perfect place for a burial. Gaudy monuments, cheek by jowl on the public highway had never appealed to her. Zoë, she told him, had returned to nature, roaming free in the rustle of trees, the rush of water and birdsong. She quoted his favourite poet, 'God pervades his whole creation and all things return to him, dissolved, restored.'

'Don't let's go in yet, my darling,' she would say, 'I want the nightingale to sing for you.'

These thoughts comforted him and, when he sat by the grave on balmy nights, he did believe he sensed his mother's presence. He wanted to set up a monument but it was unthinkable to do that without Lucius, who composed the citation, designed the stele and would come in person to dedicate it.

Spring was now fulfilled in all its sweet radiance, the countryside overlaid with the creamy foam of cow parsley and spiced with broom. Nerysa ran barefoot across the springy meadow to the shed, learning to match the number of fleece to the number of sheep and to milk goats without getting kicked. She pressed curds in wicker baskets, taking them to a trestle, set up under a holm oak, for the goatherd's woman to salt and mix with olives and cobnuts. Each time she brought a full tray, the woman looked at her intently, finally lowering her eyes and scratching the soil with her toe. Nerysa looked down and the cheeses slipped from her grasp as the sign of the fish swam before her eyes. Groping under the table, scooping curds back into baskets, her words came in a low rush. 'Even here, you know about the new god?'

'What god do you mean?'

'I heard about a god, higher above this world than Olympian Zeus, who hid himself in human flesh so he could share its misery. That's a god I could worship with my whole soul.'

'You're in the right place. Half the rural family is Christian. Didn't they tell you at the domus?'

'I...stopped going to meetings in Rome. I...did something to embarrass them – but it was because I didn't understand and I never would again.'

'You're welcome to come to ours.'

'One of my women...watches me.'

'We know. We could get you books.'

'Leave them in the top attic inside the formularies.'

She returned to the shed elated, as if she'd been bidden to a higher plane of being, just as Iris emerged from behind it, face flushed, tunic hitched up and legs splayed. Nerysa saw the ploughmen swaggering off in the opposite direction and hot rage swept over her.

'Our noble master ought to know how you behave.' she hissed. 'In front of the children too. Someone should be telling tales about *you*.'

'Do you think he only cares for prudes? Your virtue's lost its charm, even for your own husband. When I'm an old hag, sitting at my cottage door weaving baskets, I want some memories to live on.'

'Just how many memories do you want?'

'As many as I can get!'

Nerysa held out her baskets of curds. 'We make cheese in my country too,' she said, 'and something else that you don't. It's rich and sweet and golden and we make it from pure cream. You can't get it from whey, no matter how long you churn it.'

Iris and Italia both preened themselves as the master's visit approached. Italia wanted to know how he was served at the domus. Nerysa explained that what he most valued was quiet. That was impossible on a farm. The noise of the workers, animals and machinery continued even through siesta time. But she must keep the children and house slaves quiet while he reclined in his day room and his meal times were sacred. She showed her how to set down dishes soundlessly and advised the flat-footed waiters to walk on tiptoe. The dining room should be so silent, the service so unobtrusive, that the lectores could read him letters and he could dictate replies without raising his voice. Italia must not lapse from complete concentration and never take her downcast eyes from his table, judging when to replace the courses. She taught her to add sweet herbs to the rinsing water and warm it to diffuse its fragrance. Italia, wide-eyed, blushed for the rough and ready service she'd been used to offer.

As a final precaution, Nerysa sent her daughter to the villa rustica with the other slave children. She, herself, would keep out of sight unless he sent for her. She dreaded that. Demetrius didn't mince his words.

'How long do you think he's going to play these games?' he demanded 'How long before he takes it out on the children? Stop agonising about right and wrong. Virtue, for you, is obedience.'

He held her while defiance drained from her, then drew back sharply so she knew, at least, that her yielding body in his arms was still a temptation.

***

Lucius knew the villa was agog to know where his favour would fall. He dangled it briefly before letting it light on Lucillus. He observed his progress minutely and with satisfaction. Back in Rome, friends would enquire and he'd be able to say that Lucillus could sit a pony and drive a goat cart. He could run, swim without a cork float, count and recite the alphabet in Latin and Greek; and all with more style and grace than any boy the world had known. He took him on his tour of the estate, accompanied by Demetrius, with Charis and Iris following on foot. No sooner had he set off than he realised that he'd made a mistake. Her absence was even more tangible than her presence would have been.

He couldn't avoid seeing her at the dedication ceremony, for all the slaves and tenants assembled to pray. She was cleanly and neatly presented, anything less would have been a punishable insult to his presence, but he couldn't flatter himself that she'd made any special effort to attract him. Ready to forgive, he waited in vain for the look or gesture that would make it possible. He asked himself, yet again, with exasperation, in what did her charm consist? She wasn't a gaudy flower. She didn't flaunt her original mind, her winning speech or her whimsical humour. The unsuspecting would pass them by. He glanced across at the modest veil and devoutly bowed head. Who would guess at her waywardness or the tenacity with which she clung to her sham marriage? It was the unpredictability, the internal contrasts that tantalised him. He'd gaze at her lips, seemingly made for kissing, until she opened them and said something so pertinent, so rational, only a man could have said it. It was as arresting as a shower of icy water on his back. And her charm was exclusively for him. Only the most perceptive could enjoy her. Demetrius, with his fabled eye for quality, had failed even to discover she was literate. He all but laughed aloud. Whatever had Severus seen in her? Not erudition certainly. She was for the connoisseur. Quintus had known that. He hadn't trumpeted his gift, simply hidden her in the house. The most subtle of tributes from one discerning aesthete to another.

Demetrius, on the other hand, had disappointed him. They'd been so close. He'd always read his mind, anticipated his needs; must see that the girl was meant for him. Had he forgotten his place? When they played harpastum, he should do his damnedest to intercept the ball but, once his master tired of the game, he was supposed to hand it back with a self-deprecating smile. Lucius thought of Alexander in his tasteless tomb. Alexander who'd once offered Theodorus ten talents for his harpist. 'But not if you love her.' he'd written. 'You needn't send her if you love her.' But Theodorus was Alexander's ally, not his slave, and did Demetrius really love her? No doubt he thought he did, or had, according to his lights. But a slave must be less sensitive than a free man. How else did he endure his condition? And how did one assay the strength of love? He'd stationed himself to watch their meeting; a bland stare from him, a demure salute from her. Stubborn she was and misguided, but virtuous. Her charm was the bait on the hook, her chastity the barb, and both embedded so deeply in him he couldn't steel himself to wrench them out. He reminded himself of all that was due to his dignity and reflected that it became the philosopher no more than the patrician, to be the slave of a slave.

The nostalgia he'd so cunningly prepared for Demetrius rebounded on him. Sitting in Lucillus' nursery, the room they'd once shared, it overwhelmed him. He was haunted by a childhood unease never quite defined. He didn't reproach his foster mother. He'd adored her and she'd given him love over and above duty. Yet between her and Demetrius he'd sensed something more, too deep for him to reach. He'd heard the second child was a girl. A pity. It should have been a boy; he could have given him to Lucillus as a slave.

He'd begun to notice children, in streets and parks and friends' houses, and could see that Lucillus was outstanding; healthier, more advanced, more poised and more loving. But his friends' children were brought up in the back bedrooms of domestics because their flighty mothers had no time for them. Lucillus was Nerysa's charge and she was a devoted mother. His villa had changed; there were roses everywhere, chosen with taste. His meals were served with precision and elegance. It was her doing. She had the gift of generosity. He need only deflect it a little more towards himself and her love and her sweet body would come tumbling, ripe fruit from the arched bough. She hadn't spurned him. She'd acted from obstinate, misguided loyalty. Two for a pair, she and Demetrius. When he'd married them, a friend had asked why he was yoking a stallion to a she-ass and he'd laughed and said he rather thought he was yoking two mules.

His plan was to make her abject for forgiveness then grant or withhold it as he felt inclined but, back in Rome, he feared she'd come home with a heart hardened in resentment, not warm with gratitude for her release. He had the harp crated up and sent to her as a peace offering. She sent a letter of thanks. It was painfully stilted, dwelling on her humble gratitude, her sense of obligation, her devotion to his interests. It had obviously been dictated by Demetrius. But it was her white hand that had pressed the paper and left faint traces of her scent. He slipped it into his slim codex of Catullus against the couplet beginning 'I hate and love'. Yet even this paradox didn't describe his complex feelings. She was hardly faithless and he didn't hate her. It was just that she tormented him.

CHAPTER LXVII

October 176 – January 177

Non ignara mali, miseris succurrere disco.

No stranger to suffering I learn to relieve it. Virgil. Aeneid I 630

Archias had been right. Nerysa's knowledge was rudimentary but she had the closest thing to medical skill in Horta. She worked in a disused attic. Only Italia and Charis dared to part trusses of melissa and southernwood trailing from the rafters, disturbing dust pungent with citron and juniper. They'd find her hunched over her scrolls or grinding camomile and anise in a cracked pestle for poultices. Or she'd be beating vine flowers and white violets into beeswax as a balm. Sealed, labelled jars of poppy seed, henbane and hellebore root stood in orderly ranks along the corbels – foot soldiers in a campaign against suffering and disease.

At first, her help was spurned. The villa had an infirmary, presided over by Italia whose brief was to discourage malingering. First aid was given in the fields. For serious injuries, Georgius could call on the ostler. The superstitious swore by a variety of charms and concoctions. But, as the mother of healthy children, she was consulted by other mothers. She sat all night beside a child with pneumonia, filling the hut with pungent steam and panting hope. Unexpectedly, the child survived. A rumour spread that she'd borne the master a son. It was forbidden to repeat this story, yet everyone knew it. Her supervision of a difficult breech delivery confirmed her ascendancy over women's ailments. But the men stuck by their old arrangements.

So it was the women, headed by the ploughboy's mother, who took her to the field. The plough stood idle, the field hands clustered round the boy, waving sticks and drowning his cries in rhythmic chants.

'What are they shouting?' she asked the mother.

'The charm for mending limbs.'

'What language is that?'

'It's not a language. It's a charm.'

She elbowed her way into the circle and saw, from the flattened contour of the boy's bare shoulder, that it was dislocated. How could anyone think you could move a bone by shouting at it?

'This is useless!' she yelled.

Seizing the boy's wrist, she thrust her foot into his armpit and pulled with all her strength. His screams redoubled, the bone didn't move and she was jostled roughly out of the circle. She wept with frustration. It was her own fault. Pain and fear had made his muscles rock hard. She should have given him a skin of wine first. They wouldn't give her a second chance. Of all the injuries she could have met, here was one she knew how to treat and no one would listen. The frenzied shouts maddened her. With every passing moment, the tissues would tighten, making the displaced bone more difficult to dislodge. At last, their enthusiasm flagged and, between screams, she made herself heard. 'The gods of our hearth can't hear you. Why not take him closer?'

Somewhat to her surprise, a burly fellow threw the boy over his shoulder. His screams were hoarse now and rhythmic, jerked out of him with each giant stride towards the yard. Panting to keep up, she said to the big man, 'Hoist him up higher. Hang him over the barn door by his arm. The gods can see it now. Call them while I hold him.'

The boy hung pale and limp. The men formed a circle, closed their eyes and stamped, chanting, 'Haut! Haut! Haut! Histasis! Histasis! Tarsis! Tarsis!' Nerysa pulled steadily on his dangling wrist, with increasing confidence as she felt the limb lengthen. There was a click as the head of the bone flipped over the rim of the joint and she felt it sucked back into the socket. She fell on her knees and praised the gods with such melodrama, the men lifted the boy down and allowed her to bandage him.

To offer help was to accept responsibility. Sometimes the outcome was not good. She'd once thought whipping the keenest pain to bear, then learned that childbirth could be worse. Now she discovered there was no pain like responsibility. She was less inclined than Demetrius to blame fate. It seemed to her that an internal logic lay at the heart of creation. Intervention must be possible in ways she either failed to discover or stumbled on by accident. The 'cause of things' was such an immense and complex puzzle it would take a thousand lifetimes to scratch its surface. Philosophy proposed plotting a path to the hub of the system by arguing from first principles. She had only a few hard bright facts; missing stones from a huge mosaic. Could the overall scheme be deduced from such? Maybe, if they were combined with a million others. But she was isolated. Letters couldn't describe the characteristic smell of a wound or the consistency of a swelling and Archias' replies seldom came in time to be of any use, except for the next time. She set herself to learn; trading the pain of failure for a wealth of experience. The best traditions inspired her. To comfort always: with a smile, a soft word or touch. To relieve, when possible, with medicine. To cure, she didn't presume, yet she sensed that, sometimes, with support, the patient's own strength could do it. At least her patients were spared the mischief of charlatans because they couldn't afford to pay them. In that respect, they were better off than the rich. Rome faded in her memory. Though Charis and Iris talked incessantly of the domus, to her, it became less and less real.

Summer grew to maturity. Herbs ripened. Italia harvested honey, preserved fruit in it and carried armfuls of lavender into the house. Reaping and threshing continued all day and Nerysa went cheerfully to the fields with rations for the slaves and hired hands. Demetrius never stood on ceremony when he worked alongside the labourers. She found him at the centre of a merry group, sitting cross-legged on a mound of wheat stalks. With his face tanned and glowing, his eyes bright and his hair shedding chaff, he looked not a day older than sixteen. She knew, with a lurch of her heart, that he was happy in Horta and knew it again from his wistful look as they watched the trails of flame and smoke from the stubble and the winking lime light of the fireflies.

***

With the harvest gathered in, Demetrius hurried back to Rome. The law courts were sitting, shipping was drawing to a close and he had the year's accounts to square. The social season was in full swing and especially brilliant because the emperors were home after five years at the front. Demetrius was gratified that Marcus had a nod of recognition, even for him.

He learned that the emperor's agents proposed to make an approach to Lucius with a view to acquiring him for the imperial civil service. His peculium, his woman and his child would be included in the deal. He was sorely tempted. Imperial slaves were salaried and soon earned their freedom. A successful commission as a tax inspector could catapult him from the bottom of the social scale to the top. He could have a career as brilliant, in its way, as Lucius' own and, in all modesty, he knew he had the talent to succeed. Yet he was thrown into an agony of indecision. He couldn't feel comfortable about leaving Lucius. Eventually, he decided to put his wife's interests first. His duty to Lucius was of longer standing, legally and morally more binding but she was more vulnerable and had committed herself totally to him. Needing her encouragement to spur his ambition, he made his first and only, unauthorised visit to Horta.

'It's your destiny.' he told her. 'Pulcher meant you for the palace. Hoping for influence rather than money, I should think. From Verus probably; Verus was always a soft touch for a pretty face and a lively mind. But he died, didn't he? And that left Marcus, the strait-laced family man with money worries. So Pulcher tossed you to Lucius in a fit of pique.'

'So Lucius would have us believe. It's extraordinary how you both claim to read his mind. I lived with him and I don't.'

Her response baffled him. She was happy in the country, couldn't face life at court and wouldn't be accepted. Palace secretaries came from Greece and Syria, Spain, Africa and Palestine; not Britain. One didn't buy clerks in Britain, only herdsmen and domestics. He explained patiently, until she couldn't fail to understand, the benefits to them all and, especially, to her. She said she wouldn't hold him back. No one knew better than she how much he deserved this chance and how brilliantly he'd succeed. No one would rejoice more when he did. But she would stay behind.

He persisted. 'The beauty of it is, Lucius can't object, he wouldn't dare show the slightest reluctance. Don't you want us to be free to love each other?'

'I wouldn't be free in the palace. I should die and, if you love me, you'd regret it. You go, and leave me here.'

He urged every argument he could muster without moving her an inch. It must be that she couldn't bear to leave Lucillus. He took both her hands, and spoke gently, knowing he must hurt her. The realisation should have come gradually. Lucillus was living a privileged life. Being raised by Lucius, he couldn't fail to become a snob, indeed a worse one than Lucius because he'd always be painfully conscious of his unfortunate birth. Would he always want to recognise a mother who was a disgraced slave, degraded out of the urban family? Her best chance of a long term relationship with him was as an imperial freedwoman. She turned on him, desperate with rage and grief. Lucillus had the truest, most loving heart. How could he believe his own child to be shallow and callous? He took her in his arms and soothed her but he didn't allow her to hide from the truth. Lucillus wasn't four years old. Who could say what he'd be at twenty-four, or even fourteen?

He went to the tax office and said that, though he was entirely at the emperor's disposal, if his own inclinations were to be considered, his choice would be to stay with his master. Lepidus had been good to him and still needed him. If it should be the emperor's pleasure to insist, he hoped his reluctance wouldn't be held against him, since the emperor would be glad to have acquired a servant whose first consideration was loyalty to the man who owned him. From the recruiting officer's expression he inferred he'd shown himself to be of unsound mind and was, therefore, of no further interest.

The emperors, father and son, celebrated their triumph in December so he couldn't leave Rome at Saturnalia. He presided with Thaïs and noted, with surprise, that Jacob seemed to be suppressing resentment. The day after the triumph, he humbled his pride and begged Lucius for a few days in Horta. He judged that the euphoria of the festivities and the emperor's inspiring company would sway him to be generous. And so they did - to the extent of granting him three days leave. He told Nerysa how Marcus seemed fitter, running beside the triumphator's chariot driven by his son but failed to convince her that their purple robes were more glorious than a field of vetch in flower. He described the gaudy decorations, massed crowds shouting, 'Hail conquerors!' until they were hoarse and hypnotised, the blasts of trumpets, the clash of cymbals and the earth shaking under the boots of ten thousand soldiers. She'd seen snowy oxen with gilded horns, garlanded with flowers and ribbons, at the May festival in Horta but she couldn't begin to imagine a thousand slaughtered in a single day. He didn't avoid describing the desperate faces of the captives, destined for execution or slavery and not knowing which. Showers of gold coins, newly minted for the occasion, were thrown to the crowd and he'd caught some in his cloak for her and the children. He was thrilled by Lucius' success at court.

'I praise my genius I never took you there. Marcus has taken one of the secretaries as his concubine. I should have lost you for sure. And yet, I could never lose you. They didn't make a clean break when they wrenched us apart. There's so much of you left in me; the way I think, the things I notice, the decisions I make; all different because of you.

Lucius needs a wife. I think Marcus intends to find him one. You know he told Marcus about you and Marcus said that, as a young man, he'd had a similar problem?'

'Problem?'

'Her name was Benedicta. She was his slave and he was burning for her but he never touched her. He's proud of that and Lucius is now immensely proud that he never touched you. The emperor offered to cure him with philosophy.'

'With philosophy?'

'Apparently the emperor said love was only a friction of innards and discharge of slime and one could bend one's mind to control the urge so as not to be troubled by it.'

'Oh good,' she snapped, snatching up her cloak, 'That makes things easy then, for all three of us!'

CHAPTER LXVIII

January 177

Nil mihi rescribes, tu tamen ipse veni.

Don't send me letters. Come yourself. Ovid. Heroides I

Nerysa strode through freezing mist to the pig man's hut and was still there the next morning, a dead child warm in her arms. Defeat and sadness weighed on her and she wept with the other women. One of them caught her hand and kissed it.

'Praise the gods for you! You care about us and we're only slaves.'

She said the words she'd never said, even to herself.

'I'm a slave too.'

'I can't believe that when I'm with you. So ladylike no one's ever seen you spit.'

She was nonplussed. It was true she detested the habit but this was an odd definition of a lady.

'Since you come here,' the woman confided, 'I've tried to puzzle out who you remind me of and tonight it come to me. Zoë, the bailiff's mother that died twenty years ago.'

'Am I like her?'

'Not a bit. She were warm and brown and you, forgive me, your hair's like copper and your face like chalk. Only when you smile, then there's something of that blessed girl again, I can't say what, it don't last long enough for me to catch hold of. But I just love to see you smile.'

'I can't smile today.' she said, laying the tiny corpse across the woman's lap and stumbling out of the hut towards the bathhouse. But she smiled a secret smile as Charis rubbed her dry. She'd found a cause! She could hardly wait to run to the house and smile for Demetrius. If she saw Lucius again, she'd scowl. Demetrius, happy to see her wreathed in smiles, warmed her hands in his.

'By Venus!' he said, 'You look bonny after a sleepless night! And our Lucius imagines you wasting away with grief and cold and pottage.'

'How ridiculous! What's more delicious than vegetable soup when you're hungry? Truffles just taste of privilege. If you couldn't get pottage, you'd pine for it. Like Lucius. He only began to want me when he'd given me away.'

'What if he didn't know the true value of what he gave? It reminds me of one of his school exercises. Beachcombers meet a poor fisherman launching his boat at Ostia. They offer to buy his catch for an agreed sum. He catches a gold ingot in his nets. To whom does it belong? Discuss.'

'What was his answer?

'Well, it was one of those days when he had better things to do. I wrote it.'

'What did you say?'

'The word 'catch' means 'catch of fish'. 'Catch' implies 'of fish'. Not one of my best efforts. He was supposed to wring the listeners' hearts with pity for the fisherman's poor wife and ailing children.'

'I don't see the connection. Lucius gave. He ought not to take back. And he oughtn't to take from a man who has so much less than he has.'

'Why ever not? That's bound to happen. Say a poor man comes by a rare jewel. It's no use to gloat over it in secret. He brings it to market. Maybe the man who buys it is no match for it either. He sells it on until it finds its level. To own anything too fine is hubris, resented by one's betters. And a slave hasn't the legal capacity to own anything. Strictly speaking, everything I have belongs to him.'

'And why are you still a slave? He hasn't been generous to you. He hasn't even been just. You've earned your freedom many times over and you've offered him the full price for it. As for me, he has my liberty, my labour and my loyalty. He's not having my self-respect as well - nor yours either.'

'Is my self-respect so important?'

'It is to me. In my heart and soul, I'm wholly yours.'

'But he's got a deed of sale for you! Watertight. I drew it up myself. How could you not be his? You fill his life, dominate his thoughts, invade his dreams. And you hurt him more than anyone in his life. I daren't guess what you said to him but I know he considered selling you.'

'To Severus?'

'Not to any personable fellow who might have won your affection, he couldn't have stood that. But he's been good, to both of us and, frankly, he takes your ingratitude very hard.'

'Yes, he's good to you; calls you brother and gives you everything of the very second best. Your couch is citrus wood, his is ivory. You wear the fine linen, he wears silk. You go to the best dinners in town - to stand behind his couch.'

'Exactly. So how can it be right for me to have the woman he wants? When I come to you, I feel I've broken down his cellar door and made myself incapably drunk on his old Falernian. I'm exhilarated by my own guilt. You've made me a bad slave.'

'"A bad master makes a bad slave."'

'No. This isn't a cruel whim of his. It's a rational choice. Where could he find another girl so faithful, who can converse in Greek and discuss literature and philosophy? Should he send to Britain for one?'

'Well, he'd find women there who are dependable and clever and an asset to their husbands but not, I think, educated in the Roman manner. But he wants a lively woman, with some independence of mind, who's nevertheless content to be passed around from one man to another like a parcel. He couldn't find one of those in Britain, or anywhere else, I should think.'

'Oh, there've been some in Rome. Cato's wife for one. Perhaps her husband was more persuasive. But you must, at least, stop making a farce of your banishment.'

'What do you mean?'

'Someone told him you'd been working the land. That distressed him terribly.'

'I plant medicinal herbs. When I need one, I don't want to depend on finding it growing by chance. I want them ready in neat rows, the way you like your fire buckets. Does he want his gardeners to plant them?'

'Why not write and ask him? I'll dictate something for you.'

'You forget, I'm a scribe. I know the form. A florid introduction addressing him by all his titles. A preamble praising his generosity in periods so labyrinthine he can scarcely tell he's being asked for something. A calculation showing he stands to lose less by the inconvenience than he'll gain from the eternal gratitude of his workers and a grovelling conclusion begging him to believe in my undying devotion to him, his genius, his ancestors and his dogs. Couldn't I just say, if his people don't have medicine, they'll die if they take the fever?'

'You will say that. But in civilised society there are *ways* of saying things.'

The old taunt. She flushed. 'Why don't you have Adrian write it? He's the prince of sycophants.'

'It's possible he's more…eloquent than me, but he's less discreet.'

'Lucius won't read my letter anyway.'

'He certainly will. He'll have it read aloud at dinner and invite the lectores to comment. They'll praise your literary style and all your other talents –'

'At tedious length I hope.'

'Most tedious. Then, they'll deplore your defiance and your ingratitude until he frowns and says, "Even so, we could perhaps indulge her in this, which seems to be for the general good." Then they'll change tack and recommend indulgence, pointing out how kindness will remind you of all his past favours, sting your conscience and make you weep over your ingratitude.'

'Demetrie! You've coached them to say all that!'

'Naturally, I use what influence I have on your behalf. But, rather than write, why not come home and ask him yourself?'

'Is that your idea or did he send you here to say it?'

'He wants you home. He misses you and the boy. Beg your discharge humbly enough and he'll make a suitable show of reluctance but he'll grant it.'

'What about my work here?'

'It's kept you amused but he has better plans for your entertainment.'

'But I'm *needed* here. Before I came, they didn't even clean wounds properly. At Galen's school, less than forty miles away, there's sanity and science. Here they're using gibberish from the time of Romulus. How can that be?'

'If you asked him, he'd buy them a doctor or a medical student. It'd be thought odd but he'd do it for you. Have you thought how much good you could do through him? Nerysa, can it be right to think of slaves when your master needs you?'

'What about the power of philosophy?'

'Perhaps philosophy could cure him, if he wanted to be cured. But he doesn't.'

'"Why should I trade my Sabine farm for a load of mammon? " as the poet says.'

'Send him such an insolent reply and I wouldn't blame him if he took your books away.'

'How could he when I know them by heart? I've made a life for myself here. I'm useful. And I won't grovel to get something I don't want.'

She didn't expect him to be so disloyal to his master as to show satisfaction. He pursed his lips with the effort.

'I'll tell His Excellency you think the country air agrees with Lucillus.'

'Do, and give him my best wishes for the new year.'

'The year of the consul Commodus! The senate didn't want Pertinax, the most capable man in the empire. What will they make of a talentless fifteen-year-old?'

'Has he no talent at all?'

'I believe he's quite good at throwing pots but, not having seen one, I can't comment. I'll draft two good men into your herb garden. But hear me. Your master sunk his pride and sent you a peace offering. You've rejected it. How do you expect him to react?'

CHAPTER LXIX

February 177

Credat amari

Let him think he is loved Ovid Amores I viii 353

Nerysa was overjoyed when Demetrius came again in March, until she heard what he came to say.

'Lucius has dealers living in Athens.' she complained. 'He doesn't need *you* there.'

'This is something new. There's a market in reproductions for modest houses in the city and the provinces and factories in Athens turning out statues by the thousand, some of them quite passable.'

'Why can't local dealers buy them up?'

'Because it's a different operation. We wouldn't put these through the fine art business. *That* trades on its reputation for authenticity. We'll start a new company.'

'Not in *Athens*?'

'I'm going to negotiate a bulk price and charter transport. Jacob will arrange storage at Ostia and open a showroom in Rome.'

'Why doesn't Lucius go?'

'I've hardly travelled since I married. He's been away for years. He waits on the emperors daily, his legal practice is growing and, frankly,' he sounded embarrassed, 'I've more of a feel for this sort of thing. I've the common touch.'

'No, you haven't; you've studied your market. He could do the same.'

'Why should he? He keeps me to do that.'

'Demetrie, you're thirty years old. Are you going to while away your life making him even richer?'

He fidgeted with his feet and looked intently at them, 'I live comfortably, for all the world like a freedman. It's easy to forget I'm his slave. I owe him service and he owes me nothing but board and lodging, a clean tunic and a serviceable pair of sandals.'

She wrung his hands, 'Ask him to take the money and free you. He promised. Hold him to it.'

'You know that's a favour a slave can't ask. I could ask some free man to broach it with him on my behalf but, if he wanted me to have it, he'd have offered. Don't you see, if he were asked and refused, it would be the end between us? The friendship, the love we've shared would be poisoned, sour even in the memory. Do you want me to risk that?'

He seemed resigned to live and die without ever tasting freedom, because of her.

'I once knew freedom.' she said. 'I want you to know it.'

'It's because you knew it that you miss it. Don't pity me. I live in luxury with the minimum of constraint. The yoke's light and my neck's hardened to it. Not like yours, so tender you feel every hump in the ground. If only I could massage your neck with goose fat, my love, to ease the stiffness.'

'So, we're nothing but an ox-team.'

'We're as surely in our master's power and as bound to do him service. But there's a difference. We're forced to be slaves but no one makes us good ones. That's our choice.'

'True, you could get away with far less than you do.'

He chuckled, 'What, lie in bed 'till noon, then set about me with a whip? Tell me then, do British kings lead their armies from behind?'

She flushed. 'Why do you do everything? What does he do?'

'He's in court every day it sits, very successfully.'

'Does he make much at it?'

'Of course not. A gentleman doesn't charge for his services. He works for honour and reputation.'

Demetrius was sick at heart. He must persuade her to give in. What would Lucius do with a slave who refused to serve him? What would he do with a shoe that pinched his foot? They'd exhausted his patience and she'd better know it. He asked, 'You can guess why he's sending me away?'

'Trust me. While he keeps you a slave, I wouldn't give in to him even if I wanted to.'

'But you must. We've no choice.'

'On the contrary, it's the only choice we have. We can make it any way we like if we can live with the consequences. So can he. When it comes to punishing us, he makes the decisions and he'll have to live with them.'

'Our whole strategy is not to push him into actions he'll regret but can't go back on. Tell me, how did you come into Quintus' hands, by private sale I suppose?'

She gave an inscrutable half-smile. 'By private arrangement, yes.'

'Then you've never seen a public auction. Imagine it. Think of yourself stripped naked on a revolving stage with a misspelled placard slung around your neck. Picture the rabble who couldn't afford the price, pretending to be in the market so they can squeeze your flesh and slobber with lust. Imagine their vile comments, the stench of their breath and filthy clothes. The hammer falls and you're the property of some vulgar freedman, too coarse to begin to appreciate you. He signs to his slaves to take you to his house in chains and saunters off about his business. Would he be as patient as our Lucius? Would you really prefer his touch? If *you* could bear it, could you bring such agony on *me*? I'd sooner share you with my brother than lose you to a jumped-up mushroom.' He steadied his voice with an effort and begged.

'Nerysa, dear soul, don't let me come home to find you gone from the house.'

He saw she didn't believe him and insisted, 'Don't flatter yourself he wouldn't do that to you. What if his love wears out? It would be too late to appease him then. Suppose he sold our daughter too? Choose that for yourself, if you must, but not for her. If you provoke him, I'll give you up and take another girl. Please him and I'll wait until he's tired of you, however long.'

'He's not the barbarian, I am. I can fend him off until you come home.'

'And if I don't come home?'

'You always come home.'

'I've only been shipwrecked once. I'm careful when I sail and who with. I'll make the usual offerings, of course, but the truth is...I made a vow in the temple of Neptune...that Lucius should have you. I never trusted myself to the sea before without making peace with the gods.'

'Would your gods drown the crew and the other passengers with you because I made you forsworn?'

'I don't know.'

'Then if Lucius should.. still want me, I won't hold out against him, I promise.'

'Don't give yourself out of duty. You have his love, let him think he has yours.'

CHAPTER LXX

March – July 177

Παν μοι καρπος, ο φερουσιν αι σαι ωραι, ω φυσις

Nature is always young. Meditations of Marcus Aurelius.

Over the year, Nerysa had come to respect Italia, whose slight frame belied her stamina. Never still, she supervised spinning and weaving, storing, preserving and cleaning. Although courteous to everyone, she allowed no slacking. She kept numbered lists of her master's possessions; ceremonial robes, ritual equipment, kitchen utensils, dry stores and tableware, and she had a place for everything, so if anything went missing, she knew immediately because its empty place reproached her. She and Nerysa worked so hard and were both so naturally reserved it was more than a year before Nerysa asked her how long she'd lived at Horta.

'The master brought me here from Sicily when I was seventeen. Too young for a housekeeper really. It's a responsibility. The men sweat blood to bring in the crop but, if we don't store it safely and use it carefully, their work goes for nothing.'

'Did you ever see the domus?'

'Once. But I'd hate to live in a city where folk need a calendar to tell the seasons. Here the frost tingles in your nose when you salt olives. You follow the plough in February; the west wind nuzzles your cheeks and the turned earth smells of turnips and vinegar. And when the dog-roses flutter in the hedgerow, can't you just taste the sweet grass in the milk? Then, it's mown hay, apricots and hot pitch for sealing jars. And one morning, at the end of summer, it's misty and you scent the vintage and the fumes of the boiling must. Then the year's over -

'And you're back to salting windfall olives!' Nerysa laughed.

'It's the same every year but nature's always new. Townies are so smug with their talk of spectacles and leftovers from banquets. But what's a finer spectacle than the sun rising over Soracte or the first bleat of a newborn lamb? What sort of dawn chorus is traffic and street criers? We send them figs and cherries in jars but who gets to eat them fresh with cream still foaming from the udder?'

Nerysa laughed. 'You don't need to convince me, I love it here. Demetrius thinks the master will come in the summer.'

'I heard the rumour. Your boy will be pleased. I shouldn't say so, of course, but I think it's the most wonderful thing to have born the master a son. I did, you know, the year after I came, but it died. I was ill after and never fell again. The gods didn't wish it. Georgius is a good man and we're a good team but I loathed his lovemaking at first.' She lowered her voice to a whisper. 'In fact, I still do. When I was given to him, I'd never known any man except the master and he's so – well, you know, of course, so sweet and gentle.'

Nerysa steeled herself to mention Demetrius.

'Oh, yes!' Italia laughed. 'In haylofts mostly, on hayricks and under them and in the woods at night, on ferns and wood anemones, all silver in the moonlight. We were young and crazy!'

Nerysa wanted to tell her the truth but she was wary of pillow talk. Italia had to think of her as a rival. Even if she was told Lucillus wasn't Lucius' child, she wouldn't believe it because he was so like him. Demetrius said he admired Lucius so much he imitated him; his gestures, his gait, his turns of phrase. He did resemble Demetrius too, if one looked for the likeness, but not as obviously as he did Lucius. And it was Lucius he asked for, though less often now and with a subdued resignation. But in August, his faith was rewarded. An advance party came to prepare the villa to receive the master for the vintage.

CHAPTER LXXI

April - August 177

Ubi ubi es, mellitissimo, meus amor, mea voluptas. Quid mihi tecum est? Amo absentem.

Where are you, my sweet love, my delight? How are things between us? I love you while you're far away. Marcus Cornelius Fronto. Letter to Marcus Aurelius circa 144 AD

D emetrius felt a sense of belonging in Greece that was like a homecoming. He was pleased to have brought Melissus. With Polybius, Philemon and Achilles and Patroclus, the two guards, they were a lively party. First, they stayed with Lucius' correspondent in the Piraeus, later they rented a flat at the foot of the Acropolis, eating out and keeping house in a spare, masculine way. He worked them hard but, as the project took shape, he unbent and took them sightseeing too, armed with his well-worn copy of Pausanias. He embraced the chance to broaden their minds at Lucius' expense and to crowd out the recurring image of him with Nerysa. The thought of them together disturbed him, though less than the fear that she'd reject him and risk the consequences.

In the evenings, while the others toured wine bars and brothels, he and Melissus caught up with the paperwork. Melissus, he discovered, was not only numerate but good company. He took him to the new theatre, donated to the city by its most famous citizen, Herodes Atticus, and they came home with plenty to discuss.

'Herodes is a colourful fellow.' Demetrius observed. 'Our Lucius knows him. He was the emperor's teacher.'

'What did he teach?'

'Rhetoric. He was the greatest orator of his generation. At least, *he* thought so. Marcus' other teacher, Cornelius Fronto, wasn't so sure. Marcus actually had to take time off from his studies to settle his masters' squabbles.'

Melissus shook his head. 'There were no such diversions at my school.'

'You went to school? Your master must have valued you. How did he come to part with you?'

'He died. The heirs had no use for me.'

The boy's eyes brightened with tears; Demetrius reverted quickly to Herodes.

'Well, Herodes' schooldays are a legend. No one caught him studying. He spent his days in pleasure and wrote his essays in the small hours, more drunk than sober - but with such flair, he put the conscientious students in the shade.'

Even as he spoke, Demetrius realised that he disapproved. Talent ought to be inherited together with application. It was wasted otherwise. Yet Herodes fascinated him.

'I'd dearly love to hear him speak,' he told Melissus, 'I just missed him in Sirmium last year. He was being prosecuted by the Quintillii. Have you heard of them?'

'Brothers aren't they, so devoted they run parallel careers and only take postings in the same province?'

'Yes, they're from Alexandria in Troas, Herodes used to call them "the Trojans".'

'Offensive from a Greek.'

'Very. No doubt they enjoyed stirring up trouble for him in Athens. It was tricky for Marcus because, naturally, he sympathised with his old teacher but the Quintillii were friends of the empress.'

'So, how did he judge between them?'

'While he was stalling, lightning struck Herodes' house and killed his two favourite slave girls. He flew into a spectacular rage, and made rather a fool of himself by blaming Marcus for the thunderbolt. Marcus made him leave court until he'd lived it down.'

'How unreasonable!'

Demetrius raised his brows. 'Unreasonable? *Marcus!* Why do you say that?'

'Marcus was pleased enough to take the credit for the lightning strike that took out an enemy catapult. Even had it commemorated on his coins. Can he choose which particular thunderbolt he wants to be responsible for?'

Demetrius suppressed a smile.

'Melisse, that's seditious. It reminds me of some of the more incautious pronouncements of my wife. I fear I must deal with you as I have with her and forbid you to discuss politics, in or out of my presence.'

'Sir, please excuse me, I didn't realise, I'm dismayed to have offended you.'

Best draw the lad out, Demetrius thought. *Find out where he got his disturbing ideas.*

He refilled the wine cups.

'Was your last owner interested in politics?' he asked gently.

'No, sir, he was interested in making a living. But some of his customers were. And we did publish underground pamphlets.'

'You'd be best to forget that, completely, from this moment. It could be highly embarrassing for Lucius Marius to keep someone on his staff who'd been involved in sedition.'

'Of course, sir, I understand.'

'You've made a good beginning with us. You wouldn't want to blight your chances of promotion.'

'May I dare to hope, sir, that I haven't already done so?'

'You'll be safe enough if you remember that, while you're young, it behoves you to listen to opinions rather than express them.'

From the film of sweat on the boy's brow, he judged he'd said enough and reverted to Herodes.

'He's a public benefactor. Everywhere you go, you trip over something financed by him. Usually the newest, grandest building in town.'

'Is that pure generosity?'

'Yes, he's generous and, yes, he's buying popularity. People haven't forgotten the scandal surrounding his wife's death.'

'The theatre's dedicated to her memory, isn't it?'

'A handsome gesture, though some say she'd have preferred to be treated kindly while she was alive. Besides, he can afford it and he says money's useless unless it keeps circulating.'

'Did he make money by spending it?'

'Well, he was born rich and married money but what really made his fortune was buying a house in Athens and finding treasure buried under the floor.'

Melissus looked down unconsciously. 'It's too bad we're on the top floor.'

'I imagine every house in Athens has had its floors ripped up and searched by now, don't you?'

'What he's famous for is extempore speaking. He likes to be challenged to speak on any subject at a moment's notice. Not like our master who goes to court with every word meticulously planned. He can't know in advance what the other side will say, so he has speeches ready for every eventuality. He's always prepared. That's why he's a brilliant lawyer, but he'd never agree to improvise.'

'That would take a special kind of skill and a certain brashness, I think.'

'What really puzzles me is how such a talented man fathered such a stupid son.'

'Do you mean Herodes or Marcus Aurelius?'

'Now, Melisse, what did I just say? Herodes, of course. He despaired of the boy learning to read. So he bought him twenty-four slaves, called them by the letters of the alphabet and made them wear boards slung round their necks with letters painted on them. Poor boys!'

'There are worse fates for a slave. Wearing boards would be more comfortable than the fork - better than the mines or the sewers.'

'More ridiculous. But the idea was creative - typical of Herodes. He hoped the lad would learn his letters as he got to know his new servants.'

'And did he?'

'Must have done. He didn't grow up illiterate. But he was a disappointment – one of many. The first son was stillborn, he lost two daughters and, of course, his wife was pregnant when she died in such unfortunate circumstances. He fostered sons who did him credit but he's survived them all. Do you know, so far, in that respect, I'm luckier than the richest man in the world?'

'Indeed you are, sir, and your wife is so kind and beautiful. We're all so glad she's coming home.'

'Coming home? Who says so?'

'Everyone, sir. At least, Polybius offered odds on her being back in Rome for Saturnalia and Philemon laughed and said he wouldn't bet against a certainty.'

It was Demetrius' turn to sweat. If the house was making a book on the master's trial of strength with his own slave girl, the stakes were high indeed. The words oozed from his lips as oil from a plump olive.

'Repeat that, Melisse, to anyone at all, and I'll have the hide off your back to stop your mouth. The same goes for your colleagues.'

The others usually brought girls home with them and, when Demetrius found one in his bed, he dismissed her cheerfully. But pretty girls were thrown in his way persistently and a deal of interest taken in his reaction to them. Towards the end of one undignified evening, he intercepted a look between Polybius and Philemon and understood. His indiscretions were to be documented and reported to Nerysa, possibly by an intermediary, perhaps by Lucius himself. This from the man who shrank from touching her body with a whip! For the first time in his life, he thought of him with contempt. But he was sobered to think how easily he might have fallen into the trap. They read him well, his orphaned body, his aching for her.

He thought they must be homesick too and, when Polybius asked for a loan to bid for a Scythian girl, he was inclined to be indulgent. At twenty-six, Polybius was no longer a boy. He lived a carefree life, serving himself gracefully to pleasure wherever he found it but he'd never inconvenienced himself to the extent of falling in love. Perhaps this was a sign of growing maturity. He urged him to negotiate a private sale before the auction but, as the dealer would have none of it, he equipped him with the cash and sent Achilles, Patroclus and Philemon to the sale with him, while he and Melissus balanced the accounts.

When a shout from below the window announced the success of the mission, he had Melissus unseal a wine jug so the homecoming of Polybius' girl would be a festive occasion. But when the purchase was carried in, he felt the stab of betrayal. Polybius hadn't fallen for the girl; he'd bought a snare for his master. She was young, about Nerysa's height and build, with bright red hair. Polybius had thought to take a tunic to cover her nakedness but her feet were still chained and chalked to show she was a novice. She looked wild and desperate, trembling like a hedge sparrow caught in the hand. Demetrius, playing along, lay back on his cushions and assumed his most avuncular manner, smacking his lips to his thumb and forefinger.

'Excellent!' he purred, 'Your taste is unerring, as ever, but you'll need to tame her and you should make a good beginning. If I were you, I'd take off those chains and let her wash her feet. What's her name?'

'Uxinia.'

He smiled. That wasn't a name, it was a direction. A part of her, at least, would not be bought and sold.

'Does she know any Latin?'

'A little Greek, sir.'

'Good, then try and discover what she likes to eat. You'll need to spend time with her at first. And be consistent so she learns what to expect of you.'

This friendly advice clearly bored Polybius, whose purpose was commercial rather than amorous, but Demetrius, thoroughly enjoying himself, persisted, 'If you'll take my advice, you'll give her time to settle down before you take her to your couch. She's a virgin, at that price, I assume?'

'Indeed, and I'm in no hurry. I should rather leave her to you at first. The hand of experience is what she needs.'

Demetrius had great difficulty keeping a straight face at this and, when Polybius had left the room, he laughed long and loud at his impudence. But other considerations sobered him. If they couldn't get a genuine report of his infidelity, they wouldn't scruple to invent one. He'd been content to stay away while events took their course but now he felt a desperate urgency to finish the business and go home.

They went briefly to Corinth, looking for reproduction bronzes. Socially, Corinth was a unique city. Roman armies had razed it and left it derelict for a hundred years until it took on a new lease of life as a colony for Julius Caesar's veterans. It was a classless city, full of self-made men and women who deferred to no one. As an unusually gifted man, trapped at the base of an hierarchical system, Demetrius should have approved of egalitarian Corinth. Perverse of him that he merely deplored its vulgarity.

He took a solitary walk up the stony path to Acrocorinth through olive groves; silver filigree above tortured trunks. From the pinnacle, he surveyed the twin gulfs and the isthmus between. Nero must have stood on that very spot when he conceived his crackbrained scheme of dividing the isthmus by canal. It looked so feasible from that distance. Nero had been wildly enthusiastic, coming in person to rouse the motley crew of convicts and slaves drafted in for the digging and wielding a golden pick axe to begin the task. But, as soon as his back was turned, realism prevailed and the hare-brained scheme was abandoned.

Demetrius didn't expect his charges to resist the fleshpots of Corinth and got used to sitting alone reading in the evenings, relieved to have the flat silent. One sultry evening, he couldn't concentrate and thought he heard faint sounds, perhaps of a baby behind the party wall. Eventually, he realised that the sound was crying and came from his own flat. Taking a lamp, he followed the sound, knowing he was looking for Uxinia and in what condition he'd find her. She'd been making clumsy attempts to attract him, he assumed because he'd treated her kindly. He flattered himself. She was under orders and her failure had been punished.

Seeing her on the floor in the corner of a room, he lit a lamp and took a good look at her, noting grimly that, although she was badly bruised, someone had taken care not to break her skin. So, if he didn't succumb to temptation, or even if he did, Polybius meant to dangle her before Lucius. If Lucius wanted her, he'd score heavily. It was a clever idea and might serve, though he doubted it. True, when he'd first seen her, the superficial likeness had caused him a pang but, almost immediately, he'd perceived the differences. Polybius had lived close to Nerysa; hadn't he seen the light in her eyes, the truth of her heart, the force of her intelligence? How could he think this insipid child anything like her? He was puzzled but not displeased. If Lucius was equally fooled she might draw him off, with happy consequences for himself.

He gave her wine, spelled out in simple words that she was not at fault and promised her kinder treatment in future. She lay in his arms as Polybius had intended. That was the moment for her to exert herself more than ever to seduce him but she was broken, capable of nothing but sobbing. In the occasional silence, he heard muffled footfall. So they weren't alone and the spies had the evidence they wanted. He looked at Uxinia, hardly more than a child, and cursed them.

Next morning, after Polybius had dressed and shaved him and served breakfast, Demetrius established that there were no just grounds for beating Uxinia and expressed his disappointment that an innocent girl had been ill-treated in his charge. Polybius shrugged in cheerful unconcern and said he hadn't beaten her, he'd only watched. Demetrius was disgusted. Polybius, who was unworthy of his master's generosity, would forfeit the girl, and he, Achilles and Patroclus would pay their master punitive damages for the injuries they'd caused. Polybius threw back his head and laughed; a grating, joyless laugh that Demetrius didn't recognise.

'You take a high tone, you who sent a maid to Surdus' house, where they more than half killed her, so our Lucius had to pay the surgeon a fortune for fear of offending her owner.'

So, Polybius thought he was immune. His actions had been sanctioned, indeed ordered, by a higher authority. Reading the situation, Demetrius could handle it calmly and spoke gently. 'You forget yourself. Lucius Marius knows what's necessary to the discipline and good order of his household. He'd never condone insolence and insubordination. Nor would he lift a finger to spare you any punishment I cared to lay on you.'

But Polybius was reckless. 'I beg you to overlook it, sir, *if* I said anything that was untrue or that otherwise offended you.'

'What offends me most of all is that you thought this paltry creature in any way comparable to my wife.'

Polybius actually sniggered, 'Indeed sir, she's younger and fresher and I'd be amazed if she weren't hotter.'

The next moment he lay unconscious on the floor and Demetrius was spitting on his own clenched fist. Polybius had served him in the most intimate way for more than twelve years. He'd never earned the mildest rebuke and Demetrius had never given him one. Kneeling over him, he made a new discovery. He'd been drinking, before the third hour of the morning. Perhaps it was the wine that kept him unconscious but Demetrius wasn't comfortable with the wait. He'd have preferred to keep the incident quiet, for both their sakes, but there was no hiding a black eye and there seemed little to be lost in handing him over to his colleagues to be cared for.

In the evening, he reported for duty, pale but for the ugly bruise, his manner still hinting at defiance. Demetrius wouldn't dispense with his services in the absence of an alternative. Back at the domus, there were any number of well-trained young men eager to step into his shoes. For the present, he had him sleep outside his door, addressed no word to him that wasn't a direct command and otherwise ignored him. It was two days before he begged the privilege of addressing his master. His manner was always insouciant but Demetrius could see he was shaken.

'Sir, you've often said that men behave badly away from home. I know, now, that it's true, in my own case at least. I beg you to pardon me because I haven't always been so.'

Demetrius put out his hand and suffered it to be kissed.

'I know what Lucius Marius wants of you.' he sighed. 'May I spare you further exertion by convincing you, you won't succeed?'

Polybius said nothing.

'Don't you believe me?'

'Perhaps, but I don't understand you, either of you. One woman's so much like another.'

'If you think that I'm sorry for you.'

Demetrius felt depressed when he dismissed him. He'd been a sweet, sensitive boy. How had he grown so coarse in a civilised house?

Achilles and Patroclus he fined and flogged, which put him in the tedious predicament of having four invalids on his hands. He and Melissus completed the business; Philomen ran errands, brought in food and doubled as infirmarian. The party returned to Athens smouldering with suppressed rancour.

CHAPTER LXXII

September 177

Tu vim putas esse solum, si homines vulnerentur?

Do you think there is no violence except where people are wounded? Marcus Aurelius

cited by Callistratus in the Digest of Justinian. IV.ii.13

Lucius didn't come as a suppliant. The look in Demetrius' eyes had told him what to expect. In her absence, philosophy had strengthened him and he believed he no longer needed her body. But he'd take it, in the interest of discipline and to allow her to purge her defiance.

He brought a large retinue, conducted the religious rites and gave audience to his manager and tenants. He played with Lucillus, heard his lessons and took him up on his horse to tour the estate. When all his business was completed, he sent for his disgraced slave mistress.

How crude Demetrius was! There was no need of a whip, only patience and the sustained application of pressure. It was nine months since she'd declined to come home. Nine months of gruelling work in Spartan conditions. She must be desperate to earn reinstatement at the domus. Curiously enough, that was the one favour he could no longer grant. But she needn't know that yet.

She knelt before him and he looked down again on that slight, white neck. He felt the hair rise on his own but he had his mantra for protection. He could hear Marcus saying, 'There's something stronger, more divine in you than lust, which would make a puppet of you. Reason is sovereign. Passion cannot master it.'

Supported by these fine words he told her to get up and asked coldly, 'What have you to say for yourself?'

***

Nerysa stood up slowly, uncertain how to begin. She was prepared for all possible arguments but not for an invitation to speak freely.

'Master,' she began, 'when I agreed to marry Demetrius, it was for your sake, not because I was afraid of you, either of you.' He quickened with interest. 'Because I saw that you loved him, as you still do, and dreaded sending him away. I didn't want you to be unhappy.'

'Then you did love me, even then?'

'I couldn't hurt you.'

'And you didn't love him.'

'That's true, but I learned to...respect him and it seemed wrong to cheat him.'

'You can't cheat a slave with his own master. You forget what he is and what you are.'

'Master, you gave me in marriage, my marriage is happy, I beg you humbly, desperately, not to poison it.'

'How could it poison your marriage? He need never know.'

How could she explain the understanding between her and Demetrius?

'He'd read it in my eyes the instant he came home.'

'Nerysa, he's in Corinth. My friend, Demades, is fond of him and will do everything he can to entertain him. Think of it, Corinth, the erotic capital of the world. Do you think he's unconsoled tonight?'

'I'm not his gaoler. We both belong to you. But what you prize in me is loyalty. If I betrayed my marriage, would you still want me?'

'Whatever has love to do with marriage? Was Catullus married to Lesbia or Ovid to Corinna or Propertius to Cynthia? Marriage is a civic duty. It doesn't concern you. You were made for love.'

He took her in his arms and kissed the tears from her face, gentle, as though wary of breaking a fragile accord. His resemblance to Demetrius, more seductive when they were apart, confused senses that swam with longing. She couldn't dissemble. Her starving body trembled for joy in a man's embrace.

'Master, I'm not important,' she gasped. 'His love means more to you than my body.'

'I want *your* love too and your body is the pledge of it. How can I be sure I have the one when you don't yield me the other?'

'It's because I love you, both of you, that I can resist you.'

He drew back. 'I understand! To love me truly in your heart and mind is enough. Philosophy teaches me to despise the body and its pitiful impulses. I have complete control over them. I could lie beside you and resist. Just to hold you, just to enter you.' She stiffened and he whispered, 'Then not that, just to hold you, would you even deny me that?'

Her knees failed. She clawed ineffectually at his gown as she slithered to the ground at his feet, breathing, 'Master, I'm your slave. I do whatever you wish.'

She was disorientated by how swiftly he changed from fond lover to overbearing victor. He had her serve his lunch and behaved with chilly hauteur, then sat in the garden through the heat of the afternoon, dictating letters at breakneck speed, raising his brows in disappointed surprise when she failed to keep up. When she took up her tablets to go and make fair copies, he told her to wash and change into something more becoming to serve his dinner.

She'd scant faith in the power of philosophy over lust. It would need help. No one thought it strange that she went to the kitchen and supervised every dish for the master's dinner; attention to detail was typical of her. She made sure the heavy wines were added to the sauces after boiling so they wouldn't lose strength. But the effects of wine alone would be crude and suspicious. With sleight of hand, she added ingredients of her own. Her heart pounded with terror. The potency of her plant and fungal extracts was variable. She'd no way of knowing how much of each dish he'd eat or with what unpredicted results the various alkaloids might combine. If the master were to die suddenly, after eating dinner, foul play would be assumed. The kitchen slaves might be tortured to death. She didn't know how she could contemplate such a risk. She looked into her heart and recoiled from the evil she uncovered; fierce, overweening pride. She'd been given once as a gift, treated as a thing. She'd never suffer that again and, in the last analysis, she didn't care whom she sacrificed to prevent it. Sure that no god, of any religion, would condone what she did, she persisted but she dared not pray for success.

A calm detachment fell on her as she served him. When she bent over his table to remove the second course, he whispered. 'Leave this to the others. Come to me when the house is asleep.'

Iris and Charis helped her to get ready. When the house fell silent they kissed her and promised to wait up. Cradling a lamp in her hand to guard the flickering flame, she groped her way down the staircase and round the atrium towards the glint of light from under his door. There was no reply to her soft scratch. In panic, she knocked hard, blew out her lamp and burst into the room.

CHAPTER LXXIII

September 177

Ει δε τι λελυπηκα, απαιτησον παρ' εμου δικας εν τω ιερω της εν αστει Αθηνας εν μυστηριοις

If I've done you wrong ask satisfaction of me in the temple at Athens during the mysteries. Marcus.Aurelius. Letter to Herodes Atticus 176 AD

D emetrius found his cargo assembled at the Piraeus and his ship lying at anchor. He supervised the lading himself, having learned long since not to trust to the solicitude of dockers. Melissus, he noticed, had also acquired a black eye and, while he didn't demean himself to arbitrate the petty squabbles of his minions, he was concerned at the level of animosity between them and moved to delay his departure long enough for them to be initiated at Eleusis. He and Lucius had seen the mysteries together and he still thought of it as the high point of his inner life. Moreover, the emperor himself had been initiated the previous year and brought it into fashion. The privilege was open to any man, slave or free, who spoke Greek and was innocent of murder.

He laid out an extortionate sum on a white sow and bought roses for Uxinia to weave into a garland. Blood from her dainty fingertips dried on the petals, no doubt as acceptable to the goddess as the blood of the beast with which it would mingle. After breakfast they locked her in the flat, garlanded their sow and processed her down to the beach. They left the priests to dispatch her and plunged into the sea for the ritual purification. Their behaviour was more riotous than devout but, if being splashed and ducked in those limpid waters had power to cleanse body and spirit, then they were all comprehensively purified.

The smoke assailed their nostrils, flooding their mouths with eager juices and, for ever after, the scent of roasting pork recalled the smoke drifting to a periwinkle sky, the tang of salt air and the pounding of waves on compacted sand. Dried in the noon sunshine and fortified with huge helpings of meat and barley wine, they joined the procession. No one hurried along the sacred way but squandered energy flailing limbs, pouring and spilling wine, singing, and shouting. The clamour of pipes and cymbals and the roaring of the crowds made shouting a necessity but the fifteen miles and six hours passed without effort and left no focused memory.

They were too drunk to shudder as they passed the menacing caves, through which the screaming Persephone had once been dragged to hell. But it did sober them to see scaffolding around the ancient temple, evidence that it had been desecrated by barbarians only seven years before and was being restored at the emperor's personal expense.

Three thousand pilgrims gathered in the marble forecourt and lit their torches beside the massive well, where King Keleos' daughters had once helped a destitute, old woman, never suspecting she was the goddess Demeter. Ascending the great propylaia, Demetrius paused and bent back his head to study the crystalline pediment, ghostly in the twilight. At its centre was an ornate, medallion portrait of his emperor and he savoured the memory of that oasis of time when he'd commanded the ear of that tortured, introspective monarch and talked to him as man to man.

Awed silence fell as the crowd filed into the windowless cavern and took their places on the terraced seats, conscious that the ritual they were about to witness was seventeen centuries old. The abduction of Persephone by the king of hell and her mother's distraught grief were re-enacted before them. Majestic themes of loss, death and renewal were confronted with crushing impact, resonating in the mind of each aspirant until he suffered an agonising catharsis of grief, terror and tremulous hope. Each soul lay flayed and quivering under the searing rays of enlightenment. Then, through the gloom and smoke and flickering torchlight, the priests spoke the ineffable words of comfort and revealed the holy secrets.

Demetrius saw the bright eyes and burnished faces of his charges with great joy. He caught Polybius by the eyes and the hand and they exchanged mute forgiveness. The mysteries inspired free men to live and die in hope but for slaves there was more. They'd been granted what Nero himself had coveted and been refused. The goddess had noted their existence and promised them a new dignity in the life to come, when even they should commune with the gods.

CHAPTER LXXIV

September 177

O me felicem! O nox mihi candida!

Oh joy! Oh wonderful night! Propertius. II 15

Lucius was reclining on a daybed reading. Without glancing up, he motioned to Nerysa to undress. He wouldn't treat her as a lover. She was a servant doing her duty, and not before time. Now that she was in his grip at last, he was torn between triumph and resentment, uncertain how to use her. A demonstration of self-control would be mortifying to her but would it be satisfying to him? He could tantalise her with piercing sweetness until she was wet and heaving and then, with the self-mastery of a stoic, dismiss her to stumble along the dark passages to her cold bed. If philosophy failed him, he'd take her; show her who was the cream and who the whey. In either case, he'd have his victory.

She hung her head until her chin brushed her chest but he saw her blush. And he saw her fingers tremble as they fumbled with the pins but, at last, she'd removed them all and her tunics pooled at her feet. He put out a hand and guided her round. Lamplight licked the scars on her back and sides, the dimple on her breast where the abscess had been drained and, on her rounded belly, the silver tracery of her pregnancies. Demetrius had left the marks of his predation on her as a fox leaves his trail on the hen house. He felt contempt for him and for her that she clung to him. But, for her, the contempt was mild, tempered by the tenderness she stirred in him. He knew, now, that he could never hurt her.

He led her to the bed. She knelt, unloosed his sandals and slipped off his gown. As they lay, she breathed the heavy, scented air in unison with him. An immense languor stole through his body. The yielding softness of her breasts absorbed the thrusting of his heart and tamed it to a steady monotony.

He felt peace as he hadn't known it since childhood. He was back in his first home, enfolded in loving arms. There was a sense of wonder, of joy and deep comfort, reconciliation with the past and confidence in the future. He lost all sense of solidity, floating like thistledown, supported only by her breasts and her soft round belly. Even her touch melted away. The boundaries of his body dissolved and his being flowed and mingled with hers. He was freed from the tyranny of fixed dimensions. Now, he was infinitely small and lost in her. Now, he was infinitely large; he enveloped her and she was a small, sweet kernel of gladness within him. Awed by the majesty of the experience, he embraced it eagerly, confident of its benign purpose and glorying in a mind more incisive than ever before. The blessed tranquillity was beyond time and space, leaving only consciousness which ebbed imperceptibly from him.

*****

Nerysa gathered him in her arms and held him as she held the children when they had the earache. The full horror of her crime burst on her. Every kindness he'd shown her rose in her mind to reproach her. His death would cause a scandal. She couldn't let the whole house suffer for it. She'd have to confess. She saw Demetrius' face as she was given to the beasts in the arena. But that wouldn't happen. He'd strangle her himself sooner than see that. She couldn't pretend that she'd acted for his sake. He hadn't wanted it. Was it pure pride or because she didn't trust herself to lie unmoved in Lucius' arms? Whatever the motive, she was unworthy to be a Christian, yet she prayed fervently, 'Dear Lord, don't let my master die, please, please, don't let my sweet master die.'

She held his body with dread watchfulness as if to corral his spirit.

When dawn light slanted through the shutters and Cyrus stirred and coughed in the anteroom, Lucius was sleeping healthily and she judged it safe to leave him. Her women found none of the rank odour of stale loving on her body but, as they washed her, she shook like an aspen in a squall. Had she satisfied him? Would he give her her freedom? Perhaps he wouldn't arrange matters like that. He might free Demetrius first, making him a present of her so he could free her himself and become her patron. She locked her arms tight around her body to contain the violence of her longing.

***

Lucius awoke in the late afternoon, unable to move or speak, bereft of a blessed place, dimly remembered yet poignantly regretted. He'd known physical release. Whether he'd discharged his molten passion into her or combined it with some ethereal vision of her he couldn't be sure and didn't want to be. What he saw, with shining clarity, was that every hurt and bitterness he'd ever felt had been neutralised. He still remembered them but they'd lost all power to distress. His mind was suffused with a blissful serenity and trust. He'd known the secret of the gods; how evil might be confronted, resolved and transformed to good. He saluted Demetrius. Did he sustain such a shattering experience often? He himself was anxious to repeat it but not straight away. Maybe in a year's time he'd be ready.

In his bath the physical torpor left him. His body was invigorated and his mind clear. He went to the atrium and watched the household bustle and Lucillus' boisterous play. Nerysa stood behind a group of women and, as he looked across at her, flame swept her face and throat so swiftly he could fancy it was firing her toes in her open sandals. Her delicacy humbled him. She'd melted from him like a vision. Any other woman would have stayed to collect a douceur or beg a favour while he was still under the spell of her body.

Nothing was further from his mind than manumission. What sane man, possessed of such an asset, would give it up? One day, he might be widowed and then, duty done, he could follow the emperor's example and contract a base alliance. Until then, country visits would be his secret solace. Before dinner, he sent for her, motioning her to stand close because he felt shy of raising his voice. His own words sounded stilted, banal.

'You've done your duty and more. As for your past obstinacy, I do forgive you from my heart.'

She sank to the ground and pressed the toe of his sandal with her lips. He looked down at her and praised his good genius he'd never harmed her.

'So hard,' he breathed, 'so hard to let you go.'

He bent and raised her, shivering, in his arms and cupped her chin in his hand. Her face was silk under his lips and he pressed it again and again, each kiss a seal on his vow to protect her. Between them his words came in disjointed whispers.

'So wilful. No one ever made me so sad. Or so angry. I forgive you. Last night. You forgave me. Even for sending you here. Why, why did you hold out on me so long? If you hadn't, I should never...'

Poor girl! he thought. *What have you done? You've wrecked your own happiness.*

And, suddenly, he knew why she'd been planted in his house and why she was his Galatea, created purposely for him. But the insight had come too late.

'You don't understand.' he said. 'Of course not. I didn't either. I knew, but I didn't understand.' He sank onto his couch pulling her down beside him. 'How much can I explain? I met Pulcher twelve years ago at my patron's house. We drank late after dinner and, as you'd expect, the conversation came round to love. I shan't offend you; you must know Pulcher's views. He mocked women in that languid, sardonic way of his. They were mercenary and shallow. Hairdressing was all they were interested in. Their deceit and their cloying scent choked him. He preferred a boy's honest sweat.

It wasn't like me to contradict my elders and I was by far the youngest of the company, but I was full of myself that night. I'd caused a stir, winning my first case and just got my commission in the seventh legion. I parodied his sneering tone. If our women were shallow, I said, it was our own fault. We didn't educate them. A dose of Euclid would crowd out vanity and idle gossip; an orator's training would help them explain their needs rationally, instead of sulking. Astronomy would give them a sense of proportion and philosophy develop their self-control. I remember the room fell suddenly silent and everyone stared. Pulcher said something patronising. Everyone laughed. I forgot about it.

But *he* didn't. When he found you, he sent you to me. As a compliment or a practical joke, I'll never know for sure but, I think, because he hoped I'd appreciate you, as no other man could. I didn't find you straight away...Zeus, that's it! You resented it. All these years, you've been punishing me and you relent when it's too late.'

'Master, I don't know what was in his mind but, as far as I'm concerned, you're mistaken. I never resented you. Please believe me.'

'Then don't resent me now. I can't bring you home but don't think of yourself as banished, just safer here, hidden away. I'll make you comfortable. Anything you want...books?'

Seized with inspiration, he threw open the door and halted the procession of slaves carrying book cases to his carriage. He identified the case and pulled out the scroll. It was his only copy. He'd nothing more precious to lend. It was worthy of her.

'You're too high-minded to crave the baubles that please other women. But you'll value these. - notes I made myself of the emperor's maxims. He shows how a noble mind can achieve detachment. Are you still involved with those Christians?'

'Master, I'm no Christian.'

'They're anathema to him. Some were found guilty of treason last year in Gaul and faced the beasts. I won't have you near them.'

'Because they died a criminal's death, does it necessarily follow they were criminals?'

'I don't claim justice never miscarries, though every lawyer I know strives his utmost that it shouldn't. But there are people, influential people, who are asking if it shouldn't be a crime just to be a Christian.'

'Surely, to commit a crime you have to *do* something, not just *be* something.'

'It's what they *don't* do. Your life is sheltered. As it should be. But I see turbulence everywhere. Order and tranquillity are gone from our world; barbarians invading Italy, plagues, natural disasters - this latest earthquake in Smyrna, for instance, so terrible the emperor wept over it. No wonder people say the gods resent our neglect.'

'With the greatest respect, master, the consensus of medical opinion is that plague is borne on foul winds.'

'Quite. And who governs the paths of the winds? We've discussed this before. You know I don't believe the gods petty and vindictive. But when their altars are deserted and there's no market for sacrificial meat, isn't it just possible they could be provoked to a show of power?'

'I think there were plagues and earthquakes and barbarians long before there were Christians.'

'Of course! They don't have a monopoly on wickedness. They're just the latest threat to the state. I don't want to hear them mentioned. Keep yourself and Lucillus away from them. That's not advice; it's an order, for your safety and his.'

He suspected his rustic family was infected with the superstition but he shrank from embarking on a domestic tribunal. Most of them, confined to the estate and kept down to their work, were unlikely to be harmed by it. But not even the shadow of possible harm must touch her or Lucillus. She needed philosophy to console her.

'Read the emperor's thoughts,' he said. 'You'll find they answer better than crude Jewish superstitions. As for our night, I shan't mention it to Demetrius or to anyone. Nor must you. I don't grudge him your love. How could I grudge him anything when I love him as a brother? Love him, by all means, but love me more because I love you more. And because I can do more for you. You shouldn't confuse love with possessiveness. If he's rough with you I'll stop him coming here.'

'He doesn't touch me, master.'

'Thank god for that! You should know I did what I could for him. If I hadn't refused food and endangered my own health, it would have been the mines or the galleys for him.'

'Master, I never blamed you but I felt he'd suffered enough. I didn't want him to suffer any more.'

'Is he your only concern? Don't other people suffer too?'

'People in my position have limited ambitions, master. I thought, if I could make one man entirely happy, I shouldn't have lived in vain.'

'Didn't you ever think you'd chosen the wrong man?'

She murmured something that might have been, 'I didn't make the choice.' But surely she couldn't have said that. She was insubordinate

411

but, since she'd been put under Demetrius' tutelage, she was no longer insolent. Best to pretend he hadn't heard.

He left the next morning, having exerted his charm to such effect no one felt relieved of a burden of work rather, they were bereft of the pleasure of serving him.

CHAPTER LXXV

October 177 – May 178

Δειται δη σου επ' εκεινα μεν ουδαμως επει δε πωγωνα εχεις βαθυν και σεμνος τις ει την προσοψιν και 'ιματιον 'Ελληνικον ευσταλως περιβεβλησαι και παντες ισασι σε φιλοσοφον, καλον αυτω δοκει αναμεμιχθαι και τοιουτον τινα τοις προιουσι και προπομπευουσιν αυτου

Because you have a long beard, a distinguished air in your Greek cloak and are known as a philosopher, it seems good to him to keep you among his followers. From Lucian *On Salaried Posts In Great Houses* 26

Engineers came from Rome to overhaul the heating system and Darius came with them. He presented Nerysa with a package and told her to open it in private. Glad that she had, she sat down abruptly on the bed, staring incredulously at an emerald necklace and earrings. Lucius must have bought them for her in Alexandria and kept them since. He had exquisite taste, they would have become her excellently well if she'd worn them but the thought was absurd. Where did he intend her to wear them, in the sheep-shearing shed or the vegetable plot? She hid them under the loose floorboard and burned his letter. It made her blush until the tips of her ears tingled and she couldn't bear Demetrius to know she'd received it. Her reply was a masterpiece worthy of Adrian himself. It couldn't fail to convince him that her gratitude, at least, was real.

Demetrius then sent her greetings from Rome. It would take some weeks to set up the retail end of the business, then he would come to Horta. Her standing in the house was now second only to his and she was able to have it filled with flowers and a pig slaughtered.

Demetrius set himself to discover what had passed between his wife and Lucius. He'd expected to find her back in Rome, heard she was still in Horta but didn't hear she was out of favour. He and Lucius dined together, a privilege he'd been long denied, and Lucius looked at him often; a long, strange look; not triumphant exactly, somewhere between awe and conspiracy.

He'd ached to see her yet, when he arrived at Horta, he needed time to brace himself before speaking to her. It was a relief that the whole estate crowded into the atrium to welcome him and recount everything that had happened during his absence and that she took her place in the queue, behind even Charis and Iris. He'd remembered her request to bring them home something pretty to wear and produced shimmering chitons of pleated silk. The first, for Charis, was shell pink at the shoulder, shading through every tint of rose to carmine at the hem; the other shot with all the humours of the sky from misty grey through azure to indigo. Both had been chosen to suit each girl so well there was no risk of jealousy.

Nerysa's turn came. Was she wary, shy, or, like him, dulled by sheer weight of emotion? Was she still his in her heart or had Lucius seduced her? Her smile blazed like sunshine from a cloudless sky. His heart tumbled, his eyes misted. Afraid to take her in his arms in case her touch belied that smile, he said, 'Whatever happened to your face? Are you ill?'

'It's not a rash! They're freckles! From the sun. My young brother used to be speckled like a quail's egg all summer.'

'Then stay indoors or wear a veil. Whatever will our Lucius think?'

'I hope he hates them.'

'Our problems start when he falls out of love. Have you heard he's going to be married?'

Nerysa reeled. It had been a well-kept secret. She took his hand and led him into the garden where the fountain was playing and there was less chance of being overheard.

'No one here knows.' she said. 'Who's his bride?'

'Annia Aurelia Fulvia. It's a splendid match; she's rich as Croesus, and related to the emperor.'

'What does it mean for us? Will he free us?'

'I wouldn't keep your teeth clenched for it but it is inconvenient for him to keep me enslaved - it unbalances the household. Other people are eligible and could afford to buy out but he can't free them and expect them to defer to me. And it's shabby for a man in his position not to have a larger following of freedmen. The wedding would be a suitable occasion. I'll have to be there, of course.'

'You don't sound enthusiastic.'

'I don't know if she'll suit him, although I hope so. She's a powerful woman by all accounts. Married twice before.'

'Why would she want to marry him? He's only an equestrian.'

'Oh, he'll be co-opted to the senate. I've got the censor's officers coming to see the books to check he satisfies the property qualification but that's a formality. Everyone knows he's got the necessary income many times over. If he goes to the senate he'll have to free me.'

'Why?'

'Money. There are many lines of business an equestrian can pursue which would be demeaning or even illegal for a senator. He can't engage in them through a slave but, at arm's length, through a freedman, he could. He's been paying dearly the last few years to keep me enslaved. There are all sorts of openings he's had to forgo for dignity's sake and I don't mean whore houses and circus artists.'

'What sort of percentage would he take as a sleeping partner?'

'A seventy thirty split, I imagine.'

'Thirty percent's a lot for doing nothing.'

'No, seventy for him - a sixty forty split in his favour and ten percent on the use of his capital. There's no need to pout as Lucillus does when the cake basket's removed. We should do comfortably on that.'

'Aurelia will do comfortably.'

'She doesn't need his money. He's an attractive proposition though - young, good looking and successful. But he needs affection. Do you know what the emperor said about him? That he was naturally affectionate, the rarest thing in Rome.'

'Does the emperor usually converse in Greek?'

'He does, but how did you guess?'

'I can't think how he'd say that in Latin.'

'Do you know, you're right! There's no word in Latin. *Amor* is passion, *pietas* is reverence, *caritas*...too impersonal.

'*Sodalitas*?'

'No, that's comradeship. There's really no word to describe the intimacy, the tenderness of affection - friendship with extra warmth.'

'I think he's been lonely estranged from you.'

'He's bereft of both of us but of Lucillus most of all. The last two years have been difficult. He's worked and studied hard.'

'He gave me a philosophy book while he was here, written by the emperor.'

'Yes, he takes stoicism seriously. He doesn't carry it to extremes - going barefoot and not washing - he keeps a sense of proportion. But he's studious. There's a professor in the house on a fat salary; a bearded fellow with staff, short cloak and tedious delivery who discourses through dinner. I think I'm supposed to be edified too.'

'He used to look such a boy. There's nothing boyish about him anymore.'

'That's the new beard.'

'Partly that, but he looks careworn.'

'He works harder than he should. Imagine, I used to think he lacked application. And he's not happy. By the way, Polybius bought himself a girl in Athens.' He studied his sandals, 'You might hear that someone saw her on my knee. I want you to know Polybius had beaten her and gone out and left her to cry. I gave her wine and soft words, nothing more.'

She didn't need to forgive, she understood. He was a passionate man who believed he ought not to touch his wife. How could she blame him? She was grateful he didn't humiliate her with indiscretions at home and that he'd told her himself and not left her to learn it from household gossip. She lowered her eyes in case he guessed that she didn't believe him.

'It's not like Polybius to beat a girl.' she said.

'I expect he got Achilles and Patroclus to do it for him.'

'But why?'

'He'd set her a task beyond her skill. She couldn't satisfy him.'

416

'Poor little thing, I'm glad you were kind to her.'

She looked up and smiled and he said abruptly, 'Why are you so cold to me?'

'I, sir, cold to you?'

'You used to be happy to see me.'

She felt faint. 'I can't begin to express how happy I am to see you nor how I dread you going away.'

'You never touch me. When I touch you, you shrink from me.'

She stared at him in disbelief. Was he mad or was she?

'But you threatened to banish me from your bed and your room. Don't you think I'd rather behave like a block of wood than suffer that?'

'I only meant you to help me make sure you don't conceive. We needn't behave as though we were indifferent to each other, need we?'

She melted into his arms with a crow of joy and showed him the extent of her indifference. It was her body that reassured him, for her women's report of Lucius' visit had been Delphic and when he'd asked her about it, she'd merely expressed herself amazed by the power of philosophy. Now she grappled him to her and harnessed him to the sweet yoke of reciprocal bliss, releasing him into her quivering hands, between her turgid, silken breasts and into her scorching, pulsating throat. With his left hand, which he didn't use to eat or sacrifice to the gods, he found ways to pleasure her. The separation Lucius imposed on them didn't lessen their affection but it kept their passion like a rich flavoured stock pot, for ever boiling over and hissing in the flames.

Lucius, in amorous mood in the run-up to his wedding, deflowered Uxinia with graceful indifference and tired of her. Polybius toyed with her in a desultory fashion, displayed her around the house, conducted a brisk auction among Lucius' friends and made a handsome profit. There was mute but mounting tension between him and Melissus, who was too young to hide the fact that he was nursing a broken heart. Demetrius felt for him. Certain small aspects of his behaviour in Greece had suggested that he thought he was expected to console his superior for the absence of his wife. Adrian was clearly the culprit. Demetrius spelled it out to him that the boy now grew down on his top lip and was no longer fair game and watched as Melissus gradually stopped holding his body braced against assault.

He reassured him that he'd visited Uxinia and that she seemed happy in her new house. Figuring that the boy had then only his own grief to bear, he worked him so long and hard he'd neither time nor energy to indulge it.

Now he had to prepare the household for a society wedding. His own celebration, seven years before, had been a minor dress rehearsal for this magnificent event, which was delayed until May because of legal complications in recovering the bride's dowry from her ex-husband and so as not to compete with the even grander wedding of the emperor Commodus. Demetrius supervised every detail with the same care that Lucius had lavished on him, when he first gave him his wife. He was not the only slave in the house who hoped that the day that brought the master wedded bliss would also bring him release from servitude.

CHAPTER LXXVI

May 178 – May 179

Coniungi invisa ac meae subiecta famulae.

Hated by my husband and less valued than a slave girl. Seneca. Octavia 104-105

Nerysa, knowing little about Lucius' hopes and nothing at all of his wife, could fantasise happily about his future; but Demetrius was dutifully hoping and praying for something he couldn't rationally expect. He wrote that two emperors had helped to bring home the bride and that everyone at the domus basked in imperial favour.

But, although donatives had been given, there had been no manumissions, a break with tradition that caused ill-feeling in the house and distaste among the guests. Most of the ill feeling was directed at Aurelia because, as a new bride, if she'd asked, Lucius could hardly have refused her. Demetrius conceded that this was unfair since she herself *had* freed a token number of her own slaves. His letters were perfunctory. He could tell her everything or nothing. It was easier, and probably wiser, to say nothing.

Aurelia took an immediate interest in him. She sent for him to hand her out of the bath and made her wishes plain. A courteous explanation that respect for his master debarred him from gratifying himself in such a flattering way only served to whet her appetite. He knew he'd finally convinced her when Lucius confided with a laugh,

'My wife thinks you're importuning her! I told her she'd mistaken the most uxorious man in the empire.'

From then on it was war. She scoured the house for minor faults, for which she blamed him personally. If Lucius dined out, she'd haul him before her guests and delight in humiliating him. His own response he could control but the household was a restive beast, balked of feasting the freedom of any of its members and resenting the persecution of its prefect even more than its own misery. Tempers smouldered. Hostility, barely submerged, broke the surface daily. He didn't risk leaving the house in June but in July he was needed at Horta. He'd never been a mere overseer but now hard labour was more than a diversion, it purged his distress. For the first time in three years, he'd been allowed to bring Polybius with him and had also brought Melissus. Georgius needed permanent help in the farm office. He hated paperwork and was inclined to put it off. Also, Demetrius had long cherished the idea of developing a banking business in nearby Narnia and needed an accountant there. Melissus was young for responsibility but bright, keen to learn and grateful to be away from the domus. Demetrius was able to prolong his own stay in Horta while he trained him.

***

Nerysa was delighted with Melissus who'd grown tall and poised. He held no flippant mask to the world as Polybius did but, in repose, his expression was sweet and reflective. The night they arrived, the three of them dined with Nerysa, Iris and Charis. Italia and her staff served them like guests and indeed, their conversation was so rational, their demeanour so grave and dignified, Nerysa looked in vain for any outward sign of that fundamental flaw, of which they were all acutely aware and which would have made them leap to their feet in the presence of any free man.

They brought amazing news from Rome. Thaïs was pregnant. She and Jacob had been close for years but she was old for childbearing. When Demetrius went out into the garden after dinner, Nerysa followed him, even though she sensed he wanted to be alone. At first, he was uncommunicative but, once she'd coaxed him to begin speaking, he couldn't stop and she was deluged with seven months' worth of pent-up news.

'Melissus says the emperor's declared a tax amnesty.'

'It's wonderful! I remember when the state was so strapped for cash Marcus held a public auction of palace furniture – that's where I bought my Demeter. Just ten years of sound management and the treasury's in such good heart all debts are cancelled and the bills burned in the forum.'

'It's as well you never went to the tax office. You'd have had nothing to do.'

'On the contrary, they must be rushed off their feet. Think of the records to be made.'

'But they're burning all the records.'

'But you have to record what you burn. How else could you prove you'd burned it?'

Since his look was tenderly indulgent of her naivety, she could only change the subject.

'How is our mistress?'

'Disgusting!'

'What did you say?'

'She's disgusting. Would you believe she keeps two slaves just to flog the rest? It must be a strange life, nothing but ripping clothes and thrashing flesh. Her people cringe if you look at them and yell long before the whip falls, as if they think they can appease her by squealing. Imagine how it distresses Lucius! Remember the days when I'd reprove a slave for clearing his throat at the wrong moment? And it's embarrassing. He'll be conducting delicate negotiations or discussing politics with grave senators when, suddenly, the peace is shattered by bloodcurdling screams.'

'Whatever do people say?'

'Nothing. They stop talking while they can't make themselves heard and, when the noise dies down, they carry on as if nothing had happened. No one wants to pain Lucius by appearing to notice. She's particularly unpleasant to the ear, which must be his most sensitive organ. Her laugh sets my teeth on edge. When it bursts out during dinner, it sounds as if some wretch has dropped a tray of glassware and people turn around to enjoy his dismay.'

'Hadn't he heard her laugh before he married her?'

'He hadn't met her often. She was the emperor's choice but I doubt even he knew her well. Her people are my problem. They're not sensible. Partly because she's so inconsistent. One day, some girl says or does something that tickles an ear-splitting laugh out of her, the next day, she tries the same thing again and earns a beating for her pains. She brought more slaves than we expected. There seem to be thousands of them looking for somewhere to put their pillows at night. She doesn't manage them and she won't let me, so most of them have nothing to do but spy on each other and pick fights with us.'

'She can't whip Lucius' slaves can she?'

'Why not? She's mistress. Dinners are a penance. There's no conversation, no intelligent company, none of Lucius' friends. Just an army of inane, pretentious socialites come to name-drop and backbite.'

'I thought she was a learned lady.'

'The emperor was a prodigy in his own family. You needn't think all his relations are scholars. Her guests are revolting. When did our slaves have to scrape vomit off the floor or bring pisspots to the table? And they have to be prompt or those who can't wait turn over and widdle into the cushions.'

Were these the sort Polybius had hinted at, so incapably drunk their wayward members had to be guided to the pot by the hands of mortified slaves, compared to whom Severus was a model of deportment. If so, it was plain from Demetrius' pursed lips that he wasn't going to tell her so.

'The guests have their own slaves with them, can't they do such things for their masters?' she asked.

'How should a slave be more civilised than his master? A slave is always a worse man than his master. How could he be otherwise?'

She lowered her eyes. It was hardly the moment to challenge his cherished beliefs.

'Of course, she's furious with Lucius because he hasn't become a senator.'

'Why hasn't he?'

'Maybe to spite her. Maybe it's something he's holding over her, a reward for good behaviour - if she were capable of it.'

'Whatever does the professor of philosophy say?'

'What Socrates said of *his* wife, she's a training exercise in self-restraint.'

'It seems we haven't been the only ones to suffer.'

'Oh, he's suffering. He hides out in his library. At meal times, he's as dumb as a jug and she insults him venomously - to sting a response out of him, I suppose. She has some cause for complaint. He makes no effort. He used to choose exquisite presents for her before they married. Now, Cyrus and Successus keep the calendar and when one's due they order something and have it delivered. If she troubled to thank him he'd be embarrassed, he never knows what he's sent her. But one thing pleases her. She hasn't any litter-bearers, so she loves to use his. Most afternoons she goes visiting. It takes hours of pantomime before she emerges from her room, surrounded by women weighed down with baggage. They halt a few paces beyond the bedroom door while some are sent back for things she's forgotten or things she says *they* forgot. She sits in the atrium, calls for her mirror and decides she doesn't like her dress or the jewellery doesn't go with it and back they all go. But not before she punishes the poor creatures who suggested the outfit. She has them whipped there and then.'

'In the *atrium*?'

'Yes, and they squawk their heads off, right outside Lucius' library.'

'Then that's why she does it, to annoy him.'

'That's an interesting suggestion, I hadn't thought her so purposeful. Meanwhile, the litter-bearers are standing to attention out in the sun for hours. Eventually, she's installed and sets off, a crowd of attendants fore and aft and she hangs out of the window, screaming at them. When they're half way there, she decides she wants to change her necklet and they have to come back home again.'

'It must amuse you to see those stiff-necked, impassive fellows discomfited.'

'That's just the point; they're impassive so you don't. I liked the house the way it used to be.'

'You're conservative. Perhaps you exaggerate. You wouldn't have liked change of any kind.'

'I shouldn't have expected sympathy from you. You're well out of it and can afford to laugh at other people's misery.'

It was unlike him to snap.

'I'm sorry; perhaps I have my own reasons for disliking the litter-bearers.'

'They were useful in Alexandria; loyal, stolid fellows, all of them. They're not sociable, I agree, but, who buys litter-bearers for their conversation?'

***

Towards the end of harvest, Lucius made an overnight visit to Horta. He came to take Lucillus to spend the summer in Baiae where he'd bought a villa. He hadn't bought it to indulge his wife, as Demetrius was quick to point out.

'See that ugly pair?' he asked. 'Hardly his choice of escort. She sent them to tell her if he chases the maids. They wouldn't tell, of course, because she'd flog them for not stopping him.'

'She's not very bright, is she?'

'She's angry. It seems he's not an eager lover.'

Lucius regarded Nerysa kindly, commended her on Lucillus' progress and enquired if it were necessary for his bags to fill two carriages.

'Master, I packed one box for him but all morning he's been bringing me other things and saying you'd ordered him to take them.'

'Ah, well, if I've ordered it, it must be done.'

'Master, leave them in Rome and tell him he can't take them to Baiae.'

'Well,' he smiled, 'Perhaps I shall.'

She knew he wouldn't.

It was natural that, as his favourite grew older, he'd enjoy his company more and want to keep him at his side. She knew that was reasonable but she'd miss Lucillus sorely. She echoed Flora's prayers to Domiduca, the goddess whose business it was to see children safely home. Iris was to go to Baiae to look after Lucillus. Disturbed to see her packing make-up and perfume not suitable for nurse maids, Nerysa reminded her that Lucius was a married man. Iris tossed her head,

'From what I hear, he wishes he weren't.'

'From what I hear, Aurelia's vicious when she's angry. Be careful.'

She begged Demetrius to send Flora instead but he said that Aurelia's rages were unpredictable and would be better vented on Iris, if she were asking for it, than on little Flora.

When Lucillus returned, it was hard to believe he'd grown so tall and mature in twelve weeks.

He announced solemnly, 'My lady took the baths and the remedies - but she's no better.'

'Of course she's not. She wasn't sick.'

'She is. My lord says she's got demons inside her.'

He took a roguish delight in imitating Aurelia; her affected walk, her laugh and her tantrums and was surprised and hurt to be discouraged by his horrified mother and tutor. Lucius, apparently, begged his performances, laughed at them until he cried and paid him a silver talent each time. He displayed his hoard proudly. Demetrius approved of his saving money but it seemed he'd also spent some, on a coral necklace for his sister.

'And,' he said, eyeing Demetrius defiantly, 'if you say it's too grand for a slave girl, she can wear it under her dress.'

Nerysa hugged and kissed him, 'Darling, it's almost too grand but I think she can wear it on feast days.'

'I bought a present for my lord too.'

'Whatever did you buy for him?'

What could Lucius want that he hadn't already got?

'He took me to this bookshop and spent ages talking to the owner. His client, I think. I was bored so I flicked through some scrolls in a basket and found one my lord had been wanting forever. I checked the title with the slave because I couldn't believe the bookseller had overlooked it - he knew my lord wanted it. I said it was a bit dirty and he let me have it cheap. I didn't give it to my lord straight away, not until after dinner. He was so pleased he gave me five gold talents so I was better off than before.'

He drew a silver bracelet from the folds of his tunic and gave it to his mother. She kissed him and thanked him but she felt for Demetrius, forced to be a mere disciplinarian and excluded from the family. She'd underestimated Lucillus. He produced a bronze toilet set; ear scoop, nail file and tweezers, clipped together and ingeniously compact. Demetrius showed delight out of all proportion to the disappointment he'd have allowed himself to feel at being left out but returned dutifully to the point of conflict.

'I can forbid you to insult your patron's wife and beat you each time you disobey but I'd rather help you understand what his favour means to you. You'll hardly enjoy cordial relations if you insult his wife. The house is full of indiscreet slaves, even the carriage isn't private. Whatever you say about her, she'll hear within the hour. If she can't be revenged on you because Lucius protects you, she'll take it out on us or your sister. Is that what you want?'

'If we're alone in a boat and my lord rows us to the middle of the lake, can I say what I think then?'

'If I don't learn of your indiscretions, I shan't be able to punish them. But never forget how foolish you'd be to lose your patron's good will.'

He seemed confident that these reasonable words would settle the matter but Nerysa was still uneasy.

'Do you suppose,' she asked 'that Lucius ever tires of Lucillus' endless chatter?'

'No, but his friends tire of hearing Lucius endlessly repeat it and none more so than his wife.'

'I hope he'll leave him here, at least until Saturnalia. I think he could be irritating to someone who didn't love him.'

'Indeed. Especially when he's trying to be.'

Lucius left him to his schoolmasters but promised to send for him at Saturnalia. Nerysa understood that he would visit his patron more often and for longer as he grew older. The separation would be gradual but the winter and summer breaks would be regular and she prepared herself to expect them calmly. Unnecessarily as it happened, for he didn't go to Baiae the next summer. By then, war had broken out again; the emperors were in Vienna and Lucius was with them.

***

Demetrius saw nothing of his wife that winter. She was in Horta with the children while he struggled to keep three hundred staff in good order and good heart, supervise a hectic social life for his master and mistress and plan his next season's trading. Aurelia had no wish to go north and Marcus had allowed her to keep her husband in Rome until the spring. In April, when Lucius had left for Vienna, Demetrius was able to go to Horta to collect rents and prepare the accounts. He'd hardly arrived when word came that Thaïs' labour had begun and Nerysa wanted to go to her.

'She's forty-three and she's never borne a child. At the very least, it won't be easy. She was so good to me when I was confined.'

'You can't go to the domus without our Lucius' express and public permission.'

'Couldn't you take me there, just for a short time, to see Thaïs, please?'

She wanted it so much. She'd had a hard time these last four years and never asked for anything for herself. He judged that, with careful planning, he could bring it off safely. She was appreciative, especially when she peered into the half-light and made out the shape of Lucius' carriage.

'We're travelling in style!'

'You mustn't risk a night at the domus. We'll need to make good speed.'

When they left the carriage at the city gate, he was glad he'd brought her. She'd been about so little, even buying a simple meal from a street vendor was an adventure. He made sure she kept her veil well down over her face as he hustled her through the postern gate and into Thaïs' room. Then he went to his office.

***

An air of weary defeat hung over the room. The crowd around the birthing chair parted as Nerysa came forward but Thaïs didn't know her. Her eyes were dull from long agony, her hair, now grey, stuck to her scalp with sweat, the skin of her face taut as cloth on a tapestry frame. She writhed and cried out and a tiny battered form hit the pillow. The midwife gave a yelp of triumph and pushed it aside. There was no ceremony for an unwanted baby. Thaïs, on the other hand, was a valuable slave. She looked up and summoned the last remnants of her strength.

'Please, don't let my baby die.' she moaned. 'Don't let my baby d...'

Nerysa reached for the pillow and slid it towards her. The child was small, like one born before its time; perfect but limp, unresponsive.

She watched in desperation. If it didn't breathe soon it never would. She snatched up the baby and blew on the wrinkled, heliotrope face, then, with blind instinct, pressed her lips to the mouth and blew again. Her hand around its tiny chest felt a juddering rise and fall. She didn't see Demetrius cross the room. She felt his hands suddenly insistently around her wrists and heard his voice, harsh with fear. 'Drop it! Drop it, now!' The pressure on her wrists numbed her hands and the baby fell back on the pillow. As he dragged her from the room, she heard a feeble cry.

'Look to the child.' she screamed over her shoulder. 'She's crying.'

He pulled her through a bewildering maze of storerooms and slave dormitories, up and down flights of stairs and into the home farm courtyard where Philomen stood holding a horse. Throwing her up in front of him, he thrust his foot into Philomen's cupped hands and jumped astride. The horse lunged forward before his seat struck the saddle. She hadn't sat a horse since childhood and had no hope of staying up unaided but his right arm was around her waist in a ferocious grip while he controlled the bridle with his left. Her head lolled back against his chest. His hard breathing and the pounding of his heart stirred her to panic.

***

They were half way to Horta before Demetrius thought to explain. 'Someone betrayed us.'

'Who?' she gasped.

'Who knows? That cursed house is full of spies and informers.'

He ran a hand down the beast's steaming neck, reined in and walked but lunged forward again as soon as he dared. He was grateful, now, for the countless times he'd ridden that road by moonlight. He knew every bend, every milestone and every wayside shrine. No one from the domus could catch him, if the horse lasted the distance. Well short of home, he left the road and cut across country. When the moon set, the hawthorn blossom, milky in the starlight, guided him between the meadows up to the villa. He tethered the horse to a holm oak, knelt and pressed his ear to the ground. No sound. He lifted Nerysa into the fork of the tree. She crouched on the slippery bark and he pulled her hands around a sturdy branch. His feet knew their own way across the bathhouse roof even without the shimmering giant moths clustered above its warmth. He breathed a swift prayer and groped for the shutter, returned and coaxed her towards it. They crept past the sleeping women and children into their own room. He lit a single lamp and chuckled.

'That shutter's been loose for twenty years.' he told her. 'We never complained about the smoke from the bathhouse. That broken shutter was too useful.'

He barred the door from inside, pulled off her boots and cloak and hid them in the clothes room. She looked incapable of the role she still had to play.

'Pretend you're asleep.' he told her, 'I'm going back down the road to wait for Aurelia's people and tail them home. When they arrive, I'll be close behind. Just let everyone hear your voice but don't open the door unless they threaten to break it down. They'll change their tune when they find you're here and I'm not.'

She looked up at him, oyster pale, her eyes dark with hurt. 'Demetrie, why?'

'You're banished. It's a criminal offence for you to put a foot over the estate boundary.'

'Lucius said I wasn't banished.'

'He didn't announce it formally. If she'd found you anywhere but here, she meant to order me to flog you in front of the household.'

'You wouldn't have obeyed her.'

'My darling, I'm afraid I would. If I'd defied her, I'd have given her the perfect excuse to sell me. With me out of the house, she'd do as she liked with you.'

'Why should she want to?'

'Someone told her she'll never have her husband's heart because he gave it to a slave and can't recover it. How they must have enjoyed telling her that!'

She flinched as he laughed. 'They must hate her.'

'With good reason. I expect no good of her but even I was shocked when she had the dwarves flogged.'

'Dwarves? What's that?'

'Small people - short legged.'

'Children?'

'No, fully grown but short'

429

'Why?'

'That's how they are, their growth was cursed. Were there none in Pulcher's house?'

'Are they beautiful?'

'Quite the opposite.'

'Then he wouldn't have had any, would he?'

She always bridled when he mentioned Quintus, as if she defied him to criticise. He shrugged.

'Well, many houses have them - masters find them diverting.'

'I think she's angry with Lucius because he hasn't become a senator. It must be demeaning for her. He must want it for himself. Why doesn't he?'

He well understood what was holding Lucius back but he could hardly explain that to her. He kissed her and left by the nursery window.

***

She heard a low whinny and the thud of hooves over the grass, then silence. Her hands clung to the mattress, as though the bed were struggling to shake her off. The insistent rhythm of hooves thundered in her ears and on the threshold of her hearing was the feeble greet of Thaïs' baby. Sleep was impossible. She knew nothing of Aurelia except what Demetrius had told her and saw now that he'd held back a great deal. The things he left unsaid and his strangely unsettled manner terrified her.

Everything fell out as he'd planned. The guards woke the household rudely. Baffled to find her alone in bed, they demanded a night's lodging of Demetrius, who arrived in their wake, and returned to Rome after a hearty breakfast. She was relieved until she saw that he was far from it.

'Aurelia doesn't like to be thwarted.' he told her. 'We've made a dangerous enemy.'

'I don't want to deceive Lucius. He knows what he told me. He knows I didn't neglect Lucillus to leave him for such a short time and that I tried to help Thaïs. I'm not afraid to tell him the truth.'

'I'll see him myself first and judge how he's likely to react.'

'He's never been unjust to me.'

'Everyone else in that wretched house is different, why shouldn't he be?'

CHAPTER LXXVII

July 179 – January 180

Ita ut meam filiam facilius ipse percusserim quam ab alio percuti viderim.

I'd sooner beat my daughter myself than watch someone else do it. Marcus Cornelius Fronto. Letter to Marcus Aurelius circa 145 AD

In July, with Lucius away, Aurelia and her hundred slaves took over the house at Baiae. The domus calmed and Demetrius arrived at Horta with the evening star. The rustic meal was long over so Nerysa brought cheese and fruit into the garden and they sat watching the pipistrelles flit in and out of the colonnade. She asked him first about Thaïs' baby, sure that it must have died.

'Aurelia says you're keeping it alive by witchcraft, to spite her. Apparently, you *were* at the domus and you summoned your demon and flew back here clinging to his tail.'

She laughed and kissed him.

'However did she guess?'

'She wouldn't have the baby in the house. She ordered it to be exposed.'

'What does it matter to her if there's a baby in the house? She needn't see it.'

'Would she want Lucius to come home and ask how it is that his old housekeeper can make a baby for his accountant when his wife can't give him an heir?'

'That's not the sort of thing our Lucius would say.'

'She judges him by herself. But don't fret, the child's with Jacob in Ostia and he has a good nurse for her. He's called her Hannah, by the way, his mother's name, I think.'

'Poor Thaïs! How can she bear to be separated from her baby?'

'She's glad it's out of Aurelia's way. She and Erinna can do no right and she's too old and senior and too poorly to be beaten.'

'She wouldn't beat Thaïs, surely?'

'She'll box anyone's ears on the slightest pretext.'

'Not yours, I'm sure.'

He grinned. 'Not yet, but I expect it any day.'

'Couldn't we poison her?'

He looked over his shoulder.

'You're being playful but jokes like that are dangerous.'

'Have you written to Lucius to tell him how things are?'

'He knows. Why do you think he stays away?'

'He must care that his people are desperate.'

'What can he do? The emperor made the match. He wouldn't disappoint him. Then, Marcus tolerated his own wife's infidelity. Lucius wouldn't want to seem more particular than the emperor.'

'Is she unfaithful too?'

There was that unpleasant, humourless laugh again. It was becoming a habit and she didn't like it.

'Unfaithful?' he asked scornfully. 'Her own relations even – worse: her slaves and freedmen, even the charming pair with the rods and thongs.'

'Are you sure? Perhaps people say spiteful things.'

'I know these fine ladies, itching to be taken by a slave – the degradation excites them and mocks their husbands.'

'Did you ever oblige them just so they could feel degraded by your touch?'

'When I was young and lustful, they used me and I used them.'

'Did you marry a kitchen slave because the shame of it excited you?'

'Of course not. You know I had no peace of mind, no hope of happiness without you.'

Her heart raced.

'A lady might feel the same.' she suggested. 'What if she felt that for a slave?'

'A woman couldn't feel that. Aurelia certainly doesn't.

She looked away. 'What does Lucius do in Vienna – besides hiding from his wife?'

'He's the emperor's assessor.'

'I know that, but what does he assess?'

'Well, Marcus is the highest court in the empire. He feels duty-bound to hear the appeals himself but he's trying to win a war at the same time. Lucius studies the papers. If the prosecution looks unlikely to succeed or the dispute can be resolved on a point of law that's been overlooked, he advises both sides and saves the emperor's time. If it proceeds, he briefs Marcus with the salient facts. In court he turns up the relevant documents and references. Marcus relies on him to know the minutiae.'

'What a vast amount of work!'

'Well, of course, he's not the only assessor. But the worst of it is that Marcus is so terribly painstaking. He couldn't bear the thought that justice had miscarried through any oversight on his own part. He's acutely sensitive to criticism and nothing makes people more angry than injustice. Do you know the story about the plaintiff who tackled Hadrian in the street? When he said he hadn't had time to look at her case she said, "If you haven't time for my case, you haven't time to be emperor!" Every beggarly citizen thinks the emperor has nothing better to do than get him justice. So Marcus lets the lawyers speak for as long as they like and, if they run out of time, he sits through the night.'

'Lucius must be worn out.'

'Everyone's worn out. Marcus is old and sick. And, when he's killed himself with work, his successor won't imitate his zeal.'

'He made Commodus co-ruler to secure the succession in a crisis. Do you think, now that times are quieter and he looks so unsuitable..?'

'He's invested with imperium. Crispina, his wife, is an Augusta. Nothing short of civil war could unseat him.' He looked up and the fear in his eyes startled her. 'Just that frail life between the empire and Commodus. I must make sure there's no rebellion in Lucius' house while he's away.'

'There couldn't be a riot in Lucius' house.'

'It's not the same house. Time was when people felt privileged to serve there and dreaded being sold away. Now most would give up their hope of freedom to get out.'

'I'm safe here. Go back to the tax office and say you've changed your mind.'

'I can't leave Lucius now, you know I couldn't. He needs me. I was born into his family. I owe them everything. In different hands I might have become a pack-carrier or a gladiator.'

'Whatever you were, you'd have been the best - because of your nature. They didn't create that, they just exploited it.'

'No, they *invested* in it. Look; say I buy timber in Leptis. It's no use to me there, however fine. It costs me money, effort and risk to bring it home and, when I've got it safely here, I expect to sell it at a profit. Why else should I have bothered with it? Now, because they raised me and educated me, I'm more useful to them and they've earned my gratitude and devotion. Are you saying they should have no reward for their pains? Whatever sort of world would it be if there were no return on investment?'

'You describe the prudent handling of a consignment of timber but you can't take a rake off a man's soul. I'm not even sure a man like you should be owned.'

'But everything of value must be owned. How else can it be managed and made to yield profitably?'

'No one owns Lucius or Severus.'

'Well, I suppose you might say they own themselves and they're responsible for making sure they're useful to the commonwealth.'

'Why can't you assume that responsibility for yourself?'

'Fate has decided I'm, in some way, unworthy of that.'

'In what way?'

He shook his head. 'I don't know.'

'But if Lucius freed you, you'd instantly become worthy?'

'Yes. But if he did, wouldn't it be because fate had ordained that he should?'

'No. It would be because his philosophy had finally overcome his jealousy.'

'I don't.. can't believe he keeps me in servitude because he's jealous of my woman.'

'He's not jealous of your woman but of what she loves. Jealous of what you are.'

'Now there, my precious, confused beloved, you must be wrong. How could he be jealous of his own property?'

***

Aurelia returned to Rome in the autumn and gave and attended dinner parties furiously all winter. Demetrius was kept hard at work ensuring the comfort of guests whom it pained him to see in Lucius' house. After Saturnalia, when everyone at the domus was exhausted and hung over, he came to Horta over roads that crunched with snow. Nerysa was proud of the welcome she gave him. The furnace roared. The villa's winter warmth was more genial than its summer heat. Instead of smoky lamps, she had candles. She decked the house in green and put on the kind of spread that only a prosperous country estate can provide.

After five long months, she sat on his couch and felt his body firm against hers. His fingers brushed hers in the sauce bowl. The children sat on a bench below, their soft brown curls pressed together over a shared secret. They were growing up study and bright. She was proud of them.

Demetrius leant forward, flicked the back of Nerissina's head with his napkin and said, 'Take your hand out of his bowl. Saturnalia's over. Black bread and pottage is what you eat.'

Lucillus looked up, his usually soulful eyes hard and bright. 'It's my food.' he said. 'I'll give it to whoever I like.'

Demetrius raised his brows and lowered his voice. 'You know what I expect. Disobey and I'll punish you.'

Lucillus took a drumstick from his bowl and held it up to his sister. She giggled. He swung it nonchalantly in front of her nose, moving it closer and then further away. He smiled playfully and, as she smiled back, showing the rosy tip of her tongue, he edged it closer. She shot a nervous glance at Demetrius. Nerysa shook her head, willing her not to disobey. The drumstick moved closer and her tongue protruded, steadied it and began to lick around the rim. Then she laughed, bared milk-white teeth and sank them into the meat.

Melissus appeared at Demetrius' shoulder in response to a summons so minimal Nerysa felt rather than saw it. Demetrius grasped each child's thumb and held them up to him.

'Bring me two three-foot vine rods. One, so thick and one so thick.'

'I'm a free man.' raged Lucillus, 'I won't submit to a slave.'

It was a cheap taunt but Demetrius didn't flinch. He waited while a slave slipped on his sandals and then stood up, saying levelly, 'I'm your tutor and I have authority over you until you come of age. By then, if I'm fortunate, you'll be wise enough to be grateful that I did my duty by you.'

Nerysa felt Lucillus had earned his beating but, when Demetrius reached for Nerissina, she threw herself between them crying, 'She didn't understand. If anyone's punished it should be me for not training her better.'

The disparity in their physical strength was mortifying. He brushed her aside as if she were a muslin drape and pulled the girl towards him saying, 'Six of the vine rod as a boy would have spared me worse later.'

It took no longer than it took Lucillus to scream, 'I hate you! She didn't put a finger in my bowl! Anyway, there's no point in teaching her to be a slave. I'm going to free her.'

'Don't count on it.' Demetrius turned and passed the rod back to Melissus. 'Because she's your sister, you won't have to wait until she's thirty, but you won't convince a magistrate you're a fit person to free a slave much before you're twenty. A lot can happen in thirteen years. And all that time you must keep your patron's favour – no easy task when you've no self-control.'

Nerissina, white and rigid, struggled to catch breath to scream. Nerysa held her close, sick with fury and bewildered that Demetrius was veering out of control. He turned on her.

'Do you think a rap on the buttocks is the worst that can happen to her? You've had it so easy you don't know how lucky you are. What do you know of chains and prisons, masters who rape, maim and brand?'

He referred to the circumstances of the girl's birth which made her very existence an affront to those who had the most power to hurt her. She must give them no excuse to justify their cruelty. By the time she went to serve in Rome, she must know, beyond a shadow of a doubt, what it meant to be a slave.

'Tomorrow,' he said, 'she starts work.'

***

When Demetrius went to the schoolroom the next morning, he found it tidy and well swept. The vine rod, as he'd suggested, was propped against the wall as a warning. Swathed in an apron with her hair bound up Nerissina looked older than her years. He was consoled to see how conscientiously she beat the floor with her besom, how quickly she ran to fetch and carry for Gisco and Macrinus, the schoolmasters. He need only keep her out of the reach of malice. Any fair-minded master or mistress would be quick to value her. He told the masters, 'Keep her down to her work and see that she's respectful and obedient.'

The rest of his stay passed gloomily. He spent the last morning briefing Melissus, finding it hard to concentrate. The office was dark. The shutters, fastened against the biting wind, creaked and rattled.

The sound of sandals shuffling across the atrium floor was almost a welcome distraction. Melissus parted the curtains and Gisco appeared followed by Macrinus, dragging Nerissina by the hand.

'Before you leave, sir, we'd be grateful if you'd clarify your orders about the girl. She's been playing with the tablets - not dusting or tidying them - scratching on them. We asked if she'd done it and she didn't deny it. When we looked at them, we told her not to tell us lies, then the boy said he'd written on them. They're impossible, sir, either they both deny something or else they both admit it.'

Demetrius opened the tablets and saw they were all covered with neat, even writing. He handed her a stylus and an empty tablet of his own, saying severely, 'If you copied the Twelve Tablets once, you'll be able to copy them again.'

She took them with a self-possession so close to insolence he was shocked. It had cost him more than he'd admit to teach her a lesson, he'd thought once and for all, and in such a short time, she was guilty, not just of defiance but deception. Gisco and Macrinus, leaning over her shoulder, looked up at him in bewilderment,

'Look, sir,' said Gisco, 'not just letters, whole words, without a master to guide her hand!'

Demetrius looked down and came close to tears. His voice broke with pity and pride.

'It would be wrong to deny her education. Put her at the back of the classroom and let her learn what she can. But you must never fail to make the proper distinctions between her and her brother.'

He took his leave of Nerysa, conscious that their precious time together had been soured. Her eyes were bright with tears and he knew she had the same regrets.

'Look to our daughter,' he told her, 'remind her how she ought to behave. If she lapses, you must take the rod to her.'

She made made no reply.

'You must not defy me in this matter.'

'It would be hard to hurt her, sir, she's a good child.'

'Would you rather leave it to Aurelia to teach her? If you can't bring yourself to do what's necessary, I'll speak to Gisco. He's thorough. I'd rather do it myself but, if I'm not here, I can't.'

'We must keep her away from Aurelia. She'll hate her because of me.'

'How do we do that? Do you think Lucius will leave her here on the land? If she's going to be a town servant she'll have to be trained at the domus. Aurelia hates all three of us and can't touch us. Who do you think is going to pay for that?'

'If you'd gone to the palace and taken her, she'd be safe. That's my fault. Why don't you say so?'

What good would it do if he said it? They both knew the decision was made and couldn't be changed.

'How long will you be away?'

Her voice was hollow, frightened. At last, she'd understood.

'I owe it to Lucius to keep his house as well ordered as I can and I may have to go to Athens in the spring.'

'Is there a problem with the statues?'

'The last ones they sent weren't the right quality. I've written to the supplier, maybe he was trying to see what he could get away with.

If the next consignment's no better I'll have to go and sort things out on the ground. I'll come here when I can. Public holidays used to be a good time. Not now with all those idle slaves prowling round the house or coming home from the games violent and over-excited.'

'Should we sell her?'

'I've thought about that but I'd have even less control of her future and she might lose the chance to be Lucillus' freedwoman. Lucius wouldn't be cruel to her if he were here but who knows how long the war will drag on? The generals keep declaring victories but they don't make an end of it. I could put her in another house but the villa in Sicily is even more rustic than this one and we only need one woman at Ostia. When the time comes, I'll look at the staffing at Baiae and Tivoli. Did you know she could write?'

'I saw her trying, I helped her.'

'Maybe we could train her for copying in the library. That's one place Aurelia never goes.'

CHAPTER LXXVIII

March/May 180

Quod vindicta Nemo magis gaudet quam femina.

No one delights in revenge more than a woman. Juvenal. Satires XIII 189

The emperor Commodus flouted his father's dying wish. Marcus had begged him not to despise his life's work but to complete it. Commodus, anxious to escape both the plague and the battlefield, replied that, with prudence, he might eventually achieve something whereas a dead man could achieve nothing. The truth of this must have been all too obvious to the dying Marcus. On the seventeenth of March, when snowdrops bobbed beneath the silver birches and tufts of snow were caught like lamb's wool in the bare hedgerow, he declined to give the password.

'Go to the rising sun,' he said, 'this one has set.' And, dragging the sheet over his head, he surrendered his charge to one he knew to be wholly unworthy of it.

The news travelled on leaden feet. Lucius Marius' slaves, in company with all the priests and citizens of Rome, were praying fervently for the emperor's recovery until the beginning of April. Then Marcus was mourned as no emperor before. His subjects knew they would never see his like again but they hoped for the best. Commodus was the undisputed heir, born to the purple, and Marcus had surrounded him with trusted advisors; Pertinax, Pompeianus, Fronto's son-in-law, Victorinus and able younger men, like Lucius Lepidus.

Demetrius changed his plans; he didn't go to Athens and he warned Nerysa by letter. Aurelia had decided to visit Horta. Her husband was coming home and she had business to settle there before she saw him again.

The staff of the villa urbana were on their mettle. A mistress' visit was different from a master's. A mistress noticed things a master didn't. They went to work with tamarisk brooms, feather dusters, sponges and polishing rags. On the day she was expected, they gathered in the atrium, excitement and curiosity at fever pitch, and ran around tweaking cushions and flicking imaginary dust from statues. They strewed fresh flowers over the threshold and sprinkled the air with rose water from a silver brush and pail. Then, they waited.

For several hours, no one dared to go and relieve himself for fear of missing her arrival. By late afternoon, spirits had flagged but, as soon as the shout went up from the outdoor slaves, the receiving line re-formed, headed by Georgius and Italia, with Nerysa towards the end, buttressed between Charis and Iris. No one wanted to stand out from the crowd so all stood shoulder to shoulder, hands behind backs, staring at fixed positions, low on the opposite wall.

Through the corner of an eye Nerysa saw Successus guiding an imposing, tower-haired personage down the line and Demetrius behind them, chewing his lip. Then she heard the laugh, exactly as he'd described it. If she'd caught his eye, she'd have giggled. She looked down and clenched her teeth. The slapping footfall approached. Aurelia stopped in front of Charis and enquired of Successus, 'Which is the steward's woman?'

Nerysa looked slyly sideways and was aghast. This was neither cat nor monkey. She wished it were. The eyes agate soft, the complexion like crust on a ripe cheese. Lucius, so sensitive, so discerning, was a sorry match for this charmless woman. The crude make-up alone must daunt him. Successus guided her on and indicated Nerysa, who looked straight ahead, avoiding the insolence of eye contact.

The laugh burst forth again, the crust cracked and cratered.

'You're teasing me! That drab little bag!'

She spat in Nerysa's face and clattered away. Behind came a crocodile of harassed-looking maids and bowed footmen. Nerysa had never been spat at. If the spittle was from the throat of a superior was it offensive to wipe it off?

Iris whispered, 'Forty trunks, how long's she staying?'

'Great ladies,' Charis assured her, 'take at least forty trunks, even for an overnight stay.'

'Then they must have them packed with rocks, no one could have enough clothes to fill forty trunks.'

'Is that our Lucius' philosopher?'

'No, it's her doctor. Archias says he's a quack.'

'That hairstyle!' hissed Charis, 'So old-fashioned!'

How like Demetrius to go half way to meet trouble Nerysa thought. *He made me think she wanted to hurt me but she only came to laugh at me after all.*

The next morning she sat in the schoolroom, with Nerissina on her lap and Lucillus at her feet, telling the story of Pandora. It was the story Quintus had told her the first night she spent in his house. She thought of Quintus. He was so rational. Of course, he was cynical and Demetrius thought him a rogue. But he was searingly honest; so sane, so reassuring. However serious the problem, he'd face it unflinchingly and be sure to identify its risible angles. She saw that satire and philosophy were both ways of coping with grief and fear, to reduce them to manageable proportions. Lucius' philosophy was earnest and sound but she preferred Quintus' humorous approach. She remembered how, in her tactless, childish way, she'd asked him why he wasn't married and he'd described women like Aurelia. She'd thought him in jest but now she saw he'd been in deadly earnest. He thought all Roman ladies were like that. Her eyes filled with tears and she felt an intense yearning for him. He wasn't far from her in space, living less than a mile from the domus. Lucius and Demetrius often saw him in the forum. Yet for her, he might as well have lived on the moon.

The children interrupted her thoughts and insisted she finish the story but Italia prevented her.

'Nerysa! You must go at once and wait on the mistress. She's furious. Didn't Demetrius tell you, you were supposed to wait on her every morning?'

'No, nor am I. I'm not house staff. I'm nursery staff.'

442

'I'd go straight away if I were you. I'll get Flora to mind the children.'

'Take them both to the villa rustica and perhaps you should tell Demetrius?'

Instinctively she smoothed her tunic, checked the hem and adjusted her hairpins. As soon as she entered the bedroom, she saw that none of the villa slaves was there, only Aurelia's own. They were mostly women but, behind the mistress' chair, stood the two floggers; ugly brutes. One had a broken nose, no doubt the result of a brawl, but the most striking feature of both was a vacant stupidity.

It was time for the arduous process of dressing the mistress' hair. The coals were smoking on the brazier, heating an assortment of tongs. A cohort of women stood ready to curl the hair, another held the pins to fix them and the largest group seemed to have no function except, perhaps, to express ecstatic admiration of the result. The crowd parted and Nerysa stood before the mistress and saluted her. She was a sorry sight without her platform shoes and make-up; a sad, sallow woman with mournful features and a scrofulous scar on her neck.

'How dare you come late! You must know senior staff attend my dressing each morning?'

'Mistress, I'm very sorry. I'm not senior staff. I work in the nursery here.'

'Insolent! Don't they call you chief slave mistress? You don't earn that rank by warming your master's bed. I expect work from you. Take the tongs and curl my hair.'

'Mistress, I'll fetch Charis or Iris, they're both clever with hair. I should only disappoint you.'

'Minx! Are you deaf? I ordered you to curl my hair.'

'Mistress, I've neither skill nor training. I beg you to excuse me and employ me in some service where I can please you.'

Aurelia looked significantly behind her. The brutish pair began to wink and grin. Nerysa could only guess what to do with the tongs, although she knew better than to use them red hot. Nervously, she grasped a pair cooling to one side of the glowing charcoal and slipped them out of the metal sheath. She lifted a strand of hair and was puzzling exactly how to wind it round the instrument when she felt a stab in her arm. She flinched and the tongs clattered to the floor. Aurelia's shrieks were prompt and eloquent.

'You wicked slut! You've burned me with the tongs.'

Nerysa looked down and stared in blank disbelief at a long bronze pin quivering in her arm. The torturers closed in, drooling and fondling their whips.

'Will you twitch down your tunic, sweetheart?' said one thickly, 'Or shall us?'

Aurelia stood up. 'No.' she said. 'Leave this to me. You may take over if I get tired but,' smiling at Nerysa, 'I don't think I shall. I feel full of energy today.'

She signalled to a maid for her mirror and turned it over thoughtfully. Fashioned from a single silver bar, it was ornate and heavy. She took Nerysa's tunics by the neck and ripped them down to her waist, jerked them off her shoulders and held her by the girdle. Nerysa looked up in mute appeal and caught the first blow on her cheekbone.

It was the day of reckoning Demetrius had dreaded. The day they should settle the account for their happiness in each other. She'd hurt Lucius and now his wife was taking revenge for him. Nerysa stood braced and silent as the blows slammed down on her head and breasts, together with loathsome obscenities. Her intimate organs were itemised, reviled and cursed in words of sickening coarseness until the gasping and coughing of unaccustomed exercise stifled the hysteria. It was a particular cough. Through a veil of pain, Nerysa heard the barking, the wet rattle and faint whoop. *She's crazed,* she thought, *because she's dying and she knows it.*

***

Demetrius stood in the doorway, knew Aurelia was taking revenge for his rejection of her and struggled with an overpowering urge to snap her neck and snuff the life out of her. He was only her husband's slave but she couldn't out-face him and he sensed her triumph change to apprehension. Holding her with his eyes, he came slowly into the room, using his softest, most respectful tone.

'Mistress, I'm sorry one of our slaves has offended you. You needn't put yourself to such exertion. Hand her over to me and I will try her and punish her legally. That's how such matters are dealt with in Lucius Marius' house.'

Aurelia bridled. 'There's no need for formalities. My people saw her burn me with the tongs. Assaulted in my husband's villa by his slave! It's outrageous! Whipping's too good for her.'

He looked at his wife. Bruises hadn't yet formed. She was shroud white, terrifyingly still.

'Mistress, it would be more suitable to your dignity to have me deal with this matter. You may depend on my devotion to your interests.'

Aurelia weakened. 'Place her under restraint.'

'Naturally, mistress. Given the seriousness of the charge, that's obvious.'

'You have an ergastulum here?'

He lowered his eyes so she shouldn't see the contempt in them.

'There was such a place mistress, it's used as a store house now.'

'If it's not secure, she must be kept in irons; fetters and a halter. I'll sell her tomorrow, to the brothel keeper in Narnia.'

'Very good, mistress.'

He thought no further than getting Nerysa out of the room. As he crossed to her, she sank on her knees and he knew she wouldn't be able to walk. He took her in his arms and carried her out, bowing to his mistress as he left.

A small group of well-wishers gathered in the ergastulum. It was a typical rural prison, largely underground, lit by windows near the top of high walls which protruded a short way above ground. The gaoler was sorting out his irons, an incomplete set fallen into disuse. Charis had a straw pallet and sheet. Iris had ice from the ice pit which she was pressing to Nerysa's face and chest. Demetrius bound her wrists and ankles with linen, placing the fetters over the bandages so they wouldn't chafe her skin. Scarred ankles were the mark of slavery. A house born slave might escape them but anyone who'd been brought in from abroad or passed through the hands of a dealer had been chained by the ankle and the scars were permanent. A freedman who'd made his fortune would give any price for an ankle job, though plastic surgery and cosmetic plasters were expensive and fooled no one. When Demetrius had lain in this same prison, he'd torn strips of rag from his tunic to protect his skin under the fetters, because scars on his back could be covered but ankle scars couldn't. Only soldiers wore boots. Everyone else slipped their bare feet into sandals. The telltale marks were the butt of offensive jokes by anyone who envied a self-made man his prosperity. Secretly, he'd delighted in his wife's shapely, white ankles. It was entirely logical that, though her face had been beaten to a pulp, he worked doggedly to preserve her ankles.

He growled, 'Our noble mistress particularly mentioned a halter.'

'The mistress will have to wait.' snapped the gaoler, 'Your wife's neck's no thicker than a child's. We don't keep halters that size. Ask the blacksmith tomorrow.'

Demetrius moved mechanically, his mind racing. The slaves were on the brink of revolt which would solve nothing and bring a scandal on Lucius. To abscond could never be an option for him. But if they were still on the estate the next morning, he'd no doubt Aurelia would carry out her threat. He'd underestimated her. He'd thought she wouldn't dare touch Nerysa and would content herself with her daughter. But she'd obviously calculated that, if Nerysa were disfigured and, above all, disgracefully used, Lucius would be disgusted and finally disenchanted with her. How little she knew her husband! Lucius would go to the ends of the earth to fetch Nerysa home, whatever degradation she'd suffered.

The only way to leave the estate legally was to flee to the protection of a free man and beg him to intercede with their master. Though Nerysa was hardly fit to travel and he was afraid of a revolt in his absence, that was what he meant to do. He dismissed Iris and Charis because their crying distracted him and they left reluctantly, weeping on each other's shoulders. He dealt with Aurelia's insolent bodyguards, come to see her instructions carried out. They indicated that she wouldn't consider a pallet a necessary comfort and he was obliged to hold his wife while they kicked straw into a meagre heap for her to lie on. Then, to his relief, they left. Aurelia needed them outside her own room.

Sitting on the stone floor, he held Nerysa's hand but had no sense of her presence. She'd been so vital and strong, nothing like the broken, unconscious wreck beside him. He couldn't let her wake alone and in chains. Useless to waste time wondering if he could have repulsed Aurelia more tactfully. He, too, believed that fate had intervened in their life. He glanced round at the sunken wine jars.

'We've plenty of good, strong wine here,' he said, 'I'm sure our master could spare some for his wife's servants.'

'And when they've had their fill,' grinned the gaoler, 'we'll finish them off – and their precious mistress. Say we tried to stop them killing her.'

There was just enough of a gleam in Demetrius' eyes to encourage him further.

'Rough up her clothes a bit and splay her legs – like it was a debauch that got out of hand.'

Demetrius pulled back from the brink.

'Nothing will be done to compromise our master's dignity. If it should happen that I'm not here to ensure that, you will give our people my orders.'

'Never fear, sir. We'll have a strong horse tethered outside the gate before dawn.'

'Make sure there's another ready for you. As soon as you've passed on my message, go to Publius Curtius' house in Narnia and say I sent you about the order for clogs. Our mistress won't wake in a forgiving mood.'

The sun was high when they arrived at Servius Blandus' villa. Demetrius took Nerysa to the infirmary of the villa rustica and persuaded the bailiff's woman to look after her. In daylight, she was a horrific sight. A rough ride, slung on her belly across a saddle, hadn't helped. Her face was purple black and so swollen her eyes wouldn't open. He could barely discern a nose beneath the swelling and she couldn't breathe through it but gasped through her mouth, bleeding where her teeth had pierced lips that seemed to snarl. As her throat was too bruised to swallow, blood-stained saliva trickled from the corners of her mouth and down her neck. Her breasts were black and distended to gross caricatures. Mercifully, she was unconscious. Unnerved, he began to laugh. Aurelia had set herself a task to sell her to a brothel keeper. Customers expected something more lively and attractive. He watched for signs of returning consciousness until the afternoon, when the bailiff came to say that his master would condescend to see him.

He hadn't chosen Servius Junius Blandus just for the distance of his estates – too far for news to spread quickly, close enough for Nerysa to stand the journey. Servius was a local landowner of substance but he had no great social standing, no political ambitions and no important connections, which led Demetrius to hope he was an independent thinker. Meeting him in the flesh, he feared he'd miscalculated. Blandus could have been fashioned like a pot from coils of soft, white clay. Pendulous belly, midriff and chest were surmounted by two soft chins and bulbous lips that never quite managed to meet. Only his fingers, like jointed sausages touched pulp to pulp. Blue eyes, pale and close together, blinked from behind further folds of flesh. His voice was surprisingly high and querulous. He reclined on a couch worrying a linen sweat cloth.

'Demetri, I could wish you'd not burdened me with this. You put me in an awkward position. His Excellency, Lucius Marius, his father and grandfather before him, have been neighbours for generations. My family's humble in comparison but we've always enjoyed excellent relations. I wouldn't offend him for the world.'

'We've come to you, sir, so you may appeal to him for us. That can't offend him surely? He holds my wife in special affection. If he were here, he'd never permit her to be ill-treated.'

Servius blustered. His voice rose a further octave.

'Demetri, you should know better than to try to control your master by putting your woman in his bed. It looks cunning but it was bound to turn out badly. You're too clever by half. I've thought so for years.'

'Sir, with respect, you misconstrue.'

'On the contrary, I see it all. New bride, finds her husband already being entertained; distressing, understandably hurt. I'd expect her to show it.'

'Believe me, sir, my wife is innocent. In Lucius Marius' absence she's been abused, unlawfully.'

A brief silence and Servius shifted his ground.

'When His Excellency left for the front, did he leave his wife jurisdiction over his property and affairs during his absence?'

'Naturally, he did, sir.'

'Did he specify, or even hint, that you or your woman were exempt from her authority?'

'No, sir.'

'Well, there we have it! How could I insult his wife by harbouring her fugitive slaves? Consider the affront to her, to her family – to the emperor himself, meHercule! I must have your word, Demetri, that you won't try to escape. Otherwise, I'll have you put under restraint.'

Demetrius closed his eyes in despair.

'I'll write to Aurelia that I'm holding her fugitive slaves and inform the local magistrate likewise. I may say one is not yet fit to travel and that I await her further instructions. I can send a letter to Lepidus at the same time.'

'Sir, your letter could be months on the road between here and Vienna. What would that hell-hag have done by then?'

'I didn't hear that, Demetri. You know better than to embarrass me with disrespect for your mistress.'

He pleaded in a whisper as though the mere voicing of such an outrage would make it more likely to happen.

'Sir, she means to sell my wife to a whoremaster.'

Blandus blinked, 'That's bad. Demeaning to Lepidus to have his girlfriend sold off for such a purpose. I could put that to her. Utmost delicacy, of course.'

He looked up sharply, exuding unease, as his wife bustled in.

'Servi, come and see the condition of this slave. It's appalling. I've never seen anything like it.'

'Now, what good would it do if I came to stare at her? Better leave the poor creature in peace.'

'Come and see for yourself why we can't send her back.'

'My dear, we must and shall send her back. The emperors clarified the law only last year; we're bound to help Aurelia recover her fugitive slaves in any way we can. We could be heavily fined.'

'Sir, we're not fugitives, we came to ask you to intercede for us.'

Demetrius had made the point already but he thought it worth making in the presence of Blandus' wife.

'How can I intercede with a man who isn't here?' snapped Blandus.

'We could offer Aurelia a fair price for her. Servi, dearest, she's a clever housekeeper, skilled in medicine, so I hear. Won't you buy her for me?'

'Aurelia wouldn't sell her to you, my lady. She has other plans. Sir, I think you'd feel easier to know Lucius Marius' mind in this matter. Trust me with a letter and I'll be in Vienna and back in a month. I once made it to Sirmium in less.'

Servius' brow cleared.

'Yes, it would be best if you tried to reach your master. Take your pick of my horses. I'll authorise it.'

Demetrius knelt and clasped the knees of his benefactor. 'Thank you, sir, my master will be for ever in your debt. My wife will be safe with you for a month, sir?'

'I'll look to her, but see you return within the month.'

Demetrius collected his baggage and took a last look at his wife. He didn't underestimate the difficulty of reaching Vienna in less than three weeks. He'd no official pass but he had money. He'd buy horses or, once in Illyria, steal them. For the return, he would surely have a pass. Inspecting the horseflesh, he heard a rider enter the stable and rub down his horse and, glancing up, saw Melissus.

'How did you know where to find me?'

'Servius Junius sent word to my mistress this morning.'

Demetrius steadied himself. Naturally, a free man couldn't betray a slave since he owed him no loyalty. No wonder he'd been gracious enough to lend a horse. As soon as he'd left, Nerysa would have been bundled into a cart and sent to Horta and he, himself, arrested at the first staging post. Melissus gripped his elbow.

'Are you well, sir? I came to tell you not to hurry home.'

He felt oddly detached, as though fate had bludgeoned him to complete passivity.

'What choice have we?'

Melissus shook his arm and said with gentle urgency, 'The mistress never got the message, sir, she left Horta this morning.'

'Left Horta?'

'She's gone back to Rome, to her father's house and sent the master notice of divorce.'

Demetrius leapt back to himself, 'Melisse, has there been a rebellion?'

'Not quite, but she knew there would be. Her people couldn't have prevented it - they weren't sober. The villa was like a military camp last night, bristling with pickaxes, mallets and scythes as well as the weapons kept for defence, rusty but serviceable. We'd shepherds and swineherds armed to the teeth and the blacksmith got up like a centurion brandishing a ploughshare. I wish you'd seen it, sir.'

Demetrius shuddered. His first instinct was to leave immediately but, distasteful as it was to stay, he dared not impose a second journey on Nerysa so soon. He sent home for a wagon and her women.

CHAPTER LXXIX

May 180 – October 180

At enim dei miles nec in dolore deseritur.

God's soldier will not be deserted in her grief. Minucius Felix. Octavius 'xvii 3

Nerysa wept with relief to be laid in her own bed. Her eyes were less swollen and she could open them slightly. The familiar room and faces comforted her but she was alarmed by the expression on peoples' faces when they looked at her and because the children didn't come. She heard Demetrius tell Charis to take away her mirror and anything else with a shiny surface. But she couldn't deal with the unknown, she had to see for herself. Charis and Iris were too alert to fool. When Flora served her wine, she struggled to move her lips.

'The rim of this cup's thick. My lips are so bruised. Bring me a silver one from the dining room.'

Flora soon scampered back, filled the silver cup and held it out to her, but even as she reached for it, it was dashed to the ground. Demetrius had Flora by the neck and dragged her, screaming, from the room. Iris came, mopped the floor, poured more wine and chattered brightly without pause. Nerysa shut her eyes and, as far as she was able, her ears. She longed for Charis but Charis, when she came, was subdued.

'You're not crying for me, are you, Charis? I've been home three days already and I'm much better.'

'Don't fret, mistress, we all have our sorrows but none as great as yours.'

'Charis, don't tease. What's the matter?'

Demetrius had beaten Flora. There seemed no end to the chain of troubles that beset them. Tears welled up in Nerysa's bloodshot eyes and stung her torn cheeks. Charis sobbed too.

'He's sorry. He spat on his hand to show he was sorry. He didn't mean to hurt her.'

'Ask him to come.'

He came but didn't speak. She forced her voice past her swollen throat and lips.

'If you let that woman's poison into this house, she's won and we've lost.'

Flora was soon on her feet again but, although Nerysa's bruises faded, she didn't recover. Her ribs had been so painful she'd breathed carefully. Now, paroxysms of harsh, dry coughing tore at her lungs and exhausted her, yet yielded only threads of rusty phlegm. She shivered and complained of cold, while burning with fever and drenched in sweat. Her thoughts were confused but she was conscious, with enough self-awareness to be amused when Charis and Italia asked what medicines to bring from the store. She was useless to herself. She'd no idea what ailed her, she only knew that she was desperately ill. Melissus rode to Rome for Archias but she thought he wouldn't come in time. In lucid moments, she looked for Demetrius. Each time she surfaced he looked more haggard and she urged herself to get the process of dying over, so he should be spared the futile agony of watching it.

***

Archias ordered infusions of fenugreek and scorching poultices for her chest. He'd bought medicines with him and took his pick from Nerysa's.

'It's a good physic garden,' he told Demetrius, 'Is it true she - ?'

'Of course not! I've two of my best men working it.'

Inactivity came hard to Demetrius, but, since he'd no alternative, he sat at the bedside, insensible of hunger or fatigue. He spared no thought for Aurelia. He thought only of the wrongs he, himself, had done his wife and remembered her saying that the most fortunate life was short and already so full of pain it made no sense for anyone to add to it. Was she, too, to be fleeting as a chicory flower? More than once, he'd prepared himself for the agony of losing her but never imagined living in a world where she no longer breathed. For hours at a time, he was conscious of nothing but the catch in her every breath and the hiss of the steam kettle, belching hyssop. He was supported by the household, who gathered in the atrium and gave the gods no peace. He thought, if ever gods were moved by the prayers of slaves, they must be moved now. Successus came from the domus and assured him the urban family were praying too. Such concern, from one whose position he'd usurped, dispelled the awkwardness he'd always felt in his presence and he grasped the proffered hand like a shipwrecked man.

'How good of you! You who've never been married and couldn't know -.'

'Sir, we all share your grief. I hesitate to trouble you with other business but I'm being pressed by the master's father-in-law about the divorce settlement. We'll have to make them some response.'

'Have you briefed lawyers?'

'Severus is in Rome but he's about take up his command in Syria. I thought you'd know best, sir, whether the master would wish you to consult him before he leaves.'

'I've written to our Lucius. But I don't expect a reply within the month.'

'They're demanding immediate repayment of the dowry.'

'That's preposterous. We haven't had the final instalment. It's not even due.'

'They want it in full – with interest and a share of the capital growth during the marriage. I haven't shown them the books, I've said only you can do that. It's a delicate matter, sir, but the lady's infidelities – there's proof. We're entitled to withhold part of the dowry.'

'Fifteen percent. But our Lucius would have to go to court with proof. He'd hate that. Besides he's out of favour with Commodus and she's his kinswoman. I'll see Severus. He can't represent him once he's in Syria but he's wily. I'd value his opinion. In the meantime we stall and pay nothing.'

'There is another matter, sir. Your wife longs for Baptism. There are those here who could administer it but, as you're always with her, they haven't thought it right, or possible, to proceed without your permission.'

'Baptism?'

'Rite of Christian initiation, sir.

'You're out of your mind! Lucius Marius wouldn't hear of it.'

In fifteen years Demetrius couldn't recall Successus having made him any reply but 'Very good, sir.' Now he challenged him with a firmness that reproached his own wavering.

'Lucius Marius' displeasure is no longer a threat to her. She must make her peace with her divine master so as to be received into his heavenly household.'

'It's too late. Can't you see she has no strength for ordeals.'

'Immersion's not necessary. It's enough to wet the head, which those who are nursing her must be doing often enough, and to say the right words with intention. It's purely a spiritual exercise, though it does sometimes happen that soul and body heal together.'

'So you're infected with this superstition.'

'I've been a Christian since boyhood, sir, and now a priest.'

'You and Timothy both. I begin to suspect there's more going on in this family than I know of.'

He hesitated. It was superstition, of course. It differed from suggestions that she be wrapped in a lion skin or stroked with a weasel's tooth only in that she herself probably believed in it. What if belief gave her the strength to fight? *It does sometimes happen that soul and body heal together.*

'How long does the "exercise" take?'

'As long as it would take you, sir, to eat some bread and meat and drink a cup of wine.'

'I don't want to know. Don't speak of it to anyone. I shall leave you for a moment.'

'You'll find a table laid outside, sir.'

The illness tightened its grip, pressing forward to the crisis which came as night yielded to dawn. The sudden silence as her breathing eased didn't alarm him because Archias had told him what to hope for. Archias was saying, 'The worst is over. With careful nursing, she should recover. Do you still think we should send for Lepidus?'

'Not in that case. If the worst had happened, it would have been wrong to keep him away. But I think, now, I would rather he didn't come here.'

As soon as Nerysa was out of danger, Demetrius returned to Rome. The domus hadn't regained its tranquillity. Hatred was entrenched. Those who'd suffered from Aurelia turned on those who'd colluded with her people. He forbade fighting and threatened severe punishment for offenders. Then he was forced to order it, often for workers he respected and trusted. It was a sorry business with limited effect. The house fell into a surly, ill-natured truce. Listening to every grievance, he pieced together a clearer picture and identified those whose behaviour was commonly held to be unforgivable. Those he sold. Then he set himself to persuade people that the time had come for reconciliation.

By October, Commodus had made a hasty, scrappy peace and awarded himself a triumph. Lucius returned to Rome for it. Demetrius made no attempt to shield him, recounting every detail of their troubles except those of her pneumonia. He could still hear those croaking breaths, synchronous with his own heart beat but he couldn't have spoken of them. He said baldly, 'Three days between life and death. Months before the swelling cleared and we were sure she wouldn't be disfigured.'

Lucius, stiff and silent, expressed neither sympathy nor regret. Demetrius had never known him so imperious or so cold.

CHAPTER LXXX

November 180 – March 183

απο χρυσης τε βασιλειας ες σιδηραν και κατιωμενην νυν καταπεσουσης της ιστοριας

For the Romans of that time, life descended from an age of gold to an age of iron and rust. Dio Cassius

The master's carriage swept up to the villa on a gusty November day. When Successus had handed her down, Thaïs stood like a column as the wind swirled dead leaves around her and whipped her hair against her cheeks. Nerysa ran across the forecourt. As she hugged her, she felt a tiny girl squirming under her cloak.

'It's wonderful to see you both! How long can you stay?'

'Until I'm well, the master says.'

'You soon will be, we'll take the greatest care of you.'

Thaïs shook her head. Her face crumpled and her body heaved sobs. Nerysa held her close, murmuring the words that comfort children. Nothing gave her such a clear insight into the misery Aurelia had wrought as the breaking of the serene, efficient Thaïs. She brewed up a sedative, put her to bed and lay beside her holding her hand and whispering over and over, 'She's gone. We're free of her. She's never, never coming back.'

But Thaïs moaned through every night. She'd cry out suddenly and back across the bed, fighting any attempt to stop her falling to the floor. Nerysa's faith in the healing power of love and reassurance began to falter. At last, the day came when they watched Hannah running round the house and Thaïs smiled. Then she laughed and began to speak.

'Our Lucius says, if she grows old enough to be useful, she'll be yours. That's only right – she'd have died but for you.'

'But she's yours, you must keep her with you.'

'No. If she's any chance, it's here. The air's so bad in the city. There are women who've had eight children and none of them lived, even to Hannah's age. Ostia's no healthier. But our Lucius will be surprised to see me back. Archias said my case was hopeless.'

'Is he angry with me for coming to the domus?'

'Our Lucius, angry with you? How could he be? He longs for you. But he daren't send for you. Once someone just mentioned you and his eyes filled up. So embarrassing.'

'It wasn't his fault.'

'Demetrius says a man should be able to control his own wife.'

Nerysa laughed. 'Where did he get that idea? Not from me, surely?'

'Did he exaggerate? I don't see any scars.'

Nerysa blushed, 'I'm using lead paste, just a little. Around my eye here and under my lip you can see something. I'm just glad I didn't end up with a nose like that man of hers. I lay in bed dreading that. Did you see something of the triumph?'

'I saw the emperor!'

'What's he like?'

'A god! Tall and muscular as Hercules with golden hair and a face that shines like a star. The crowds went mad for him; I never knew you could find so many flowers in October. The streets were ankle deep. He can do no wrong for me – except I wish he'd give our master an appointment.'

'Hasn't he got anything yet?'

'He's been waiting since March. He felt it when Severus got a legionary command straight away. Since Maecianus died, there's no one to put in a word for him. I suppose Severus might find him something in Syria, especially since Pertinax is his governor. They say Pertinax thinks well of our Lucius.'

When Nerysa related this to Demetrius he snorted, 'Golden god indeed! Did she tell you he had Saoterus, his boyfriend, in the triumphator's chariot with him and he kept turning round to drool kisses on him? It was blatant enough to look innocent to the unsuspecting but, to those in the know, it was disgusting. And it's not just kisses the fellow gets but real influence over matters that shouldn't concern him.

'It looks as if Lucius won't get an official post but he's got plenty of legal work so he'll hold the fort in Rome while I catch up abroad. Athens is urgent and Spain; the south coast for fish sauce then up the silver trail to the mines. From there, it's just a hop to Britain to see if I can trade wine for oysters.'

To Nerysa's surprise and pleasure he was impressed with London; its efficient port and cosmopolitan business community. He'd heard educated Greek on London Bridge, struck up a conversation and made useful contacts. She was puzzled. This wasn't the Britain she remembered. London would be no safer than Rome for fugitives, but Anglesey or Ireland? It was a wild thought. She knew how difficult it was to make a life outside one's sphere. She couldn't have done it without him. Could he? Would he want to? She looked at his smooth chin and manicured hands.

'I suppose you couldn't live without baths and books?'

'Well, they make life liveable, don't they? I loved your country, Nerysa, as green as the eyes of bright Minerva, even in September, and that turbulent grey-green sea. It reminded me of your beautiful eyes.'

***

Lucius no longer tried to keep Demetrius away from Horta. He wanted to go himself but stayed away, doubtful of a sincere welcome at his own farm. Homecoming had brought him no joy. His house was bleak and he felt a stranger to it. Few of his dogs recognised him. His slaves were wary. His pet boys, whose affection had consoled him, were adolescent and must be sent away and trained for work. He bought others but he was too emotionally drained to invest in new relationships, he needed to fall back on old ones. His house was still full of women but he no longer wanted variety. Rather he needed someone as pliant as last year's sandals. He found the girl who'd serviced him in the dark days of his marriage and settled back into a half-hearted routine with her. His steward's diligence was most poignant of all for he was perceptive enough to know that it was now prompted solely by a sense of duty. Nerysa haunted his thoughts. For months, her blessed vision would return as he fell asleep, fainter each time until it faded to an elusive memory. He'd waited patiently for her to see him as her protector. But he'd utterly failed to protect her. How would she believe any promise he made her? She would not reproach him but he couldn't endure that frank gaze or to look down on her white neck and bowed head, and feel her contempt of his weakness.

Lucillus wasn't a pet; he was a son in all but name; as dear as any natural son could have been. How could he think of uprooting him to assuage his own loneliness? To have him brought to Baiae for the summer break and to Rome for a month each winter was as much as he could do.

Moving between houses like an ambassador, purveying merry tales and goodwill, Lucillus detected the drop in temperature between his patron and his tutor and was obviously pained by it. Lucius had always talked freely to him but couldn't bring himself to discuss the unacknowledged rift between himself and Demetrius. Having raised him to treat his tutor with deference, he now indicated that some shift in the balance of the relationship would be appropriate. Lucillus was free. Demetrius was not. Albeit with tact and consideration, that fact must be recognised.

The political situation was dismaying. For Lucius, government meant Marcus. From before Lucius was born, Marcus had been emperor; first, assisting the gentle Pius; next jointly with his colourful son-in-law, Verus; then as sole ruler and, lastly, with his son. Lucius had heard of Nero, Caligula and Domitian but they were ghosts from a distant past, almost mythical. He lived in the modern age; an age of philosophy, reason and the rule of law; heir to five reigns and ninety years of sane government. The reign of Commodus was an histrionic melodrama – a throwback to horrors the empire thought it had outgrown. When Lucius dreamed of the bleak expanse of the frozen Danube he mourned not only a friend and mentor but the passing of a whole age of enlightenment.

His clients flooded back to him, accompanying him in droves to the forum, the baths and the law courts. Each workday morning he sallied forth from his sumptuous house; tunic and toga dazzling white, fragrant and intricately pleated; beard trimmed; hair curled, combed and pomaded; skin oiled and perfumed; manicured and pedicured, shod in scented leather. His legal papers were drafted, corrected, copied, checked, packed and carried. Before the world he was the visible pinnacle of a great pyramid of talent and devotion; the public face of six households.

He defended desperate men, fallen foul of Commodus and facing trumped-up charges. He hadn't been among the reckless on the battlefield but danger in the courtroom exhilarated him. Even Commodus had to live within the letter of the law and, of that, Lucius was a master. He had no royal favour to lose. He'd been divorced by Commodus' cousin, Commodus resented his reputation and disliked him of old.

Socially, he kept a low profile. On days when the courts didn't sit, he went walking with his freedmen; the intellectuals at his side, the brawny ones on the outside of the group with the guards and slaves. He wasn't alone in this. Men no longer walked the streets in twos and threes but in cohorts.

In September, on a day when a brilliant cobalt sky looked infinitely distant and everything under it sharply distinct, he went down to the Pompey gardens. Plane trees along the main avenue were woven into a lofty, vaulted corridor leading down to the nymphaeum. Gilt leaves glittered among the green; some lay on the gravel walk like scattered coin. Sunlight filtered through the canopy, glancing off the mosaicked trunks as shards of gold.

Lucius drew a deep breath and stopped in his tracks. Attar of rose always caused his heart to race. It reminded him of Nerysa. He turned and saw Quintus Pulcher close behind him. Their two parties coalesced, encircling them and pressing them forward. Lucius was on his guard as he took Quintus' jewelled hand. Quintus sent him mixed messages, treating him at some times with deference and at others with amused condescension. Besides, the nobility were shunning him at present, unless they were in trouble.

'Lepide, my dear fellow! What an unexpected pleasure! We don't see you at the palace these days.'

'How kind of you to notice.'

'Come! You're a patriot, I think. What of your vows to the dying Marcus?'

Lucius searched the lean face, etched deep from nose to chin. As usual, he couldn't decide if he was being mocked.

'Shouldn't you be more attentive to his orphaned successor?' Pulcher persisted, 'Barely twenty and not, if I may say so, the brightest star in the firmament. Where are all the friends of Marcus? Retired, gone abroad, suffering from strange diseases that leave them hale and hearty in the country but too ill to attend the senate?'

Lucius shrugged. 'The father's cronies don't appeal to the son. His own freedmen are more accommodating. But you've changed your habit, too. It seems you *do* go to court. Do you dine there?'

'Oh, very droll. It's true, you know, he really does mix turds into the food. His idea of humour. What a charmer!'

'You oughtn't to suffer such indignities at your time of life. Why go?'

'To keep an eye on my boys – his boys now. Saoterus commandeered them, you know. Well brought up they were, modest little boys. Now they strut and waddle like cheap tarts, mouths like sewers and minds to match. All they dream of is replacing Saoterus!'

'The job has its perks, I suppose; bribes, selling posts and pardons.'

'Oh that doesn't impress. They want to run the empire!'

Lucius winced. It distressed him less that the empire was run by a pimp than that slave boys knew it.

'The keeper of the imperial piss pot has more influence over his majesty than the entire senate.' Pulcher's lip curled. 'The boys took me backstage. A wing of the palace has been converted into a brothel run by Saoterus. Commodus likes to watch and be watched.'

'Where does he find all these depraved people?' Lucius voiced a question that had exercised him for some time. 'In Marcus' day, everyone you met was rational and urbane. Now, suddenly, everyone's a rent boy or a circus juggler.'

'In government, yes, not in this brothel. They're not all slaves either. I saw youths and girls of all classes, even noble families, and respectable matrons pressed into service. But it's the dregs of the slave pen who run the show – and the empire.'

'There was a prophesy doing the rounds in Alexandria when I was there, that the empire was about to fall. Nonsense, of course, but I sometimes think. The modern world is Rome. Civilization is Rome. Without it, what would there be but chaos and confusion?'

They'd reached the nymphaeum. Nude nereids poured water into the marble basin from ever flowing urns. Pulcher spoke softly into the roar. 'There are people, people in high places, who think the rot should be stopped.'

'Who in high places?'

'The emperor's sister for one.'

'Lucilla?'

'And Paternus and Julianus even. Would you like to do your bit?'

'My dear Pulcher, you're surely not suggesting I should bump off the c... er... the young gentleman?'

'Horses for courses, Lepide. Lucilla has a son-in-law and a stepson keen to oblige.'

'The two Q's?'

'Just so. Paternus will bring over the guards, he's their commanding officer, after all. The emperor's secretary is sounding out the provincial governors but a personal letter from you - not through official channels – to Severus, would be very useful. He could approach Pertinax. We need his answer within the month.'

'I don't see why. You've enough clout to kill Saoterus without calling on the legions. I should have thought Paternus had other things on his mind, by the way. I'm bidden to his daughter's wedding.'

'To Julianus' son. So perhaps you follow me now. What those two don't suspect is that Lucilla isn't exerting herself to instal Julianus. Much as she hates Pompeianus, she'd sooner see him emperor than anyone else. Think, what does an emperor's widow want but to be an emperor's wife again? But Pompeianus won't move without a nod from his old friend and client Pertinax.'

Lucius' heart was pounding. He heard himself stammer like a schoolboy.

'Forgive me. Didn't hear you clearly - don't understand you at all. Hold me excused. Pressing business. Leaving this afternoon - for Sicily.'

***

Demetrius understood his master's reluctance to betray the son of Marcus but his analysis, as he paced the tablinum, was strictly pragmatic. If the coup succeeded, Lucius would be guilty of nothing worse than inertia but to be implicated in a failed plot was treason. His judgement was that it would fail. Commodus was still the idol of the common people and Pompeianus and Pertinax, stern disciplinarians both, weren't popular with the military.

'They want Pertinax's answer within the month. So, before the Augustan games.'

'Public games?' Lucius objected, 'Quadratus and Quintillian are close to Commodus, they'll pick him off in the palace, surely.'

'Paternus is to bribe the guards. Which ones? Commodus' personal bodyguard would mean the palace. But Paternus is prefect of the Praetorians, who provide the guard for official functions. The two Q's will be in his train wherever he goes.'

'Zeus, you're right! It will be the Augustan Games.'

'Shall you go?'

'I meant to. I don't get many invitations to the imperial box these days. Besides, if something were to happen and I'd stayed away, it might look suspicious.'

'Commodus always goes backstage, doesn't he, rubbing shoulders with the gladiators. A fine place for a murder, that warren beneath the arena.'

Lucius shook his head. 'It'd be a bad business. And unnecessary. Get rid of Saoterus and Commodus would be manageable, don't you think?'

'Saoterus isn't unique.'

'Not in his vices but in his influence over Commodus he is. He's looked after him since he was a child.'

'You're not inclined to warn the authorities?'

'Who are they, these days? The senior senators I might approach all seem to be in the plot.'

***

Lucius showed his token to the guard and paused under the marble gateway of the imperial box. He bowed to the royal ladies; Crispina beside the vacant throne, the broad-faced Lucilla and her chubby teenage daughter a little below her. He noted that their husbands; the victim, his proposed successor and the assassin were absent, but Julianus and Paternus were bending solicitously over Lucilla. He took his place - the last of the marble seats on the back row, accepted a cup of wine and made it last until those around him had downed their fifth.

'The crowd's restive.' yawned his neighbour. 'He makes them wait so, when he does come, they go wild.'

Lucius grunted non-committally. If Commodus never emerged into the sunlight, he would feign surprise to rival that of the most innocent bystander. The skin around his mouth tingled as he looked back and forth from Lucilla and Julianus to the doorways opening onto the arena, from any one of which Demetrius might send the pre-arranged signal. In the shimmering heat, he fancied he saw a giant patchwork quilt. The people were random splashes of colour fluttering among awnings and pennants. Below them the fourteen rows of knights in their white togas formed the fringe of a sheet. His neighbour began to snore. The variegated scene below was slipping in and out of focus when the trumpets suddenly blared and a shower of rose petals floated down. The patchwork was rent to strips as the crowd surged to its feet and the stone structure quivered with its roar. Lucius pulled himself to his feet, his eyes fixed on the centre of the balustrade. Between the gleaming helmets of the guards was that unmistakable golden head and, above it, arms stretched wide to embrace the crowd. Commodus stayed a long time immobile, head thrust back, drinking adulation. Lucius felt embarrassed; a voyeur of the incontinent love affair between Commodus and the plebs. *That's it then*, he thought. *We were wrong.*

But, as Commodus prowled along the front of the box, scowling and pausing now and then to turn and bare his teeth, Lucius saw he was a ghastly grey and that the golden hair stood on end. His eyes were wild and Lucius smelled fear. Something had happened in the bowels of the building. But what?

He mustn't see me sweat, Lucius thought, drawing his draped left elbow over his face. He looked up, straight into the eyes of Commodus who threw back his head and laughed. 'Why, it's Lepidus,' he drawled, 'pious Lepidus, the model for Roman youth. How's your slave-born bastard?'

Lucius bowed low. 'My Lord Emperor is so gracious to enquire.'

Ironic, he thought. Commodus couldn't know that the taunt wounded him to the soul. Not because Lucillus was his bastard, but because he wasn't.

'Amusing. I'll give you that. The rumpus in your town house when your slaves threw your wife's slaves into the street. Best laugh I'd had all year! Keep it up!'

Pulling him toward him, he kissed him; once on each cheek and once on the lips and, as he moved away, Lucius tasted an emperor's sweat.

***

Lucius was not at home to callers. The great bronze doors were shut and Hypnos turned visitors away. Demetrius sat in the locked tablinum, head in hands.

'Fatuous!' he groaned. 'To kill someone, you come from behind with your dagger under wraps and slide it between his ribs before he knows you're there. Quintillian should have got his slave to do it. "See what the senate has sent you!" indeed! How could anyone make a speech at a time like that? The guards may have been bribed but what were they to do, stand there gawping while Quintillian did his declaiming practice?'

'I suppose,' Lucius complained, 'you'd no choice either.'

'Quadratus broke and ran. When the guards chased him round the corner, they'd have recognised me as your slave and asked themselves what I was doing there. Not that I worked that out at the time, my foot shot out of its own accord.'

'So. Now there are two on the rack to blab my name.'

'Their slaves perhaps. Not the two Q's. They're part of the royal family.'

'Read your history books, Demetrie. Forget how Marcus dealt with Cassius. Commodus was always stupid and vicious. Now he's shit scared. The two Q's will be racked until they name ten more and those ten until they name ten apiece. That's how tyrants operate. That's why every good emperor starts his reign by vowing to banish informers and crucify slaves who denounce their masters. Make no mistake, this business will empty the senate faster than the plague.'

It won't be comfortable for us either, Demetrius thought. *Under the hammer; pretty ones to the palace brothel; the rest on the land.*

'And,' he said aloud, 'as a traitor's estate is forfeit to the emperor and Commodus is broke, he's no incentive to believe in anyone's innocence.'

'Of course, my name may not be mentioned.'

'And until it is, master, you'd best behave as though you'd nothing to fear.'

So the great bronze doors swung open again and visitors streamed in, agog with news. The two 'Q's' were executed, Lucilla exiled. No conspirator was brought before any court. The law was useless against summary justice so, to his relief, Lucius wasn't called upon to defend the accused. He breathed more easily when Pompeianus, on whose behalf the plot had been conceived, was, inexplicably, left untouched. Pompeianus was the patron of his patrons, Pertinax and Severus. He trembled again when these two were sacked from their posts in Syria but, by the spring, the spate of executions had slowed to a trickle. Then Quintus Pulcher sent for him. *Is he mad?* Lucius thought. *Or is he trying to implicate me?*

'He might be being watched,' Demetrius observed, 'I'll go and see him.'

'Don't be stupid, Demetrie. You're as recognisable as I am.'

***

Lucius paced his garden, wrestling with his better self. The blow, if it fell, would fall suddenly. To prevent Demetrius and Nerysa going under the hammer as confiscate property, he should free them. But he couldn't bring himself to give up his last hold over them. He could sign back-dated manumissions and hide them in the shrine. No poison could kill fast enough to prevent him leaving Demetrius a message. He thought of them living on together after his death and ground his teeth. As if that thought were not provoking enough, he seemed to have an intruder in the garden. An Egyptian priest, to judge from his dazzling white, pleated robe, girded around the breast. He looked vaguely familiar. He must have come late for the morning reception and strayed into the private apartments by mistake. Lucius could have called the guards but the fellow seemed harmless enough so he strolled over to put him right. The priest wouldn't listen. He broke into a frenzied dance, chanted and shook his rattles menacingly. Lucius turned to call for him to be removed and heard Demetrius say, 'If *you* don't know me master, who will?'

Lucius stared at him, aghast. 'Demetrie! Whatever happened to you? You're as bald as an egg!'

'It was only hair, master. Which is why I opted to serve Isis. Cybele asked too great a sacrifice. Shall I go and pray with Quintus?'

Lucius was amused. It was a brilliant idea. The more disappointing when it failed.

'He did see me briefly, master.' Demetrius said. 'But he wouldn't give me any message except that you're not in danger and he needs to speaks to you, personally. I think he means to jump before he's pushed. That would allow him to choose his time and pass his estate to his nephew in an orderly fashion. Anyway, he suggests we buy a beaten-up litter from a cab service and fit some heavy curtains. Hired hands take you up in a quiet street, drop you back there afterwards and dump the litter. What do you think?'

'I'll go tomorrow. The day after that, I'm going to Horta. No, not with you. When I get back you can go there, or to Ostia – wherever you like.'

He struggled for a light tone but the resentment of nine years finally erupted.

'Did you ever consider me? What sort of life I may have managed to hold onto! Thirty-five and what have I got? No career, no heir, not even the woman I love. I shared everything I had with you. What luxury did I ever refuse you?'

The question was rhetorical yet he waited. Demetrius stayed silent, head bowed.

'Quintus groomed her, created her for me and hid her in my house for me to find. What business did you have, grabbing her for yourself and poisoning her against me on the pretext that my father treated you badly? Well, if I owe you anything, I'll compensate you - money and freedom. Not the woman I love. Since when does a slave cut out his master?'

Demetrius looked up then, eyes dark and brilliant.

'Master, if she's difficult, at first, you won't be cruel to her?'

'I'll do the same as you; whatever it takes to make her obey me. She can come here of her own free will or in chains. Whichever she likes. When I've won her, let's see if I can woo her. But you stay away until she's settled down. I'm not having you fill her head with ideas of loyalty to you or putting Lucillus up to beg her freedom because you know I couldn't refuse him. Later, when I marry again, she can come back to you, richer than she left. We'll all benefit. You'll come to see that in time.'

CHAPTER LXXXI

March 183

αν αφεθω, ευθυς πασα ευροια, ουδενος επιστρεφομαι, πασιν ως ισος και ομοιος
λαλω, πορευομαι οπου θελω, ερχομαι οθεν θελω και οπου θελω.

If I were free, I'd be completely happy. I wouldn't defer to anyone. I'd address everyone
as an equal, and come and go just as I pleased. Epictetus IV i 33-39

When Charis flew out of the house to find her, Nerysa was helping Italia pull turnips for pickling, wind-tangled hair straggling from under a kerchief, mud-spattered tunic hitched above her knees.

'The master's here asking for you.' shouted Charis, 'Demetrius is with him and his head's shaved.'

Merciful God! Nerysa thought, *he's taken a fever.* She fidgeted impatiently as Charis washed her, bundled her into clean tunics and sandals and tugged a comb through her hair. She had elegant dresses, for Demetrius loved to indulge her, but she wouldn't risk provoking her master by any show of pretension. The uniform of the villa rustica was drab and couldn't be got to drape becomingly but it was clean and suitable for the life he'd assigned to her.

It was more than four years since she'd seen him but he looked older by more than that. He looked up from the papyrus, pens and rod ranged before him, in a way she could only call furtive. *He's looking for my scars,* she thought. She glanced round for Demetrius and saw him slumped in a corner of the room, looking so ill she rushed towards him. He stopped her in her tracks with a look that tore at her heart;

reproachful, unbelieving, as if she'd turned on him and dealt him a mortal wound. Lucius spoke into his beard and kept his eyes down on his papers.

'Yesterday, I saw Quintus Fabius Pulcher. He asked to be remembered to you.'

She stayed calm. Quintus had no reason to unmask her after so many years.

'What have you to say?'

'I trust His Excellency, Quintus Fabius, is in good health, master?'

'As a matter of fact, he's dying. That's why he sent for me. To tell me the truth about you.'

Her heart slammed against her ribs, her hands clawed and stretched. The years rolled back and fate returned to claim her.

'He told me you lived in his house six years. Legally you were a hostage, entrusted, before her death, to the care of his mother, but informally, you were his beloved daughter. He didn't even engage teachers for you but educated you himself. You were of high rank among your own people. A princess, he said. which, in view of your shameless behaviour, I find hard to believe.'

'What do you mean, master?'

'Do the kings of your northern race honour their word, madam, or do they cheat their allies and boast of their cunning?'

She drew herself up to retort, then, remembering her father's inexplicable betrayal of her, she faltered, lowering her eyes.

'We don't like cheats.'

'Then why deceive me for twelve years and suffer me to offer you indignities that make me burn with shame to think of?'

'Master —'

'Don't call me that!'

'My people broke their treaty and my life was forfeit. I was eighteen. Was it so wicked to refuse to die, before I'd begun to live? Had Quintus educated me so carefully just so I could become a heap of bleached bones in his mausoleum?'

'I suppose I wasn't worthy of the chance to protect you.'

'You're a Roman knight, my husband is a Roman slave. Would I expect you to commit treason for me?'

He raised his brows at Demetrius and she fired at the implied criticism of Quintus.

'He couldn't save me! Do you think he didn't try? He stopped the soldiers taking me away for execution. In fact, they didn't want to. It's supposed to be bad luck to kill a virgin. He persuaded them to let him see to it. The lightest slick on the wrists he said and a slow fading. I'd die blissfully and he wouldn't leave me until the end. He didn't want slavery for me. He'd have preferred death, of course, but I was desperate to live. He made the arrangements. I don't know who's in that funerary urn but it's not me. I was inflicted on you.'

She remembered the meticulous planning, the fearful risk, his faith in the young man he'd chosen to dupe. *Why do all that only to expose her now?*

***

Lucius conceded that Quintus had judged him shrewdly. He never considered betraying her. It was a wretched situation. The slaughter of hostages was a harsh necessity. To have forced her into cohabitation with a slave was an atrocity unworthy of the Roman people. How far might he be held to blame for it? Now he must protect her secret and dignify her condition as far as discretion allowed. He flinched as she flung defiance at him.

'You despise me for choosing slavery rather than death. I don't care what you think. I had to stay alive, wherever, however I could. I'm not sorry. I stole twelve years. I'll gladly pay for them. Before I was a slave, I'd only lived in books. I'd never seen or done anything real. Now I've lived a useful life and known the love of husband and children. I can die without rancour or regret.'

She stood with her head thrown back, body braced against attack, as he remembered her on her wedding day. He saw she'd rejected his love because she'd never, for a moment, believed in it. Bewildered and too drained to protest, he set out the position as he might have summed up a case.

'Britain was passive for years. At one time, our diplomats would have been pleased to give your people news of you. Now, of course, there's war in Britain again. I believe it will be over soon and Pulcher thinks your tribe's not involved but this isn't the time to try and rehabilitate you. The emperor's a capricious madman and my patron slung out of office and out of favour. When Marcus was alive, I could have got you a free pardon with honour and privilege.'

'Do you mean, master, that you won't give me up?'

'What have I ever done to make you think I would?'

'Then I can stay as I am?'

He shook his head.

'Consorting with Demetrius could have made you legally a slave. Do you think I haven't wished a thousand times that I'd freed him before his wedding? I've brought lawyers with me, experts on status claims, but I doubt if anything can be done without revealing your identity. A freedwoman is all I can make of you. If you'd only spoken, Lucillus would have been freeborn. I could have adopted him and made him my heir. How could I forgive you? For his sake alone, I couldn't.'

He hadn't meant to sound bitter. It wasn't dignified. He didn't expect gratitude but she should appreciate the skill and care he was exercising. The case wasn't entirely straightforward; she, like Demetrius, had once been chained in his prison, a disgrace which could make them ineligible for citizenship. He must observe every legal nicety to ensure that their status could never be challenged.

'I'll perform the ceremony now.' he said. Demetrius nodded and went out.

***

Alone with Lucius, Nerysa knew neither what to say nor where to look. She and Quintus had used him cynically. He'd deserved better. She felt shabby and, at the same time, resentful. He could afford the luxury of handsome behaviour whereas she was one of the downtrodden hordes whose only recourse was to wheedle and deceive.

Demetrius returned with two lawyers. One of them laid the rod on her head and said, 'I declare that this slave is free.'

Lucius took her by the elbows and gently turned her round, saying in his beautiful voice the sweetest words she'd ever heard, 'And I confirm that this slave is free.'

He released her and, the next instant, held her hand in the strong, warm clasp of friendship. It was rough from heavy work and his tone betrayed annoyance – or distaste.

'Congratulations on your freedom, Maria Nerysa.'

'Thank you.'

It was only as Demetrius stood up that she realised the significance of his having been sitting down. He must have been freed. He took her hand and spoke without meeting her eye. 'Congratulations on your freedom, Maria Nerysa.'

'Thank you. Congratulations on *your* freedom, sir.'

They spoke the words they'd yearned to speak with a constraint they could never have imagined. The lawyers congratulated her. Lucius paid over the manumission tax and offered them the use of his library to complete their records. As soon as they left, the mood changed. Lucius rubbed his hands exclaiming, 'Well, now we're all free, who's going to serve the wine?'

Nerysa made to oblige them but he shouted merrily, 'No, let me!'

She giggled. 'This is just like Saturnalia.'

She and Demetrius laughed, realising in the same instant that, next Saturnalia, it would be their duty to impersonate slaves. They were middle-aged and didn't insist that their dreams come true in every detail. Lucius, who had, perhaps, the most to regret, seemed the most elated. It was as if he'd set down a heavy load. Nerysa felt a pang for the years that had been wasted but they didn't matter now. Life was beginning again for all of them.

'Your daughter!' Lucius shouted, 'MeHercule! We've forgotten the girl. Demetri, be so kind as to trouble the worthy magistrates a third time.'

The whole of her daughter's short life had been overshadowed by fear. Nerysa couldn't immediately shake free of it. She stood before Lucius; the child whose name could never be mentioned in his presence; feet apart, arms thrust behind her. There was nothing in her eager face, dusky curls and violet eyes to provoke hostility. Nothing but the circumstances of her birth.

'Remind me,' he said softly, 'how old are you?'

'Eight, master.'

'Then you've been my slave for eight years? That seems long enough to me. This gentleman is going to touch you with a rod but he won't hurt you. Will you keep still?'

The brief ceremony over, Demetrius lifted her in his arms.

'Congratulations on your freedom, darling.'

Her eyes searched his face anxiously until he said, 'Yes, you can congratulate me too.'

Nerysa added, 'Yes, darling, and me.'

As Demetrius set her down she began to cry and Lucius frowned.

'Aren't you pleased with your freedom, little girl? Then I'd better write your certificate quickly, before you persuade me to change my mind.'

She stood by his chair, watching him write. His gentle laugh and his hand over hers calmed her. At the end of each line, he looked up and smiled and when he'd finished, he drew her onto his knee. To Nerysa's horror, she threw her dimpled arms around his neck and kissed him, full on the lips. He seemed startled but not displeased and asked what she wanted as a present to mark the occasion. She slid from his knee, grave and earnest.

'Can it be something I already have?'

'That would be a waste, wouldn't it?'

'No. I think you don't know I share my brother's lessons. My father said it was allowed but I'd like you to tell me so yourself.'

'What are you studying?'

'The same as everyone, of course; Latin, Greek, mathematics and philosophy.'

'You're a philosopher, little one! Which philosophers do you study?'

'Socrates, sir, and the great seven.' She ticked them off on her hand in a sing-song voice.

'Bias, Chilo, Cleobulus, Periander, Pittacus, Solon and Thales. I need to know them thoroughly before I study Epictetus and Musonius.'

'Yes,' he agreed, 'I'd certainly advise you to do that. And you should mention Musonius first because he was the master. Epictetus was his pupil.'

'But, comparing their work, sir, don't you consider that the pupil outshone his master?'

Lucius shot Demetrius a bemused look while the girl tugged at his sleeve.

'Sir?'

'Yes, little philosopher.'

'Is Lucillus going to live with you in Rome?'

'Not until he's twelve, that will be two years at least.'

'If you take Gisco and Macrinus with him there'll be no one here to teach me.'

'I'll engage masters for him in Rome. Gisco and Macrinus may stay and teach you all they can before it's time for you to be married.'

She laughed, 'Oh, no one will have me, sir. Men don't want to marry scholars.'

'Well, as your patron, it will fall to me to find a husband for you. I'll give it my best shot and may even succeed. But isn't it past your bedtime?'

'What an extraordinary child!' he said when Charis had taken her out. 'We must send her to the university in Alexandria. I wanted to give you these in private. Pulcher sent them.'

He emptied a leather bag onto the table, whistling softly as she unwrapped a gold torque. She hadn't seen it since she'd worn it to court and had forgotten how magnificent it was. Neither Roman could have seen finer craftsmanship anywhere in the world. But it was an impersonal ornament, a masterpiece from a royal treasury. She felt nothing for it but a detached admiration whereas the plain gold locket on a worn leather strap made her eyes sting.

'My bulla! I wore it from when I went to live with Quintus and for far too long. He thought thirteen too young for marriage. He wanted every girl to be a child until her sixteenth birthday. But, by then, the political situation was bad. He didn't dare try to arrange a marriage for me. He kept me quietly at home and hoped I'd been forgotten. But I hadn't.'

More poignant still was a delicate portrait on ivory. Quintus had painted it himself. He'd sometimes asked her to sit still for long periods and very tedious she'd found it.

'I should like to see Pulcher if he's well enough to receive me.'

'He's not, Nerysa.'

'He would have watched by my death bed, why shouldn't I comfort him on his?'

Lucius put his arm around her, looking troubled.

'It's too great a risk. Slaves might recognise you. To be linked with Pulcher could be dangerous and you shouldn't join your fortunes to those of your tribe again. You're a Roman citizen, be content.'

How strange! Romans were her enemies. Fate might easily have destined her to lead her people into battle against them. Now they calmly told her that she was one of them.

'Couldn't I go veiled?'

'Believe me, it's out of the question.'

She'd spent twelve years being trained in strict obedience and gave in, knowing she'd always regret it.

'Please don't tell him I married unwillingly, or that your wife... hurt me. It would distress him. Please tell him I've been happy.'

'I'll see him and give him your greetings. I shall say nothing...to distress him. I urge you, too, to say nothing, even to your children; but when it comes to duplicity, I suspect *you* can teach *me*.'

She was wounded by his manner and by the fact that he and Demetrius distanced themselves from her and turned to each other. Deceived and hurt, they'd slammed together like the valves of a clam, locking her out. She watched them strolling in the moonlit garden, arms linked, no longer as master and slave but, for the first time, as friends. They stood under the window and haggled over the price of twelve amphora of wine, which Demetrius bought from the store to feast his freedom. The slave family spent an uproarious evening while she was left alone with her tearful reminiscences and her outgrown possessions.

There were pieces of jewellery Quintus had given her, books, amber balls, crystal jars, ivory combs and a gold toilet set. The girl they'd belonged to didn't seem to have anything to do with her. The dresses she'd worn in Quintus' house weren't suited to a matron and she put them away for her daughter. She felt a pang of regret for the filmy gauze dresses Demetrius had bought her. He'd now insist on the soberest garb for her and he'd become the stateliest citizen ever encumbered by a toga. They'd be the most respectable couple in

Etruria, an achievement which, she supposed, would be a greater satisfaction to him than to her.

Among the belongings, in a twist of paper, she found her wedding ring. Her hands had swollen from pregnancy and manual labour so it no longer fitted the base of her finger but she thrust it onto the middle joint with resolution.

CHAPTER LXXXII

March 183 – August 183

Discet nurus Etiam viro probante, meliorem sequi.

A woman is well advised, provided her husband agrees, to follow a better man.
Seneca. Hercules Furens

Schooling was no longer a favour for Nerissina to beg but a norm to which she must submit and it wasn't her patron's idea of a suitable present to mark the occasion of her manumission. He chose amethysts for her; the sort of present he'd expected her to ask for before he knew her better. For Nerysa, he made a generous dowry provision and for Demetrius, he bought the adjoining farm. Once seized with enthusiasm, he traced the heirs, persuaded them to sell and paid with the half million Demetrius insisted on paying for his freedom; a circular arrangement which satisfied everyone's pride and left money to spare for stock and slaves. The farm was their common project. To justify his choice rather than inform it, Lucius pored over textbooks, jabbing his finger at the scroll and informing Demetrius, 'It says, "Check the water supply, the road and the neighbours." Well, there's nothing wrong with the stream or the road and who would you prefer as a neighbour?'

When Demetrius replied that he was equally concerned with the quality of the soil, they set off to dig trenches and take samples from all levels, crumbling it through their fingers and mixing it with water to taste. They inspected the equipment and buildings and drew up a list of repairs. Lucius rhapsodised over the forest, the lake and the charm of the villa from the distant hills, seeing it as it would be when Demetrius had tamed it.

Nerysa felt edged out. She'd dreamed of Demetrius as a free man; of watching him grow into his new status. She understood why he was resentful of her but not why he seemed unsure of himself, or why he shrank from her touch. Lucius was stiff and formal. Both took her deception as a personal insult. The awkwardness was made worse by having to call each other by new names. He'd become Lucius Marius Demetrius and she was Maria Nerysa. They had to remember not to address Lucius as 'master' but as 'Your Excellency' in public and 'Carissime Lepide' in private. What she and Demetrius called each other was another problem. She couldn't call him Lucius. For her, there was only one Lucius.

'That's ridiculous.' he objected. 'Every fourth man in the empire is called Lucius.'

'But I don't know every fourth man in the empire.'

Then she could call him Demetrius, now his official nickname. She did, when she remembered, but she'd called him 'sir' since the second time they'd met and the habit died hard.

She didn't share their enthusiasm for the farm. There was an old adage that a farm should be weaker than the farmer. The size and state of this one bid fair to overwhelm him. But the farmhouse, though derelict, had been well built. The pride of the villa rustica was a great kitchen with chestnut rafters too high to catch fire. She saw it as the hub of life in the villa; a warm, good smelling place where the slave family could congregate.

She took a team of women to the villa urbana, scraped down swathes of cobwebs and recovered mosaic floors from beneath layers of mud and weeds. Serviceable furniture, found in the house, was aired and mended. There were rich finds in the attics. A prudent retainer had folded away hangings and bedding, strewn with herbs and carefully wrapped. Pottery and hundreds of clay lamps were packed in straw in osier baskets. There was an assortment of cooking pots and six bronze braziers for cooking and heating. These they rubbed with citron and salt until they saw their own smiling faces reflected in them. They scoured everything useful, found a place for them all and compiled an inventory.

Demetrius was cheerfully realistic, undeterred by acres of shoulder high nettles. Nettle soup was nourishing and, besides, they were proof of his soil's fertility. He would spread the cinders of every weed he could harvest. He saw coolly that there wasn't an intact fence on the entire estate and the drains were silted up, so standing water had rotted the wooden walls of his sheds. Thistles sprouted through the crumbling threshing floor, cisterns were cracked and ploughshares rusted away. He wasn't even daunted at the thought of uprooting and replanting the neglected vineyard, a back-breaking task. None of this weighed against the single, overwhelming attraction of the place - that it was his.

He was lonely as a freedman. There was a barrier between him and his former colleagues. They'd long been his subordinates but now the difference between them was one of kind rather than degree. For all his worldly experience, he was uncertain how to behave. He wouldn't make himself ridiculous by giving himself airs but he was conscious of a new dignity, which it was a responsibility, rather than a satisfaction to maintain. He mustn't be arrogant nor yet too familiar and was never quite sure on which side of the balance he erred. In a lawfully married wife he could have had kin – his only kin for, legally, his daughter was a fellow freedwoman. He'd dreamed of freeing Nerysa himself and becoming her patron and husband – had even imagined those comfortable words carved on their tombstone. But that was impossible. It was beneath her dignity to be the freedwoman of an illustrious Roman knight, unthinkable she should be the dependant of an obscure freedman.

His home consoled him. Its mosaics were cracked and uneven but, when they were spotless, he had the curious thought that he preferred their soft gleam to the brilliance of a new floor. The quaint Etruscan pillars of painted wood pleased him more than porphyry. But, when Lucius' plasterer and painter had restored the frescoes, he was less happy.

'The house looks as if it's been tricked out by some vulgar new man.' he complained to Nerysa.

'Let's try washing mud over them.' she suggested and he sent for barrels of it.

What he loved about the house was its maturity and, above all, its past. It had a pedigree that he hadn't. Maybe he'd been too contemptuous of the nouveau riches who bought houses and assumed ownership of the ancestors in the shrines. He understood their yearning for background, for a sense of continuity.

The rooms of the villa urbana were gracious and well-proportioned and he could afford the necessary repairs. He wasn't tempted to be extravagant; he needed to build on a modest bathhouse and was looking to buy the best farm manager he could afford. As a partner in the trading company, he'd be travelling. The farm wouldn't make a good profit for years and would have to be subsidised by everything he could earn from commerce. The master's eye was the best fertiliser of any soil but, failing that, he needed a bailiff he could trust.

Lucius had given him Polybius, Darius and Melissus, Charis and Iris for his household and workers for the farm. He took cash in lieu of Philemon, unable to justify the luxury of a personal secretary, and he told Polybius he would place him in a patrician house in the capital. Polybius hadn't expected the rejection. He'd shadowed Demetrius so long he needed no training to be the perfect major domo.

'Master,' he said, in a shaking voice, 'that sad business in Corinth has made you think me disloyal. Perhaps you haven't considered the pressure I was put under?'

'Polybi, you're not suitable for rough country life. You're a highly trained and valuable city servant.'

'I understand. You'll buy twenty labourers for the price I can command. Under the circumstances, I couldn't expect you to consider my feelings.'

'That's unworthy of you. I'm considering your *interests*. I'll place you in a noble house where you'll live in luxury with every hope of advancement. When could I offer you freedom, if ever? Get off the floor and don't be ridiculous! I don't bear grudges. It's simply that you're too fine to serve a poor freedman camping out on a derelict farm. How would you live without town glamour?'

'I don't want *glamour*, as you call it. I want to live in a house like the domus used to be before you and my mistress left.'

'Since you call her mistress, I assume I'll never again hear you speak of her in such disrespectful terms as you did in Corinth.'

If he'd ever wished for revenge, he had it more completely now, in Polybius' dismay, than in the blow he'd dealt him.

'I should live for her, master, and if necessary, I'd be happy to die for her.'

'Let's hope such exhibitionism won't be required of you.'

'Then you'll keep me?'

'For as long as you wish it. If you're not content, be good enough to tell me and I'll make other arrangements. I want no unwilling service of you.'

Polybius knelt and kissed his hand. But when he heard Philemon was wandering the domus asking everyone he met, 'What did I do? Whatever did I do wrong?' Demetrius hardened his heart. Survival was more than sentiment.

CHAPTER LXXXIII

August 183 – June 184

Cum digno digna fuisse ferar

Let it be said that I was a worthy woman with a worthy man Tibullus 3.13

While the villa was made ready, Lucius entertained them in Rome. To be back at the domus was an emotional experience for Nerysa. It seemed even grander than she remembered and Lucillus smiled at her from every wall; the faces of the cupids had been painted over and each was a portrait of him. Demetrius came to her room to survey her wedding clothes; pleated chiffon, embroidered silk and gilded pumps.

'Very fine.' he observed.

'Too fine for a farmer's wife.'

'But not too fine for you.'

The compliment was banal and she didn't quite like the way he said it. It seemed that their servile past, previously held to be the provision of an all-wise providence, was to be expunged as though it had never been. Over dinner, she confided with a giggle, 'I polished this couch so often it feels like sacrilege to sit on it.'

He flushed and deliberately turned his back, leaving her to make conversation with two charming law students on her other side. Next morning, he told her he was returning to Horta to see to the farm.

'I'll be back,' he said, 'for the wedding.'

'I'll go with you. We can come back together.'

He turned towards her, suave and formal.

'Lepidus has asked me to say that, for the sake of your dignity, he would be the most suitable person to have care of you. He wouldn't now offer you less than marriage.'

'What do you want me to say to him?'

'I suggest you talk to him, he is a fit person to advise you.'

'Well, at least *he* looks me in the eye. But how can he tell me how you feel?'

'Oh, I wish you insane.'

'What do you mean?'

'I'd like you to reject a Roman knight and choose a poor farmer, a Roman since yesterday. Yes, it'd suit me if you were a crazy woman.'

'But I *have* chosen you! That's what I'm here for - to be legally married.'

'To be legally married, certainly.'

'Not to you?'

'High born ladies can't marry freedmen. There's a law against it.'

'If I'm a high born lady there's a law against my being alive.'

'Not this way. Lucius is offering you the ancient right; a marriage solemnised in the presence of the Pontifex Maximus. With this form of marriage, there is no possibility of divorce because, by it, you become part of Lucius' family as if you had been born into it. It restores you freeborn status – something he can never do for Lucillus. He can only do it for you and only in this way. The arrangement is not equal to your birth but it's a start.'

'And what would it say of me? That I was held in subjection by a slave and bore children for a man who wasn't worthy to be my husband? Or that I chose to love my man and still live with him in faith and honour? Does any girl choose a husband? Aren't we all traded for money or alliance? Of course, I didn't choose you at first. But later, once I knew what I was doing, I did.

'Lepidus makes too much of my birth. My father, if he's alive, is a head taller than his fellow tribesmen and has a bigger stockade. They send their sons to serve him, would follow if he called them to war. I used to think he had a tenacity and astuteness above the rest that justified their trust in him. But that doesn't make me Cleopatra! Is that why Lepidus bobs up and down when I come into a room and speaks in that oily voice he uses for family prayers?'

'He cannot but be acutely conscious of what is due to your consequence, especially since he was ignorant for so long, through no fault of his own. He's ashamed of treating you with disrespect.'

'He could respect me now though; by not deceiving me and allowing me some say in my own future.'

'He would if he could trust your judgement. But your attitude proves that you need guidance.'

'So does he. The way he fawns on me looks suspicious. He'll betray me.'

At last, he flashed her a look she recognised; one of swift, grave understanding.

'I'll speak to him.'

'Get him to treat me like his other freedwomen; a vague condescending smile and that click of the fingers behind his back to have Petosiris come and remind him what my name is.'

'We'll be more careful.'

'In Pulcher's house, I had slaves to wait on me. I looked at them and saw machines, not people. Shame on me for that! I'd been taught it, but shame on me, even so! When you took me, I admit I felt soiled. Then I found that for wit, courage and kindness I was more than evenly matched. I know, now, a slave's no different from anyone else, it's a label they hang round your neck to justify abusing you.'

'But there is,' he said in a small, urgent voice, 'a difference.'

'I can't convince you. Then, for the sake of argument, let's suppose you *are* unworthy. Love covers that, that's what love is. Whatever inequality there is, love fills and smoothes it, just as it did when I was a kitchen maid and you were a steward. Only love me, my sweetness. If you'd only hold me, everything would be as it used to be between us.'

His eyes kindled. He made her a stilted bow.

'If that's your wish, my lady, I believe I couldn't be blamed for obliging you. Naturally, my body is at your service.'

She no longer needed to imagine his demeanour with Aurelia. She'd seen it. She swayed on her feet, blind with rage.

'You worm!' she cried, 'You...you servile...thing! Find yourself a gutter and a kitchen slut to squat over you. Do you think I want your craven obedience?'

He looked uneasily over his shoulder as slaves began to drift across the atrium towards the open bedroom door and she saw how to get herself sent back to Horta. Lucius couldn't bear scenes. She understood his scruples. A slave could be coerced. The daughter of a royal house, even an obscure, barbarian one, couldn't. Once she was in Horta, he wouldn't kidnap her. Away from Lucius and on his own ground, Demetrius would be himself again. She screamed at the top of her voice, 'Can't you see, you stupid, stubborn man, the only thing standing between us and happiness is your own, absurd underrating of yourself?'

Lucius appeared in the doorway. The reproachful look he gave Demetrius inspired her. Throwing back her head, she laughed, softly at first but with mounting shrillness until she achieved Aurelia's laugh in all its hysteria and hatred. With each breath, the laugh grew wilder until she lost control in an explosion of grief, sobbing, 'Take me home. Just take me home!'

Slowly, perhaps involuntarily, Demetrius' arms came up around her, his hands gentle on her back, in her hair. Lucius signed to a slave to pull the doors to, his voice tender as his freedman's touch.

'Demetrie, this is an aberration. High-born persons, you know, have an inborn sense of their own dignity. I think it never deserted her until now. It will come back. But no one should see her like this. Take her to your place until she's well. Hold her in trust for me, a sacred trust.'

It was a sombre homecoming. Demetrius was courteous, even kind, but he'd disengaged from her. 'A sacred trust.' Lucius had said. She'd no wish to be a pensioner or farmed-out invalid nor an added burden to him at a difficult time. But he had work she could do. She set out to make herself essential to the running of his house, succeeding so well he left her in sole charge while he visited Rome and Marseilles. When he returned, the barrier between them had lifted. They were forced to discuss the farm and house and, united in common effort, couldn't fail to appreciate each other.

'I've found the ideal farm manager,' he told her. 'The owner would sell him as a single lot but he has a woman and a two-year-old child. I can't afford them. I can barely afford him.'

'Could you buy him now and try to acquire them later?'

'No, the estate's being broken up. If I don't take them, they'll be sold elsewhere. I'm sorely tempted.'

'Why do you want him so much?'

'He's intelligent.'

'Is that so important for a farmer? I should have thought health and strength mattered most.'

'The manuals say the manager should be almost as intelligent as his master without realising he is.'

'Does this one realise?'

'If he does then, naturally, he's too bright to show it. He's just the man for me. After all, if I don't buy him, someone else will and there's no guarantee they'd take the woman and child.'

She thought of the two valuables he possessed. He'd never sell the portrait but the bronzes? It would hurt him to part with them. She didn't care to suggest it. His brow cleared.

'That's it! I'll sell the bronzes. If the farm prospers, I'll buy others. If it doesn't, I deserve to lose them.'

They were taken to Rome and sold. Jacob sent the cash with the next cargo bound for Marseilles and Commatus the Gaul came to Horta with his woman and boy, his brother Arecomus, a skilled vine dresser, and four hunting dogs.

Demetrius installed the gods of his hearth - a lar to protect the house and penates to guard the food store. He acquired a Priapus, whose impossible proportions provoked incredulous laughter from Nerysa and, his pride and joy, a marble bust of the deified Marcus Aurelius.

He followed his usual habit in stocking the farm. He didn't buy slaves under the hammer or from dealers but from people he respected. Good labourers didn't often come up for sale. He looked for men born and bred on farms who were, through no fault of their own, surplus to requirements. He believed the old wisdom that those who were unruly were those with the most initiative. It could be a good plan to buy such men to harness their energy but work them in a chain gang with no chance to misbehave. Perhaps he could even manage them without chains using a judicious mix of fear and incentive. But he'd take no risks with discipline, one bad apple would infect the rest. He and Commatus examined each man. First they decided whether, even if he had a bad report, he could, with good handling, be capable of loyalty and hard work. Next they had him stripped and tried the strength of his shoulders and legs, for stamina was as important as temperament. Bringing his land into good heart was work for the strongest and most willing, working all hours in all weathers.

More and more he valued Nerysa's capable housekeeping. Slowly, steadily, she'd become indispensable. He didn't like to think about the time when she'd leave him for a life more fitted to her station. It wasn't just that he'd miss her labour but that her presence doubled his own strength. Only because she asked, he agreed to have a pleasure garden. She mentioned the gardener at the domus who'd said he wanted to end his days in Horta. Lucius could certainly spare him for he must be past heavy work. It was his knowledge she wanted. Labouring could be done by boys under his direction.

'You'll be working in the fields all day.' she said, 'I want somewhere sweet and cool where you can rest in the evening. But I'd like to know the old man's happy to come.'

He laughed, 'Too bad if he isn't. It's the first time you've asked Lepidus for anything for yourself. You'll certainly get it.'

'Why do you laugh?'

'I was thinking of Roxana. Do you remember her? The little minx made a fortune out of him. He won't sell the man or even give him because he's too old to have any value but he'll lend him for as long as you want. And he's giving me a cook.'

'I hoped we'd get Argos. He's itching for promotion and he'll never get it at Lepidus' villa because the head cook's so young.'

'Oh I'm not getting Argos, he's sending Epicurus from the domus.'

'Epicurus! Whatever shall we do with him? He'll hate it here; he's no idea of country fare.'

'But Lepidus intends to dine here often. He thinks we're the only congenial company in the neighbourhood.'

'And he won't want to eat bread and wild garlic! He'll bring Lucillus with him, I hope?'

'You'll miss Lucillus.'

'Did Lepidus put pressure on him to go to Rome?'

'So you'd follow? Probably, but he didn't need to, Lucillus wants to go.'

'Before he goes, I want him to know who his father is.'

To her surprise, he agreed without argument. It was a cruel deprivation, he said, not to know one's father and Lucillus could be trusted to keep the secret. Of course, it pleased him to think of the golden opportunities the lad would have in Rome but he saw difficulties that Lucius didn't in thrusting him among freeborn, well-heeled boys. He needed to know how a freedman should conduct himself in society, the difference between deference and servility, how to give way gracefully to other boys and fall in with their suggestions. It would be improper, for instance, for him to strike a freeborn youth but, if an argument was forced on him, he could deflect it onto one of their slaves or freedmen and fight them so doughtily that no one would care to challenge him afterwards.

It troubled Nerysa that Demetrius meant to take this task upon himself. It would be a blow to Lucillus to learn that he was the son of a slave, not a Roman knight. She would have given much to shield Demetrius from the mortification of seeing it. But he was forearmed and braced himself for the pain. Most poignant, for them both, was Lucillus' brave attempt to hide his dismay.

Epicurus arrived and his comical sulks made Nerysa reflect on what an odd assortment of servants they had. He, Polybius and Charis belonged in city mansions. The only sensible course would have been to sell them and buy labourers – and a competent housekeeper. Demetrius had chosen Commatus but not Matugena his woman. Italia briefed her and left notes; instructions, timetables and household hints. Matugena listened attentively, thanked her and put away the tablets carefully. She was a good practical housekeeper but she seemed to have decided to ignore some of Italia's directions. Nerysa gave her the inventory, explained that they must agree that all the items were in place before she assumed responsibility for them and proposed checking it straight away.

'If you please, mistress,' she said, 'I'll do it later. It's time I went round the dormitories in case anyone's skulking in bed.'

When she broached the subject again, Matugena's eyes were inflamed and she couldn't see clearly. Wet, southerly winds in spring were well known to cause conjunctivitis so, fearing an epidemic, Nerysa boiled up an infusion of eyebright and, when she was better, mentioned the inventory.

'I did it myself yesterday, mistress. It's all correct.'

Nerysa was annoyed and complained to Demetrius. Nerissina observed, 'She says reading hurts her eyes, I'm not surprised. She makes it difficult for herself. Why hold the tablets upside down?'

It was dismaying to have an illiterate housekeeper but infinitely worse to keep a deceitful one. Nerysa sat in her high-backed chair, assumed her sternest expression and sent for her. Matugena was an imposing woman, towering over her as she saluted. Charis handed her a shopping list and Nerysa said coldly, 'Matugena, I want you to read the list to me - aloud.'

Matugena paled. Her mouth opened and closed but no sound came. Fascinated, Nerysa watched as beads of sweat erupted on her brow. She fell to the ground and, looking down at her, Nerysa understood what it would mean to her to be sold apart from her man. She told her, 'None of us was born reading and writing. We've all had to learn and so must you.'

She couldn't expect Commatus to teach her, he was never home in daylight. She steeled herself to take on the burden but couldn't spare the time. Lessons were always interrupted or postponed because of housework. None of the women had time. She decided to ask her daughter. The idea didn't appeal to Nerissina. Elementary education didn't interest her and she resented the interruption to her own studies. Every morning she worked with her schoolmasters. In the evenings she wrote essays Lucius set her. They had to include a bulletin on her health signed by her nurse, were sent by courier and returned annotated in his own hand. When Nerysa explained the difficulties of having a housekeeper who couldn't keep records, she agreed but she'd no idea how to teach reading and writing, never having been taught herself. That Matugena learned was a tribute to the determination of both, rather than the aptitude of either.

On the first day of his summer visit, Lucius appeared. He liked to combine Nerissina's instruction in philosophy with a country walk and had prepared the lesson as carefully as his cooks had prepared the picnic. It would be an intimate occasion. He knew better than to overwhelm a child with his consequence and had taken care not to bring a large entourage; only two boys to carry scrolls, two secretaries to organize them, three kitchen slaves to carry the basket and flasks and three of his female staff as chaperones. When Nerissina explained she couldn't come until she'd finished teaching herself, they all repaired cheerfully to the garden to wait. But when her parents heard she'd kept her patron cooling his heels for an hour while she gave a reading lesson to a slave, they were appalled. In vain she insisted that he hadn't minded. Didn't she realise that a gentleman was too dignified to show annoyance at the insolence of an inferior or that a freedwoman who wasn't obsequious to her patron could be summarily re-enslaved? Did she imagine anyone, from shopkeeper to senator, would treat the splendid one with such contempt?

'Epictetus was a slave. I suppose we're all glad someone taught him to read.'

'You're not at fault for teaching the slave but you do it in your own time, not in your patron's time. Isn't it enough that your mother tries his patience but that you must be doing it too?'

Nerissina puzzled over these words and the bitterness of her father's tone. She thought of Lucius as he was to her; his winsome smile and gentle manner, his sensitivity to her wishes and the pains he took over studies. It was hard to believe her parents were talking of the same Lucius. Yet her father had been his slave for thirty-five years, her mother for twelve. They must know him better than she. She treated him with circumspection afterwards so he, in his turn, puzzled over what he'd done to frighten her. He planned a lengthy course of study, beginning with Solon and guiding her through seven centuries of thought, tracing the thread of enlightenment from age to age so, when he taught her the precepts of his divine emperor, he could present them as the final flowering of the human intellect.

CHAPTER LXXXIV

June 183 – August 184

O fortunatos nimium sua si bona norint agricolas.

Farmers, if you only knew how fortunate you are!Virgil. Georgics II 438-9

It was usual to write a letter of congratulation to a slave who'd gained his freedom. Demetrius was a popular man and letters descended on Horta from Rome and Ostia, from Athens and Corinth, from Alexandria and Leptis, from Marseilles, Cadiz and even London. The same people also wrote to Lucius to applaud his decision. No one was so ungracious as to ask why he'd been so long about it; all praised him for having chosen exactly the right moment to change Demetrius' condition and allow him to be their friend.

After the letters came presents; signet rings and goblets, silver plate and statuettes. His neighbours were more practical. He was delighted to be presented with well sharpened tools, a mare in foal, twenty yearling lambs and their shepherd. But most well-wishers hit on the ingenious idea of sending him a toga. He'd need to wear one for formal occasions. It was easy to pack and unbreakable. An incredible number were parcelled up and slipped into cargoes around the world. He and Nerysa surveyed their toga mountain in consternation.

'I'll only need to wear one when I attend on Lucius. Three or four of his cast-offs would last me a lifetime and there are so many other things I need.'

'Let's sell them.' she said.' We'll remember the people who sent them. We'll label everything we buy. "This cauldron was the gift of Demetrius, merchant of Tarsus" or "This wine jug was given by Commius, shipwright in London".'

He shook his head and refused to show such ingratitude to any of the donors. She sighed and strewed them with insect-repelling herbs, packed them in linen cloths and stowed them in the attic. Then she thought again.

'You need ceremonial robes for yourself and your slaves to wear on feast days. No one would be offended, surely, if their gift were reshaped and used to honour the gods.'

He agreed. He needed divine favour with so many mouths to feed and bodies to clothe. In the villa urbana, he had house slaves. Twenty workers and their dependents lived in the villa rustica, not so much a house as a complex. There was the great kitchen, slave bedrooms around it and outbuildings shared by herdsmen and their animals.

Commatus, the gigantic, sweaty Gaul with straggly blond hair and moustache, presided there. He had rooms adjoining the entrance, well placed for checking on everyone who came and went. Demetrius had provided a couch so he had the dignity of reclining to eat in the evening. He was allowed to reward the best workers by inviting them to dine with him, a privilege they worked hard to deserve. As time passed, encouraged by his wife, he became less unkempt, went every now and then to the bathhouse and began to imitate the manners of the villa urbana. But he never discarded his outlandish trousers in favour of a tunic.

Demetrius visited his tenants. He wasn't responsible for their upkeep but it grieved him to see them scratching subsistence from exhausted soil. There was no point in demanding rent arrears or holding them to the letter of their contracts but he did insist that his land be carefully tilled so it would yield enough to pay the rent and feed the farmer's family. He instigated the digging of manure pits and urged that no weed or excrement should go to waste. His standards were too high for one cottager who came up to the farm office with his children. Demetrius heard him out in deepening disgust.

'These are your own, freeborn children and you want to sell them into slavery?'

'I can trust them to you sir. I've another son, their half-brother, who's completed twenty- five years military service. He's being settled in the colony of Colchester, in Britain and I've got the chance to join him. I can't take these two. I raised them alone and now I'm too old to be responsible for them. The money will pay my passage to Britain. They won't disappoint you, sir, they're good children.'

The boy was around fifteen and the girl a little younger, both strong and comely. The girl looked at the ground and blushed rosily but the boy gave him a cool, fearless gaze. He asked him, 'What is your name?'

'Sextus.'

'What can you do?'

'Look after animals, sir; oxen, sheep, pigs, dogs and so on.'

'He's good with sick animals, sir,' said the old man, 'he has a gift.'

'I'll take you and your sister and pay your father the going rate. Give me good service and I'll release you after fifteen years, when you're thirty and can become a citizen. Is that agreeable to you?'

'It is.'

'Then from now on you call me 'master'.'

'Very good, master.'

He gave the girl, Perpenna, to Arecomus as his woman, and handed her over still a virgin, which overwhelmed Arecomus, was the talk of the community and humiliated the girl.

He and Nerysa dined regularly at Lucius' villa and he watched Lucius watching her, as he did himself, trying to gauge whether she'd recovered her judgement. Lucius conveyed, with gentle condescension, that the provision Demetrius made for her fell short of what was suitable. The expressions of deference and gratitude Demetrius was quick to offer, which he would once have disavowed, he accepted blandly, never failing to ask if Demetrius could use a loan or to say airily as he left, 'Anything you need; tools or hands, just speak to Georgius.'

Demetrius began to find his generosity oppressive and the gratitude he knew he ought to feel for it was replaced by a determination to do without.

But introspection was a luxury he couldn't afford. His first harvest was due. Winter vegetables had done well. Commatus had taken a surplus to market. The orchard had bloomed and set fruit. There'd be no vintage for several years for the vineyard had not been replanted; but the olive grove, weeded and fertilised, promised to yield at the end of the year. He bought meat in town when he entertained his patron. He wouldn't slaughter his own beasts until he'd built up his herds; and there was no need; Epicurus had invented ten new and delicious ways to serve spelt porridge. But the corn harvest was his people's staple diet for the coming year. When he convened prayers twice a day and proposed sacrificing a ram, Nerysa pointed out that the fields were white with corn already and asked why he was anxious.

'Can you feel how still the air is?' he replied. 'Stagnant air around the rising of the dog threatens storms. Last night I saw the bright star in the breast of Leo, another bad sign. The wheat's all but ready. Georgius has begun his harvest. He'd rather let it ripen in the shed than rot in the field. But I don't have the labour to make a short job of it and I can't afford to hire it in.'

'Don't the tenants have to help?'

'They're only bound to give me two days. How would it help if they lost their own crop and couldn't pay the rent? We'll have to make a start tomorrow and pray the rain holds off.'

'Can women help?'

'Well, the land girls bind the stooks.'

'I mean me and the other women in the villa.'

'You couldn't ask women like Charis and Iris and Matugena to labour in the fields. As for you, Lepidus would think I'd taken leave of my senses.'

She laughed. 'He wouldn't, he knows I'm wayward. When the girls understand what's at stake, they'll want to help. Melissus and Darius will enjoy it and they're both young and strong. Epicurus needn't be left out, we shan't want him to cook during harvest. But I shouldn't trouble to ask the exquisite Polybius.'

'I shan't need to. He's already volunteered. We'll leave Hannah and Commatillus up at the villa to keep house and greet our noble patron, should he call.'

Lucius did call, accompanied only by Lucillus for he, too, was short-staffed at harvest time and his town servants were busy unpacking. Hannah and Commatillus seized his hands and skipped him down to the cornfields. There he found Demetrius, lying propped against an elm with Nerysa, straw hatted, ruddy-cheeked beside him. They were surrounded by their slaves, male and female, all recumbent in their master's presence. Polybius, sun-bleached hair and taut, bronzed torso, sat on a tree stump with Charis on his knee. Lucius had never liked her. She was pretty enough; he'd sent for her soon after she came to the house and she'd behaved with perfect docility whilst giving the clear impression that her mind was elsewhere. Piqued, he'd withheld the customary douceur and humiliated her publicly by never sending for her again. Now he turned away, took in Epicurus snoring among the poppies, portly body glazed with sweat, and blenched at the sprawling forms of two massive Gauls, felled colossi in fancy dress. It was unthinkable that these rustics shouldn't stand and salute him but, not entirely sure they would, he judged it expedient to sit down on a fallen log.

At once, Nerissina was at his elbow with a wine jug and a stammered apology because she hadn't finished her essay. The scene was primitive and unseemly but, four pints and some bread and salt olives later, it had become delightful. He blinked into the dappled light and inhaled the heavy, perfumed air. Droning insects lulled him until he wondered drowsily why anyone consented to live in a city.

Then Demetrius sprang to his feet and his people after him. Lucius saw, with a pang, that he was lean and tanned and possessed of furious energy. He snatched up a scythe and matched him, stroke for flamboyant stroke. Friendly rivalry spurred Demetrius and the two of them worked like demons until every last grain had been stored. Then the rain spilled down the hillside, flattening the reed beds, overflowing Demetrius' carefully cleared channels and gouging its own across the churned soil.

Bread tasted special that year. The slaves boasted that every ear of wheat had been gathered, personally, by the master's noble patron.

CHAPTER LXXXV

September 184

Eum, qui se libertinum esse fatetur, nec adoptando patronus ingenuum facere potuit.

If a man confesses he is a freedman his patron cannot give him freeborn status even by adopting him.

Ulpian Digest of Justinian I on status

Lucius had intended to educate Lucillus at home but, while he was looking out the best teachers, he sent him to a grammar school, the best in the city. The masters soon complained to him that his freedman, who'd impressed at first, had ceased to give of his best. Lucius sent for his boy and he sent for the rod but, before laying it on, he spoke to him and probed for the cause of his lack-lustre performance.

Lucillus was tight-lipped and obstinate at first but, when Lucius said how disappointed he felt that his beloved boy no longer cared to please him, he broke down and explained that quickness of study was resented in a freedman. Lucius replaced the pedagogues with brawnier ones in greater numbers and Lucillus was left in peace. As his fellows got to know him, they found him engagingly modest and grew to respect him and accept his help. If he'd sought a liaison with one of their sisters, they'd have known how to put him in his place, but at their age such complications didn't arise. His school days were a success and he learned more than the Latin and Greek language and literature on the curriculum. He studied the most complex of balancing acts - how to survive gracefully in a class-ridden society as that most stateless and despised of beings, a freedman.

He lacked none of the trappings of patrician boyhood; his books and equipment, his sports gear and attendants were the finest in the city. He was exquisitely turned out in the most fashionable colours and had everything money could buy except the plain, red-bordered toga of freeborn boyhood which Lucius, to his anguished regret, could never give him. The moment when he could have secured him that had passed and could never come again.

When school was out, the classmates went to a cook shop. They usually went on to the baths for ball-games, wrestling and swimming. Towards the end of the afternoon, Lucillus would have his slaves arrange his clothes before he made his way to the law courts, accompanied by his friends. The vast Basilica Julia was curtained off into several courts, which proceeded simultaneously. Lucius sensed precisely when to look up and see the pedagogues struggling to keep up with Lucillus as he manoeuvred his way through the crowds to get the best view of his patron in action. Lucillus would know the speech by heart, having sat on the library floor while it was rehearsed. He would listen avidly, watching the opposition, the judges and the water clocks and, whenever Lucius made a telling point he would mutter, 'Effecta! Euge!' and clench his fist in triumph.

Lucius was the leading exponent of the minimalist school of oratory. He seldom raised his voice, used economical gesture and had never been known to stamp his foot. Unfailing courtesy was instinct and policy, his power a piquant mixture of sweetness and devastating acuity. In his youth, when an opponent had hired a claque to drown out his well-modulated voice, he'd stayed poised to speak while his slaves mounted the dais and marked the water level in the clock with charcoal. When the hecklers were hoarse and the din subsided, he'd suggested affably that a similar measure be decanted from his opponents' clock and added to his own. He won the argument and the case.

At the end of the day, they'd walk home together. The anteambulares went ahead, clearing a way with their elbows and shouting, 'Make way! Make way for my master!' Lucius, his victorious client and Lucillus followed, surrounded by clients and students with the pedagogues bringing up the rear.

When they'd come home in this happy way, Lucillus would hang the victory wreath on the door. They took their bath and he helped Lucius with the prayers and sacrifice. Then came dinner, a relaxed, convivial occasion lasting several hours. Sometimes there was a formal dinner party, sometimes a select gathering of friends and colleagues. If it was just the two of them, Lucillus asked about his schoolwork or the day's proceedings in court and Lucius shared his knowledge generously. The boy looked at him with adoration and copied his every word and movement, adding to his own natural grace, the bearing of a Roman aristocrat. Lucius had lavished care on him but he'd tilled fertile soil and saw his efforts rewarded. His friends had educated their sons with equal care and cherished high hopes of them but they'd all disappointed. Some had succumbed to illness, some showed early signs of dissipation, some were merely mediocre. Lucius couldn't see Lucillus' brilliance and charm in any of them and knew that none was as devoted to his father as Lucillus was to him. He thrilled with pride in him, not least in the secret knowledge of his royal blood. Love and pride didn't blind him to the stigma of his base birth but the implications of that were too painful to dwell on.

CHAPTER LXXXVI

September 184

Alterum insaniae genus est, quod spatium longius recipit. Consistit in tristitia, quam videtur bilis atra contrahere. Galen

There is another kind of madness, which follows a lengthy course; it consists of sadness and is caused by a gathering of black bile.

The last present to arrive was from the manager of the Spanish mine. It was delivered personally by Jacob and presented very prettily by Hannah. When he and Nerysa were alone, Demetrius unwrapped it carefully, revealing an ornate, solid silver figure of a youth holding a cornucopia. *Oh God*, thought Nerysa, *another god!* But she asked respectfully, 'Which god is that, sir?'

He laughed, 'This isn't a god! This is my genius, my spirit.'

'Demetrie!' she said. His face softened, as it always did when she spoke his name.

'This figure's newly cast. Had you no spirit before it was made?'

'Yes, all men, slave and free, have a genius from birth. Two, in fact, a good and a bad genius. If you insist on the precision of a lawyer, this statue *represents* my genius. What do you think of it?'

'That, as a figurine, it's exquisite but as the embodiment of your spirit, compared with the original, it lacks a certain verve.'

He shook his head. 'I ought never to have let those Christians corrupt you.'

'What's it to do with them?'

'The distaste you have for the images of the gods seems Jewish to me.'

'Christians aren't Jews.'

'I know. Jews are a little singular perhaps but the ones I know are good family men and clever businessmen. I respect them. Christians are troublemakers and hold disgusting orgies.'

'I've never been to a Christian orgy. I've never even heard of one.'

'Precisely. You're not worldly wise. That's why you should let yourself be guided by those who know about such things.'

'Will they send the bad genius later?'

'Don't be ridiculous. I don't want to worship him, only to ignore him if I can. The bad genius prompts one to do evil.'

She threw her arms around him.

'Then I am sure you've never had one.'

'You know I've done things I'm ashamed of.'

She didn't want to hear confessions of infidelity.

'I don't know of anything you should be ashamed of.'

'But you do.' he persisted, 'I whipped you, I broke my vow to Lucius, and, worst of all, I forced you into marriage with a slave.'

'But, my dearest love, when you did those things, you did them for the best.'

'Even marriage! I wanted to protect you and better your condition.' He choked on bitter laughter.

'I know that, I'm grateful - for everything you did for me.'

As if stunned, he said, 'I did wrong.'

He looked stricken and she couldn't coax him back to serenity. It seemed to her that from that moment, his spirit had taken up residence in the silver statue, leaving him empty. All his enthusiasm was lost. He could visit correspondents, mechanically following ongoing business but he'd no new ideas, his spring of creativity had dried up. A schedule of tasks set out in the farming manual he could follow to the letter but he'd no inspiration. Though he went to bed exhausted, he woke long before dawn, sick with dread of the new day, scheming what to do in the event of flood, drought or plague. He castigated himself for every wrong he'd ever done until he convinced himself he wasn't worthy to live. To rise betimes was a welcome relief from these torments and he went earlier and earlier to the fields, to less and less effect. He couldn't concentrate but flitted from one insoluble problem to the next without ever reaching a decision. He'd no enjoyment in the present and no hope in the future. To her eager loving, he was humiliatingly unresponsive. And he was unreasonable, accusing her of sarcasm if, from long habit, she called him 'sir'. He questioned her endlessly about Quintus, more jealous of the dead man than he'd ever shown himself of Lucius. She tried desperately, but neither logic nor loving kindness reached him. She clung to him and cried, 'I'm your woman, Demetrie. As for Pulcher, I was the centrepiece of his private art collection. You're my real life.'

She thought it unjust that he could take no satisfaction in his own success. The careful plans he'd laid were carried out energetically by Commatus and Polybius and proved excellent. Everything prospered but he couldn't see that it did.

***

Demetrius felt a useless burden to everyone. Epicurus despaired of tempting him to eat. When fresh figs came into season, he asked for some. His people ran to fetch them for they would gladly have done anything to bring him comfort. But, when he bit into the first, it didn't taste as he remembered. It was sand in his mouth and he pushed the dish aside.

If he'd thought the world order arbitrary or absurd he could never have submitted so patiently to it. He knew there was something intrinsically inferior about those who were slaves, otherwise fate wouldn't have destined them for servitude. He believed in an orderly structure; slaves at the bottom, then freedmen whose merit had earned them release from bondage but not the full dignity of freeborn manhood. Next came the freeborn; poor then rich, then knights and senators. Kings and emperors were supreme and so were princesses, even barbarian ones. He'd desecrated what he was unworthy to touch. She'd been a virgin too. Perhaps in Britain, as in Rome, princes were also priests. He didn't know what sacred precincts he'd profaned.

Though he longed to end his misery, to take his own life would be ungrateful and insulting to his patron. He suspected Nerysa would become her patron's wife as soon as decency allowed and that she'd be the happier for it. But his farm would be sold and his slaves would go under the hammer. He couldn't do that to them.

***

Nerysa saw it was useless to reason with him. She could only make sure he was never left alone because Polybius had seen him testing the edges of scythes with his thumb and staring at the river in spate. She thought that each hour, each day, each month she stayed must help to convince him that she meant to stay for good. But the months dragged on with no sign of improvement. She often knelt in tears before the hated silver god and begged him to release her husband's spirit and restore him to himself. She prayed to her own God too, for though her husband was a pagan, he was an upright man and the God she worshipped didn't harden his heart against good men. She considered melting the malign object in the fire or hurling it into the river. But then she wouldn't be able to appease it with incense, libations of the best wine and bitter tears. So it stayed smugly in its shrine and mocked them both.

CHAPTER LXXXVII

December 184 – December 185

Rem divinam ne faciat.........Haruspicem, augurem, hariolum, Chaldaeum nequem consuluisse velit.

The bailiff must not perform religious rites or divinations. Marcus Porcius Cato. De Agri Cultura V 3

In desperation, Nerysa wrote to Archias who came, examined Demetrius and pronounced him physically fit. He talked to him for many long hours but Demetrius' conversations were circular and always came round to the same assertions of impending doom. It was natural to think of consulting Lucius but, whenever Lucius came, Demetrius rallied, borrowing energy and cheerfulness from future days. He made it so plain that he didn't want Lucius to know about his melancholy, she felt it would be disloyal to reveal it. Lucius only saw swelling grain, streams turbid with fish, stone walls black and heaving with swarms. The local farmers told him Demetrius' sheep never gave birth to singletons and all his cows calved twice a year.

Demetrius only saw that he'd no reserve. An untimely frost, a drought, a freak hailstorm and he'd be dependent on a loan from Lucius. He'd made ends meet so far but he was worried by unexplained loss of stock.

At intervals, hens went missing and ducks disappeared from the pond. There were no fox trails. Bands of brigands were active further north but he could think of no reason why they should consistently raid his farm in preference to Lucius' richer one. His slaves all denied theft and he shrank from torturing confessions out of them because he didn't believe them guilty.

A happier train of thought was prompted by Nerysa who told him Charis was pregnant and Polybius was responsible. He approved of Charis. He knew she'd loved Polybius from the moment she'd arrived at the domus and resented Nerysa because she lived close to him. Yet, he reflected, she'd shared her exile and never breathed a word about her own loss.

He interviewed Polybius and was as generous as he felt able, offering him all the privileges of contubernium; to be quartered with her and never sold separately. Polybius' ingratitude disappointed him. He cared no more for Charis than for any other girl and had no wish to be yoked to her. Nor had he any interest in children, even one he supposed was his own. Marriage was for free men, fidelity an absurdity for anyone. He begged his master to attend to more important matters.

'Commatus would be grateful, master, for advice on a religious matter.'

'What is the problem?'

'Eumaeus, master.'

'My pigman has a religious question for me? Let's hope I'm equal to it.'

'This morning, master, he looked down on the farrowing pens and counted each sow's piglings, just as he does many times a day. Two were missing. He counted the ones in the other pens just in case, though the partitions are too high for them to climb over. He called the boy to help him turn the sows but there were none overlain.'

'It's not unheard of for a breeding sow to eat her young. It's not regarded as a portent. You can reassure the men.'

'Master, I'm no countryman, as you know, but does a sow devour her young without leaving a spot of blood or a single hair?'

'I've no doubt a hungry sow could swallow a suckling whole.'

'If Eumaeus kept your breeding sows hungry, master, Commatus would know. That's not all. Several slaves report seeing vapours drifting from the woods. There's talk of phantoms and mystic music.'

'Have you seen anything?'

'No master, but then, I'm -'

'Not a rustic. Tell Commatus I sent the piglings to my neighbour as a present and, if he keeps the slaves' eyes down on their work, they'll see nothing to alarm them.'

Exploring the wood alone, he found a flat stone, charred and cracked and an icy draught lifted his hair. Someone was making sacrifices to appease the spirits of the place. He wasn't alone in sensing their hostility. The spirits were pursuing him because he kept a woman he'd no right to keep. He couldn't ignore the signs nor conceal them from Nerysa. Her distress burst forth in a mocking tirade.

'I'm out of patience with your stupid gods! You think me too ignorant to understand religion but I do know one thing; the strong-minded interpret portents to suit themselves or else they make sure to get favourable ones. Listen! One of the men goes hunting which he's not allowed to do. If he bags a hare he daren't bring it home so he roasts it in the forest. Perhaps people see smoke or perhaps they see swirls of mist off the lake. The wind in the reeds sounds like strange music. Imagination and superstition do the rest. Think! With the world in the state it's in, have your gods no more pressing business than us? My God tends his universe which he made out of nothing. With the force of His mind He keeps its myriad parts moving in sweet order. Do you think He has time to hop round sow pens, stealing sucking pigs?'

'Has your god no slaves, then, to be about his business?'

'Yes! Us! If we accept his yoke. He sends us to help the wretched, comfort widows and orphans, to bind up wounds and broken hearts. Imagine what the world will be like when everyone stops taking and starts giving.'

For a fleeting moment, he caught her vision of what such a world might be. But he soon saw the implausibility of it and his face fell back into the familiar folds of defeat. Her arm stole around his waist and her head pressed against his heart.

'Demetrie,' she murmured, 'can't your gods forgive? How can they be gods when they're less forgiving than you are yourself?'

'Why should gods be forgiving?'

'Because it's the most difficult thing to be, I suppose. The psalms say "We revere the Lord *because* of his mercy".'

'You can't make yourself gods as you'd like them to be. They aren't to be questioned, they just are.'

'Go and placate them then! Hang garlands round their stiff necks and scrub the bird-lime off them. That should please them since they can't do it for themselves.'

He couldn't remonstrate or even look at her. She put both arms around him.

'These fears torment you because you're ill. You wouldn't believe such nonsense if you were well.'

Melissus suggested a spiritual healing and Nerysa and Polybius took Demetrius to the shrine of Aesclepius in the northern hills. They duly sacrificed a sheep and he lay on the pelt on the temple floor all night. The cure, or inspiration as to how he could be cured, was supposed to come to him in a dream but, since he couldn't sleep, he didn't dream. The next day, the priests advised him on diet and exercise and prayed with him. There was no instant cure but he improved steadily from then on until he thought he worked as well as ever. But he couldn't recapture the eagerness and energy that had been so characteristic of him.

***

Nerysa's pleasure garden was established and, though modest, it fulfilled her purpose admirably. It was a place of cool and contrast. Lucius' gardener had created a copybook display of topiary. Precision-trimmed evergreens threw crisp, grey shadows on the stone paths. Lavender, rosemary and white roses diffused an elusive fragrance. She'd persuaded Demetrius he could live with one or two reproduction statues damaged in transit and, in his garden, they did look less crude than when crowded together in the warehouse at Ostia. He'd have preferred one small, genuine work of art but a serviceable olive-press was a higher priority.

As the shadows lengthened and cicadas began their companionable trilling, she had wine served, and, watching the day's care slip from him, chose her moment carefully.

'Does Charis belong to you or to me?'

There was wistfulness in his slow smile.

'Perhaps she belongs to *us*.'

'I've been thinking I'd like to give her her freedom. I always planned to do it eventually but I'd rather do it now. When she gives birth it will give her strength to know her child will be born a free man.'

He frowned in a way that told her he meant to indulge her. He said, 'It's early days yet to be freeing slaves. A harsh winter and we'll be selling. Then there's the tax, five percent of her value remember, and she's quality goods.'

'I'm not asking you to pay that, I've got savings. And we shan't lose her. She wouldn't even move from my anteroom to be with Polybius, although she loves him dearly. She wants to put the baby out to nurse. Nothing would change except that her child would be freeborn.'

'Then take her to the magistrate in Narnia while she can still travel. Polybius can escort you, that should make him squirm.'

But the suave Polybius behaved impeccably. If he felt bitterness, he didn't give anyone the satisfaction of seeing it. Nor did Iris show jealousy. The one who might have rewarded her with freedom was Lucius, whose agent she'd always been, but he'd given her to Nerysa, to pay for her disloyalty with a lifetime of servitude.

Maria Charis' son was born during the Saturnalia but it was pain and fear, not the license of the season, that released her inhibition and allowed her to speak of her past. During her pains, she fixed her gaze intently on Nerysa's face. Between them she gasped out her mind as through a window lately broken and soon to be boarded up.

'You wept for me once before, mistress.'

'Dearest Charis, you're such a happy girl, why would I have wept for you?'

'When you watched me being beaten.'

'Oh Charis! Forgive me that. Forgive me for forgetting I ordered it.'

'I was raised by a dealer, you know. There were more than twenty of us lost children in his house - so crowded and chaotic I'm surprised none of us fell on the fire. I never fitted in. My owner wasn't cruel, he didn't want to scar me. He knew something of my birth and fancied, when I was grown, I'd make his fortune. But I was never punished without seeing a gleam of satisfaction in everyone's eyes – until I saw tears in yours.'

She broke off with a look of puzzled enquiry, grunting like a startled sow. Matugena carried her to the birthing chair. Nerysa crouched on the floor, eased the child into the world and lifted him into his mother's eager arms with tears of relief.

Iris chose the wrong moment to intrude.

'If you please, mistress, the master wants you in the yard.'

'Not now, Iris, tell the master I'll come later.'

Gaius Marius Andreus was being bathed when Hannah tumbled through the curtain screaming shrilly. Nerysa was now very angry.

'Matugena, this is intolerable. Why does no one look to the children?'

Nerissina appeared in the open doorway.

'Mother, you must come. The slaves have gone mad.'

There were ten men spread around the perimeter of the yard. None was doing anything effective. She stepped out over a boy crouched on the ground, whimpering and warding off invisible foes with shaking hands. A crazed fellow was stamping up and down chanting and jabbing the air with a pitchfork. So far, everyone had been agile enough to keep out of range but if he hurled the fork, as he was threatening to, there would be mayhem. Commatus and Demetrius circled him in opposite directions carrying a chain. Iris sidled her way along the wall to Nerysa who whispered, 'Fetch the hellebore and a jar of wine and ask Sextus for the horn he uses to dose the cattle.'

Having encircled their quarry with the chain, Demetrius and Commatus pulled it taut, hobbling him and knocking him off balance. As he hit the ground, they set him rolling over the chain until it swaddled him from neck to ankle. Then they forced the horn down his throat. Impressed by his heaving and spluttering, the boy in the doorway took his own dose quietly. Nerysa looked anxiously at Demetrius.

'Disgraceful, I agree, but it *is* Saturnalia.'

He turned to her, his face ashen. 'Nerysa, these men aren't drunk. They've seen ghosts.'

'Have the small storeroom cleared and confine them there. Keep it dark - that will be soothing. If they wake no calmer, dose them again. We must purify the land to reassure our people.'

'Maybe you're right and there's a rational explanation. But the slaves won't believe it.'

He prayed, purified his land and made sacrifices. Nerysa helped him. Although she'd no faith in the old religion, its lore and ritual were integral to the science of farming and she wouldn't undermine him. He forbade the slaves to talk about the haunted field but no threat of his could persuade anyone to work it.

CHAPTER LXXXVIII

February 186

Pater ipse colendi haud facilem esse viam voluit.

God himself willed that the farmer's way should not be easy. Virgil. Georgics I 121-122

The unexplained loss of stock increased during the winter. Demetrius took to patrolling the estate at night with Commatus or Arecomus and the dogs. When he didn't return for breakfast one blustery March morning, Nerysa sent to the villa rustica to enquire for Commatus. He hadn't returned either but he'd sent for Arecomus and a band of men armed with cudgels to go to the haunted field. Nerysa fretted and was about to send men after them when Demetrius returned alone, looking for her. His voice vibrated with suppressed excitement.

'The poachers are slaves who used to work this farm. I bought the estate including workers but we thought they'd disappeared; absconded or dead of the plague. We stalked one ruffian back to his hideout and found fifty of them living rough. They're starving. Spitting blood some of them. Things looked ugly for a time but we have them cornered now. The stench of them takes away our stomach for a fight and desperation gives them strength.'

'What will you do with them?'

'What *must* I do with them? If I don't feed them, they'll die. If I don't work them they'll grow vicious from idleness. Once they're stronger, they'll have to be sternly disciplined because they outnumber us.'

'Demetri, they can't stay here! They're useless for work and we can't feed them.'

'We can give them something. Their labour's not worth much as they are but we can find them something useful to do.'

'But they'll pollute our stream and foul the land! We'll have epidemics among the animals, plague and phthisis among our workers and our workers' children. Is that what you want? Some of our women are pregnant. How could you bring such trouble on us?'

'What do you want me do with them?'

'Turn them loose, put up high fences to keep them out. Commatus is very cunning at making fences. Punish intruders as an example to the rest.'

His jaw tightened.

'They belong to me. I can't abandon them. If I turn them out, they'll steal from my neighbours and end by getting themselves crucified.'

'Then free them so they can claim the dole.'

'Nerysa, I know nothing about these men. I can't make Roman citizens of them. That would be irresponsible.'

'Very well. But I won't stay here and watch you destroy everything we've struggled to build. I'll take our daughter and Charis and Gaius to Rome and ask Lucius for shelter.'

'You'd better send to him for an escort. There are bandits on the roads.'

She watched him turn away and knew he wouldn't try to dissuade her. He'd always expected her to go to Lucius. He'd stay to do his duty and find that it wasn't so easy without her.

Packing her bags, she racked her brain for something that seemed to be eluding her. Why had her heart leapt at the very sight of him? Because his eyes shone with eagerness for the first time in two years. His melancholy had lifted! She had a cart loaded with bread and vegetables, oil and wine, cauldrons and long handled besoms and Darius drove her to the field.

She thought she'd never get over what she saw there. The wretches were huddled together, guarded by dogs and overseers with stout vine rods. They represented the youngest and toughest of the abandoned slaves; the rest had perished; of cold, plague and starvation. Each was a chrysalis of filthy wrinkled skin, pouting running sores. She could identify every one of their protruding bones. All stared dully at her out of sunken eyes. The sight and smell of them turned over her stomach repeatedly. Some of the walking ghosts were women. When she saw children and a skeletal baby, she could no longer choke back her tears. Heedless of her own advice, she sprang from the cart and ran to Demetrius.

'Sir, these people must be bathed. At once!'

He looked at her in bewilderment.

'Shouldn't they be fed?'

'Promise them food after the bath so they'll submit. How many men can you spare?'

He looked at her gratefully, though still doubtful.

'As many as you need.'

She sent Darius back to the villa for hip baths, buckets and clean clothes. The men kindled fires and she directed them to throw infested rags on them and sling cauldrons of water above them. When the aroma of cooking vegetables began to rise from the pot, the starving sprang to life and surged towards it. Demetrius tightened the ring of guards standing with rods uplifted to prevent disorder.

One by one, each wretch was prodded forward from the herd. Their heads, brows and bodies were shaved and each was stood in a bath of fresh herb water and scrubbed from scalp to toe. Their wounds were dressed and patchwork tunics were handed out. As they lined up to be given bread and a bowl of pottage, she heard another cart creak to a halt. Recognizing Lucius' blacksmith and seeing, with horror, that the men were being chained together, she cried out, 'No! That's disgusting!' then bit her lip and blushed. Later, in private, she apologized.

'I should never have questioned your judgement in front of your slaves. I'm sorry.'

He drew her onto the couch and into his arms.

'I don't blame you. I'm horrified by what's necessary but it *is* necessary as I shall persuade you.'

'But these people escaped detection for years. They could have carried on but they virtually gave themselves up. Why restrain them if they wanted to be caught?'

'They're desperate but desperation won't make them manageable. You know the life of a countrywoman in a villa but not the life of a labourer. The work's incessant and backbreaking. They're encouraged by the support of their master, of course, but mainly they bear it because they're inured to it from childhood. Nature's rhythms and her remorseless demands are seared into their bodies and souls. Now these men have spent years in idleness and indiscipline. They no longer have the habit of work or the habit of obedience and they must be brought back to both; not with cruelty, I hope, but with complete firmness. Commatus will watch them. As soon as any of them proves he's reliable, we'll release him. We'll absorb them into the family one by one.'

'The mother and baby should come to the villa now and we ought to foster the orphans with trusted slaves who can train them.'

'I'll have them sent up to you. The building they've been hiding in must be made secure. The rest can live there until we're more sure of them. Tomorrow I'll question each one and find out what he used to do. I'll work them gently from the next day.'

'Demetri, some of them can hardly stand, how could they work?'

'They must accept that food is the reward of their labour. We shan't expect much from them at first, just to help relieve their own want. They can collect the acorns we'll grind to eke out their flour and they can help repair their own shelter. I can't spare men to do it, I'll have to hire contractors in Narnia. It ought to be fairly easy to secure. It's the old ergastulum.'

She shuddered and he tightened his arms around her momentarily. Then he lay back on his cushions and stared at the ceiling.

'The difficulty is, I've no ready money. What I had, I lent out at ten percent and I can't call it in without notice. How am I going to feed fifty extra mouths through next winter? I've calculated the rations to the last scoop of grain.'

'And no one can do that better than you. But we might have enough windfall olives and fig paste, and pomegranates. We could get extra grain and vegetables from Lepidus, he usually has a surplus.'

515

'At the market price. I won't be his pensioner.'

'So, when his men bring me an injured worker on a stretcher, do you want me to send him a bill?'

'Hermes! I should think I can be self-reliant without your being offensive.'

Sobered but undeterred, he said to the ceiling, 'I shall manage. Though, at present, I don't see how.'

She fetched the emeralds from her room and held them out to him. He turned them over in his hand and her heart ached for him. But she couldn't say she'd drugged her master and risked his life. If he knew that, he must reject her, thinking her either mad or depraved. He looked up sharply.

'Where did you get them?' he asked, although, of course, he knew.

'Lepidus sent them to me after he spent the night here when you were in Corinth.'

His jaw stiffened almost imperceptibly. Then his eyes gleamed.

'You probably don't realise but these are worth a king's ransom. They'll fetch even more in Rome than he gave for them in Egypt. We could feed the slaves and dower our daughter handsomely.'

She lowered her eyes.

'Marry me and I'll give them to you.'

He shook his head.

'A freedwoman can't marry to defy her patron. If we asked a magistrate to register a citizen marriage, the first thing he'd ask to see would be Lepidus' written permission.'

'Then will you dictate me a letter? Say since I came into his power, all I've ever wanted was to be his dutiful slave and freedwoman. Tell him I beg him tearfully, on my knees, not to exclude me from his family by refusing me marriage with his dependant, the one to whom he gave my virginity. Say my grateful heart will lie at his feet for ever and whatever else you think might move him, and, just for once, add your pleas to mine!'

She took down his dictation verbatim without comment and signed it.

Then she said, 'Christians say one shouldn't swear and flatter. If you always speak your mind, people learn to value your plain word above other men's oaths.'

He shook his head.

'Wouldn't work. A slave may work ten years in a family before the master addresses him. If, then, his reply is curt and ungracious, why should he notice him again?'

He rolled the paper and sealed it.

'I think I should take this to Rome myself, tomorrow.'

'Then sell the emeralds while you're there.'

He took up his tablets and stylus, never far from his hand.

'What should I buy?'

'The outdoor workers must be properly clothed and shod. Leather tunics and hoods, wooden clogs, thick cloaks and mittens.'

'Undertunics?'

'No, we'll make patchwork ones at home.'

'They'll freeze in that prison in winter. They should have bedding.'

'If their bodies ache from hard labour, I think they should have pallets, if we can afford it, and each man will need a bowl and a drinking cup.'

The final list filled a diptych. He slid the jewellery into his wallet and gave her a piercing look.

'Didn't you fall pregnant?'

'No.'

'Remarkable!' was all he said but she thought he looked smug.

CHAPTER LXXXIX

February - 186

Operarios parandos esse, qui laborem ferre possint, ne minores annorum XXII et ad agri culturam dociles. Eam coniecturam fieri posse ex aliarum rerum imperatis, et in eo eorum e noviciis requisitione, ad priorem dominum quid factitarint.

You should choose those who can bear heavy work, at least 22 years old, and who have an aptitude for farming. Judge them by how they cary out other tasks and, in the case of new recruits, by asking them what they used to do for their former master. M. Terentius Varro *Rerum Rusticarum* I vii 3

The next morning saw Demetrius seated in state in the ergastulum, his wretched property paraded before him in four ranks of ten. To his amusement, Polybius insisted that it was beneath his master's dignity to address this scum directly. He had Commatus question them while he relayed their replies to Demetrius and made notes.

'This one's sixteen, master.'

'He doesn't look it.'

Polybius shrugged. 'His family died of plague seven years ago. He's not been trained for anything, being only a boy when the farm was abandoned. Until he was ten he minded sheep. He says he can play pipes.'

'What's his name?'

'The thankless wretch won't say, master.'

'Don't strike him. Ask his fellows. Or I'll give him a name. A new name for a new beginning. Next!'

'This man is Stentor. He's thirty and was a ploughman.'

That was laughable. Ploughing was the most strenuous work of all and he had barely strength to stand. Unstooped, he was probably tall enough. It was just possible to imagine what he might once have been.

'Is that his child?'

'No, master, his sister's child. She died last winter.'

'Where have they buried their dead?'

'At the edge of the estate, sir.'

'Do they recall the place exactly? Is it close to the road?'

'Yes, against the boundary.'

'The boundary must be moved so the burial is outside the estate. Tell them I'll set up a suitable monument.'

'Next one's forty, a beekeeper.'

'He looks to be an honest type, bring him forward.'

With Arecomus' foot in his back, the cadaverous wretch tottered forward. Commatus lowered his cudgel between him and Demetrius but Demetrius pushed it aside.

'What I want to understand,' he said, 'is why you starved rather than make yourselves known to us. When you saw the wilderness shrinking and more and more land under the plough, you must have known you had a new master. Why hide?'

'What master would want us? We knew you'd turn us out.'

'If you thought I wouldn't want you, why didn't you go free?'

The man looked puzzled.

'We were born here.' he said.

When all forthcoming details had been recorded, bread and olive paste was given out. Demetrius hardly recognised Polybius, the town dandy, in Polybius the country bailiff. He strutted down the ranks, thrusting his rod under each man's chin in turn and barking, 'Heads up, eyes down! You're the slaves of Lucius Marius Demetrius. If you're obedient, hard-working and respectful you'll be well treated. If not, you'll be punished. In five years from now, this will be the best farm in Etruria, in twenty years the best in Italy. Be grateful to belong here.'

The shackled crew limped off behind their overseers and began work.

***

Nerysa waited impatiently for a reply from Lucius but Demetrius came back from Rome without one.

'Lepidus will consider your position and take advice. He'll write to you in due course.'

They began rehabilitating the new slaves. Some died, but, as they died in the makeshift infirmary of the ergastulum under her own care, Demetrius rejected Nerysa's protests that the regime was too strict and the work too hard. The most cooperative of them joined the family of the villa rustica, integrated well and were accepted. But there was a hard core of renegades who troubled him.

'Over the working day, I drain every last dram of energy from them. They owe me that. They're well fed and clothed; when they're ill, I send them to the infirmary and I know you treat them with loving care. They ought to feel grateful and work because they want to please, not because they're forced. Then they'll be welcome in the villa to enjoy the warmth of the kitchen and the company of the women. On holidays, they'll have the freedom of the estate and leisure for their own activities. I'm more anxious to give them all that than some of them are to earn it.'

'I don't understand why they try your patience.'

'Starvation disturbed their reason. There's one, a shepherd boy, who snarls and bites like an animal. The only thing he responds to is the rod. He's only fit for the mines or the galleys and not yet strong enough for either.'

'How old is he?'

'They say he's sixteen but he looks the same age as Lucillus.'

Nerysa's curiosity was aroused but Demetrius didn't allow chained slaves to have contact with the women except in the infirmary so her mind dwelt on him though she never saw him.

CHAPTER XC

June 186

O matris pulchrae filia pulchrior.

More beautiful daughter of a beautiful mother. Horace. Odes XVI

Lucius and Lucillus had their own duties to perform at Saturnalia and no time to visit Horta in the spring. Lucillus graduated with honours from the grammar school and began to study rhetoric with private tutors. Lucius, busier than ever professionally, coached him and took him about; to the law courts, to the rhetors' schools and to hear the best orators debate. They both missed Horta and Lucius decided to spend the summer there instead of Baiae. Lucillus needn't be idle, he'd a reading list and Gisco still had something to offer him in mathematics. Lucius himself was grateful to relax. He and Demetrius toured both estates together and gave each other plenty of good-natured advice.

Waking one morning full of energy, Lucius decided to walk the three miles to his freedman's villa. Approaching through the garden, he dismissed his escorts and entered the back of the house. A stray duck followed him in and Matugena shooed it out before she saluted and told him the 'master and mistress' were not at home. She set a chair and a tray with wine and limpid honey on wedges of barley bread, and withdrew. The recesses of the atrium were airy and cool. Against the walls and around the green fluted pillars stood stone jars full of white oleander and roses, deadnettle, hogweed and ivy. He suspected this eclectic mixture defied some rubric of good taste, yet he had to admit that its effect was magnificent. Beyond the parted tablinum curtains, he saw Demetrius' familiar chest with the portrait of Demeter above.

The principal bedrooms were swept and neat with nothing to indicate whether both were in use. He wandered from room to room without inhibition. His freedman's house was, to all intents and purposes, his own and hadn't he paid for it?

He found nothing to despise. The house was simply appointed but beautifully kept and vibrant with atmosphere. In their absence, their house was redolent, not of each individually, but of the alchemy of the bonded pair. To have bought it wasn't enough; he wanted to put something inside it. He'd buy them a present; statue, vase, citrus wood table; it didn't matter what, so long as it was the grandest piece in the house.

He was beyond jealousy now but it still seemed wrong that Nerysa's learning and liveliness should be buried in obscurity. How did she stand it? Two days of the country folk and their rumbustious good humour was enough to bore him to tears. She'd been a success in Rome. He'd had to intercept presents and poems that might have embarrassed her. He imagined her presiding over a salon of his elegant friends. Every talented man in Rome would have aspired to be her lover. Married to him, would she have stayed so obstinately chaste? That would have seemed slow and old-fashioned, undermining her popularity with the smart set. Yet, had he been her husband, he thought he could have borne that philosophically.

His passion for her had been his companion for so long he hardly knew how to live without it, yet even that began to desert him as he reflected on how completely she'd outmanoeuvred him. He'd banished her to the country to bring her sharply to heel. Ten years later, here she still was; purposeful and happy – happier than him by far.

And she'd made him a poisonous gift; a child to break his heart. A son who could never be his son, whose natural gifts fitted him for the highest office but whose birth debarred him from it. Her strength of character repelled him. He didn't wish, ever again, to be dominated by a woman.

Only the girl was pure delight. He'd realised early on that he couldn't teach her as he taught law students. If her efforts didn't satisfy him, her eyes sparkled tears. A hint of sarcasm, the mildest rebuke devastated her. She was exquisitely receptive, drinking wisdom from his mind in deep shuddering draughts like an orphaned lamb at the shepherd's bottle. The only reward she wanted was his praise, which seemed to clothe her in a gentle radiance and spur her to greater effort. He praised her often and when, in honesty, he couldn't, he confined himself to the observation that he knew she could do even better.

He decided to visit the school room unannounced and see her and Lucillus at their studies. Sprinting up the stairs two at a time, he stopped short, hearing the unmistakable slap of birch twigs on flesh – a sound distressingly familiar from his own schooldays. Feeling a stab of disappointment that Lucillus, a graduate of the best school in the capital, should fail to satisfy a provincial school master, he drew back the curtain and saw the girl dangling by her wrists, draped over Macrinus' back in an obscene parody of a pick-a-back ride. She quivered with each blow but made no protest. Tears had matted her hair and plastered it to her face. He followed the lines of her body and saw that womanhood had begun to stir in her. Breasts were forming, tense and pointed as buds on the vine in spring. Suffocating with rage, he signalled stiffly and the sickening noise stopped.

'Why are you beating my freedwoman?'

Gisco laid down the birch twigs and held out a tablet. Lucius scanned it and shook his head.

'Disgraceful! A theorem familiar to every graduate. Eleven years old and she still hasn't mastered it!'

Settling himself in the master's chair, he beckoned the girl to his side as, unconscious of irony, Gisco and Macrinus hung their heads and dragged her tunic over her head.

'Remind me, little one,' he said softly, 'what does Pythagoras say about right-angled triangles?'

'That the s-square on the side s-subtending the right-angle equals the squares of the other sides.'

'Good! Now, if you were building a temple you'd want it to be exactly rectangular so the corners should be –'

'Square?'

'Exactly. You wouldn't want any crooked corners, would you? But it's difficult to measure an angle and a small mistake would show over

523

a big area. Supposing you could get that corner angle right just by making it part of a triangle with sides of certain lengths? Lengths are easy to measure.'

She blinked back her tears. He handed her a fresh tablet and a stylus.

'To find suitable lengths for our triangle, we need to find a square number that is, itself, the sum of two other squares. Take your stylus and make a dot. Just one. One is the first uneven number, and isn't it also the first square number? Now, a dot beside it, one below it and one to finish the square.'

She drew them promptly.

'How many dots is that?'

'Four, sir.'

'Four. Isn't that the next square number? And how many did you add to one to make four?'

'Three.'

'Three. The next uneven number after one. Now more dots, to the right of your square and below and one at the corner. See, a larger square. How many dots in this one?'

'Nine, sir.'

'The next square after four. And how many did you add?'

'Five, sir.'

'The next uneven number to three. Now, is that a coincidence?'

The violet eyes danced.

'I think, sir, that if it were, you wouldn't be at such pains to point it out.'

'You're shrewd! I say when you add successive uneven numbers to successive square numbers, you make the next square.'

'Always?'

'Always. Try it for yourself later.'

He ached to squeeze her tiny waist in the crook of his arm but remembered, just in time, that she was bruised.

'Now, consult your figure. For a square of side a, how many dots will you need to make the next square?'

'Twice a and an extra one for the corner.'

'So 2a + 1. And we want that to be a square number too – say the square of N.'

'You mean let 2a + 1 be N squared?'

'Exactly! And so what is a?'

'Half N squared minus one.'

'And one plus a?'

Her brow creased. 'One plus a half of N squared minus one?'

'There you have it!'

His words came in a rush of enthusiasm as he seized the tablet and stylus.

'So! N squared plus a half N squared minus one all squared, equals one plus a half N squared minus 1 all squared! And since you worked it out for yourself, you can never forget it!'

Insight broke over her wet face like sun bursting through cloud. He flashed Gisco a look of triumph.

'That's how to do it! Simple! Explain things and make them plain to her. Nothing more. Never beat her again. Do you think she makes mistakes on purpose?'

Demetrius, he remembered, had had remarkable facility in adding columns of figures without an abacus when they were boys. That the girl had his able mind there was no doubt. He wondered what a child of his own body would have been like. But he didn't repine. No son of his own could have been more to his mind than Lucillus. He'd meant to give these two dolts their freedom when Lucillus came of age. They'd never get it now, not even in his will. The girl drew back from him, crying wildly as though her heart would break.

But sir, she choked out, 'you said – you said – you *promised*.'

'Whatever did I *promise*?'

'That I could study just like my brother. If the masters can't beat me, they won't take me seriously and then how will I learn?'

'Do you think that's the only way to learn? Boys have to be beaten because they're unwilling and easily distracted. But you want to learn. Harsh treatment isn't suitable for you.'

She shook her head mutinously.

'I want to be the same as my brother.'

'How could you be that?'

He lifted her carefully in his arms and carried her to the high window.

'Do you see the bulrushes growing along the dyke? They're like Lucillus; sturdy and straight. But you're like a pale poppy. Can you see them, too, swaying by the edge of the cornfield? If I don't look to you, you'll be caught in the ploughshare or trampled by a clumsy ox.'

Gisco ventured, 'Master, maybe her father?'

'She's my freedwoman. No one else may touch the hem of her dress.'

'But you're never here!' she cried, 'Must I save up my beatings and take them all at once?'

'For something so important, little one, I'll come straight away, whatever I'm doing.'

'Then Euclid was wrong about one thing, sir, there *is* a royal road to geometry.'

'If there is, little one, I shall carpet it and set your feet on it.'

When he'd carried her out of the room, he stopped, because he had no idea where to go.

'Tell me,' he said, 'where to find your nurse. You'll need some ointment.'

Nerissina smiled. 'My mother makes ointment from violets and lavender. It makes you feel better just to smell it.'

'Then I've a mind to have Gisco beat *me* so I can try it.'

'No need,' she laughed, 'she'd give you some if you asked.'

'Perhaps, if *you* asked for me?'

He groaned aloud as he went downstairs.

Merciful gods! he thought, *can lightning strike twice in the same place?*

She usually sat on his couch at dinner, delighting him with her lively talk and artless kisses but that evening he told her not to neglect her parents. If he were to kiss her now he'd frighten her. In future, he'd be uneasy to be too close to her. Besides, the opposite couch was a better place to observe her from and he needed to analyse his complex feelings; rage, joy, astonishment, liberation, caution. He seemed to have spent his life waiting and thought he must be getting rather good at it. Now he would wait again and watch her grow up. His slaves must talk to Demetrius' slaves and find out about her; her disposition, her habits and her faults. Lucius was too old for rash judgements and too jaded for a second mistake.

CHAPTER XCI

August 186

Nam utrumque maxime servare debet, ut et quem paterfamiliae tali poena multaverit, vilicus nisi eiusdem permissu compedibus non eximat, et quem ipsesua sponte vinxerit, antequam dominus, non resolvat.

The overseer must be punctilious as regards both these points ; he must not release anyone whom the master has ordered to be chained or free anyone who he, himself has chained, without the master's knowledge. Columella *De Re Rustica* 1. viii. 16

In August, Demetrius was in the horn of Africa. Jacob had been in Berenice to buy spices and discovered that ivory and tortoiseshell fetched lower prices the further south you found them. The slaves missed Demetrius but they were very proud, saying importantly, 'Our master is in *Cinnamonia* or *Scythia* or *Arabia*.' Having no idea where such places might be, the more exotic their master's destination the more they were impressed, marvelling that one so expert with mattcock and plough could find his way to the ends of the earth and parley with savages.

Nerysa was apprehensive. This was the first time he'd been outside the bounds of the empire and she suspected the expedition was more dangerous than he admitted. Because of resettling the new slaves, he'd delayed his departure too late in the year. It was safest to be back in port by September and foolhardy to sail after October, yet he wouldn't want to be kicking his heels in Egypt until the spring. Lucius had sent no reply to her letter. It seemed he meant to ignore it. Lonely and anxious, she felt in need of a project and remembered the shepherd boy.

She went with Melissus to see the gang at work in the fields. Melissus spoke to the foreman, who was doubtful. The mistress had full authority in the absence of the master and, naturally, might speak to anyone she chose but he advised her to keep her distance. So she offered the boy her herb tonic at arm's length.

'Take it.' she said. 'It will help you grow strong.'

He took it, looked at her and flung the liquid in her face, then hurled the cup to the ground. Overseers closed in to thrash him but she didn't move to give them room.

'That wasn't very sensible.' she said. 'Can't you think of a better way to insult people than depriving yourself? It doesn't please me that you should go thirsty. I imagine it doesn't please you. So far we can agree.'

She forbade the foreman to punish him, then left. The next day she came later, leaving him time to build up a more powerful thirst. He took the cup and she smiled encouragement. He seemed to hesitate, swilling the liquid around his mouth. At last he swallowed the mouthful and downed the rest of the cup. Nerysa put out her hand and took it back.

'I'll come again tomorrow.' she said. 'If you can say, "Thank you, mistress," I'll give you cake. And, if you tell me any of these men has been kind to you, I'll give *him* cake as well.'

She came regularly at the same time so the boy began to look for her. He was never gracious and his general behaviour didn't improve. The day came when she didn't find him at work. Upon no provocation, apparently, he'd attacked his overseer, who, politely reproachful, showed her several gaping bites and admitted to others which, for reasons of modesty, he couldn't show. Sweeping his modesty aside, she took him to the infirmary and salved his wounds and his pride. Then she loaded her ointments into a basket and proposed to do the same for his assailant whom he claimed to have beaten senseless.

The boy was in a separate, locked cell in the ergastulum where he would stay, until the master returned and disposed of him. His bread was thrown to him through a high window. The guard wouldn't let her in.

'Mistress, it's not safe. He's raving.'

'He won't rave at me since I've done nothing to hurt him.'

'With respect mistress, he's not sane. He'll savage anyone within reach.'

'I thought he was chained?'

'He is, mistress, weighed down with chains.'

'Then surely I can keep out of his reach?'

'Suppose he bursts his chains? They say madmen have superhuman strength.'

'The master's orders are that injured slaves must have medical attention.'

The muscular guard paled and broke out in a sweat.

'Mistress, I daren't go in there.'

She narrowed her eyes. 'Do you want to join him there until the master returns? Give me the key!'

He hung his head and squirmed but he dropped the key into her hand.

She was relieved to find the prison so humane. It was lofty and well-aired, lit by small windows all at inaccessible height. The boy had a pallet. He had had a skinful of water and one of wine but had emptied them on the floor in a futile gesture of defiance. He'd been cruelly beaten. She salved his wounds but couldn't lift his spirits, which were more bruised than his body. All the pains she'd taken to reach him had been lost. She scolded him, for the beating was thoroughly deserved. Then she asked, 'What's your name?'

He wouldn't say.

'Then I'll call you Corin. Corin, why do you behave so badly? It's true you hurt your master and mistress, because you frustrate their wish to treat you kindly, but you hurt yourself much more and it's so unnecessary. Lucius Demetrius is a good master and one who understands your difficulties for the best of reasons. He was once a slave himself.'

She saw his eyes flicker interest and she spoke softly. 'And so was I.'

'Not chained on the land, mistress.'

'That's true. I worked in the scullery at first, scouring pots. Then I was given in marriage and had to serve my husband by night and my master by day. I bore children, one for the master and one for my husband. I struggled to be obedient because it didn't come easily to me, any more than it does to you, but, in the end, I did please my master and I earned my freedom, which is far sweeter to me now than if I'd never lost it. You might do the same.'

'No, I couldn't. House slaves often get their freedom. Labourers don't.'

'Could you do anything else? The master would try you out if you'd only behave well.'

'What does a farmer want with a flute player?'

'Can you play the flute?'

'The last eight years I practised day and night. There was nothing else to do and people said it made them happy. One night last winter, we had two chickens between us. The smell of them roasting drove us crazy. I stole more than my share and the men stamped on my flute and threw the pieces on the fire. I make reed pipes but I can't get them in tune. Now I can't even get reeds.'

The fierce defiant looked down at his shackled legs and wept like a girl. She put out her hand and stroked his hair. He looked up, returned her smile and whispered, 'Corin loves you, mistress.'

'Of course he does. I shall be like a mother to him and he's my son.'

He squirmed and sighed, shielding his crotch with his bound hands.

'You don't understand. I bit the bastard because he said... something foul about me...and you.'

'Corin, it's you who doesn't understand, you're young and you're confused. I'm old enough to be your mother, I wish I had been. But we can be like mother and son, nothing else would be suitable. Would you like to go to Narnia tomorrow and buy a flute? Then try to sleep now, so you'll be strong enough.'

She laughed when she came out of the cell to confront a rescue party assembled round the door, holding clubs.

She said, 'I've dressed his wounds as the master would wish. Take him food and wine, and then I think he'll sleep.'

The next morning, she told Melissus that Commatus had agreed that the boy could be brought to the infirmary at the villa. He was doubtful. Was she sure? Knowing Commatus was working a field at the other end of the estate and that Polybius was away inspecting tenancies, she challenged him to consult either or both and succeeded in embarrassing him so much that he gave in. He regretted it immediately and told her to send word if the prisoner gave any trouble in the infirmary. The mule cart was waiting. The driver, at least, didn't question her command to drive them to Narnia.

CHAPTER XCII

October 186

Sive in extremos penetrabit Indos horribilesque ultimosque Britannos.

Whether you penetrate the furthest Indies or to the horrible Britons at the end of the earth. Catullus XI

Demetrius arrived overland from Brundisium as Lucius and Lucillus were going to their bath. He planned to change horses and head home but they prevailed on him to break his journey. Lucillus, jigging up and down with excitement, was irresistible.

'When you hear the dinner gong,' he said, 'look across the peristyle and you'll see the *consul*, Pertinax, and two *senators*.'

Lucius laughed.

'You'll do more than see him. He's not above meeting freedmen. Between ourselves, they say his father was one. Besides, he's on his way to Britain, where I've never been.'

As good as his word, he lent Demetrius a dinner gown, sent Lucillus to bring him to the atrium and swept him forward.

'Excellency, allow me to present my freedman, Demetrius.'

The stately, silver-haired general extended his hand cordially.

'So, Demetri, we meet again! But you don't recognise me from Sirmium, ten years ago? There were so many of us around Marcus. This is Valerianus, my friend and colleague, and Severus, who also knows you.'

Valerianus smiled affably. Severus, more careful of his dignity, managed the brief nod a freedman would be honoured to receive from a senator. Strange, thought Demetrius. Without Lucius' briefing, he'd have taken Marcus Aurelius for a palace secretary. Severus, swarthy and weasel-eyed, looked coarse until you knew he was a governor-elect. But Pertinax, the freedman's son, looked every inch the emperor.

'Do you join us for dinner?'

Demetrius hesitated over the hand. Should he shake or kiss it? He grasped it, combining a self-effacing smile with regret worthy of a sincere invitation.

'You're too kind, Excellency, but I'm travelling; not even a napkin with me! You'll excuse me?'

Lucius frowned, 'His Excellency didn't ask for the pleasure of hearing you refuse, Demetrie. This is a private dinner; your coyness is out of place.'

Flushing as if Lucius had struck him, he fell in behind as they processed to the triclinium. Shielded between Lucius and Lucillus, he kept his head down, his fingers circumspect and his ears pricked. Freedmen should be seen and not heard and, if the service left anything to be desired, he wouldn't want to embarrass Successus by appearing to notice. Six tables were drawn up to the couch by six waiters and he recognized the one assigned to him as Philo - the team's newest recruit had drawn the short straw. But Philo seemed to find the presence of an ex-slave at a consul's table highly satisfactory. He gave no sign of recognition but Demetrius sensed solidarity in every officious twitch of the cloth and every assiduous flick of the crumb brush. Philo put heart into him. He did know how to comport himself as a gentleman and he could be as silent and observant from on the couch as he'd always been from behind it.

'What do you make of the political situation, Demetrie?' Pertinax asked him.

His hand froze above a dish of saffron pheasant while he framed a suitable reply; respectful, brief yet not perfunctory. Lucius sped to the rescue.

'Excuse him, Excellency; he's only just got back from Africa.'

'I can see that. He's almost as brown as Severus here. But he must know the public enemy, Perennis, is dead; torn to pieces in the heart of Rome by rogue British soldiers.'

'Indeed, Excellency, even before I disembarked I'd heard that.'

'And here am I, tossed up by fortune's wheel and, who knows, perhaps Lepidus with me.'

Lucius shook his head and waved the suggestion away.

'I applaud your caution in avoiding the senate,' Pertinax persisted, 'but there are interesting equestrian posts in Britain now and, unless the emperor's change of heart is permanent, it could be safer than Rome. Yes, I know my predecessor was recalled and barely escaped with his life but he was incompetent, remember?

'Then how about a legal post? Not much scope for disgrace and execution there, surely?'

'Permit me to offer my congratulations, Excellency, on your recent appointment.'

'Governor of Britain? Better offer me luck! I was there the last time the natives swarmed over the wall. Thanks to my predecessor's lack of resolution, they're at it again. You've been there, Demetrie. What did you make of it?'

'I was only there for the summer, Excellency. London, five years ago. I seem to remember they were building a city wall.'

'The way things are going they'll be glad of it. The country's a basket case. Impossible to say who's more unpredictable – the natives or the garrison. Something happens to legionaries when they get there. They go as wild as the Brits.'

Lucius nodded. 'They're extraordinary. You won't have heard this, Demetrie, but they set on Priscus and proclaimed him emperor – he escaped their clutches in his underwear –. Commodus, understandably nervous, sacked all the senatorial legates and replaced them with equestrians.'

'No, Lepide,' sighed Pertinax. 'Commodus does nothing but fondle concubines and overturn chariots. Perennis ran the show. Not content with treason, they deserted their posts and marched on Rome to complain to Commodus about Perennis.'

Demetrius shook his head. 'That's been tried before. Great way to get yourself burned alive.'

'So you'd think. But they were two thousand strong. I owe them my good fortune I suppose, they destroyed my enemy and created chaos that I'm called up to deal with. But we can't have the legions deserting post, lodging complaints and setting themselves up as kingmakers. Firmness is the only thing that benighted province understands. That's what it's going to get from me.'

'And the native kings,' Lucius asked, 'are they passive?'

'In the south but it'll take generations before they're reliable. Remember Cassius, descended from kings of Syria, romanized for generations. Scratch the surface and you find all the old tribal loyalties.'

Severus, looked up, eyes like beads of mercury, rolling in all directions. 'My dear Pertinax, not even Marcus blamed the Syrians for *Cassius*.'

It was the first time he'd spoken. For a lawyer he was oddly reticent. Less than fully confident of his Greek perhaps or conscious of the Punic lisp he'd never managed to lose. While the waiters were replacing the pheasant with jugged hare and gingered venison he darted looks at Lucius, as if trying to catch his eye. As they stepped back, he said abruptly, 'Remember that little Brit you had?' He ruffled Lucillus' hair. 'Left you this pledge of her affection didn't she? What became of her?'

Lucius hardly hesitated before saying smoothly, 'Her? I gave her to my freedman here.'

'*Gave* her, by Zeus! snarled Severus, 'You wouldn't sell her to me.'

All eyes turned on Demetrius. Lucius shrugged and said ruefully, 'He caught me in a weak moment.'

Severus' lisp was softly menacing.

'Your master indulges you, Demetrie. No wonder you slighted the divine Marcus for him.'

'I'm always Sensible, Excellency, of my *patron's* goodness.'

'You could have explained that to my brother, Geta, and spared him some exertion on your behalf.'

'I don't understand you, sir. I did have the honour of meeting your brother - in Aquileia, years ago, fifteen maybe.'

'Having brought yourself to his attention as a result of some trifling service, you induced him to recommend you to the imperial civil service. Then you declined their offer and made him look a fool.'

'Some misunderstanding surely.' said Lucius suavely. 'No one would approach my slave without my permission.'

Demetrius floundered in a bath of cold sweat.

'I must confess, sir…there was an approach. I didn't know who to thank for it – whether, perhaps the emperor –'

'I grant Marcus took no persuading but the suggestion came from my brother.'

'It might be thought good form,' observed Lucius, 'before procuring a slave for the state, to mention the matter to the owner.'

Severus shrugged. 'I've no doubt he would've done. In the event there was no need, and since he's now discharged whatever obligation he may have felt towards your ex-slave, there'll be none.'

Demetrius, wanting to sink through the cushions, watched Lucillus wave his wine cup at his waiter and copied him mechanically. Lucillus should be holding back, the serious drinking wouldn't start until after the meal, but with Lucius' eye, fond and indulgent, also on him, it wasn't a tutor's place to interfere.

'Have you any appointments, Demetrie?' asked Pertinax, 'A public priesthood perhaps? Where's your farm?'

'Horta, Excellency, on the Tiber.'

'Oh, Valerianus and I know Etruria well. That's where we did our ten year stint in the classroom. What would be your nearest city, Narnia or Ferrentum, I guess? We must see if we can bring you on.'

'Your Excellency is too good.'

'Did Lepidus warn you about Maternus' brigands? Have they reached Horta yet?'

'There've been a few isolated incidents on the roads.' said Lucius. 'Difficult to say if they're connected with Maternus.'

'He'll be a headache for Severus when he gets to Gaul.'

'Gaul?' Lucillus butted in, pushing out his cup again. 'I heard Maternus was in Spain.'

'He may be on the Rhine or the Rhone or in Spain or anywhere between but his army of deserters and runaway slaves is everywhere.' replied Pertinax. 'If he's in Gaul, or even if he isn't, Severus had better catch him. The last time he and I failed to get our man we got the sack.'

'Condianus?' Lucius asked. 'I did wonder. Dismissing you both from Syria, and so abruptly seemed a strange decision, even by today's standards.'

'Condianus?' Lucillus interrupted again. 'Wasn't he related to the Quintilii brothers - a nephew or son?'

'As you say, boy, son to the one, nephew to the other. After they were executed, we got a warrant for his arrest but, as he'd had a fatal accident, we filed it. Then a rumour started he'd faked his own death. It was said he'd drunk hare's blood, fallen off his horse and vomited it up. Once he'd been carried inside, the story went, he'd had a goat carcass burned in a fancy coffin and ridden off to Parthia!'

Valerianus laughed. 'Every day some wretch was dragged before us accused of looking like Condianus. None of them was him – Pertinax here knew him well.'

'Our successors were busier. They sent Commodus a whole series of severed heads but they weren't so recognisable parted from their shoulders and sent on long journeys. We'll never know the truth of it.'

Demetrius looked up and saw Pertinax looking thoughtfully from him to Lucillus.

'So, my boy, your mother's from Britain, is she?'

'Born there, Excellency, but she never speaks of it. I only know what's in Strabo's Geography and what Tacitus thought of my ferocious ancestors.' He smiled his winning smile; a less ferocious youth was difficult to imagine. 'And Caesar's description of the cliffs and sands of the south coast.'

'Caesar would have deplored your grammar, young man.' said Pertinax, 'He taught that sand can't be plural. Like grain and sky, it's always singular.'

'Correct.' agreed Lucius, 'I've heard the divine Marcus say that.'

'And I heard his teacher, Fronto, tell him so.'

Lucillus muttered into his cup, '"The victor gazed on the Libyan sands"'

There was an uncomfortable silence. Lucius might well bite his lip Demetrius thought. This was the result of making too much of a child and not keeping him in his place. He slid a foot towards Lucillus and dug a toenail into his shin.

Valerianus laughed, 'Metamorphoses book 4. Well spotted, lad!'

Lucillus drew back his leg and drained his cup defiantly.

'"The sea foamed the sands".' Aeneid book 1; and what's that bit of Propertius..?'

Demetrius choked on his pear. Propertius! What could be more unsuitable? That's what came of letting boys loose in libraries.

'"Rejoice if you can on the grimy sands." ' Lucillus quoted defiantly, wagging his snail spoon under the consul's nose. 'You can't call that poetic license because it would scan just as well in the singular. The cobbler should stick to his last and Gaius Julius return to his barracks.'

Demetrius glowered at the cup-bearers as, eyes glittering, oblivious of his patron's discomfort, Lucillus held forth. Whereas Caesar was a mere soldier, he announced, Ovid was a wordsmith. On a question of linguistic taste, one surely preferred the judgement of a poet. Pertinax regarded him thoughtfully.

'As one who was a "mere" schoolmaster before becoming a "mere" soldier, I'm inclined to agree. But I could show you commanders in our army today whose Latin would make you weep and who have no Greek at all. We need them because of the war and the uncomfortable fact is, they're just as capable of giving the enemy a bloody nose as we educated men. Valeri, what would we have done with a boy like this one in our class?'

'A taste of the rod, I think, to teach him respect for his elders.'

'And a quiet word with his father, recommending teachers in Rome who might cope with his precocity. Who has the challenge of directing your studies, my boy?'

'Antistius.' gulped Lucillus, whose face had turned green.

'And for Greek?'

'Hic. Hadrianus!' Torn between leaving a consul's presence without permission and vomiting in his face, Lucillus rolled his eyes in despair.

'Lepidus couldn't have done better by you. And who's your tutor?'

Hand to his mouth, Lucillus looked helplessly at Demetrius and so did everyone else.

'Ah! So *he* was responsible for bringing you up to modesty and sober habits?'

Lucillus nodded or, perhaps, ducked, snatching a cushion to his face.

'I expect he has something to say to you in private.' said Pertinax. 'We'll excuse you so as not to keep him waiting.'

Lucillus lunged for the door and Demetrius signed for his sandals. A boy appeared behind the couch and another in front and Philo swept away his table. As he was about to stand, Lucius leaned towards him and said in a low voice, 'Adrian has a letter I've dictated for Maria Nerysa. Would you be so kind as to deliver it?'

Demetrius bowed his assent, bowed again to the guests and followed the heaving Lucillus with a considered combination of speed and decorum. Severus turned to Lucius.

'My condolences, Lepide, on the death of your wife.'

'Thank you. It grieves me to have to offer the same to you.'

'At this point in our careers, the right marriage should apply maximum leverage. I wouldn't mind casting my eye around on your behalf. Nor would Pertinax, I'm sure.'

Demetrius passed through the doorway and flatted himself against the outer wall.

He heard the unease in Lucius' short laugh.

'As a matter of fact, Severe, I do mean to marry in the spring. But I married once before on advice from the highest quarter. This time I'm choosing for myself and you'd better brace yourselves for a scandal.'

He said something else Demetrius didn't catch and Pertinax laughed.

'Don't distress yourself, Lepide, Valerianus and I know all about boys.'

'They put themselves forward these days.' said Severus. 'It seems to be the fashion. But *that* boy ought not to.'

Two of Lucillus' slaves were coming out of his room, one bearing a silver bowl, discreetly covered with a white napkin and the other a glass and carafe. They stood aside as Demetrius entered. Lucillus, standing in the centre of the room, looked at him with cold dislike.

'The usual chastisement? Let's get it over. I want to go to bed.'

Demetrius shook his head.

'If Lucius wants to raise you as a graceless whelp with no sense of when to keep your mouth shut, that's his choice but I won't be his hired rod any longer. I've always opposed his absurd indulgence because I thought it would ruin you. It will and I'll be sorry to see it because I care more for you than you'd ever want to believe.'

Lucillus hand shot to his mouth again. Demetrius emptied the gold fruit bowl and held it under his chin, steadying his forehead with his free hand as the boy sobbed and retched. He felt an agony of pity for him. *So brilliant; so many hard lessons to learn.*

He called for the slaves who took the bowl, dabbed their young master's face with a linen cloth and gave him a drink. Demetrius turned to slip away.

Lucillus said, 'Don't go.' His teeth chattered. He struggled. 'Thank you…..for everything.'

'No need. By the way, you forgot Lucan.'

Lucillus frowned. 'Pharsalia?' His eyes brightened. 'Yes, of course, chapter three, no two, "The Nile floods the Egyptian sands".'

'You see, you may well know more than your so-called betters but they don't need to know you know. Let that be one more thing you know that they don't.'

He'd get home, take out the plough and break a new field. If he wanted to leave at first light, he should collect Nerysa's letter before he went to bed. It was substantial, several sheets of papyrus tightly rolled and sealed. It lay like lead in his hand. How could Lucius be so confident of its effect as to announce his forthcoming marriage? He had one last hold over her. He could threaten to betray her to the authorities. What if she called his bluff? Lucius might be sure she wouldn't but Demetrius thought he knew otherwise. It was his turn to feel sick to the stomach. She wouldn't be safe anywhere in the empire. Where could he take her? Sub-Saharan Africa? Persia? Scythia? Could they, perhaps, make a life among her people? If he knew the letter contained that threat, he could make plans. She could send a reply playing for time and they would make for Marseille and then Milford Haven. Would he make the success of himself in her world as she had done in his? He turned the scroll over in his hand and studied the seal.

CHAPTER XCIII

October 186

Auguror, uxoris fidos optabis amores..nec tibi malueristotum quaecumque per orbem fortis arat valido rusticus arva bove nec tibi gemmarum quidquid felicibus Indis nascitur

I divine you will pray for your wife's true love. You'd prefer that to all the land in the whole world and to all the pearls of India Tibullus II 2

Corin rejected the lascivious throb of the aulos for a plain wooden transverse flute with a clear, pure sound. Nerysa was thrilled by his musicianship. She hadn't miscalculated, he was extraordinary. She bought the instrument he chose, making no quibble over the price, and he played without stopping as they drove home. For safe keeping, she took it from him as the cart lumbered to a halt. In the last rays of the setting sun, slanting down on the villa, she saw six horses in the courtyard and slaves running to and fro with saddles and torches. Melissus came and handed her down, his expression wooden.

'Mistress, the master's home. He's waiting for you.'

It was Demetrius' old trick of arriving without warning. She turned and saw Corin thrown out of the cart and chained.

They were no longer steward and slave mistress as Demetrius acknowledged by having a chair placed for her by his couch, before dismissing the slaves. He maintained his usual calm, though not without noticeable effort. He didn't wish to hear her account but to ask questions so as to confirm or dismiss what he'd already heard and piece together his own assessment. When she'd answered, promptly and honestly, he was silent for some time before saying, 'What have you done? You've made a fool of Melissus, who's spent the day racked with anxiety and you've completely undermined Commatus. What would you say if he came up to the villa and countermanded your orders in the kitchen and infirmary? No one is released from chains until I command it. Do you know why that is?'

'Because you're the master.'

'No, it's for the worker's own protection. Commatus may imprison or chain a worker in my absence but he may not release him. That means he can't confine anyone without acquainting me with the facts, so he daren't do it unjustly or for any reason of his own that doesn't bear directly on the management of my farm. But you – you take it on yourself to unloose a madman and drive off with him! How is anyone to respect my authority when you make it plain that you don't?'

'That's unfair, you know I respect you and all your people know it too.'

'The boy's vicious and unpredictable. Don't you see how alarmed we were? Setting out to search and fearing we'd find you injured or worse?'

'I wasn't in danger. You don't understand. The boy would be manageable if he were kindly treated. You can't imagine the horror of the life you've led him.'

He sprang up looming over her. His fist crashed down on the back of her chair with such force she was surprised it didn't break.

'You know nothing! Don't dare tell me I don't understand! I know better than you, better than anyone, what that life is because I was worked in chains myself. Did I behave like him? No! I forced my pride down my throat and gave my master the best that was in me.'

He'd told her. The secret he'd dreaded her knowing. She watched him shake with shame and rage.

'Now you know what I am and how you demean yourself to live with me! But I haven't sought the honour of caring for you. You foist yourself on me, flout my authority and make a fool of me. You belong with your own kind but, if you insist on staying here, I'm prepared to give you control over the house and the infirmary. I shall endorse your decisions and not question your judgement. But, for your part, you will not go to my fields and byres unless you're invited. Nor will you will undermine the authority of my overseers by questioning their decisions, let alone overruling them. I don't underestimate the deference due to your birth but it's better for all concerned that this farm is run by someone who understands agriculture. You should reflect that what's not good for the hive is no good for the bee.'

She spoke evenly as though to steady him with her voice alone.

'Like any sensible woman, I would rather defer to a clever man than dominate a fool. I did what I did because you said that, if any of your men was capable of something better, you'd put him to it. How can you judge without hearing him?'

The boy was brought, fettered but with unbound hands. She gave him the flute and her sweetest smile.

'Corin, it would make me very happy if you would play for the master.'

He looked surly. She prayed he wouldn't throw away his last chance with a stupid show of defiance. But the feel of the instrument seemed to calm him. He handled it lovingly and, as he coaxed the sweet sound from it, resentment fell away and he was lost in enchantment, as was his audience. Cascades of haunting, liquid melody rippled from him, caught up in whirlpools of elegant ornament. She took her harp and found chords to accompany him.

***

The beauty of the music took Demetrius by surprise. He didn't know why it had more power to lift the skin on his spine than any he'd heard. He knew it wasn't technical brilliance; the flying fingers and fluttering tongue. Nor was it the crisp, insistent rhythm or the shapely phrasing, more telling than speech. Above the snatched breaths and the husky throat of the pipe, there hovered a fiery sweetness that resonated in the depths of his being yet drew him toward mysteries beyond his knowing. He didn't miss the tender rapport between the musicians. By the time they fell silent he knew two things; the boy was a genius and he was in the very desperation of love for his master's wife. He struck the gong for the houseboy and sent for Polybius and Melissus, Commatus and the boy's overseer. The two outdoor workers were uneasy in the house, conscious of the dirt clinging to their unshod feet. As they listened, tears streaked their muddy cheeks. The boy fell silent, absently worrying his scalp with the tip of the flute. Demetrius saw him with disgust. *Better get his head shaved again.*

He said, 'It pleased the mistress to excuse this boy from duty so he could practise his music. To my mind, she did right. He's not suited to farm work.'

He ordered Polybius to unchain him and give him good clothes and food but to keep him under lock and key until he'd decided what to do with him. He didn't apologise to Nerysa for his anger but he thought he should explain it. He'd been beside himself with worry and disappointed in her that her judgement had erred. Now he saw that it hadn't. He had good news of his voyage.

'If this deal comes off,' he told her, 'I could keep you in reasonable style in the short term.'

'Why only the short term?'

'Because once people know what we're about, they'll follow us and the market will be spoilt. I shan't complain, we'll have done well.'

'Are you happy with the building work?'

'The work's well enough. It seems to be taking a long time.'

'If there's stone and cement left over, could the men build some dining couches in the garden?'

'Dining couches in the garden? I may have cut a good deal but I'm a poor farmer not a sybarite.'

'Indeed, you're very poor. And too thrifty to waste good stone and cement, or risk damaging your furniture having it moved in and out of the garden all summer.'

'If there are any materials left, I'll see if I can spare the labour.'

'If we have couches, I think you'd be pleased to have an oven too.'

'A brick oven I'll allow, on condition you don't remind me of anything else I require.'

He drew a scroll from his tunic.

'I've a letter for you, from Lepidus.'

'Oh, my dearest, has he refused us?'

He gave an inscrutable half smile.

'How would I know? Look, the seal's unbroken.'

'Break it quickly and tell me! I can't bear to read it.'

'Lepidus to Maria, his freedwoman, greeting, Ah! Ill advised... headstrong disobedience... obstinacy.. ingratitude...apparently that's all too painful to dwell on but your callous indifference to your children's social standing has shocked and grieved him...that he goes into, at some length...will spare no efforts, however, at the right time, to establish your freeborn status in the hope of improving their condition but, in view of your...'

'Demetri! Don't tease! Why are you grinning and what are those loose papers?'

'He earnestly hopes that wiser counsels will prevail but, in case they shouldn't, he sends his written permission and a draft on his bankers for the first instalment of your dowry. So, if you still wanted....but you're too tired to go to Narnia again tomorrow, surely?'

'I've waited so long already, how can I possibly wait 'till tomorrow? Can Epicurus make us a feast?'

'Eumaeus shall kill a pig and your flute boy can play for us.'

Their second wedding was a rustic parody of their first. Demetrius, sure that only divine favour could have singled him out for such happiness, sacrificed the pig and stared long and hard at the entrails. They appeared unremarkable. He and Nerysa rode to Narnia early and, in the manner of the most vulgar freedwoman, she gave herself away. They returned in the afternoon to find the house festooned with hops and honeysuckle and full of happy people. All Lucius' slaves had come, bringing their own rations besides extra wine and presents. The feast wasn't lavish but there was bread, sauce, a portion of crisp hog meat and salad leaves for everyone and soft cheese and blackberries crammed into baskets, dripping juice. The tables were cut from turf and the guests sat on freshly cropped grass, sunlight dappling their faces under garlands of mallow and meadow saffron. Nerysa wound the doorpost with wool and smeared it with lard in the traditional way. Demetrius carried her over the flower-strewn threshold and she admonished him as every Roman wife to her husband, 'Tu Gaius, ego Gaia.' 'Wherever you are master, I shall be mistress'. When they and their slaves had danced the night away she asked him, 'You were so sure it was wrong. Does it feel wrong now?'

'I figured, if you'd give your body to a scrubby flute boy, then why not to me?'

'If that's what you thought, no wonder you were angry. Yes, I love him, but not in that way. I had a son, remember? Now Lucius has him. I've found one for myself.'

That was a different matter. If she loved the ruffian as a son, he must not be allowed to disappoint her. He sent for him again, baffled that the muse should have singled out such an unworthy object. The boy was loutish until he played and then it was as though heaven rained gold on him.

He told him sternly, 'Corin, you're my slave and, therefore, my responsibility. If you displease me, I'll punish you but I'll continue to support and educate you. In return, I shall take your loyalty, your obedience and all the strength and skill that is in you, to my service. I've apprenticed you to a master musician in Narnia and agreed a contract with him that releases you to play for me on festival days and whenever else I need. At all other times, you will serve him diligently and submit to his reasonable discipline. I've enrolled you in the flautists' guild, which entitles you to all the benefits of membership. What are you scowling at?'

'Why not hire me out to perform and earn you money?'

'In good time. There's more to being a master musician than playing the flute. You must learn to manage a troupe, arrange a programme and contract for business, and you must know how to keep all the instruments in good repair and your players hard at work.'

'So when I'm trained you can sell me at a profit.'

'*If* I sold you because I found you unfit for any purpose, I should be lucky to recoup my investment since, in all honesty, I couldn't foist onto any other man, a slave I couldn't handle myself. Give me good service and I'll never sell you to better my own position without, at the same time, improving yours.'

'But you're sending me away.'

'Corin, you have a talent no sane man would hide in the country. If you'd proved yourself loyal, I'd be well pleased with this arrangement. As it is, it's impossible for me to place that confidence in you that I could wish.'

'I'm sorry, master.' was barely audible.

'Abscond and you'll have no means of support other than theft and you'll end by being crucified. If you're recognised as my slave, you'll be brought back here to whatever punishment I care to impose. The blacksmith will fit you with an iron collar, showing my name and direction. When you've proved to me that this precaution is no longer necessary for your own protection, I'll have it removed.'

The master musician had also recommended that a ring be fitted to the boy's foreskin so dissipation shouldn't sap his genius. Demetrius proposed to order that only if it proved necessary but thought he should give him a timely warning.

'The muse who has so greatly favoured you is a jealous goddess. If you consort with Venus, she'll desert you.'

Corin assured him he'd no appetite for the brothels of Narnia and he had no difficulty believing him.

CHAPTER XCIV

NOVEMBER 186 – April 187

Puella tenellulo delicatior haedo Asservanda nigerrimis diligentius uvis.

A girl so tender and delicate must be handled more gently than ripe grapes. Catullus XVII

Lucius and his favourite lingered over their meal, relaxed and happy in each other's company. They lay side by side, toying with wine, fruit and cakes, discussing the day's business. Lucius steered the conversation to a favourite topic.

'I never saw your sister play with dolls. Did she have any?'

'She only ever wanted one - Socrates. She was devoted to him. I think she still takes him to bed. He made her very anxious at one time.'

'Why was that?'

'Well, she watched the slave women's babies and it seemed to her that Socrates wasn't growing or developing as he should. When she'd had him two years, he still couldn't crawl or sit on the pot. She came to our mother and confided that her baby was witless.'

Lucillus chortled at the memory.

'Mother said a person didn't need to be clever to be loveable and loving and Nerissina said she quite saw his slowness wasn't his fault and she ought to love him all the more because of it.'

Lucillus seemed to find this hilarious. Lucius tried to see its humorous side but the laughter died in his throat. He resented Socrates. Lucillus wiped his eyes on his napkin.

'I shouldn't laugh at her. You know I love her dearly. I've met many ladies in Rome but there's not one I rate as highly as my own sister. She's better educated than any society lady and there's a directness about her that pleases me more than archness.'

'When do you think she'll be ready to know a man?'

Lucillus looked up into his patron's eyes. Love and intuition guided him to his mind.

Overawed, he asked, 'Sir, would you make my sister a lady?'

'Would that be a good idea?'

Lucillus grinned. 'Her parents spent the first eight years of her life beating her to make her a good slave. Now they're making a modest, thrifty freedwoman of her. If you want her to be a lady, I think you should say so soon, before she gets confused.'

'What will Demetrius think?'

'He'll be dismayed because he'll think her unworthy of you. I don't. To my mind, she's worthy of the emperor himself.'

'Don't wish that depraved monster on her.'

'I don't. I only meant she'd be a blessing to any man. Still, he'll be pleased not to have to find a dowry for her, he grudges every penny that's not spent on the farm.'

'Why shouldn't she need a dowry?'

'I assume you'll make her your official concubine, sir?'

'I shall not.'

Lucillus flushed.

'I see. Forgive me, My Lord, I thought you intended to dignify her with that status.'

Lucius wound his arms around the stiff shoulders and kissed his favourite on the lips.

'Lucille, your sister will be my wife.'

The boy had something of his natural father's provoking impassivity. If he was stunned, he didn't show it.

'It's as well you won't need Demetrius' blessing for that.'

'Why not?'

'You'd never get it. He couldn't bear you to demean yourself.'

Lucius lay back on his cushions.

'I feel closer than ever to Marcus.' he said. 'His precepts guide me even more than when he was alive. When people questioned his judgement in making Pertinax, a freedman's son, consul, or when he married his eldest daughter to a knight, he used to say, "I choose strictly on merit".'

Lucilla had been a widow of nineteen, Lucius reflected, Pompeianus well into his fifties and it had been a fruitful marriage. The poor girl was dead now though - executed for treason. Her elder statesman husband had been unable to save her - had been lucky to save himself. Lucius felt Lucillus touch his hand. He chased the ghosts from his mind and spoke with decision.

'I'll tell Demetrius I've chosen his daughter on merit. He'll hardly want to quarrel with that.'

The marriage would be disapproved of but it would be legal. He'd never taken senatorial rank because, as a senator, it would have been illegal for him to marry a freedwoman and he'd never stopped hoping that, in some way, Nerysa would become available. Now his caution was rewarded. His people's reports of Nerissina were favourable. The only fault found against her was that she lacked humour. She was earnest and serious, her pleasures were books and learning. Naturally strong-willed, she'd been schooled to patience and submission. Her father had, indeed, amassed a generous dowry for her, genuinely fearing she'd be difficult to place. Who wanted a doctissima to wife? Certainly not the freedman shopkeepers of Narnia.

Lucius rode purposefully to Horta. Fourteen years before, he'd taken Demetrius' son from him. Now he was going to have his daughter.

***

Demetrius was indeed dismayed. But not for the reason Lucillus had predicted. He had a secret he'd intended to take to the grave. Now he would have to reveal it. He cursed his own meddlesome curiosity.

It had always troubled him that, though Lucius could trace his ancestry back more than two hundred years, he, himself, never knew from which loins he'd sprung. Of his mother's family he knew something. He knew, for instance, that he had blood relatives in Athens, although he wouldn't have dreamed of mortifying them by making contact.

While he still supervised Lucius' farm, it was his practice to visit sick workers and make a judgement as to whether they should be moved to the infirmary. The old shepherd wanted to stay in his hut; he knew he was dying and the infirmary had no remedy for age and exhaustion. Demetrius asked him how old he was. The old man smiled.

'Ten years older than your mother would be now, sir, if she'd lived.'

'You remember my mother?'

'Remember her? She's not been out of my thoughts these twenty years.'

Could this man be his father? Feeling as though he were climbing a narrow, springy gangplank swaying over a swirling sea, Demetrius searched the weather-battered face for any familiar feature. His thoughts must have been transparent.

'Oh no! She wasn't for the likes of me. The old master kept her for himself. But, if anyone had spoken of that, he'd have been flogged to death.'

Demetrius pieced together the details of his mother's life. The newly enslaved merchant's daughter had caught her master's eye. Being already betrothed, to a lady of irreproachable virtue, he rusticated her immediately for discretion's sake. She warmed his country bed, sharpened his lust and rehearsed him for his marriage. He'd given her a son and then sent his own son to take her milk and her love. Years later, on a summer visit, he'd noticed her again and rekindled his youth in her embrace.

Demetrius needed to know if Marcus Marius had known him for a son. His ugly look as he pronounced what should have been a death sentence was branded into his mind for ever. Everything fell into place. He knew. That was the reason for his loathing. Demetrius was more puzzled than hurt. How could a man feel no pity for his own child? He considered all he felt, had always felt, for Lucillus, but which it would be unseemly for him to show. He couldn't confide in his wife but he went to their bed for the comfort of her body. Sensing his desolation, although he didn't tell her the reason for it, she held him and consoled him with her touch, so that by morning he could work normally.

Legally, his daughter was Lucius' freedwoman. He demeaned himself to marry her but the marriage would be lawful - just. Biologically, he was her uncle and he'd have to know it. The relationship had no social or legal significance but, as a stockman, Demetrius knew it wasn't good for breeding and, though Lucius was marrying for love, he needed an heir. He couldn't deceive him but he was afraid to tell him, not knowing if he would be angry, incredulous, demeaned or disgusted. Whatever his reaction, it would be hurtful.

Lucius said he wasn't surprised, he thought that, in some part of himself, he'd always known. It was neither seemly nor necessary that anyone else should know. It was their own secret.

The bride's mother was not so easily reconciled, maintaining that her daughter was far too young for marriage, that any girl was too young before sixteen. She warned that children born to very young girls were invariably sickly and hardly ever survived and that a girl taken too young felt resentment towards her husband and made him an unloving wife.

'Your wedding night wasn't happy for you, was it Nerysa?'

She looked down not daring to answer. She couldn't be so disloyal to Demetrius.

'God's thunder, what a fool I was! It should have been me.'

'If you still think that, Lepide, should you marry my daughter?'

'I'm allowed to regret my past because my present and my future reconcile me to it.'

'She loves you desperately and she's so vulnerable.'

'She's safe with me. And I lie in the palm of her hand.'

'You won't consummate the marriage before she's sixteen?'

'Haven't I given my word?' He smiled indulgently, 'Are you going to be an interfering mother-in-law, Nerysa?'

'I hope not, though you couldn't have one who cares more about your happiness.'

'She'll have her own rooms where she can live four years in maiden bliss.'

She recoiled, 'Lepide, not that room with those paintings!'

'Of course not. I'll have it repainted. She can have portraits of Plato and Aristotle and the great seven.'

'Or maybe flowers and birds?'

'The groves of Academe! I shall design it myself.'

In general, the bride's parents were baffled and apprehensive rather than smug, especially Demetrius, who'd expected to have to pay over the odds to palm off his beloved bookworm onto some reluctant freedman. They tried to help each other understand. Demetrius mused, 'He says he chose her for her intelligence. I thought that odd at first but then it struck me that that's why I chose you.'

'You chose me for my defiance. It was a novelty.'

'No, it was the first moment I saw you, before you snubbed me. I knew straight away you were different. I didn't want to enjoy you for a day or a year. I wanted to lock you up and keep you to myself for ever.'

'Then Lucius must have hurt you very much.'

'If it had been anyone else...and yet I loved him too and he wanted you in the same way I did. When I saw you meant to deprive him I couldn't help but grieve for him. To be thwarted of his dearest wish - nothing in his life had prepared him for that. It would have been easier by far for me, though painful enough. There was a time when I thought we could share you and be happy all three together.'

'You can't have considered my feelings.'

'But I did. He had so much to offer you.'

'Is that what you thought would make me happy? To be garlanded like a sacrificial ox and carted round the town to visit silly socialites?'

'No, but he didn't need your unquestioning obedience. He'd have given you the dignity of freedom and love without harshness. We must make our daughter understand how fortunate she is.'

Nerysa did think of her own wedding night and couldn't contemplate such an experience for her daughter. Nerissina herself had no fear of Lucius. She couldn't wait to rush headlong into marriage, the implications of which she couldn't suspect. Nerysa trembled for her. She was bright and over-educated but not mature. All might be well if she stayed that way and Lucius forever enchanted with his child bride. But Nerissina would grow into a formidable woman. Her arguments were forceful already.

'Lucius can talk with me all day and never tell me anything I already know. And there's so much more to him than learning. He's elegant and urbane. He's travelled the world and has experience and wisdom that I'll never have.'

'Yes, but marriage is more than a philosophical discussion. There's another side to it that you're too young to understand or desire.'

'Mother, I know that. It's everywhere; chickens and rams and houseboys.'

'What of your father and I?'

'I shouldn't care to be like you and father - more like friends or partners. Your dealings are too...too equal. I can never be Lucius' equal. He's a god to me.'

'Your father is like a god to me.'

'Then he's a god who worships his own priestess!'

'What can you mean?'

'He watches you all the time. He never makes a decision without you.'

'Yes, he's considerate but he always does as he thinks right nevertheless. Have you thought that, when you're my age, Lucius will be sixty. He'll be an old man.'

'And how old is Jove?'

'Jove is immortal.'

'He has a grey beard and immense wisdom, and so will Lucius.'

Nerysa declined to mention that Jove was a byword for infidelity. The idealism of youth was like dawn dew on the orchard. No need to busy oneself to dispel it. It would vanish soon enough in the heat of the day.

'Had you thought any more about being a Christian?'

'It's not for me. Socrates wasn't a Christian, nor was Aristotle. Epictetus could have been if he'd thought it right. They understood as much as a man can about the meaning of life and how it should be lived.'

'But don't the Lord's teachings embrace theirs and crown them with a spirituality, a more certain, more joyful hope?'

'No, your Galilean's sayings seem homespun compared to their arguments.'

Nerysa put her arms around her little girl.

'Do you know that you're young and small? Do you know that a husband must break your body to enter it?'

She gazed down in horror at her daughter's exultant face.

'Mother, how long must I wait?'

Lucius came on the first day of the Floralia, bringing a gold ring fashioned as clasped hands, promising marriage. He pushed it onto her tiny, eager finger and thought his breast would rupture with tenderness and joy.

CHAPTER XCV

May 187

Cras amet qui nunquam amavit. Quiquam amavit cras amet.

May those who've not yet loved, love tomorrow. And those who've always loved, still love tomorrow. Pervigilium Veneris

Lucius was pressing for his marriage to be celebrated in June.

'There's no need to cram her with knowledge for a lifetime.' he pointed out, 'She won't stop learning just because she's married. As to the running of my own house, it might, perhaps, be thought that I could teach her that myself.'

That was almost too preposterous to be amusing. He hadn't the remotest idea of the running of his house. The mechanics of it would only have impinged on his consciousness if they'd been at fault and he had two hundred slaves whose business it was to see that they weren't.

Her parents worked with renewed fervour to prepare Nerissina to please him. She had so much to learn in so little time. It was his wish that, young as she was, she would be absolute mistress of his house and that everyone should recognise her as such. Painstakingly, they taught her the geography of the domus and the duties of everyone who served there, what shortcomings to look for in everyone and how to point them out so as to secure better service without provoking resentment. If her husband's linen was not immaculate or his favourite food didn't appear on the menu, the fault might well lie with someone else but the responsibility would be hers. When attending or hosting dinner parties with him she shouldn't voice her opinion but listen and concentrate on remembering people's names and faces so she wouldn't disgrace herself by not knowing them or saying something inappropriate when she next met them. Of course, the nomenclator was supposed to help her with that but to rely on slaves was to put yourself in their power. No one understood that better than Demetrius.

She studied Lucius' family tree in all its ramifications. She visited his villa, gazed at the busts of his ancestors and reflected that a child of her body must be the worthy successor to so many great men. She was sobered. This wasn't the life Lucius had proposed to her. He hadn't said she would be a supernumerary housekeeper, overseer of slaves and hostess. He'd only hinted vaguely that their existence would be suspended in a time warp of mutual adoration.

She learned about his hectic daily schedule; rise at dawn, receive clients and freedmen, morning and sometimes afternoon in the law courts, business meetings, consulting with Successus, Thaïs and Jacob on domestic and commercial matters, teaching students, giving legal advice to anyone who called to ask, visiting and receiving friends. She wondered if she'd ever see him at all.

Her parents laid stress on modesty. Lucius would appoint women to attend her. She must make sure they were never out of her company, except when he himself was with her. Only then, could her reputation be safe. As the great day approached, her eagerness drained away. Thoroughly apprised of her unworthiness, terrified of failure and gripped by mounting panic, she made a decision.

Nerysa heard a wail go up from the women's quarters and hurried to the staircase where she met Charis running down looking pale and shocked.

'Oh, mistress, the young mistress won't marry His Excellency after all!'

Nerysa grabbed the stair rail to steady herself not knowing if she was horrified or relieved.

'We must comfort her. She loves him so. But she's young. She'll recover. It was too great an honour to hope for, perhaps.'

'No, mistress, it's not him, it's her. She says she refuses to marry him.'

'But she can't! She can't insult him and hurt him so.'

Demetrius threatened dire punishments that would descend on her and her whole family. That she could contemplate such an affront to her patron showed that she'd no gratitude, no sense of duty, no piety whatever. She stood wild eyed and shuddering as the women shrieked and tore their hair over her trousseau, her mother pleaded and her father ranted. But she would not change her mind.

Into the pandemonium came Lucius; Lucius boyish and clean shaven, intoxicated with happiness. Undeterred by his host's unease and evasiveness, he strode across the atrium and up the stairs after his vanishing betrothed. Slaves wrung their hands under his nose, the boldest looked up at him beseechingly as he passed, some even looked as though they would have spoken had they dared. Maids stood stolidly across the threshold of her bedchamber barring his way until he waved his hand in dismissal and they fled.

Nerissina, pale and steely eyed, stood her ground as he crossed the room, took the hand that wore his ring and lifted it to his lips. Then her body fell limp against his, her hands clutched at his robe and she sobbed. He lifted her in his arms like a baby and walked up and down the room pressing her to him, absorbing the force of her grief. When she seemed calmer he sat on the bed and held her on his lap. Her feet didn't reach the ground yet he barely felt the weight of her. In sudden terror, he whispered, 'Are you ill, beloved?'

She shook her head, pressing it harder into his chest.

'Unhappy, then?' No response. 'Dearest pupil, I fear you're not being philosophical. Have you forgotten how Socrates faced prison and hemlock?'

She squirmed in his lap and turned to look at him, a look more fearful than vexed. He cast around in his mind. *What made little girls cry?* The room seemed bare to him, he saw no doll, no toys, only the bed and a bench where the maids had left untidy piles of linen.

'Do your parents constrain you in some matter?' he probed, 'Do they seem harsh to you?' Silence. *Those doltish schoolmasters again?* 'Gisco? Macrinus?' No response. 'Are your slaves neglectful? No? Then it must be that you want something you can't have – something important, since it's disturbed your peace of mind. Will you tell me what it is?'

The shake of the head was obdurate.

He said gently, 'Then I can only advise you in general terms.'

He stroked a strand of hair from her wet cheek and tucked it behind her ear, murmuring,

'Oh, my bright thinker, why did you study philosophy? Was it so you should lose your nerve at the first test of strength? These trials of daily life are like school exercises. Don't we make use of them as a gladiator uses his sparring partner? How can you progress in virtue if the gods send you nothing to bear? Whatever the trouble, let's bring up our reinforcements against it, the arguments we polished like steel. What do we philosophers say is the only real cause of pain?'

'Wanting something you can't have.'

She didn't speak with the zeal of a convert, more as a sullen schoolboy repeats his lesson.

'That's right! God has showered you with blessings but the best of them is your ability to judge between them. After all, what are jewels compared with yourself, you who are a spark of the divine fire? What clothes compare with that inner tunic, the sweet flesh that houses your spirit?'

She was achingly close. He bent and caught the scent of her baby skin. His voice came thick.

'All these things; clothes, jewels, pretty slaves, you can have them all. Everything in my power to give you, you can have. But I wish I could teach you not to pine for them. The day may come when I can't buy your every desire, any more than I can guarantee your health or my own or our children's health or the emperor's favour. These are beyond our control. They are none of our business. What is our business?'

'Virtue.'

'Of course, because that's all that matters and it's completely within our own control. Zeus has given your shining spirit into your own care to keep safe and pure. Now do you really think you are less worthy for the want of a bauble, or any less honest or rational because there are no gold threads in your dress? Sweet soul, what sort of teacher have I been that you hanker after fripperies like a woman, not like a philosopher? We don't study philosophy so we can change our fate. What is the only thing we can change?'

'Our attitude.'

'Exactly. And you've been learning how to keep your will in harmony with whatever god sends. So, if you take god as your sovereign and align your wishes with his, how can anything dismay you, since everything that happens to you is in accordance with his will? And how could you fail?'

She looked straight at him, her eyes enormous and inscrutable. He didn't think his words had moved her but it seemed to be himself that fascinated her. And, at last, she said wonderingly, 'I think with you – *for* you, I *could* be perfect.'

'Of course,' he said, patting her thigh, 'because you already are.'

CHAPTER XCVI

May 187

Domus et placens uxor

A home and an amiable wife. Horace. Odes II iv

On the feast of his patroness in May, Demetrius stood before his household as their priest, a fold of his toga drawn over his head in the ancient manner. He'd set up an altar on a hillock and he'd spared a perfect, white sow for sacrifice. She rootled placidly around the altar, garland awry, ears twitching towards the music and the shouts of the children.

The crowd, bathed, anointed and dressed in white robes, stood with their heads reverently bowed. As he gave the ritual command, 'Favete linguis', his eyes rested for an instant on each person. A gratifying number of the women appeared to be pregnant. He saw them all; those born and bred on his land, the city servants, his Spanish cook, Charis from Lesbos, Hannah with parents from the Levant, the African schoolmasters, the blond Gauls who towered over everyone, two houseboys he'd bought in Britain and Corin, whose music had led the procession.

A few were still shackled because, to his disappointment, they'd not yet convinced him they were fit to release. He was especially tender of them. Their helplessness left them vulnerable to oppression and he'd not forgotten how it felt to be so filthy, ragged and broken by toil and abuse that one's essential humanity was barely apparent to oneself, let alone to anyone else. All these disparate souls must be welded together into the familia of Lucius Marius Demetrius. On this day, sacred to his patroness, he'd given orders that no work need be done except essential care of the animals, so that his whole family could feast together.

He reviewed his life from the moment he learned he was a slave and made it his ambition to be free. Now the slaves under his care were his own and so was the land they tilled. His children were provided for. He didn't aspire to the civic honours Pertinax had proposed and could safely be relied on to forget. All that mattered was to make his farm flourish. He belonged to it as much as it to him, who'd been born into slavery a stone's throw from it.

His domain extended beyond the dim blue of the distant hills. He saw them scarred by ravines, stone bridges spanning winding streams and the naked chalk of ancient caves. He saw smaller, faint patches of white that could have been spray from distant waterfalls or the backs of his fat sheep. They were too far away for him to tell. Poplars projected like dark towers from the wooded slopes, which gave way to the dappled lime of his hazel coppice and the rippling of the reed beds bordering his lake.

Below him in the valley lay his lush meadows, bright with asphodel and the ploughed fields shooting green. The rising land was dimpled with knolls of beech and ilex and dissected by the glint of ditches and ruined Etruscan watercourses; square-cut stones knit with saxifrage and bell flowers. To his left was the verdant anarchy of the old vine and to his right, the green and silver chequerboard of his olive grove and the stippled rose and white of his orchard. Soft, golden light played on the orchard wall, on the ordered docility of his garden and the mellow stones of his house.

He looked across at his wife, taken from a world away, still dazed by the paradox that made her presence in his house and his heart seem natural and right. He would make a haven for her; each year an increment more comfortable, more elegant, more secure. He would harness the force of nature to the soil's fertility and wrest a living from them. At forty, he was at the height of his powers, secure in her loyalty and affection. With the gods' blessing, there was nothing he couldn't achieve. Stretching out his hands, palms upwards, he prayed, 'Gracious goddess, I pray and beseech you to be willing to accept this sacrifice and look with favour on me, my household and my slaves. I pray you to purify our land, our houses and ourselves and to protect us, our animals and crops, from disease, unrest and harm. Give health and vigour to me and to all of us. Unite us as one family, so that all may benefit from the care and diligence of each, and so we may serve you in piety, plenty and peace. To this end, great goddess, I pray you, bless my sacrifice.'

He scattered the grains on the sow's head and gave the order. Commatus led the sow forward until her head was poised over the pail. As Demetrius lifted his arm, the shadow of the knife flashed across the bright water. The sow raised her head in alarm so it seemed to the congregation that she offered her neck to the knife. Commatus stunned her with a single blow. Demetrius opened her throat, caught the gushing blood in his silver bowl and poured it on the altar. The flames leapt clear and bright, and his prayer soared heavenwards.

CAST LIST

(historical figures in italics)

Achilles slave of Lucius. Body guard.

Acte slave of Lucius. Assistant cook.

Adrian slave of Lucius. Chief secretary in business office.

Aglae slave of Lucius. Atriensis (receptionist).

Amemone slave of Lucius. Land girl on Lucius' estates at Horta.

Annia Aurelia Fulvia relative of Marcus Aurelius, wife of Lucius.

Antistius (Titus Aius) Latin teacher of Commodus.

Apicius slave of Lucius. chief cook at Lucius' town house in Rome.

Archias (Marcus Marius Archias) freedman of Lucius' father. A doctor.

Arecomus slave of Demetrius at Horta; vine dresser. Consort of Perpenna, brother of Commatus.

Argos slave of Lucius, deputy head cook at the villa at Horta.

Arminia Slave of Lucius. Prefect of the back kitchen.

Aura slave of Lucius. Scullery maid.

Bibulus (Marcus Marius) Freedman of Lucius' father and client of Lucius.

Boletus slave of Lucius. Vegetable cook at the town house.

Bulbus slave of Lucius. Vegetable cook at the town house.

Carbo slave of Lucius. Thermidospor (Barbecue specialist).

Cassius (*Gaius Avidius*) Governor of Syria. Proclaimed himself emperor in 175. Thought by some to have been the lover of the empress Faustina.

Cato (*Marcus Porcius* the younger) Gave his wife to his friend, Hortensius, in marriage and remarried her when Hortensius died.

Charis slave of Lucius, atriensis (receptionist) and later slave of Nerysa. Later freedwoman of Nerysa. Mother of Gaius Marius Andreus.

Charisius slave of Lucius. Librarian.

Cheimone slave of Lucius. Scullery maid afterwards wife of a freedman of Lucius

Chione slave of Lucius. Scullery maid.

Cineas slave of Lucius. Thermidospor (Barbecue specialist).

Commatillus slave of Demetrius. Son of Commatus. qv.

Commatus slave vilicus (farm manager) to Demetrius.

Commodus (*Lucius Aurelius*). Roman emperor. Son of Marcus Aurelius qv.

Condianus (*Sextus Quintilius* the younger) condemmed by Commodus.

Corin slave of Demetrius. Flautist.

Crispina (*Bruttia Crispina*) empress.Wife of Commodus. Exiled then executed for adultery

Cynthia slave of Lucius semstress and infirmarian.

Cyrus slave of Lucius. Cubicularius Valet

Darius slave of Lucius. Cubicularius. Valet.

Demetrius slave, later freedman of Lucius. Steward. Husband of Nerysa qv.

Dion slave of Lucius. personal servant.

Epictetus Greek Philosopher. Ex-slave. Had a permanent limp as a result of his master's violence.

Epicurus slave of Lucius and later of Demetrius. Meat cook specialising in overelaborate dishes.

Erinna slave of Lucius. Niece of Thaïs.

Erotion slave of Lucius. Launderess. Consort of Apicius.

Eumaus slave of Demetrius. Swine herd.

Faustina Empress, wife of Marcus Aurelius, daughter of the emperor Antoninus Pius.

Faustinianus (*Calvisius*) son of Statianus Governor of Egypt. Exiled for treason in 175.

Filix slave of Lucius and later of Nerysa. Identical twin of Flora. Daughter of Apicius.

Flora slave of Lucius and later of Nerysa. Identical twin of Filix. Daughter of Apicius.

Fronto (*Marcus Cornelius*) orator. Teacher of Marcus Aurelius. Friend of Statianus and Faustinianus. Consul 143.

Gaius (Julius) Caesar Roman general and dictator. Led an expediton to Britain. Murdered 44BC

Gaius Marius Andreus freeborn son of Charis.

Galen celebrated doctor. His writings influenced western medicine until the 19ᵗʰ century.

Georgius slave of Lucius. Vilicus (Farm manager) at Horta. Consort of Italia.

Geta (*Publius Septimius*) brother of **Severus** qv. Governor of Moesia Inferior (Modern Romania.)

Gisco slave of Lucius. Teacher of mathematics.

Gluco slave of Lucius. Pastry cook at the town house.

Hadrianus of Tyre Professor of rhetoric at Rome.

Hannah slave of Lucius and later of Nerysa. Daughter of Thaïs and Jacob.

Hermes slaves of Lucius. Messengers. Six all called by the same name and numbered.

Herodes Atticus Greek orator and philanthropist. Teacher of Marcus Aurelius. He lost his temper with his wife, who was a wealthy heiress and he ordered his freedman to beat her. She died of the beating which caused a scandal.

Idumeus underslave of Demetrius at the town house.

Iris slave of Lucius. Scullery maid. Afterwards slave of Nerysa at Horta.

Italia slave of Lucius. Vilica (farm housekeeper) at Horta consort of Georgius.

Jacob slave of Lucius. Accoutant at the shipping office in Ostia.

Julianus (*Publius Salvius*) Army commander. Plotted to overthrow Commodus and become emperor. Executed 182.

Linus slave of Lucius. sauce chef at the town house.

Lucian Greek satirical writer.

Lucilla eldest surviving daughter of Marcus Aurelius, married firstly to Lucius Verus qv. and afterwards to Claudius Pompeianus qv. Exiled and later executed for plotting to murder her brother, the emperor Commodus qv.

Lucillus Marius Sciens freedman of Lucius and presumed to be his natural son. Son of Nerysa and Demetrius.

Lucius Marius Lepidus. Roman knight and jurist.

Lucullus slave of Lucius. Meat cook at the town house.

Macrinus slave of Lucius. Grammaticus (Teacher of language and literature).

Maecianus (*Lucius Volusius*) Jurist.

Marcus Aurelius Antoninus Roman emperor and philosopher. His published writings include the Meditations.

Martius Verus (Publius) consul 179 governor of Cappadocia (modern Turkey).

Maternus brigand and leader of a slave rebellion.

Matugena slave of Demetrius. Vilica (farm housekeeper) at Horta, consort of Commatus and mother of Commatillus.

Melissus slave of Lucius. Scribe in the business office. Natural son of his master and sold on after his master's death.

Musonius Rufus philosopher from Bolsena.

Nerysa princess of the Ordovicii. Guest and client of Quintus. Slave and later freedwoman of Lucius. Underslave and later wife of Demetrius.

Nerissina slave and later freedwoman of Lucius. Daughter of Nerysa and Demetrius.

Nephele slave of Lucius. Scullery maid.

Olympia slave of Lucius. Seamstress and infirmarian.

Paternus (*Publius Taruttienus*) prefect of Praetorian Guard murdered by Commodus.

Patroclus slave of Lucius. Body guard.

Perpenna daughter of a tenant of Demetrius. Sold into slavery by her father. Consort of Arecomus.

Perennis (*Sextus Tigidius*) prefect of Praetorian Guard, sole prefect and virtual ruler of the empire from 182 until executed by Commodus in 185.

Pertinax (*Publius Helvius*) Son of a freedman. Rose to be consul.

Petosiris slave of Lucius. Nomenclator. Master of ceremonies

Phago slave of Lucius. Sausage cook.

Philemon slave of Lucius. Demetrius' secretary.

Philodespotes slave of Lucius. Pet and later meat cooks' assistant.

Phoebe visiting hairdresser.

Polybius underslave of Demetrius. Valet and barber.

Pompeianus (*Titus Claudius*) Roman knight.. Son in law of Marcus Aurelius (married to his eldest daughter Lucilla qv.) General. Consul in 173. Patron of Septimius Severus qv.

Priscus legionary legate in Britain.

Publius Cornelius Surdus neighbour of Lucius in Rome.

Quadratus (*Marcus Umidius)* stepson of the empress Lucilla.

Quintinianus (*Claudius*) Lucilla's son in law, lover and nephew of her husband.

Quintilii brothers (Sextus Quintilius Maximus and Sextus Quintilian Condianus) consuls in the same year in 151.

Quintus Fabius Pulcher Roman patrician and poet. Host and patron of Nerysa.

Rhea slave of Lucius. Cook.

Roxana slave of Lucius and, at one time, his mistress.

Saoterus chamberlain and favourite of the emperor Commodus.

Servius Junius Blandus landowner, neighbour of Lucius at Horta.

Severus (*Lucius Septimius*) senator and jurist. Later governor of Gaul.

Sextus Perpennus slave of Demetrius at Horta. Brother of Perpenna. Sold into slavery by his father. Herdsman and veterinary.

Sikon slave of Lucius. Sauce assistant at the town house.

Simo (Quintus Fabius) freedman steward of Quintus Pulcher.

Statianus (*Calvisius*) Roman knight, Governor of Egypt.

Stephanos Christian. Friend of Tomothy qv.

Stimula slave of Lucius. Server in the dining room.

Suavo slave of Lucius. Pastry cook.

Successus slave of Lucius. Deputy steward. Christian priest.

Stentor slave of Demetrius. Former ploughman.

Talos slave of Lucius. Carpenter.

Thaïs slave of Lucius. Housekeeper at the town house. Consort of Jacob qv, and mother of Hannah qv.

Thya slave of Lucius. Cook's assistant at the town house.

Timothy (Marcus Marius) freedman of Lucius' father. Christian priest.

Uxinia slave of Lucius. Bought at auction in Athens.

Verus (*Lucius Aelius Verus*) adopted son of the emperoro Antoninus Pius and adopted brother of Marcus Aurelius, with whom he ruled jointly, until his death in 169.

Vibia Sabina. youngest daughter of Marcus Aurelius.

Vulcan slave of Lucius. Boilerman at the town house.

Xenia slave of Lucius. Nurse to Lucius' father and later nursery worker.

Zoe slave of Lucius' father. Mother of Demetrius and wet nurse of Lucius.

AGE OF GOLD GLOSSARY

Ab epistulis head of the secretariat.

As low value coin.

Aesclepius god of medicine.

Alexandria first city of Roman Egypt.

Anteambulares slaves and others who walked in front of an important man to clear his path.

Antinous lover of the emperor Hadrian. Drowned in the Nile. Many statues commemorated him.

Antipho character in Terence's play *The Eunuch*.

Aphrodite/Venus goddess of love and sex.

Apicius at least two writers of cookery books bore this name.

Aquileia a town in north Italy at the head of the Adriatic.

Archimagirus head chef.

Argus a legendary figure with a hundred eyes, of which only two slept at any one time.

Athens a city state in Greece later part of the Roman empire.

Atlantes pillars supporting a building carved as figures of young men.

Atriensis a receptionist in the atrium.

Atrium main reception hall of a Roman house.

Baiae (modern Baia) a seaside resort near Naples famed for licentiousness.

Basilica Julia large public building in Rome which housed, among other things, the civil law courts.

Brundisium modern Brindisi a port in southeast Italy.

Cappadocia Roman province roughly the area of modern Turkey.

Carnuntum Roman military base near modern Vienna.

Centumviral court chancery court of Rome.

China called Seres by the Romans. Marcus Aurelius was the first Roman emperor to send a trade mission to China in 166.

Client a dependent who looked for protection from a more powerful man who was his patron. In exchange he provided services such as escorting and political support. The relationship often continued from generation to generation in families and a freedman usually became the client of his former master.

Columbarium monument equipped with rows of niches to hold funerary urns.

Concubine a woman in a recognised legal relationship with a man who does not marry her because she is of lower social status. It was not possible to keep a wife and a concubine at the same time but the children of the union were not considered legitimate.

Consul in republican times joint ruler of Rome (there were usually two at any one time) During the empire it had less of an executive role but was the highest honour.

Cuba goddess responsible for keeping children peaceful in their cots.

Cubicularius chamberlain.

Cybele Eastern goddess whose priests were castrated.

Demeter Goddess of agriculture. Known to Romans as Ceres, hence our word cereal.

Diptych two writing tablets joined together.

Domiduca goddess responsible for seeing children safely home from their travels.

Domus town house.

Donative a hand out to get people to do or support something.

Dowry a woman's portion given in trust to her husband who was supposed to grow it during the course of the marriage and hand it back if the marriage was dissolved.

Eleusis a town near Athens famous for its Mysteries; a religious festival in honour of the goddess Demeter.

Equestrian Roman knight.

Emancipation release form paternal power. A Roman father had power over his sons and control over their money until his death. He could release them from his power by emancipation.

Ergastulum rural underground prison where chained slaves were kept.

Euclid Greek mathematician known as the father of geometry.

Exposure the practice of leaving unwanted infants in certain open places in the city so they would starve or be collected by persons wanting babes (usually slave dealers).

Falernian highly prized superior wine which aged well.

Familia everyone living in the house of a Roman citizen; not just his wife, unmarried daughters and sons and daughters in law but also slaves and freedmen.

Floralia flower festival in honour of the goddess Flora.

Freedman/woman someone who has been a slave and has been set free by due legal process.

Fugitive a slave who absconds.

Genius the guardian soul or spirit of a Roman man. The female equivalent was a Juno.

Grammaticus teacher of language and literature.

Groves of Academe A grove outside Athens where Plato used to teach.

Hadrian was Roman emperor from 117 to 138.

Harpastum game played with a small hard ball.

Haruspices persons trained to practise divination from the entrails of ritually slaughtered animals and birds.

Hercules Greek demigod famous for superhuman strength.

Horta (modern Orte) a river port on the Tiber about forty miles from Rome.

Hymen god of marriage.

Hymettus mountain near Athens famous for honey produced there.

Hyperborean mythical people who lived 'beyond the north wind'.

Hypnos god of sleep.

Ides the 15th of March, May, July and October and the 13th of the other months.

Impluvium a pool in the centre of the atrium which collected rainwater entering through an opening in the ceiling.

Insula a block of flats.

Isis Egyptian goddess whose priests shaved their heads.

Juno wife of Zeus/Jove. Also the guardian soul or spirit of a Roman woman.

Kos a Greek island famous for silk markets.

Lares domestic gods of the hearth of a Roman home.

Laser a culinary herb. The original (silphium) came from Cyrene and had been harvested to extinction in the second century BC. Thereafter, inferior 'Persian laser' was used.

Leptis (Magna) town in North Africa birthplace of Septimius Severus qv.

Lucina goddess presiding over childbirth.

Manumission act of freeing a slave.

Matronalia celebration to honour mothers when it was usual for mistresses to offer food to their female slaves.

Mausoleum of Augustus family tomb of the emperor Augustus.

Mediastina low grade of household slave.

Minerva goddess of wisdom equivalent of Greek Athena.

Mercury/Hermes messenger god. Patron of commerce.

Messina a city in Sicily.

Mona Roman name for Anglesey.

Narnia (modern Narni) a town in Umbria.

Neptune god of the sea.

Nomenclator usher in a Roman house who announced guests.

Nymphaeum a fountain adorned with statues.

Ordinarii high grade of household slave.

Ostia port of Rome.

Palatine the most exclusive and up-market hill of the seven on which Rome was built. It is the origin of our word *palace.*

Parthenon temple in Athens dedicated to Athena.

Patron either a man who had obligations to protect a less powerful man or the ex master of a freedman.

Parthian Persian.

Pedagogue a slave who accompanied a child to school to see he wasn't molested on the way.

Penates domestic gods of a Roman house who protected the food supply.

Persephone daughter of Demeter. She was stolen by the god of the underworld. The distraught Demeter sought her everywhere and a compromise was reached; she could return to earth for six months of each year (spring and summer).

Peristyle garden of a Roman house usually bordered by a colonnade.

Piraeus port of Athens.

Praetor a judge.

Praxitiles Athenian sculptor of fourth century BC.

Priapus god with a large phallus who protected houses and gardens from thieves.

Primary school children of all social classes could go to school, both sexes together up to the age of ten.

Procurator someone who runs a household, a business or a province.

Pygmalion legendary sculpter whose statue of a young woman was miraculously brought to life by the gods.

Quirinal one of the seven hills on which Rome was built.

Rhegium modern Reggio di Calabria; Italian city facing Messina across the straits between Italy and Sicily.

Romulus legendary founder of Rome.

Rubicon a river outside Rome. By crossing it, Julius Caesar committed himself to civil war.

Saepta exclusive shopping street in Rome.

Sanctuary an altar to a god or a statue of the emperor. A fugitive who clung to it was protected from summary justice.

Saturnalia festival in December.

Senator highest ranking Roman aristocrat.

Sestertius a coin worth four as.

Silentarii slaves kept in large households to keep other slaves quiet.

Sirmium modern Sremska Mitrovika thirty miles west of Belgrade.

Styx river between this world and the underworld.

Suburra red light district of Rome.

Sisyphean a task as fruitless of that of Sisyphus who was condemned to roll a huge boulder up a hill only to have it roll down when it neared the top.

Tablinum a private room off the atrium sometimes created by screens which could be folded back to merge it with the atrium.

Tepidarium the warm room of a Roman bathhouse.

Tivoli town near Rome where Hadrian and many other notables had villas.

Tribune of the plebs in the republic, the representative of the common people. During the empire, an honorary role.

Triclinium dining room, so called because it was normally furnished with three couches.

Triumph a victory parade.

Triumphator the general granted permission to hold a victory parade.

Tutor not a teacher but a man responsible for the care of a child, usually teamed up with a nurse.

Twelve tablets original Roman law code from the fifth century BC.

Tyana town in Cappadocia (modern Turkey).

Tyroism a form of shorthand developed by Cicero's slave secretary, Tiro.

Verna a slave born in the house as opposed to one that has been acquired

Via Appia main road from Rome to Brindisi.

Via Aurelia main road from Rome to Pisa and Aquileia.

Via Flaminia main road from Rome to Ancona.

Villa Roman country estate. **Villa urbana**; the master's house, the **villa rustica**; the slave and animal quarters, **Villa Fructuaria** storehouses.

Vulcan god of fire and metal working.

Zeus/Jove/Jupiter chief god.

THE URBAN FAMILIA OF LUCIUS MARIUS LEPIDUS

DECURIA 1

Secretariat

Adrian dispensor (head of secretariat)

Philemon ab epistolis (secretary)

Calamus ab epistolis (secretary)

Accuratus pariator (accountant)

Cito notarius (stenographer)

Thriambius scribus (copier)

Melissus scribus (copier)

Columbus tabellarius (courier)

Hirundu tabellarius (courier)

Irus tabellarius (courier)

DECURIA 11

Library

Charisius curator (chief librarian)

Levius a bibliotheca (assisatant libarian)

Nicolaus a studiis (curator of text books)

Sosia (glutinator) bookbinder

Argutus lector (reader)

Chrysostom lector (reader)

Tiro ab epistolis (seretary)

Tachos scribus (copier)

Aquilus scribus (copier)

Apellicon (archivist)

Chairos (letter carrier)

Trexo (letter carrier)

DECURIA 111

Reception staff

Petosiris nomenclator (announcer)

DECURIA 1V

Banqueting staff

Dionysius cellarius (butler)

Xenius (chief hospitaler)
**Aglae, Cypris, Lydia,
    Hermione, Larissa,
Felicitas, Elissa, Ariadne, Ida,
    Delia.**
atrienses (reception staff)
Priscus a statuis
(keeper of gods and imagines)
Maturus buccinator (keeper of
    water clock) and to announce
    the time

Philodepotes pocilator (cup
    bearer)
Ganymede pocilator (cup bearer)
Calamis scissor (carver)
Serenus scissor (carver)
Iucundus ministrator (waiter)
Comus ministrator (waiter)
Phrates ministrator (waiter)
Carus structor (table layer)
Triambius structor (table layer)
Hebe ministrator (waitress)
Io ministrator (waitress)
Hilarus ministrator (waiter)

DECURIA V

Dining room staff
Felix Triclinarchus (maitre d)
Hesperus lamplighter
Hespera lamplighter
Amadogus table polisher
Mys silver polisher
Lua glass polisher
Pyrrha florist
Anthea florist
Sybaris, Corinna, Chloe
    lectisterniatores
(attendants to wash hands and
    remove shoes of guests)

DECURI VI

Master's bedroom staff
Cyrus cubicularius (valet)
Papias cubicularius (assistant
    valet)
Syloson cosmeta (wardrobe
    master)
Phratus plicator (toga folder)
Licinus tonsor (barber)
Cinnamus cincitor (barber's
    assistant)
Formosus ciniflo (hairdresser)
Ion ciniflo (hairdresser)
Fidus Sardonyx (jewel keeper)
Nardus unctor (masseur)
Myrina unctor (masseuse)
Favorinus, Cyrus capsarii (bath
    attendants)

DECURIA VII

Vicarii (underslaves)
Polybius for Demetrius
Philemon for Demetrius
Darius for Demetrius
Niobe for Thaïs
Lycozius for Successus
Patro for Charisius
Sinhoë for Petosiris
Sinnaces for Felix
Idumeus for Adrian

DECURIA IX

Litter-bearers – lectarii
Atlas
Dion
Mysius
Antigonus
Calius
Calpas
Bryazorius
Pausias
Ajax
Disciplinarians – silentarii
Chilon
Tacitus

DECURIA XI

Kitchens (bread and pastry)
Apicius Archimagirus head chef
Juda pistor (baker)

DECURIA VIII

Escorts and porters
Hypnos ostiarius (door keeper)
Leon lanternarius (lantern bearer)
Hermes 1-6 nuntii (messengers)
Achaeus pedesequus (attendant)
Agathan pedesequus (attendant)
Andreas and **Cleon** antambulares
  (walk in front of master)
Chelidonion and **Eros**
  salutigeruli (errand boys)

DECURIA X

Guards - custodii
Achilles
Patroclus
Alexander
Mimus
Jason
Hunnius
Noricus
Hierax

DECURIA XII

Kitchens (meat and fish)
Epicurus coquus (meat cook)
Sikon condimentarius (sauce
  maker)

Josephus pistor (baker)
Otys pistor (baker)
Strymo pistor (baker)
Callistus (dulciarius sweetmaker)
Gluco dulciarius (pastry cook)
Suavo dulciarius (pastry cook)
Alcimus dulciarius (pastry cook)

Linus condimentarius (sauce maker)
Lucullus coquus (meat cook)
Fumosus botularius (sauasage smoker)
Hillarus botularius (sausage smoker)
Carbo thermidospor barbecuer
Cineas thermidospor barbecuer
Phago botularius (sausage maker)
Sudor boy to turn the spit
Torris boy to turn the spit
Psychrus fish cook

DECURIA XIII

(Vegetables and fruit)
Bulbo coquus (cook)
Boletus coquus
Lotus coquus
Satrus coquus
Scempsia coquua
Thya coquua
Acte coquua
Rhea coquua
Pomona coquua
Citron coquus

DECURIA XIV

Scullery (culina)
Arminia praefecta supervisor
Cheimone ancilla (maid)
Chiona ancilla (maid)
Iris ancilla (maid)
Aura ancilla (maid)
Nephele ancilla (maid)
Nerysa ancilla (maid)

DECURIA XV

Laundry
Erotion curator (supervisor)
Candidus
Helvetius
Cogamus
Flora

DECURIA XVI

Linen room
Stimula praefecta (supervisor)
Syrinx
Damalis
Dorcas
Crino

Dathus
Simo
Avius
Blandina
Filix

Felicitas
Sidonia plicator (cloth folder)
Sipte plicator (cloth folder)
Olympia sutrix & a valetudinaria (seamstress and infirmarian)
Cynthia sutrix & a valetudinaria (seamstress and infirmarian)-

DECURIA XVII

Cleaning staff
Margiatilla
Carina
Ida
Philotis
Rigdulla
Doris
Lanice
Logamus
Linus
Phylo

DECURIA XVIII

Maintenance
Biton machinator (chief engineer)
Vulcan (boilerman)
Pyrodes (assistant boilerman)
Fons aquarius (fountain engineer)
Herogenes albarius (plasterer)
Glycon artifex plumbarius (plumber)
Phryx balneator (bathhouse engineer)
Talos faber lignarius (carpenter)
Ichmalius faber lignarius (carpenter)
Tychius pictor (painter)
Apelles pictor (painter)

DECURIA XIX

Garden
Rigodolus hortulanus (gardener)
Petros hortulanus (gardener)
Davos hortulanus (gardener)
Coelus hortulanus (gardener)
Conditor hortulanus (gardener)
Sariton hortulanus (gardener)

DECURIA XX

Home Farm

Ixion agaso (Head groom)
Flavus agaso (groom)
Geta agaso (groom)
Sedunius equarius (stable lad)
Scorpus equarius (stable lad)

Fontus topiarus (hedge trimmer)

Liber topiarus (hedge trimmer)

Diocles equarius (stable lad)

Olidus subulcus (pig man)

Gallus gallinarius (poultry man)

Capriolus caprarius (goatherd)

Gyes a gliraria (in charge of dormice)

Porus a coclearia (in charge of snails)

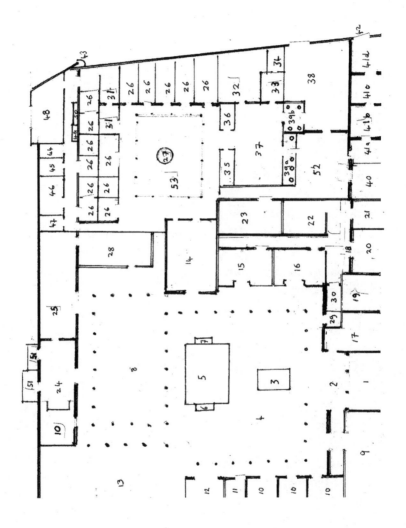

Plan of the Domus

583

Key to Plan of Domus

1 Portico
2 Vestibule
3 Implvium
4 Atrium
5 Tablinum
6 Imagines (death masks of family members)
7 Shrine
8 Peristyle (Garden)
9 Library
10 Cubiculum (Bedroom)
11 Visitors' room
12 Master's day sitting room
13 Summer Triclinium (dining room)
14 Winter Triclinium (dining room)
15 Principal guest bedroom
16 Master's bedroom
17 Porter's room
18 Bathhouse
19 Tepidarium (warm bath)
20 Caldarium (hot bath)
21 Frigidarium (cold bath)
22 Boiler room
23 Linen room
24 Demetrius' bedroom
25 Demetrius' office
26 Slave bedrooms
27 Well
28 Secretaries' office
29 Fire equipment
30 Latrine
31 Apicius' rooms
32 Back kitchen
33 Meat room
34 Smoke house
35 Head cook's office

36 Store
37 Kitchen
38 Laundry
39 Latrines a) men's b) women's
40 Preserving room
41 Stores a) fruit and vegetables b) grain c) wine d) oil
42 Service gate
43 Postern gate
44 Saddlery
45 Tool shed
46 Poultry
47 Pigsty
48 Stable
49 Dormice and snails
50 Rabbit hutches
51 Washroom
52 Laundry yard
53 Yard

Edwards Brothers Malloy
Oxnard, CA USA
September 10, 2015